# A TREASURY OF
# CIVIL WAR
# STORIES

# A Treasury of
# Civil War
# Stories

*Edited by*

## Martin H. Greenberg
## and Bill Pronzini

BONANZA BOOKS
New York

Published 1985 by Bonanza Books,
distributed by Crown Publishers, Inc.,
One Park Avenue, New York, New York 10016

Printed & bound in the United States of America

Library of Congress Cataloging in Publication Data
Main entry under title:
A Treasury of Civil War stories.
    1. United States—History—Civil War, 1861-1865—
Fiction. 2. War stories, American. I. Greenberg,
Martin Harry. II. Pronzini, Bill
PS648.C54T74 1985     813′.01′08358     85-4138
ISBN 0-517-46781X

h g f e d c b a

# CONTENTS

# ACKNOWLEDGMENTS

*Faulkner*—Copyright 1935 and copyright renewed © 1963 by William Faulkner. Reprinted from *The Unvanquished*, by William Faulkner, by permission of Random House, Inc.

*Fitzgerald*—"The Night Before Chancellorsville" Copyright 1950 by Francis Scott Fitzgerald Smith, copyright © renewed 1978 Charles Scribner's Sons in *Taps at Reveille*. Reprinted with the permission of Charles Scribner's Sons.

*Wolfe*—"Chickamauga" from *The Hills Beyond* by Thomas Wolfe. Copyright 1939 by Maxwell Perkins. Reprinted by permission of Harper & Row, Publishers, Inc.

*Benét*—"The Die-Hard" from *The Selected Works of Stephen Vincent Benét*. Copyright, 1942 by Stephen Vincent Benét. Copyright renewed © 1966 by Thomas C. Benét, Stephanie B. Mahin & Rachel Benét Lewis. Reprinted by permission of Brandt & Brandt Literary Agents, Inc.

*Mitchell*—Copyright 1911 by Mary E. Mitchell as first published in *The Atlantic Monthly*. Reprinted with permission.

*Benét*—"Jack Ellyat at Gettysburg" from: *The Selected Works of Stephen Vincent Benét*, Holt, Rinehart & Winston, Inc. Copyright renewed 1955, © 1956 by Rosemary Carr Benét. Reprinted by permission of Brandt & Brandt Literary Agents, Inc.

*Dowdey*—Copyright 1943 by The Curtis Publishing Company. Reprinted by permission of Harold Ober Associates, Inc.

*Bellah*—Copyright 1953 by The Curtis Publishing Company. Reprinted by permission of the agents for the author's Estate, the Scott Meredith Literary Agency, Inc., 845 Third Avenue, New York, NY 10022.

*Foote*—Copyright 1954 by Shelby Foote; copyright renewed © 1982. Reprinted by permission of the author.

*Marquand*—Copyright 1932, copyright renewed © 1960 by John P. Marquand. By permission of Little, Brown and Company in association with the Atlantic Monthly Press.

*Jones*—Reprinted from *The Saturday Evening Post;* © 1956 by The Curtis Publishing Company.

*Alter*—Copyright © 1985 by Sande Alter Kakuba. Reprinted by permission of Larry Sternig.

*Alter*—Copyright © 1968 by Robert Edmund Alter. Reprinted by permission of Larry Sternig.

# INTRODUCTION

THE WAR BETWEEN THE STATES was the most traumatic event in American history. Had its outcome been different, the entire course of our nation's domestic and international life would have been radically altered. The bloodiest war in the American experience was also in many ways the first modern war—a conflict that saw the use of massed artillery, ironclad ships, and the extensive use of railways for military purposes.

It is not surprising that such an event would become a major theme for books, magazines, songs, and, later, motion pictures. We believe that this volume is the largest and most comprehensive collection of Civil War fiction ever published, a book that combines the work of such titans of American literature as Herman Melville, Mark Twain, F. Scott Fitzgerald, William Faulkner, Thomas Wolfe, and O. Henry, as well as stars of "slick" magazines such as *Collier's* and the *Saturday Evening Post*—men like John P. Marquand, Stephen Vincent Benét, James Warner Bellah, and the tragic Robert Edmond Alter, who died of cancer at the age of forty at the height of his powers but before he could break out of the magazines and establish the national reputation he deserved.

A number of the authors represented in this book are also known for important novels about the Civil War. For example, Joseph A. Altsheler wrote at least ten books about the battles and personalities of the war, including *The Guns of Bull Run* and *The Sword of Antietam*. James Warner Bellah is the author of *The Valiant Virginians*, one of the best fictional accounts of the fighting in the Shenandoah Valley. The notable and mysterious Ambrose Bierce is known for his *Tales of Soldiers and Civilians*, published in 1891 yet still one of the very finest collections of Civil War stories. The greatly underrated Clifford Dowdey wrote four Civil War novels, two of them—*Bugles Blow No More* and *Tidewater*—focusing on the role in the war and fate of the city of Richmond.

Shelby Foote's *Shiloh* remains one of the great "double viewpoint" war novels, with the battle seen through the eyes of soldiers from both sides. And finally, we must mention one of William Faulkner's best books, *The Unvanquished*, with its tales of Mississippi during the war and its depiction of the passing of a way of life; and Stephen Crane, America's greatest writer on the war, here represented by two stories, including the classic short novel *The Red Badge of Courage*.

In these pages you will relive the great battles of the Civil War—Gettysburg, Chickamauga, Antietam, Shiloh, and Chancellorsville, among many others. You will meet or hear about the great military figures on the Union side, men such as Gen. Ulysses S. Grant, who accepted the surrender of the Confederacy and later became president of the United States; Gen. George B. McClellan, commander of the Army of the Potomac; Gen. George Meade, commander of the forces at Gettysburg; Gen. Philip Sheridan, commander of the Army of the Shenandoah; and, of course, William T. Sherman, who took Atlanta and made the immortal statement, "War is Hell."

And on the Confederate side, there are brave soldiers such as Gen. "Stonewall" Jackson, who died at Chancellorsville and fought Sheridan in the battles of the Shenandoah Valley; the gallant and greatly loved Robert E. Lee, who lost the decisive struggle at Gettysburg; Gen. George E. Pickett, who led the ill-fated charge that was the turning point of the war; and J.E.B. Stuart, perhaps the most famous cavalry officer of all time.

Return with us, then, to those deadly yet glorious years of 1860 to 1865, when the men of the Blue and the Gray determined the fate of a nation.

MARTIN H. GREENBERG
BILL PRONZINI

1985

# WILLIAM FAULKNER

## *Skirmish at Sartoris*

# 1

WHEN I THINK of that day, of Father's old troop on their horses drawn up facing the house, and Father and Drusilla on the ground with that Carpet Bagger voting box in front of them, and opposite them the women—Aunt Louisa, Mrs. Habersham and all the others—on the porch and the two sets of them, the men and the women, facing one another like they were both waiting for a bugle to sound the charge, I think I know the reason. I think it was because Father's troop (like all the other Southern soldiers too), even though they had surrendered and said that they were whipped, were still soldiers. Maybe from the old habit of doing everything as one man; maybe when you have lived for four years in a world ordered completely by men's doings, even when it is danger and fighting, you don't want to quit that world: maybe the danger and the fighting are the reasons, because men have been pacifists for every reason under the sun except to avoid danger and fighting. And so now Father's troop and all the other men in Jefferson, and Aunt Louisa and Mrs. Habersham and all the women in Jefferson were actually enemies for the reason that the men had given in and admitted that they belonged to the United States but the women had never surrendered.

I remember the night we got the letter and found out at last where Drusilla was. It was just before Christmas in 1864, after the Yankees had burned Jefferson and gone away, and we didn't even know for sure if the war was still going on or not. All we knew was that for three years the country had been full of Yankees, and then all of a sudden they were gone and there were no men there at all anymore. We hadn't even heard from Father since July, from Carolina, so that now we lived in a world of burned towns and houses and ruined plantations and fields inhabited only by women. Ringo and I were fifteen then; we felt almost exactly like we had to eat and sleep and change our clothes in a hotel built only for ladies and children.

The envelope was worn and dirty and it had been opened once and then glued back, but we could still make out *Hawkhurst, Gihon County, Alabama* on it even though we did not recognise Aunt Louisa's hand at first. It was addressed to Granny; it was six pages cut with scissors from wallpaper and written on both sides with pokeberry juice and I thought of that night eighteen months ago when Drusilla and I stood outside the cabin at Hawkhurst and listened to the niggers passing in the road, the night when she told me about the dog, about keeping the dog quiet, and then asked me to ask Father to let her join his troop and ride with him. But I didn't tell Father. Maybe I forgot it. Then the Yankees went away, and Father and his troop went away too. Then, six months later, we had a letter from him about how they were fighting in Carolina, and a month after that we had one from Aunt Louisa that Drusilla was gone too, a short letter on the wallpaper that you could see where Aunt Louisa had cried in the pokeberry juice about how she did not know where Drusilla was but that she had expected the worst ever since Drusilla had deliberately tried to unsex herself by refusing to feel any natural grief at the death in battle not only of her affianced husband but of her own father and that she took it for granted that Drusilla was with us and though she did not expect Drusilla to take any steps herself to relieve a mother's anxiety, she hoped that Granny would. But we didn't know where Drusilla was either. She had just vanished. It was like the Yankees in just passing through the South had not only taken along with them all living men blue and gray and white and black, but even one young girl who happened to try to look and act like a man after her sweetheart was killed.

So then the next letter came. Only Granny wasn't there to read it because she was dead then (it was the time when Grumby doubled back past Jefferson and so Ringo and I spent one night at home and found the letter when Mrs. Compson had sent it out) and so for a while Ringo and I couldn't make out what Aunt Louisa was trying to tell us. This one was on the same wallpaper too, six pages this time, only Aunt Louisa hadn't cried in the pokeberry juice this time: Ringo said because she must have been writing too fast:

> *Dear Sister:*
>     *I think this will be news to you as it was to me though I both hope and pray it will not be the heartrending shock to you it was to me as*

*naturally it cannot since you are only an aunt while I am the mother. But it is not myself I am thinking of since I am a woman, a mother, a Southern woman, and it has been our lot during the last four years to learn to bear anything. But when I think of my husband who laid down his life to protect a heritage of courageous men and spotless women looking down from heaven upon a daughter who had deliberately cast away that for which he died, and when I think of my half-orphan son who will one day ask of me why his martyred father's sacrifice was not enough to preserve his sister's good name—*

That's how it sounded. Ringo was holding a pineknot for me to read by, but after a while he had to light another pineknot and all the farther we had got was how when Gavin Breckbridge was killed at Shiloh before he and Drusilla had had time to marry, there had been reserved for Drusilla the highest destiny of a Southern woman—to be the bride-widow of a lost cause—and how Drusilla had not only thrown that away, she had not only become a lost woman and a shame to her father's memory but she was now living in a word that Aunt Louisa would not even repeat but that Granny knew what it was, though at least thank God that Father and Drusilla were not actually any blood kin, it being Father's wife who was Drusilla's cousin by blood and not Father himself. So then Ringo lit the other pineknot and then we put the sheets of wallpaper down on the floor and then we found out what it was: how Drusilla had been gone for six months and no word from her except she was alive, and then one night she walked into the cabin where Aunt Louisa and Denny were (and now it had a line drawn under it, like this:) in the garments not alone of a man but of a common private soldier and told them how she had been a member of Father's troop for six months, bivouacking at night surrounded by sleeping men and not even bothering to put up the tent for her and Father except when the weather was bad, and how Drusilla not only showed neither shame nor remorse but actually pretended she did not even know what Aunt Louisa was talking about; how when Aunt Louisa told her that she and Father must marry at once, Drusilla said, "Can't you understand that I am tired of burying husbands in this war? That I am riding in Cousin John's troop not to find a man but to hurt Yankees?" and how Aunt Louisa said:

"At least don't call him *Cousin* John where strangers can hear you."

# 2

THE THIRD LETTER did not come to us at all. It came to Mrs. Compson. Drusilla and Father were home then. It was in the spring and the war was over now, and we were busy getting the cypress and oak out of the bottom to build the house and Drusilla working with Joby and Ringo and Father and me like another man, with her hair shorter than it had been at Hawkhurst and her face sunburned from riding in the weather and her body thin from living like soldiers lived. After Granny died Ringo and Louvinia and I all slept in the cabin, but after Father came Ringo and Louvinia moved back to the other cabin with Joby and now Father and I slept on Ringo's and my pallet and Drusilla slept in the bed behind the quilt curtain where Granny used to sleep. And so one night I remembered Aunt Louisa's letter and I showed it to Drusilla and Father, and Father found out that Drusilla had not written to tell Aunt Louisa where she was and Father said she must, and so one day Mrs. Compson came out with the third letter. Drusilla and Ringo and Louvinia too were down in the bottom at the sawmill and I saw that one too, on the wallpaper with the pokeberry juice and the juice not cried on this time either, and this the first time Mrs. Compson had come out since Granny died and not even getting out of her surrey but sitting there holding to her parasol with one hand and her shawl with the other and looking around like when Drusilla would come out of the house or from around the corner it would not be just a thin sunburned girl in a man's shirt and pants but maybe something like a tame panther or bear. This one sounded just like the others: about how Aunt Louisa was addressing a stranger to herself but not a stranger to Granny and that there were times when the good name of one family was the good name of all and that she naturally did not expect Mrs. Compson to move out and live with Father and Drusilla because even that would be too late now to preserve the appearance of that which had never existed anyway. But that Mrs. Compson was a woman too, Aunt Louisa believed, a Southern woman too, and had suffered too, Aunt Louisa didn't doubt, only she did hope and pray that Mrs. Compson had been spared the sight of her own daughter if Mrs. Compson had one flouting and outraging all Southern principles of purity and womanhood that our husbands had died for, though Aunt Louisa hoped again that Mrs. Compson's husband (Mrs. Compson was a good deal older than Granny and the only husband she had ever had had been locked up for crazy a long time ago because in the slack part of the afternoons he would gather up eight or ten little niggers from the quarters and line them up across the creek from him with sweet potatoes on their heads and he would shoot the potatoes off with a rifle; he would tell them he might miss a potato but he wasn't going to miss a nigger, and so they would stand mighty still) had not made one of the number. So I couldn't make any sense out of that one too and I still didn't know what Aunt Louisa was talking about and I didn't believe that Mrs. Compson knew either.

Because it was not her: it was Mrs. Habersham, that never had been out here before and that Granny never had been to see that I knew of. Because Mrs. Compson didn't stay, she didn't even get out of the surrey, sitting there kind of drawn up under the shawl and looking at me and then at the cabin like she didn't know just what might come out of it or out from behind it. Then she begun to tap the nigger driver on his head with the parasol and they went away, the two old horses going pretty fast back down the drive and and back down the road to town. And the next afternoon when I came out of the bottom to go to the spring with the water bucket there were five surreys and buggies in front of the cabin and inside the cabin there were fourteen of them that had come the four miles out from Jefferson, in the Sunday clothes that the Yankees and the war had left them, that had husbands dead in the war or alive back in Jefferson helping Father with what he was doing, because they were strange times then. Only like I said, maybe times are never strange to women: that it is just one continuous monotonous thing full of the repeated follies of their menfolks. Mrs. Compson was sitting in Granny's chair, still holding the parasol and drawn up under her shawl and looking like she had finally seen whatever it was she had expected to see, and it had been the panther. It was Mrs. Habersham who was holding back the quilt for the others to go in and look at the bed where Drusilla slept and then showing them the pallet where Father and I slept. Then she saw me and said, "And who is this?"

"That's Bayard," Mrs. Compson said.

"You poor child," Mrs. Habersham said. So I didn't stop. But I couldn't help but hear them. It sounded like a ladies' club meeting with Mrs. Habersham running it, because every now and then Mrs. Habersham would forget to whisper: "—Mother should come, be sent for at once. But lacking her presence . . . we, the ladies of the community, mothers ourselves . . . child probably taken advantage of by gallant romantic . . . before realising the price she must—" and

Mrs. Compson said "Hush! Hush!" and then somebody else said, "Do you really suppose—" and then Mrs. Habersham forgot to whisper good: "What else? What other reason can you name why she should choose to conceal herself down there in the woods all day long, lifting heavy weights like logs and—".

Then I went away. I filled the bucket at the spring and went back to the log-yard where Drusilla and Ringo and Joby were feeding the bandsaw and the blindfolded mule going round and round in the sawdust. And then Joby kind of made a sound and we all stopped and looked and there was Mrs. Habersham, with three of the others kind of peeping out from behind her with their eyes round and bright, looking at Drusilla standing there in the sawdust and shavings, in her dirty sweated overalls and shirt and brogans, with her face sweat-streaked with sawdust and her short hair yellow with it. "I am Martha Habersham," Mrs. Habersham said. "I am a neighbor and I hope to be a friend." And then she said, "You poor child."

We just looked at her; when Drusilla finally spoke, she sounded like Ringo and I would when Father would say something to us in Latin for a joke. "Ma'am?" Drusilla said. Because I was just fifteen; I still didn't know what it was all about; I just stood there and listened without even thinking much, like when they had been talking in the cabin. "My condition?" Drusilla said. "My—"

"Yes," Mrs. Habersham said. "No mother, no woman to . . . forced to these straits—" kind of waving her hand at the mules that hadn't stopped and at Joby and Ringo goggling at her and the three others still peeping around her at Drusilla. "—to offer you not only our help, but our sympathy."

"My condition," Drusilla said. "My con . . . Help and sym—" Then she began to say, "Oh. Oh. Oh." standing there, and then she was running. She began to run like a deer, that starts to run and then decides where it wants to go; she turned right in the air and came toward me, running light over the logs and planks, with her mouth open, saying "John, John" not loud; for a minute it was like she thought I was Father until she waked up and found I was not; she stopped without even ceasing to run, like a bird stops in the air, motionless yet still furious with movement. "Is that what you think too?" she said. Then she was gone. Every now and then I could see her footprints, spaced and fast, just inside the woods, but when I came out of the bottom, I couldn't see her. But the surreys and buggies were still in front of the cabin and I could see Mrs. Compson and the other ladies on the porch, looking out across the pasture toward the bottom, so I did not go there. But before I came to the other cabin, where Louvinia and Joby and Ringo lived, I saw Louvinia come up the hill from the spring, carrying her cedar water bucket and singing. Then she went into the cabin and the singing stopped short off and so I knew where Drusilla was. But I didn't hide. I went to the window and looked in and saw Drusilla just turning from where she had been leaning her head in her arms on the mantel when Louvinia came in with the water bucket and a gum twig in her mouth and Father's old hat on top of her head rag. Drusilla was crying. "That's what it is then," she said. "Coming down there to the mill and telling me that in my condition—sympathy and help—Strangers; I never saw any of them before and I don't care a damn what they—But you and Bayard. It that what you believe? that John and I—that we—" Then Louvinia moved. Her hand came out quicker than Drusilla could jerk back and lay flat on the belly of Drusilla's overalls, then Louvinia was holding Drusilla in her arms like she used to hold me and Drusilla was crying hard. "That John and I—that we—And Gavin dead at Shiloh and John's home burned and his plantation ruined, that he and I—We went to the war to hurt Yankees, not hunting women!"

"I knows you ain't," Louvinia said. "Hush now. Hush."

And that's about all. It didn't take them long. I don't know whether Mrs. Habersham made Mrs. Compson send for Aunt Louisa or whether Aunt Louisa just gave them a deadline and then came herself. Because we were busy, Drusilla and Joby and Ringo and me at the mill, and Father in town; we wouldn't see him from the time he would ride away in the morning until when he would get back, sometimes late, at night. Because they were strange times then. For four years we had lived for just one thing, even the women and children who could not fight: to get Yankee troops out of the country; we thought that when that happened, it would be all over. And now that had happened, and then before the summer began I heard Father say to Drusilla, "We were promised Federal troops; Lincoln himself promised to send us troops. Then things will be all right." That, from a man who had commanded a regiment for four years with the avowed purpose of driving Federal troops from the country. Now it was as though we had not surrendered at all, we had joined forces with the men who had been our enemies against a new foe whose means we could not always fathom but whose aim we could always dread. So he was busy in town all day long. They were bulding Jefferson back, the courthouse and the stores, but it was more than that which Father and the other men were doing; it was something which he would not let

Drusilla or me or Ringo go into town to see. Then one day Ringo slipped off and went to town and came back and he looked at me with his eyes rolling a little.

"Do you know what I ain't?" he said.

"What?" I said.

"I ain't a nigger any more. I done been abolished." Then I asked him what he was, if he wasn't a nigger any more and he showed me what he had in his hand. It was a new scrip dollar; it was drawn on the United States Resident Treasurer, Yoknapatawpha County, Mississippi, and signed "Cassius Q. Benbow, Acting Marshal" in a neat clerk's hand, with a big sprawling X under it.

"Cassius Q. Benbow?" I said.

"Co-rect," Ringo said. "Uncle Cash that druv the Benbow carriage twell he run off with the Yankees two years ago. He back now and he gonter be elected Marshal of Jefferson. That's what Marse John and the other white folks is so busy about."

"A nigger?" I said. "A nigger?"

"No," Ringo said. "They ain't no more niggers, in Jefferson nor nowhere else." Then he told me about the two Burdens from Missouri, with a patent from Washington to organize the niggers into Republicans, and how Father and the other men were trying to prevent it. "Naw, suh," he said. "This war ain't over. Hit just started good. Used to be when you seed a Yankee you knowed him because he never had nothing but a gun or a mule halter or a handful of hen feathers. Now you don't even know him and stid of the gun he got a clutch of this stuff in one hand a a clutch of nigger voting tickets in the yuther."

So we were busy; we just saw Father at night and sometimes then Ringo and I and even Drusilla would take one look at him and we wouldn't ask him any questions. So it didn't take them long, because Drusilla was already beaten; she was just marking time without knowing it from that afternoon when the fourteen ladies got into the surreys and buggies and went back to town until one afternoon about two months later when we heard Denny hollering even before the wagon came in the gates, and Aunt Louisa sitting on one of the trunks (that's what beat Drusilla: the trunks. They had her dresses in them that she hadn't worn in three years; Ringo never had seen her in a dress until Aunt Louisa came) in mourning even to the crepe bow on her umbrella handle, that hadn't worn mourning when we were at Hawkhurst two years ago though Uncle Dennison was just as dead then as he was now. She came to the cabin and got out of the wagon, already crying and talking just like the letters sounded, like even when you listened to her you had to skip around fast to make any sense:

"I have come to appeal to them once more with a mother's tears though I don't think it will do any good though I had prayed until the very last that this boy's innocence might be spared and preserved but what must be must be and at least we can all three bear our burden together"; sitting in Granny's chair in the middle of the room, without even laying down the umbrella or taking her bonnet off, looking at the pallet where Father and I slept and then at the quilt nailed to the rafter to make a room for Drusilla, dabbing at her mouth with a handerchief that made the whole cabin smell like dead roses. And then Drusilla came in from the mill, in the muddy brogans and the sweaty shirt and overalls and her hair sunburned and full of sawdust, and Aunt Louisa looked at her once and begun to cry again, saying, "Lost, lost. Thank God in His mercy that Dennison Hawk was taken before he lived to see what I see."

She was already beaten. Aunt Louisa made her put on a dress that night; we watched her run out of the cabin in it and down the hill toward the spring while we were waiting for Father. And he came and walked into the cabin where Aunt Louisa was still sitting in Granny's chair with the handkerchief before her mouth. "This is a pleasant surprise, Miss Louisa," Father said.

"It is not pleasant to me, Colonel Sartoris," Aunt Louisa said. "And after a year, I suppose I cannot call it surprise. But it is still a shock." So Father came out too and we went down to the spring and found Drusilla hiding behind the big beech, crouched down like she was trying to hide the skirt from Father even while he raised her up. "What's a dress?" he said. "It don't matter. Come. Get up, soldier."

But she was beaten, like as soon as she let them put the dress on her she was whipped; like in the dress she could neither fight back nor run away. And so she didn't come down to the log-yard any more, and now that Father and I slept in the cabin with Joby and Ringo, I didn't even see Drusilla except at mealtime. And we were busy getting the timber out, and now everybody was talking about the election and how Father had told the two Burdens before all the men in town that the election would never be held with Cash Benbow or any other nigger in it and how the Burdens had dared him to stop it. And besides, the other cabin would be full of Jefferson ladies all day; you would have thought that Drusilla was Mrs. Habersham's daughter and not Aunt Louisa's. They would begin to arrive right after breakfast and stay all day, so that at supper Aunt Louisa would sit in her black mourning except for the bonnet and umbrella, with a wad of some kind of black knitting she carried around with her and that never got finished and the folded handkerchief handy in her belt (only she ate fine; she ate more than Father even because the election was just a week off and I reckon he was thinking about the Burdens) and refusing to speak to anybody except Denny; and Drusilla trying to eat, with her face strained and thin and her eyes like somebody's that had been whipped a long time now and is going just on nerve.

Then Drusilla broke; they beat her. Because she was strong; she wasn't much older than I was, but she had let Aunt Louisa and Mrs. Habersham choose the game and she had beat them both until that night when Aunt Louisa went behind her back and chose a game she couldn't beat. I was coming up to supper; I heard them inside the cabin before I could stop: "Can't you believe me?" Drusilla said. "Can't you understand that in the troop I was just another man and not much of one at that, and since we came home here I am just another mouth for John to feed, just a cousin of John's wife and not much older than his own son?" And I could almost see Aunt Louisa sitting there with that knitting that never progressed:

"You wish to tell me that you, a young woman, associated with him, a still young man, day and night for a year, running about the country with no guard nor check of any sort upon—Do you take me for a complete fool?" So that night Aunt Louisa beat her; we had just sat down to supper when Aunt Louisa looked at me like she had been waiting for the noise of the bench to stop: "Bayard, I do not ask your forgiveness for this because it is your burden too; you are an innocent victim as well as Dennison and I——" Then she looked at Father, thrust back in Granny's chair (the only chair we had) in her black dress, the black wad of knitting beside her plate. "Colonel Sartoris," she said, "I am a woman; I must request what the husband whom I have lost and the man son which I have not would demand, perhaps at the point of a pistol.—Will you marry my daughter?"

I got out. I moved fast; I heard the light sharp sound when Drusilla's head went down between her flungout arms on the table, and the sound the bench made when Father got up too; I passed him standing beside Drusilla with his hand on her head. "They have beat you, Drusilla," he said.

# 3

MRS. HABERSHAM got there before we had finished breakfast the next morning. I dont' know how Aunt Louisa got word in to her so quick. But there she was, and she and Aunt Louisa set the wedding for the day after tomorrow. I don't reckon they even knew that that was the day Father had told the Burden's Cash Benbow would never be elected marshal in Jefferson. I don't reckon they paid any more attention to it than if all the men had decided that day after tomorrow all the clocks in Jefferson were to be set back or up an hour. Maybe they didn't even know there was to be an election, that all the men in the county would be riding toward Jefferson tomorrow with pistols in their pockets, and that the Burdens already had their nigger voters camped in a cotton gin on the edge of town under guard. I don't reckon they even cared. Because like Father said, women cannot believe that anything can be right or wrong or even be very important that can be decided by a lot of little scraps of scribbled paper dropped into a box.

It was to be a big wedding; all Jefferson was to be invited and Mrs. Habersham planning to bring the three bottles of Madeira she had been saving for five years now when Aunt Louisa began to cry again. But they caught on quick now; now all of them were patting Aunt Louisa's hands and giving her vinegar to smell and Mrs. Habersham saying, "Of course. You poor thing. A public wedding now, after a year, would be a public notice of the . . . " So they decided it would be a reception, because Mrs. Habersham said how a reception could be held for a bridal couple at any time, even ten years later. So Drusilla was to ride into town, meet Father and be married as quick and quiet as possible, with just me and one other for witnesses to make it legal; none of the ladies themselves would even be present. Then they would come back home and we would have the reception.

So they began to arrive early the next morning, with baskets of food and tablecloths and silver like for a church supper. Mrs. Habersham brought a veil and a wreath and they all helped Drusilla to dress, only Aunt Louisa made Drusilla put on Father's big riding cloak over the veil and wreath too, and Ringo brought the horses up, all curried and brushed, and I helped Drusilla on with Aunt Louisa and the others all watching from the porch. But I didn't know that Ringo was missing when we started, not even when I heard Aunt Louisa hollering for Denny while we rode down the drive. It was Louvinia that told about it, about how after we left the ladies set and decorated the table and spread the wedding breakfast and how they were all watching the gate and Aunt Louisa still hollering for Denny now and then when they saw Ringo and Denny come up the drive riding double on one of the mules at a gallop, with Denny's eyes round as doorknobs and already hollering, "They kilt um! They kilt um!"

"Who?" Aunt Louisa hollered. "Where have you been?"

"To town!" Denny hollered. "Them two Burdens! They kilt um!"

"Who killed them?" Aunt Louisa hollered.

"Drusilla and Cousin John!" Denny hollered. Then Louvinia said how Aunt Louisa hollered sure enough.

"Do you mean to tell me that Drusilla and that man are not married yet?"

Because we didn't have time. Maybe Drusilla and Father would have, but when we came into the square we saw the crowd of niggers kind of huddled beyond the hotel door with six or eight strange white men herding them, and then all of a sudden I saw the Jefferson men, the men that I knew, that Father knew, running across the square toward the hotel with each one holding his hip like a man runs with a pistol in his pocket. And then I saw the men who were Father's troop lined up before the hotel door, blocking it off. And then I was sliding off my horse too and watching Drusilla struggling with George Wyatt. But he didn't have hold of her, he just had hold of the cloak, and then she was through the line of them and running toward the hotel with her wreath on one side of her head and the veil streaming behind. But George held me. He threw the cloak down and held me. "Let go," I said. "Father."

"Steady, now," George said, holding me. "John's just gone in to vote."

"But there are two of them!" I said. "Let me go!"

"John's got two shots in the derringer," George said. "Steady, now."

But they held me. And then we heard the three shots and we all turned and looked at the door. I don't know how long it was. "The last two was that derringer," George said. I don't know how long it was. The old nigger that was Mrs. Holston's porter, that was too old even to be free, stuck his head out once and said "Gret Gawd" and ducked back. Then Drusilla came out, carrying the ballot box, the wreath on one side of her head and the veil twisted about her arm, and then

Father came out behind her, brushing his new beaver hat on his sleeve. And then it was loud; I could hear them when they drew in their breath like when the Yankees used to hear it begin:

"Yaaaaa—" But Father raised his hand and they stopped. Then you couldn't hear anything.

"We heard a pistol too," George said. "Did they touch you?"

"No," Father said. "I let them fire first. You all heard. You boys can swear to my derringer."

"Yes," George said. "We all heard." Now Father looked at all of them, at all the faces in sight, slow.

"Does any man here want a word with me about this?" he said. But you could not hear anything, not even moving. The herd of niggers stood like they had when I first saw them, with the Northern white men herding them together. Father put his hat on and took the ballot box from Drusilla and helped her back onto her horse and handed the ballot box up to her. Then he looked around again, at all of them. "This election will be held out at my home," he said. "I hereby appoint Drusilla Hawk voting commissioner until the votes are cast and counted. Does any man here object?" But he stopped them again with his hand before it had begun good. "Not now, boys," he said. He turned to Drusilla. "Go home, I will go to the sheriff, and then I will follow you."

"Like hell you will," George Wyatt said. "Some of the boys will ride out with Drusilla. The rest of us will come with you."

But Father would not let them. "Don't you see we are working for peace through law and order?" he said. "I will make bond and then follow you. You do as I say." So we went on; we turned in the gates with Drusilla in front, the ballot box on her pommel—us and Father's men and about a hundred more, and rode on up the the cabin where the buggies and surreys were standing, and Drusilla passed the ballot box to me and got down and took the box again and was walking toward the cabin when she stopped dead still. I reckon she and I both remembered at the same time and I reckon that even the others, the men, knew all of a sudden that something was wrong. Because like Father said, I reckon women don't ever surrender: not only victory, but not even defeat. Because that's how we were stopped when Aunt Louisa and the other ladies came out on the porch, and then Father shoved past me and jumped down beside Drusilla. But Aunt Louisa never even looked at him.

"So you are not married," she said.

"I forgot," Drusilla said.

"You forgot? You *forgot*?"

"I . . . " Drusilla said. "We . . . "

Now Aunt Louisa looked at us; she looked along the line of us sitting there in our saddles; she looked at me too just like she did at the others, like she had never seen me before. "And who are these, pray? Your wedding train of forgetters? Your groomsmen of murder and robbery?"

"They came to vote," Drusilla said.

"To vote," Aunt Louisa said. "Ah. To vote. Since you have forced your mother and brother to live under a roof of license and adultery you think you can also force them to live in a polling booth refuge from violence and bloodshed, do you? Bring me that box." But Drusilla didn't move, standing there in her torn dress and the ruined veil and the twisted wreath hanging from her hair by a few pins. Aunt Louisa came down the steps; we didn't know what she was going to do: we just sat there and watched her snatch the polling box from Drusilla and fling it across the yard. "Come into the house," she said.

"No," Drusilla said.

"Come into the house. I will send for a minister myself."

"No," Drusilla said. "This is an election. Don't you understand? I am voting commissioner."

"So you refuse?"

"I have to. I must." She sounded like a little girl that has been caught playing in the mud. "John said that I—"

Then Aunt Louisa began to cry. She stood there in the black dress, without the knitting and for the first time that I ever saw it, without even the handkerchief, crying, until Mrs. Habersham came and led her back into the house. Then they voted. That didn't take long either. They set the box on the sawchunk where Louvinia washed, and Ringo got the pokeberry juice and an old piece of window shade, and they cut it into ballots. "Let all who want the Honorable Cassius Q. Benbow to be Marshal of Jefferson write Yes on his ballot; opposed, No," Father said.

"And I'll do the writing and save some more time," George Wyatt said. So he made a pack of the ballots and wrote them against his saddle and fast as he would write them the men would take them and drop them into the box and Drusilla would call their names out. We could hear Aunt Louisa still crying inside the cabin and we could see the other ladies watching us through the window. It didn't take long. "You needn't bother to count them," George said. "They all voted No."

And that's all. They rode back to town then, carrying the box, with Father and Drusilla in the torn wedding dress and the crooked wreath and veil standing beside ths sawchunk, watching them. Only this time even Father could not have stopped them. It came back high and thin and ragged and fierce, like when the Yankees used to hear it out of the smoke and the galloping:

"Yaaaaay, Drusilla!" they hollered. "Yaaaaaay, John Sartoris! Yaaaaaaay!"

# F. SCOTT FITZGERALD
## *The Night Before Chancellorsville*

I TELL YOU I didn't have any notion what I was getting into or I wouldn't of gone down there. They can have their army—it seems to me they were all acting like a bunch of yellow bellies. But my friend Nell said to me:

"Look here, Nora, Philly is as dead as Baltimore and we've got to eat this summer." She'd just got a letter from a girl that said they were living fine down there in "old Virginia." The soldiers were getting big pay offs and figuring maybe they'd stay there all summer, till the Johnny Rebs gave up. They got their pay regular too, and a good clean-looking girl could ask—well, I forget now, because after what happened to us I guess you can't expect me to remember anything.

I've always been used to decent treatment—somehow when I meet a man, no matter how fresh he is in the beginning, he comes to respect me in the end and I've never had things done to me like some girls, getting left in a strange town or had my purse stolen.

Well, I started to tell you how I went down to the army in "old Virginia." Never again! Wait till you hear.

I'm used to travelling nice—once when I was a little girl my daddy took me on the cars to Baltimore—we lived in York, Pa.—and we couldn't have been more comfortable; we had pillows and the men came through with baskets of oranges and apples, you know, singing out:

"Want to buy some oranges or apples—or beer."

You know what they sell—but I never took any beer because—

Oh I know, I'll go on—You only want to talk about the war, like all you men. But if that's their idea what a war is—

Well, they stuck us all in one car and a fresh guy took our tickets and winked and said:

"Oh, you're going down to Hooker's army."

The lights was terrible in the car, smoky and not cleaned so

21

everything looked sort of yellow. And say that car was so old it was falling to pieces.

There must have been forty girls in it, a lot of them from Baltimore and Philly. Only there were three or four that weren't gay—I mean they were more, oh you know, rich people that sat up front; every once in a while an officer would pop in his head from the next car and ask them if they wanted anything. I was in the seat behind with Nell and we heard him whisper:

"You're in pretty terrible company but we'll be there in a few hours and we'll go right to headquarters, and I'll promise you solid comfort."

I never will forget that night. None of us had any food except some girls behind us had some sausage and bread, and they gave us what they had left. There was a spigot you turned but no water came out. After about two hours, stopping every two minutes it seemed to me, a couple of lieutenants, loaded to the gills, came in from the next car and offered Nell and me some whisky out of a bottle. Nell took some and I pretended to and they sat on the side of our seats. One of them started to make up to her but just then the officer that had spoken to the women, pretty high up I guess, a major or a general, came back again and asked:

"You all right? Anything I can do?"

One of the ladies kind of whispered to him, and he turned to the drunk that was talking to Nell and made him go back in the other car. After that there was only one officer with us; he wasn't really so drunk, just feeling sick.

"This certainly is a jolly looking gang," he says. "It's good you can hardly see them in this light. They look as if their best friend just died."

"What if they do," Nell answered back. "How would you look yourself if you come all the way from Philly and then climbed in a car like this?"

"I come all the way from the Seven Days, Sister," he answered; pretty soon he left and said he'd try and get us some water or coffee, which was what we wanted.

The car kept rocking and it made us both feel funny. Some of the girls was sick and some was sound asleep on each other's shoulders.

"Hey, where is this army?" Nell demanded. "Down in Mexico?"

I was kind of half asleep myself by that time and didn't answer.

The next thing I knew I was woke up by a storm, the car was stopped again and I said, "It's raining."

"Raining!" said Nell. "That's cannon—they're having a battle."

"Oh. Well, after *this* ride I don't care who wins."

It seemed to be getting louder all the time, but out the windows you couldn't see anything on account of the mist.

In about half an hour another officer came in the car—he looked pretty messy as if he'd just crawled out of bed: his coat was still unbuttoned and he kept hitching up his trousers as if he didn't have any suspenders.

"All you ladies outside," he said, "we need this car for wounded."

"What?"

"Hey!"

"We paid for our tickets, didn't we?"

"I don't care. We need all the cars for the wounded and the other cars are about filled up."

"Hey! We didn't come down to fight in any battle!"

"It doesn't matter what you came down for—you're in a battle, a hell of a battle."

I was scared I can tell you. I thought maybe the Rebs would capture us and send us down to one of those prisons you hear about where they starve you to death unless you sing Dixie all the time and kiss niggers.

"Hurry up now!"

But another officer had come in who looked more nice.

"Stay where you are, ladies," he said, and then he said to the officer, "What do you want to do, leave them standing on the siding! If Sedgewick's Corps is broken like they say the Rebs may come up in this direction!" Some of the girls began crying out loud. "These are northern women after all."

"These are—"

"Oh shut up—go back to your command. I'm detailed to this transportation job, and I'm taking these girls to Washington with us."

I thought they were going to hit each other but they both walked off together, and we sat wondering what we were going to do.

What happened next I don't quite remember. The cannon were sometimes very loud and then sometimes more far away, but there was firing of shots right near us and a girl down the car had her window smashed. I heard a whole bunch of horses gallop by our windows but I still couldn't see anything.

This went on for half an hour—galloping and more shots. We couldn't tell how far away but they sounded like up by the engine.

Then it got quiet and two guys came into our car—we all knew right away they were rebels, not officers, just plain private ones with guns. One had on a brown blouse and one a blue blouse and I was surprised because I thought they always wore grey. They were disgusting looking and very dirty; one had a big pot of jam he'd smeared all over his face and the other had a box of crackers.

"Hi, Ladies."

"What you gals doin' down here?"

"Kaint you see, Steve, this is old Joe Hooker's staff."

"Reckin we ought to take 'em back to the General?"

They talked outlandish like that—I could hardly understand they talked so funny.

One of the girls got hysterical, she was so scared and that made them kind of shy. They were just kids I guess, under those beards, and one of them tipped his hat or whatever the old thing was:

"We're not fixin' to hurt you."

At that moment there was a whole bunch more shooting down by the engine and the rebs turned and ran. We were glad I can tell you.

Then about fifteen minutes later in came one of our officers. This was another new one.

"You better duck down!" he shouted to us, "they may shell this train. We're starting you off as soon as we load two more ambulances on board."

Half of us was on the floor already. The rich women sitting ahead of Nell and me went up into the car ahead where the wounded were—I heard one of them say to see if they could do anything. Nell thought she'd look in too, but she came back holding her nose—she said it smelled awful in there.

It was lucky she didn't go in because two of the girls did try and see if they could help, but the nurses sent them right back, as if they was dirt under their feet.

After I don't know how long the train began to move. A soldier came in and poured the oil out of all our lights except one and took it into the wounded car, so now we could hardly see at all.

If the trip down was slow the trip back was terrible. The wounded began groaning and we could hear in our car, so nobody couldn't get a decent sleep. We stopped everywhere.

When we got in Washington at last there was a lot of people in the station and they were all anxious about what had happened to the army, but I said you can search me. All I wanted was my little old room and my little old bed. I never been treated like that in my life. One of the girls said she was going to write to President Lincoln about it.

And in the papers next day they never said anything about how our train got attacked or about us girls at all! Can you beat it?

# THOMAS WOLFE
## *Chickamauga*

ON THE SEVENTH day of August, 1861, I was nineteen years of age. If I live to the seventh day of August this year I'll be ninety-five years old. And the way I feel this mornin' I intend to live. Now I guess you'll have to admit that that's goin' a good ways back.

I was born up at the Forks of the Toe River in 1842. Your grandpaw, boy, was born at the same place in 1828. His father, and mine, too, Bill Pentland—your great-grandfather, boy—moved into that region way back right after the Revolutionary War and settled at the Forks of Toe. The real Indian name fer hit was Estatoe, but the white men shortened hit to Toe, and hit's been known as Toe River ever since.

Of course hit was all Indian country in those days. I've heared that the Cherokees helped Bill Pentland's father build the first house he lived in, where some of us was born. I've heared, too, that Bill Pentland's grandfather came from Scotland back before the Revolution, and that thar was three brothers. That's all the Pentlands that I ever heared of in this country. If you ever meet a Pentland anywheres you can rest assured he's descended from one of those three.

Well, now, as I was tellin' you, upon the seventh day of August, 1861, I was nineteen years of age. At seven-thirty in the mornin' of that day I started out from home and walked the whole way in to Clingman. Jim Weaver had come over from Big Hickory where he lived the night before and stayed with me. And now he went along with me. He was the best friend I had. We had growed up alongside of each other: now we was to march alongside of each other fer many a long and weary mile—how many neither of us knowed that mornin' when we started out.

Hit was a good twenty mile away from where we lived to Clingman, and I reckon young folks nowadays would consider twenty mile a right smart walk. But fer people in those days hit wasn't anything at all. All of us was good walkers. Why Jim Weaver could keep going' without stoppin' all day long.

Jim was big and I was little, about the way you see me know, except that I've shrunk up a bit, but I could keep up with him anywhere he went. We made hit into Clingman before twelve o'clock—hit was a hot day, too—and by three o'clock that afternoon we had both joined up with the Twenty-ninth. That was my regiment from then on, right on to the end of the war. Anyways, I was an enlisted man that night, the day that I was nineteen years of age, and I didn't see my home again fer four long years.

Your Uncle Bacchus, boy, was already in Virginny: we knowed he was thar because we'd had a letter from him. He joined up right at the start with the Fourteenth. He'd already been at First Manassas and I reckon from then on he didn't miss a big fight in Virginny fer the next four years, except after Antietam he got wounded and was laid up fer four months.

Even way back on those days your Uncle Bacchus had those queer religious notions that you've heard about. The Pentlands are good people, but everyone who ever knowed 'em knows they can go queer on religion now and then. That's the reputation that they've always had. And that's the way Back was. He was a Russellite even in those days: accordin' to his notions the world was comin' to an end and he was goin' to be right in on hit when hit happened. That was the way he had hit figgered out. He was always prophesyin' and predictin' even back before the war, and when the war came, why Back just knowed that this was hit.

Why law! He wouldn't have missed that war fer anything. Back didn't go to war because he wanted to kill Yankees. He didn't want to kill nobody. He was as tender-hearted as a baby and as brave as a lion. Some fellers told hit on him later how they'd come on him at Gettysburg, shootin' over a stone wall, and his rifle bar'l had got so hot he had to put hit down and rub his hands on the seat of his pants because they got so blistered. He was singin' hymns, they said, with tears a-streamin' down his face—that's the way they told hit, any-way—and every time he fired he'd sing another verse. And I reckon he killed plenty because when Back had a rifle in his hands he didn't miss.

But he was a good man. He didn't want to hurt a fly. And I reckon the reason that he went to war was because he thought he'd be at Armageddon. That's the way he had hit figgered out, you know. When the war came, Back said: ''Well, this is hit, and I'm a-goin' to be thar. The hour has come," he said, "when the Lord is goin' to set up His Kingdom here on earth and separate the sheep upon the right hand and the goats upon the left—jest like hit was predicted long ago—and I'm a-goin' to be thar when hit happens."

Well, we didn't ask him which side *he* was goin' to be on, but we all knowed which side without havin' to ask. Back was goin' to be on the *sheep* side—that's the way *he* had hit figgered out. And that's the way he had hit figgered out right up to the day of his death ten years ago. He kept prophesyin' and predictin' right up to the end. No matter what happened, no matter what mistakes he made, he kept right on predictin'. First he said the war was goin' to be the Armageddon day. And when that didn't happen he said hit was goin' to come along in the eighties. And when hit didn't happen then he moved hit up to the nineties. And when the war broke out in 1914 and the whole world had to go, why Bacchus knowed that that was hit.

And no matter how hit all turned out, Back never would give in or own up he was wrong. He'd say he'd made a mistake in his figgers somers, but that he'd found out what hit was and that next time he'd be right. And that's the way he was up to the time he died.

I had to laugh when I heared the news of his death, because of course, accordin' to Back's belief, after you die nothin' happens to you fer a thousand years. You jest lay in your grave and sleep until Christ comes and wakes you up. So that's why I had to laugh. I'd a-give anything to've been there the next mornin' when Back woke up and found himself in heaven. I'd've give any thing just to've seen the expression on his face. I may have to wait a bit but I'm goin' to have some fun with him when I see him. But I'll bet you even then he won't give in. He'll have some reason fer hit, he'll try to argue he was right but that he made a little mistake about hit somers in his figgers.

But Back was a good man—a better man than Bacchus Pentland never lived. His only failin' was the failin' that so many Pentlands have—he went and got queer religious notions and he wouldn't give them up.

Well, like I say then, Back was in the Fourteenth. Your Uncle Sam and Uncle George was with the Seventeenth, and all three of them was in Lee's army in Virginny. I never seed nor heared from either Back or Sam fer the next four years. I never knowed what had happened to them or whether they was dead or livin' until I got back home in '65. And of course I never heared from George again until they wrote me after Chancellorsville. And then I knowed that he was dead. They told hit later when I came back home that hit took seven men to take him. They asked him to surrender. And then they had to kill him because he wouldn't be taken. That's the way he was. He never would give up. When they got to his dead body they told how they had to crawl over a whole heap of dead Yankees before they found him. And then they knowed hit was George. That's the way he was, all right. He never would give in.

He is buried in the Confederate cemetery at Richmond, Virginny. Bacchus went through thar more than twenty years ago on his way to the big reunion up at Gettysburg. He hunted up his grave and found out where he was.

That's where Jim and me thought that we'd be too. I mean with Lee's men, in Virginny. That's where we thought that we was goin' when we joined. But, like I'm goin' to tell you now, hit turned out different from the way we thought.

Bob Saunders was our Captain; L. C. McIntyre our Major; and Leander Briggs the Colonel of our regiment. They kept us thar at Clingman fer two weeks. Then they marched us into Altamont and drilled us fer the next two months. Our drillin' ground was right up and down where Parker Street now is. In those days thar was nothing thar but open fields. Hit's all built up now. To look at hit today you'd never know thar'd ever been an open field thar. But that's where hit was, all right.

Late in October we was ready and they moved us on. The day they marched us out, Martha Patton came in all the way from Zebulon to see Jim Weaver before we went away. He'd known her fer jest two months; he'd met her the very week we joined up and I was with him when he met her. She came from out along Cane River. Thar was a camp revival meetin' goin' on outside of Clingman at the time, and she was visitin' this other gal in Clingman while the revival lasted; and that was how Jim Weaver met her. We was walkin' along one evenin' toward sunset and we passed this house where she was stayin' with this other gal. And both of them was settin' on the porch as we went past. The other gal was fair, and she was dark: she had black hair and eyes, and she was plump and sort of little, and she had the pertiest complexion, and the pertiest white skin and teeth you ever seed; and when she smiled there was a dimple in her cheeks.

Well, neither of us knowed these gals, and so we couldn't stop and talk to them, but when Jim saw the little 'un he stopped short in his tracks like he was shot, and then looked at her so hard she had to turn her face. Well, then, we walked on down the road a piece and Jim stopped and turned and looked again, and when he did, why, sure enough, he caught her lookin' at him too. And then her face got red—she looked away again.

Well, that was where she landed him. He didn't say a word, but Lord! I felt him jerk there like a trout upon the line—and I knowed right then and thar she had him hooked. We turned and walked on down the road a ways, and then he stopped and looked at me and said:

"Did you see that gal back thar?"

"Do you mean the light one or the dark one?"

"You know damn good and well which one I mean," said Jim.

"Yes, I seed her—what about her?" I said.

"Well, nothin'—only I'm a-goin' to marry her," he said.

I knowed then that she had him hooked. And yet I never believed at first that hit would last. Fer Jim had had so many gals—I'd never had a gal in my whole life up to that time, but Lord! Jim would have him a new gal every other week. We had some fine-lookin' fellers in our company, but Jim Weaver was the handsomest feller that you ever seed. He was tall and lean and built just right, and he carried himself as straight as a rod: he had black hair and coal-black eyes, and when he looked at you he could burn a hole through you. And I reckon he'd burned a hole right through the heart of many a gal before he first saw Martha Patton. He could have had his pick of the whole lot—a born lady-killer if you ever seed one—and that was why I never thought that hit'd last.

And maybe hit was a pity that hit did. Fer Jim Weaver until the day that he met Martha Patton had been the most happy-go-lucky feller that you ever seed. He didn't have a care in the whole world—full of fun—ready fer anything and into every kind of devilment and foolishness. But from that moment on he was a different man. And I've always thought that maybe hit was a pity that hit hit him when hit did—that hit had to come jest at that time. If hit had only come a few years later—if hit could only have waited till the war was over! He'd wanted to go so much—he'd looked at the whole thing as a big lark—but now! Well she had him, and he had her: the day they marched us out of town he had her promise, and in his watch he had her picture and a little lock of her black hair, and as they marched us out, and him beside me, we passed her, and she looked at him, and I felt him jerk again and knowed the look she gave him had gone through him like a knife.

From that time on he was a different man; from that time on he was like a man in hell. Hit's funny how hit all turns out—how none of hit is like what we expect. Hit's funny how war and a little black-haired gal will change a man—but that's the story that I'm goin' to tell you now.

The nearest rail head in those days was eighty mile away at Locust Gap. They marched us out of town right up the Fairfield Road along the river up past Crestville, and right across the Blue Ridge there, and down the mountain. We made Old Stockade the first day's march and camped thar fer the night. Hit was twenty-four miles of marchin' right across the mountain, with the roads the way they was in those days, too. And let me tell you, fer new men with only two months' trainin' that was doin' good.

We made Locust Gap in three days and a half, and I wish you'd seed the welcome that they gave us! People were hollerin' and shoutin' the whole way. All the women folk and childern were lined up along the road, bands a-playing', boys runnin' along beside us, good shoes, new uniforms, the finest-lookin' set of fellers that you ever seed—Lord! You'd a-thought we was goin' to a picnic from the way hit looked. And I reckon that was the way most of us felt about hit, too. We thought we was goin' off to have a lot of fun. If anyone had knowed what he was in fer or could a-seed the passel o' scarecrows that came limpin' back barefoot and half naked four years later, I reckon he'd a-thought twice before he 'listed up.

Lord, when I think of hit! When I try to tell about hit thar jest ain't words enough tell what hit was like. And when I think of the way I was when I joined up—and the way I was when I came back four years later! When I went away I was an ignorant country boy, so tender-hearted that I wouldn't harm a rabbit. And when I came back after the war was over I could a-stood by and seed a man murdered right before my eyes with no more feelin' than I'd have had fer a stuck hog. I had no more feelin' about human life than I had fer the life of a sparrer. I'd seed a ten-acre field so thick with dead men that you could have walked all over hit without steppin' on the ground a single time.

And that was where I made my big mistake. If I'd only knowed a little more, if I'd only waited jest a little longer after I got home, things would have been all right. That's been the big regret of my whole life. I never had no education, I never had a chance to git one before I went away. And when I came back I could a-had my schoolin' but I didn't take hit. The reason was I never knowed no better: I'd seed so much fightin' and killin' that I didn't care fer nothin'. I jest felt dead and numb like all the brains had been shot out of me. I jest wanted to git me a little patch of land somewheres and settle down and fergit about the world.

That's where I made my big mistake. I didn't wait long enough. I got married too soon, and after that the childern came and hit was root, hawg, or die: I had to grub fer hit. But if I'd only waited jest a little while hit would have been all right. In less'n a year hit all cleared up. I got my health back, pulled myself together and got my feet back on the ground, and had more mercy and understandin' in me, jest on account of all the sufferin' I'd seen, than I ever had. And as fer my head, why hit was better than hit ever was: with all I'd seen and knowed I could a-got a schoolin' in no time. But you see I wouldn't wait. I didn't think that hit'd ever come back. I was jest sick of livin'.

But as I say—they marched us down to Locust Gap in less'n four days' time, and then they put us on the cars fer Richmond. We got to Richmond on the mornin' of one day, and up to that very moment we had thought that they was sendin' us to join Lee's army in the north. But the next mornin' we got our orders—and they was sendin' us out west. They had been fightin' in Kentucky: we was in trouble thar; they sent us out to stop the Army of the Cumberland. And that was the last I ever saw of old Virginny. From that time on we fought it out thar in the west and south. That's where we war, the Twenty-ninth, from then on to the end.

We had no real big fights until the spring of '62. And hit takes a fight to make a soldier of a man. Before that, thar was skirmishin' and raids in Tennessee and in Kentucky. That winter we seed hard marchin' in the cold and wind and rain. We learned to know what hunger was, and what hit was to have to draw your belly in to fit your rations. I reckon by that time we knowed hit wasn't goin' to be a picnic like we thought that hit would be. We was a-learnin' all the time, but we wasn't soldiers yet. It takes a good big fight to make a soldier, and we hadn't had one yet. Early in '62 we almost had one. They marched us to the relief of Donelson—but law! They had taken her before we got thar—and I'm goin' to tell you a good story about that.

U. S. Grant was thar to take her, and we was marchin' to relieve her before old Butcher could git in. We was seven mile away, and hit was comin' on to sundown—we'd been marchin' hard. We got the order to fall out and rest. And that was when I heared the gun and knowed that Donelson had fallen. Thar was no sound of fightin'. Everything was still as Sunday. We was sittin' thar aside the road and then I heared a cannon boom. Hit boomed five times, real slow like—

Boom!—Boom!—Boom!—Boom!—Boom! And the moment that I heared hit, I had a premonition. I turned to Jim and I said: "Well, thar you are! That's Donelson—and she's surrendered!"

Cap'n Bob Saunders heared me, but he wouldn't believe me and he said: "You're wrong!"

"Well," said Jim, "I hope to God he's right. I wouldn't care if the whole damn war had fallen through. I'm ready to go home."

"Well, he's wrong," said Captain Bob, "and I'll bet money on hit that he is."

Well, I tell you, that jest suited me. That was the way I was in those days—right from the beginnin' of the war to the very end. If thar was any fun or devilment goin' on, any card playin' or gamblin', or any other kind of foolishness, I was right in on hit. I'd a-bet a man that red was green or that day was night, and if a gal had looked at me from a persimmon tree, why, law! I reckon I'd a-clumb the tree to git her. That's jest the way hit was with me all through the war. I never made a bet or played a game of cards in my life before the war or after hit was over, but while the war was goin' on I was ready fer anything.

"How much will you bet?" I said.

"I'll bet you a hundred dollars even money," said Bob Saunders, and no sooner got the words out of his mouth than the bet was on.

We planked the money down right thar and gave hit to Jim to hold the stakes. Well, sir, we didn't have to wait half an hour before a feller on a horse came ridin' up and told us hit was no use goin' any father—Fort Donelson had fallen.

"What did I tell you?" I said to Cap'n Saunders, and I put the money in my pocket.

Well, the laugh was on him then. I wish you could a-seen the expression on his face—he looked mighty sheepish, I tell you. But he admitted hit, you know, he had to own up.

"You were right," he said. "You won the bet. But—I'll tell you what I'll do!" He put his hand into his pocket and pulled out a roll of bills. "I've got a hundred dollars left—and with me hit's all or nothin'! We'll draw cards fer this last hundred, mine against yorn—high card wins!"

Well, I was ready fer him. I pulled out my hundred, and I said, "Git out the deck!"

So they brought the deck out then and Jim Weaver shuffled hit and held hit while we drawed. Bob Saunders drawed first and he drawed the eight of spades. When I turned my card up I had one of the queens.

Well, sir, you should have seen the look upon Bob Saunders' face. I tell you what, the fellers whooped and hollered till he looked like he was ready to crawl through a hole in the floor. We all had some fun with him, and then, of course, I gave the money back. I never kept a penny in my life I made from gamblin'.

But that's the way hit was with me in those days—I was ready fer hit—fer anything. If any kind of devilment or foolishness came up I was right in on hit with the ringleaders.

Well then, Fort Donelson was the funniest fight that I was ever in because hit was all fun fer me without no fightin'. And that jest suited me. And Stone Mountain was the most peculiar fight that I was in because—well, I'll tell you a strange story and you can figger fer yourself if you ever heared about a fight like that before.

Did you ever hear of a battle in which one side never fired a shot and yet won the fight and did more damage and more destruction to the other side than all the guns and cannon in the world could do? Well, that was the battle of Stone Mountain. Now, I was in a lot of battles. But the battle of Stone Mountain was the queerest one of the whole war.

I'll tell you how hit was.

We was up on top of the Mountain and the Yankees was below us tryin' to drive us out and take the Mountain. We couldn't git our guns up thar, we didn't try to—we didn't have to git our guns up thar. The only gun I ever seed up thar was a little brass howitzer that we pulled up with ropes, but we never fired a shot with hit. We didn't git a chance to use hit. We no more'n got hit in position before a shell exploded right on top of hit and split that little howitzer plumb in two. Hit jest fell into two parts: you couldn't have made a neater job of hit if you'd cut hit down the middle with a saw. I'll never fergit that little howitzer and the way they split hit plumb in two.

As for the rest of the fightin' on our side, hit was done with rocks and stones. We gathered together a great pile of rocks and stones and boulders all along the top of the Mountain, and when they attacked we waited and let 'em have hit.

The Yankees attacked in three lines, one after the other. We waited until the first line was no more'n thirty feet below us—until we could see the whites of their eyes, as the sayin' goes—and then we let 'em have hit. We jest rolled those boulders down on 'em, and I tell you what, hit was an awful thing to watch. I never saw no worse destruction than that with guns and cannon during the whole war.

You could hear 'em screamin' and hollerin' until hit made your blood run cold. They kept comin' on and we mowed 'em down by the hundreds. We mowed 'em down without firin' a single shot. We crushed them, wiped them out—jest by rollin' those big rocks and boulders down on them.

There was bigger battles in the war, but Stone Mountain was the queerest one I ever seed.

Fort Donelson came early in the war, and Stone Mountain came later toward the end. And one was funny and the other was peculiar, but thar was fightin' in between that wasn't neither one. I'm goin' to tell you about that.

Fort Donelson was the first big fight that we was in—and as I say, we wasn't really in hit because we couldn't git to her in time. And after Donelson that spring, in April, thar was Shiloh. Well—all that I can tell you is, we was thar on time at Shiloh. Oh Lord, I reckon that we was! Perhaps we had been country boys before, perhaps some of us still made a joke of hit before—but after Shiloh we wasn't country boys no longer. We didn't make a joke about hit after Shiloh. They wiped the smile off of our faces at Shiloh. And after Shiloh we was boys no longer: we was vet'ran men.

From then on hit was fightin' to the end. That's where we learned what hit was like—at Shiloh. From then on we knowed what hit would be until the end.

Jim got wounded thar at Shiloh. Hit wasn't bad—not bad enough to suit him anyways—fer he wanted to go home fer good. Hit was a flesh wound in the leg, but hit was some time before they could git to him, and he was layin' out thar in the field and I reckon that he lost some blood. Anyways, he was unconscious when they picked him up. They carried him back and dressed his wound right thar upon the field. They cleaned hit out, I reckon, and they bandaged hit—thar was so many of 'em they couldn't do much more than that. Oh, I tell you what, in those days thar wasn't much that they could do. I've seed the surgeons workin' underneath an open shed with meat-saws, choppin' off the arms and legs and throwin' 'em out thar in a pile like they was sticks of wood, sometimes without no chloroform or nothin', and the screamin' and the hollerin' of the men was enough to make your head turn gray. And that was as much as anyone could do. Hit was live or die and take your chance—and thar was so many of 'em wounded so much worse than Jim that I reckon he was lucky they did anything fer him at all.

I heared 'em tell about hit later, how he came to, a-lyin' stretched out thar on an old dirty blanket on the bare floor, and an army surgeon seed him lookin' at his leg all bandaged up and I reckon thought he'd cheer him up and said: "Oh, that ain't nothin'—you'll be up and fightin' Yanks again in two weeks' time."

Well, with that, they said, Jim got to cursin' and a-takin' on something terrible. They said the language he used was enough to make your hair stand up on end. They said he screamed and raved and reached down thar and jerked that bandage off and said—"Like hell I will!" They said the blood spouted up thar like a fountain, and they said that army doctor was so mad he throwed Jim down upon his back and sat on him and he took that bandage, all bloody as hit was, and he tied hit back around his leg again and he said: "Goddam you, if you pull that bandage off agian, I'll let you bleed to death."

And Jim, they said, came ragin' back at him until you could have heared him fer a mile, and said: "Well, by God, I don't care if I do; I'd rather die than stay here any longer."

They say they had hit back and forth thar until Jim got so weak he couldn't talk no more. I know that when I come to see him a day or two later he was settin' up and I asked him: "Jim, how is your leg? Are you hurt bad?"

And he answered: "Not bad enough. They can take the whole damn leg off," he said, "as far as I'm concerned, and bury hit here at Shiloh if they'll only let me go back home and not come back again. Me and Martha will git along somehow," he said. "I'd rather be a cripple the rest of my life than have to come back and fight in this damn war."

Well, I knowed he meant hit too. I looked at him and seed how much he meant hit, and I knowed thar wasn't anything that I could do. When a man begins to talk that way, thar hain't much you can say to him. Well, sure enough, in a week or two, they let him go upon a two months' furlough and he went limpin' away upon a crutch. He was the happiest man I ever seed. "They gave me two months' leave," he said, "but if they jest let me git back home old Bragg'll have to send his whole damn army before he gits me out of thar again."

Well, he was gone two months or more, and I never knowed what happened—whether he got ashamed of himself when his wound healed up all right, or whether Martha talked him out of hit. But he was back with us again by late July—the grimmest, bitterest-lookin' man you ever seed. He wouldn't talk to me about hit, he wouldn't tell me what had happened, but I knowed from that time on he'd never draw his breath in peace until he left the army and got back home fer good.

Well, that was Shiloh, that was the time we didn't miss, that was where we lost our grin, where we knowed at last what hit would be until the end.

I've told you of three battles now, and one was funny, one was strange, and one was—well, one showed us what war and fightin' could be like. But I'll tell you of a fourth one now. And the fourth one was the greatest of the lot.

We seed some big fights in the war. And we was in some bloody battles. But the biggest fight we fought was Chickamauga. The bloodiest fight I ever seed was Chickamauga. Thar was big battles in the war, but thar never was a fight before, thar'll never be a fight again, like Chickamauga. I'm goin' to tell you how hit was at Chickamauga.

All through the spring and summer of that year Old Rosey follered us through Tennessee.

We had him stopped the year before, the time we whupped him at Stone's River at the end of '62. We tard him out so bad he had to wait. He waited thar six months at Murfreesboro. But we knowed he was a-comin' all the time. Old Rosey started at the end of June and drove us out to Shelbyville. We fell back on Tullahoma in rains the like of which you never seed. The rains that fell the last week in June that year was terrible. But Rosey kept a-comin' on.

He drove us out of Tullahoma too. We fell back across the Cumberland, we pulled back behind the mountain, but he follered us.

I reckon thar was fellers that was quicker when a fight was on, and when they'd seed just what hit was they had to do. But when it came to plannin' and a-figgerin', Old Rosey Rosecrans took the cake. Old Rosey was a fox. Fer sheer natural cunnin' I never knowed the beat of him.

While Bragg was watchin' him at Chattanooga to keep him from gittin' across the Tennessee, he sent some fellers forty mile up stream. And then he'd march 'em back and forth and round the hill and back in front of us again where we could look at 'em, until you'd a-thought that every Yankee in the world was there. But laws! All that was just a dodge! He had fellers a-sawin't and a-hammerin', a-buildin' boats, a-blowin' bugles and a-beatin' drums, makin' all the noise they could—you could hear 'em over yonder gittin' ready—and all the time Old Rosey was fifty mile or more down stream, ten mile past Chattanooga, a-fixin' to git over way down thar. That was the kind of feller Rosey was.

We reached Chattanooga early in July and waited fer two months. Old Rosey hadn't caught up with us yet. He still had to cross the Cumberland, push his men and pull his trains across the ridges and through the gaps before he got to us. July went by, we had no news of him. "Oh Lord!" said Jim, "perhaps he ain't a-comin'!" I knowed he was a-comin', but I let Jim have his way.

Some of the fellers would git used to hit. A feller'd git into a frame of mind where he wouldn't let hit worry him. He'd let termorrer look out fer hitself. That was the way hit was with me.

With Jim hit was the other way around. Now that he knowed Martha Patton he was a different man. I think he hated the war and army life from the moment that he met her. From that time he was livin' only fer one thing—to go back home and marry that gal. When mail would come and some of us was gittin' letters he'd be the first in line; and if she wrote him why he'd walk away like someone in a dream. And if she failed to write he'd jest go off somers and set down by himself: he'd be in such a state of misery he didn't want to talk to no one. He got the reputation with the fellers fer bein' queer—unsociable—always a-broodin' and a-frettin' about somethin' and a-wantin' to be left alone. And so, after a time, they let him be. He wasn't popular with most of them—but they never knowed what was wrong, they never knowed that he wasn't really the way they thought he was at all. Hit was jest that he was hit so desperate hard, the worst-in-love man that I ever seed. But law! I knowed what was the trouble from the start.

Hit's funny how war took a feller. Before the war I was the serious one, and Jim had been the one to play.

I reckon that I'd had to work too hard. We was so poor. Before the war hit almost seemed I never knowed the time I didn't have to work. And when the war came, why I only thought of all the fun and frolic I was goin' to have; and then at last, when I knowed what hit was like, why I was used to hit and didn't care.

I always could git used to things. And I reckon maybe that's the reason that I'm here. I wasn't one to worry much, and no matter how rough the goin' got I always figgered I could hold out if the others could. I let termorrer look out fer hitself. I reckon that you'd have to say I was an optimist. If things got bad, well, I always figgered that they could be worse; and if they got so bad they couldn't be no worse, why then I'd figger that they couldn't last this way ferever, they'd have to git some better sometime later on.

I reckon toward the end thar, when they got so bad we didn't think they'd ever git no better, I'd reached the place where I jest didn't care. I could still lay down and go to sleep and not worry over what was goin' to come termorrer, because I never knowed what was to come and so I didn't let hit worry me. I reckon you'd have to say that was the Pentland in me—our belief in what we call predestination.

Now, Jim was jest the other way. Before the war he was happy as a lark and thought of nothin' except havin' fun. But then the war came and hit changed him so you wouldn't a-knowed he was the same man.

And, as I say, hit didn't happen all at once. Jim was the happiest man I ever seed that mornin' that we started out from home. I reckon he thought of the war as we all did, as a big frolic. We gave hit jest about six months. We figgered we'd be back by then, and of course all that jest suited Jim. I reckon that suited all of us. It would give us all a chance to wear a uniform and to see the world, to shoot some Yankees and to run 'em north, and then to come back home and lord it over those who hadn't been and be a hero and court the gals.

That was the way hit looked to us when we set out from Zebulon. We never thought about the winter. We never thought about the mud and cold and rain. We never knowed what hit would be to have to march on an empty belly, to have to march barefoot with frozen feet and with no coat upon your back, to have to lay down on bare ground and try to sleep with no coverin' above you, and thankful half the time if you could find dry ground to sleep upon, and too tard the rest of hit to care. We never knowed or thought about such things as these. We never knowed how hit would be there in the cedar thickets beside Chickamauga Creek. And if we had a-knowed, if someone had a-told us, why I reckon that none of us would a-cared. We was too young and ignorant to care. And as fer knowin't—law! The only trouble about knowin' is that you've got to know what knowin's like before you know what knowin' is. Thar's no one that can tell you. You've got to know hit fer yourself.

Well, like I say, we'd been fightin' all this time and still thar was no

sign of the war endin'. Old Rosey jest kept a-follerin' us and—
"Lord!" Jim would say, "will it never end?"

I never knowed myself. We'd been fightin' fer two years, and I'd
given over knowin' long ago. With Jim hit was different. He'd been
a-praying and a-hopin' from the first that soon hit would be over and
that he could go back and get that gal. And at first, fer a year or more, I
tried to cheer him up. I told him that it couldn't last forever. But after a
while hit wasn't no use to tell him that. He wouldn't believe me any
longer.

Because Old Rosey kept a-comin' on. We'd whup him and we'd
stop him fer a while, but then he'd git his wind, he'd be on our trail
again, he'd drive us back.—"Oh Lord!" said Jim, "will hit never
stop?"

That summer I been tellin' you about, he drove us down through
Tennessee. He drove us out of Shelbyville, and we fell back on
Tullahoma, to the passes of the hills. When we pulled back across the
Cumberland I said to Jim: "Now we've got him. He'll have to cross
the mountains now to git at us. And when he does, we'll have him.
That's all that Bragg's been waitin' fer. We'll whup the daylights out
of him this time," I said, "and after that thar'll be nothin' left of him.
We'll be home by Christmas, Jim—you wait and see."

And Jim just looked at me and shook his head and said: "Lord,
Lord, I don't believe this war'll ever end!"

Hit wasn't that he was afraid—or, if he was, hit made a wildcat of
him in the fightin'. Jim could get fightin' mad like no one else I ever
seed. He could do things, take chances no one else I ever knowed
would take. But I reckon hit was jest because he was so desperate. He
hated hit so much. He couldn't git used to hit the way the others could.
He couldn't take hit as hit came. Hit wasn't so much that he was afraid
to die. I guess hit was that he was still so full of livin'. He didn't want
to die because he wanted to live so much. And he wanted to live so
much because he was in love.

. . . So, like I say, Old Rosey finally pushed us back across the
Cumberland. He was in Chattanooga in July, and fer a few weeks hit
was quiet thar. But all the time I knowed that Rosey would keep
comin' on. We got wind of him again along in August. He had started
after us again. He pushed his trains across the Cumberland, with the
roads so bad, what with the rains, his wagons sunk down to the axle
hubs. But he got 'em over, came down in the valley, then across the
ridge, and early in September he was on our heels again.

We cleared out of Chattanooga on the eighth. And our tail end was pullin' out at one end of the town as Rosey came in through the other. We dropped down around the mountain south of town and Rosey thought he had us on the run again.

But this time he was fooled. We was ready fer him now, a-pickin' out our spot and layin' low. Old Rosey follered us. He sent McCook around down toward the south to head us off. He thought he had us in retreat but when McCook got thar we wasn't thar at all. We'd come down south of town and taken our positions along Chickamauga Creek. McCook had gone too far. Thomas was follerin' us from the north and when McCook tried to git back to join Thomas, he couldn't pass us, fer we blocked the way. They had to fight us or be cut in two.

We was in position on the Chickamauga on the seventeenth. The Yankees streamed in on the eighteenth, and took their position in the woods a-facin' us. We had our backs to Lookout Mountain and the Chickamauga Creek. The Yankees had their line thar in the woods before us on a rise, with Missionary Ridge behind them to the east.

The Battle of Chickamauga was fought in a cedar thicket. That cedar thicket, from what I knowed of hit, was about three miles long and one mile wide. We fought fer two days all up and down that thicket and to and fro across hit. When the fight started that cedar thicket was so thick and dense you could a-took a butcher knife and drove hit in thar anywhere and hit would a-stuck. And when that fight was over that cedar thicket had been so destroyed by shot and shell you could a-looked in thar anywheres with your naked eye and seed a black snake run a hundred yards away. If you'd a-looked at that cedar thicket the day after that fight was over you'd a-wondered how a hummin' bird the size of your thumbnail could a-flown through thar without bein' torn into pieces by the fire. And yet more than half of us who went into that thicket came out of hit alive and tole the tale. You wouldn't have thought that hit was possible. But I was thar and seed hit, and hit was.

A little after midnight—hit may have been about two o'clock that mornin', while we lay there waitin' for the fight we knowed was bound to come next day—Jim woke me up. I woke up like a flash— you got used to hit in those days—and though hit was so dark you could hardly see your hand a foot away, I knowed his face at once. He was white as a ghost and he had got thin as a rail in that last year's campaign. In the dark his face looked white as paper. He dug his hand into my arm so hard hit hurt. I roused up sharp-like; then I seed him and knowed who hit was.

"John!" he said—"John!"—and he dug his fingers in my arm so hard he made hit ache—"John! I've seed him! He was here again!"

I tell you what, the way he said hit made my blood run cold. They say we Pentlands are a superstitious people, and perhaps we are. They told hit how they say my brother George a-comin' up the hill one day at sunset, how they all went out upon the porch and waited fer him, how everyone, the children and the grown-ups alike, all seed him as he clumb the hill, and how he passed behind a tree and disappeared as if the ground had swallered him—and how they got the news ten days later that he'd been killed at Chancellorsville on that very day and hour. I've heared these stories and I know the others all believe them, but I never put no stock in them myself. And yet, I tell you what! The sight of that white face and those black eyes a-burnin' at me in the dark—the way he said hit and the way hit was—fer I could feel the men around me and hear somethin' movin' in the wood—I heared a trace chain rattle and hit was enough to make your blood run cold! I grabbed hold of him—I shook him by the arm—I didn't want the rest of 'em to hear—I told him to hush up—

"John, he was here!" he said.

I never asked him what he meant—I knowed too well to ask. It was the third time he'd seed hit in a month—a man upon a horse. I didn't want to hear no more—I told him that hit was a dream and I told him to go back to sleep.

"I tell you, John, hit was no dream!" he said. "Oh John I heared hit—and I heared his horse—and I seed him sittin' thar as plain as day—and he never said a word to me—he jest sat thar lookin' down, and then he turned and rode away into the woods. . . . John, John, I heared him and I don't know what hit means!"

Well, whether he seed hit or imagined hit or dreamed hit, I don't know. But the sight of his black eyes a-burnin' holes through me in the dark made me feel almost as if I'd seed hit, too. I told him to lay down by me—and still I seed his eyes a-blazin' thar. I know he didn't sleep a wink the rest of that whole night. I closed my eyes and tried to make him think that I was sleepin' but hit was no use—we lay thar wide awake. And both of us was glad when mornin' came.

The fight began upon our right at ten o'clock. We couldn't find out what was happenin': the woods thar was so close and thick we never knowed fer two days what had happened, and we didn't know fer certain then. We never knowed how many we was fightin' or how many we had lost. I've heared them say that even Old Rosey himself didn't know jest what had happened when he rode back into town next day, and didn't know that Thomas was still standin' like a rock. And if Old Rosey didn't know no more than this about hit, what could a common soldier know? We fought back and forth across that cedar thicket for two days, and thar was times when you would be right up on top of them before you even knowed that they was thar. And that's the way the fightin' went—the bloodiest fightin' that was ever knowed, until that cedar thicket was soaked red with blood, and thar was hardly a place left in thar where a sparrer could have perched.

And as I say, we heared 'em fightin' out upon our right at ten o'clock, and then the fightin' came our way. I heared later that this fightin' started when the Yanks come down to the Creek and run into a bunch of Forrest's men and drove 'em back. And then they had hit back and forth until they got drove back themselves, and that's the way we had hit all day long. We'd attack and we'd beat them off. And that was the way hit went from mornin' till night. We piled up there upon their left: they mowed us down with canister and grape until the very grass was soakin' with our blood, but we kept comin' on. We must have charged a dozen times that day—I was in four of 'em myself. We fought back and forth across that wood until there wasn't a piece of hit as big as the palm of your hand we hadn't fought on. We busted through their right at two-thirty in the afternoon and got way over past the Widder Glenn's, where Rosey had his quarters, and beat 'em back until we got the whole way 'cross the Lafayette Road and took possession of the road. And then they drove us out again. And we kept comin' on, and both sides were still at hit after darkness fell.

We fought back and forth across that road all day with first one side and then the t'other holdin' hit until that road itself was soaked in blood. They called that road the Bloody Lane, and that was jest the name fer it.

We kept fightin' an hour or more after hit had gotten dark, and you could see the rifles flashin' in the woods, but then hit all died down. I tell you what, that night was somethin' to remember and to marvel at as long as you live. The fight had set the wood afire in places, and you could see the smoke and flames and hear the screamin' and the hollerin' of the wounded until hit made your blood run cold. We got as many as we could—but some we didn't even try to git—we jest let 'em lay. It was an awful thing to hear. I reckon many a wounded man was jest left to die or burn to death because we couldn't git 'em out.

You could see the nurses and the stretcher-bearers movin' through the woods, and each side huntin' fer hits dead. You could see them movin' in the smoke an' flames, an' you could see the dead men layin' there as thick as wheat, with their corpse-like faces 'n black powder on their lips, an' a little bit of moonlight comin' through the trees, and all of hit more like a nightmare out of hell than anything I ever knowed before.

But we had other work to do. All through the night we could hear the Yanks a-choppin' and a-thrashin' round, and we knowed that they was fellin' trees to block us when we went fer them next mornin'. Fer we knowed the fight was only jest begun. We figgered that we'd had the best of hit, but we knowed no one had won the battle yet. We knowed the second day would beat the first.

Jim knowed hit too. Poor Jim, he didn't sleep that night—he never seed the man upon the horse that night he jest sat there, a-grippin' his knees and starin', and a-sayin'; "Lord God, Lord God, when will hit ever end?"

Then mornin' came at last. This time we knowed jest where we was and what hit was we had to do. Our line was fixed by that time. Bragg knowed at last where Rosey had his line, and Rosey knowed where we was. So we waited there, both sides, till mornin' came. Hit was a foggy mornin' with mist upon the ground. Around ten o'clock when the mist began to rise, we got the order and we went chargin' through the wood again.

We knowed the fight was goin' to be upon the right—upon our right, that is—on Rosey's left. And we knowed that Thomas was in charge on Rosey's left. And we all knowed that hit was easier to crack a flint rock with your teeth than to make old Thomas budge. But we went after him, and I tell you what, that was a fight! The first day's fight had been like playin' marbles when compared to this.

We hit old Thomas on his left at half-past ten, and Breckenridge came sweepin' round and turned old Thomas's flank and came in at his back, and then we had hit hot and heavy. Old Thomas whupped his men around like he would crack a raw-hide whup and drove Breckenridge back around the flank again, but we was back on top of him before you knowed the first attack was over.

The fight went ragin' down the flank, down to the center of Old

Rosey's army and back and forth across the left, and all up and down old Thomas's line. We'd hit him right and left and in the middle, and he'd come back at us and throw us back again. And we went ragin' back and forth thar like two bloody lions with that cedar thicket so tore up, so bloody and so thick with dead by that time, that hit looked as if all hell had broken loose in thar.

Rosey kept a-whuppin' men around off of his right, to help old Thomas on the left to stave us off. And then we'd hit old Thomas left of center and we'd bank him in the middle and we'd hit him on his left again, and he'd whup those Yankees back and forth off of the right into his flanks and middle as we went fer him, until we run those Yankees ragged. We had them gallopin' back and forth like kangaroos, and in the end that was the thing that cooked their goose.

The worst fightin' had been on the left, on Thomas's line, but to hold us thar they'd thinned their right out and had failed to close in on the center of their line. And at two o'clock that afternoon when Longstreet seed the gap in Wood's position on the right, he took five brigades of us and poured us through. That whupped them. That broke their line and smashed their whole right all to smithereens. We went after them like a pack of ragin' devils. We killed 'em and we took 'em by the thousands, and those we didn't kill and take right thar went streamin' back across the Ridge as if all hell was at their heels.

That was a rout if ever I heared tell of one! They went streamin' back across the Ridge—hit was each man fer himself and the devil take the hindmost. They caught Rosey comin' up—he rode into them—he tried to check 'em, face 'em round, and get 'em to come on again—hit was like tryin' to swim the Mississippi upstream on a boneyard mule! They swept him back with them as if he'd been a wodden chip. They went streamin' into Rossville like the rag-tag of creation—the worst whupped army that you ever seed, and Old Rosey was along with all the rest!

He knowed hit was all up with him, or thought he knowed hit, for everybody told him the Army of the Cumberland had been blowed to smithereens and that hit was a general rout. And Old Rosey turned and rode to Chattanooga, and he was a beaten man. I've heared tell that when he rode up to his headquarters thar in Chattanooga they had to help him from his horse, and that he walked into the house all dazed and fuddled-like, like he never knowed what had happened to him— and that he jest sat thar struck dumb and never spoke.

This was at four o'clock of that same afternoon. And then the news was brought to him that Thomas was still thar upon the field and wouldn't budge. Old Thomas stayed thar like a rock. We'd smashed the right, we'd sent it flyin' back across the Ridge, the whole Yankee right was broken into bits and streamin' back to Rossville for dear life. Then we bent old Thomas back upon his left. We thought we had him, he'd have to leave the field or else surrender. But old Thomas turned and fell back along the Ridge and put his back against the wall thar, and he wouldn't budge.

Longstreet pulled us back at three o'clock when we had broken up the right and sent them streamin' back across the Ridge. We thought that hit was over then. We moved back stumblin' like men walkin' in a dream. And I turned to Jim—I put my arm around him, and I said: "Jim, what did I say? I knowed hit, we've licked 'em and this is the end!" I never even knowed if he heard me. He went stumblin' on beside me with his face as white as paper and his lips black with the powder of the cartridge-bite, mumblin' and mutterin' to himself like someone talkin' in a dream. And we fell back to position, and they told us all to rest. And we leaned thar on our rifles like men who hardly knowed if they had come out of that hell alive or dead.

"Oh Jim, we've got 'em and this is the end!" I said.

He leaned thar swayin' on his rifle, starin' through the wood. He jest leaned and swayed thar, and he never said a word, and those great eyes of his a-burnin' through the wood.

"Jim, don't you hear me?"—and I shook him by the arm. "Hit's over, man! We've licked 'em and the fight is over!—Can't you understand?"

And then I heared them shoutin' on the right, the word came down the line again, and Jim—poor Jim!—he raised his head and listened, and "Oh God!" he said, "we've got to go again!"

Well, hit was true. The word had come that Thomas had lined up on the Ridge, and we had to go fer him again. After that I never exactly knowed what happened. Hit was like fightin' in a bloody dream—like doin' somethin' in a nightmare—only the nightmare was like death and hell. Longstreet threw us up that hill five times, I think, before darkness came. We'd charge up to the very muzzles of their guns, and they'd mow us down like grass, and we'd come stumblin' back—or what was left of us—and form again at the foot of the hill, and then come on again. We'd charge right up the Ridge and drive 'em through the gap and fight 'em with cold steel, and they'd come back again and we'd brain each other with the butt end of our guns. Then they'd throw us back and we'd re-form and come on after 'em again.

The last charge happened jest at dark. We came along and stripped the ammunition off the dead—we took hit from the wounded—we had nothin' left ourselves. Then we hit the first line—and we drove them back. We hit the second and swept over them. We were goin' up to take the third and last—they waited till they saw the color of our eyes before they let us have hit. Hit was like a river of red-hot lead had poured down on us: the line melted thar like snow. Jim stumbled and spun round as if somethin'. had whupped him like a top. He fell right toward me, with his eyes wide open and the blood a-pourin' from his mouth. I took one look at him and then stepped over him like he was a log. Thar was no more to see or think of now—no more to reach— except that line. We reached hit and they let us have hit—and we stumbled back.

And yet we knowed that we had won a victory. That's what they told us later—and we knowed hit must be so because when daybreak came next mornin' the Yankees was all gone. They had all retreated into town, and we was left there by the Creek at Chickamauga in possession of the field.

I don't know how many men got killed. I don't know which side lost the most. I only know you could have walked across the dead men without settin' foot upon the ground. I only know that cedar thicket which had been so dense and thick two days before you could've drove a knife into hit and hit would of stuck, had been so shot to pieces that you could've looked in thar on Monday mornin' with your naked eye and seed a black snake run a hundred yards away.

I don't know how many men we lost or how many of the Yankees we may have killed. The Generals on both sides can figger all that out to suit themselves. But I know that when that fight was over you could have looked in thar and wondered how a hummin' bird could've flown through that cedar thicket and come out alive. And yet that happened, yes, and something more than hummin' birds—fer men came out, alive.

And on that Monday mornin', when I went back up the Ridge to where Jim lay, thar just beside him on a little torn piece of bough, I heard a redbird sing. I turned Jim over and got his watch, his pocket-knife, and what few papers and belongin's that he had, and some letters that he'd had from Martha Patton. And I put them in my pocket.

And then I got up and looked around. It all seemed funny after hit had happened, like something that had happened in a dream. Fer Jim had wanted so desperate hard to live, and hit had never mattered half so much to me, and now I was a-standin' thar with Jim's watch and Martha Patton's letters in my pocket and a-listenin' to that little redbird sing.

And I would go all through the war and go back home and marry Martha later on, and fellers like poor Jim was layin' thar at Chickamauga Creek.

Hit's all so strange now when you think of hit. Hit all turned out so different from the way we thought. And that was long ago, and I'll be ninety-five years old if I am livin' on the seventh day of August, of this present year. Now that's goin' back a long ways, hain't hit? And yet hit all comes back to me as clear as if hit happened yesterday. And then hit all will go away and be as strange as if hit happened in a dream.

But I have been in some big battles I can tell you. I've seen strange things and been in bloody fights. But the biggest fight that I was ever in—the bloodiest battle anyone has ever fought—was at Chickamauga in that cedar thicket—at Chickamauga Creek in that great war.

# HERMAN MELVILLE

## *Fort Donelson*

# DONELSON

*(February, 1862)*

THE BITTER CUP
   Of that hard countermand
Which gave the Envoys up,
Still was wormwood in the mouth,
   And clouds involved the land,
When, pelted by sleet in the icy street,
   About the bulletin board a band
Of eager, anxious people met,
And every wakeful heart was set
On latest news from West or South.
"No seeing here," cries one—"don't crowd"—
"You tall man, pray you, read aloud."

IMPORTANT.
     *We learn that General Grant,*
     *Marching from Henry overland,*
*And joined by a force up the Cumberland sent*
     *(Some thirty thousand the command),*
     *On Wednesday a good position won—*
     *Began the siege of Donelson.*

     *This stronghold crowns a river-bluff,*
       *A good broad mile of leveled top;*
     *Inland the ground rolls off*
       *Deep-gorged, and rocky, and broken up—*
     *A wilderness of trees and brush.*
       *The spaded summit shows the roods*
       *Of fixed intrenchments in their hush;*
       *Breast-works and rifle-pits in woods*
       *Perplex the base.—*

*The welcome weather*
*Is clear and mild; 'tis much like May.*
*The ancient boughs that lace together*
*Along the stream, and hang far forth,*
   *Strange with green mistletoe, betray*
*A dreamy contrast to the North.*

*Our troops are full of spirits—say*
   *The siege won't prove a creeping one.*
*They purpose not the lingering stay*
*Of old beleaguerers; not that way;*
   *But, full of* vim *from Western prairies won,*
   *They'll make, ere long, a dash at Donelson.*
Washed by the storm till the paper grew
Every shade of a streaky blue,
That bulletin stood. The next day brought
A second.

LATER FROM THE FORT.
   *Grant's investment is complete—*
      *A semicircular one.*
*Both wings the Cumberland's margin meet,*
*Then, backward curving, clasp the rebel seat.*
   *On Wednesday this good work was done;*
   *But of the doers some lie prone.*
*Each wood, each hill, each glen was fought for;*
*The bold inclosing line we wrought for*
*Flamed with sharpshooters. Each cliff cost*
*A limb or life. But back we forced*
*Reserved and all; made good our hold;*
*And so we rest.*

                  *Events unfold.*
*On Thursday added ground was won,*
   *A long bold steep: we near the Den.*
*Later the foe came shouting down*
      *In sortie, which was quelled; and then*
   *We stormed them on their left.*
   *A chilly change in the afternoon;*

The sky, late clear, is now bereft
Of sun. Last night the ground froze hard—
Rings to the enemy as they run
Within their works. A ramrod bites
The lip it meets. The cold incites
To swinging of arms with brisk rebound.
Smart blows 'gainst lusty chests resound.

Along the outer line we ward
    A crackle of skirmishing goes on,
Our lads creep round on hand and knee,
    They fight from behind each trunk and stone;
    And sometimes, flying for refuge, one
Finds 'tis an enemy shares the tree.
Some scores are maimed by boughs shot off
    In the glades by the Fort's big gun.
    We mourn the loss of Colonel Morrison,
    Killed while cheering his regiment on.
Their far sharpshooters try our stuff;
And ours return them puff for puff;
'Tis diamond-cutting-diamond work.
    Woe on the rebel cannoneer
Who shows his head. Our fellows lurk
    Like Indians that waylay the deer
By the wild salt-spring.—The sky is dun,
Foredooming the fall of Donelson.

Stern weather is all unwonted here.
    The people of the country own
We brought it. Yea, the earnest North
Has elementally issued forth
    To storm this Donelson.
FURTHER.
                    A yelling rout
Of ragamuffins broke profuse
    To-day from out the Fort.
    Sole uniform they wore, a sort
Of patch, or white badge (as you choose)
    Upon the arm. But leading these,

*Or mingling, were men of face*
*And bearing of patrician race,*
*Splendid in courage and gold lace—*
   *The officers. Before the breeze*
*Made by their charge, down went our line;*
*But, rallying, charged back in force,*
*And broke the sally; yet with loss.*
*This on the left; upon the right*
*Meanwhile there was an answering fight;*
   *Assailants and assailed reversed.*
*The charge too upward, and not down—*
*Up a steep ridge-side, toward its crown,*
*A strong redoubt. But they who first*
*Gained the fort's base, and marked the trees*
*Felled, heaped in horned perplexities,*
   *And shagged with brush; and swarming there*
*Fierce wasps whose sting was present death—*
*They faltered, drawing bated breath,*
   *And felt it was in vain to dare;*
*Yet still, perforce, returned the ball,*
*Firing into the tangled wall*
*Till ordered to come down. They came;*
*But left some comrades in their fame,*
*Red on the ridge in icy wreath*
*And hanging gardens of cold Death.*
   *But not quite unavenged these fell;*
*Our ranks once out of range, a blast*
   *Of shrapnel and quick shell*
*Burst on the rebel horde, still massed,*
   *Scattering them pell-mell.*
      *(This fighting—judging what we read—*
      *Both charge and countercharge,*
      *Would seem but Thursday's told at large*
      *Before in brief reported. Ed.)*
*Night closed in about the Den*
   *Murky and lowering. Ere long, chill rains.*
*A night not soon to be forgot,*
   *Reviving old rheumatic pains*
*And longings for a cot.*
   *No blankets, overcoats, or tents.*

*Coats thrown aside on the warm march here—*
*We looked not then for changeful cheer;*
*Tents, coats, and blankets too much care.*
  *No fires; a fire a mark presents;*
  *Near by, the tree shows bullet-dents.*
*Rations were eaten cold and raw.*
  *The men well soaked, came snow; and more—*
*A midnight sally. Small sleeping done—*
      *But such is war;*
*No matter, we'll have Fort Donelson.*


              "Ugh! Ugh!
'Twill drag along—drag along,"
Growled a cross patriot in the throng,
His battered umbrella like an ambulance-cover
Riddled with bullet-holes, spattered all over.
"Hurrah for Grant!" cried a stripling shrill;
Three urchins joined him with a will,
And some of taller stature cheered.
Meantime a Copperhead passed; he sneered.
  "Win or lose," he pausing said,
"Caps fly the same; all boys, mere boys;
Any thing to make a noise.
  Like to see the list of the dead;
These *'craven Southerners'* hold out;
Ay, ay, they'll give you many a bout."
  "We'll beat in the end, sir,"
Firmly said one in staid rebuke,
A solid merchant, square and stout.
  "And do you think it that way tend, sir?"
Asked the lean Copperhead, with a look
Of splenetic pity. "Yes, I do."
His yellow death's head the croaker shook:
"The country's ruined, that I know."
A shower of broken ice and snow,
  In lieu of words, confuted him;
They saw him hustled round the corner go,
  And each by-stander said—Well suited him.

Next day another crowd was seen
In the dark weather's sleety spleen.
Bald-headed to the storm came out
A man, who, 'mid a joyous shout,
Silently posted this brief sheet:

GLORIOUS VICTORY OF THE FLEET!

FRIDAY'S GREAT EVENTS!

THE ENEMY'S WATER-BATTERIES BEAT!

WE SILENCED EVERY GUN!

THE OLD COMMODORE'S COMPLIMENTS SENT
PLUMP INTO DONELSON!

"Well, well, go on!" exclaimed the crowd
To him who thus much read aloud.
"That's all," he said. "What! nothing more?"
"Enough for a cheer, though—hip, hurrah!
"But here's old Baldy come again—
"More news!"—And now a different strain.

*(Our own reporter a dispatch compiles,*
    *As best he may, from varied sources.)*

*Large re-enforcements have arrived—*
    *Munitions, men, and horses—*
*For Grant, and all debarked, with stores.*

    *The enemy's field-works extend six miles—*
*The gate still hid; so well contrived.*
*Yesterday stung us; frozen shores*
    *Snow-clad, and through the drear defiles*

*And over the desolate ridges blew*
*A Lapland wind.*
                    *The main affair*
    *Was a good two hours' steady fight*

Between our gun-boats and the Fort.
  The Louisville's wheel was smashed outright.
A hundred-and-twenty-eight-pound ball
Came planet-like through a starboard port,
Killing three men, and wounding all
The rest of that gun's crew,
(The captain of the gun was cut in two);
Then splintering and ripping went—
Nothing could be its continent.
  In the narrow stream the Louisville,
Unhelmed, grew lawless; swung around,
  And would have thumped and drifted, till
All the fleet was driven aground,
But for the timely order to retire.

Some damage from our fire, 'tis thought,
Was done the water-batteries of the Fort.

Little else took place that day,
  Except the field artillery in line
Would now and then—for love, they say—
      Exchange a valentine.

The old sharpshooting going on.
Some plan afoot as yet unknown;
So Friday closed round Donelson.

LATER.
        Great suffering through the night—
A stinging one. Our heedless boys
  Were nipped like blossoms. Some dozen
  Hapless wounded men were frozen.
  During day being struck down out of sight,
And help-cries drowned in roaring noise,
They were left just where the skirmish shifted—
Left in dense underbrush snow-drifted.
Some, seeking to crawl in crippled plight,
So stiffened—perished
                        Yet in spite
Of pangs for these, no heart is lost.

*Hungry, and clothing stiff with frost,*
*Our men declare a nearing sun*
*Shall see the fall of Donelson.*
  *And this they say, yet not disown*
*The dark redoubts round Donelson,*
    *And ice-glazed corpses, each a stone—*
      *A sacrifice to Donelson;*
*They swear it, and swerve not, gazing on*
*A flag, deemed black, flying from Donelson.*
*Some of the wounded in the wood*
  *Were cared for by the foe last night,*
*Though he could do them little needed good,*
  *Himself being all in shivering plight.*
*The rebel is wrong, but human yet;*
*He's got a heart, and thrusts a bayonet.*
*He gives us battle with wondrous will—*
*This bluff's a perverted Bunker Hill.*

The stillness stealing through the throng
The silent thought and dismal fear revealed;
          They turned and went,
        Musing on right and wrong
        And mysteries dimly sealed—
Breasting the storm in daring discontent;
The storm, whose black flag showed in heaven,
As if to say no quarter there was given
        To wounded men in wood,
  Or true hearts yearning for the good—
All fatherless seemed the human soul.
But next day brought a bitterer bowl—
  On the bulletin-board this stood:
  *Saturday morning at 3 A. M.*
    *A stir within the Fort betrayed*
  *That the rebels were getting under arms;*
    *Some plot these early birds had laid.*
  *But a lancing sleet cut him who stared*
  *Into the storm. After some vague alarms,*
  *Which left our lads unscared,*
  *Out sallied the enemy at dim of dawn,*
    *With cavalry and artillery, and went*
    *In fury at our environment.*

*Under cover of shot and shell*
 *Three columns of infantry rolled on,*
 *Vomited out of Donelson—*
*Rolled down the slopes like rivers of hell,*
 *Surged at our line, and swelled and poured*
*Like breaking surf. But unsubmerged*
 *Our men stood up, except where roared*
*The enemy through one gap. We urged*
*Our all of manhood to the stress,*
*But still showed shattered in our desperateness.*
  *Back set the tide,*
*But soon afresh rolled in;*
 *And so it swayed from side to side—*
*Far batteries joining in the din,*
*Though sharing in another fray—*
 *Till all became an Indian fight,*
*Intricate, dusky, stretching far away,*
*Yet not without spontaneous plan*
 *However tangled showed the plight:*
*Duels all over 'tween man and man,*
*Duels on cliff-side, and down in ravine,*
 *Duels at long range, and bone to bone;*
*Duels every where flitting and half unseen,*
 *Only by courage good as their own,*
*And strength outlasting theirs,*
 *Did our boys at last drive the rebels off.*
*Yet they went not back to their distant lairs*
 *In strong-hold, but loud in scoff*
*Maintained themselves on conquering ground—*
*Uplands; built works, or stalked around.*
*Our right wing bore this onset. Noon*
*Brought calm to Donelson.*


The reader ceased; the storm beat hard;
 'Twis day, but the office-gas was lit;
Nature retained her sulking-fit,
 In her hand the shard.
Flitting faces took the hue
Of that washed bulletin-board in view,
And seemed to bear the public grief
As private, and uncertain of relief;

Yea, many an earnest heart was won,
　　As broodingly he plodded on,
To find in himself some bitter thing,
Some hardness in his lot as harrowing
　　　　　　As Donelson.
That night the board stood barren there,
　　Oft eyed by wisful people passing,
　　Who nothing saw but the rain-beads chasing
Each other down the wafered square,
As down some storm-beat grave-yard stone.
But next day showed—

MORE NEWS LAST NIGHT

STORY OF SATURDAY AFTERNOON

VICISSITUDES OF THE WAR

*　　The damaged gun-boats can't wage fight*
*For days; so says the Commodore.*
*Thus no diversion can be had.*
*Under a sunless sky of lead*
*　　Our grim-faced boys in blackened plight*
*Gaze toward the ground they held before,*
*And then on Grant. He marks their mood,*
*·And hails it, and will turn the same to good.*
*Spite all that they have undergone,*
*Their desperate hearts are set upon*
*This winter fort, this stubborn fort,*
*This castle of the last resort,*
*　　　　　This Donelson.*

*1 P.M.*
*　　　　　　　　An order given*
*　　Requires withdrawal from the front*
*Of regiments that bore the brunt*
*Of regiments that bore the brunt*
*Are being replaced by fresh, strong men.*
*Great vigilance in the foreman's Den;*
*He snuffs the stormers. Need it is*
*That for that fell assault of his,*

*That rout inflicted, and self-scorn—*
*Immoderate in noble natures, torn*
*By sense of being through slackness overborne—*
*The rebel be given a quick return:*
*The kindest face looks now half stern.*
*Balked of their prey in airs that freeze,*
*Some fierce ones glare like savages.*
*And yet, and yet, strange moments are—*
*Well—blood, and tears, and anguished War!*
*The morning's battle-ground is seen*
    *In lifted glades, like meadows rare;*
    *The blood-drops on the snow-crust there*
*Like clover in the white-weed show—*
    *Flushed fields of death, that call again—*
    *Call to our men, and not in vain,*
*For that way must the stormers go.*

*3 P.M.*
                    *The work begins.*
*Light drifts of men thrown forward, fade*
    *In skirmish-line along the slope,*
*Where some dislodgments must be made*
    *Ere the stormer with the strong-hold cope.*

*Lew Wallace, moving to retake*
*The heights late lost—*
                    *(Herewith a break,*
    *Storms at the West derange the wires.*
    *Doubtless, ere morning, we shall hear*
    *The end; we look for news to cheer—*
    *Let Hope fan all her fires.)*

Next day in large bold hand was seen
The closing bulletin:

        VICTORY!
            *Our troops have retrieved the day*
        *By one grand surge along the line;*
        *The spirit that urged them was divine.*
            *The first works flooded, naught could stay*
        *The stormers: on! still on!*

*Bayonets for Donelson!*
*Over the ground that morning lost*
*Rolled the blue billows, tempest-tossed,*
*Following a hat on the point of a sword.*
*Spite shell and round-shot, grape and cannister,*
*Up they climbed without rail or banister—*
*Up the steep hill-sides long and broad*
*Driving the rebel deep within his works.*
*'Tis nightfall; not an enemy lurks*
*In sight. The chafing men*
*Fret for more fight:*
*"To-night, to-night let us take the Den!"*
*But night is treacherous, Grant is wary;*
*Of brave blood be a little chary.*
*Patience! the Fort is good as won;*
*To-morrow, and into Donelson.*

LATER AND LAST.
THE FORT IS OURS.
*A flag came out at early morn*
*Bringing surrender. From their towers*
*Floats out the banner late their scorn.*
*In Dover, hut and house are full*
*Of rebels dead or dying.*
*The National flag is flying*
*From the crammed court-house pinnacle.*
*Great boat-loads of our wounded go*
*To-day to Nashville. The sleet-winds blow;*
*But all is right: the fight is won,*
*The winter-fight for Donelson.*
*Hurrah!*
*The spell of old defeat is broke,*
*The habit of victory begun;*
*Grant strikes the war's first sounding stroke*
*At Donelson.*
*For lists of killed and wounded, see*
*The morrow's dispatch: to-day 'tis victory.*

The man who read this to the crowd
Shouted as the end he gained;

And though the unflagging tempest rained,
    They answered him aloud.
And hand grasped hand, and glances met
In happy triumph; eyes grew wet.
O, to the punches brewed that night
Went little water. Windows bright
Beamed rosy on the sleet without,
And from the deep street came the frequent shout;
While some in prayer, as these in glee,
Blessed heaven for the winter-victory.
But others were who wakeful laid
    In midnight beds, and early rose,
      And, feverish in the foggy snows,
      Snatched the damp paper—wife and maid.
    The death-list like a river flows
      Down the pale sheet,
And there the whelming waters meet.

    Ah, God! may Time with happy haste
    Bring wail and triumph to a waste,
      And war be done
    The battle flag-staff fall altwart
    The curs'd ravine, and wither; naught
      Be left of trench or gun;
    The bastion, let it ebb away,
    Washed with the river bed; and Day
      In vain seek Donelson.

# STEPHEN CRANE

## *The Red Badge of Courage*

# 1

THE COLD PASSED reluctantly from the earth, and the retiring fogs revealed an army stretched out on the hills, resting. As the landscape changed from brown to green, the army awakened, and began to tremble with eagerness at the noise of rumors. It cast its eyes upon the roads, which were growing from long troughs of liquid mud to proper thoroughfares. A river, amber-tinted in the shadow of its banks, purled at the army's feet; and at night, when the stream had become of a sorrowful blackness, one could see across it the red, eyelike gleam of hostile camp fires set in the low brows of distant hills.

Once a certain tall soldier developed virtues and went resolutely to wash a shirt. He came flying back from a brook waving his garment banner-like. He was swelled with a tale he had heard from a reliable friend, who had heard it from a truthful cavalryman, who had heard it from his trustworthy brother, one of the orderlies at division headquarters. He adopted the important air of a herald in red and gold.

"We're goin' t' move t'-morrah—sure," he said pompously to a group in the company street. "We're goin' 'way up the river, cut across, an' come around in behint 'em."

To his attentive audience he drew a loud and elaborate plan of a very brilliant campaign. When he had finished, the blue-clothed men scattered into small arguing groups between the rows of squat brown huts. A negro teamster who had been dancing upon a cracker box with the hilarious encouragement of twoscore soldiers was deserted. He sat mournfully down. Smoke drifted lazily from a multitude of quaint chimneys.

"It's a lie! that's all it is—a thunderin' lie!" said another private loudly. His smooth face was flushed, and his hands were thrust sulkily into his trousers' pockets. He took the matter as an affront to him. "I don't believe the derned old army's every going to move. We're set. I've got ready to move eight times in the last two weeks, and we ain't moved yet."

The tall soldier felt called upon to defend the truth of a rumor he himself had introduced. He and the loud one came near to fighting over it.

A corporal began to swear before the assemblage. He had just put a costly board floor in his house, he said. During the early spring he had refrained from adding extensively to the comfort of his environment because he had felt that the army might start on the march at any moment. Of late, however, he had been impressed that they were in a sort of eternal camp.

Many of the men engaged in a spirited debate. One outlined in a peculiarly lucid manner all the plans of the commanding general. He was opposed by men who advocated that there were other plans of campaign. They clamored at each other, numbers making futile bids for the popular attention. Meanwhile, the soldier who had fetched the rumor bustled about with much importance. He was continually assailed by questions.

"What's up, Jim?"

"Th' army's goin' t' move."

"Ah, what yeh talkin' about? How yeh know it is?"

"Well, yeh kin b'lieve me er not, jest as yeh like. I don't care a hang. [I tell yeh what I know an' yeh kin take it er leave it. Suit yourselves. It don't make no different t' me.]"

There was much food for thought in the manner in which he replied. He came near to convincing them by disdaining to produce proofs. They grew much excited over it.

There was a youthful private who listened with eager ears to the words of the tall soldier and to the varied comments of his comrades. After receiving a fill of discussions concerning marches and attacks, he went to his hut and crawled through an intricate hole that served it as a door. He wished to be alone with some new thoughts that had lately come to him.

He lay down on a wide bunk that stretched across the end of the room. In the other end, cracker boxes were made to serve as furniture. They were grouped about the fireplace. A picture from an illustrated weekly was upon the log walls, and three rifles were paralleled on pegs. Equipments hung on handy projections, and some tin dishes lay upon a small pile of firewood. A folded tent was serving as a roof. The sunlight, without, beating upon it, made it glow a light yellow shade. A small window shot an oblique square of whiter light upon the cluttered floor. The smoke from the fire at times neglected the clay chimney and wreathed into the room, and this flimsy chimney of clay and sticks made endless threats to set ablaze the whole establishment.

The youth was in a little trance of astonishment. So they were at last going to fight. On the morrow, perhaps, there would be a battle, and he would be in it. For a time he was obliged to labor to make himself believe. He could not accept with assurance an omen that he was about to mingle in one of those great affairs of the earth.

He had, of course, dreamed of battles all his life—of vague and bloody conflicts that had thrilled him with their sweep and fire. In visions he had seen himself in many struggles. He had imagined peoples secure in the shadow of his eagle-eyed prowess. But awake he had regarded battles as crimson blotches on the pages of the past. He had put them as things of the bygone with his thought-images of heavy crowns and high castles. There was a portion of the world's history which he had regarded as the time of wars, but it, he thought, had been long gone over the horizon and had disappeared for ever.

From his home his youthful eyes had looked upon the war in his own country with distrust. It must be some sort of a play affair. He had long despaired of witnessing a Greek like struggle. Such would be no more, he had said. Men were better, or more timid. Secular and religious education had effaced the throat-grappling instinct, or else firm finance held in check the passions.

He had burned several times to enlist. Tales of great movements shook the land. They might not be distinctly Homeric, but there seemed to be much glory in them. He had read of marches, sieges, conflicts, and he had longed to see it all. His busy mind had drawn from him large pictures extravagant in color, lurid with breathless deeds.

But his mother had discouraged him. She had affected to look with some contempt upon the quality of his war ardor and patriotism. She could calmly seat herself, and with no apparent difficulty give him many hundreds of reasons why he was of vastly more importance on the farm than on the field of battle. She had had certain ways of expression that told him that her statements on the subject came from deep conviction. Moreover, on her side, was his belief that her ethical motive in the argument was impregnable.

At last, however, he had made firm rebellion against this yellow light thrown upon the color of his ambitions. The newspapers, the gossip of the village, his own picturing, had aroused him to an uncheckable degree. They were in truth fighting finely down there. Almost every day the newspapers printed accounts of a decisive victory.

One night, as he lay in bed, the winds had carried to him the clangoring of the church bell as some enthusiast jerked the rope

frantically to tell the twisted news of a great battle. This voice of the
people rejoicing in the night had made him shiver in a prolonged
ecstasy of excitement. Later, he had gone down to his mother's room
and had spoken thus: "Ma, I'm going to enlist."

"Henry, don't you be a fool," his mother had replied. She had then
covered her face with the quilt. There was an end to the matter for that
night.

Nevertheless, the next morning he had gone to a town that was near
his mother's farm and had enlisted in a company that was forming
there. When he had returned home his mother was milking the brindle
cow. Four others stood waiting. "Ma, I've enlisted," he had said to
her diffidently. There was a short silence. "The Lord's will be done,
Henry," she had finally replied, and had then continued to milk the
brindle cow.

When he had stood in the doorway with his soldier's clothes on his
back, and with the light of excitement and expectancy in his eyes
almost defeating the glow of regret for the home bonds, he had seen
two tears leaving their trails on his mother's scarred cheeks.

Still, she had disappointed him by saying nothing whatever about
returning with his shield or on it. He had privately primed himself for
a beautiful scene. He had prepared certain sentences which he thought
could be used with touching effect. But her words destroyed his plans.
She had doggedly peeled potatoes and addressed him as follows:
"You watch out, Henry, an' take good care of yerself in this here
fighting business—you watch out, an take good care of yerself. Don't
go a-thinkin' you can lick the hull rebel army at the start, because yeh
can't. Yer jest one little feller amongst a hull lot of others, and yeh've
got to keep quiet an' do what they tell yeh. I know how you are,
Henry.

"I've knet yeh eight pair of socks, Henery, and I've put in all yer
best shirts, because I want my boy to be jest as warm and comf'able as
anybody in the army. Whenever they get holes in 'em, I want yeh to
send 'em right-away back to me, so's I kin dern 'em.

"An' allus be careful an' choose yer comp'ny. There's lots of bad
men in the army, Henry. The army makes 'em wild, and they like
nothing better than the job of leading off a young feller like you, as
ain't never been away from home much and has allus had a mother,
an' a-learning 'em to drink and swear. Keep clear of them folks,
Henry. I don't want yeh to ever do anything, Henry, that yeh would be
'shamed to let me know about. Jest think as if I was a-watchin' yeh. If
yeh keep that in yer mind allus, I guess yeh'll come out about right.

"Young fellers in the army get awful careless in their ways, Henry. They're away f'm home and they don't have nobody to look after 'em. I'm 'feard fer yeh about that. Yeh ain't never been used to doing for yerself. So yeh must keep writing to me how yer clothes are lasting.

"Yeh must allus remember yer father, too, child, an' remember he never drunk a drop of licker in his life, and seldom swore a cross oath.

"I don't know what else to tell yeh, Henry, excepting that yeh must never do no shirking, child, on my account. If so be a time comes when yeh have to be kilt or do a mean thing, why, Henry, don't think of anything 'cept what's right, because there's many a woman has to bear up 'ginst sech things these times, and the Lord'll take keer of us all. Don't fergit to send your socks to me the minute they git holes in 'em, and here's a little Bible I want yeh to take along with yeh, Henry. I don't presume yeh'll be a-setting reading it all day long, child, ner nothin' like that. Many a time, yeh'll fergit yeh got it, I don't doubt. But there'll be many a time, too, Henry, when yeh'll be wanting advice, boy, and all like that, and there'll be nobody round, perhaps, to tell yeh things. Then if yeh take it out, boy, yeh'll find wisdom in it—wisdom in it, Henry—with little or no searching. Don't forgit about the socks and the shirts, child; and I've put a cup of blackberry jam with yer bundle, because I know yeh like it above all things. Good-by, Henry. Watch out, and be a good boy."

He had, or course, been impatient under the ordeal of this speech. It had not been quite what he expected, and he had borne it with an air of irritation. He departed feeling vague relief.

Still, when he had looked back from the gate, he had seen his mother kneeling among the potato parings. Her brown face, upraised, was stained with tears, and her spare form was quivering. He bowed his head and went on, feeling suddenly ashamed of his purposes.

From his home he had gone to the seminary to bid adieu to many schoolmates. They had thronged about him with wonder and admiration. He had felt the gulf now between them and had swelled with calm pride. He and some of his fellows who had donned blue were quite overwhelmed with privileges for all of one afternoon, and it had been a very delicious thing. They had strutted.

A certain light-haired girl had made vivacious fun at his martial spirit, but there was another and darker girl whom he had gazed at steadfastly, and he thought she grew demure and sad at sight of his blue and brass. As he had walked down the path between the rows of oaks, he had turned his head and detected her at a window watching his departure. As he perceived her, she had immediately begun to stare up through the high tree branches at the sky. He had seen a good deal of flurry and haste in her movement as she changed her atttitude. He often thought of it.

On the way to Washington his spirit had soared. The regiment was fed and caressed at station after station until the youth had believed that he must be a hero. There was a lavish expenditure of bread and cold meats, coffee, and pickles and cheese. As he basked in the smiles of the girls and was patted and complimented by the old men, he had felt growing within him the strength to do mighty deeds of arms.

After complicated journeyings with many pauses, there had come months of monotonous life in a camp. He had had the belief that real war was a series of death struggles with small time in between for sleep and meals; but since his regiment had come to the field the army had done little but sit still and try to keep warm.

He was brought then gradually back to his old ideas. Greek like struggles would be no more. Men were better, more timid. Secular and religious education had effaced the throat-grappling instinct, or else firm finance held in check the passions.

He had grown to regard himself merely as a part of a vast blue demonstration. His province was to look out, as far as he could, for his personal comfort. For recreation he would twiddle his thumbs and speculate on the thoughts which must agitate the minds of the generals. Also, he was drilled and drilled and reviewed, and drilled and drilled and reviewed.

The only foes he had seen were some pickets along the river bank. They were a sun-tanned, philosophical lot, who sometimes shot reflectively at the blue pickets. When reproached for this afterwards, they usually expressed sorrow, and swore by their gods that the guns had exploded without their permission. The youth, on guard duty one night, conversed across the stream with one of them. He was a slightly ragged man, who spat skilfully between his shoes and possessed a great fund of bland and infantile assurance. The youth like him personally.

"Yank," the other had informed him, "yer a right dum good feller." This sentiment, floating to him upon the still air, had made him temporarily regret war.

Various veterans had told him tales. Some talked of gray, be-whiskered hordes who were advancing with relentless curses, and chewing tobacco with unspeakable valor—tremendous bodies of fierce soldiery who were sweeping along like the Hung. Others spoke of tattered and eternally hungry men who fired despondent powders. "They'll charge through hell's fire an' brimstone t' git a holt on a haversack, an' sech stomachs ain't a-lastin' long," he was told. From the stories, the youth imagined the red, live bones sticking out through slits in the faded uniforms.

Still, he could not put a whole faith in veterans' tales, for recruits were their prey. They talked much of smoke, fire, and blood, but he could not tell how much might be lies. They persistently yelled "Fresh fish!" at him, and were in no wise to be trusted.

However, he perceived now that it did not greatly matter what kind of soldiers he was going to fight, so long as they fought, which fact no one disputed. There was a more serious problem. He lay in his bunk pondering upon it. He tried to mathematically prove to himself that he would not run from a battle.

Previously he had never felt obliged to wrestle too seriously with this question. In his life he had taken certain things for granted, never challenging his belief in ultimate success, and bothering little about means and roads. But here he was confronted with a thing of moment. It had suddenly appeared to him that perhaps in a battle he might run. He was forced to admit that as far as war was concerned he knew nothing of himself.

A sufficient time before he would have allowed the problem to kick its heels at the outer portals of his mind, but now he felt compelled to give serious attention to it.

A little panic-fear grew in his mind. As his imagination went forward to a fight, he saw hideous possibilities. He contemplated the lurking menaces of the future, and failed in an effort to see himself standing stoutly in the midst of them. He recalled his visions of broken-bladed glory, but in the shadow of the impending tumult he suspected them to be impossible pictures.

He sprang from the bunk and began to pace nervously to and fro. "Good Lord, what's th' matter with me?" he said aloud.

He felt that in this crisis his laws of life were useless. Whatever he had learned of himself was here of no avail. He was an unknown quantity. He saw that he would again be obliged to experiment as he had in early youth. He must accumulate information of himself, and meanwhile he resolved to remain close upon his guard lest those qualities of which he knew nothing should everlastingly disgrace him. "Good Lord!" he repeated in dismay.

After a time the tall soldier slid dexterously through the hole. The loud private followed. They were wrangling.

"That's all right," said the tall soldier as he entered. He waved his hand expressively. "You can believe me or not, jest as you like. All you got to do is to sit down and wait as quiet as you can. Then pretty soon you'll find out I was right."

His comrade grunted stubbornly. For a moment he seemed to be searching for a formidable reply. Finally he said: "Well, you don't know everything in the world, do you?"

"Didn't say I knew everything in the world," retorted the other sharply. He began to stow various articles snugly into his knapsack.

The youth, pausing in his nervous walk, looked down at the busy figure. "Going to be a battle, sure, is there, Jim?" he asked.

"Of course there is," replied the tall soldier. "Of course there is. You jest wait 'til to-morrow, and you'll see one of the biggest battles ever was. You jest wait."

"Thunder!" said the youth.

"Oh, you'll see fighting this time, my boy, what'll be regular out-and-out fighting," added the tall soldier, with the air of a man who is about to exhibit a battle for the benefit of his friends.

"Huh!" said the loud one from a corner.

"Well," remarked the youth, "like as not this story'll turn out jest like them others did."

"Not much it won't," replied the tall soldier, exasperated. "Not much it won't. Didn't the cavalry all start this morning?" He glared about him. No one denied his statement. "The cavalry started this morning," he continued. "They say there ain't hardly any cavalry left in camp. They're going to Richmond, or some place, while we fight all the Johnnies. It's some dodge like that. The regiment's got orders, too. A feller what seen 'em go to headquarters told me a little while ago. And they're raising blazes all over camp—anybody can see that."

"Shucks!" said the loud one.

The youth remained silent for a time. At last he spoke to the tall soldier. "Jim!"

"What?"

"How do you think the reg'ment'll do?"

"Oh, they'll fight all right, I guess, after they once get into it," said the other, with cold judgment. He made a fine use of the third person. "There's been heaps of fun poked at 'em because they're new, of course, and all that; but they'll fight all right, I guess."

"Think any of the boys'll run?" persisted the youth.

"Oh, there may be few of 'em run, but there's them kind in very regiment, 'specially when they first goes under fire," said the other in a tolerant way. "Of course it might happen that the hull kit-and-boodle might start and run, if some big fighting came first-off, and then again they might stay and fight like fun. But you can't bet on nothing. Of course they ain't never been under fire yet, and it ain't likely they'll lick the hull rebel army all-to-oncet the first time; but I think they'll fight better than some, if worse than others. That's the way I figger. They call the reg'ment 'Fresh fish' and everything; but the boys come of good stock, and most of 'em'll fight like sin after they oncet git shootin'," he added, with a mighty emphasis on the last four words.

"Oh, you think you know——" began the loud soldier with scorn.

The other turned savagely upon him. They had a rapid altercation, in which they fastened upon each other various strange epithets.

The youth at last interrupted them. "Did you ever think you might run yourself, Jim?" he asked. On concluding the sentence he laughed as if he had meant to aim a joke. The loud soldier also giggled.

The tall private wave his hand. "Well," said he profoundly, "I've thought it might get too hot for Jim Conklin in some of them scrimmages, and if a whole lot of the boys started and run, why, I s'pose I'd start and run. And if I once started to run, I'd run like the devil, and no mistake. But if everybody was a-standing and a-fighting, why, I'd stand and fight. Be jiminey, I would. I'll bet on it."

"Huh!" said the loud one.

The youth of this tale felt gratitude for these words of his comrade. He had feared that all of the untried men possessed a great and correct confidence. He now was in a measure reassured.

## 2

THE NEXT MORNING the youth discovered that his tall comrade had been the fast-flying messenger of a mistake. There was much scoffing at the latter by those who had yesterday been firm adherents of his views, and there was even a little sneering by men who had never believed the rumor. The tall one fought with a man from Chatfield Corners and beat him severely.

The youth felt, however, that his problem was in no wise lifted from him. There was, on the contrary, an irritating prolongation. The tale had created in him a great concern for himself. Now, with the newborn question in his mind, he was compelled to sink back into his old place as part of a blue demonstration.

For days he made ceaseless calculations, but they were all wondrously unsatisfactory. He found that he could establish nothing. He finally concluded that the only way to prove himself was to go into the blaze, blood, and danger, even as a chemist requires this, that, and the other. So he fretted for an opportunity.

Meanwhile he continually tried to measure himself by his comrades. The tall soldier, for one, gave him some assurance. This man's serene unconcern dealt him a measure of confidence, for he had known him since childhood, and from his intimate knowledge he did not see how he could be capable of anything that was beyond him, the youth. Still, he thought that his comrade might be mistaken about himself. Or, on the other hand, he might be a man heretofore doomed to peace and obscurity, but, in reality, made to shine in war.

The youth would have liked to have discovered another who suspected himself. A sympathetic comparison of mental notes would have been a joy to him.

He occasionally tried to fathom a comrade with seductive sentences. He looked about to find men in the proper mood. All attempts failed to bring forth any statement which looked in any way like a confession to those doubts which he privately acknowledged in himself. He was afraid to make an open declaration of his concern, because he dreaded to place some unscrupulous confidant upon the high plane of the unconfessed from which elevation he could be derided.

In regard to his companions his mind wavered between two opinions, according to his mood. Sometimes he inclined to believing them all heroes. In fact, he usually admitted in secret the superior development of the higher qualities in others. He could conceive of men going very insignificantly about the world bearing a load of courage unseen, and although he had known many of his comrades through boyhood, he began to fear that his judgment of them had been blind. Then, in other moments, he flouted these theories, and assured himself that his fellows were all privately wondering and quaking.

His emotions made him feel strange in the presence of men who talked excitedly of a prospective battle as of a drama they were about to witness, with nothing but eagerness and curiosity apparent in their faces. It was often that he suspected them to be liars.

He did not pass such thoughts without severe condemnation of himself. He dinned reproaches at times. He was convicted by himself of many shameful crimes against the gods of traditions.

In his great anxiety his heart was continually clamoring at what he considered the intolerable slowness of the generals. They seemed content to perch tranquilly on the river bank, and leave him bowed down by the weight of a great problem. He wanted it settled forthwith. He could not long bear such a load, he said. Sometimes his anger at the commanders reached an acute stage, and he grumbled about the camp like a veteran.

One morning, however, he found himself in the ranks of his prepared regiment. The men were whispering speculations and recounting the old rumors. In the gloom before the break of the day their uniforms glowed a deep purple hue. From across the river the red eyes were still peering. In the eastern sky there was a yellow patch like a rug laid for the feet of the coming sun; and against it, black and patternlike, loomed the gigantic figure of the colonel on a gigantic horse.

From off in the darkness came the trampling of feet. The youth could occasionally see dark shadows that moved like monsters. The regiments stood at rest for what seemed a long time. The youth grew impatient. It was unendurable the way these affairs were managed. He wondered how long they were to be kept waiting.

As he looked all about him and pondered upon the mystic gloom, he began to believe that at any moment the ominous distance might be aflare, and the rolling crashes of an engagement come to his ears. Staring once at the red eyes across the river, he conceived them to be growing larger, as the orbs of a row of dragons advancing. He turned toward the colonel and saw him lift his gigantic arm and calmly stroke his mustache.

At last he heard from along the road at the foot of the hill the clatter of a horse's galloping hoofs. It must be the coming of orders. He bent forward, scarce breathing. The exciting clickety-click, as it grew louder and louder, seemed to be beating upon his soul. Presently a horseman with jangling equipment drew rein before the colonel of the regiment. The two held a short, sharp-worded conversation. The men in the foremost ranks craned their necks.

As the horseman wheeled his animal and galloped away he turned to shout over his shoulder, "Don't forget that box of cigars!" The colonel mumbled in reply. The youth wondered what a box of cigars had to do with war.

A moment later the regiment went swinging off into the darkness. It was now like one of those moving monsters wending with many feet. The air was heavy, and cold with dew. A mass of wet grass, marched upon, rustled like silk.

There was an occasional flash and glimmer of steel from the backs of all these huge crawling reptiles. From the road came creakings and grumblings as some surly guns were dragged away.

The men stumbled along still muttering speculations. There was a subdued debate. Once a man fell down, and as he reached for his rifle a comrade, unseeing, trod upon his hand. He of the injured fingers swore bitterly and aloud. A low, tittering laugh went among his fellows.

Presently they passed into a roadway and marched forward with easy strides. A dark regiment moved before them, and from behind also came the tinkle of equipments on the bodies of marching men.

The rushing yellow of the developing day went on behind their backs. When the sunrays at last struck full and mellowingly upon the earth, the youth saw that the landscape was streaked with two long, thin, black columns which disappeared on the brow of a hill in front, and rearward vanished in a wood. They were like two serpents crawling from the cavern of the night.

The river was not in view. The tall soldier burst into praises of what he thought to be his powers of perception.

Some of the tall one's companions cried with emphasis that they, too, had evolved the same thing, and they congratulated themselves upon it. But there were others who said that the tall one's plan was not the true one at all. They persisted with other theories. There was a vigorous discussion.

The youth took no part in them. As he walked along in careless line he was engaged with his own eternal debate. He could not hinder himself from dwelling upon it. He was despondent and sullen, and threw shifting glances about him. He looked ahead, often expecting to hear from the advance the rattle of firing.

But the long serpents crawled slowly from hill to hill without bluster of smoke. A dun-colored cloud of dust floated away to the right. The sky overhead was of a fairy blue.

The youth studied the faces of his companions, ever on the watch to detect kindred emotions. He suffered disappointment. Some ardor of the air which was causing the veteran commands to move with glee—almost with song—had infected the new regiment. The men began to speak of victory as of a thing they knew. Also, the tall soldier received his vindication. They were certainly going to come around in behind the enemy. They expressed commiseration for that part of the army which had been left upon the river bank, felicitating themselves upon being a part of a blasting host.

The youth, considering himself as separated from the others, was saddened by the blithe and merry speeches that went from rank to rank. The company wags all made their best endeavors. The regiment tramped to the tune of laughter.

The blatant soldier often convulsed whole files by his biting sarcasms aimed at the tall one.

And it was not long before all the men seemed to forget their mission. Whole brigades grinned in unison, and regiments laughed.

A rather fat soldier attempted to pilfer a horse from a dooryard. He planned to load his knapsack upon it. He was escaping with his prize when a young girl rushed from the house and grabbed the animal's mane. There followed a wrangle. The young girl, with pink cheeks and shining eyes, stood like a dauntless statue.

The observant regiment, standing at rest in the roadway, whooped at once, and entered whole-souled upon the side of the maiden. The men became so engrossed in this affair that they entirely ceased to remember their own large war. They jeered the piratical private, and called attention to various defects in his personal appearance; and they were wildly enthusiastic in support of the young girl.

To her, from some distance, came bold advice, "Hit him with a stick."

There were crows and catcalls showered upon him when he retreated without the horse. The regiment rejoiced at his downfall. Loud and vociferous congratulations were showered upon the maiden, who stood panting and regarding the troops with defiance.

At nightfall the column broke into regimental pieces, and the fragments went into the fields to camp. Tents sprang up like strange plants. Camp fires, like red, peculiar blossoms, dotted the night.

The youth kept from intercourse with his companions as much as circumstances would allow him. In the evening he wandered a few paces into the gloom. From this little distance the many fires, with the black forms of men passing to and fro before the crimson rays, made weird and satanic effects.

He lay down in the grass. The blades pressed tenderly against his cheek. The moon had been lighted and was hung in a treetop. The liquid stillness of the night enveloping him made him feel vast pity for himself. There was a caress in the soft winds; and the whole mood of the darkness, he thought, was one of sympathy for himself in his distress.

He wished, without reserve, that he was at home again making the endless rounds from the house to the barn, from the barn to the house. He remembered he had often cursed the brindle cow and her mates, and had sometimes flung milking stools. But, from his present point of view, there was a halo of happiness about each of their heads, and he would have sacrificed all the brass buttons on the continent to have been enabled to return to them. He told himself that he was not formed for a soldier. And he mused seriously upon the radical differences between himself and those men who were dodging imp-like around the fires.

As he mused thus he heard the rustle of grass, and, upon turning his head, discovered the loud soldier. He called out, "Oh, Wilson!"

The latter approached and looked down. "Why hello, Henry; is it you? What you doing here?"

"Oh, thinking," said the youth.

The other sat down and carefully lighted his pipe. "You're getting blue, my boy. You're looking thundering peeked. What the dickens is wrong with you?"

"Oh, nothing," said the youth.

The loud soldier launched then into the subject of the anticipated fight. "Oh, we've got 'em now!" As he spoke his boyish face was wreathed in a gleeful smile, and his voice had an exultant ring. "We've got 'em now. At last, by the eternal thunders, we'll lick 'em good!"

"If the truth was known," he added more soberly, "*they've* licked *us* about every clip up to now; but this time—this time—we'll lick 'em good!"

"I thought you was objecting to this march a little while ago," said the youth coldly.

"Oh, it wasn't that," explained the other. "I don't mind marching, if there's going to be fighting at the end of it. What I hate is this getting moved here and moved there, with no good coming of it, as far as I can see, excepting sore feet and damned short rations."

"Well, Jim Conklin says we'll get aplenty of fighting this time."

"He's right for once, I guess, though I can't see how it come. This time we're in for a big battle, and we've got the best end of it, certain sure. Gee rod! how we will thump 'em!"

He arose and began to pace to and fro excitedly. The thrill of his enthusiasm made him walk with an elastic step. He was sprightly, vigorous, fiery in his belief in success. He looked into the future with clear, proud eye, and he swore with the air of an old soldier.

The youth watched him for a moment in silence. When he finally spoke his voice was as bitter as dregs. "Oh, you're going to do great things I s'pose!"

The loud soldier blew a thoughtful cloud of smoke from his pipe. "Oh, I don't know," he remarked with dignity; "I don't know. I s'pose I'll do as well as the rest. I'm going to try like thunder." He evidently complimented himself upon the modesty of this statement.

"How do you know you won't run when the time comes?" asked the youth.

"Run?" said the loud one; "run?—of course not!" He laughed.

"Well," continued the youth. "lots of good-a-'nough men have thought they was going to do great things before the fight, but when the time come they skedaddled."

"Oh, that's all true, I s'pose," replied the other; "but I'm not going to skedaddle. The man that bets on my running will lose his money, that's all." He nodded confidently.

"Oh, shucks!" said the youth. "You ain't the bravest man in the world, are you?"

"No, I ain't," exclaimed the loud soldier indignantly; "and I didn't say I was the bravest man in the world, neither. I said I was going to do my share of fighting—that's what I said. And I am, too. Who are you, anyhow? You talk as if you thought you was Napoleon Bonaparte." He glared at the youth for a moment, and then strode away.

The youth called in a savage voice after his comrade: "Well, you needn't git mad about it!" But the other continued on his way and made no reply.

He felt alone in space when his injured comrade had disappeared. His failure to discover any mite of resemblance in their view points made him more miserable than before. No one seemed to be wrestling with such a terrific personal problem. He was a mental outcast.

He went slowly to his tent and stretched himself on a blanket by the side of the snoring tall soldier. In the darkness he saw visions of a thousand-tongued fear that would babble at his back and cause him to flee, while others were going coolly about their country's business. He admitted that he would not be able to cope with this monster. He felt that every nerve in his body would be an ear to hear the voices, while other men would remain stolid and deaf.

And as he sweated with the pain of these thoughts, he could hear low, serene sentences. "I'll bid five." "Make it six." "Seven." "Seven goes."

He stared at the red, shivering reflection of a fire on the white wall of his tent until, exhausted and ill from the monotony of his suffering, he fell asleep.

# 3

WHEN ANOTHER NIGHT came the columns, changed to purple streaks, filed across two pontoon bridges. A glaring fire wine-tinted the waters of the river. Its rays, shining upon the moving masses of troops, brought forth here and there sudden gleams of silver or gold. Upon the other shore a dark and mysterious range of hills was curved against the sky. The insect voices of the night sang solemnly.

After this crossing the youth assured himself that at any moment they might be suddenly and fearfully assaulted from the caves of the lowering woods. He kept his eyes watchfully upon the darkness.

But his regiment went unmolested to a camping place, and its soldiers slept the brave sleep of wearied men. In the morning they were routed out with early energy, and hustled along a narrow road that led deep into the forest.

It was during this rapid march that the regiment lost many of the marks of a new command.

The men had begun to count the miles upon their fingers, and they grew tired. "Sore feet an' damned short rations, that's all," said the loud soldier. There was perspiration and grumblings. After a time they began to shed their knapsacks. Some tossed them unconcernedly down; others hid them carefully, asserting their plans to return for them at some convenient time. Men extricated themselves from thick shirts. Presently few carried anything but their necessary clothing, blankets, haversacks, canteens, and arms and ammunition. "You can now eat and shoot," said the tall soldier to the youth. "That's all you want to do. What you want to do—carry a hotel?"

There was sudden change from the ponderous infantry of theory to the light and speedy infantry of practice. The regiment, relieved of a burden, received a new impetus. But there was much loss of valuable knapsacks, and, on the whole, very good shirts.

But the regiment was not yet veteran like in appearance. Veteran regiments in the army were likely to be very small aggregations of men. Once, when the command had first come to the field, some perambulating veterans, noting the length of their column, had accosted them thus: "Hey, fellers, what brigade is that?" And when the men had replied that they formed a regiment and not a brigade, the older soldiers had laughed, and said, "O Gawd!"

Also, there was too great a similarity in the hats. The hats of a regiment should properly represent the history of headgear for a period of years. And, moreover, there were no letters of faded gold speaking from the colors. They were new and beautiful, and the color-bearer habitually oiled the pole.

Presently the army again sat down to think. The odor of the peaceful pines was in the men's nostrils. The sounds of monotonous axe blows rang through the forest, and the insects, nodding upon their perches, crooned like old women. The youth returned to his theory of a blue demonstration.

One gray dawn, however, he was kicked in the leg by the tall soldier, and then, before he was entirely awake, he found himself running down a wood road in the midst of men who were panting from the first effects of speed. His canteen banged rhythmically upon his thigh, and his haversack bobbed softly. His musket bounded a trifle from his shoulder at each stride and made his cap feel uncertain upon his head.

He could hear the men whisper jerky sentences: "Say—what's all this—about?" "What th' thunder—we—skedaddlin' this way fer?" "Billie—keep off m' feet. Yeh run—like a cow." And the loud soldier's shrill voice could be heard: "What th' devil they in sich a hurry for?"

The youth thought the damp fog of early morning moved from the rush of a great body of troops. From the distance came a sudden spatter of firing.

He was bewildered. As he ran with his comrades he strenuously tried to think, but all he knew was that if he fell down those coming behind would tread upon him. All his faculties seemed to be needed to guide him over and past obstructions. He felt carried along by a mob.

The sun spread disclosing rays, and, one by one, regiments burst into view like armed men just born of the earth. The youth perceived that the time had come. He was about to be measured. For a moment he felt in the face of his great trial like a babe, and the flesh over his heart seemed very thin. He seized time to look about him calculatingly.

But he instantly saw that it would be impossible for him to escape from the regiment. It enclosed him. And there were iron laws of tradition and law on four sides. He was in a moving box.

As he perceived this fact it occurred to him that he had never wished to come to the war. He had not enlisted of his free will. He had been dragged by the merciless government. And now they were taking him out to be slaughtered.

The regiment slid down a bank and wallowed across a little stream. The mournful current moved slowly on, and from the water, shaded black, some white bubble eyes looked at the men.

As they climbed the hill on the farther side artillery began to boom. Here the youth forgot many things as he felt a sudden impulse of curiosity. He scrambled up the bank with a speed that could not be exceeded by a bloodthirsty man.

He expected a battle scene.

There were some little fields girted and squeezed by a forest. Spread over the grass and in among the tree trunks, he could see knots and waving lines of skirmishers who were running hither and thither and firing at the landscape. A dark battle line lay upon a sun struck clearing that gleamed orange color. A flag fluttered.

Other regiments floundered up the bank. The brigade was formed in line of battle, and after a pause started slowly through the woods in the rear of the receding skirmishers, who were continually melting into the scene to appear again farther on. They were always busy as bees, deeply absorbed in their little combats.

The youth tried to observe everything. He did not use care to avoid trees and branches, and his forgotten feet were constantly knocking against stones or getting entangled in briers. He was aware that these battalions with their commotions were woven red and startling into the gentle fabric of softened greens and browns. It looked to be a wrong place for a battlefield.

The skirmishers in advance fascinated him. Their shots into thickets and at distant and prominent trees spoke to him of tragedies— hidden, mysterious, solemn.

Once the line encountered the body of a dead soldier. He lay upon his back staring at the sky. He was dressed in an awkward suit of yellowish brown. The youth could see that the soles of his shoes had been worn to the thinness of writing paper, and from a great rent in one the dead foot projected piteously. And it was as if fate had betrayed the soldier. In death it exposed to his enemies that poverty which in life he had perhaps concealed from his friends.

The ranks opened covertly to avoid the corpse. The invulnerable dead man forced a way for himself. The youth looked keenly at the ashen face. The wind raised the tawny beard. It moved as if a hand were stroking it. He vaguely desired to walk around and around the body and stare; the impulse of the living to try to read in dead eyes the answer to the Question.

During the march the ardor which the youth had acquired when out of view of the field rapidly faded to nothing. His curiosity was quite easily satisfied. If an intense scene had caught him with its wild swing as he came to the top of the bank, he might have gone roaring on. This advance upon Nature was too calm. He had opportunity to reflect. He had time in which to wonder about himself and to attempt to probe his sensations.

Absurd ideas took hold upon him. He thought that he did not relish the landscape. It threatened him. A coldness swept over his back, and it is true that his trousers felt to him that they were no fit for his legs at all.

A house standing placidly in distant fields had to him an ominous look. The shadows of the woods were formidable. He was certain that in this vista there lurked fierce-eyed hosts. The swift thought came to him that the generals did not know what they were about. It was all a trap. Suddenly those close forests would bristle with rifle barrels. Iron like brigades would appear in the rear. They were all going to be sacrificed. The generals were stupids. The enemy would presently swallow the whole command. He glared about him, expecting to see the stealthy approach of his death.

He thought that he must break from the ranks and harangue his comrades. They must not all be killed like pigs; and he was sure it would come to pass unless they were informed of these dangers. The generals were idiots to send them marching into a regular pen. There was but one pair of eyes in the corps. He would step forth and make a speech. Shrill and passionate words came to his lips.

The line, broken into moving fragments by the ground, went calmly on through fields and woods. The youth looked at the men nearest him, and saw, for the most part, expressions of deep interest, as if they were investigating something that had fascinated them. One or two stepped with over valiant airs as if they were already plunged into war. Others walked as upon thin ice. The greater part of the untested men appeared quiet and absorbed. They were going to look at war, the red animal—war, the blood-swollen god. And they were deeply engrossed in this march.

As he looked the youth gripped his outcry at his throat. He saw that even if the men were tottering with fear they would laugh at his warning. They would jeer him, and, if practicable, pelt him with missiles. Admitting that he might be wrong, a frenzied declamation of the kind would turn him into a worm.

He assumed, then, the demeanor of one who knows that he is doomed alone to unwritten responsibilities. He lagged, with tragic glances at the sky. He was surprised presently by the young lieutenant of his company, who began heartily to beat him with a sword, calling out in a loud and insolent voice: "Come, young man, get up into the ranks there. No skulking'll do here." He mended his pace with suitable haste. And he hated the lieutenant, who had no appreciation of fine minds. He was a mere brute.

After a time the brigade was halted in the cathedral light of a forest. The busy skirmishers were still popping. Through the aisles of the wood could be seen the floating smoke from their rifles. Sometimes it went up in little balls, white and compact.

During this halt many men in the regiment began erecting tiny hills in front of them. They used stones, sticks, earth, and anything they thought might turn a bullet. Some built comparatively large ones, while others seemed content with little ones.

This procedure caused a discussion among the men. Some wished to fight like duellists, believing it to be correct to stand erect and be, from their feet to their foreheads, a mark. They said they scorned the devices of the cautious. But the others scoffed in reply, and pointed to the veterans on the flanks who were digging at the ground like terriers. In a short time there was quite a barricade along the regimental fronts. Directly, however, they were ordered to withdraw from that place.

This astounded the youth. He forgot his stewing over the advance movement. "Well, then, what did they march us out here for?" he demanded of the tall soldier. The latter with calm faith began a heavy explanation, although he had been compelled to leave a little protection of stones and dirt to which he had devoted much care and skill.

When the regiment was aligned in another position each man's regard for his safety caused another line of small entrenchments. They ate their noon meal behind a third one. They were moved from this one also. They were marched from place to place with apparent aimlessness.

The youth had been taught that a man became another being in a battle. He saw his salvation in such a change. Hence this waiting was an ordeal to him. He was in a fever of impatience. He considered that there was denoted a lack of purpose on the part of the generals. He began to complain to the tall soldier. "I can't stand this much longer," he cried. "I don't see what good it does to make us wear out our legs for nothin'." He wished to return to camp, knowing that this affair was a blue demonstration; or else to go into battle and discover that he had been a fool in his doubts, and was, in truth, a man of traditional courage. The strain of present circumstances he felt to be intolerable.

The philosophical tall soldier measured a sandwich of cracker and pork and swallowed it in a nonchalant manner. "Oh, I suppose we must go reconnoitering around the country jest to keep 'em from getting too close, or to develop 'em, or something."

"Huh!" said the loud soldier.

"Well," cried the youth, still fidgeting, "I'd rather do anything 'most than go tramping 'round the country all day doing no good to nobody and jest tiring ourselves out."

"So would I," said the loud soldier. "It ain't right. I tell you if anybody with any sense was a-runnin' this army it——"

"Oh, shut up!" roared the tall private. "You little fool. You little damn' cuss. You ain't had that there coat and them pants on for six months, and yet you talk as if——"

"Well, I wanta do some fighting anyway," interrupted the other. "I didn't come here to walk. I could 'ave walked to home—'round an' 'round the barn, if I jest wanted to walk."

The tall one, red-faced, swallowed another sandwich as if taking poison in despair.

But gradually, as he chewed, his face became again quiet and contented. He could not rage in fierce argument in the presence of such sandwiches. During his meals he always wore an air of blissful contemplation of the food he had swallowed. His spirit seemed then to be communing with the viands.

He accepted new environment and circumstance with great coolness, eating from his haversack at every opportunity. On the march he went along with the stride of a hunter, objecting to neither gait nor distance. And he had not raised his voice when he had been ordered away from three little protective piles of earth and stone, each of which had been an engineering feat worthy of being made sacred to the name of his grandmother.

In the afternoon the regiment went out over the same ground it had taken in the morning. The landscape then ceased to threaten the youth. He had been close to it and become familiar with it.

When, however, they began to pass into a new region, his old fears of stupidity and incompetence reassailed him, but this time he doggedly let them babble. He was occupied with his problem, and in his desperation he concluded that the stupidity did not greatly matter.

Once he thought he had concluded that it would be better to get killed directly and end his troubles. Regarding death thus out of the corner of his eye, he conceived it to be nothing but rest, and he was filled with a momentary astonishment that he should have made an extraordinary commotion over the mere matter of getting killed. He would die; he would go to some place where he would be understood. It was useless to expect appreciation of his profound and fine senses from such men as the lieutenant. He must look to the grave for comprehension.

The skirmish fire increased to a long clattering sound. With it was mingled far-away cheering. A battery spoke.

Directly the youth would see the skirmishers running. They were pursued by the sound of musketry fire. After a time the hot, dangerous flashes of the rifles were visible. Smoke clouds went slowly and insolently across the fields like observant phantoms. The din became crescendo, like the roar of an oncoming train.

A brigade ahead of them and on the right went into action with a rending roar. It was as if it had exploded. And thereafter it lay stretched in the distance behind a long gray wall, that one was obliged to look twice at to make sure that it was smoke.

The youth, forgetting his neat plan of getting killed, gazed spellbound. His eyes grew wide and busy with the action of the scene. His mouth was a little ways open.

Of a sudden he felt a heavy and sad hand laid upon his shoulder. Awakening from his trance of observation he turned and beheld the loud soldier.

"It's my first and last battle, old boy," said the latter, with intense gloom. He was quite pale, and his girlish lip was trembling.

"Eh?" murmured the youth in great astonishment.

"It's my first and last battle, old boy," continued the loud soldier. "Something tells me——"

"What?"

"I'm a gone coon this first time and—and I w-want you to take these here things—to—my—folks." He ended in a quavering sob of pity for himself. He handed the youth a little packet done up in a yellow envelope.

"Why, what the devil——" began the youth again.

But the other gave him a glance as from the depths of a tomb, and raised his limp hand in a prophetic manner and turned away.

# 4

THE BRIGADE WAS halted in the fringe of a grove. The men crouched among the trees and pointed their restless guns out at the fields. They tried to look beyond the smoke.

Out of this haze they could see running men. Some shouted information and gestured as they hurried.

The men of the new regiment watched and listened eagerly, while their tongues ran on in gossip of the battle. They mouthed rumors that had flown like birds out of the unknown.

"They say Perry has been driven in with big loss."

"Yes, Carrott went t' th' hospital. He said he was sick. That smart lieutenant is commanding 'G' Company. The' boys say they won't be under Carrott no more if they all have t' desert. They allus knew he was a——"

"Hannises' batt'ry is took."

"It ain't either. I saw Hannises' batt'ry off on th' left not more'n fifteen minutes ago."

"Well——"

"Th' general, he ses he is goin' t' take th' hull command of th'

304th when we go inteh action, an' then he ses we'll do sech fightin'
as never another one reg'ment done.''

"They say we're catchin' it over on th' left. They say th' enemy
driv' our line inteh a devil of a swamp an' took Hannises' batt'ry.''

"No sech thing. Hannises' batt'ry was 'long here 'bout a minute
ago.''

"That young Hasbrouck, he makes a good off'cer. He ain't afraid
'a nothin'.''

"I met one of th' 148th Maine boys an' he ses his brigade fit th' hull
rebel army fer four hours over on th' turnpike road an' killed about
five thousand of 'em. He ses one more sech fight as that an' th' war'll
be over.''

"Bill wasn't scared either. No, sir! It wasn't that. Bill ain't a-gittin'
scared easy. He was jest mad, that's what he was. When that feller
trod on his hand, he up an' sed that he was willin' t' give his hand t' his
country, but he be dumbed if he was goin' t' have every dumb
bushwhacker in th' kentry walkin' 'round on it. So he went t' th'
hospital disregardless of th' fight. Three fingers was crunched. Th'
dern doctor wanted t' amputate 'm, an' Bill, he raised a heluva row, I
hear. He's a funny feller.''

"Hear that what th' ol' colonel ses, boys? He ses he'll shoot the first
man what'll turn an' run.''

"He'd better try it. I'd like t' see him shoot at *me*.''

"He wants t' look fer his *own* self. He don't wanta go 'round talkin'
big.''

"They say Perry's division's a-givin' 'em thunder.''

"Ed Williams over in Company A, he ses the rebs 'll all drop their
guns an' run an' holler if we onct give 'em one good lickin'.''

"Oh, thunder, Ed Williams, what does he know? Ever since he got
shot at on picket he's been runnin' th' war.''

"Well, he——''

"Hear the news, boys? Corkright's crushed th' hull rebel right an'
captured two hull divisions. We'll be back in winter quarters by a
short cut t'-morrah.''

"I tell yeh I've been all over that there kentry where th' rebel right
is an' it's th' nastiest part th' rebel line. It's all mussed up with hills an'
little damn creeks. I'll bet m' shirt Corkright never harmed 'em down
there.''

"Well, he's a fighter an' if they could be licked, he'd lick 'em.''

The din in front swelled to a tremendous chorus. The youth and his
fellows were frozen to silence. They could see a flag that tossed in the
smoke angrily. Near it were the blurred and agitated forms of troops.

There came a turbulent stream of men across the fields. A battery changing positions at a frantic gallop scattered the stragglers right and left.

A shell screaming like a storm banshee went over the huddled heads of the reserves. It landed in the grove, and exploding redly flung the brown earth. There was a little shower of pine needles.

Bullets began to whistle among the branches and nip at the trees. Twigs and leaves came sailing down. It was as if a thousand axes, wee and invisible, were being wielded. Many of the men were constantly dodging and ducking their heads.

The lieutenant of the youth's company was shot in the hand. He began to swear so wondrously, that a nervous laugh went along the regimental line. The officer's profanity sounded conventional. It relieved the tightened senses of the new men. It was as if he had hit his fingers with a tack hammer at home.

He held the wounded member carefully away from his side so that the blood would not drip upon his trousers.

The captain of the company, tucking his sword under his arm, produced a handkerchief and began to bind with it the lieutenant's wound. And they disputed as to how the binding should be done.

The battle flag in the distance jerked about madly. It seemed to be struggling to free itself from an agony. The billowing smoke was filled with horizontal flashes.

Men running swiftly emerged from it. They grew in numbers until it was seen that the whole command was fleeing. The flag suddenly sank down as if dying. Its motion as it fell was a gesture of despair.

Wild yells came from behind the walls of smoke. A sketch in gray and red dissolved into a moblike body of men who galloped like wild horses.

The veteran regiments on the right and left of the 304th immediately began to jeer. With the passionate song of the bullets and the banshee shrieks of shells were mingled loud catcalls and bits of facetious advice concerning places of safety.

But the new regiment was breathless with horror. "Gawd! Saunders's got crushed!" whispered the man at the youth's elbow. They shrank back and crouched as if compelled to await a flood.

The youth shot a swift glance along the blue ranks of the regiment. The profiles were motionless, carven; and afterward he remembered that the color sergeant was standing with his legs apart, as if he expected to be pushed to the ground.

The following throng went whirling around the flank. Here and there were officers carried along in the stream like exasperated chips.

They were striking about them with their swords and with their left fists, punching every head they could reach. They cursed like highwaymen.

A mounted officer displayed the furious anger of a spoiled child. He raged with his head, his arms, and his legs.

Another, the commander of the brigade, was galloping about bawling. His hat was gone and his clothes were awry. He resembled a man who has come from bed to go to a fire. The hoofs of his horse often threatened the heads of the running men, but they scampered with singular fortune. In this rush they were apparently all deaf and blind. They heeded not the largest and longest of the oaths that were thrown at them from all directions.

Frequently over this tumult could be heard the grim jokes of the critical veterans; but the retreating men apparently were not even conscious of the presence of an audience.

The battle reflection that shone for an instant in the faces on the mad current made the youth feel that forceful hands from heaven would not have been able to have held him in place if he could have got intelligent control of his legs.

There was an appalling imprint upon these faces. The struggle in the smoke had pictured an exaggeration of itself on the bleached cheeks and in the eyes wild with one desire.

The sight of this stampede exerted a floodlike force that seemed able to drag sticks and stones and men from the ground. They of the reserves had to hold on. They grew pale and firm, and red and quaking.

The youth achieved one little thought in the midst of this chaos. The composite monster which had caused the other troops to flee had not then appeared. He resolved to get a view of it, and then, he thought he might very likely run better than the best of them.

## 5

THERE WERE MOMENTS of waiting. The youth thought of the village street at home before the arrival of the circus parade on a day in the spring. He remembered how he had stood, a small, thrillful boy, prepared to follow the dingy lady upon the white horse, or the band in its faded chariot. He saw the yellow road, the lines of expectant people, and the sober houses. He particularly remembered an old fellow who used to sit upon a cracker box in front of the store and feign to despise such exhibitions. A thousand details of color and form surged in his mind. The old fellow upon the cracker box appeared in middle prominence.

Some one cried, "Here they come!"

There was rustling and muttering among the men. They displayed a feverish desire to have every possible cartridge ready to their hands. The boxes were pulled around into various positions, and adjusted with great care. It was as if seven hundred new bonnets were being tried on.

The tall soldier, having prepared his rifle, produced a red handkerchief of some kind. He was engaged in knitting it about his throat with exquisite attention to its position, when the cry was repeated up and down the line in a muffled roar of sound.

"Here they come! Here they come!" Gun locks clicked.

Across the smoke-infested fields came a brown swarm of running men who were giving shrill yells. They came on, stooping and swinging their rifles at all angles. A flag, tilted forward, sped near the front.

As he caught sight of them the youth was momentarily startled by a though that perhaps his gun was not loaded. He stood trying to rally his faltering intellect so that he might recollect the moment when he had loaded, but he could not.

A hatless general pulled his dripping horse to a stand near the colonel of the 304th. He shook his fist in the other's face. "You've got to hold 'em back!" he shouted savagely; "you've got to hold 'em back!"

In his agitation the colonel began to stammer. "A-all r-right, General, all right, by Gawd! We-we'll do our—we-we'll d-d-do—do our best, General." The general made a passionate gesture and galloped away. The colonel, perchance to relieve his feelings, began to scold like a wet parrot. The youth, turning swiftly to make sure that the rear was unmolested, saw the commander regarding his men in a highly resentful manner, as if he regretted above everything his association with them.

The man at the youth's elbow was mumbling, as if to himself: "Oh, we're in for it now! oh, we're in for it now!"

The captain of the company had been pacing excitedly to and fro in the rear. He coaxed in schoolmistress fashion, as to a congregation of boys with primers. His talk was an endless repetition. "Reserve your fire, boys—don't shoot till I tell you—save your fire—wait till they get close up—don't be damned fools——"

Perspiration streamed down the youth's face, which was soiled like that of a weeping urchin. He frequently, with a nervous movement, wiped his eyes with his coat sleeve. His mouth was still a little way open.

He got the one glance at the foe-swarming field in front of him, and instantly ceased to debate the question of his piece being loaded. Before he was ready to begin—before he had announced to himself that he was about to fight—he threw the obedient, well-balanced rifle into position and fired a first wild shot. Directly he was working at his weapon like an automatic affair.

He suddenly lost concern for himself, and forgot to look at a menacing fate. He was not a man but a member. He felt that something of which he was a part—a regiment, an army, a cause, or a country—was in a crisis. He was welded into a common personality which was dominated by a single desire. For some moments he could not flee no more than a little finger can commit a revolution from a hand.

If he had thought the regiment was about to be annihilated, perhaps he could have amputated himself from it. But its noise gave him assurance. The regiment was like a firework that, once ignited, proceeds superior to circumstances until its blazing vitality fades. It wheezed and banged with a mighty power. He pictured the ground before it as strewn with the discomfited.

There was a consciousness always of the presence of his comrades about him. He felt the subtle battle brotherhood more potent even than the cause for which they were fighting. It was a mysterious fraternity born of the smoke and danger of death.

He was at a task. He was like a carpenter who has made many boxes, making still another box, only there was furious haste in his movements. He, in his thought, was careering off in other places, even as the carpenter who as he works whistles and thinks of his friend or his enemy, his home or a saloon. And these jolted dreams were never perfect to him afterward, but remained a mass of blurred shapes.

Presently he began to feel the effects of the war atmosphere—a blistering sweat, a sensation that his eyeballs were about to crack like hot stones. A burning roar filled his ears.

Following this came a red rage. He developed the acute exasperation of a pestered animal, a well-meaning cow worried by dogs. He had a mad feeling against his rifle, which could only be used against one life at a time. He wished to rush forward and strangle with his fingers. He craved a power that would enable him to make a world-sweeping gesture and brush all back. His impotency appeared to him, and made his rage into that of a driven beast.

Buried in the smoke of many rifles his anger was directed not so much against the men whom he knew were rushing toward him as against the swirling battle phantoms which were choking him, stuffing their smoke robes down his parched throat. He fought frantically for respite for his senses, for air, as a babe being smothered attacks the deadly blankets.

There was a blare of heated rage mingled with a certain expression of intentness on all faces. Many of the men were making low-toned noises with their mouths, and these subdued cheers, snarls, imprecations, prayers, made a wild, barbaric song that went as an undercurrent of sound, strange and chantlike, with the resounding chords of the war march. The man at the youth's elbow was babbling. In it there was something soft and tender like the monologue of a babe. The tall soldier was swearing in a loud voice. From his lips came a black procession of curious oaths. Of a sudden another broke out in a querulous way, like a man who has mislaid his hat. "Well, why don't they support us? Why don't they send supports? Do they think——"

The youth in his battle sleep heard this as one who dozes hears.

There was a singular absence of heroic poses. The men bending and surging in their haste and rage were in every impossible attitude. The steel ramrods clanked and clanged with incessant din as the men pounded them furiously into the hot rifle barrels. The flaps of the cartridge boxes were all unfastened, and bobbed idiotically with each movement. The rifles, once loaded, were jerked to the shoulder and fired without apparent aim into the smoke or at one of the blurred and shifting forms which upon the field before the regiment had been growing larger and larger like puppets under a magician's hands.

The officers, at their intervals, rearward, neglected to stand in picturesque attitudes. They were bobbing to and fro roaring directions and encouragements. The dimensions of their howls were extraordinary. They expended their lungs with prodigal wills. And often they nearly stood upon their heads in their anxiety to observe the enemy on the other side of the tumbling smoke.

The lieutenant of the youth's company had encountered a soldier who had fled screaming at the first volley of his comrades. Behind the lines these two were acting a little isolated scene. The man was blubbering and staring with sheeplike eyes at the lietuenant, who had seized him by the collar and was pommelling him. He drove him back into the ranks with many blows. The soldier went mechanically, dully, with his animal-like eyes upon the officer. Perhaps there was to him a divinity expressed in the voice of the other—stern, hard, with no reflection of fear in it. He tried to reload his gun, but his shaking hands prevented. The lieutenant was obliged to assist him.

The men dropped here and there like bundles.

The captain of the youth's company had been killed in an early part of the action. His body lay stretched out in the position of a tired man resting, but upon his face there was an astonished and sorrowful look, as if he thought some friend had done him an ill turn. The babbling man was grazed by a shot that made the blood stream widely down his face. He clasped both hands to his head. "Oh!" he said, and ran. Another grunted suddenly as if he had been struck by a club in the stomach. He sat down and gazed ruefully. In his eyes there was mute, indefinite reproach. Further up the line a man, standing behind a tree, had had his knee joint splintered by a ball. Immediately he had dropped his rifle and gripped the tree with both arms. And there he remained, clinging desperately and crying for assistance, that he might withdraw his hold upon the tree.

At last an exultant yell went along the quivering line. The firing dwindled from an uproar to a last vindictive popping. As the smoke slowly eddied away, the youth saw that the charge had been repulsed. The enemy were scattered into reluctant groups. He saw a man climb to the top of the fence, straddle the rail, and fire a parting shot. The waves had receded, leaving bits of dark *débris* upon the ground.

Some in the regiment began to whoop frenziedly. Many were silent. Apparently they were trying to contemplate themselves.

After the fever had left his veins, the youth thought that at last he was going to suffocate. He became aware of the foul atmosphere in which he had been struggling. He was grimy and dripping like a laborer in a foundry. He grasped his canteen and took a long swallow of the warmed water.

A sentence with variations went up and down the line. "Well, we've helt 'em back. We've helt 'em back; derned if we haven't." The men said it blissfully, leering at each other with dirty smiles.

The youth turned to look behind him and off to the right and off to the left. He experienced the joy of a man who at last finds leisure in which to look about him.

Underfoot there were a few ghastly forms motionless. They lay twisted in fantastic contortions. Arms were bent and heads were turned in incredible ways. It seemed that the dead men must have fallen from some great height to get into such positions. They looked to be dumped out upon the ground from the sky.

From a position in the rear of the grove a battery was throwing shells over it. The flash of the guns startled the youth at first. He thought they were aimed directly at him. Through the trees he watched the black figures of the gunners as they worked swiftly and intently. Their labor seemed a complicated thing. He wondered how they could remember its formula in the midst of confusion.

The guns squatted in a row like savage chiefs. They argued with abrupt violence. It was a grim pow-wow. Their busy servants ran hither and thither.

A small procession of wounded men were going drearily toward the rear. It was a flow of blood from the torn body of the brigade.

To the right and to the left were the dark lines of other troops. Far in front he thought he could see lighter masses protruding in points from the forest. They were suggestive of unnumbered thousands.

Once he saw a tiny battery go dashing along the line of the horizon. The tiny riders were beating the tiny horses.

From a sloping hill came the sounds of cheerings and clashes. Smoke welled slowly through the leaves.

Batteries were speaking with thunderous oratorical effort. Here and there were flags, the red in the stripes dominating. They splashed bits of warm color upon the dark lines of troops.

The youth felt the old thrill at the sight of the emblem. They were like beautiful birds strangely undaunted in a storm.

As he listened to the din from the hillside, to a deep pulsating thunder that came from afar to the left, and to the lesser clamors which came from many directions, it occurred to him that they were fighting, too, over there, and over there, and over there. Heretofore he had supposed that all the battle was directly under his nose.

As he gazed around him the youth felt a flash of astonishment at the blue, pure sky and the sun gleaming on the trees and fields. It was surprising that Nature had gone tranquilly on with her golden process in the midst of so much devilment.

# 6

THE YOUTH AWAKENED slowly. He came gradually back to a position from which he could regard himself. For moments he had been scrutinizing his person in a dazed way as if he had never before seen himself. Then he picked up his cap from the ground. He wriggled in his jacket to make a more comfortable fit, and kneeling replaced his shoe. He thoughtfully mopped his reeking features.

So it was all over at last! The supreme trial had been passed. The red, formidable difficulties of war had been vanquished.

He went into an ecstasy of self-satisfaction. He had the most delightful sensations of his life. Standing as if apart from himself, he viewed that last scene. He perceived that the man who had fought thus was magnificent.

He felt that he was a fine fellow. He saw himself even with those ideals which he had considered as far beyond him. He smiled in deep gratification.

Upon his fellows he beamed tenderness and good will. "Gee! ain't it hot, hey?" he said affably to a man who was polishing his streaming face with his coatsleeves.

"You bet!" said the other, grinning sociably. "I never seen sech dumb hotness." He sprawled out luxuriously on the ground. "Gee yes! An' I hope we don't have no more fightin' till a week from Monday."

There were some handshakings and deep speeches with men whose features were familiar, but with whom the youth now felt the bonds of tied hearts. He helped a cursing comrade to bind up a wound of the shin.

But, of a sudden, cries of amazement broke out along the ranks of the new regiment. "Here they come ag'in! Here they come ag'in!" The man who had sprawled upon the ground started up and said, "Gosh!"

The youth turned quick eyes upon the field. He discerned forms begin to swell in masses out of a distant wood. He again saw the tilted flag speeding forward.

The shells, which had ceased to trouble the regiment for a time, came swirling again, and exploded in the grass or among the leaves of the trees. They looked to be strange war flowers bursting into fierce bloom.

The men groaned. The luster faded from their eyes. Their smudged countenances now expressed a profound dejection. They moved their stiffened bodies slowly, and watched in sullen mood the frantic approach of the enemy. The slaves toiling in the temple of this god began to feel rebellion at his harsh tasks.

They fretted and complained each to each. "Oh, say, this is too much of a good thing! Why can't somebody send us supports?"

We ain't never goin' to stand this second banging. I didn't come here to fight the hull damn' rebel army."

There was one who raised a doleful cry. "I wish Bill Smithers had trod on my hand, insteader me treddin' on his'n." The sore joints of the regiment creaked as it painfully floundered into position to repulse.

The youth stared. Surely, he thought, this impossible thing was not about to happen. He waited as if he expected the enemy to suddenly stop, apologize, and retire bowing. It was all a mistake.

But the firing began somewhere on the regimental line and ripped along in both directions. The level sheets of flame developed great clouds of smoke that tumbled and tossed in the mild wind near the ground for a moment, and then rolled through the ranks as through a gate. The clouds were tinged an earth-like yellow in the sunrays and in the shadow were a sorry blue. The flag was sometimes eaten and lost in this mass of vapor, but more often it projected, sun-touched, resplendent.

Into the youth's eyes there came a look that one can see in the orbs of a jaded horse. His neck was quivering with nervous weakness and the muscles of his arms felt numb and bloodless. His hands, too, seemed large and awkward as if he was wearing invisible mittens. And there was a great uncertainty about his knee joints.

The words that comrades had uttered previous to the firing began to recur to him. "Oh, say, this is too much of a good thing! What do they take us for—why don't they send supports? I didn't come here to fight the hull damned rebel army."

He began to exaggerate the endurance, the skill, and the valor of those who were coming. Himself reeling from exhaustion, he was astonished beyond measure at such persistency. They must be machines of steel. It was very gloomy struggling against such affairs, wound up perhaps to fight until sundown.

He slowly lifted his rifle and catching a glimpse of the thick-spread field he blazed at a cantering cluster. He stopped then and began to peer as best he could through the smoke. He caught changing views of the ground covered with men who were all running like pursued imps, and yelling.

To the youth it was an onslaught of redoubtable dragons. He became like the man who lost his legs at the approach of the red and green monster. He waited in a sort of a horrified, listening attitude. He seemed to shut his eyes and wait to be gobbled.

A man near him who up to this time had been working feverishly at his rifle suddenly stopped and ran with howls. A lad whose face had borne an expression of exalted courage, the majesty of he who dares give his life, was, at an instant, smitten abject. He blanched like one who has come to the edge of a cliff at midnight and is suddenly made aware. There was a revelation. He, too, threw down his gun and fled. There was no shame in his face. He ran like a rabbit.

Others began to scamper away through the smoke. The youth turned his head, shaken from his trance by this movement as if the regiment was leaving him behind. He saw the few fleeting forms.

He yelled then with fright and swung about. For a moment, in the great clamor, he was like a proverbial chicken. He lost the direction of safety. Destruction threatened him from all points.

Directly he began to speed toward the rear in great leaps. His rifle and cap were gone. His unbuttoned coat bulged in the wind. The flap of his cartridge box bobbed wildly, and his canteen, by its slender cord, swung out behind. On his face was all the horror of those things which he imagined.

The lieutenant sprang foward bawling. The youth saw his features wrathfully red, and saw him make a dab with his sword. His one thought of the incident as that the lieutenant was a peculiar creature to feel interested in such matters upon this occasion.

He ran like a blind man. Two or three times he fell down. Once he knocked his shoulder so heavily against a tree that he went headlong.

Since he had turned his back upon the fight his fears had been wondrously magnified. Death about to thrust him between the shoulderblades was far more dreadful than death about to smite him between the eyes. When he thought of it later, he conceived the impression that it is better to view the appalling than to be merely within hearing. The noises of the battle were like stones; he believed himself liable to be crushed.

As he ran on he mingled with others. He dimly saw men on his right and on his left, and he heard footsteps behind him. He thought that all the regiment was fleeing, pursued by these ominous crashes.

In his flight the sound of these following footsteps gave him his one meager relief. He felt vaguely that death must make a first choice of the men who were nearest; the initial morsels for the dragons would be then those who were following him. So he displayed the zeal of an insane sprinter in his purpose to keep them in the rear. There was a race.

As he, leading, went across a little field, he found himself in a region of shells. They hurtled over his head with long wild screams. As he listened he imagined them to have rows of cruel teeth that grinned at him. Once one lit before him and the livid lightning of the explosion effectually barred the way in his chosen direction. He grovelled on the ground and then springing up went careering off through some bushes.

He experienced a thrill of amazement when he came within view of a battery in action. The men there seemed to be in conventional moods, altogether unaware of the impending annihilation. The battery was disputing with a distant antagonist and the gunners were wrapped in admiration of their shooting. They were continually bending in coaxing postures over the guns. They seemed to be patting them on the back and encouraging them with words. The guns, stolid and undaunted, spoke with dogged valor.

The precise gunners were cooly enthusiastic. They lifted their eyes every chance to the smoke-wreathed hillock from whence the hostile battery addressed them. The youth pitied them as he ran. Methodical idiots! Machine-like fools! The refined joy of planting shells in the midst of the other battery's formation would appear a little thing when the infantry came swooping out of the woods.

The face of a youthful rider, who was jerking his frantic horse with an abandon of temper he might display in a placid barnyard, was impressed deeply upon his mind. He knew that he looked upon a man who would presently be dead.

Too, he felt a pity for the guns, standing, six good comrades, in a bold row.

He saw a brigade going to the relief of its pestered fellows. He scrambled upon a wee hill and watched it sweeping finely, keeping formation in difficult places. The blue of the line was crusted with steel color, and the brilliant flags projected. Officers were shouting.

This sight also filled him with wonder. The brigade was hurrying briskly to be gulped into the infernal mouths of the war god. What manner of men were they, anyhow? Ah, it was some wondrous breed! Or else they didn't comprehend—the fools.

A furious order caused commotion in the artillery. An officer on a bounding horse made maniacal motions with his arms. The teams went swinging up from the rear, the guns were whirled about, and the battery scampered away. The cannon with their noses poked slantingly at the ground grunted and grumbled like stout men, brave but with objections to hurry.

The youth went on, moderating his pace since he had left the place of noises.

Later he came upon a general of division seated upon a horse that pricked its ears in an interested way at the battle. There was a great gleaming of yellow and patent leather about the saddle and bridle. The quiet man astride looked mouse-colored upon such a splendid charger.

A jingling staff was galloping hither and thither. Sometimes the general was surrounded by horsemen and at other times he was quite alone. He looked to be much harassed. He had the appearance of a business man whose market is swinging up and down.

The youth went slinking around this spot. He went as near as he dared trying to overhear words. Perhaps the general, unable to comprehend chaos, might call upon him for information. And he could tell him. He knew all concerning it. Of a surety the force was in a fix, and any fool could see that if they did not retreat while they had opportunity—why——

He felt that he would like to thrash the general, or at least approach and tell him in plain words exactly what he thought him to be. It was criminal to stay calmly in one spot and make no effort to stay destruction. He loitered in a fever of eagerness for the division commander to apply to him.

As he warily moved about he heard the general call out irritably: "Tompkins, go over an' see Taylor, an' tell him not t' be in such an all-fired hurry; tell him t' halt his brigade in th' edge of th' woods; tell him t' detach a reg'ment—say I think th' center'll break if we don't help it out some; tell him t' hurry up."

A slim youth on a fine chestnut horse caught these swift words from the mouth of his superior. He made his horse bound into a gallop almost from a walk in his haste to go upon his mission. There was a cloud of dust.

A moment later the youth saw the general bounce excitedly in his saddle.

"Yes, by heavens, they have!" The officer leaned forward. His face was aflame with excitement. "Yes, by heavens, they've held 'im! They've held 'im!"

He began blithely to roar at his staff: "We'll wallop 'im now. We'll wallop 'im now. We've got 'em sure." He turned suddenly upon an aid: "Here—you—Jones—quick—ride after Tompkins—see Taylor—tell him t' go in—everlastingly—like blazes—anything."

As another officer sped his horse after the first messenger, the general beamed upon the earth like a sun. In his eyes was a desire to chant a pæan. He kept repeating, "They've held 'em, by heavens!"

His excitement made his horse plunge, and he merrily kicked and swore at it. He held a little carnival of joy on horseback.

# 7

THE YOUTH CRINGED as if discovered in a crime. By heavens, they had won after all! The imbecile line had remained and become victors. He could hear cheering.

He lifted himself upon his toes and looked in the direction of the fight. A yellow fog lay wallowing on the treetops. From beneath it came the clatter of musketry. Hoarse cries told of an advance.

He turned away amazed and angry. He felt that he had been wronged.

He had fled, he told himself, because annihilation approached. He had done a good part in saving himself, who was a little piece of the army. He had considered the time, he said, to be one in which it was the duty of every little piece to rescue itself if possible. Later the officers could fit the little pieces together again, and make a battle front. If none of the little pieces were wise enough to save themselves from the flurry of death at such a time, why, then, where would be the army? It was all plain that he had proceeded according to very correct and commendable rules. His actions had been sagacious things. They had been full of strategy. They were the work of a master's legs.

Thoughts of his comrades came to him. The brittle blue line had withstood the blows and won. He grew bitter over it. It seemed that the blind ignorance and stupidity of those little pieces had betrayed him. He had been overturned and crushed by their lack of sense in holding the position, when intelligent deliberation would have convinced them that it was impossible. He, the enlightened man who looks afar in the dark, had fled because of his superior perceptions and knowledge. He felt a great anger against his comrades. He knew it could be proved that they had been fools.

He wondered what they would remark when later he appeared in camp. His mind heard howls of derision. Their density would not enable them to understand his sharper point of view.

He began to pity himself acutely. He was ill used. He was trodden beneath the feet of an iron injustice. He had proceeded with wisdom and from the most righteous motives under heaven's blue only to be frustrated by hateful circumstances.

A dull, animal-like rebellion against his fellows, war in the abstract, and fate grew within him. He shambled along with bowed head, his brain in a tumult of agony and despair. When he looked lowering up, quivering at each sound, his eyes had the expression of those of a criminal who thinks his guilt and his punishment great, and knows that he can find no words; who, through his suffering, thinks that he peers into the core of things and sees that the judgment of man is thistledown in wind.

He went from the fields into a thick wood, as if resolved to bury himself. He wished to get out of hearing of the crackling shots which were to him like voices.

The ground was cluttered with vines and bushes, and the trees grew close, and spread out like bouquets. He was obliged to force his way with much noise. The creepers, catching against his legs, cried out harshly as their sprays were torn from the barks of trees. The swishing saplings tried to make known his presence to the world. He could not conciliate the forest. As he made his way, it was always calling out protestations. When he separated embraces of trees and vines the disturbed foliages waved their arms and turned their face leaves toward him. He dreaded lest these noisy motions and cries should bring men to look at him. So he went far, seeking dark and intricate places.

After a time the sound of musketry grew faint and the cannon boomed in the distance. The sun, suddenly apparent, blazed among the trees. The insects were making rhythmical noises. They seemed to be grinding their teeth in unison. A woodpecker stuck his impudent head around the side of a tree. A bird flew on lighthearted wing.

Off was the rumble of death. It seemed now that Nature had no ears.

This landscape gave him assurance. A fair field holding life. It was the religion of peace. It would die if its timid eyes were compelled to see blood. He conceived Nature to be a woman with a deep aversion to tragedy.

He threw a pine cone at a jovial squirrel, and he ran with chattering fear. High in a treetop he stopped, and poking his head cautiously from behind a branch, looked down with an air of trepidation.

The youth felt triumphant at this exhibition. There was the law, he said. Nature had given him a sign. The squirrel, immediately upon recognizing danger, had taken to his legs without ado. He did not stand stolidly baring his furry belly to the missile, and die with an upward glance at the sympathetic heavens. On the contrary, he had fled as fast as his legs could carry him; and he was but an ordinary squirrel, too—doubtless no philosopher of his race. The youth wended, feeling that Nature was of his mind. She re-enforced his argument with proofs that lived where the sun shone.

Once he found himself almost into a swamp. He was obliged to walk upon bog tufts, and watch his feet to keep from the oily mire. Pausing at one time to look about him he saw, out at some black water, a small animal pounce in and emerge directly with a gleaming fish.

The youth went again into the deep thickets. The brushed branches made a noise that drowned the sounds of cannon. He walked on, going from obscurity into promises of a greater obscurity.

At length he reached a place where the high, arching boughs made a chapel. He softly pushed the green doors aside and entered. Pine needles were a gentle brown carpet. There was a religious half light.

Near the threshold he stopped, horror-stricken at the sight of a thing.

He was being looked at by a dead man, who was seated with his back against a columnlike tree. The corpse was dressed in a uniform that once had been blue, but was now faded to a melancholy shade of green. The eyes, staring at the youth, had changed to the dull hue to be seen on the side of a dead fish. The mouth was open. Its red had changed to an appalling yellow. Over the gray skin of the face ran little ants. One was trundling some sort of bundle along the upper lip.

The youth gave a shriek as he confronted the thing. He was for moments turned to stone before it. He remained staring into the liquid-looking eyes. The dead man and the living man exchanged a long look. Then the youth cautiously put one hand behind him and brought it against a tree. Leaning upon this he retreated, step by step, with his face still toward the thing. He feared that if he turned his back the body might spring up and stealthily pursue him.

The branches, pushing against him, threatened to throw him over upon it. His unguided feet, too, caught aggravatingly in brambles; and with it all he received a subtle suggestion to touch the corpse. As he thought of his hand upon it he shuddered profoundly.

At last he burst the bonds which had fastened him to the spot and fled, unheeding the underbrush. He was pursued by a sight of the black ants swarming greedily upon the gray face and venturing horribly near to the eyes.

After a time he paused, and, breathless and panting, listened. He imagined some strange voice would come from the dead throat and squawk after him in horrible menaces.

The trees about the portal of the chapel moved soughingly in a soft wind. A sad silence was upon the little guarding edifice.

# 8

THE TREES BEGAN softly to sing a hymn of twilight. The sun sank until slanted bronze rays struck the forest. There was a lull in the noises of insects as if they had bowed their beaks and were making a devotional pause. There was silence save for the chanted chorus of the trees.

Then, upon this stillness, there suddenly broke a tremendous clangor of sounds. A crimson roar came from the distance.

The youth stopped. He was transfixed by this terrific medley of all noises. It was as if worlds were being rended. There was the ripping sound of musketry and the breaking crash of the artillery.

His mind flew in all directions. He conceived the two armies to be at each other panther fashion. He listened for a time. Then he began to run in the direction of the battle. He saw that it was an ironical thing for him to be running thus toward that which he had been at such pains to avoid. But he said, in substance, to himself that if the earth and the moon were about to clash, many persons would doubtless plan to get upon the roofs to witness the collision.

As he ran, he became aware that the forest had stopped its music, as if at last becoming capable of hearing the foreign sounds. The trees hushed and stood motionless. Everything seemed to be listening to the crackle and clatter and ear-shaking thunder. The chorus pealed over the still earth.

It suddenly occured to the youth that the fight in which he had been was, after all, but perfunctory popping. In the hearing of this present din he was doubtful if he had seen real battle scenes. This uproar explained a celestial battle; it was tumbling hordes a-struggle in the air.

Reflecting, he saw a sort of humor in the point of view of himself and his fellows during the late encounter. They had taken themselves and the enemy very seriously and had imagined that they were deciding the war. Individuals must have supposed that they were cutting the letters of their names deep into everlasting tables of brass, or enshrining their reputations for ever in the hearts of their country-men, while, as to fact, the affair would appear in printed reports under a meek and immaterial title. But he saw that it was good, else, he said, in battle every one would surely run save forlorn hopes and their ilk.

He went rapidly on. He wished to come to the edge of the forest that he might peer out.

As he hastened, there passed through his mind pictures of stupen-dous conflicts. His accumulated thought upon such subjects was used to form scenes. The noise was as the voice of an eloquent being, describing.

Sometimes the brambles formed chains and tried to hold him back. Trees, confronting him, stretched out their arms and forbade him to pass. After its previous hostility this new resistance of the forest filled him with a fine bitterness. It seemed that Nature could not be quite ready to kill him.

But he obstinately took roundabout ways, and presently he was where he could see long gray walls of vapor where lay battle lines. The voices of cannon shook him. The musketry sounded in long irregular surges that played havoc with his ears. He stood regardant for a moment. His eyes had an awestruck expression. He gawked in the direction of the fight.

Presently he proceeded again on his forward way. The battle was like the grinding of an immense and terrible machine to him. Its complexities and powers, its grim processes, fascinated him. He must go close and see it produce corpses.

He came to a fence and clambered over it. On the far side, the ground was littered with clothes and guns. A newspaper, folded up, lay in the dirt. A dead soldier was stretched with his face hidden in his arm. Farther off there was a group of four or five corpses keeping mournful company. A hot sun had blazed upon the spot.

In this place the youth felt that he was an invader. This forgotten part of the battleground was owned by the dead men, and he hurried, in the vague apprehension that one of the swollen forms would rise and tell him to begone.

He came finally to a road from which he could see in the distance dark and agitated bodies of troops, smoke-fringed. In the lane was a bloodstained crowd streaming to the rear. The wounded men were cursing, groaning, and wailing. In the air, always, was a mighty swell of sound that it seemed could sway the earth. With the courageous words of the artillery and the spiteful sentences of the musketry mingled red cheers. And from this region of noises came the steady current of the maimed.

One of the wounded men had a shoeful of blood. He hopped like a schoolboy in a game. He was laughing hysterically.

One was swearing that he had been shot in the arm through the commanding general's mismanagement of the army. One was marching with an air imitative of some sublime drum major. Upon his features was an unholy mixture of merriment and agony. As he marched he sang a bit of doggerel in a high and quavering voice:

> "Sing a song 'a vic'try,
> A pocketful 'a bullets,
> Five an' twenty dead men
> Baked in a—pie."

Parts of the procession limped and staggered to this tune.

Another had the gray seal of death already upon his face. His lips were curled in hard lines and his teeth were clinched. His hands were bloody from where he had pressed them upon his wound. He seemed to be awaiting the moment when he should pitch headlong. He stalked like the specter of a soldier, his eyes burning with the power of a stare into the unknown.

There were some who proceeded sullenly, full of anger at their wounds, and ready to turn upon anything as an obscure cause.

An officer was carried along by two privates. He was peevish. "Don't joggle so, Johnson, yeh fool," he cried. "Think m' leg is made of iron? If yeh can't carry me decent, put me down an' let someone else do it."

He bellowed at the tottering crowd who blocked the quick march of his bearers. "Say, make way there, can't yeh? Make way, dickens take it all."

They sulkily parted and went to the roadsides. As he was carried past they made pert remarks to him. When he raged in reply and threatened them, they told him to be damned.

The shoulder of one of the tramping bearers knocked heavily against the spectral soldier who was staring into the unknown.

The youth joined this crowd and marched along with it. The torn bodies expressed the awful machinery in which the men had been entangled.

Orderlies and couriers occasionally broke through the throng in the roadway, scattering wounded men right and left, galloping on followed by howls. The melancholy march was continually disturbed by the messengers, and sometimes by bustling batteries that came swinging and thumping down upon them, the officers shouting orders to clear the way.

There was a tattered man, fouled with dust, blood and powder stain from hair to shoes, who trudged quietly at the youth's side. He was listening with eagerness and much humility to the lurid descriptions of a bearded sergeant. His lean features wore an expression of awe and admiration. He was like a listener in a country store to wondrous tales told among the sugar barrels. He eyed the story-teller with unspeakable wonder. His mouth was agape in yokel fashion.

The sergeant, taking note of this, gave pause to his elaborate history while he administered a sardonic comment. "Be keerful, honey, you'll be a-ketchin' flies," he said.

The tattered man shrank back abashed.

After a time he began to sidle near to the youth, and in a different way try to make him a friend. His voice was gentle as a girl's voice and his eyes were pleading. The youth saw with surprise that the soldier had two wounds, one in the head, bound with a blood-soaked rag, and the other in the arm, making that member dangle like a broken bough.

After they had walked together for some time the tattered man mustered sufficient courage to speak. "Was pretty good fight, wa'n't it?" he timidly said. The youth, deep in thought, glanced up at the bloody and grim figure with its lamblike eyes. "What?"

"Was pretty good fight, wa'n't it?"

"Yes," said the youth shortly. He quickened his pace.

But the other hobbled industriously after him. There was an air of apology in his manner, but he evidently thought that he needed only to talk for a time, and the youth would perceive that he was a good fellow.

"Was pretty good fight, wa'n't it?" he began in a small voice, and then he achieved the fortitude to continue. "Dern me if I ever see fellers fight so. Laws, how they did fight! I knowed th' boys'd like when they onct got square at it. Th' boys ain't had no fair chanct up t' now, but this time they showed what they was. I knowed it'd turn out this way. Yeh can't lick them boys. No, sir! They're fighters, they be."

He breathed a deep breath of humble admiration. He had looked at the youth for encouragement several times. He received none, but gradually he seemed to get absorbed in his subject.

"I was talkin' 'cross pickets with a boy from Georgie, onct, an' that boy, he ses, 'Your fellers'll all run like hell when they onct hearn a gun,' he ses. 'Mebbe they will,' I ses, 'but I don't b'lieve none of it,' I ses; 'an' b'jiminey,' I ses back t' 'um, 'mebbe your fellers'll all run like hell when they once hearn a gun,' I ses. He larfed. Well, they didn't run t'-day, did they, hey? No, sir! They fit, an' fit, an' fit."

His homely face was suffused with a light of love for the army which was to him all things beautiful and powerful.

After a time he turned to the youth. "Where yeh hit, ol' boy?" he asked in a brotherly tone.

The youth felt instant panic at this question, although at first its full import was not borne in upon him.

"What?" he asked.

"Where yeh hit?" repeated the tattered man.

"Why," began the youth, "I—I—that is—why—I——"

He turned away suddenly and slid through the crowd. His brow was heavily flushed, and his fingers were picking nervously at one of his buttons. He bent his head and fastened his eyes studiously upon the button as if it were a little problem.

The tattered man looked after him in astonishment.

# 9

THE YOUTH FELL back in the procession until the tattered soldier was not in sight. Then he started to walk on with the others.

But he was amid wounds. The mob of men was bleeding. Because of the tattered soldier's question he now felt that his shame could be viewed. He was continually casting sidelong glances to see if the men were contemplating the letters of guilt he felt burned into his brow.

At times he regarded the wounded soldiers in an envious way. He conceived persons with torn bodies to be peculiarly happy. He wished that he, too, had a wound, a little red badge of courage.

The spectral soldier was at his side like a stalking reproach. The man's eyes were still fixed in a stare into the unknown. His gray, appalling face had attracted attention in the crowd, and men, slowing to his dreary pace, were walking with him. They were discussing his plight, questioning him and giving him advice. In a dogged way he repelled them, signing to them to go on and leave him alone. The shadows of his face were deepening and his tight lips seemed holding in check the moan of great despair. There could be seen a certain stiffness in the movements of his body, as if he were taking infinite care not to arouse the passion of his wounds. As he went on he seemed always looking for a place, like one who goes to choose a grave.

Something in the gesture of the man as he waved the bloody and pitying soldiers away made the youth start as if bitten. He yelled in horror. Tottering forward he laid a quivering hand upon the man's arm. As the latter slowly turned his wax-like features toward him, the youth screamed:

"Gawd! Jim Conklin!"

The tall soldier made a little commonplace smile. "Hello Henry," he said.

The youth swayed on his legs and glared strangely. He stuttered and stammered. "Oh, Jim—oh, Jim—oh, Jim——"

The tall soldier held out his gory hand. There was a curious red and black combination of new blood and old blood upon it. "Where yeh been, Henry?" he asked. He continued in a monotonous voice. "I thought mebbe yeh got keeled over. There's been thunder t' pay t'-day. I was worryin' about it a good deal."

The youth still lamented. "Oh, Jim—oh, Jim—oh, Jim——"

"Yeh know," said the tall soldier, "I was out there." He made a careful gesture. "An', Lord, what a circus! An' b'jiminey, I got shot—I got shot. Yes, b'jiminey, I got shot." He reiterated this fact in a bewildered way, as if he did not know how it came about.

The youth put forth anxious arms to assist him, but the tall soldier went firmly on as if propelled. Since the youth's arrival as a guardian for his friend, the other wounded men had ceased to display much interest. They occupied themselves again in dragging their own tragedies toward the rear.

Suddenly, as the two friends marched on, the tall soldier seemed to be overcome by a terror. His face turned to a semblance of gray paste. He clutched the youth's arm and looked all about him, as if dreading to be overheard. Then he began to speak in a shaking whisper:

"I tell yeh what I'm 'fraid of, Henry—I'll tell yeh what I'm 'fraid of. I'm 'fraid I'll fall down—an' then yeh know—them damned artillery wagons—they like as not'll run over me. That's what I'm 'fraid of——"

The youth cried out to him hysterically: "I'll take care of yeh, Jim! I'll take care of yeh! I swear t' Gawd I will!"

"Sure—will yeh, Henry?" the tall soldier beseeched.

"Yes—yes—I tell yeh—I'll take care of yeh, Jim!" protested the youth. He could not speak accurately because of the gulpings in this throat.

But the tall soldier continued to beg in a lowly way. He now hung babelike to the youth's arm. His eyes rolled in the wildness of his terror. "I was allus a good friend t' yeh, wa'n't I, Henry? I've allus been a pretty good feller, ain't I? An' it ain't much t' ask, is it? Jest t' pull me along outer th' road? I'd do it fer you, wouldn't I, Henry?"

He paused in piteous anxiety to await his friend's reply.

The youth had reached an anguish where the sobs scorched him. He strove to express his loyalty, but he could only make fantastic gestures.

However, the tall soldier seemed suddenly to forget all those fears. He became again the grim, stalking specter of a soldier. He went stonily forward. The youth wished his friend to lean upon him, but the other always shook his head and strangely protested. "No—no—no—leave me be—leave me be——"

His look was fixed again upon the unknown. He moved with mysterious purpose, and all of the youth's offers he brushed aside. "No—no—leave me be—leave me be——"

The youth had to follow.

Presently the latter heard a voice talking softly near his shoulder. Turning he saw that it belonged to the tattered soldier. "Ye'd better take 'im outa th' road, pardner. There's a batt'ry comin' helitywhoop down th' road an' he'll git runned over. He's a goner anyhow in about five minutes—yeh kin see that. Ye'd better take 'im outa th' road. Where th' blazes does he git his stren'th from?"

"Lord knows!" cried the youth. He was shaking his hands helplessly.

He ran forward presently and grasped the tall soldier by the arm. "Jim! Jim!" he coaxed, "come with me."

The tall soldier weakly tried to wrench himself free. "Huh," he said vacantly. He stared at the youth for a moment. At last he spoke as if dimly comprehending. "Oh! Inteh th' fields? Oh!"

He started blindly through the grass.

The youth turned once to look at the lashing riders and jouncing guns of the battery. He was startled from this view by a shrill outcry from the tattered man.

"Gawd! He's runnin'!"

Turning his head swiftly, the youth saw his friend running in a staggering and stumbling way toward a little clump of bushes. His heart seemed to wrench itself almost free from his body at this sight. He made a noise of pain. He and the tattered man began a pursuit. There was a singular race.

When he overtook the tall soldier he began to plead with all the words he could find. "Jim—Jim—what are you doing—what makes you do this way—you'll hurt yerself."

The same purpose was in the tall soldier's face. He protested in a dulled way, keeping his eyes fastened on the mystic place of his intentions. "No—no—don't tech me—leave me be—leave me be——"

The youth, aghast, and filled with wonder at the tall soldier, began quaveringly to question him. "Where yeh goin', Jim? What you thinking about? Where you going? Tell me, won't you, Jim?"

The tall soldier faced about as upon relentless pursuers. In his eyes there was a great appeal. "Leave me be, can't yeh? Leave me be fer a minnit."

The youth recoiled. "Why, Jim," he said, in a dazed way, "what's the matter with you?"

The tall soldier turned and, lurching dangerously, went on. The youth and the tattered soldier followed, sneaking as if whipped, feeling unable to face the stricken man if he should again confront them. They began to have thoughts of a solemn ceremony. There was something rite-like in these movements of the doomed soldier. And there was a resemblance in him to a devotee of a mad religion, blood-sucking, muscle-wrenching, bone-crushing. They were awed and afraid. They hung back lest he have at command a dreadful weapon.

At last, they saw him stop and stand motionless. Hastening up, they perceived that his face wore an expression telling that he had at last found the place for which he had struggled. His spare figure was erect; his bloody hands were quietly at his side. He was waiting with patience for something that he had come to meet. He was at the rendezvous. They paused and stood, expectant.

There was a silence.

Finally, the chest of the doomed soldier began to heave with a strained motion. It increased in violence until it was as if an animal was within and was kicking and tumbling furiously to be free.

This spectacle of gradual strangulation made the youth writhe, and once as his friend rolled his eyes, he saw something in them that made him sink wailing to the ground. He raised his voice in a last supreme call.

"Jim—Jim—Jim——"

The tall soldier opened his lips and spoke. He made a gesture. "Leave me be—don't tech me—leave me be——"

There another silence while he waited.

Suddenly, his form stiffened and straightened. Then it was shaken by a prolonged ague. He stared into space. To the two watchers there was a curious and profound dignity in the firm lines of his awful face.

He was invaded by a creeping strangeness that slowly enveloped him. For a moment the tremor of his legs caused him to dance a sort of hideous hornpipe. His arms beat wildly about his head in expression of implike enthusiasm.

His tall figure stretched itself to its full height. There was a slight rending sound. Then it began to swing forward, slow and straight, in the manner of a falling tree. A swift muscular contortion made the left shoulder strike the ground first.

The body seemed to bounce a little way from the earth. "God!" said the tattered soldier.

The youth had watched, spellbound, this ceremony at the place of meeting. His face had been twisted into an expression of every agony he had imagined for his friend.

He now sprang to his feet and, going closer, gazed upon the pastelike face. The mouth was open and the teeth showed in a laugh.

As the flap of the blue jacket fell away from the body, he could see that the side looked as if it had been chewed by wolves.

The youth turned, with sudden, livid rage, toward the battlefield. He shook his fist. He seemed about to deliver a philippic.

"Hell——"

The red sun was pasted in the sky like a fierce wafer.


# 10

THE TATTERED MAN STOOD MUSING.

"Well, he was reg'lar jim-dandy fer nerve, wa'n't he," said he finally in a little awestruck voice. "A reg'lar jim-dandy." He thoughtfully poked one of the docile hands with his foot. "I wonner where he got 'is stren'th from? I never seen a man do like that before. It was a funny thing. Well, he was a reg'lar jim-dandy."

The youth desired to screech out his grief. He was stabbed, but his tongue lay dead in the tomb of his mouth. He threw himself again upon the ground and began to brood.

The tattered man stood musing.

"Look-a-here, pardner," he said after a time. He regarded the corpse as he spoke. "He's up an' gone, ain't 'e, an' we might as well begin t' look out fer ol' number one. This here thing is all over. He's up an' gone, ain't 'e? An' he's all right here. Nobody won't bother 'im. An' I must say I ain't enjoying any great health m'self these days."

The youth, awakened by the tattered soldier's tone, looked quickly up. He saw that he was swinging uncertainly on his legs and that his face had turned to a shade of blue.

"Good Lord!" he cried, "you ain't goin' t'—not you, too."

The tattered man waved his hand. "Nary die," he said. "All I want is some pea soup an' a good bed. Some pea soup," he repeated dreamfully.

The youth arose from the ground. "I wonder where he came from. I left him over there." He pointed. "And now I find 'im here. And he was coming from over there, too." He indicated a new direction. They both turned toward the body as if to ask of it a question.

"Well," at length spoke the tattered man, "there ain't no use in our stayin' here an' tryin' t' ask him anything."

The youth nodded an assent wearily. They both turned to gaze for a moment at the corpse.

The youth murmured something.

"Well, he was a jim-dandy, wa'n't he?" said the tattered man as if in response.

They turned their backs upon it and started away. For a time they stole softly, treading with their toes. It remained laughing there in the grass.

"I'm commencin' t' feel pretty bad," said the tattered man, suddenly breaking one of his little silences. "I'm commencin' t' feel pretty damn' bad."

The youth groaned. "O Lord!" He wondered if he was to be the tortured witness of another grim encounter.

But his companion waved his hand reassuringly. "Oh, I'm not goin' t' die yit! There too much dependin' on me fer me t' die yit. No, sir! Nary die! I *can't*! Ye'd oughta see th' swad a' chil'ren I've got, an' all like that."

The youth glancing at his companion could see by the shadow of a smile that he was making some kind of fun.

As they plodded on the tattered soldier continued to talk. "Besides, if I died, I wouldn't die th' way that feller did. That was th' funniest thing. I'd jest flop down, I would. I never seen a feller die th' way that feller did.

"Yeh know Tom Jamison, he lives next door t' me up home. He's a nice feller, he is, and we was allus good friends. Smart, too. Smart as a steel trap. Well, when we was a-fightin' this afternoon, all-of-a-sudden he begin t' rip up an' cuss an' beller at me. 'Yer shot, yeh blamed infernal tooty-tooty-tooty-too'—he swear horrible—he ses t' me. I put up m' hand t' m' head an' when I looked at m' fingers, I seen, sure 'nough, I was shot. I give a holler an' begin t' run, but b'fore I could git away another one hit me in th' arm an' whirl' me clean 'round. I got skeared when they was all a-shootin' b'hind me an' I run t' beat all, but I cotch it pretty bad. I've an idee I'd 'a' been fightin' yit, if 'twasn't fer Tom Jamison.''

Then he made a calm announcement: "There's two of 'em—little ones—but they're beginnin' t' have fun with me now. I don't b'lieve I kin walk much furder.''

They went slowly on in silence. "Yeh look pretty peek-ed yer-self,'' said the tattered man at last. "I bet yeh've got a worser one than yeh think. Ye'd better take keer of yer hurt. It don't do t' let sech things go. It might be inside mostly, an' them plays thunder. Where is it located?'' But he continued his harangue without waiting for a reply. "I see a feller git hit plum in th' head when my reg'ment was a-standin' at ease onct. An' everybody yelled out to 'im: 'Hurt, John? Are yeh hurt much?' 'No,' ses he. He looked kinder surprised, an' he went on tellin' 'em how he felt. He sed he didn't feel nothin'. But, by dad, th' first thing that feller knowed he was dead. Yes, he was dead—stone dead. So, yeh wanta watch out. Yeh might have some queer kind 'a hurt yerself. Yeh can't never tell. Where is your'n located?''

The youth had been wriggling since the introduction of this topic. He now gave a cry of exasperation and made a furious motion with his hand. "Oh, don't bother me!'' he said. He was enraged against the tattered man, and could have strangled him. His companions seemed ever to play intolerable parts. They were ever upraising the ghost of shame on the stick of their curiosity. He turned toward the tattered man as one at bay. "Now, don't bother me'' he repeated with desperate menace.

"Well, Lord knows I don't wanta bother anybody,'' said the other. There was a little accent of despair in his voice as he replied, "Lord knows I've gota 'nough m' own t' tend to.''

The youth, who had been holding a bitter debate with himself and casting glances of hatred and contempt at the tattered man, here spoke in a hard voice. "Good-by,'' he said.

The tattered man looked at him in gaping amazement. "Why—why, pardner, where yeh goin''' he asked unsteadily. The youth looking at him, could see that he, too, like that other one, was beginning to act dumb and animal-like. His thoughts seemed to be floundering about in his head. "Now—now—look—a—here, you Tom Jamison—now—I won't have this—this here won't do. Where—where yeh goin'?"

The youth pointed vaguely. "Over there," he replied.

"Well, now look—a—here—now," said the tattered man, rambling on in idiot fashion. His head was hanging forward and his words were slurred. "This thing won't do, now, Tom Jamison. It won't do. I know yeh, yeh pig-headed devil. Yeh wanta go trompin' off with a bad hurt. It ain't right—now—Tom Jamison—it ain't. Yeh wanta leave me take keer of yeh, Tom Jamison. It ain't—right—it ain't— fer yeh t' go—trompin' off—with a bad hurt—it ain't—ain't—ain't right—it ain't."

In reply the youth climbed a fence and started away. He could hear the tattered man bleating plaintively.

Once he faced about angrily. "What?"

"Look—a—here, now, Tom Jamison—now—it ain't——"

The youth went on. Turning at a distance he saw the tattered man wandering about helplessly in the field.

He now thought that he wished he was dead. He believed that he envied those men whose bodies lay strewn over the grass of the fields and on the fallen leaves of the forest.

The simple questions of the tattered man had been knife thrusts to him. They asserted a society that probes pitilessly at secrets until all is apparent. His late companion's chance persistency made him feel that he could not keep his crime concealed in his bosom. It was sure to be brought plain by one of those arrows which cloud the air and are constantly pricking, discovering, proclaiming those things which are willed to be forever hidden. He admitted that he could not defend himself against this agency. It was not within the power of vigilance.


# 11

HE BECAME AWARE that the furnace roar of the battle was growing louder. Great brown clouds had floated to the still heights of air before him. The noise, too, was approaching. The woods filtered men and the fields became dotted.

As he rounded a hillock, he perceived that the roadway was now a crying mass of wagons, teams, and men. From the heaving tangle issued exhortations, commands, imprecations. Fear was sweeping it all along. The cracking whips bit and horses plunged and tugged. The white-topped wagons strained and stumbled in their exertions like fat sheep.

The youth felt comforted in a measure by this sight. They were all retreating. Perhaps, then, he was not so bad after all. He seated himself and watched the terror-stricken wagons. They fled like soft, ungainly animals. All the roarers and lashers served to help him to magnify the dangers and horrors of the engagement that he might try to prove to himself that the thing with which men could charge him was in truth a symmetrical act. There was an amount of pleasure to him in watching the wild march of this vindication.

Presently the calm head of a forward-going column of infantry appeared in the road. It came swiftly on. Avoiding the obstructions gave it the sinuous movements of a serpent. The men at the head butted mules with their musket stocks. They prodded teamsters, indifferent to all howls. The men forced their way through parts of the dense mass by strength. The blunt head of the column pushed. The raving teamsters swore many strange oaths.

The commands to make way had the ring of a great importance in them. The men were going forward to the heart of the din. They were to confront the eager rush of the enemy. They felt the pride of their onward movement when the remainder of the army seemed trying to dribble down this road. They tumbled teams about with a fine feeling that it was no matter so long as their column got to the front in time. This importance made their faces grave and stern. And the backs of the officers were very rigid.

As the youth looked at them the black weight of his woe returned to him. He felt that he was regarding a procession of chosen beings. The separation was as great to him as if they had marched with weapons of flame and banners of sunlight. He could never be like them. He could have wept in his longings.

He searched about in his mind for an adequate malediction for the indefinite cause, the thing upon which men turn the words of final blame. It—whatever it was—was responsible for him, he said. There lay the fault.

The haste of the column to reach the battle seemed to the forlorn young man to be something much finer than stout fighting. Heroes, he thought, could find excuses in that long seething lane. They could retire with perfect self-respect and make excuses to the stars.

He wondered what those men had eaten that they could be in such haste to force their way to grim chances of death. As he watched his envy grew until he thought that he wished to change lives with one of them. He would have like to have used a tremendous force, he said, throw off himself and become a better. Swift pictures of himself, apart, yet in himself, came to him—a blue desperate figure leading lurid charges with one knee forward and a broken blade high—a blue, determined figure standing before a crimson and steel assault, getting calmly killed on a high place before the eyes of all. He thought of the magnificent pathos of his dead body.

These thoughts uplifted him. He felt the quiver of war desire. In his ears, he heard the ring of victory. He knew the frenzy of a rapid successful charge. The music of the trampling feet, the sharp voices, the clanking arms of the column near him made him soar on the red wings of war. For a few moments he was sublime.

He thought that he was about to start for the front. Indeed, he saw a picture of himself, dust-stained, haggard, panting, flying to the front at the proper moment to seize and throttle the dark, leering witch of calamity.

Then the difficulties of the thing began to drag at him. He hesitated, balancing awkwardly on one foot.

He had no rifle; he could not fight with his hands, said he resentfully to his plan. Well, rifles could be had for the picking. They were extraordinarily profuse.

Also, he continued, it would be a miracle if he found his regiment. Well, he could fight with any regiment.

He started forward slowly. He stepped as if he expected to tread upon some explosive thing. Doubts and he were struggling.

He would truly be a worm if any of his comrades should see him returning thus, the marks of his flight upon him. There was a reply that the intent fighters did not care for what happened rearward saving that no hostile bayonets appeared there. In the battle-blur his face would, in a way be hidden, like the face of a cowled man.

But then he said that his tireless fate would bring forth, when the strife lulled for a moment, a man to ask of him an explanation. In imagination he felt the scrutiny of his companions as he painfully labored through some lies.

Eventually, his courage expended itself upon these objections. The debates drained him of his fire.

He was not cast down by this defeat of his plan, for, upon studying the affair carefully, he could not but admit that the objections were very formidable.

Furthermore, various ailments had begun to cry out. In their presence he could not persist in flying high with the wings of war; they rendered it almost impossible for him to see himself in a heroic light. He tumbled headlong.

He discovered that he had a scorching thirst. His face was so dry and grimy that he thought he could feel his skin crackle. Each bone of his body had an ache in it, and seemingly threatened to break with each movement. His feet were like two sores. Also, his body was calling for food. It was more powerful than a direct hunger. There was a dull, weight like feeling in his stomach, and, when he tried to walk, his head swayed and he tottered. He could not see with distinctness. Small patches of green mist floated before his vision.

While he had been tossed by many emotions, he had not been aware of ailments. Now they beset him and made clamor. As he was at last compelled to pay attention to them, his capacity for self-hate was multiplied. In despair, he declared that he was not like those others. He now conceded it to be impossible that he should ever become a hero. He was a craven loon. Those pictures of glory were piteous things. He groaned from his heart and went staggering off.

A certain mothlike quality within him kept him in the vicinity of the battle. He had a great desire to see, and to get news. He wished to know who was winning.

He told himself that, despite his unprecedented suffering, he had never lost his greed for a victory, yet, he said, in a half-apologetic manner to his conscience, he could not but know that a defeat for the army this time might mean many favorable things for him. The blows of the enemy would splinter regiments into fragments. Thus, many men of courage, he considered, would be obliged to desert the colors and scurry like chickens. He would appear as one of them. They would be sullen brothers in distress, and he could then easily believe he had not run any farther or faster than they. And if he himself could believe in his virtuous perfection, he conceived that there would be small trouble in convincing all others.

He said, as if in excuse for this hope, that previously the army had encountered great defeats and in a few months had shaken off all blood and tradition of them, emerging as bright and valiant as a new one; thrusting out of sight the memory of disaster, and appearing with the valor and confidence of unconquered legions. The shrilling voices of the people at home would pipe dismally for a time, but various generals were usually compelled to listen to these ditties. He of course felt no compunctions for proposing a general as a sacrifice. He could not tell who the chosen for the barbs might be, so he could center no direct sympathy upon him. The people were afar and he did not conceive public opinion to be accurate at long range. It was quite probable they would hit the wrong man who, after he had recovered from his amazement would perhaps spend the rest of his days in writing replies to the songs of his alleged failure. It would be very unfortunate, no doubt, but in this case a general was of no consequence to the youth.

In a defeat there would be a roundabout vindication of himself. He thought it would prove, in a manner, that he had fled early because of his superior powers of perception. A serious prophet upon predicting a flood should be the first man to climb a tree. This would demonstrate that he was indeed a seer.

A moral vindication was regarded by the youth as a very important thing. Without salve, he could not, he thought, wear the sore badge of his dishonor through life. With his heart continually assuring him that he was despicable, he could not exist without making it, through his actions, apparent to all men.

If the army had gone gloriously on he would be lost. If the din meant that now his army's flags were tilted forward he was a condemned wretch. He would be compelled to doom himself to isolation. If the men were advancing, their indifferent feet were trampling upon his chances for a successful life.

As these thoughts went rapidly through his mind, he turned upon them and tried to thrust them away. He denounced himself as a villain. He said that he was the most unutterably selfish man in existence. His mind pictured the soldiers who would place their defiant bodies before the spear of the yelling battle fiend, and as he saw their dripping corpses on an imagined field, he said that he was their murderer.

Again he thought that he wished he was dead. He believed that he envied a corpse. Thinking of the slain, he achieved a great contempt for some of them, as if they were guilty for thus becoming lifeless. They might have been killed by lucky chances, he said, before they had had opportunities to flee or before they had been really tested. Yet they would receive laurels from tradition. He cried out bitterly that their crowns were stolen and their robes of glorious memories were shams. However, he still said that it was a great pity he was not as they.

A defeat of the army had suggested itself to him as a means of escape from the consequences of his fall. He considered now, however, that it was useless to think of such a possibility. His education had been that success for that mighty blue machine was certain; that it would make victories as a contrivance turns out buttons. He presently discarded all his speculations in the other direction. He returned to the creed of soldiers.

When he perceived again that it was not possible for the army to be defeated, he tried to bethink him of a fine tale which he could take back to his regiment, and with it turn the expected shafts of derision.

But, as he mortally feared these shafts, it became impossible for him to invent a tale he felt he could trust. He experimented with many schemes, but threw them aside one by one as flimsy. He was quick to see vulnerable places in them all.

Furthermore, he was much afraid that some arrow of scorn might lay him mentally low before he could raise his protecting tale.

He imagined the whole regiment saying: "Where's Henry Fleming? He run, didn't 'e? Oh, my!" He recalled various persons who would be quite sure to leave him no peace about it. They would doubtless question him with sneers, and laugh at his stammering hesitation. In the next engagement they would try to keep watch of him to discover when he would run.

Wherever he went in camp, he would encounter insolent and lingeringly-cruel stares. As he imagined himself passing near a crowd of comrades, he could hear some one say, "There he goes!"

Then, as if the heads were moved by one muscle, all the faces were turned toward him with wide, derisive grins. He seemed to hear some one make a humorous remark in a low tone. At it the others all crowed and cackled. He was a slang phrase.

# 12

THE COLUMN THAT had butted stoutly at the obstacles in the roadway was barely out of the youth's sight before he saw dark waves of men come sweeping out of the woods and down through the fields. He knew at once that the steel fibers had been washed from their hearts. They were bursting from their coats and their equipments as from entanglements. They charged down upon him like terrified buffaloes.

Behind them blue smoke curled and clouded above the tree-tops, and through the thickets he could sometimes see a distant pink glare. The voices of the cannon were clamoring in interminable chorus.

The youth was horror-stricken. He stared in agony and amazement. He forgot that he was engaged in combating the universe. He threw aside his mental pamphlets on the philosophy of the retreated and rules for the guidance of the damned. He lost concern for himself.

The fight was lost. The dragons were coming with invincible strides. The army, helpless in the matted thickets and blinded by the overhanging night, was going to be swallowed. War, the red animal, war, the blood-swollen god, would have bloated fill.

Within him something bade to cry out. He had the impulse to make a rallying speech, to sing a battle hymn, but he could only get his tongue to call into the air: "Why—why—what—what's th' matter?"

Soon he was in the midst of them. They were leaping and scampering all about him. Their blanched faces shone in the dusk. They seemed, for the most part, to be very burly men. The youth turned from one to another of them as they galloped along. His incoherent questions were lost. They were heedless of his appeals. They did not seem to see him.

They sometimes gabbled insanely. One huge man was asking of the sky: "Say, where de plank road? Where de plank road!" It was as if he had lost a child. He wept in his pain and dismay.

Presently, men were running hither and thither in all ways. The artillery booming, forward, rearward, and on the flanks made jumble of ideas of direction. Landmarks had vanished into the gathered gloom. The youth began to imagine that he had got into the center of the tremendous quarrel, and he could perceive no way out of it. From the mouths of the fleeing men came a thousand wild questions, but no one made answers.

The youth, after rushing about and throwing interrogations at the heedless bands of retreating infantry, finally clutched a man by the arm. They swung around face to face.

"Why—why——" stammered the youth, struggling with his balking tongue.

The man screamed, "Let go me! Let go me!" His face was livid and his eyes were rolling uncontrolled. He was heaving and panting. He still grasped his rifle, perhaps having forgotten to release his hold upon it. He tugged frantically, and the youth being compelled to lean forward was dragged several paces.

"Let go me! Let go me!"

"Why—why——" stuttered the youth.

"Well, then!" bawled the man in a lurid rage. He adroitly and fiercely swung his rifle. It crushed upon the youth's head. The man ran on.

The youth's fingers had turned to paste upon the other's arm. The energy was smitten from his muscles. He saw the flaming wings of lightning flash before his vision. There was a deafening rumble of thunder within his head.

Suddenly his legs seemed to die. He sank writhing to the ground. He tried to arise. In his efforts against the numbing pain he was like a man wrestling with a creature of the air.

There was a sinister struggle.

Sometimes he would achieve a position half erect, battle with the air for a moment, and then fall again, grabbing at the grass. His face was of a clammy pallor. Deep groans were wrenched from him.

At last, with a twisting movement, he got upon his hands and knees, and from thence, like a babe trying to walk, to his feet. Pressing his hands to his temples, he went lurching over the grass.

He fought an intense battle with his body. His dulled senses wished him to swoon and he opposed them stubbornly, his mind portraying unknown dangers and mutilations if he should fall upon the field. He went tall soldier fashion. He imagined secluded spots where he could fall and be unmolested. To search for one he strove against the tide of his pain.

Once he put his hand to the top of his head and timidly touched the wound. The scratching pain of the contact made him draw a long breath through his clenched teeth. His fingers were dabbled with blood. He regarded them with a fixed stare.

Around him he could hear the grumble of jolted cannon as the scurrying horses were lashed toward the front. Once, a young officer on a besplashed charger nearly ran him down. He turned and watched the mass of guns, men, and horses sweeping in a wide curve toward a gap in a fence. The officer was making excited motions with a gauntleted hand. The guns followed the teams with an air of unwillingness, of being dragged by the heels.

Some officers of the scattered infantry were cursing and railing like fishwives. Their scolding voices could be heard above the din. Into the unspeakable jumble in the roadway rode a squadron of cavalry. The faded yellow of their facings shone bravely. There was a mighty altercation.

The artillery were assembling as if for a conference.

The blue haze of evening was upon the field. The lines of forest were long purple shadows. One cloud lay along the western sky partly smothering the red.

As the youth left the scene behind him, he heard the guns suddenly roar out. He imagined them shaking in black rage. They belched and howled like brass devils guarding a gate. The soft air was filled with the tremendous remonstrance. With it came the shattering peal of opposing infantry. Turning to look behind him, he could see sheets of orange light illumine the shadowy distance. There were subtle and sudden lightnings in the far air. At times he thought he could see heaving masses of men.

He hurried on in the dusk. The day had faded until he could barely distinguish place for his feet. The purple darkness was filled with men who lectured and jabbered. Sometimes he could see them gesticulating against the blue and somber sky. There seemed to be a great ruck of men and munitions spread about in the forest and in the fields.

The little narrow roadway now lay lifeless. There were overturned wagons like sun-dried bowlders. The bed of the former torrent was choked with the bodies of horses and splintered parts of war machines.

It had come to pass that his wound pained him but little. He was afraid to move rapidly, however, for dread of disturbing it. He held his head very still and took many precautions against stumbling. He was filled with anxiety, and his face was pinched and drawn in anticipation of the pain of any sudden mistake of his feet in the gloom.

His thoughts, as he walked, fixed intently upon his hurt. There was a cool, liquid feeling about it and he imagined blood moving slowly down under his hair. His head seemed swollen to a size that made him think his neck to be inadequate.

The new silence of his wound made much worriment. The little blistering voices of pain that had called out from his scalp were, he thought, definite in their expression of danger. By them he believed that he could measure his plight. But when they remained ominously silent he became frightened and imagined terrible fingers that clutched into his brain.

Amid it he began to reflect upon various incidents and conditions of the past. He bethought him of certain meals his mother had cooked at home, in which those dishes of which he was particularly fond had occupied prominent positions. He saw the spread table. The pine walls of the kitchen were glowing in the warm light from the stove. Too, he remembered how he and his companions used to go from the schoolhouse to the bank of the shaded pool. He saw his clothes in disorderly array upon the grass of the bank. He felt the swash of the fragrant water upon his body. The leaves of the overhanging maple rustled with melody in the wind of youthful summer.

He was overcome presently by a dragging weariness. His head hung forward and his shoulders were stooped as if he were bearing a great bundle. His feet shuffled along the ground.

He held continuous arguments as to whether he should lie down and sleep at some near spot, or force himself on until he reached a certain haven. He often tried to dismiss the question, but his body persisted in rebellion and his senses nagged at him like pampered babies.

At last he heard a cheery voice near his shoulder: "Yeh seem t' be in a pretty bad way, boy?"

The youth did not look up, but he assented with thick tongue. "Uh!"

The owner of the cheery voice took him firmly by the arm. "Well," he said, with a round laugh, "I'm goin' your way. Th' hull gang is goin' your way. An' I guess I kin give yeh a lift." They began to walk like a drunken man and his friend.

As they went along, the man questioned the youth, and assisted him with the replies like one manipulating the mind of a child. Sometimes he interjected anecdotes. "What reg'ment do yeh b'long teh? Eh? What's that? Th' 304th N' York? Why, what corps is that in? Oh, it is? Why, I thought they wasn't engaged t'-day—they're 'way over in th' center. Oh, they was, eh? Well, pretty nearly everybody got their share 'a fightin' t'-day. By dad, I give myself up fer dead any number 'a times. There was shootin' here an' shootin' there, an' hollerin' here an' hollerin' there, in th' damn' darkness, until I couldn't tell t' save m' soul which side I was on. Sometimes I thought I was sure 'nough from Ohier, an' other times I could 'a swore I was from th' bitter end of Florida. It was th' most mixed up dern thing I ever see. An' these here hull woods is a reg'lar mess. It'll be a miracle if we find our reg'ments t'-night. Pretty soon, though, we'll meet a-plenty of guards an' provost-guards, an' one thing an' another. Ho! there they go with an off'cer, I guess. Look at his hand a-draggin'. He's got all th' war he wants, I bet. He won't be talkin' so big about his reputation an' all when they go t' sawin' off his leg. Poor feller! My brother's got whiskers jest like that. How did yeh git 'way over here, anyhow? Your reg'ment is a long way from here, ain't it? Well, I guess we can find it. Yeh know there was a boy killed in my comp'ny t'-day that I thought th' world an' all of. Jack was a nice feller. By ginger, it hurt like thunder t' see ol' Jack jest git knocked flat. We was a-standin' purty peaceable fer a spell, 'thought there was men runnin' ev'ry way all 'round us, an' while we was a-standin' like that, 'long come a big fat feller. He began t' peck at Jack's elbow, an' he says: 'Say, where's th' road t' th' river?' An' Jack he never paid no attention, an' th' feller kept on a-peckin' at his elbow an' sayin': 'Say, where's th' road t' th' river?' Jack was a-lookin' ahead all th' time tryin' t' see th' Johnnies comin' through th' woods, an' he never paid no attention t' this big fat feller fer a long time, but at last he turned 'round an' he ses: 'Ah, go t' hell an' find th' road t' th' river!' An' jest then a shot slapped him bang on th' side th' head. He was a sergeant, too. Them was his last words. Thunder, I wish we was sure 'a findin' our reg'ments t'-night. It's goin' t' be long huntin'. But I guess we kin do it.''

In the search which followed, the man of the cheery voice seemed to the youth to possess a wand of a magic kind. He threaded the mazes of the tangled forest with a strange fortune. In encounters with guards and patrols he displayed the keenness of a detective and the valor of a gamin. Obstacles fell before him and became of assistance. The youth, with his chin still on his breast, stood woodenly by while his companion beat ways and means out of sullen things.

The forest seemed a vast hive of men buzzing about in frantic circles, but the cheery man conducted the youth without mistakes, until at last he began to chuckle with glee and self-satisfaction. "Ah, there yeh are! See that fire?''

The youth nodded stupidly.

"Well, there's where your reg'ment is. An' now good-by, ol' boy, good luck t' yeh.''

A warm and strong hand clasped the youth's languid fingers for an instant, and then he heard a cheerful and audacious whistling as the man strode away. As he who had so befriended him was thus passing out of his life, it suddenly occurred to the youth that he had not once seen his face.

# 13

THE YOUTH WENT slowly toward the fire indicated by his departed friend. As he reeled, he bethought him of the welcome his comrades would give him. He had a conviction that he would soon feel in his sore heart the barbed missiles of ridicule. He had no strength to invent a tale; he would be a soft target.

He made vague plans to go off into the deeper darkness and hide, but they were all destroyed by the voices of exhaustion and pain from his body. His ailments, clamoring, forced him to seek the place of food and rest, at whatever cost.

He swung unsteadily toward the fire. He could see the forms of men throwing black shadows in the red light, and as he went nearer it became known to him in some way that the ground was strewn with sleeping men.

Of a sudden he confronted a black and monstrous figure. A rifle barrel caught some glinting beams. "Halt! halt!" He was dismayed for a moment, but he presently thought that he recognized the nervous voice. As he stood tottering before the rifle barrel, he called out: "Why, hello, Wilson, you—you here?"

The rifle was lowered to a position of caution and the loud soldier came slowly forward. He peered into the youth's face. "That you, Henry?"

"Yes, it's—it's me."

"Well, well, ol' boy," said the other, "by ginger, I'm glad t' see yeh! I give yeh up fer a goner. I thought yeh was dead sure enough." There was husky emotion in his voice.

The youth found that now he could barely stand upon his feet. There was a sudden sinking of his forces. He thought he must hasten to produce his tale to protect him from the missiles already at the lips of his redoubtable comrades. So, staggering before the loud soldier, he began: "Yes, yes. I've—I've had an awful time. I've been all over. Way over on th' right. Ter'ble fightin' over there. I had an awful time. I got separated from th' reg'ment. Over on th' right I got shot. In th' head. I never see sech fightin'. Awful time. I don't see how I could 'a got separated from th' reg'ment. I got shot, too."

His friend had stepped forward quickly. "What? Got shot? Why didn't yeh say so first? Poor ol' boy, we must—hol' on a minnit; what am I doin'. I'll call Simpson."

Another figure at that moment loomed in the gloom. They could see that it was the corporal. "Who yeh talkin' to, Wilson?" he demanded. His voice was anger-toned. "Who yeh talkin' to? Yeh th' derndest sentinel—why—hello, Henry, you here? Why, I thought you was dead four hours ago! Great Jerusalem, they keep turnin' up every ten minutes or so! We thought we'd lost forty-two men by straight count, but if they keep on a-comin' this way, we'll git th' comp'ny all back by mornin' yit. Where was yeh?"

"Over on th' right. I got separated—" began the youth with considerable glibness.

But his friend had interrupted hastily. "Yes, an' he got shot in th' head an' he's in a fix, an' we must see t' him right away." He rested his rifle in the hollow of his left arm and his right around the youth's shoulder.

"Gee, it must hurt like thunder!" he said.

The youth leaned heavily upon his friend. "Yes, it hurts—hurts a good deal," he replied. There was a faltering in his voice.

"Oh," said the corporal. He linked his arm in the youth's and drew him forward. "Come on, Henry. I'll take keer 'a yeh."

As they went on together the loud private called out after them: "Put 'im t' sleep in my blanket, Simpson. An'—hol' on a minnit—here's my canteen. It's full 'a coffee. Look at his head by th' fire an' see how it looks. Maybe it's a pretty bad un. When I git relieved in a couple 'a minnits, I'll be over an' see t' him."

The youth's senses were so deadened that his friend's voice sounded from afar and he could scarcely feel the pressure of the corporal's arm. He submitted passively to the latter's directing strength. His head was in the old manner hanging forward upon his breast. His knees wobbled.

The corporal led him into the glare of the fire. "Now, Henry," he said, "let's have a look at yer ol' head."

The youth sat down obediently and the corporal, laying aside his rifle, began to fumble in the bushy hair of his comrade. He was obliged to turn the other's head so that the full flush of the firelight would beam upon it. He puckered his mouth with a critical air. He drew back his lips and whistled through his teeth when his fingers came in contact with the splashed blood and the rare wound.

"Ah, here we are!" he said. He awkwardly made further investigation. "Jest as I thought," he added presently. "Yeh've been grazed by a ball. It's raised a queer lump jest as if some feller had lammed yeh on th' head with a club. It stopped a-bleedin' long time ago. Th' most about it is that in th' mornin' yeh'll feel that a number ten hat wouldn't fit yeh. An' your head'll be all het up an' feel as dry as burnt pork. An' yeh may git a lot 'a other sicknesses, too, by mornin'. Yeh can't never tell. Still, I don't much think so. It's jest a damn' good belt on th' head, and nothin' more. Now, you jest sit here an' don't move, while I go rout out th' relief. Then I'll send Wilson t' take keer 'a yeh.''

The corporal went away. The youth remained on the ground like a parcel. He stared with a vacant look into the fire.

After a time he aroused, for some part, and the things about him began to take form. He saw that the ground in the deep shadows was cluttered with men, sprawling in every conceivable posture. Glancing narrowly into the more distant darkness, he caught occasional glimpses of visages that loomed pallid and ghostly, lit with a phosphorescent glow. These faces expressed in their lines the deep stupor of the tired soldiers. They made them appear like men drunk with wine. This bit of forest might have appeared to an ethereal wanderer as a scene of the result of some frightful debauch.

On the other side of the fire the youth observed an officer asleep, seated bolt upright, with his back against a tree. There was something perilous in his position. Badgered by dreams, perhaps, he swayed with little bounces and starts, like an old, toddy-stricken grandfather in a chimney corner. Dust and stains were upon his face. His lower jaw hung down as if lacking strength to assume its normal position. He was the picture of an exhausted soldier after a feast of war.

He had evidently gone to sleep with his sword in his arms. These two had slumbered in an embrace, but the weapon had been allowed in time to fall unheeded to the ground. The brass-mounted hilt lay in contact with some parts of the fire.

Within the gleam of rose and orange light from the burning sticks were other soldiers, snoring and heaving, or lying deathlike in slumber. A few pairs of legs were stuck forth, rigid and straight. The shoes displayed the mud or dust of marches and bits of rounded trousers, protruding from the blankets, showed rents and tears from hurried pitchings through the dense brambles.

The fire crackled musically. From it swelled light smoke. Overhead the foliage moved softly. The leaves, with their faces turned toward the blaze, were colored shifting hues of silver, often edged with red. Far off to the right, through a window in the forest could be seen a handful of stars lying, like glittering pebbles, on the black level of the night.

Occasionally, in this low-arched hall, a soldier would arouse and turn his body to a new position, the experience of his sleep having taught him of uneven and objectionable places upon the ground under him. Or, perhaps, he would lift himself to a sitting posture, blink at the fire for an unintelligent moment, throw a swift glance at his prostrate companion, and then cuddle down again with a grunt of sleepy content.

The youth sat in a forlorn heap until his friend the loud young soldier came, swinging two canteens by their light strings. "Well, now, Henry, ol' boy," said the latter, "we'll have yeh fixed up in jest about a minnit."

He had the bustling ways of an amateur nurse. He fussed around the fire and stirred the sticks to brilliant exertions. He made his patient drink largely from the canteen that contained the coffee. It was to the youth a delicious draught. He tilted his head afar back and held the canteen long to his lips. The cool mixture went caressingly down his blistered throat. Having finished, he sighed with comfortable delight.

The loud young soldier watched his comrade with an air of satisfaction. He later produced an extensive handkerchief from his pocket. He folded it into a manner of bandage and soused water from the other canteen upon the middle of it. This crude arrangement he bound over the youth's head, tying the ends in a queer knot at the back of the neck.

"There," he said, moving off and surveying his deed, "yeh look like th' devil, but I bet yeh feel better."

The youth contemplated his friend with grateful eyes. Upon his aching and swelling head the cold cloth was like a tender woman's hand.

"Yeh don't holler ner say nothin'," remarked his friend approvingly. "I know I'm a blacksmith at takin' keer 'a sick folks, an' yeh never squeaked. Yer a good un, Henry. Most 'a men would 'a' been in th' hospital long ago. A shot in th' head ain't foolin' business."

The youth made no reply, but began to fumble with the buttons of his jacket.

"Well, come, now," continued his friend, "come on. I must put yeh t' bed an' see that yeh git a good night's rest."

The other got carefully erect, and the loud young soldier led him among the sleeping forms lying in groups and rows. Presently he stooped and picked up his blankets. He spread the rubber one upon the ground and placed the woollen one about the youth's shoulders.

"There now," he said, "lie down and git some sleep."

The youth, with his manner of doglike obediance, got carefully down like a crone stooping. He stretched out with a murmur of relief and comfort. The ground felt like the softest couch.

But of a sudden he ejaculated: "Hol' on a minnit! Where you goin' t' sleep?"

His friend waved his hand impatiently. "Right down there by yeh."

"Well, but hol' on a minnit," continued the youth. "What yeh goin' t' sleep in? I've got your——"

The loud young soldier snarled: "Shet up an' go on t' sleep. Don't be makin' a damn' fool 'a yerself," he said severely.

After the reproof the youth said no more. An exquisite drowsiness had spread through him. The warm comfort of the blanket enveloped him and made a gentle languor. His head fell forward on his crooked arm and his weighted lids went softly down over his eyes. Hearing a splatter of musketry from the distance, he wondered indifferently if those men sometimes slept. He gave a long sigh, snuggled down into his blanket, and in a moment was like his comrades.

# 14

WHEN THE YOUTH awoke it seemed to him that he had been asleep for a thousand years, and he felt sure that he opened his eyes upon an unexpected world. Gray mists were slowly shifting before the first efforts of the sun rays. An impending splendor could be seen in the eastern sky. An icy dew had chilled his face, and immediately upon arousing he curled farther down into his blanket. He stared for a while at the leaves overhead, moving in a heraldic wind of the day.

The distance was splintering and blaring with the noise of fighting. There was in the sound an expression of a deadly persistency, as if it had not begun and was not to cease.

About him were the rows and groups of men that he had dimly seen the previous night. They were getting a last draught of sleep before the awakening. The gaunt, careworn features and dusty figures were made plain by this quaint light at the dawning, but it dressed the skin of the men in corpselike hues and made the tangled limbs appear pulseless and dead. The youth started up with a little cry when his eyes first swept over this motionless mass of men, thick-spread upon the ground, pallid, and in strange postures. His disordered mind interpreted the hall of the forest as a charnel place. He believed for an instant that he was in the house of the dead, and he did not dare to move lest these corpses start up, squalling and squawking. In a second, however, he achieved his proper mind. He swore a complicated oath at himself. He saw that this somber picture was not a fact of the present, but a mere prophecy.

He heard then the noise of a fire crackling briskly in the cold air, and, turning his head, he saw his friend pottering busily about a small blaze. A few other figures moved in the fog, and he heard the hard cracking of axe blows.

Suddenly there was a hollow rumble of drums. A distant bugle sang faintly. Similar sounds, varying in strength, came from near and far over the forest. The bugles called to each other like brazen gamecocks. The near thunder of the regimental drums rolled.

The body of men in the woods rustled. There was a general uplifting of heads. A murmuring of voices broke upon the air. In it there was much bass of grumbling oaths. Strange gods were addressed in condemnation of the early hours necessary to correct war. An officer's peremptory tenor rang out and quickened the stiffened movement of the men. The tangled limbs unravelled. The corpse-hued faces were hidden behind fists that twisted slowly in the eye sockets. It was the soldier's bath.

The youth sat up and gave vent to an enormous yawn. "Thunder!" he remarked petulantly. He rubbed his eyes, and then putting up his hand felt carefully for the bandage over his wound. His friend, perceiving him to be awake, came from the fire. "Well, Henry, ol' man, how do yeh feel this mornin'?" He demanded.

The youth yawned again. Then he puckered his mouth to a little pucker. His head, in truth, felt precisely like a melon, and there was an unpleasant sensation at his stomach.

"Oh Lord, I feel pretty bad," he said.

"Thunder!" exclaimed the other. "I hoped ye'd feel all right this mornin'. Let's see th' bandage—I guess it's slipped." He began to tinker at the wound in rather a clumsy way until the youth exploded.

"Gosh-dern it!" he said in sharp irritation; "you're the hangdest man I ever saw! You wear muffs on your hands. Why in good thunderation can't you be more easy? I'd rather you'd stand off an' throw guns at it. Now, go slow, an' don't act as if you was nailing down carpet.''

He glared with insolent command at his friend, but the latter answered soothingly. ''Well, well, come now, an' git some grub,'' he said. ''Then, maybe, yeh'll feel better.''

At the fireside the loud young soldier watched over his comrade's wants with tenderness and care. He was very busy marshalling the little black vagabonds of tin cups and pouring into them the steaming, iron colored mixture from a small and sooty tin pail. He had some fresh meat, which he roasted hurriedly upon a stick. He sat down then and contemplated the youth's appetite with glee.

The youth took note of a remarkable change in his comrade since those days of camp life upon the river bank. He seemed no more to be continually regarding the proportions of his personal prowess. He was not furious at small words that pricked his conceits. He was no more a loud young soldier. There was about him now a fine reliance. He showed a quiet belief in his purposes and his abilities. And this inward confidence evidently enabled him to be indifferent to little words of other men aimed at him.

The youth reflected. He had been used to regarding his comrade as a blatant child with an audacity grown from his inexperience, thought-less, headstrong, jealous, and filled with a tinsel courage—a swag-gering babe accustomed to strut in his own dooryard. The youth wondered where had been born those new eyes; when his comrade had made the great discovery that there were many men who would refuse to be subjected by him. Apparently, the other had now climbed a peak of wisdom from which he could perceive himself as a very wee thing. And the youth saw that ever after it would be easier to live in his friend's neighborhood.

His comrade balanced his ebony coffee-cup on his knee. ''Well, Henry,'' he said, ''what d'yeh think th' chances are? D'yeh think we'll wallop 'em?''

The youth considered for a moment. ''Day-b'fore-yesterday,'' he finally replied, with boldness, ''you would 'a' bet you'd lick the hull kit-an'-boodle all by yourself.''

His friend looked a trifle amazed. ''Would I?'' he asked. He pondered. ''Well, perhaps I would,'' he decided at last. He stared humbly at the fire.

The youth was quite disconcerted at this surprising reception of his remarks. "Oh, no, you wouldn't either," he said hastily trying to retrace.

But the other made a deprecating gesture. "Oh, yeh needn't mind, Henry," he said. "I believe I was a pretty big fool in those days." He spoke as after a lapse of years.

There was a little pause.

"All th' officers say we've got th' rebs in a pretty tight box," said the friend, clearing his throat in a commonplace way. "They all seem t' think we've got 'em jest where we want 'em."

"I don't know about that," the youth replied. "What I seen over on th' right makes me think it was th' other way about. From where I was, it looked as if we was gettin' a good poundin' yestirday."

"D'yeh think so?" inquired the friend. "I thought we handled 'em pretty rough yestirday."

"Not a bit," said the youth. "Why, lord, man, you didn't see nothing of the fight. Why!" Then a sudden thought came to him. "Oh! Jim Conklin's dead."

His friend started. "What? Is he? Jim Conklin?"

The youth spoke slowly. "Yes, He's dead. Shot in th' side."

"Yeh don't say so. Jim Conklin . . . poor cuss!"

All about them were other small fires surrounded by men with their little black utensils. From one of these near came sudden sharp voices in a row. It appeared that two light-footed soldiers had been teasing a huge, bearded man, causing him to spill coffee upon his blue knees. The man had gone into a rage and had sworn comprehensively. Stung by his language, his tormentors had immediately bristled at him with a great show of resenting unjust oaths. Possibly there was going to be a fight.

The friend arose and went over to them, making pacific motions with his arms. "Oh, here now, boys, what's th' use?" he said. "We'll be at th' rebs in less'n an hour. What's th' good fightin' 'mong ourselves?"

One of the light-footed soldiers turned upon him, red-faced and violent. "Yeh needn't come around here with yer preachin'. I s'pose yeh don't approve 'a fightin' since Charley Morgan licked yeh; but I don't see what business this here is 'a yours or anybody else."

"Well, it ain't," said the friend mildly. "Still I hate t' see——"

There was a tangled argument.

"Well, he——" said the two, indicating their opponent with accusative forefingers.

The huge soldier was quite purple with rage. He pointed at the two soldiers with his great hand, extending clawlike. "Well, they——"

But during this argumentative time the desire to deal blows seemed to pass, although they said much to each other. Finally the friend returned to his old seat. In a short while the three antagonists could be seen together in an amiable bunch.

"Jimmie Rogers ses I'll have t' fight him after th' battle t'-day," announced the friend as he again seated himself. "He ses he don't allow no interferin' in his business. I hate t' see th' boys fightin' 'mong themselves."

The youth laughed. "Yer changed a good bit. Yeh ain't at all like yeh was. I remember when you an' that Irish feller——" He stopped and laughed again.

"No, I didn't use t' be that way," said his friend thoughtfully. "That's true 'nough."

"Well, I didn't mean——"began the youth.

The friend made another deprecatory gesture. "Oh, yeh needn't mind, Henry."

There was another little pause.

"Th' reg'ment lost over half th' men yestirday," remarked the friend eventually. "I thought 'a course they was all dead, but, laws, they kep' a-comin' back last night until it seems, after all, we didn't lost but a few. They'd been scattered all over, wanderin' around in th' woods, fightin' with other reg'ments, an' everything. Jest like you done."

"So?" said the youth.

# 15

THE REGIMENT WAS standing at order arms at the side of a lane, waiting for the command to march, when suddenly the youth remembered the little packet enwrapped in a faded yellow envelope which the loud young soldier with lugubrious words had entrusted to him. It made him start. He uttered an exclamation and turned toward his comrade.

"Wilson!"

"What?"

His friend, at his side in the ranks, was thoughtfully staring down the road. From some cause his expression was at that moment very meek. The youth, regarding him with sidelong glances, felt impelled to change his purpose. "Oh, nothing," he said.

His friend turned his head in some surprise. "Why, what was yeh goin' t' say?"

"Oh, nothing," repeated the youth.

He resolved not to deal the little blow. It was sufficient that the fact made him glad. It was not necessary to knock his friend on the head with the misguided packet.

He had been possessed of much fear of his friend, for he saw how easily questionings could make holes in his feelings. Lately, he had assured himself that the altered comrade would not tantalize him with a persistent curiosity, but he felt certain that during the first period of leisure his friend would ask him to relate his adventures of the previous day.

He now rejoiced in the possession of a small weapon with which he could prostrate his comrade at the first signs of a cross-examination. He was master. It would now be he who could laugh and shoot the shafts of derision.

The friend had, in a weak hour, spoken with sobs of his own death. He had delivered a melancholy oration previous to his funeral, and had doubtless in the packet of letters presented various keepsakes to relatives. But he had not died, and thus he had delivered himself into the hands of the youth.

The latter felt immensely superior to his friend, but he inclined to condescension. He adopted towards him an air of patronizing good humor.

His self-pride was now entirely restored. In the shade of its flourishing growth he stood with braced and self-confident legs, and since nothing could now be discovered he did not shrink from an encounter with the eyes of judges, and allowed no thoughts of his own to keep him from an attitude of manfulness. He had performed his mistakes in the dark, so he was still a man.

Indeed, when he remembered his fortunes of yesterday, and looked at them from a distance, he began to see something fine there. He had license to be pompous and veteranlike.

His panting agonies of the past he put out of his sight. The long tirades against nature he now believed to be foolish compositions born of his condition. He did not altogether repudiate them because he did not remember all that he had said. He was inclined to regard his past rebellions with an indulgent smile. They were all right in their hour, perhaps.

In the present, he declared to himself that it was only the doomed and the damned who roared with sincerity at circumstance. Few but they ever did it. A man with a full stomach and the respect of his fellows had no business to scold about anything that he might think to be wrong in the ways of the universe, or even with the ways of society. Let the unfortunates rail; the others may play marbles.

Since he was comfortable and contented, he had no desire to set things straight. Indeed, he no more contended that they were not straight. How could they be crooked when he was restored to a requisite amount of happiness? There was a slowly developing conviction that in all his red speeches he had been ridiculously mistaken. Nature was a fine thing moving with a magnificent justice. The world was fair and wide and glorious. The sky was kind, and smiled tenderly, full of encouragement, upon him.

Some poets now received his scorn. Yesterday, in his misery, he had thought of certain persons who had written. Their remembered words, broken and detached, had come piecemeal to him. For these people he had then felt a glowing, brotherly regard. They had wandered in paths of pain and they had made pictures of the black landscape that others might enjoy it with them. He had, at that time, been sure that their wise, contemplating spirits had been in sympathy with him, had shed tears from the clouds. He had walked alone, but there had been pity, made before a reason for it.

But he was now, in a measure, a successful man, and he could no longer tolerate in himself a spirit of fellowship for poets. He abandoned them. Their songs about black landscapes were of no importance to him, since his new eyes said that his landscape was not black. People who called landscapes black were idiots.

He achieved a mighty scorn for such a snivelling race.

He felt that he was the child of the powers. Through the peace of his heart, he saw the earth to be a garden in which grew no weeds of agony. Or, perhaps, if there did grow a few, it was in obscure corners where no one was obliged to encounter them unless a ridiculous search was made. And, at any rate, they were tiny ones.

He returned to his old belief in the ultimate, astounding success of his life. He, as usual, did not trouble about processes. It was ordained, because he was a fine creation. He saw plainly that he was the chosen of some gods. By fearful and wonderful roads he was to be led to a crown. He was, of course, satisfied that he deserved it.

He did not give a great deal of thought to these battles that lay directly before him. It was not essential that he should plan his ways in regard to them. He had been taught that many obligations of a life were easily avoided. The lessons of yesterday had been that retribution was a laggard and blind. With these facts before him he did not deem it necessary that he should become feverish over the possibilities of the ensuing twenty-four hours. He could leave much to chance. Besides, a faith in himself had secretly blossomed. There was a little flower of confidence growing within him. He was now a man of experience. He had been out among the dragons, he said, and he assured himself that they were not so hideous as he had imagined them. Also they were inaccurate; they did not sting with precision. A stout heart often defied, and defying, escaped.

And, furthermore, how could they kill him who was the chosen of gods and doomed to greatness?

He remembered how some of the men had run from the battle. As he recalled their terror-struck faces, he felt a scorn for them. They had surely been more fleet and more wild than was absolutely necessary. They were weak mortals. As for himself, he had fled with discretion and dignity.

He was aroused from his reverie by his friend, who, having hitched about nervously and blinked at the trees for a time, suddenly coughed in an introductory way, and spoke.

"Fleming!"

"What?"

The friend put his hand up to his mouth and coughed again. He fidgeted in his jacket.

"Well," he gulped at last, "I guess yeh might as well give me back them letters." Dark, prickling blood had flushed into his cheeks and brow.

"All right, Wilson," said the youth. He loosened two buttons of his coat, thrust in his hand, and brought forth the packet. As he extended it to his friend the latter's face was turned from him.

He had been slow in the act of producing the packet because during it he had been trying to invent a remarkable comment upon the affair. He could conjure nothing of sufficient point. He was compelled to allow his friend to escape unmolested with his packet. And for this he took unto himself considerable credit. It was a generous thing.

His friend at his side seemed suffering great shame. As he contemplated him, the youth felt his heart grow more strong and stout. He had never been compelled to blush in such manner for his acts; he was an individual of extraordinary virtues.

He reflected, with condescending pity: "Too bad! Too bad! The poor devil, it makes him feel tough!"

After this incident, and as he reviewed the battle pictures he had seen, he felt quite competent to return home and make the hearts of the people glow with stories of war. He could see himself in a room of warm tints telling tales to listeners. He could exhibit laurels. They were insignificant; still, in a district where laurels were infrequent, they might shine.

He saw his gaping audience picturing him as the central figure in blazing scenes. And he imagined the consternation and the ejaculations of his mother and the young lady at the seminary as they drank his recitals. Their vague feminine formula for beloved ones doing brave deeds on the field of battle without risk of life would be destroyed.

# 16

A SPUTTERING OF musketry was always to be heard. Later, the cannon had entered the dispute. In the fog-filled air their voices made a thudding sound. The reverberations were continued. This part of the world led a strange, battleful existence.

The youth's regiment was marched to relieve a command that had lain long in some damp trenches. The men took positions behind a curving line of rifle pits that had been turned up, like a large furrow, along the line of woods. Before them was a level stretch, people with short, deformed stumps. From the woods beyond came the dull popping of the skirmishers and pickets, firing in the fog. From the right came the noise of a terrific fracas.

The men cuddled behind the small embankment and sat in easy attitudes awaiting their return. Many had their backs to the firing. The youth's friend lay down, buried his face in his arms, and almost instantly, it seemed, he was in a deep sleep.

The youth leaned his breast against the brown dirt and peered over at the woods and up and down the line. Curtains of trees interfered with his ways of vision. He could see the low line of trenches but for a short distance. A few idle flags were perched on the dirt hills. Behind them were rows of dark bodies with a few heads sticking curiously over the top.

Always the noise of skirmishers came from the woods on the front and left, and the din on the right had grown to frightful proportions. The guns were roaring without an instant's pause for breath. It seemed that the cannon had come from all parts and were engaged in a stupendous wrangle. It became impossible to make a sentence heard.

The youth wished to launch a joke—a quotation from newspapers. He desired to say, "All quiet on the Rappahannock," but the guns refused to permit even a comment upon their uproar. He never successfully concluded the sentence. But at last the guns stopped, and among the men in the rifle pits rumors again flew, like birds, but they were now for the most part black creatures who flapped their wings drearily near to the ground and refused to rise on any wings of hope. The men's faces grew doleful from the interpreting of omens. Tales of hesitation and uncertainty on the part of those high in place and responsibility came to their ears. Stories of disaster were borne into their minds with many proofs. This din of musketry on the right, growing like a released genie of sound, expressed and emphasized the army's plight.

The men were disheartened and began to mutter. They made gestures expressive of the sentence: "Ah, what more can we do?" And it could always be seen that they were bewildered by the alleged news and could not fully comprehend a defeat.

Before the gray mists had been totally obliterated by the sun rays, the regiment was marching in a spread column that was retiring carefully through the woods. The disordered, hurrying lines of the enemy could sometimes be seen down through the groves and little fields. They were yelling, shrill and exultant.

At this sight the youth forgot many personal matters and became greatly enraged. He exploded in loud sentences. "B'jiminey, we're generalled by a lot 'a lunkheads."

"More than one feller has said that t'day," observed a man.

His friend, recently aroused, was still very drowsy. He looked behind him until his mind took in the meaning of the movement. Then he sighed. "Oh, well, I s'pose we got licked," he remarked sadly.

The youth had a thought that it would not be handsome for him to freely condemn other men. He made an attempt to restrain himself, but the words upon his tongue were too bitter. He presently began a long and intricate denunciation of the commander of the forces.

"Mebbe it wa'n't all his fault—not all together. He did th' best he knowed. It's our luck t' git licked often," said his friend in a weary tone. He was trudging along with stooped shoulders and shifting eyes like a man who has been caned and kicked.

"Well, don't we fight like the devil? Don't we do all that men can?" demanded the youth loudly.

He was secretly dumbfounded at this sentiment when it came from his lips. For a moment his face lost its valor, and he looked guiltily about him. But no one questioned his right to deal in such words, and presently he recovered his air of courage. He went on to repeat a statement he had heard going from group to group at the camp that morning. "The brigadier said he never saw a new reg'ment fight the way we fought yestirday, didn't he? And we didn't do better than many other reg'ment, did we? Well, then, you can't say it's th' army's fault, can you?"

In his reply, the friend's voice was stern. "'A course not," he said. "No man dare say we don't fight like th' devil. No man will ever dare say it. Th' boys fight like hell-roosters. But still—still, we don't have no luck."

"Well, then, if we fight like the devil an' don't ever whip, it must be the general's fault," said the youth grandly and decisively. "And I don't see any sense in fighting and fighting and fighting, yet always losing through some derned old lunkhead of a general."

A sarcastic man who was tramping at the youth's side, then spoke lazily. "Mebbe yeh think yeh fit th' hull battle yestirday, Fleming," he remarked.

The speech pierced the youth. Inwardly he was reduced to an abject pulp by these chance words. His legs quaked privately. He cast a frightened glace at the sarcastic man.

"Why, no,' he hastened to say in a conciliating voice, "I don't think I fought the whole battle yesterday."

But the other seemed innocent of any deeper meaning. Apparently, he had no information. It was merely his habit. "Oh!" he replied in the same tone of calm derision.

The youth, nevertheless, felt a threat. His mind shrank from going near to the danger, and thereafter he was silent. The significance of the sarcastic man's words took from him all loud moods that would make him appear prominent. He became suddenly a modest person.

There was low-toned talk among the troops. The officers were impatient and snappy, their countenances clouded with the tales of misfortune. The troops, sifting through the forest, were sullen. In the youth's company once a man's laugh rang out. A dozen soldiers turned their faces quickly toward him and frowned with vague displeasure.

The noise of firing dogged their footsteps. Sometimes, it seemed to be driven a little way, but it always returned again with increased insolence. The men muttered and cursed, throwing black looks in its direction.

In a clear space the troops were at last halted. Regiments and brigades, broken and detached through their encounters with thickets, grew together again and lines were faced toward the pursuing bark of the enemy's infantry.

This noise, following like the yellings of eager, metallic hounds, increased to a loud and joyous burst, and then, as the sun went serenely up the sky throwing illuminating rays into the gloomy thickets, it broke forth into prolonged pealings. The woods began to crackle as if afire.

"Whoop-a-dadee," said a man, "here we are! Everybody fightin'. Blood an' destruction."

"I was willin' t' bet they'd attack as soon as th' sun got fairly up," savagely asserted the lieutenant who commanded the youth's company. He jerked without mercy at his little moustache. He strode to and fro with dark dignity in the rear of his men, who were lying down behind whatever protection they had collected.

A battery had trundled into position in the rear and was thoughtfully shelling the distance. The regiment, unmolested as yet, awaited the moment when the gray shadows of the woods before them should be slashed by the lines of flame. There was much growling and swearing.

"Good Gawd," the youth grumbled, "we're always being chased around like rats! It makes me sick. Nobody seems to know where we go or why we go. We just get fired around from pillar to post and get licked here and get licked there, and nobody knows what it's done for. It makes a man feel like a damn' kitten in a bag. Now, I'd like to know what the eternal thunders we was marched into these woods for anyhow, unless it was to give the rebs a regular pot shot at us. We came in here and got our legs all tangled up in these cussed briers, and then we begin to fight and the rebs had an easy time of it. Don't tell me it's just luck! I know better. It's this derned old———"

The friend seemed jaded, but he interrupted his comrade with a voice of calm confidence. "It'll turn out all right in th' end," he said.

"Oh, the devil it will! You always talk like a dog-hanged parson. Don't tell me! I know——"

At this time there was an interposition by the savage-minded lieutenant, who was obliged to vent some of his inward dissatisfaction upon his men. "You boys shut right up! There's no need 'a your wasting your breath in long-winded arguments about this an' that an' th' other. You've been jawin' like a lot 'a old hens. All you've got t' do is to fight, an' you'll get plenty 'a that t' do in about ten minutes. Less talkin' and more fightin' is what's best for you boys. I never saw sech gabbling jackasses."

He paused, ready to pounce upon any man who might have the temerity to reply. No words being said, he resumed his dignified pacing.

"There's too much chin music and too little fightin' in this war, anyhow," he said to them, turning his head for a final remark.

The day had grown more white, until the sun shed his full radiance upon the thronged forest. A sort of a gust of battle came sweeping toward that part of the line where lay the youth's regiment. The front shifted a trifle to meet it squarely. There was a wait. In this part of the field there passed slowly the intense moments that precede the tempest.

A single rifle flashed in a thicket before the regiment. In an instant it was joined by many others. There was a mighty song of clashes and crashes that went sweeping through the woods. The guns in the rear, aroused and enraged by shells that had been thrown burr-like at them, suddenly involved themselves in a hideous altercation with another band of guns. The battle roar settled to a rolling thunder, which was a single, long explosion.

In the regiment there was a peculiar kind of hesitation denoted in the attitudes of the men. They were worn, exhausted, having slept but little and labored much. They rolled their eyes toward the advancing battle as they stood awaiting the shock. Some shrank and flinched. They stood as men tied to stakes.

# 17

THIS ADVANCE OF the enemy had seemed to the youth like a ruthless hunting. He began to fume with rage and exasperation. He beat his foot upon the ground, and scowled with hate at the swirling smoke that was approaching like a phantom flood. There was a maddening quality in this seeming resolution of the foe to give him no rest, to give him no time to sit down and think. Yesterday he had fought and had fled rapidly. There had been many adventures. For to-day he felt that he had earned opportunities for contemplative repose. He could have enjoyed portraying to uninitiated listeners various scenes at which he had been a witness or ably discussing the processes of war with other proved men. Too, it was important that he should have time for physical recuperation. He was sore and stiff from his experiences. He had received his fill of all exertions, and he wished to rest.

But those other men seemed never to grow weary; they were fighting with their old speed. He had a wild hate for the relentless foe. Yesterday, when he had imagined the universe to be against him, he had hated it, little gods and big gods; to-day he hated the army of the foe with the same great hatred. He was not going to be badgered of his life, like a kitten chased by boys, he said. It was not well to drive men into final corners; at those moments they could all develop teeth and claws.

He leaned and spoke into his friend's ear. He menaced the woods with a gesture. "If they keep on chasing us, by Gawd they'd better watch out. Can't stand *too* much."

The friend twisted his head and made a calm reply. "If they keep on a-chasin' us they'll drive us all inteh th' river."

The youth cried out savagely at this statement. He crouched behind a little tree, with his eyes burning hatefully, and his teeth set in a cur-like snarl. The awkward bandage was still about his head, and upon it, over his wound, there was a spot of dry blood. His hair was wondrously tousled, and some straggling, moving locks hung over the cloth of the bandage down toward his forehead. His jacket and shirt were open at the throat, and exposed his young bronzed neck. There could be seen spasmodic gulpings at his throat.

His fingers twined nervously about his rifle. He wished that it was an engine of annihilating power. He felt that he and his companions were being taunted and derided from sincere convictions that they were poor and puny. His knowledge of his inability to take vengeance for it made his rage into a dark and stormy specter, that possessed him and made him dream of abominable cruelties. The tormentors were flies sucking insolently at his blood, and he thought that he would have given his life for a revenge of seeing their faces in pitiful plights.

The winds of battle had swept all about the regiment, until the one rifle, instantly followed by others, flashed in its front. A moment later the regiment roared forth its sudden and valiant retort. A dense wall of smoke settled slowly down. It was furiously slit and slashed by the knifelike fire from the rifles.

To the youth the fighters resembled animals tossed for a death struggle into a dark pit. There was a sensation that he and his fellows, at bay, were pushing back, always pushing fierce onslaughts of creatures who were slippery. Their beams of crimson seemed to get no purchase upon the bodies of their foes; the latter seemed to evade them with ease, and come through, between, around, and about with unopposed skill.

When, in a dream, it occurred to the youth that his rifle was an impotent stick, he lost sense of everything but his hate, his desire to smash into pulp the glittering smile of victory which he could feel upon the faces of his enemies.

The blue smoke-swallowed line curled and writhed like a snake stepped upon. It swung its end to and fro in an agony of fear and rage.

The youth was not conscious that he was erect upon his feet. He did not know the direction of the ground. Indeed, once he even lost the habit of balance and fell heavily. He was up again immediately. One thought went through the chaos of his brain at the time. He wondered if he had fallen because he had been shot. But the suspicion flew away at once. He did not think more of it.

He had taken up a first position behind the little tree, with a direct determination to hold it against the world. He had not deemed it possible that his army could that day succeed, and from this he felt the ability to fight harder. But the throng had surged in all ways, until he lost directions and locations, save that he knew where lay the enemy.

The flames bit him, and the hot smoke broiled his skin. His rifle barrel grew so hot that ordinarily he could not have borne it upon his palms; but he kept on stuffing cartridges into it, and pounding them with his clanking, bending ram-rod. If he aimed at some charging form through the smoke, he pulled his trigger with a fierce grunt, as if he were dealing a blow of the fist with all his strength.

When the enemy seemed falling back before him and his fellows, he went instantly forward, like a dog who, seeing his foes lagging, turns and insists upon being pursued. And when he was compelled to retire again, he did it slowly, sullenly, taking steps of wrathful despair.

Once he, in his intense hate, was almost alone, and was firing when all those near him had ceased. He was so engrossed in his occupation that he was not aware of a lull.

He was recalled by a hoarse laugh and a sentence that came to his ears in a voice of contempt and amazement. "Yeh infernal fool, don't yeh know enough t' quit when there ain't anything t' shoot at? Good Gawd!"

He turned then and, pausing with his rifle thrown half into position, looked at the blue line of his comrades. During this moment of leisure they seemed all to be engaged in staring with astonishment at him. They had become spectators. Turning to the front again he saw, under the lifted smoke, a deserted ground.

He looked bewildered for a moment. Then there appeared upon the glazed vacancy of his eyes a diamond point of intelligence. "Oh," he said, comprehending.

He returned to his comrades and threw himself upon the ground. He sprawled like a man who had been thrashed. His flesh seemed strangely on fire, and the sounds of the battle continued in his ears. He groped blindly for his canteen.

The lieutenant was crowing. He seemed drunk with fighting. He called out to the youth: "By heavens, if I had ten thousand wild cats like you, I could tear th' stomach outa this war in less'n a week!" He puffed out his chest with large dignity as he said it.

Some of the men muttered and looked at the youth in awestruck ways. It was plain that as he had gone on loading and firing and cursing without proper intermission, they had found time to regard him. And they now looked upon him as a war devil.

The friend came staggering to him. There was some fright and dismay in his voice. "Are yeh all right, Fleming? Do yeh feel all right? There ain't nothin' th' matter with yeh, Henry, is there?"

"No," said the youth with difficulty. His throat seemed full of knobs and burrs.

These incidents made the youth ponder. It was revealed to him that he had been a barbarian, a beast. He had fought like a pagan who defends his religion. Regarding it, he saw that it was fine, wild, and in some ways, easy. He had been a tremendous figure, no doubt. By this struggle he had overcome obstacles which he had admitted to be mountains. They had fallen like paper peaks, and he was now what he called a hero. And he had not been aware of the process. He had slept and, awakening, found himself a knight.

He lay and basked in the occasional stares of his comrades. Their faces were varied in degrees of blackness from the burned powder. Some were utterly smudged. They were reeking with perspiration, and their breaths came hard and wheezing. And from these soiled expanses they peered at him.

"Hot work! Hot work!" cried the lieutenant deliriously. He walked up and down, restless and eager. Sometimes his voice could be heard in a wild, incomprehensible laugh.

When he had a particularly profound thought upon the science of war he always unconsciously addressed himself to the youth.

There was some grim rejoicing by the men. "By thunder, I bet this army'll never see another new reg'ment like us!"

"You bet!"

> *"'A dog, a woman, an' a walnut tree,*
> *Th' more yeh beat' em, th' better they be!'*

That's like us."

"Lost a piler men, they did. If an ol' woman swep' up th' woods she'd git a dustpanful."

"Yes, an' if she'll come around ag'in in 'bout an hour she'll git a pile more."

The forest still bore its burden of clamor. From off under the trees came the rolling clatter of the musketry. Each distant thicket seemed a strange porcupine with quills of flame. A cloud of dark smoke, as from smoldering ruins, went up toward the sun now bright and gay in the blue, enamelled sky.

# 18

THE RAGGED LINE had respite for some minutes, but during its pause the struggle in the forest became magnified until the trees seemed to quiver from the firing and the ground to shake from the rushing of the men. The voices of the cannon were mingled in a long and interminable row. It seemed difficult to live in such an atmosphere. The chests of the men strained for a bit of freshness, and their throats craved water.

There was one shot through the body, who raised a cry of bitter lamentation when came this lull. Perhaps he had been calling out during the fighting also, but at that time no one had heard him. But now the men turned at the woeful complaints of him upon the ground.

"Who is it? Who is it?"

"It's Jimmie Rogers. Jimmie Rogers."

When their eyes first encountered him there was a sudden halt, as if they feared to go near. He was thrashing about in the grass, twisting his shuddering body into many strange postures. He was screaming loudly. This instant's hesitation seemed to fill him with a tremendous, fantastic contempt, and he damned them in shrieked sentences.

The youth's friend had a geographical illusion concerning a stream, and he obtained permission to go for some water. Immediately canteens were showered upon him. "Fill mine, will yeh?" "Bring me some, too." "And me, too." He departed, laden. The youth went with his friend, feeling a desire to throw his heated body into the stream and, soaking here, drink quarts.

They made a hurried search for the supposed stream, but did not find it. "No water here," said the youth. They turned without delay and began to retrace their steps.

From their position as they again faced toward the place of the fighting, they could of course comprehend a greater amount of the battle than when their visions had been blurred by the hurling smoke of the line. They could see dark stretches winding along the land, and on one cleared space there was a row of guns making gray clouds, which were filled with large flashes of orange-colored flame. Over some foliage they could see the roof of a house. One window, glowing a deep murder red, shone squarely through the leaves. From the edifice a tall leaning tower of smoke went far into the sky.

Looking over their own troops, they saw mixed masses slowly getting into regular form. The sunlight made twinkling points of the bright steel. To the rear there was a glimpse of a distant roadway as it curved over a slope. It was crowded with retreating infantry. From all the interwoven forest arose the smoke and bluster of the battle. The air was always occupied by a blaring.

Near where they stood shells were flip-flapping and hooting. Occasional bullets buzzed in the air and spanged into tree trunks. Wounded men and other stragglers were slinking through the woods.

Looking down an aisle of the grove, the youth and his companion saw a jangling general and his staff almost ride upon a wounded man, who was crawling on his hands and knees. The general reined strongly at his charger's opened and foamy mouth and guided it with dexterous horsemanship past the man. The latter scrambled in wild and torturing haste. His strength evidently failed him as he reached a place of safety. One of his arms suddenly weakened, and he fell, sliding over upon his back. He lay stretched out, breathing gently.

A moment later the small, creaking cavalcade was directly in front of the two soldiers. Another officer, riding with the skilful abandon of a cowboy. galloped his horse to a position directly before the general. The two unnoticed foot soldiers made a little show of going on, but they lingered near in the desire to overhear the conversation. Perhaps they thought some great inner historical things would be said.

The general, whom the boys knew as the commander of their division, looked at the other officer and spoke coolly, as if he were criticizing his clothes. "Th' enemy's formin' over there for another charge," he said. "It'll be directed against Whiterside, an' I fear they'll break through there unless we work like thunder t' stop them."

The other swore at his restive horse, and then cleared his throat. He made a gesture toward his cap. "It'll be hell t' pay stoppin' them," he said shortly.

"I presume so," remarked the general. Then he began to talk rapidly and in a lower tone. He frequently illustrated his words with a pointing finger. The two infantrymen could hear nothing until finally he asked: "What troops can you spare?"

The officer who rode like a cowboy reflected for an instant. "Well," he said, "I had to order in th' 12th to help th' 76th, an' I haven't really got any. But there's th' 304th. They fight like a lot 'a mule drivers. I can spare them best of any."

The youth and his friend exchanged glances of astonishment.

The general spoke sharply. "Get 'em ready, then. I'll watch developments from here, an' send you word when t' start them. It'll happen in five minutes."

As the other officer tossed his fingers toward his cap and wheeling his horse, started away, the general called out to him in a sober voice: "I don't believe many of your mule drivers will get back."

The other shouted something in reply. He smiled.

With scared faces, the youth and his companion hurried back to the line.

These happenings had occupied an incredibly short time, yet the youth felt that in them he had been made aged. New eyes were given

to him. And the most startling thing was to learn suddenly that he was
very insignificant. The officer spoke of the regiment as if he referred
to a broom. Some part of the woods needed sweeping, perhaps, and
he merely indicated a broom in a tone properly indifferent to its fate. It
was war, no doubt, but it appeared strange.

As the two boys approached the line, the lieutenant perceived them
and swelled with wrath. "Fleming—Wilson—how long does it take
yeh to git water, anyhow—where yeh been to?"

But his oration ceased as he saw their eyes, which were large with
great tales. "We're goin' t' charge—we're goin' t' charge!" cried the
youth's friend, hastening with his news.

"Charge?" said the lieutenant. "Charge? Well, b'Gawd! Now,
this is real fightin'." Over his soiled countenance there went a
boastful smile. "Charge? Well, b'Gawd!"

A little group of soldiers surrounded the two youths. "Are we, sure
'nough? Well, I'll be derned! Charge? What fer? What at? Wilson,
you're lyin'."

"I hope to die," said the youth, pitching his tones to the key of
angry remonstrance. "Sure as shooting, I tell you."

And his friend spoke in re-enforcement. "Not by a blame sight, he
ain't lyin'. We heard 'em talkin'."

They caught sight of two mounted figures a short distance from
them. One was the colonel of the regiment and the other was the
officer who had received orders from the commander of the division.
They were gesticulating at each other. The soldier, pointing at them,
interpreted the scene.

One man had a final objection: "How could yeh hear 'em talkin'?"
But the men, for a large part, nodded, admitting that previously the
two friends had spoken truth.

They settled back into reposeful attitudes with airs of having
accepted the matter. And they mused upon it, with a hundred varieties
of expression. It was an engrossing thing to think about. Many
tightened their belts carefully and hitched at their trousers.

A moment later the officers began to bustle among the men,
pushing them into a more compact mass and into a better alignment.
They chased those that straggled and fumed at a few men who seemed
to show by their attitudes that they had decided to remain at that spot.
They were like critical shepherds struggling with sheep.

Presently, the regiment seemed to draw itself up and heave a deep
breath. None of the men's faces were mirrors of large thoughts. The
soldiers were bended and stooped like sprinters before a signal. Many
pairs of glinting eyes peered from the grimy faces toward the curtains

of the deeper woods. They seemed to be engaged in deep calculations of time and distance.

They were surrounded by the noises of the monstrous altercation between the two armies. The world was fully interested in other matters. Apparently the regiment had its small affair to itself.

The youth, turning, shot a quick inquiring glance at his friend. The latter returned to him the same manner of look. They were the only ones who possessed an inner knowledge. "Mule drivers—hell t' pay—don't believe many will get back." It was an ironical secret. Still, they saw no hesitation in each other's faces, and they nodded a mute and unprotesting assent when a shaggy man near them said in a meek voice, "We'll git swallowed."

# 19

THE YOUTH STARED at the land in front of him. Its foliages now seemed to veil powers and horrors. He was unaware of the machinery of orders that started the charge, although from the corners of his eyes he saw an officer, who looked like a boy a-horseback, come galloping, waving his hat. Suddenly he felt a straining and heaving among the men. The line fell slowly forward like a toppling wall, and, with a convulsive gasp that was intended for a cheer, the regiment began its journey. The youth was pushed and jostled for a moment before he understood the movement at all, but directly he lunged ahead and began to run.

He fixed his eye upon a distant and prominent clump of trees where he had concluded the enemy were to be met, and he ran toward it as toward a goal. He had believed throughout that it was a mere question of getting over an unpleasant matter as quickly as possible, and he ran desperately, as if pursued for a murder. His face was drawn hard and tight with the stress of his endeavor. His eyes were fixed in a lurid glare. And with his soiled and disordered dress, his red and inflamed features surmounted by the dingy rag with its spot of blood, his wildly swinging rifle and banging accouterments, he looked to be an insane soldier.

As the regiment swung from its position out into a cleared space the woods and thickets before it awakened. Yellow flames leaped toward it from many directions. The forest made a tremendous objection.

The line lurched straight for a moment. Then the right wing swung forward; it in turn was surpassed by the left. Afterward the center careered to the front until the regiment was a wedge-shaped mass, but an instant later the opposition of the bushes, trees, and uneven places on the ground split the command and scattered it into detached clusters.

The youth, light-footed, was unconsciously in advance. His eyes still kept note of the clump of trees. From all places near it the clannish yell of the enemy could be heard. The little flames of rifles leaped from it. The song of the bullets was in the air and shells snarled among the tree-tops. One tumbled directly into the middle of a hurrying group and exploded in crimson fury. There was an instant's spectacle of a man, almost over it, throwing up his hands to shield his eyes.

Other men, punched by bullets, fell in grotesque agonies. The regiment left a coherent trail of bodies.

They had passed into a clearer atmosphere. There was an effect like a revelation in the new appearance of the landscape. Some men working madly at a battery were plain to them, and the opposing infantry's lines were defined by the gray walls and fringes of smoke.

It seemed to the youth that he saw everything. Each blade of the green grass was bold and clear. He thought that he was aware of every change in the thin, transparent vapor that floated idly in sheets. The brown or gray trunks of the trees showed each roughness of their surfaces. And the men of the regiment, with their starting eyes and sweating faces, running madly, or falling, as if thrown headlong, to queer, heaped-up corpses—all were comprehended. His mind took a mechanical but firm impression, so that afterward everything was pictured and explained to him, save why he himself was there.

But there was a frenzy made from this furious rush. The men, pitching forward insanely, had burst into cheerings, moblike and barbaric, but tuned in strange keys that can arouse the dullard and the stoic. It made a mad enthusiasm that, it seemed, would be incapable of checking itself before granite and brass. There was the delirium that encounters despair and death, and is heedless and blind to the odds. It is a temporary but sublime absence of selfishness. And because it was of this order was the reason, perhaps, why the youth wondered, afterward, what reasons he could have had for being there.

Presently the straining pace ate up the energies of the men. As if by agreement, the leaders began to slacken their speed. The volleys directed against them had had a seeming windlike effect. The regiment snorted and blew. Among some stolid trees it began to falter and hesitate. The men, staring intently, began to wait for some of the distant walls of smoke to move and disclose to them the scene. Since much of their strength and their breath had vanished, they returned to caution. They were become men again.

The youth had a vague belief that he had run miles, and he thought, in a way, that he was now in some new and unknown land.

The moment the regiment ceased its advance the protesting splutter of musketry became a steadied roar. Long and accurate fringes of smoke spread out. From the top of a small hill came level belchings of yellow flame that caused an inhuman whistling in the air.

The men, halted, had opportunity to see some of their comrades, dropping with moans and shrieks. A few lay under foot, still or wailing. And now for an instant the men stood, their rifles slack in their hands, and watched the regiment dwindle. They appeared dazed and stupid. This spectacle seemed to paralyze them, overcome them with a fatal fascination. They stared woodenly at the sights, and lowering their eyes, looked from face to face. It was a strange pause, and a strange silence.

Then, above the sounds of the outside commotion, arose the roar of the lieutenant. He strode suddenly forth, his infantile features black with rage.

"Come on, yeh fools!" he bellowed. "Come on! Yeh can't stay here. Yeh must come on." He said more, but much of it could not be understood.

He started rapidly forward, with his head turned toward the men. "Come on," he was shouting. The men stared with blank and yokel-like eyes at him. He was obliged to halt and retrace his steps. He stood then with his back to the enemy and delivered gigantic curses into the faces of the men. His body vibrated from the weight and force of his imprecations. And he could string oaths with the facility of a maiden who strings beads.

The friend of the youth aroused. Lurching suddenly forward and dropping to his knees, he fired an angry shot at the persistent woods. This action awakened the men. They huddled no more like sheep. They seemed suddenly to bethink them of their weapons, and at once commenced firing. Belabored by their officers, they began to move forward. The regiment, involved like a cart involved in mud and muddle, started unevenly with many jolts and jerks. The men stopped now every few paces to fire and load, and in this manner moved slowly on from trees to trees.

The flaming opposition in their front grew with their advance until it seemed that all forward ways were barred by the thin leaping

tongues, and off to the right an ominous demonstration could sometimes be dimly discerned. The smoke lately generated was in confus-
ing clouds that made it difficult for the regiment to proceed with
intelligence. As he passed through each curling mass the youth
wondered what would confront him on the farther side.

The command went painfully forward until an open space in-
terposed between them and the lurid lines. Here, crouching and
cowering behind some trees, the men clung with desperation, as if
threatened by a wave. They looked wild-eyed, and as if amazed at this
furious disturbance they had stirred. In the storm there was an ironical
expression of their importance. The faces of the men, too, showed a
lack of a certain feeling of responsibility for being there. It was as if
they had been driven. It was the dominant animal failing to remember
in the supreme moments the forceful causes of various superficial
qualities. The whole affair seemed incomprehensible to many of
them.

As they halted thus the lieutenant again began to bellow profanely.
Regardless of the vindictive threats of the bullets, he went about
coaxing, berating, and bedamning. His lips, that were habitually in a
soft and childlike curve, were now writhed into unholy contortions.
He swore by all possible deities.

Once he grabbed the youth by the arm. "Come on, yeh lunkhead!"
he roared. "Come on! We'll all git killed if we stay here. We've on'y
got t' go across that lot. An' then"—the remainder of his idea
disappeared in a blue haze of curses.

The youth stretched forth his arm. "Cross there?" His mouth was
puckered in doubt and awe.

"Certainly. Jest 'cross th' lot! We can't stay here," screamed the
lieutenant. He poked his face close to the youth and waved his
bandaged hand. "Come on!" Presently he grappled with him as if for
a wrestling bout. It was as if he planned to drag the youth by the ear on
to the assault.

The private felt a sudden unspeakable indignation against his officer. He wrenched fiercely and shook him off.

"Come on yerself, then," he yelled. There was a bitter challenge
in his voice.

They galloped together down the regimental front. The friend
scrambled after them. In front of the colors the three men began to
bawl: "Come on! come on!" They danced and gyrated like tortured
savages.

The flag, obedient to these appeals, bended its glittering form and swept toward them. The men wavered in indecision for a moment, and then with a long, wailful cry the dilapidated regiment surged forward and began its new journey.

Over the field went the scurrying mass. It was a handful of men splattered into the faces of the enemy. Toward it instantly sprang the yellow tongues. A vast quantity of blue smoke hung before them. A mighty banging made ears valueless.

The youth ran like a madman to reach the woods before a bullet could discover him. He ducked his head low, like a football player. In his haste his eyes almost closed, and the scene was a wild blur. Pulsating saliva stood at the corners of his mouth.

Within him, as he hurled himself forward, was born a love, a despairing fondness for this flag which was near him. It was a creation of beauty and invulnerability. It was a goddess, radiant, that bended its form with an imperious gesture to him. It was a woman, red and white, hating and loving, that called him with the voice of his hopes. Because no harm could come to it he endowed it with power. He kept near, as if it could be a saver of lives, and an imploring cry went from his mind.

In the mad scramble he was aware that the color sergeant flinched suddenly, as if struck, by a bludgeon. He faltered, and then became motionless, save for his quivering knees.

He made a spring and a clutch at the pole. At the same instant his friend grabbed it from the other side. They jerked at it, stout and furious, but the color sergeant was dead, and the corpse would not relinquish its trust. For a moment there was a grim encounter. The dead man, swinging with bended back, seemed to be obstinately tugging, in ludicrous and awful ways, for the possession of the flag.

It was past in an instant of time. They wrenched the flag furiously from the dead man, and, as they turned again, the corpse swayed forward with bowed head. One arm swung high, and the curved hand fell with heavy protest on the friend's unheeding shoulder.

# 20

WHEN THE TWO youths turned with the flag they saw that much of the regiment had crumbled away, and the dejected remnant was coming slowly back. The men, having hurled themselves in projectile fashion, had presently expended their forces. They slowly retreated, with their faces still toward the spluttering woods, and their hot rifles still replying to the din. Several officers were giving orders, their voices keyed to screams.

"Where in hell yeh goin'?" the lieutenant was asking in a sarcastic howl. And a red-bearded officer, whose voice of triple brass could plainly be heard, was commanding: "Shoot into 'em! Shoot into 'em, Gawd damn their souls!" There was a *mêlée* of screeches, in which the men were ordered to do conflicting and impossible things.

The youth and his friend had a small scuffle over the flag. "Give it t' me!" "No, let me keep it!" Each felt satisfied with the other's possession of it, but each felt bound to declare, by an offer to carry the emblem, his willingness to further risk himself. The youth roughly pushed his friend away.

The regiment fell back to the stolid trees. There it halted for a moment to blaze at some dark forms that had begun to steal upon its track. Presently it resumed its march again, curving among the tree trunks. By the time the depleted regiment had again reached the first open space they were receiving a fast and merciless fire. There seemed to be mobs all about them.

The greater part of the men, discouraged, their spirits worn by the turmoil, acted as if stunned. They accepted the pelting of the bullets with bowed and weary heads. It was of no purpose to strive against walls. It was of no use to batter themselves against granite. And from this consciousness that they had attempted to conquer an unconquerable thing there seemed to arise a feeling that they had been betrayed. They glowered with bent brows, but dangerously, upon some of the officers, more particularly upon the red-bearded one with the voice of triple brass.

However, the rear of the regiment was fringed with men, who continued to shoot irritably at the advancing foes. They seemed resolved to make every trouble. The youthful lieutenant was perhaps the last man in the disordered mass. His forgotten back was toward the enemy. He had been shot in the arm. It hung straight and rigid. Occasionally he would cease to remember it, and be about to emphasize an oath with a sweeping gesture. The multiplied pain cause him to swear with incredible power.

The youth went along with slipping, uncertain feet. He kept watchful eyes rearward. A scowl of mortification and rage was upon his face. He had thought of a fine revenge upon the officer who had referred to him and his fellows as mule drivers. But he saw that it could not come to pass. His dreams had collapsed when the mule drivers, dwindling rapidly, had wavered and hesitated on the little clearing, and then had recoiled. And now the retreat of the mule drivers was a march of shame to him.

A dagger-pointed gaze from without his blackened face was held toward the enemy, but his greater hatred was riveted upon the man, who, not knowing him, had called him a mule driver.

When he knew that he and his comrades had failed to do anything in successful ways that might bring the little pangs of a kind of remorse upon the officer, the youth allowed the rage of the baffled to possess him. This cold officer upon a monument, who dropped epithets unconcernedly down, would be finer as a dead man, he thought. So grievous did he think it that he could never possess the secret right to taunt truly in answer.

He had pictured red letters of curious revenge. "We *are* mule drivers, are we?" And now he was compelled to throw them away.

He presently wrapped his heart in the cloak of his pride and kept the flag erect. He harangued his fellows, pushing against their chests with his free hand. To those he knew well he made frantic appeals, beseeching them by name. Between him and the lieutenant, scolding and near to losing his mind with rage, there was felt a subtle fellow-ship and equality. They supported each other in all manner of hoarse, howling protests.

But the regiment was a machine run down. The two men babbled at a forceless thing. The soldiers who had heart to go slowly were continually shaken in their resolves by a knowledge that comrades were slipping with speed back to the lines. It was difficult to think of reputation when others were thinking of skins. Wounded men were left crying on this black journey.

The smoke fringes and flames blustered always. The youth, peer-ing once through a sudden rift in a cloud, saw a brown mass of troops, interwoven and magnified until they appeared to be thousands. A fierce-hued flag flashed before his vision.

Immediately, as if the uplifting of the smoke had been prearranged, the discovered troops burst into a rasping yell, and a hundred flames jetted toward the retreating band. A rolling gray cloud again in-terposed as the regiment doggedly replied. The youth had to depend again upon his misused ears, which were trembling and buzzing from the *mêlée* of musketry and yells.

The way seemed eternal. In the clouded haze men became panic-stricken with the thought that the regiment had lost its path, and was proceeding in a perilous direction. Once the men who headed the wild procession turned and came pushing back against their comrades, screaming that they were being fired upon from points which they had considered to be toward their own lines. At this cry a hysterical fear and dismay beset the troops. A soldier, who heretofore had been ambitious to make the regiment into a wise little band that would proceed calmly amid the huge-appearing difficulties, suddenly sank down and buried his face in his arms with an air of bowing to a doom. From another a shrill lamentation ran out filled with profane allusions to a general. Men ran hither and thither, seeking with their eyes roads of escape. With serene regularity, as if controlled by a schedule, bullets buffed into men.

The youth walked stolidly into the midst of the mob, and with his flag in his hands took a stand as if he expected an attempt to push him to the ground. He unconsciously assumed the attitude of the color bearer in the fight of the preceding day. He passed over his brow a hand that trembled. His breath did not come freely. He was choking during this small wait for the crisis.

His friend came to him. "Well, Henry, I guess this is good-bye-John."

"Oh, shut up, you damned fool!" replied the youth, and he would not look at the other.

The officers labored like politicians to beat the mass into a proper circle to face the menaces. The ground was uneven and torn. The men curled into depressions and fitted themselves snugly behind whatever would frustrate a bullet.

The youth noted with vague surprise that the lieutenant was standing mutely with his legs far apart and his sword held in the manner of a cane. The youth wondered what had happened to his vocal organs that he no more cursed.

There was something curious in this little intent pause of the lieutenant. He was like a babe which, having wept its fill, raises its eyes and fixes them upon a distant toy. He was engrossed in this contemplation, and the soft underlip quivered from self-whispered words.

Some lazy and ignorant smoke curled slowly. The men, hiding from the bullets, waited anxiously for it to lift and disclose the plight of the regiment.

The silent ranks were suddenly thrilled by the eager voice of the youthful lieutenant bawling out: "Here they come! Right onto us, b'Gawd!" His further words were lost in a roar of wicked thunder from the men's rifles.

The youth's eyes had instantly turned in the direction indicated by the awakened and agitated lieutenant, and he had seen the haze of treachery disclosing a body of soldiers of the enemy. They were so near that he could see their features. There was a recognition as he looked at the types of faces. Also he perceived with dim amazement that their uniforms were rather gay in effect, being light gray, accented with a brilliant-hued facing. Moreover, the clothes seemed new.

These troops had apparently been going forward with caution, their rifles held in readiness, when the youthful lieutenant had discovered them and their movement had been interrupted by the volley from the blue regiment. From the moment's glimpse, it was derived that they had been unaware of the proximity of their dark-suited foes, or had mistaken the direction. Almost instantly they were shut utterly from the youth's sight by the smoke from the energetic rifles of his companions. He strained his vision to learn the accomplishment of the volley, but the smoke hung before him.

The two bodies of troops exchanged blows in the manner of a pair of boxers. The fast angry firings went back and forth. The men in blue were intent with the despair of their circumstances and they seized upon the revenge to be had at close range. Their thunder swelled loud and valiant. Their curving front bristled with flashes and the place resounded with the clangor of their ramrods. The youth ducked and dodged for a time and achieved a few unsatisfactory views of the enemy. There appeared to be many of them and they were replying swiftly. They seemed moving toward the blue regiment, step by step. He seated himself gloomily on the ground with his flag between his knees.

As he noted the vicious, wolf-like temper of his comrades he had a sweet thought that if the enemy was about to swallow the regimental broom as a large prisoner, it could at least have the consolation of going down with bristles forward.

But the blows of the antagonist began to grow more weak. Fewer bullets ripped the air, and finally, when the men slackened to learn of the fight, they could see only dark, floating smoke. The regiment lay still and gazed. Presently some chance whim came to the pestering blur, and it began to coil heavily away. The men saw a ground vacant of fighters. It would have been an empty stage if it were not for a few corpses that lay thrown and twisted into fantasitc shapes upon the sward.

At sight of this tableau, many of the men in blue sprang from behind their covers and made an ungainly dance of joy. Their eyes burned and a hoarse cheer of elation broke from their dry lips.

It had begun to seem to them that events were trying to prove that they were impotent. These little battles had evidently endeavored to demonstrate that the men could not fight well. When on the verge of submission to these opinions, the small duel had showed them that the proportions were not impossible, and by it they had revenged themselves upon their misgivings and upon the foe.

The impetus of enthusiasm was theirs again. They gazed about them with looks of uplifted pride, feeling new trust in the grim, always confident weapons in their hands. And they were men.

# 21

PRESENTLY THEY KNEW that no firing threatened them. All ways seemed once more opened to them. The dusty blue lines of their friends were disclosed a short distance away. In the distance there were many colossal noises, but in all this part of the field there was sudden stillness.

They perceived that they were free. The depleted band drew a long breath of relief and gathered itself into a bunch to complete its trip.

In this last length of journey the men began to show strange emotions. They hurried with nervous fear. Some who had been dark and unfaltering in the grimmest moments now could not conceal an anxiety that made them frantic. It was perhaps that they dreaded to be killed in insignificant ways after the times for proper military deaths had passed. Or, perhpas, they thought it would be too ironical to get killed at the portals of safety. With backward looks of perturbation, they hastened.

As they approached their own lines there was some sarcasm exhibited on the part of a gaunt and bronzed regiment that lay resting in the shade of trees. Questions were wafted to them.

"Where th' hell yeh been?"

"What yeh comin' back fer?"

"Why didn't yeh stay there?"

"Was it warm out there, sonny?"

"Goin' home now, boys?"

One shouted in taunting mimicry: "Oh, mother, come quick an' look at th' sojers!"

There was no reply from the bruised and battered regiment, save that one man made broadcast challenges to fist fights and the red-bearded officer walked rather near and glared in great swashbuckler style at a tall captain in the other regiment. But the lieutenant suppressed the man who wished to fist fight, and the tall captain, flushing at the little fanfare of the red-bearded one, was obliged to look intently at some trees.

The youth's tender flesh was deeply stung by these remarks. From under his creased brows he glowered with hate at the mockers. He meditated upon a few revenges. Still, many in the regiment hung their heads in criminal fashion, so that it came to pass that the men trudged with sudden heaviness, as if they bore upon their bended shoulders the coffin of their honor. And the youthful lieutenant, recollecting himself, began to mutter softly in black curses.

They turned when they arrived at their old position to regard the ground over which they had charged.

The youth in this contemplation was smitten with a large astonishment. He discovered that the distances, as compared with the brilliant measurings of his mind, were trivial and ridiculous. The stolid trees, where much had taken place, seemed incredibly near. The time, too, now that he reflected, he saw to have been short. He wondered at the number of emotions and events that had been crowded into such little spaces. Elfin thoughts must have exaggerated and enlarged everything, he said.

It seemed, then, that there was bitter justice in the speeches of the gaunt and bronzed veterans. He veiled a glance of disdain at his fellows who strewed the ground, choking with dust, red from perspiration, misty-eyed, dishevelled.

They were gulping at their canteens, fierce to wring every mite of water from them, and they polished at their swollen and watery features with coat sleeves and bunches of grass.

However, to the youth there was a considerable joy in musing upon his performance during the charge. He had had very little time previously in which to appreciate himself, so that there was now much satisfaction in quietly thinking of his actions. He recalled bits of color that in the flurry had stamped themselves unawares upon his engaged senses.

As the regiment lay heaving from its hot exertions the officer who had named them as mule drivers came galloping along the line. He had lost his cap. His tousled hair streamed wildly, and his face was dark with vexation and wrath. His temper was displayed with more clearness by the way in which he managed his horse. He jerked and wrenched savagely at his bridle, stopping the hard-breathing animal with a furious pull near the colonel of the regiment. He immediately exploded in reproaches which came unbidden to the ears of the men. They were suddenly alert, being always curious about black words between officers.

"Oh, thunder, MacChesnay, what an awful bull you made of this thing!" began the officer. He attempted low tones, but his indignation caused certain of the men to learn the sense of his words. "What an awful mess you made! Good Lord, man, you stopped about a hundred feet this side of a very pretty success! If your men had gone a hundred feet farther you would have made a great charge, but as it is—what a lot of mud diggers you've got anyway!"

The men, listening with bated breath, now turned their curious eyes upon the colonel. They had a ragamuffin interest in this affair.

The colonel was seen to straighten his form and put one hand forth in oratorical fashion. He wore an injured air; it was as if a deacon had been accused of stealing. The men were wiggling in an ecstasy of excitement.

But of a sudden the colonel's manner changed from that of a deacon to that of a Frenchman. He shrugged his shoulders. "Oh, well, general, we went as far as we could," he said calmly.

"As far as you could? Did you, b'Gawd?" snorted the other. "Well, that wasn't very far, was it?" he added, with a glance of cold contempt into the other's eyes. "Not very far, I think. You were intended to make a diversion in favor of Whiterside. How well you succeeded your own ears can now tell you." He wheeled his horse and rode stiffly away.

The colonel, bidden to hear the jarring noises of an engagement in the woods to the left, broke out in vague damnations.

The lieutenant, who had listened with an air of impotent rage to the interview, spoke suddenly in firm and undaunted tones. "I don't care what a man is—whether he is a general or what—if he says th' boys didn't put up a good fight out there he's a damned fool."

"Lieutenant,' began the colonel severely, "this is my own affair, and I'll trouble you——"

The lieutenant made an obedient gesture. "All right colonel, all right," he said. He sat down witn an air of being content with himself.

The news that the regiment had been reproached went along the line. For a time the men were bewildered by it. "Good thunder!" they ejaculated, staring at the vanishing form of the general. They conceived it to be a huge mistake.

Presently, however, they began to believe that in truth their efforts had been called light. The youth could see this conviction weigh upon the entire regiment until the men were like cuffed and cursed animals, but withal rebellious.

The friend, with a grievance in his eye, went to the youth. "I wonder what he does want," he said. "He must think we went out there an' played marbles! I never seed sech a man!"

The youth developed a tranquil philosophy for these moments of irritation. "Oh, well," he rejoined, "he probably didn't see nothing of it at all and got mad as blazes, and concluded we were a lot of sheep, just because we didn't do what he wanted done. It's a pity old Grandpa Henderson got killed yestirday—he'd have known that we did our best and fought good. It's just our awful luck, that's what."

"I should say so," replied the friend. He seemd to be deeply wounded at an injustice. "I should say we did have awful luck! There's no fun in fightin' fer people when everything yeh do—no matter what—ain't done right. I have a notion t' stay behind next time an' let 'em take their ol' charge an' go t' th' devil with it."

The youth spoke soothingly to his comrade. "Well, we both did good. I'd like to see the fool what'd say we both didn't do as good as we could!"

"Of course we did," declared the friend stoutly. "An' I'd break th' feller's neck if he was as big as a church. But we're all right, anyhow, for I heard one feller say that we two fit th' best in th' reg'ment, an' they had a great argument 'bout it. Another feller, 'a course, he had t' up an' say it was a lie—he seen all what was goin' on an' he never seen us from th' beginnin' t' th' end. An' a lot more struck in an' ses it wasn't a lie—we did fight like thunder, an' they give us quite a send-off. But this is what I can't stand—these everlastin' ol' soldiers, titterin' an' laughin', an' then that general, he's crazy."

The youth exclaimed with sudden exasperation: "He's a lunkhead! He makes me mad. I wish he'd come along next time. We'd show 'im what——"

He ceased because several men had come hurrying up. Their faces expressed a bringing of great news.

"O Flem, yeh jest oughta heard!" cried one, eagerly.

"Heard what?" said the youth.

"Ye jest oughta heard!" repeated the other, and he arranged himself to tell his tidings. The others made an excited circle. "Well, sir, th' colonel met your lieutenant right by us—it was damnedest thing I ever heard—an' he ses: 'Ahem! ahem!' he ses. 'Mr. Hasbrouck!' he ses, 'by th' way, who was that lad what carried th' flag?' he ses. There, Flemin', what d' yeh think 'a that? 'Who was th' lad what carried th' flag?' he ses, an' th' lieutenant, he speaks up right away: 'That's Flemin', an' he's a jimhickey,' he ses, right away. What? I say he did. 'A jimhickey,' he ses—those 'r his words. He did, too. I say he did. If you kin tell this story better than I kin, go ahead an' tell it. Well, then, keep yer mouth shet. Th' lieutenant, he ses: 'He's a jimhickey,' an' th' colonel, he ses: 'Ahem! ahem! he is, indeed, a very good man t' have, ahem! He kep' th' flag 'way t' th' front. I saw 'im. He's a good un,' ses th' colonel. 'You bet,' ses th' lieutenant, 'he an' a feller named Wilson was at th' head 'a th' charge, an' howlin' like Indians all th' time,' he ses. 'Head 'a th' charge all th' time,' he ses. 'A feller named Wilson,' he ses. There, Wilson, m' boy, put that in a letter an' send it hum t' yer mother, hey? 'A feller named Wilson,' he ses. An' th' colonel, he ses: 'Were they, indeed? Ahem! ahem! My sakes!' he ses. 'At th' head 'a th' reg'ment?' he ses. 'They were,' says the lieutenant. 'My sakes!' ses th' colonel. He ses: 'Well, well, well,' he ses, 'those two babies?' 'They were,' ses th' lieutenant. 'Well, well,' ses th' colonel, 'they deserve t' be major-generals,' he ses. 'They deserve t' be major-generals.'"

The youth and his friend had said: "Huh!" "Yer lyin', Thompson." "Oh, go t' blazes!" "He never sed it." "Oh, what a lie!" "Huh!" But despite these youthful scoffings and embarrassments, they knew that their faces were deeply flushing from thrills of pleasure. They exchanged a secret glance of joy and congratulation.

They speedily forgot many things. The past held no pictures of error and disappointment. They were very happy, and their hearts swelled with grateful affection for the colonel and the youthful lieutenant.

# 22

WHEN THE WOODS again began to pour forth the dark-hued masses of the enemy the youth felt serene self-confidence. He smiled briefly when he saw men dodge and duck at the long screechings of shells that were thrown in giant handfuls over them. He stood, erect and tranquil, watching the attack begin against a part of the line that made a blue curve along the side of an adjacent hill. His vision being unmolested by smoke from the rifles of his companions, he had opportunities to see parts of the hard fight. It was a relief to perceive at last from whence came some of these noises which had been roared into his ears.

Off a short way he saw two regiments fighting a little separate battle with two other regiments. It was in a cleared space, wearing a set-apart look. They were blazing as if upon a wager, giving and taking tremendous blows. The firings were incredibly fierce and rapid. These intent regiments apparently were oblivious of all larger purposes of war, and were slugging each other as if at a matched game.

In another direction he saw a magnificent brigade going with the evident intention of driving the enemy from a wood. They passed in out of sight and presently there was a most awe-inspiring racket in the wood. The noise was unspeakable. Having stirred this prodigious uproar, and, apparently, finding it too prodigious, the brigade, after a little time, came marching airily out again with its fine formation in nowise disturbed. There were no traces of speed in its movements. The brigade was jaunty and seemed to point a proud thumb at the yelling wood.

On a slope to the left there was a long row of guns, gruff and maddened, denouncing the enemy, who, down through the woods, were forming for another attack in the pitiless monotony of conflicts. The round red discharges from the guns made a crimson flare and a high, thick smoke. Occasional glimpses could be caught of groups of the toiling artillerymen. In the rear of this row of guns stood a house, calm and white, amid bursting shells. A congregation of horses, tied to a long railing, were tugging frenziedly at their bridles. Men were running hither and thither.

The detached battle between the four regiments lasted for some time. There chanced to be no interference, and they settled their dispute by themselves. They struck savagely and powerfully at each other for a period of minutes, and then the lighter-hued regiments faltered and drew back, leaving the dark-blue lines shouting. The youth could see the two flags shaking with laughter amid the smoke remnants.

Presently there was a stillness, pregnant with meaning. The blue lines shifted and changed a trifle and stared expectantly at the silent woods and fields before them. The hush was solemn and churchlike, save for a distant battery that, evidently unable to remain quiet, sent a faint rolling thunder over the ground. It irritated, like the noises of unimpressed boys. The men imagined that it would prevent their perched ears from hearing the first words of the new battle.

Of a sudden the guns on the slope roared out a message of warning. A spluttering sound had begun in the woods. It swelled with amazing speed to a profound clamor that involved the earth in noises. The splitting crashes swept along the lines until an interminable roar was developed. To those in the midst of it, it became a din fitted to the universe. It was the whirring and thumping of gigantic machinery, complications among the smaller stars. The youth's ears were filled up. They were incapable of hearing more.

On an incline over which a road wound he saw wild and desperate rushes of men perpetually backward and forward in riotous surges. These parts of the opposing armies were two long waves that pitched upon each other madly at dictated points. To and fro they swelled. Sometimes, one side by its yells and cheers would proclaim decisive blows, but a moment later the other side would be all yells and cheers. Once the youth saw a spray of light forms go in houndlike leaps toward the waving blue lines. There was much howling, and presently it went away with a vast mouthful of prisoners. Again, he saw a blue wave dash with such thunderous force against a gray obstruction that it seemed to clear the earth of it and leave nothing but trampled sod. And always in their swift and deadly rushes to and fro the men screamed and yelled like maniacs.

Particular pieces of fence or secure positions behind collections of trees were wrangled over, as gold thrones or pearl bedsteads. There were desperate lunges at these chosen spots seemingly every instant, and most of them were bandied like light toys between the contending forces. The youth could not tell from the battle-flags flying like crimson foam in many directions which color of cloth was winning.

His emaciated regiment bustled forth with undiminished fierceness when its time came. When assaulted again by bullets, the men burst out in a barbaric cry of rage and pain. They bent their heads in aims of intent hatred behind the projected hammers of their guns. Their ramrods clanged loud with fury as their eager arms pounded the cartridges into the rifle barrels. The front of the regiment was a smoke-wall penetrated by the flashing points of yellow and red.

Wallowing in the fight, they were in an astonishingly short time resmudged. They surpassed in stain and dirt all their previous appearances. Moving to and fro with strained exertion, jabbering the while, they were, with their swaying bodies, black faces, and glowing eyes, like strange and ugly fiends jigging heavily in the smoke.

The lieutenant, returning from a tour after a bandage, produced from a hidden receptacle of his mind new and portentous oaths suited to the emergency. Strings of expletives he swung lashlike over the backs of his men, and it was evident that his previous efforts had in nowise impaired his resources.

The youth, still the bearer of the colors, did not feel his idleness. He was deeply absorbed as a spectator. The crash and swing of the great drama made him lean forward, intent-eyed, his face working in small contortions. Sometimes he prattled, words coming unconsciously from him in grotesque exclamations. He did not know that he breathed; that the flag hung silently over him, so absorbed was he.

A formidable line of the enemy came within dangerous range. They could be seen plainly—tall, gaunt men with excited faces running with long strides toward a wandering fence.

At sight of this danger the men suddenly ceased their cursing monotone. There was an instant of strained silence before they threw up their rifles and fired a plumping volley at the foes. There had been no order given; the men, upon recognizing the menace, had immediately let drive their flock of bullets without waiting for word of command.

But the enemy were quick to gain the protection of the wandering line of fence. They slid down behind it with remarkable celerity, and from this position they began briskly to slice up the blue men.

These latter braced their energies for a great struggle. Often, white clinched teeth shone from the dusky faces. Many heads surged to and fro, floating upon a pale sea of smoke. Those behind the fence frequently shouted and yelped in taunts and gibelike cries, but the regiment maintained a stressed silence. Perhaps, at this new assault the men recalled the fact that they had been named mud diggers, and it made their situation thrice bitter. They were breathlessly intent upon keeping the ground and thrusting away the rejoicing body of the enemy. They fought swiftly and with a despairing savageness denoted in their expressions.

The youth had resolved not to budge whatever should happen. Some arrows of scorn that had buried themselves in his heart had generated strange and unspeakable hatred. It was clear to him that his final and absolute revenge was to be achieved by his dead body lying, torn and glittering upon the field. This was to be a poignant retaliation upon the officer who had said "mule drivers," and later "mud diggers," for in all the wild graspings of his mind for a unit responsible for his sufferings and commotions he always seized upon the man who had dubbed him wrongly. And it was his idea, vaguely formulated, that his corpse would be for those eyes a great and salt reproach.

The regiment bled extravagantly. Grunting bundles of blue began to drop. The orderly sergeant of the youth's company was shot through the cheeks. Its supports being injured, his jaw hung afar down, disclosing in the wide cavern of his mouth a pulsing mass of blood and teeth. And with it all he made attempts to cry out. In his endeavor there was a dreadful earnestness, as if he conceived that one great shriek would make him well.

The youth saw him presently go rearward. His strength seemed in nowise impaired. He ran swiftly, casting wild glances for succor.

Others fell down about the feet of their companions. Some of the wounded crawled out and away, but many lay still, their bodies twisted into impossible shapes.

The youth looked once for his friend. He saw a vehement young man, powder-smeared and frowzled, whom he knew to be him. The lieutenant, also, was unscathed in his position at the rear. He had continued to curse, but it was now with the air of a man who was using his last box of oaths.

For the fire of the regiment had begun to wane and drip. The robust voice, that had come strangely from the thin ranks, was growing rapidly weak.

# 23

THE COLONEL CAME running along back of the line. There were other officers following him. "We must charge 'm!" they shouted. "We must charge 'm!" they cried with resentful voices, as if anticipating a rebellion against this plan by the men.

The youth, upon hearing the shouts, began to study the distance between him and the enemy. He made vague calculations. He saw that to be firm soldiers they must go forward. It would be death to stay in the present place, and with all the circumstances to go backward would exalt too many others. Their hope was to push the galling foes away from the fence.

He expected that his companions, weary and stiffened, would have to be driven to this assault, but as he turned toward them he perceived with a certain surprise that they were giving quick and unqualified expressions of assent. There was an ominous, clanging overture to the charge when the shafts of the bayonets rattled upon the rifle barrels. At the yelled words of command the soldiers sprang forward in eager leaps. There was new and unexpected force in the movement of the regiment. A knowledge of its faded and jaded condition made the charge appear like a paroxysm, a display of the strength that comes before a final feebleness. The men scampered in insane fever of haste, racing as if to achieve a sudden success before an exhilarating fluid should leave them. It was a blind and despairing rush by the collection of men in dusty and tattered blue, over a green sward and under a sapphire sky, toward a fence, dimly outlined in smoke, from behind which spluttered the fierce rifles of enemies.

The youth kept the bright colors to the front. He was waving his free arm in furious circles, the while shrieking mad calls and appeals, urging on those that did not need to be urged, for it seemed that the mob of blue men hurling themselves on the dangerous group of rifles were again grown suddenly wild with an enthusiasm of unselfishness. From the many firings starting toward them, it looked as if they would merely succeed in making a great sprinkling of corpses on the grass between their former position and the fence. But they were in a state of frenzy, perhaps because of forgotten vanities, and it made an exhibition of sublime recklessness. There was no obvious questioning, nor figurings, nor diagrams. There was, apparently, no considered loopholes. It appeared that the swift wings of their desires would have shattered against the iron gates of the impossible.

He himself felt the daring spirit of a savage religion mad. He was capable of profound sacrifices, a tremendous death. He had no time for dissections, but he knew that he thought of the bullets only as things that could prevent him from reaching the place of his endeavor. There were subtle flashings of joy within him that thus should be his mind.

He strained all his strength. His eyesight was shaken and dazzled by the tension of thought and muscle. He did not see anything excepting the mist of smoke gashed by the little knives of fire, but he knew that in it lay the aged fence of a vanished farmer protecting the snuggled bodies of the gray men.

As he ran a thought of the shock of contact gleamed in his mind. He expected a great concussion when the two bodies of troops crashed together. This became a part of his wild battle madness. He could feel the onward swing of the regiment about him and he conceived of a thunderous, crushing blow that would prostrate the resistance and spread consternation and amazement for miles. The flying regiment was going to have a catapultian effect. This dream made him run faster among his comrades, who were giving vent to hoarse and frantic cheers.

But presently he could see that many of the men in gray did not intend to abide the blow. The smoke, rolling, disclosed men who ran, their faces still turned. These grew to a crowd, who retired stubbornly. Individuals wheeled frequently to send a bullet at the blue wave.

But at one part of the line there was a grim and obdurate group that made no movement. They were settled firmly down behind posts and rails. A flag, ruffled and fierce, waved over them, and their rifles dinned fiercely.

The blue whirl of men got very near, until it seemed that in truth there would be a close and frightful scuffle. There was an expressed disdain in the opposition of the little group, that changed the meaning of the cheers of the men in blue. They became yells of wrath, directed, personal. The cries of the two parties were now in sound an interchange of scathing insults.

They in blue showed their teeth; their eyes shone all white. They launched themselves as at the throats of those who stood resisting. The space dwindled to an insignificant distance.

The youth had centered the gaze of his soul upon that other flag. Its possession would be high pride. It would express bloody minglings, near blows. He had a gigantic hatred for those who made great difficulties and complications. They caused it to be as a craved treasure of mythology, hung amid tasks and contrivances of danger.

He plunged like a mad horse at it. He was resolved it should not escape if wild blows and darings of blows could seize it. His own emblem, quivering and aflare, was winging toward the other. It seemed there would shortly be an encounter of strange beaks and claws, as of eagles.

The swirling body of blue men came to a sudden halt at close and disastrous range and roared a swift volley. The group in gray was split and broken by this fire, but its riddled body still fought. The men in blue yelled again and rushed in upon it.

The youth, in his leapings, saw, as through a mist, a picture of four or five men stretched upon the ground or writhing upon their knees with bowed heads as if they had been stricken by bolts from the sky. Tottering among them was the rival color-bearer, whom the youth saw had been bitten vitally by the bullets of the last formidable volley. He perceived this man fighting a last struggle, the sturggle of one whose legs are grasped by demons. It was a ghastly battle. Over his face was the bleach of death, but set upon it was the dark and hard lines of desperate purpose. With this terrible grin of resolution he hugged his precious flag to him and was stumbling and staggering in his design to go the way that led to safety for it.

But his wounds always made it seem that this feet were retarded, held, and he fought a grim fight, as with invisible ghouls fastened greedily upon his limbs. Those in advance of the scampering blue men, howling cheers, leaped at the fence. The despair of the lost was in his eyes as he glanced back at them.

The youth's friend went over the obstruction in a tumbling heap and sprang at the flag as a panther at prey. He pulled at it and, wrenching it free, swung up its red brilliancy with a mad cry of exultation even as the color bearer, gasping, lurched over in a final throe and, stiffening convulsively, turned his dead face to the ground. There was much blood upon the grass blades.

At the place of success there began more wild clamorings of cheers. The men gesticulated and bellowed in an ecstasy. When they spoke it was as if they considered their listener to be a mile away. What hats and caps were left to them they often slung high in the air.

At one part of the line four men had been swooped upon, and they now sat as prisoners. Some blue men were about them in an eager and curious circle. The soldiers had trapped strange birds, and there was an examination. A flurry of fast questions was in the air.

One of the prisoners was nursing a superficial wound in the foot. He cuddled it, baby-wise, but he looked up from it often to curse with a astonishing utter abandon straight at the noses of his captors. He consigned them to red regions; he called upon the pestilential wrath of strange gods. And with it all he was singularly free from recognition of the finer points of the conduct of prisoners of war. It was as if a clumsy clod had trod upon his toe and he conceived it to be his privilege, his duty, to use deep, resentful oaths.

Another, who was a boy in years, took his plight with great calmness and apparent good nature. He conversed with the men in blue, studying their faces with his bright and keen eyes. They spoke of battles and conditions. There was an acute interest in all their faces during this exchange of view points. It seemed a great satisfaction to hear voices from where all had been darkness and speculation.

The third captive sat with a morose countenance. He preserved a stoical and cold attitude. To all advances he made one reply without variation, "Ah, go t' hell!"

The last of the four was always silent and, for the most part, kept his face turned in unmolested directions. From the views the youth received he seemed to be in a state of absolute dejection. Shame was upon him, and with it profound regret that he was, perhaps, no more to be counted in the ranks of his fellows. The youth could detect no expression that would allow him to believe that the other was giving a thought to his narrowed future, the pictured dungeons, perhaps, and starvations and brutalities, liable to the imagination. All to be seen was shame for captivity and regret for the right to antagonize.

After the men had celebrated sufficiently they settled down behind the old rail fence, on the opposite side to the one from which their foes had been driven. A few shot perfunctorily at distant marks.

There was some long grass. The youth nestled in it and rested, making a convenient rail support the flag. His friend, jubilant and glorified, holding his treasure with vanity, came to him there. They sat side by side and congratulated each other.

# 24

THE ROARINGS THAT had stretched in a long line of sound across the face of the forest began to grow intermittent and weaker. The stentorian speeches of the artillery continued in some distant encounter, but the crashes of the musketry had almost ceased. The youth and his friend of a sudden looked up, feeling a deadened form of distress at the waning of these noises, which had become a part of life. They could see changes going on among the troops. There were marchings this way and that way. A battery wheeled leisurely. On the crest of a small hill was the thick gleam of many departing muskets.

The youth rose. "Well, what now, I wonder?" he said. By his tone he seemed to be preparing to resent some new monstrosity in the way of dins and smashes. He shaded his eyes with his grimy hand and gazed over the field.

His friend also arose and stared. "I bet we're goin' t' git along out of this an' back over th' river," said he.

"Well, I swan!" said the youth.

They waited, watching. Within a little while the regiment received orders to retrace its way. The men got up grunting from the grass, regretting the soft repose. They jerked their stiffened legs, and stretched their arms over their heads. One man swore as he rubbed his eyes. They all groaned, "O Lord!" They had as many objections to this change as they would have had to a proposal for a new battle.

They trampled slowly back over the field across which they had run in a mad scamper. The fence, deserted, resumed with its careening posts and disjointed bars, an air of quiet rural depravity. Beyond it, there lay spread a few corpses. Conspicuous was the contorted body of the color-bearer in gray whose flag the youth's friend was now bearing away.

The regiment marched until it had joined its fellows. The reformed brigade, in column, aimed through a wood at the road. Directly they were in a mass of dust-covered troops, and were trudging along in a way parallel to the enemy's lines as these had been defied by the previous turmoil.

They passed within view of a stolid white house, and saw in front of it groups of their comrades lying in wait behind a neat breastwork. A row of guns were booming at a distant enemy. Shells thrown in reply were raising clouds of dust and splinters. Horsemen dashed along the line of entrenchments.

As they passed near other commands, men of the dilapidated regiment procured the captured flag from the youth's friend, and tossing it high in the air, cheered tumultuously as it turned, with apparent reluctance, over and over.

At this point of its march the division curved away from the field and went winding off in the direction of the river. When the significance of this movement had impressed itself upon the youth he turned his head and looked over his shoulder toward the trampled and *débris*-strewed ground. He breathed a breath of new satisfaction. He finally nudged his friend. "Well, it's all over," he said to him.

His friend gazed backward. "B'Gawd, it is," he assented. They mused.

For a time the youth was obliged to reflect in a puzzled and uncertain way. His mind was undergoing a subtle change. It took moments for it to cast off its battleful ways and resume its accustomed course of thought. Gradually his brain emerged from the clogged clouds, and at last he was enabled to more closely comprehend himself and circumstance.

He understood then that the existence of shot and counter-shot was in the past. He had dwelt in a land of strange, squalling upheavals and had come forth. He had been where there was red of blood and black of passion, and he was escaped. His first thoughts were given to rejoicings at this fact.

Later he began to study his deeds, his failures, and his achievements. Thus, fresh from scenes where many of his usual machines of reflection had been idle, from where he had proceeded sheep-like, he struggled to marshal all his acts.

At last they marched before him clearly. From this present viewpoint he was enabled to look upon them in spectator fashion and to criticize them with some correctness, for his new condition had already defeated certain sympathies.

His friend, too, seemed engaged with some retrospection, for he suddenly gestured and said: "Good Lord!"

"What?" asked the youth.

"Good Lord!" repeated his friend. "Yeh know Jimmie Rogers? Well, he—gosh, when he was hurt I started t' git some water fer 'im an' thunder, I ain't seen him from that time 'til this. I clean forgot what I—say, has anybody seen Jimmie Rogers?"

"Seen 'im? No! He's dead," they told him.

His friend swore.

Regarding his procession of memory he felt gleeful and unregretting, for in it his public deeds were paraded in great and shining prominence. Those performances which had been witnessed by his fellows marched now in wide purple and gold having various deflections. They went gaily with music. It was pleasure to watch these things. He spent delightful minutes viewing the gilded images of memory.

He saw that he was good. He recalled with a thrill of joy the respectful comments of his fellows upon his conduct. He said to himself again the sentence of the insane young lieutenant: "If I had ten thousand wildcats like you, I could tear th' stomach outa this war in less 'n a week." It was a little coronation.

Nevertheless, the ghost of his flight from the first engagement appeared to him and danced. Echoes of his terrible combat with the arrayed forces of the universe came to his ears. There were small shoutings in his brain about these matters. For a moment he blushed, and the light of his soul flickered with shame.

However, he presently procured an explanation and an apology. He said that those tempestuous movements were of the wild mistakes and ravings of a novice who did not comprehend. He had been a mere man railing at a condition, but now he was out of it and could see that it had been very proper and just. It had been necessary for him to swallow swords that he might have a better throat for grapes. Fate had in truth been kind to him; she had stabbed him with benign purpose and diligently cudgelled him for his own sake. In his rebellion, he had been very portentous, no doubt, and sincere, and anxious for humanity, but now that he stood safe, with no lack of blood, it was suddenly clear to him that he had been wrong not to kiss the knife and bow to the cudgel. He had foolishly squirmed.

But the sky would forget. It was true, he admitted, that in the world it was the habit to cry devil at persons who refused to trust what they could not trust, but he thought that perhaps the stars dealt differently. The imperturbable sun shines on insult and worship.

As he was thus fraternizing again with nature, a specter of reproach came to him. There loomed the dogging memory of the tattered soldier—he who, gored by bullets and faint for blood, had fretted concerning an imagined wound in another; he who had loaned his last strength and intellect for the tall soldier; he who, blind with weariness and pain, had been deserted in the field.

For an instant a wretched chill of sweat was upon him at the thought that he might be detected in the thing. As he stood persistently before his vision, he gave vent to a cry of sharp irritation and agony.

His friend turned. "What's the matter, Henry?" he demanded. The youth's reply was an outburst of crimson oaths.

As he marched along the little branch-hung roadway among his prattling companions this vision of cruelty brooded over him. It clung near him always and darkened his view of these deeds in purple and gold. Whichever way his thoughts turned they were followed by the somber phantom of the desertion in the fields. He looked stealthily at his companions, feeling sure that they must discern in his face evidences of this pursuit. But they were plodding in ragged array, discussing with quick tongues the accomplishments of the late battle.

"Oh, if a man should come up an' ask me, I'd say we got a dum good lickin'."

"Lickin'—in yer eye! We ain't licked, sonny. We're goin' down here always, swing aroun', an' come in behint 'em.''

"Oh, hush, with your comin' in behint 'em. I've seen all 'a that I wanta. Don't tell me about comin' in behint——''

"Bill Smithers, he ses he'd rather been in ten hundred battles than been in that heluva hospital. He ses they got shootin' in th' night-time, an' shells dropped plum among 'em in th' hospital. He ses sech hollerin' he never see.''

"Hasbrouck? He's th' best off'cer in this here reg'ment. He's a whale.''

"Didn't I tell yeh we'd come aroun' in behint 'em? Didn't I tell yeh so? We——''

"Oh, shet yeh mouth!''

"You make me sick.''

"G' home, yeh fool.''

For a time this pursuing recollection of the tattered man took all elation from the youth's veins. He saw his vivid error, and he was afraid that it would stand before him all his life. He took no share in the chatter of his comrades, nor did he look at them or know them, save when he felt sudden suspicion that they were seeing his thoughts and scrutinizing each detail of the scene with the tattered soldier.

Yet gradually he mustered force to put the sin at a distance. And then he regarded it with what he thought to be great calmness. At last he concluded that he saw in it quaint uses. He exclaimed that its importance in the aftertime would be great to him if it even succeeded in hindering the workings of his egotism. It would make a sobering balance. It would become a good part of him. He would have upon him often the consciousness of a great mistake. And he would be taught to deal gently and with care. He would be a man.

This plan for the utilization of a sin did not give him complete joy, but it was the best sentiment he could formulate under the circumstances, and when it was combined with his successes, or public deeds, he knew that he was quite contented.

And at last his eyes seemed to be opened to some new ways. He found that he could look back upon the brass and bombast of his earlier gospels and see them truly. He was gleeful when he discovered that he now despised them.

He was emerged from his struggles with a large sympathy for the machinery of the universe. With his new eyes, he could see that the secret and open blows which were being dealt about the world with such heavenly lavishness were in truth blessings. It was a deity laying about him with the bludgeon of correction.

His loud mouth against these things had been lost as the storm ceased. He could no more stand upon places high and false, and denounce the distant planets. He beheld that he was tiny but not inconsequent to the sun. In the spacewide whirl of events no grain like him would be lost.

With this conviction came a store of assurance. He felt a quiet manhood, nonassertive but of sturdy and strong blood. He knew that he would no more quail before his guides wherever they should point. He had been to touch the great death, and found that, after all, it was but the great death and was for others. He was a man.

So it came to pass that as he trudged from the place of blood and wrath his soul changed. He came from hot plowshares to prospects of clover tranquilly, and it was as if hot plowshares were not. Scars faded as flowers.

It rained. The procession of weary soldiers became a bedraggled train, despondent and muttering, marching with churning effort in a trough of liquid brown mud under a low, wretched sky. Yet the youth smiled, for he saw that the world was a world for him, though many discovered it to be made of oaths and walking sticks, He had rid himself of the red sickness of battle. The sultry nightmare was in the past. He had been an animal blistered and sweating in the heat and pain of war. He turned now with a lover's thirst to images of tranquil skies, fresh meadows, cool brooks—an existence of soft and eternal peace.

Over the river a golden ray of sun came through the hosts of leaden rain clouds.

# MARK TWAIN

## *The Private History of*
## *A Campaign that Failed*

YOU HAVE HEARD from a great many people who did something in the war; is it not fair and right that you listen a little moment to one who started out to do something in it, but didn't. Thousands entered the war, got just a taste of it, and then stepped out again permanently. These, by their very numbers, are respectable, and are therefore entitled to a sort of voice—not a loud one, but a modest one; not a boastful one, but an apologetic one. They ought not to be allowed much space among better people—people who did something. I grant that; but they ought at least to be allowed to state why they didn't do anything, and also to explain the process by which they didn't do anything. Surely this kind of light must have a sort of value.

Out West there was a good deal of confusion in men's minds during the first months of the great trouble—a good deal of unsettledness, of leaning first this way, then that, then the other way. It was hard for us to get our bearings. I call to mind an instance of this. I was piloting on the Mississippi when the news came that South Carolina had gone out of the Union on the 20th of December, 1860. My pilot mate was a New Yorker. He was strong for the Union; so was I. But he would not listen to me with any patience; my loyalty was smirched, to his eye, because my father had owned slaves. I said, in palliation of this dark fact, that I had heard my father say, some years before he died, that slavery was a great wrong, and that he would free the solitary Negro he then owned if he could think it right to give away the property of the family when he was so straitened in means. My mate retorted that a mere impulse was nothing—anybody could pretend to a good impulse; and went on decrying my Unionism and libeling my ancestry. A month later the secession atmosphere had considerably thickened on the Lower Mississippi, and I became a rebel; so did he. We were together in New Orleans the 26th of January, when Louisiana went out of the Union. He did his full share of the rebel shouting, but was bitterly opposed to

letting me do mine. He said that I came of bad stock—of a father who
had been willing to set slaves free. In the following summer he was
piloting a Federal gunboat and shouting for the Union again, and I was
in the Confederate army. I held his note for some borrowed money.
He was one of the most upright men I ever knew, but he repudiated
that note without hesitation becaue I was a rebel and the son of a man
who owned slaves.

In that summer—of 1861—the first wash of the wave of war broke
upon the shores of Missouri. Our State was invaded by the Union
forces. They took possession of St. Louis, Jefferson Barracks, and
some other points. The Governor, Claib Jackson, issued his proclamation calling out fifty thousand militia to repel the invader.

I was visiting in the small town where my boyood had been
spent—Hannibal, Marion County. Several of us got together in a
secret place by night and formed ourselves into a military company.
One Tom Lyman, a young fellow of a good deal of spirit but of no
military experience, was made captain; I was made second lieutenant.
We had no first lieutenant; I do not know why; it was long ago. There
were fifteen of us. By the advice of an innocent connected with the
organization we called ourselves the Marion Rangers. I do not remember that anyone found fault with the name. I did not; I thought it
sounded quite well. The young fellow who proposed this title was
perhaps a fair sample of the kind of stuff we were made of. He was
young, ignorant, good-natured, well-meaning, trivial, full of romance, and given to reading chivalric novels and singing forlorn
love-ditties. He had some pathetic little nickel-plated aristocratic
instincts, and detested his name, which was Dunlap; detested it, partly
because it was nearly as common in that region as Smith, but mainly
because it had a plebian sound to his ear. So he tried to ennoble it by
writing it in this way: *d'Unlap*. That contented his eye, but left his ear
unsatisfied, for people gave the new name the same old pronun-
ciation—emphasis on the front end of it. He then did the bravest thing
that can be imagined—a thing to make one shiver when one remem-
bers how the world is given to resenting shams and affectations; he
began to write his name so: *d'Un Lap*. And he waited patiently
through the long storm of mud that was flung at this work of art, and he
had his reward at last; for he lived to see that name accepted, and the
emphasis put where he wanted it by people who had known him all his
life, and to whom the tribe of Dunlaps had been as familiar as the rain
and the sunshine for forty years. So sure of victory at last is the

courage that can wait. He said he had found, by consulting some ancient French chronicles, that the name was rightly and originally written d'Un Lap; and said that if it were translated into English it would mean Peterson: *Lap* Latin or Greek, he said, for stone or rock, same as the French *pierre*, that is to say, Peter; *d'*, of or from a stone or a Peter; that is to say, one who is the son of a stone, the son of a Peter—Peterson. Our militia company were not learned, and the explanation confused them; so they called him Peterson Dunlap. He proved useful to us in his way; he named our camps for us and he generally struck a name that was "no slouch," as the boys said.

That is one sample of us. Another was Ed Stevens, son of the town jeweler—trim-built, handsome, graceful, neat as a cat; bright, educated, but given over entirely to fun. There was nothing serious in life to him. As far as he was concerned, this military expedition of ours was simply a holiday. I should say that about half of us looked upon it in the same way; not consciously perhaps, but unconsciously. We did not think; we were not capable of it. As for myself, I was full of unreasoning joy to be done with turning out of bed at midnight and four in the morning for a while; grateful to have a change, new scenes, new occupations, a new interest. In my thoughts that was as far as I went; I did not go into the details; as a rule, one doesn't at twenty-four.

Another sample was Smith, the blacksmith's apprentice. This vast donkey had some pluck, of a slow and sluggish nature, but a soft heart; at one time he would knock a horse down for some impropriety, and at another he would get homesick and cry. However, he had one ultimate credit to his account which some of us hadn't: he stuck to the war, and was killed in battle at last.

Jo Bowers, another sample, was a huge, good-natured, flax-headed lubber; lazy, sentimental, full of harmless brag, a grumbler by nature; an experienced, industrious, ambitious, and often quite picturesque liar, and yet not a successful one, for he had had no intelligent training, but was allowed to come up just any way. This life was serious enough to him, and seldom satisfactory. But he was a good fellow anyway, and the boys all liked him. He was made orderly sergeant; Stevens was made corporal.

These samples will answer—and they are quite fair ones. Well, this herd of cattle started for the war. What could you expect of them? Nothing, I should say. That is what they did.

We waited for a dark night, for caution and secrecy were necessary; then, toward midnight, we stole in couples and from various directions to the Griffith place, beyond the town; from that point we set out together on foot. Hannibal lies at the extreme southeastern corner of Marion County, on the Mississippi River; our objective point was the hamlet of New London, ten miles away, in Ralls County.

The first hour was all fun, all idle nonsense and laughter. But that could not be kept up. The steady trudging came to be like work; the play had somehow oozed out of it; the stillness of the woods and the somberness of the night began to throw a depressing influence over the spirits of the boys, and presently the talking died out and each person shut himself up in his own thoughts. During the last half of the second hour nobody said a word.

Now we approached a log farmhouse where, according to report, there was a guard of five Union soldiers. Lyman called a halt; and there, in the deep gloom of the overhanging branches, he began to whisper a plan of assault upon the house, which made the gloom more depressing than it was before. It was a crucial moment; we realized, with a cold suddenness, that here was no jest—we were standing face to face with actual war. We were equal to the occasion. In our reponse there was no hesitation, no indecision: we said that if Lyman wanted to meddle with those soldiers, he could go ahead and do it; but if he waited for us to follow him, he would wait a long time.

Lyman urged, pleaded, tried to shame us, but it had no effect. Our course was plain, our minds were made up: we would flank the farmhouse—go out around. And that was what we did.

We struck into the woods and entered upon a rough time, stumbling over roots, getting tangled in vines, and torn by briers. At last we reached an open place in a safe region, and sat down, blown and hot, to cool off and nurse our scratches and bruises. Lyman was annoyed, but the rest of us were cheerful; we had flanked the farmhouse, we had made our first military movement, and it was a success; we had nothing to fret about, we were feeling just the other way. Horse-play and laughing began again; the expedition was become a holiday frolic once more.

Then we had two more hours of dull trudging and ultimate silence and depression; then, about dawn, we straggled into New London, soiled, heel-blistered, fagged with our little march, and all of us except Stevens in a sour and raspy humor and privately down on the war. We stacked our shabby old shotguns in Colonel Ralls's barn, and then went in a body and breakfasted with that veteram of the Mexican War. Afterwards he took us to a distant meadow, and there in the shade of a tree we listened to an old-fashioned speech from him, full of gunpowder and glory, full of that adjective-piling, mixed metaphor, and windy declamation which were regarded as eloquence in that ancient time and that remote region; and then he swore us on the Bible to be faithful to the State of Missouri and drive all invaders from her soil, no matter whence they might come or under what flag they might march. This mixed us considerably, and we could not make out just what service we were embarked in; but Colonel Ralls, the practiced politician and phrase-juggler, was not similarly in doubt; he knew quite clearly that he had invested us in the cause of the Southern Confederacy. He closed the solemnities by belting around me the sword which his neighbor, Colonel Brown, had worn at Buena Vista and Molino del Rey; and he accompanied this act with another impressive blast.

Then we formed in a line of battle and marched four miles to a shady and pleasant piece of woods on the border of the far-reaching expanses of a flowery prairie. It was an enchanting region for war—our kind of war.

We pierced the forest about half a mile, and took up a strong position, with some low, rocky, and wooded hills behind us, and a purling, limpid creek in front. Straightway half the command were in swimming and the other half fishing. The ass with the French name gave this position a romantic title, but it was too long, so the boys shortened and simplified it to Camp Ralls.

We occupied an old maple sugar camp, whose half-rotted troughs were still propped against the trees. A long corn-crib served for sleeping quarters for the battalion. On our left, half a mile away, were Mason's farm and house; and he was a friend to the cause. Shortly after noon the farmers began to arrive from several directions, with mules and horses for our use, and these they lent us for as long as the war might last, which they judged would be about three months. The animals were of all sizes, all colors, and all breeds. They were mainly young and frisky, and nobody in the command could stay on them long at a time; for we were town boys, and ignorant of horsemanship. The creature that fell to my share was a very small mule, and yet so quick and active that it could throw me without difficulty; and it did this whenever I got on it. Then it would bray—stretching its neck out, laying its ears back, and spreading its jaws till you could see down to its works. It was a disagreeable animal in every way. If I took it by the bridle and tried to lead it off the grounds, it would sit down and brace

back, and no one could budge it. However, I was not entirely destitute
of military resources, and I did presently manage to spoil this game;
for I had seen many a steamboat aground in my time, and knew a trick
or two which even a grounded mule would be obliged to respect.
There was a well by the corn-crib; so I substituted thirty fathom of
rope for the bridle, and fetched him home with the windlass.

I will anticipate here sufficiently to say that we did learn to ride,
after some days' practice, but never well. We could not learn to like
our animals; they were not choice ones, and most of them had
annoying pecularities of one kind or another. Stevens's horse would
carry him, when he was not noticing, under the huge excrescences
which form on the trunks of oak trees, and wipe him out of the saddle;
in this way Stevens got several bad hurts. Sergeant Bowers's horse was
very large and tall, with slim, long legs, and looked like a railroad
bridge. His size enabled him to reach all about, and as far as he wanted
to, with his head; so he was always biting Bowers's legs. On the
march, in the sun, Bowers slept a good deal; and as soon as the horse
recognized that he was asleep he would reach around and bite him on
the leg. His legs were black and blue with bites. This was the only
thing that could ever make him swear, but this always did; whenever
his horse bit him he always swore, and of course Stevens, who
laughed at everything, laughed at this, and would even get into such
convulsions over it as to lose his balance and fall off his horse; and
then Bowers, already irritated by the pain of the horse-bite, would
resent the laughter with hard language, and there would be a quarrel;
so that horse made no end of trouble and bad blood in the command.

However I will get back to where I was—our first afternoon in the
sugar-camp. The sugar-troughs came very handy as horse-troughs,
and we had plenty of corn to fill them with. I ordered Sergeant Bowers
to feed my mule; but he said that if I reckoned he went to war to be a
dry-nurse to a mule, it wouldn't take me very long to find out my
mistake. I believed that this was insubordination, but I was full of
uncertainties about everything military, and so I let the thing pass, and
went and ordered Smith, the blacksmith's apprentice, to feed the
mule; but he merely gave me a large, cold sarcastic grin, such as an
ostensibly seven-year-old horse gives you when you lift his lip and
find he is fourteen, and turned his back on me. I then went to the
captain, and asked if it was not right and proper and military for me to
have an orderly. He said it was, but as there was only one orderly in
the corps, it was but right that he himself should have Bowers on his

staff. Bowers said he wouldn't serve on anybody's staff; and if anybody thought he could make him, let him try it. So, of course, the thing had to be dropped; there was no other way.

Next, nobody would cook; it was considered a degradation; so we had no dinner. We lazied the rest of the pleasant afternoon away, some dozing under the trees, some smoking cob-pipes and talking sweethearts and war, some playing games. By late supper-time all hands were famished; and to meet the difficulty all hands turned to, on an equal footing, and gathered wood, built fires, and cooked the meal. Afterwards everything was smooth for a while; then trouble broke out between the corporal and the sergeant, each claiming to rank the other. Nobody knew which was the higher office; so Lyman had to settle the matter by making the rank of both officers equal. The commander of an ignorant crew like that has many troubles and vexations which probably do not occur in the regular army at all. However, with the song-singing and yarn-spinning around the campfire, everything presently became serene again; and by and by we raked the corn down level in one end of the crib, and all went to bed on it, tying a horse to the door, so that he would neigh if anyone tried to get in. *

We had some horsemanship drill every forenoon; then, afternoons, we rode off here and there in squads a few miles, and visited the farmers' girls, and had a youthful good time, and got an honest good dinner or supper, and then home again to camp, happy and content.

For a time life was idly delicious, it was perfect; there was nothing to mar it. Then came some farmers with an alarm one day. They said it was rumored that the enemy were advancing in our direction from over Hyde's prairie. The result was a sharp stir among us, and general consternation. It was a rude awakening from our pleasant trance. The rumor was but a rumor—nothing definite about it; so, in the confusion, we did not know which way to retreat. Lyman was for not retreating at all in these uncertain circumstances; but he found that if he tried to maintain that attitude he would fare badly, for the com-

---

* It was always my impression that that was what the horse was there for, and I know that it was also the impression of at least one other of the command, for we talked about it at the time, and admired the military ingenuity of the device; but when I was out West, three years ago, I was told by Mr. A. G. Fuqua, a member of our company, that the horse was his; that the leaving him tied at the door was a matter of mere forgetfulness, and that to attribute it to intelligent invention was to give him quite too much credit. In support of his position he called my attention to the suggestive fact that the artifice was not employed again. I had not thought of that before.

mand were in no humor to put up with insubordination. So he yielded the point and called a council of war—to consist of himself and the three other officers; but the privates made such a fuss about being left out that we had to allow them to remain, for they were already present, and doing the most of the talking too. The question was, which way to retreat; but all were so flurried that nobody seemed to have even a guess to offer. Except Lyman. He explained in a few calm words that, inasmuch as the enemy were approaching from over Hyde's prairie, our course was simple; all we had to do was not to retreat *toward* him; any other direction would answer our needs perfectly. Eveybody saw in a moment how true this was, and how wise; so Lyman got a great many compliments. It was now decided that we should fall back on Mason's farm.

It was after dark by this time, and as we could not know how soon the enemy might arrive, it did not seem best to try to take the horses and things with us; so we only took the guns and ammunition, and started at once. The route was very rough and hilly and rocky, and presently the night grew very black and rain began to fall; so we had a troublesome time of it, struggling and stumbling along in the dark; and soon some person slipped and fell, and then the next person behind stumbled over him and fell, and so did the rest, one after the other; and then Bowers came with the keg of powder in his arms, while the command were all mixed together, arms and legs, on the muddy slope; and so he fell, of course, with the keg, and this started the whole detachment down the hill in a body, and they landed in the brook at the bottom in a pile, and each that was undermost pulling the hair and scratching and biting those that were on top of him; and those that were being scratched and bitten scratching and biting the rest in their turn, and all saying they would die before they would ever go to war again if they ever got out of this brook this time, and the invader might rot for all they cared, and the country along with him—and all such talk as that, which was dismal to hear and take part in, in such smothered, low voices, and such a grisly dark place and so wet, and the enemy, maybe, coming any moment.

The keg of powder was lost, and the guns, too; so the growling and complaining continued straight along while the brigade pawed around the pasty hillside and slopped around in the brook hunting for these things; consequently we lost considerable time at this; and then we heard a sound, and held our breath and listened, and it seemed to be the enemy coming, though it could have been a cow; but we did not wait, but left a couple of guns behind and struck out for Mason's again as briskly as we could scramble along in the dark. But we got lost presently among the rugged little ravines, and wasted a deal of time finding the way again, so it was after nine when we reached Mason's stile at last; and then before we could open our mouths to give the countersign several dogs came bounding over the fence, with great riot and noise, and each of them took a soldier by the slack of his trousers and began to back away with him. We could not shoot the dogs without endangering the persons they were attached to; so we had to look on helpless, at what was perhaps the most mortifying spectacle of the Civil War. There was light enough, and to spare, for the Masons had now run out on the porch with candles in their hands. The old man and his son came and undid the dogs without difficulty, all but Bowers's; but they couldn't undo his dog, they didn't know his combination; he was of the bull kind, and seemed to be set with a Yale time-lock; but they got him loose at last with some scalding water, of which Bowers got his share and returned thanks. Peterson Dunlap afterwards made up a fine name for this engagement, and also for the night march which preceded it, but both have long ago faded out of my memory.

We now went into the house, and they began to ask us a world of questions, whereby it presently came out that we did not know anything concerning who or what we were running from; so the old gentleman made himself very frank, and said we were a curious breed of soldiers, and guessed we could be depended on to end up the war in time, because no government could stand the expense of the shoe-leather we should cost it trying to follow us around. "Marion *Rangers*! good name, b'-gosh!" said he. And wanted to know why we hadn't had a picket-guard at the place where the road entered the prairie, and why we hadn't sent out a scouting party to spy out the enemy and bring us an account of his strength, and so on, before jumping up and stampeding out of a strong position upon a mere vague rumor—and so on, and so forth, till he made us all feel shabbier than the dogs had done, not half so enthusiastically welcome. So we went to bed shamed and low-spirited; except Stevens. Soon Stevens began to devise a garment for Bowers which could be made to automatically display his battle-scars to the grateful, or conceal them from the envious, according to his occasions; but Bowers was in no humor for this, so there was a fight, and when it was over Stevens had some battle-scars of his own to think about.

Then we got a little sleep. But after all we had gone through, our activities were not over for the night; for about two o'clock in the morning we heard a shout of warning from down the lane, accompanied by a chorus from all the dogs, and in a moment everybody was up and flying around to find out what the alarm was about. The alarmist was a horseman who gave notice that a detachment of Union soldiers was on its way from Hannibal with orders to capture and hang any bands like ours which it could find, and said we had no time to lose. Farmer Mason was in a flurry this time himself. He hurried us out of the house with all haste, and sent one of his Negroes with us to show us where to hide ourselves and our telltale guns among the ravines half a mile away. It was raining heavily.

We struck down the lane, then across some rocky pasture-land which offered good advantages for stumbling; consequently we were down in the mud most of the time, and every time a man went down he blackguarded the war, and the people that started it, and everybody connected with it, and gave himself the master dose of all for being so foolish as to go into it. At last we reached the wooded mouth of a ravine, and there we huddled ourselves under the streaming trees, and sent the negro back home. It was a dismal and heart-breaking time. We were like to be drowned with the rain, deafened with the howling wind and the booming thunder, and blinded by the lightning. It was, indeed, a wild night. The drenching we were getting was misery enough, but a deeper misery still was the reflection that the halter might end us before we were a day older. A death of this shameful sort had not occurred to us as being among the possibilities of war. It took the romance all out of the campaign, and turned our dreams of glory into a repulsive nightmare. As for doubting that so barbarous an order had been given, not one of us did that.

The long night wore itself out at last, and then the Negro came to us with the news that the alarm had manifestly been a false one, and that breakfast would soon be ready. Straightway we were light-hearted again, and the world was bright, and life as full of hope and promise as ever—for we were young then. How long ago that was! Twenty-four years.

The mongrel child of philology named the night's refuge Camp Devastation, and no soul objected. The Masons gave us a Missouri country breakfast, in Missourian abundance, and we needed it: hot biscuits; hot "wheat bread," prettily criss-crossed in a lattice pattern on top; hot corn pone; fried chicken; bacon, coffee, eggs, milk, buttermilk, etc.; and the world may be confidently challenged to furnish the equal of such a breakfast, as it is cooked in the South.

We stayed several days at Mason's; and after all these years the memory of the dullness, and stillness, and lifelessness of that slumberous farmhouse still oppresses my spirit as with a sense of the presence of death and mourning. There was nothing to do, nothing to think about; there was no interest in life. The male part of the household were away in the fields all day, the women were busy and out of our sight; there was no sound but the plaintive wailing of a spinning-wheel, forever moaning out from some distant room—the most lonesome sound in nature, a sound steeped and sodden with home-sickness and the emptiness of life. The family went to bed about dark every night, and as we were not invited to intrude any new customs we naturally followed theirs. Those nights were a hundred years long to youths accustomed to being up till twelve. We lay awake and miserable till that hour every time, and grew old and decrepit waiting through the still eternities for the clock-strikes. This was no place for town boys. So at last it was with something very like joy that we received news that the enemy were on our track again. With a new birth of the old warrior spirit we sprang to our place in line of battle and fell back on Camp Ralls.

Captain Lyman had taken a hint from Mason's talk, and he now gave orders that our camp should be guarded against surprise by the posting of pickets. I was ordered to place a picket at the forks of the road in Hyde's prairie. Night shut down black and threatening. I told Sergeant Bowers to go out to that place and stay till midnight; and, just as I was expecting, he said he wouldn't do it. I tried to get others to go, but all refused. Some excused themselves on account of the weather; but the rest were frank enough to say they wouldn't go in any kind of weather. This kind of thing sounds odd now, and impossible, but there was no surprise in it at the time. On the contrary, it seemed a perfectly natural thing to do. There were scores of little camps scattered over Missouri where the same thing was happening. These camps were composed of young men who had been born and reared to a sturdy independence, and who did not know what it meant to be ordered around by Tom, Dick, and Harry, whom they had known familiarly all their lives, in the village or on the farm. It is quite within the probabilities that this same thing was happening all over the South. James Redpath recognized the justice of this assumption, and furnished the following instance in support of it. During a short stay in

East Tennessee he was in a citizen colonel's tent one day talking, when a big private appeared at the door, and, without salute or other circumlocution, said to the colonel:

"Say, Jim, I'm a-goin' home for a few days."

'What for?''

"Well, I hain't b'en there for a right smart while, and I'd like to see how things is comin' on."

"How long are you going to be gone?"

" 'Bout two weeks."

"Well, don't be gone longer than that; and get back sooner if you can."

That was all, and the citizen officer resumed his conversation where the private had broken it off. This was in the first months of the war, of course. The camps in our part of Missouri were under Brigadier-General Thomas H. Harris. He was a townsman of ours, a first-rate fellow, and well liked; but we had all familiarly known him as the sole and modest-salaried operator in our telegraph office, where he had to send about one dispatch a week in ordinary times, and two when there was a rush of business; consequently, when he appeared in our midst one day, on the wing, and delivered a military command of some sort, in a large military fashion, nobody was surprised at the response which he got from the assembled soldiery:

"Oh, now, what'll you take to *don't*, Tom Harris?"

It was quite the natural thing. One might justly imagine that we were hopeless material for war. And so we seemed, in our ignorant state; but there were those among us who afterwards learned the grim trade; learned to obey like machines; became valuable soldiers; fought all through the war, and came out at the end with excellent records. One of the very boys who refused to go out on picket duty that night, and called me an ass for thinking he would expose himself to danger in such a foolhardy way, had become distinguished for intrepidity before he was a year older.

I did secure my picket that night—not by authority, but by diplomacy. I got Bowers to go by agreeing to exchange ranks with him for the time being, and go along and stand the watch with him as his subordinate. We stayed out there a couple of dreary hours in the pitchy darkness and the rain, with nothing to modify the dreariness but Bowers's monotonous growlings at the war and the weather; then we began to nod, and presently found it next to impossible to stay in the saddle; so we gave up the tedious job, and went back to the camp without waiting for the relief guard. We rode into camp without interruption or objection from anybody, and the enemy could have done the same, for there were no sentries. Everybody was asleep; at midnight there was nobody to send out another picket, so none was sent. We never tried to establish a watch at night again, as far as I remember, but we generally kept a picket out in the daytime.

In that camp the whole command slept on the corn in the big corn-crib; and there was usually a general row before morning, for the place was full of rats, and they would scramble over the boys' bodies and faces, annoying and irritating everybody; and now and then they would bite someone's toe, and the person who owned the toe would start up and magnify his English and begin to throw corn in the dark. The ears were half as heavy as bricks, and when they struck they hurt. The persons struck would respond, and inside of five minutes every man would be locked in a death-grip with his neighbor. There was a grievous deal of blood shed in the corn-crib, but this was all that was spilled while I was in the war. No, that is not quite true. But for one circumstance it would have been all. I will come to that now.

Our scares were frequent. Every few days rumors would come that the enemy were approaching. In these cases we always fell back on some other camp of ours; we never stayed where we were. But the rumors always turned out to be false; so at last even we began to grow indifferent to them. One night a Negro was sent to our corn-crib with the same old warning: the enemy was hovering in our neighborhood. We all said let him hover. We resolved to stay still and be comfortable. It was a fine warlike resolution, and no doubt we all felt the stir of it in our veins—for a moment. We had been having a very jolly time, that was full of horse-play and school-boy hilarity; but that cooled down now, and presently the fast-waning fire of forced jokes and forced laughs died out altogether, and the company became silent. Silent and nervous. And soon uneasy—worried— apprehensive. We had said we would stay, and we were committed. We could have been persuaded to go, but there was nobody brave enough to suggest it. An almost noiseless movement presently began in the dark by a general but unvoiced impulse. When the movement was completed each man knew that he was not the only person who had crept to the front wall and had his eye at a crack between the logs. No, we were all there; all there with our hearts in our throats, and staring out toward the sugar-troughs where the forest footpath came through. It was late, and there was a deep woodsy stillness everywhere. There was a veiled moonlight, which was only just strong enough to enable us to mark the general shape of objects. Presently a muffled sound caught our ears, and we recognized it as the hoof-beats of a horse or horses. And right away a figure appeared in the forest path; it could have been made of smoke, its mass had so little sharpness of outline. It was a man on horseback, and it seemed to me that there were others behind him. I got hold of a gun in the dark, and pushed it through a crack between the logs, hardly knowing what I was doing, I was so dazed with fright. Somebody said, "Fire!" I pulled the trigger. I seemed to see a hundred flashes and hear a hundred reports; then I saw the man fall down out of the saddle. My first feeling was of surprised gratification; my first impulse was an apprentice-sportsman's impulse to run and pick up his game. Somebody said, harldy audibly, "Good—we've got him!—wait for the rest." But the rest did not come. We waited— listened—still no more came. There was not a sound, not the whisper of a leaf; just perfect stillness; an uncanny kind of stillness, which was all the more uncanny on account of the damp, earthy, late-night smells now rising and pervading it. Then, wondering, we crept stealthily out, and approached the man. When we got to him the moon revealed him distinctly. He was lying on his back, with his arms abroad; his mouth was open and his chest heaving with long gasps, and his white shirtfront was all splashed with blood. The thought shot through me that I was a murderer; that I had killed a man—a man who had never done me any harm. That was the coldest sensation that ever went through my marrow. I was down by him in a moment, helplessly stroking his forehead; and I would have given anything then—my own life freely—to make him again what he had been five minutes before. And all the boys seemed to be feeling in the same way; they hung over him, full of pitying interest, and tried all they could to help him, and said all sorts of regretful things. They had forgotten all about the enemy; they thought only of this one forlorn unit of the foe. Once my imagination persuaded me that the dying man gave me a reproach-ful look out of his shadowy eyes, and it seemd to me that I could rather he had stabbed me than done that. He muttered and mumbled like a dreamer in his sleep about his wife and his child; and I thought with a new despair, "This thing that I have done does not end with him; it falls upon *them* too, and they never did me any harm, any more than he."

In a little while the man was dead. He was killed in war; killed in fair and legitimate war; killed in battle, as you may say; and yet he was as sincerely mourned by the opposing force as if he had been their brother. The boys stood there a half-hour sorrowing over him, and recalling the details of the tragedy, and wondering how he might be, and if he were a spy, and saying that if it were to do over again they would not hurt him unless he attacked them first. It soon came out that mine was not the only shot fired; there were five others—a division of the guilt which was a great relief to me, since it in some degree lightened and diminished the burden I was carrying. There were six shots fired at once; but I was not in my right mind at the time, and my heated imagination had magnified my one shot into a volley.

The man was not in uniform, and was not armed. He was a stranger in the country; that was all we ever found out about him. The thought of him got to preying upon me every night; I could not get rid of it. I could not drive it away, the taking of that unoffending life seemed such a wanton thing. And it seemed an epitome of war; that all war must be just that—the killing of strangers against whom you feel no personal animosity; strangers whom, in other circumstances, you would help if you found them in trouble, and who would help you if you needed it. My campaign was spoiled. It seemed to me that I was not rightly equipped for this awful business; that war was intended for men, and I for a child's nurse. I resolved to retire from this avocation of sham soldiership while I could save some remnant of my self-respect. These morbid thoughts clung to me against reason; for at bottom I did not believe I had touched that man. The law of probabilities decreed me guiltless of his blood; for in all my small experience with guns I had never hit anything I had tried to hit, and I knew I had done my best to hit him. Yet there was no solace in the thought. Against a diseased imagination demonstration goes for nothing.

The rest of my war experience was of a piece with what I have already told of it. We kept monotonously falling back upon one camp or another, and eating up the country. I marvel now at the patience of the farmers and their families. They ought to have shot us; on the contrary, they were as hospitably kind and courteous to us as if we had deserved it. In one of these camps we found Ab Grimes, an Upper Mississippi pilot, who afterwards became famous as a dare-devil rebel spy, whose career bristled with desperate adventures. The look and style of his comrades suggested that they had not come into the war to play, and their deeds made good the conjecture later. They were fine horsemen and good revolver shots; but their favorite arm was the lasso. Each had one at his pommel, and could snatch a man out of the saddle with it every time, on a full gallop, at any reasonable distance.

In another camp the chief was a fierce and profane old blacksmith of sixty, and he had furnished his twenty recruits with gigantic home-made bowie-knives, to be swung with two hands, like the *machetes* of the Isthmus. It was a grisly spectacle to see that earnest band practicing their murderous cuts and slashes under the eye of that remorseless old fanatic.

The last camp which we fell back upon was in a hollow near the village of Florida, where I was born—in Monroe County. Here we were warned one day that a Union colonel was sweeping down on us with a whole regiment at his heel. This looked decidedly serious. Our boys went apart and consulted; then we went back and told the other companies present that the war was a disappointment to us, and we were going to disband. They were getting ready themselves to fall back on some place or other, and were only waiting for General Tom Harris, who was expected to arrive at any moment; so they tried to persuade us to wait a little while, but the majority of us said no, we were accustomed to falling back, and didn't neeed any of Tom Harris's help; we could get along perfectly well without him—and save time, too. So about half of our fifteen, including myself, mounted and left on the instant; the others yielded to persuasion and stayed—stayed through the war.

An hour later we met General Harris on the road, with two or three people in his company—his staff, probably, but we could not tell; none of them were in uniform; uniforms had not come into vogue among us yet. Harris ordered us back; but we told him there was a Union colonel coming with a whole regiment in his wake, and it looked as if there was going to be a disturbance; so we had concluded to go home. He raged a little, but it was of no use; our minds were made up. We had done our share; had killed one man, exterminated one army, such as it was; let him go and kill the rest, and that would end the war. I did not see that brisk young general again until last year; then he was wearing white hair and whiskers.

In time I came to know that Union colonel whose coming frightened me out of the war and crippled the Southern cause to that extent—General Grant. I came within a few hours of seeing him when he was as unknown as I was myself; at a time when anybody could have said, "Grant? Ulysses S. Grant? I do not remember hearing the name before." It seems difficult to realize that there was once a time when such a remark could be rationally made; but there *was*, and I was within a few miles of the place and the occasion, too, though proceeding in the other direction.

The thoughtful will not throw this war paper of mine lightly aside as being valueless. It has this value: it is a not unfair picture of what went on in many and many a militia camp in the first months of the rebellion, when the green recruits were without discipline, without the steadying and heartening influence of trained leaders; when all their circumstances were new and strange, and charged with exaggerated terrors, and before the invaluable experience of actual collision in the field has turned them from rabbits into soldiers. If this side of the picture of that early day has not before been put into history, then history has been to that degree incomplete, for it had and has its rightful place there. There was more Bull Run material scattered through the early camps of this country than exhibited itself at Bull Run. And yet it learned its trade presently, and helped to fight the great battles after. I could have become a soldier myself if I had waited. I had got part of it learned; I knew more about retreating than the man that invented retreating.

# JOHN
# WILLIAM DeFOREST

*The Brigade Commander*

THE COLONEL WAS the idol of his bragging old regiment and of the bragging brigade which for the last six months he had commanded.

He was the idol, not because he was good and gracious, not because he spared his soldiers or treated them as fellow-citizens, but because he had led them to victory and made them famous. If a man will win battles and give his brigade a right to brag loudly of its doings, he may have its admiration and even its enthusiastic devotion, though he be as pitiless and as wicked as Lucifer.

"It's nothin' to me what the Currnell is in prrivit, so long as he shows us how to whack the rrebs," said Major Gahogan, commandant of the "Old Tenth." "Moses saw God in the burrnin' bussh, an' bowed down to it, an' worrshipt it. It wasn't the bussh he worrshipt; it was his God that was in it. An' I worrship this villin of a Currnell (if he is a villin) because he's almighty and gives us the vict'ry. He's nothin' but a human burrnin' bussh, perhaps, but he's got the god of war in um. Adjetant Wallis, it's a——long time between dhrinks, as I think ye was sayin', an' with rayson. See if ye can't confiscate a canteen of whiskee somewhere in the camp. Bedad, if I can't buy it I'll stale it. We're goin' to fight tomorry, an' it may be it's the last chance we'll have for a dhrink, unless there's more lik'r now in the other worrld than Dives got."

The brigade was bivouacked in some invisible region, amid the damp, misty darkness of a September night. The men lay in their ranks, each with his feet to the front and his head rearward, each covered by his overcoat and pillowed upon his haversack, each with his loaded rifle nestled close beside him. Asleep as they were, or dropping placidly into slumber, they were ready to start in order to their feet and pour out the red light and harsh roar of combat. There were two lines of battle, each of three regiments of infantry, the first some two hundred yards in advance of the second. In the space between them lay two four-gun batteries, one of them brass twelve-pounder "Napoleons," and the other rifled Parrotts. To the rear of the infantry were the recumbent troopers and picketed horses of a regiment of cavalry. All around, in the far, black distance, invisible and inaudible, paced or watched stealthily the sentinels of the grand guards.

There was not a fire, nor a torch, nor a star-beam in the whole bivouac to guide the feet of Adjutant Wallis in his pilgrimage after whiskey. The orders from brigade headquarters had been strict against illuminations, for the Confederates were near at hand in force, and a surprise was purposed as well as feared. A tired and sleepy youngster, almost dropping with the heavy somnolence of wearied adolescence, he stumbled on through the trials of an undiscernible and unfamiliar footing, lifting his heavy riding-boots sluggishly over imaginary obstacles, and fearing the while lest his toil were labor misspent. It was a dry camp, he felt dolefully certain, or there would have been more noise in it. He fell over a sleeping Sergeant, and said to him hastily, "Steady, man—a friend!" as the half-roused soldier clutched his rifle. Then he found a Lieutenant, and shook him in vain; further on a Captain, and exchanged saddening murmurs with him; further still a camp-follower of African extraction, and blasphemed him.

"It's a God-forsaken camp, and there isn't a horn in it," said Adjutant Wallis to himself as he pursued his groping journey. "Bet you I don't find the first drop," he continued, for he was a betting boy, and frequently argued by wagers, even with himself. "Bet you two to one I don't. Bet you three to one—ten to one."

Then he saw, an indefinite distance beyond him, burning like red-hot iron through the darkness, a little scarlet or crimson gleam, as of a lighted cigar.

"That's Old Grumps, of the Bloody Fourteenth," he thought. "I've raided into his happy sleeping-grounds. I'll draw on him."

But Old Grumps, otherwise Colonel Lafayette Gildersleeve, had no rations—that is, no whiskey.

"How do you suppose an officer is to have a drink, Lieutenant?" he grumbled.

"Don't you know that our would-be Brigadier sent all the commissary to the rear day before yesterday? A canteenful can't last two days. Mine went empty about five minutes ago."

"Oh, thunder!" groaned Wallis, saddened by that saddest of all thoughts, "Too late!" "Well, least said soonest mended. I must wobble back to my Major."

"He'll send you off to some other camp as dry as this one. Wait ten minutes, and he'll be asleep. Lie down on my blanket and light your pipe. I want to talk to you about official business—about our would-be Bridagier."

"Oh, *your* turn will come some day," mumbled Wallis, remembering Gildersleeve's jealousy of the brigade commander—a jealousy which only gave tongue when aroused by "commissary." "If you do as well as usual tomorrow you can have your own brigade."

"I suppose you think we are all going to do well to-morrow," scoffed Old Grumps, whose utterance by this time stumbled. "I suppose you expect to whip and to have a good time. I suppose you brag on fighting and enjoy it."

"I like it well enough when it goes right; and it generally does go right with this brigade. I should like it better if the rebs would fire higher and break quicker."

"That depends on the way those are commanded whose business it is to break them," growled Old Grumps. "I don't say but what we are rightly commanded," he added, remembering his duty to superiors. "I concede and acknowledge that our would-be Brigadier knows his military business. But the blessing of God, Wallis! I believe in Waldron as a soldier. But as a man and a Christian, faugh!"

Gildersleeve had clearly emptied his canteen unassisted; he never talked about Christianity when perfectly sober.

"What was your last remark?" inquired Wallis, taking his pipe from his mouth to grin. Even a superior officer might be chaffed a little in the darkness.

"I made no last remark," asserted the Colonel with dignity. "I'm not a-dying yet. If I said anything last it was a mere exclamation of disgust—the disgust of an officer and gentleman. I suppose you know something about our would-be Brigadier. I suppose you think you know something about him."

"Bet you I know *all* about him," affirmed Wallis. "He enlised in the old Tenth as a common soldier. Before he had been a week in camp they found that he knew his biz, and they made him a Sergeant. Before we started for the field the Governor got his eye on him and shoved him into a Lieutenancy. The first battle h'isted him to a

Captain. And the second—bang! whiz! he shot up to Colonel, right over the heads of everybody, line and field. Nobody in the old Tenth grumbled. They saw that he knew his biz. I know *all* about him. What'll you bet?''

"I'm not a betting man, Lieutenant, except in a friendly game of poker,'' sighed Old Grumps. "You don't know anything about your Brigadier,'' he added in a sepulchral murmur, the echo of an empty canteen. "I have only been in this brigade a month, and I know more than you do, far, very far more, sorry to say it. He's a reformed clergyman. He's an apostatized minister.'' The Colonel's voice as he said this was solemn and sad enough to do credit to an undertaker. "It's a bad sort, Wallis,'' he continued, after another deep sigh, a very highly pefumed one, the sigh of a bar-keeper. "When a clergyman falls, he falls for life and eternity, like a woman or an angel. I never knew a backslidden shepherd to come to good. Sooner or later he always goes to the devil, and takes down whomsoever hangs to him.''

"He'll take down the old Tenth, then,'' asserted Wallis. "It hangs to him. Bet you two to one he takes it along.''

"You're right, Adjutant; spoken like a soldier,'' swore Gildersleeve. "And the Bloody Fourteenth, too! It will march into the burning pit as far as any regiment; and the whole brigade, yes sir!. But a backslidden shepherd, my God! Have we come to that? I often say to myself, in the solemn hours of the night, as I remember my Sabbath-school days, 'Great Scott, have we come to that?' A reformed clergyman! An apostatized minister! Think of it, Wallis, think of it! Why, sir, his very wife ran away from him. They had but just buried their first boy,'' pursued Old Grumps, his hoarse voice sinking to a whimper. "They drove home from the burial-place, where lay the new-made grave. Arrived at the door, *he* got out and extended his hand to help *her* out. Instead of accepting, instead of throwing herself into his arms and weeping there, she turned to the coachman and said, 'Driver, drive me to my father's house.' That was the end of their wedded life, Wallis.''

The Colonel actually wept at this point, and the maudlin tears were not altogether insincere. His own wife and children he heartily loved, and remembered them now with honest tenderness. At home he was not a drinker and a rough; only amid the hardships and perils of the field.

"That was the end of it, Wallis,'' he repeated. "And what was it while it lasted? What does a woman leave her husband for? Why does she separate from him over the grave of her innocent first-born? There are twenty reasons, but they must all of them be good ones. I am sorry to give it as my decided opinion, Wallis, in perfect confidence, that they must all be whopping good ones. Well, that was the beginning; only the beginning. After that he held on for a while, breaking the bread of life to a skedaddling flock, and then he bolted. The next known of him, three years later, he enlisted in your regiment, a smart but seedy recruit, smelling strongly of whisky.''

"I wish I smelt half as strong of it myself," grumbled Wallis. "It might keep out the swamp fever."

"That's the true story of Col. John James Waldron," continued Old Grumps, with a groan which was very somnolent, as if it were a twin to a snore. "That's the true story."

"I don't believe the first word of it—that is to say, Colonel, I think you have been misinformed—and I'll bet you two to one on it. If he was nothing more than a minister, how did he know drill and tactics?"

"Oh, I forgot to say, he went through West Point—that is, nearly through. They graduated him in his third year by the back door, Wallis."

"Oh, that was it, was it? He was a West Pointer, was he? Well, then, the backsliding was natural, and oughtn't to count against him. A member of Benny Havens' church has a right to backslide any-where, especially as the Colonel doesn't seem to be any worse than some of the rest of us, who haven't fallen from grace the least particle, but took our stand at the start just where we are now. A fellow that begins with a handful of trumps has a right to play a risky game."

"I know what euchered him, Wallis. It was the old Little Joker; and there's another of the same on hand now."

"On hand where? What are you driving at, Colonel?"

"He looks like a boy. I mean she looks like a boy. You know what I mean, Wallis; I mean the boy that makes believe wait on him. And her brother is in camp, got here to-night. There'll be an explanation to-morrow, and there'll be bloodshed."

"Good-night, Colonel, and sleep it off," said Wallis, rising from the side of a man whom he believed to be sillily drunk and altogether untrustworthy. "You know we get after the rebs at dawn."

"I know it—goo-night, Adjutant—gawblessyou," mumbled Old Grumps. "We'll lick those rebs, won't we?" he chuckled. "Goo-night, ole fellow, an' gawblessyou."

Whereupon Old Grumps fell asleep, very absurdly overcome by

liquor, we extremely regret to concede, but nobly sure to do his soldierly duty as soon as he should awake.

Stumbling wearily blanketward, Wallis found his Major and regimental commander, the genial and gallant Gahogan, slumbering in a peace like that of the just. He stretched himself a-near, put out his hand to touch his sabre and revolver, drew his caped great-coat over him, moved once to free his back of a root or pebble, glanced languidly at a single struggling star, thought for an instant of his far-away mother, turned his head with a sigh, and slept. In the morning he was to fight, and perhaps to die; but the boyish veteran was too seasoned, and also too tired, to mind that; he could mind but one thing—nature's pleading for rest.

In the iron-gray dawn, while the troops were falling dimly and spectrally into line, and he was mounting his horse to be ready for orders, he remembered Gildersleeve's drunken tale concerning the commandant, and laughed aloud. But turning his face toward brigade headquarters (a sylvan region marked out by the branches of a great oak), he was surprised to see a strange officer, a fair young man in Captain's uniform, riding slowly toward it.

"Is that the Boy's brother?" he said to himself; and in the next instant he had forgotten the whole subject; it was time to form and present the regiment.

Quietly and without tap of drum the small, battleworn battalions filed out of their bivouacs into the highway, ordered arms and waited for the word to march. With a dull rumble the field-pieces trundled slowly after, and halted in rear of the infantry. The cavalry trotted off circuitously through the fields, emerged upon the road in advance and likewise halted, all but a single company, which pushed on for half a mile, spreading out as it went into a thin line of skirmishers.

Meanwhile a strange interview took place near the great oak which had sheltered brigade headquarters. As the unknown officer, whom Wallis had noted, approached it, Col. Waldron was standing by his horse ready to mount. The commandant was a man of medium size, fairly handsome in person and features, and apparently about twenty-eight years of age. Perhaps it was the singular breadth of his forehead which made the lower part of his face look so unusually slight and feminine. His eyes were dark hazel, as clear, brilliant, and tender as a girl's, and brimming full of a pensiveness which seemed both loving and melancholy. Few persons, at all events few women, who looked upon him ever looked beyond his eyes. They were very fascinating, and in a man's countenance very strange. They were the kind of eyes which reveal passionate romances, and which make them.

By his side stood a boy, a singularly interesting and beautiful boy, fair-haired and blue-eyed, and delicate in color. When this boy saw the stranger approach he turned as pale as marble, slid away from the brigade commander's side, and disappeared behind a group of staff officers and orderlies. The new-comer also became deathly white as he glanced after the retreating youth. Then he dismounted, touched his cap slightly and, as if mechanically, advanced a few steps, and said hoarsely, "I believe this is Colonel Waldron. I am captain Fitz Hugh, of the —th Delaware."

Waldron put his hand to his revolver, withdrew it instantaneously, and stood motionless.

"I am on leave of absence from my regiment, Colonel," continued Fitz Hugh, speaking now with an elaborate ceremoniousness of utterance significant of struggle to suppress violent emotion. "I suppose you can understand why I made use of it in seeking you."

Waldron hesitated; he stood gazing at the earth with the air of one who represses pain; at last, after a profound sigh, he raised his eyes and answered.

"Captain, we are on the eve of battle. I must attend to my public duties first. After the battle we will settle our private affair."

"There is but one way to settle it, Colonel."

"You shall have your way if you will. You shall do what you will. I ony ask what good will it do to *her*?"

"It will do good to *me*, Colonel," whispered Fitz Hugh, suddenly turning crimson. "You forget *me*."

Waldron's face also flushed, and an angry sparkle shot from under his lashes in reply to this utterance of hate, but it died out in an instant.

"I have done a wrong, and I will accept the consequences," he said. "I pledge you my word that I will be at your disposal if I survive the battle. Where do you propose to remain meanwhile?"

"I will take the same chance, Sir. I propose to do my share in the fighting if you will use me."

"I am short of staff officers. Will you act as my aid?"

"I will, Colonel," bowed Fitz Hugh, with a glance which expressed surprise, and perhaps admiration, at this confidence.

Waldron turned, beckoned his staff officers to approach, and said, "Gentlemen, this is Captain Fitz Hugh of the —th Delaware. He has volunteered to join us for the day, and will act as my aid. And now,

Captain, will you ride to the head of the column and order it forward? There will be no drum beat and no noise. When you have given your order and seen it executed, you will wait for me.''

Fitz Hugh saluted, sprang into his saddle and galloped away. A few minutes later the whole column was plodding on silently toward its bloody goal. To a civilian, unaccustomed to scenes of war, the tranquillity of these men would have seemed very wonderful. Many of the soldiers were still munching the hard bread and raw pork of their meagre breakfasts, or drinking the cold coffee with which they had filled their canteens the day previous. Many more were chatting in an undertone, grumbling over their sore feet and other discomfits, chaffing each other, and laughing. The general bearing, however, was grave, patient, quietly enduring, and one might almost say stolid. You would have said, to judge by their expressions, that these sunburnt fellows were merely doing hard work and thoroughly commonplace work, without a prospect of adventure, and much less of danger. The explanation of this calmness, so brutal perhaps to the eye of a sensitive soul, lies mainly in the fact that they were all veterans, the survivors of marches, privations, maladies, sieges, and battles. Not a regiment present numbered four hundred men, and the average was not above three hundred. The whole force, including artillery and cavalry, might have been about twenty-five hundred sabres and bayonets.

At the beginning of the march Waldron fell into the rear of his staff and mounted orderlies. Then the Boy who had fled from Fitz Hugh dropped out of the tramping escort, and rode up to his side.

"Well, Charlie," said Waldron, casting a pitying glance at the yet pallid face and anxious eyes of the youth, "you have had a sad fright. I make you very miserable.''

"He has found us at last," murmured Charlie in a tremulous soprano voice. "What did he say?''

"We are to talk to-morrow. He acts as my aide-de-camp to-day. I ought to tell you frankly that he is not friendly.''

"Of course, I knew it," sighed Charlie, while the tears fell.

"It is only one more trouble—one more danger, and perhaps it may pass. So many *have* passed.''

"Did you tell him anything to quiet him? Did you tell him that we were married?''

"But we are not married yet, Charlie. We shall be, I hope.''

"But you ought to have told him that we were. It might stop him from doing something—mad. Why didn't you tell him so? Why didn't you think of it?''

"My dear little child, we are about to have a battle. I should like to carry some honor and truth into it."

"Where is he?" continued Charlie, unconvinced and unappeased. "I want to see him. Is he at the head of the column? I want to speak to him, just one word. He won't hurt me."

She suddenly spurred her horse, wheeled into the fields, and dashed onward. Fitz Hugh was lounging in his saddle, and sombrely surveying the passing column, when she galloped up to him.

"Carrol!" she said, in a choked voice, reining in by his side, and leaning forward to touch his sleeve.

He threw one glance at her—a glance of aversion, if not of downright hatred, and turned his back in silence.

"He is my husband, Carrol" she went on rapidly. "I knew you didn't understand it. I ought to have written you about it. I thought I would come and tell you before you did anything absurd. We were married as soon as he heard that his wife was dead."

"What is the use of this?" he muttered hoarsely, "She is not dead. I heard from her a week ago. She was living a week ago."

"Oh, Carrol!" stammered Charlie. "It was some mistake then. Is it possible! And he was so sure! But he can get a divorce, you know. She abandoned him. Or *she* can get one. No, *he* can get it—of course, when she abandoned him. But, Carrol, she *must* be dead—he was *so* sure."

"She is *not* dead, I tell you. And there can be no divorce. Insanity bars all claim to a divorce. She is in an asylum. She had to leave him, and then she went mad."

"Oh, no, Carrol, it is all a mistake; it is not so, Carrol," she murmured in a voice so faint that he could not help glancing at her, half in fury and half in pity. She was slowly falling from her horse. He sprang from his saddle, caught her in his arms, and laid her on the turf, wishing the while that it covered her grave. Just then one of Waldron's orderlies rode up and exclaimed: "What is the matter with the—the Boy? Hullo, Charlie."

Fitz Hugh stared at the man in silence, tempted to tear him from his horse. "The boy is ill," he answered when he recovered his self-command. "Take charge of him yourself." He remounted, rode onward out of sight beyond a thicket, and there waited for the brigade commander, now and then fingering his revolver. As Charlie was being placed in an ambulance by the orderly and a sergeant's wife, Waldron came up, reined in his horse violently, and asked in a furious voice, "Is that boy hurt?"

"Ah—fainted," he added immediately. "Thank you, Mrs. Gunner. Take good care of him—the best of care, my dear woman, and don't let him leave you all day."

Further on, when Fitz Hugh silently fell into his escort, he merely glanced at him in a furtive way, and then cantered on rapidly to the head of the cavalry. There he beckoned to the tall, grave, iron-gray Chaplain of the Tenth, and rode with him for nearly an hour, apart, engaged in low and seemingly impassioned discourse. From this interview Mr. Colquhoun returned to the escort with a strangely solemnized, tender countenance, while the commandant, with a more cheerful air than he had yet worn that day, gave himself to his martial duties, inspecting the landscape incessantly with his glass, and sending frequently for news to the advance scouts. It may properly be stated here that the Chaplain never divulged to any one the nature of the conversation which he had held with his Colonel.

Nothing further of note occurred until the little army, after two hours of plodding march, wound through a sinuous, wooded ravine, entered a broad, bare, slightly undulating valley, and for the second time halted. Waldron galloped to the summit of a knoll, pointed to a long eminence which faced him some two miles distant, and said tranquilly, "There is our battle-ground."

"Is that the enemy's position?" returned Captain Ives, his Adjutant-General. "We shall have a tough job if we go at it from here."

Waldron remained in deep thought for some minutes, meanwhile scanning the ridge and all its surroundings.

"What I want to know," he observed, at last, "is whether they have occupied the wooded knolls in front of their right and around their right flank."

Shortly afterward the commander of the scouting squadron came riding back at a furious pace.

"They are on the hill, Colonel," he shouted.

"Yes, of course," nodded Waldron; "but have they occupied the woods which veil their right front and flank?"

"Not a bit of it; my fellows have cantered all through, and up to the base of the hill."

"Ah!" exclaimed the brigade commander, with a rush of elation. "Then it will be easy work. Go back, Captain, and scatter your men through the wood, and hold it, if possible. Adjutant, call up the regimental commanders at once. I want them to understand my plan fully."

In a few minutes Gahogan, of the Tenth; Gildersleeve, of the Fourteenth; Peck, of the First; Thomas, of the Seventh; Taylor, of the Eighth, and Colburn, of the Fifth, were gathered around their commander. There, too, was Bradley, the boyish, red-cheeked chief of the artillery; and Stilton, the rough, old, bearded regular, who headed the cavalry. The staff was at hand, also, including Fitz Hugh, who sat his horse a little apart, downcast and sombre and silent, but nevertheless keenly interested. It is worthy of remark, by the way, that Waldron took no special note of him, and did not seem conscious of any disturbing presence. Evil as the man may have been, he was a thoroughly good soldier, and just now he thought but of his duties.

"Gentlemen," he said, "I want you to see your field of battle. The enemy occupy that long ridge. How shall we reach it?"

"I think, if we go at it straight from here, we shan't miss it," promptly judged Old Grumps, his red-oak countenance admirably cheerful and hopeful, and his jealousy all dissolved in the interest of approaching combat.

"Nor they won't miss us nuther," laughed Major Gahogan. "Bether slide our infantree into thim wuds, push up our skirmishers, play away wid our guns for an hour, an' thin rowl in a couple o' col'ms."

There was a general murmur of approval. The limits of volunteer invention in tactics had been reached by Gahogan. The other regimental commanders looked upon him as their superior in the art of war.

"That would be well, Major, if we could do nothing better," said Waldron. "But I do not feel obliged to attack the front seriously at all. The rebels have been thoughtless enough to leave that long semicircle of wooded knolls unoccupied, even by scouts. It stretches from the front of their centre clear around their right flank. I shall use it as a veil to cover us while we get into position. I shall throw out a regiment, a battery, and five companies of cavalry, to make a feint against their centre and left. With the remainder of the brigade I shall skirt the woods, double around the right of the position, and close in upon it front and rear."

"Loike scissors blades upon a snip o' paper," snorted Gahogan, in delight. Then he turned to Fitz Hugh, who happened to be nearest him, and added, "I tell ye he's got the God o' War in um. He's the burrnin' bussh of humanity, wid a God o' Battles inside on't."

"But how if they come down on our thin right wing?" asked a cautious officer, Taylor, of the Eighth. "They might smash it and seize our line of retreat."

"Men who have taken up a strong position, a position obviously chosen for defense, rarely quit it promptly for an attack," replied Waldron. "There is not one chance in ten that these gentlemen will make a considerable forward movement early in the fight. Only the greatest geniuses jump from the defensive to the offensive. Besides, we must hold the wood. So long as we hold the wood in front of their centre we save the road."

Then came personal and detailed instructions. Each regimental commander was told whither he should march, the point where he should halt to form line, and the direction by which he should attack. The mass of the command was to advance in marching column toward a knoll where the highway entered and traversed the wood. Some time before reaching it Taylor was to deploy the Eighth to the right, throw out a strong skirmish line and open fire on the enemy's centre and left, supported by the battery of Parrotts, and, if pushed, by five companies of cavalry. The remaining troops would reach the knoll, file to the left under cover of the forest, skirt it for a mile as rapidly as possible, enfold the right of the Confederate position, and then move upon it concentrically. Counting from the left, the Tenth, the Seventh, and the Fourteenth were to constitute the first line of battle, while five companies of cavalry, then the First, and then the Fifth formed the second line. Not until Gahogan might have time to wind into the enemy's right rear should Gildersleeve move out of the wood and commence the real attack.

You will go straight at the front of their right," said Waldron, with a gay smile, to this latter Colonel. "Send up two companies as skirmishers. The moment they are clearly checked, lead up the other eight in line. It will be rough work. But keep pushing. You won't have fifteen minutes of it before Thomas, on your left, will be climbing the end of the ridge to take the rebels in flank. In fifteen minutes more Gahogan will be running in on their backs. Of course they will try to change front and meet us. But they have extended their line a long way in order to cover the whole ridge. They will not be quick enough. We shall get hold of their right, and we shall roll them up. Then, Colonel Stilton, I shall expect to see the troopers jumping into the gaps and making prisoners."

"All right, Colonel," answered Stilton in that hoarse growl which is apt to mark the old cavalry officer. "Where shall we find you if we want a fresh order?"

"I shall be with Colburn, in rear of Gildersleeve. That is our centre. But never mind me; you know what the battle is to be, and you know how to fight it. The whole point with the infantry is to fold around the enemy's right, go in upon it concentrically, smash it, and roll up their line. The cavalry will watch against the infantry being flanked, and when the latter have seized the hill, will charge for prisoners. The artillery will reply to the enemy's guns with shell, and fire grape at any offensive demonstration. You all know your duties, now, gentlemen. Go to your commands, and march!''

The Colonels saluted and started off at a gallop. In a few minutes twenty-five hundred men were in simultaneous movement. Five companies of cavalry wheeled into column of companies, and advanced at a trot through the fields, seeking to gain the shelter of the forest. The six infantry regiments slid up alongside of each other, and pushed on in six parallel columns of march, two on the right of the road and four on the left. The artillery, which alone left the highway, followed at a distance of two or three hundred yards. The remaining cavalry made a wide detour to the right, as if to flank the enemy's left.

It was a mile and a quarter—it was a march of fully twenty minutes—to the edge of the woodland, the proposed cover of the column. Ten minutes before this point was reached a tiny puff of smoke showed on the brow of the hostile ridge; then, at an interval of several seconds, followed the sound of a distant explosion; then, almost immediately, came the screech of a rifled shell. Every man who heard it swiftly asked himself, ''Will it strike *me*?'' But even as the words were thought out it had passed, high in air, clean to the rear, and burst harmlesssly. A few faces turned upward and a few eyes glanced backward, as if to see the invisible enemy. But there was no pause in the column; it flowed onward quietly, eagerly, and with business-like precision; it gave forth no sound but the trampling of feet and the muttering of the officers, ''Steady, men! Forward, men.''

The Confederates, however, had got their range. A half minute later four puffs of smoke dotted the ridge, and a flight of hoarse humming shrieks tore the air. A little aureole cracked and splintered over the First, followed by loud cries of anguish and a brief, slight confusion. The voice of an officer rose sharply out of the flurry, ''Close up, Company A! Forward, men!'' The battalion column resumed its even formation in an instant, and tramped unitedly onward, leaving behind it two quivering corpses and a wounded man who tottered rearward.

Then came more screeches, and a shell exploded over the high road, knocking a gunner lifeless from his carriage. The brigade commander glanced anxiously along his batteries, and addressed a few words to his chief of artillery. Presently the four Napoleons set forward at a gallop for the wood, while the four Parrotts wheeled to the right, deployed, and advanced across the fields, inclining toward the left of the enemy. Next, Taylor's regiment (the Eighth) halted, fronted, faced to the right, and filed off in a column of march at a double-quick until it had gained the rear of the Parrotts, when it fronted again, and pushed on in support. A quarter of a mile further on these guns went into battery behind the brow of a little knoll, and opened fire. Four companies of the English spread out to the right as skirmishers, and commenced stealing toward the ridge, from time to time measuring the distance with rifle-balls. The remainder of the regiment lay down in line between the Parrotts and the forest. Far away to the right, five companies of cavalry showed themselves, maneuvering as if they proposed to turn the left flank of the Southerners. The attack on this side was in form and in operation.

Meantime the Confederate fire had divided. Two guns pounded away at Taylor's feint, while two shelled the main column. The latter was struck repeatedly; more than twenty men dropped silent or groaning out of the hurrying files; but the survivors pushed on without faltering, and without even caring for the wounded. At last a broad belt of green branches rose between the regiments and the ridge; and the rebel gunners, unable to see their foe, dropped suddenly into silence.

Here it appeared that the road divided. The highway traversed the forest, mounted the slope beyond and dissected the enemy's position, while a branch road turned to the left and skirted the exterior of the long curve of wooded hillocks. At the fork the battery of Napoleons had halted, and there it was ordered to remain for the present in quiet. There, too, the Fourteenth filed in among the dense greenery, threw out two companies of skirmishers toward the ridge, and pushed slowly after them into the shadows.

"Get sight of the enemy at once!" was Waldron's last word to Gildersleeve. "If they move down the slope, drive them back. But don't commence your attack under half an hour."

Next he filed the Fifth into the thickets, saying to Colburn, "I want you to halt a hundred yards to the left and rear of Gildersleeve. Cover his flank if he is attacked; but otherwise lie quiet. As soon as he charges, move forward to the edge of the wood, and be ready to support him. But make no assault yourself until further orders."

The next two regiments—the Seventh and First—he placed in

*échelon*, in like manner, a quarter of a mile further along. Then he galloped forward to the cavalry, and had a last word with Stilton. "You and Gahogan must take care of yourselves. Push on four or five hundred yards, and then face to the right. Whatever Gahogan finds let him go at it. If he can't shake it, help him. You two *must* reach the top of the ridge. Only, look out for your left flank. Keep a squadron or two in reserve on that side."

"Currnel, if we don't raich the top of the hill, it'll be because it hasn't got wan," answered Gahogan. Stilton only laughed and rode forward.

Waldron now returned toward the fork of the road. On the way he sent a staff officer to the Seventh with renewed orders to attack as soon as possible after Gildersleeve. Then another staff officer was hurried forward to Taylor with directions to push his feint strongly, and drive his skirmishers as far up the slope as they could get. A third staff officer set the Parrotts in rear of Taylor to firing with all their might. By the time that the commandant had returned to Colburn's ambushed ranks, no one was with him but his enemy, Fitz Hugh.

"You don't seem to trust me with duty, Colonel," said the young man.

"I shall use you only in case of extremity, Captain," replied Waldron. "We have business to settle to-morrow."

"I ask no favors on that account. I hope you will offer me none."

"In case of need I shall spare no one," declared Waldron.

Then he took out his watch, looked at it impatiently, put it to his ear, restored it to his pocket, and fell into an attitude of deep attention. Evidently his whole mind was on this battle, and he was waiting, watching, yearning for its outburst.

"If he wins this fight," thought Fitz Hugh, "how can I do him a harm? And yet," he added, "how can I help it?"

Minutes passed. Fitz Hugh tried to think of his injury, and to steel himself against his chief. But the roar of battle on the right, and the suspense and imminence of battle on the left, absorbed the attention of even this wounded and angry spirit, as, indeed, they might have absorbed that of any being not more or less than human. A private wrong, insupportable though it might be, seemed so small amid that deadly clamor and awful expectation! Moreover, the intellect which worked so calmly and vigorously by his side, and which alone of all things near appeared able to rule the coming crisis, began to dominate him, in spite of his sense of injury. A thought crossed him to the effect that the great among men are too valuable to be punished for their evil deeds. He turned to the absorbed brigade commander, now not only his ruler but even his protector, with a feeling that he must accord him a word of peace, a proffer in some form of possible forgiveness and friendship. But the man's face was clouded and stern with responsibility and authority. He seemed at that moment too lofty to be approached with a message of pardon. Fitz Hugh gazed at him with a message of profound respect and smothered hate. He gazed, turned away, and remained silent.

Minutes more passed. Then a mounted orderly dashed up at full speed, with the words, "Colonel, Major Gahogan has fronted."

"Has he?" answered Waldron, with a smile which thanked the trooper and made him happy. "Ride on through the thicket here, my man, and tell Colonel Gildersleeve to push up his skirmishers."

With a thud of hoofs and a rustling of parting foliage the cavalryman disappeared amid the underwood. A minute or two later a thin, dropping rattle of musketry, five hundred yards or so to the front, announced that the sharpshooters of the Fourteenth were at work. Almost immediately there was an angry response, full of the threatenings and execution of death. Through the lofty leafage tore the screech of a shell, bursting with a sharp crash as it passed overhead, and scattering in humming slivers. Then came another, and another, and many more, chasing each other with hoarse hissings through the trembling air, a succession of flying serpents. The enemy doubtless believed that nearly the whole attacking force was massed in the wood around the road, and they had brought at least four guns to bear upon that point, and were working them with the utmost possible rapidity. Presently a large chestnut, not fifty yards from Fitz Hugh, was struck by a shot. The solid trunk, nearly three feet in diameter, parted asunder as if it were the brittlest of vegetable matter. The upper portion started aside with a monstrous groan, dropped in a standing posture to the earth, and then toppled slowly, sublimely prostrate, its branches crashing and all its leaves wailing. Ere long, a little further to the front, another Anak of the forest went down; and, mingled with the noise of its sylvan agony, there arose sharp cries of human suffering. Then Colonel Colburn, a broadchested and ruddy man of thirty-five, with a look of indignant anxiety in his iron-gray eyes, rode up to the brigade commander.

"This is very annoying, Colonel," he said. "I am losing my men without using them. That last tree fell into my command."

"Are they firing toward our left?" asked Waldron.

"Not a shot."

"Very good," said the chief, with a sigh of contentment. "If we can only keep them occupied in this direction! By the way, let your men lie down under the fallen tree, as far as it will go. It will protect them from others."

Colburn rode back to his regiment. Waldron looked impatiently at his watch. At that moment a fierce burst of line firing arose in front, followed and almost overborne by a long-drawn yell, the scream of charging men. Waldron put up his watch, glanced excitedly at Fitz Hugh, and smiled.

"I must forgive or forget," the latter could not help saying to himself. "All the rest of life is nothing compared with this."

"Captain," said Waldron, "ride off to the left at full speed. As soon as you hear firing at the shoulder of the ridge, return instantly and let me know."

Fitz Hugh dashed away. Three minutes carried him into perfect peace, beyond the whistling of ball or the screeching of shell. On the right was a tranquil, wide waving of foliage, and on the left a serene landscape of cultivated fields, with here and there an embowered farm-house. Only for the clamor of artillery and musketry far behind him, he could not have believed in the near presence of battle, of blood and suffering and triumphant death. But suddenly he heard to his right, assaulting and slaughtering the tranquillity of nature, a tumultuous outbreak of file-firing, mingled with savage yells. He wheeled, drove spurs into his horse and flew back to Waldron. As he re-entered the wood he met wounded men streaming through it, a few marching alertly upright, many more crouching and groaning, some clinging to their less injured comrades, but all haggard in face and ghastly.

"Are we winning?" he hastily asked of one man who held up a hand with three fingers gone and the bones projecting in sharp spikes through mangled flesh.

"All right, Sir; sailing in," was the answer.

"Is the brigade commander all right?" he inquired of another who was winding a bloody handkerchief around his arm.

"Straight ahead, Sir; hurrah for Waldron!" responded the soldier, and almost in the same instant fell lifeless with a fresh ball through his head.

"Hurrah for him!" Fitz Hugh answered frantically, plunging in through the underwood. He found Waldron with Colburn, the two conversing tranquilly in their saddles amid hissing bullets and dropping branches.

"Move your regiment forward now," the brigade commander was saying; "but halt it in the edge of the wood."

"Shan't I relieve Gildersleeve if he gets beaten?" asked the subordinate officer eagerly.

"No. The regiments on the left will help him out. I want your men and Peck's for the fight on top of the hill. Of course the rebels will try to retake it; then I shall call for you."

Fitz Hugh now approached and said, "Colonel, the Seventh has attacked in force."

"Good!" answered Waldron, with that sweet smile of his which thanked people who brought him pleasant news. "I thought I heard his fire. Gahogan will be on their right rear in ten minutes. Then we shall get the ridge. Ride back now to Major Bradley, and tell him to bring his Napoleons through the wood, and set two of them to shelling the enemy's centre. Tell him my idea is to amuse them, and keep them from changing front."

Again Fitz Hugh galloped off as before on a comfortably safe errand, safer at all events than many errands of that day. "This man is sparing my life," he said to himself. "Would to God I knew how to spare his!"

He found Bradley lunching on a gun caisson, and delivered his orders. "Something to do at last, eh?" laughed the rosy-cheeked youngster. "The smallest favors thankfully received. Won't you take a bite of rebel chicken, Captain? This rebellion must be put down. No? Well, tell the Colonel I am moving on, and John Brown's soul not far ahead."

When Fitz Hugh returned to Waldron he found him outside of the wood, at the base of the long incline which rose into the rebel position. About the slope were scattered prostrate forms, most numerous near the bottom, some crawling slowly rearward, some quiescent. Under the brow of the ridge, decimated and broken into a mere skirmish line sheltered in knots and singly, behind rocks and knolls and bushes, lay the Fourteenth Regiment, keeping up a steady, slow fire. From the edge above, smokily dim against a pure, blue heaven, answered another rattle of musketry, incessant, obstinate, and spiteful. The combatants on both sides were lying down; otherwise neither party could have lasted ten minutes. From Fitz Hugh's point of view not a

Confederate uniform could be seen. But the smoke of their rifles made a long gray line, which was disagreeably visible and permanent; and the sharp *whit! whit!* of their bullets continually passed him, and cheeped away in the leafage behind.

"Our men can't go another inch," he ventured to say to his commander. "Wouldn't it be well for me to ride up and say a cheering word?"

"Every battle consists largely in waiting," replied Waldron thoughtfully. "They have undoubtedly brought up a reserve to face Thomas. But when Gahogan strikes the flank of the reserve, we shall win."

"I wish you would take shelter," begged Fitz Hugh. "Everything depends on your life."

"My life has been both a help and a hurt to my fellow-creatures," sighed the brigade commander. "Let come what will to it."

He glanced upward with an expression of profound emotion; he was evidently fighting two battles, an outward and an inward one.

Presently he added, "I think the musketry is increasing on the left. Does it strike you so?"

He was all eagerness again, leaning forward with an air of earnest listening, his face deeply flushed and his eye brilliant. Of a sudden the combat rose and swelled into higher violence. There was a clamor far away—it seemed nearly a mile away—over the hill. Then the nearer musketry, first Thomas' on the shoulder of the ridge, next Gildersleeve's in front, caught fire and raged with new fury.

Waldron laughed outright. "Gahogan has reached them," he said to one of his staff who had just rejoined him. "We shall all be up there in five minutes. Tell Colburn to bring on his regiment slowly."

Then, turning to Fitz Hugh, he added, "Captain, we will ride forward."

They set off at a walk, now watching the smoking brow of the eminence, now picking their way among dead and wounded. Suddenly there was a shout above them and a sudden diminution of the firing; and looking upward, they saw the men of the Fourteenth running confusedly toward the summit. Without a word the brigade commander struck spurs into his horse and dashed up the long slope at a run, closely followed by his enemy and aid. What they saw when they overtook the straggling, running, panting, screaming pell-mell of the Fourteenth was victory!

The entire right wing of the Confederates, attacked on three sides at once, placed at enormous disadvantage, completely outgeneraled, had given way in confusion, was retreating, breaking, and flying. There were lines yet of dirty gray or butternut; but they were few, meagre, fluctuating, and recoiling, and there were scattered and scurrying men in hundreds. Three veteran and gallant regiments had gone all to wreck under the shock of three similar regiments far more intelligently directed. A strong position had been lost because the heroes who held it could not perform the impossible feat of forming successively two fresh fronts under a concentric fire of musketry. The inferior brain power had confessed the superiority of the stronger one.

On the victorious side there was wild, clamorous, fierce exultation. The hurrying, shouting, firing soldiers, who noted their commander riding among them swung their rifles or their tattered hats at him and screamed "Hurrah!" No one thought of the Confederate dead under foot, nor of the Union dead who dotted the slope behind. "What are you here for, Colonel?" shouted rough old Gildersleeve, one leg of his trousers dripping blood. "We can do it alone."

"It is a battle won," laughed Fitz Hugh, almost worshipping the man whom he had come to slay.

"It is a battle won, but not used," answered Waldron. "We haven't a gun yet, nor a flag. Where is the cavalry? Why isn't Stilton here? He must have got afoul of the enemy's horse, and been obliged to beat it off. Can anybody hear anything of Stilton?"

"Let him go," roared Old Grumps. "The infantry don't want any help."

"Your regiment has suffered, Colonel," answered Waldron, glancing at the scattered files of the Fourteenth. "Halt it and re-organize it, and let it fall in with the right of the First when Peck comes up. I shall replace you with the Fifth. Send your Adjutant back to Colburn and tell him to hurry along. Those fellows are making a new front over there," he added, pointing to the centre of the hill. "I want the Fifth, Seventh, and Tenth in *échelon* as quickly as possible. And I want that cavalry. Lieutenant," turning to one of his staff, "ride off to the left and find Colonel Stilton. Tell him that I need a charge in ten minutes."

Presently canon opened from that part of the ridge still held by the Confederates, the shells tearing through or over the dissolving groups of their right wing, and cracking viciously above the heads of the victorious Unionists. The explosions followed each other with stunning rapidity, and the shrill whirring of the splinters was ominous.

Men began to fall again in the ranks or to drop out of them wounded. Of all this Waldron took no further note than to ride hastily to the brow of the ridge and look for his own artillery.

"See how he attinds to iverything himself," said Major Gahogan, who had cantered up to the side of Fitz Hugh. "It's just a matther of plain business, an' he looks after it loike a business man. Did ye see us, though, Captin, whin we come in on their right flank? By George, we murthered um. There's more'n a hundred lyin' in hapes back there. As for old Stilton, I just caught sight of um behind that wood to our left, an' he's makin' for the enemy's right rair. He'll have lots o' prisoners in half an hour."

When Waldron returned to the group he was told of his cavalry's whereabouts, and responded to the information with a smile of satisfaction.

"Bradley is hurrying up," he said, "and Taylor is pushing their left smartly. They will make one more tussle to recover their line of retreat; but we shall smash them from end to end and take every gun."

He galloped now to his infantry, and gave the word "Forward!" The three regiments which composed the *échelon* were the Fifth on the right, the Seventh fifty yards to the rear and left of the Fifth, the Tenth to the rear and left of the Seventh. It was behind the Fifth, that is the foremost battalion, that the brigade commander posted himself.

"Do *you* mean to stay here, Colonel?" asked Fitz Hugh, in surprise and anxiety.

"It is a certain victory now," answered Waldron with a singular glance upward. "My life is no longer important. I prefer to do my duty to the utmost in the sight of all men."

"I shall follow you and do mine, Sir," said the Captain, much moved, he could scarcely say by what emotions, they were so many and conflicting.

"I want you other wheres. Ride to Colonel Taylor at once, and hurry him up the hill. Tell him the enemy have greatly weakened their left. Tell him to push up everything, infantry, and cavalry, and artillery, and to do it in haste."

"Colonel, this is saving my life against my will," remonstrated Fitz Hugh.

"Go!" ordered Waldron, imperiously. "Time is precious."

Fitz Hugh dashed down the slope to the right at a gallop. The brigade commander turned tranquilly, and followed the march of his *échelon*. The second and decisive crisis of the little battle was approaching, and to understand it we must glance at the ground on which it was to be fought. Two hostile lines were marching toward each other along the broad, gently rounded crest of the hill and at right angles to its general course. Between these lines, but much the nearest to the Union troops, a spacious road came up out of the forest in front, crossed the ridge, swept down the smooth decline in rear, and led to a single wooden bridge over a narrow but deep rivulet. On either hand the road was hedged in by a close board fence, four feet or so in height. It was for the possession of this highway that the approaching lines were about to shed their blood. If the Confederates failed to win it, all their artillery would be lost, and their army captured or dispersed.

The two parties came on without firing. The soldiers on both sides were veterans, cool, obedient to orders, intelligent through long service, and able to reserve all their resources for a short-range and final struggle. Moreover, the fences as yet partially hid them from each other, and could have rendered all aim for the present vague and uncertain.

"Forward, Fifth!" shouted Waldron. "Steady. Reserve your fire." Then, as the regiment came up to the fence, he added, "Halt; right dress. Steady, men."

Meantime he watched the advancing array with an eager gaze. It was a noble sight, full of moral sublimity, and worthy of all admiration. The long, lean, sunburned, weatherbeaten soldiers in ragged gray stepped forward, superbly, their ranks loose, but swift and firm, the men leaning forward in their haste, their tattered slouch hats pushed backward, their whole apsect business-like and virile. Their line was three battalions strong, fair outflanking the Fifth, and at least equal to the entire *échelon*. When within thirty or forty yards of the further fence they increased their pace to nearly a double-quick, many of them stooping low in hunter fashion, and a few firing. Then Waldron rose in his stirrups and yelled, "Battalion! ready—aim— aim low. Fire!"

There was a stunning roar of three hundred and fifty rifles, and a deadly screech of bullets. But the smoke rolled out, the haste to reload was intense, and none could mark what execution was done. Whatever the Confederates may have suffered, they bore up under the volley, and they came on. In another minute each of those fences, not more than twenty-five yards apart, was lined by the shattered fragment of a regiment, each firing as fast as possible into the face of the other. The Fifth bled fearfully: it had five of its ten company commanders shot dead in three minutes; and its loss in other officers and in men fell scarcely short of this terrible ratio. On its left the Seventh and the Tenth were up, pouring in musketry, and receiving it in a fashion hardly less sanguinary. No one present had ever seen, or ever afterward saw, such another close and deadly contest.

But the strangest thing in this whole wonderful fight was the conduct of the brigade commander. Up and down the rear of the lacerated Fifth Waldron rode thrice, spurring his plunging and wounded horse close to the yelling and fighting file-closers, and shouting in a piercing voice encouragement to his men. Stranger still, considering the character which he had borne in the army, and considering the evil deed for which he was to account on the morrow, were the words which he was distinctly and repeatedly heard to utter. "Stand steady, men—God is with us!" was the extraordinary battle-cry of this backslidden clergyman, this sinner above many.

And it was a prophecy of victory. Bradley ran up his Napoleons on the right in the nick of time, and, although only one of them could be brought to bear, it was enough; the grape raked the Confederate left, broke it, and the battle was over. In five minutes more their whole array was scattered, and the entire position open to galloping cavalry, seizing guns, standards, and prisoners.

It was in the very moment of triumph, just as the stubborn Southern line reeled back from the fence in isolated clusters, that the miraculous impunity of Waldron terminated and he received his death wound. A quarter of an hour later Fitz Hugh found a sorrowful group of officers gazing from a little distance upon their dying commander.

"Is the Colonel hit?" he asked, shocked and grieved, incredible as the emotion may seem.

"Don't go near him," called Gildersleeve, who, it will be remembered, knew or guessed his errand in camp. "The Chaplain and surgeon are there. Let him alone."

"He's going to render his account," added Gahogan. "An' whativer he's done wrong, he's made it square to-day. Let um lave it to his brigade."

Adjutant Wallis, who had been blubbering aloud, who had cursed the rebels and the luck energetically, and who had also been trying to pray inwardly, groaned out, "This is our last victory. You see if it ain't. Bet you two to one."

"Hush, man!" replied Gahogan. "We'll win our share of um. though we'll have to work harder for it. We'll have to do more ourselves, an' get less done for us in the way of tactics."

"That so, Major," whimpered a drummer, looking up from his

duty of attending to a wounded comrade. "He knowed how to put his men in the right place, and his men knowed when they was in the right place. But it's goin' to be uphill through the steepest part of hell the rest of the way."

Soldiers, some of them weeping, some of them bleeding, arrived constantly to inquire after their commander, only to be sent quietly back to their ranks or to the rear. Around lay other men—dead men, and senseless, groaning men—all for the present unnoticed. Everything, except the distant pursuit of the cavalry, waited for Waldron to die. Fitz Hugh looked on silently, with the tears of mingled emotions in his eyes, and with hopes and hatreds expiring in his heart. The surgeon supported the expiring victor's head, while Chaplain Colquhoun knelt beside him, holding his hand and praying audibly. Of a sudden the petition ceased, both bent hastily toward the wounded man, and after what seemed a long time exchanged whispers. Then the Chaplain rose, came slowly toward the now advancing group of officers, his hands outspread toward heaven in an attitude of benediction, and tears running down his haggard white face.

"I trust, dear friends," he said, in a tremulous voice, "that all is well with our brother and commander. His last words were, 'God is with us.'"

"Oh! but, man, *that* isn't well," broke out Gahogan, in a groan. "What did ye pray for his sowl for? Why didn't ye pray for his loife?"

Fitz Hugh turned his horse and rode silently away. The next day he was seen journeying rearward by the side of an ambulance, within which lay what seemed a strangely delicate boy, insensible, and, one would say, mortally ill.

# STEPHEN VINCENT BENÉT

## *The Die-Hard*

THERE WAS A TOWN called Shady, Georgia, and a time that's gone, and a boy named Jimmy Williams who was curious about things. Just a few years before the turn of the century it was, and that seems far away now. But Jimmy Williams was living in it, and it didn't seem far away to him.

It was a small town, Shady, and sleepy, though it had two trains a day and they were putting through a new spur to Vickery Junction.

They'd dedicated the War Memorial in the Square, but, on market days, you'd still see oxcarts on Main Street. And once, when Jimmy Williams was five, there'd been a light fall of snow and the whole town had dropped its business and gone out to see it. He could still remember the feel of the snow in his hands, for it was the only snow he'd ever touched or seen.

He was a bright boy—maybe a little too bright for his age. He'd think about a thing till it seemed real to him—and that's a dangerous gift. His father was the town doctor, and his father would try to show him the difference, but Doctor Williams was a right busy man. And the other Williams children were a good deal younger and his mother was busy with them. So Jimmy had more time to himself than most boys—and youth's a dreamy time.

I reckon it was that got him interested in Old Man Cappalow, in the first place. Every town has its legends and characters, and Old Man Cappalow was one of Shady's. He lived out of town, on the old Vincey place, all alone except for a light-colored Negro named Sam that he'd brought from Virginia with him; and the local Negroes wouldn't pass along that road at night. That was partly because of Sam, who was supposed to be a conjure, but mostly on account of Old Man Cappalow. He'd come in the troubled times, right after the end of the war, and ever since then he'd kept himself to himself. Except that once a month he went down to the bank and drew money that came in a letter from Virginia. But how he spent it, nobody knew. Except that he had a treasure—every boy in Shady knew that.

Now and then, a gang of them would get bold and they'd rattle sticks along the sides of his fence and yell, "Old Man Cappalow! Where's your money?" But then the light-colored Negro, Sam, would come out on the porch and look at them, and they'd run away. They didn't want to be conjured, and you couldn't be sure. But on the way home, they'd speculate and wonder about the treasure, and each time they speculated and wondered, it got bigger to them.

Some said it was the last treasure of the Confederacy, saved right up to the end to build a new "Alabama," and that Old Man Cappalow had sneaked it out of Richmond when the city fell and kept it for himself; only now he didn't dare spend it, for the mark of Cain was on every piece. And some said it came from the sea islands, where the pirates had left it, protected by h'ants and devils, and Old Man Cappalow had had to fight devils for it six days and six nights before he could take it away. And if you looked inside his shirt, you could see the long white marks where the devils had clawed him. Well, sir, some said one thing and some said another. But they all agreed it was there, and it got to be a byword among the boys of the town.

It used to bother Jimmy Williams tremendously. Because he knew his father worked hard, and yet sometimes he'd only get fifty cents a visit, and often enough he'd get nothing. And he knew his mother worked hard, and that most folks in Shady weren't rich. And yet, all the time, there was that treasure, sitting out at Old Man Cappalow's. He didn't mean to steal it exactly. I don't know just what he did intend to do about it. But the idea of it bothered him and stayed at the back of his mind. Till, finally, one summer when he was turned thirteen, he started making expeditions to the Cappalow place.

He'd go in the cool of the morning or the cool of the afternoon, and sometimes he'd be fighting Indians and Yankees on the way, because he was still a boy, and sometimes he was thinking what he'd be when he grew up, for he was starting to be a man. But he never told the other boys what he was doing—and that was the mixture of both. He'd slip from the road, out of sight of the house, and go along by the fence. Then he'd lie down in the grass and the weeds, and look at the house.

It had been quite a fine place once, but now the porch was sagging and there were mended places in the roof and paper pasted over broken windowpanes. But that didn't mean much to Jimmy Williams; he was used to houses looking like that. There was a garden patch at the side, neat and well-kept, and sometimes he'd see the Negro, Sam, there, working. But what he looked at mostly was the side porch. For Old Man Cappalow would be sitting there.

He sat there, cool and icy-looking, in his white linen suit, on his cane chair, and now and then he'd have a leather-bound book in his hand, though he didn't often read it. He didn't move much, but he sat straight, his hands on his knees and his black eyes alive. There was something about his eyes that reminded Jimmy Williams of the windows of the house. They weren't blind, indeed they were bright, but there was something living behind them that wasn't usual. You didn't expect them to be so black, with his white hair. Jimmy Williams had seen a governor once, on Memorial Day, but the governor didn't look half as fine. This man was like a man made of ice—ice in the heat of the South. You could see he was old, but you couldn't tell how old, or whether he'd ever die.

Once in a great while he'd come out and shoot at a mark. The mark was a kind of metal shield, nailed up, on a post, and it had been painted once, but the paint had worn away. He'd hold the pistol very steady, and the bullets would go "whang, whang" on the metal, very loud in the stillness. Jimmy Williams would watch him and wonder if that was the way he'd fought with his devils, and speculate about all kinds of things.

All the same, he was only a boy, and though it was fun and scary to get so near Old Man Cappalow without being seen, and he'd have a grand tale to tell the others, if he ever decided to tell it, he didn't see any devils or any treasure. And probably he'd have given the whole business up in the end, boylike, if something hadn't happened.

He was lying in the weeds by the fence, one warm afternoon, and, boylike, he fell asleep. And he was just in the middle of a dream where Old Man Cappalow was promising him a million dollars if he'd go to the devil to get it, when he was wakened by a rustle in the weeds and a voice that said, "White boy."

Jimmy Williams rolled over and froze. For there, just half a dozen steps away from him, was the light-colored Negro, Sam, in his blue jeans, the way he worked in the garden patch, but looking like the butler at the club for all that.

I reckon if Jimmy Williams had been on his feet, he'd have run. but he wasn't on his feet. And he told himself he didn't mean to run, though his heart began to pound.

"White boy," said the light-colored Negro, "Marse John see you from up at the house. He send you his obleegances and say will you step that way." He spoke in a light, sweet voice, and there wasn't a thing in his manners you could have objected to. But just for a minute, Jimmy Williams wondered if he was being conjured. And then he didn't care. Because he was going to do what no boy in Shady had ever done. He was going to walk into Old Man Cappalow's house and not be scared. He wasn't going to be scared, though his heart kept pounding.

He scrambled to his feet and followed the line of the fence till he got to the driveway, the light-colored Negro just a little behind him. And when they got near the porch, Jimmy Williams stopped and took a leaf and wiped off his shoes, though he couldn't have told you why. The Negro stood watching while he did it, perfectly at ease. Jimmy Williams could see that the Negro thought better of him for wiping off his shoes, but not much. And that made him mad, and he wanted to say, "I'm no white trash. My father's a doctor," but he knew better than to say it. He just wiped his shoes and the Negro stood and waited. Then the Negro took him around to the side porch, and there was Old Man Cappalow, sitting in his cane chair.

"White boy here, Marse John," said the Negro, in his low, sweet voice.

The old man lifted his head, and his black eyes looked at Jimmy Williams. It was a long stare and it went to Jimmy Williams' backbone.

"Sit down, boy," he said, at last, and his voice was friendly enough, but Jimmy Williams obeyed it. "You can go along, Sam," he said, and Jimmy Williams sat on the edge of a cane chair and tried to feel comfortable. He didn't do very well at it, but he tried.

"What's your name, boy?" said the old man, after a while.

"Jimmy Williams, sir," said Jimmy Williams. "I mean James Williams, Junior, sir."

"Williams," said the old man, and his black eyes glowed. "There was a Colonel Williams with the Sixty-fifth Virginia—or was it the Sixty-third? He came from Fairfax County and was quite of my opinion that we should have kept to primogeniture, in spite of Thomas Jefferson. But I doubt if you are kin."

"No, sir," said Jimmy Williams. "I mean, father was with the Ninth Georgia. And he was a private. They were aiming to make him a corporal, he says, but they never got around to it. But he fit—he fought lots of Yankees. He fit tons of 'em. And I've seen his uniform. But now he's a doctor instead."

The old man seemed to look a little queer at that. "A doctor?" he said. "Well, some very reputable gentlemen have practiced medicine. There need be no loss of standing."

"Yes, sir," said Jimmy Williams. Then he couldn't keep it back any longer: "Please, sir, were you ever clawed by the devil?" he said.

"Ha-hrrm!" said the old man, looking startled. "You're a queer boy. And suppose I told you I had been?"

"I'd believe you," said Jimmy Williams, and the old man laughed. He did it as if he wasn't used to it, but he did it.

"Clawed by the devil!" he said. "Ha-hrrm! You're a bold boy. I didn't know they grew them nowadays. I'm surprised." But he didn't look angry, as Jimmy Williams had expected him to.

"Well," said Jimmy Williams, "if you had been, I thought maybe you'd tell me about it. I'd be right interested. Or maybe let me see the claw-marks. I mean, if they're there."

"I can't show you those," said the old man, "though they're deep and wide." And he stared fiercely at Jimmy Williams. "But you weren't afraid to come here and you wiped your shoes when you came. So I'll show you something else." He rose and was tall. "Come into the house," he said.

So Jimmy Williams got up and went into the house with him. It was a big, cool, dim room they went into, and Jimmy Williams didn't see much at first. But then his eyes began to get used to the dimness.

Well, there were plenty of houses in Shady where the rooms were cool and dim and the sword hung over the mantelpiece and the old furniture was worn. It wasn't that made the difference. But stepping into this house was somehow like stepping back into the past, though Jimmy Williams couldn't have put it that way. He just knew it was full of beautiful things and grand things that didn't quite fit it, and yet all belonged together. And they knew they were grand and stately, and yet there was dust in the air and a shadow on the wall. It was peaceful enough and handsome enough, yet it didn't make Jimmy Williams feel comfortable, though he couldn't have told you why.

"Well," said the old man, moving about among shadows, "how do you like it, Mr. Williams?"

"It's—I never saw anything like it," said Jimmy Williams.

The old man seemed pleased. "Touch the things, boy," he said. "Touch the things. They don't mind being touched."

So Jimmy Williams went around the room, staring at the miniatures and the pictures, and picking up one thing or another and putting it down. He was very careful and he didn't break anything. And there were some wonderful things. There was a game of chess on a table—carved-ivory pieces—a game that people had started, but hadn't finished. He didn't touch those, though he wanted to, because he felt the people mightn't like it when they came back to finish their game. And yet, at the same time, he felt that if they ever did come back, they'd be dead, and that made him feel queerer. There were silvermounted pistols, long-barreled, on a desk by a big silver inkwell; there was a quill pen made of a heron's feather, and a silver sandbox beside it—there were all sorts of curious and interesting things. Finally Jimmy Williams stopped in front of a big, tall clock.

"I'm sorry, sir," he said, "but I don't think that's the right time."

"Oh, yes, it is," said the old man. "It's always the right time."

"Yes, sir," said Jimmy Williams, "but it isn't running."

"Of course not," said the old man. "They say you can't put the clock back, but you can. I've put it back and I mean to keep it back. The others can do as they please. I warned them—I warned them in 1850, when they accepted the Compromise. I warned them there could be no compromise. Well, they would not be warned."

"Was that bad of them, sir?" asked Jimmy Williams.

"It was misguided of them," said the old man. "Misguided of them all." He seemed to be talking more to himself than to Jimmy, but Jimmy Williams couldn't help listening. "There can be no compromise with one's class or one's breeding or one's sentiments," the old man said. "Afterwards—well, there were gentlemen I knew who went to Guatemala or elsewhere. I do not blame them for it. But mine is another course." He paused and glanced at the clock. Then he spoke in a different voice. "I beg your pardon," he said. "I fear I was growing heated. You will excuse me. I generally take some refreshment around this time in the afternoon. Perhaps you will join me, Mr. Williams?"

It didn't seem to Jimmy Williams as if the silver hand bell in the old man's hand had even stopped ringing before the Negro, Sam, came in with a tray. He had a queer kind of old-fashioned long coat on now, and a queer old-fashioned cravat, but his pants were the pants of his blue jeans. Jimmy Williams noticed that, but Old Man Cappalow didn't seem to notice.

"Yes," he said, "there are many traitors. Men I held in the greatest esteem have betrayed their class and their system. They have accepted ruin and domination in the name of advancement. But we will not speak of them now." He took the frosted silver cup from the tray and motioned to Jimmy Williams that the small fluted glass was for him. "I shall ask you to rise, Mr. Williams," he said. "We shall drink a toast." He paused for a moment, standing straight. "To the Confederate States of America and damnation to all her enemies!" he said.

Jimmy Williams drank. He'd never drunk any wine before, except blackberry cordial, and this wine seemed to him powerfully thin and sour. But he felt grown up as he drank it, and that was a fine feeling.

"Every night of my life," said the old man, "I drink that toast. And usually I drink it alone. But I am glad of your company, Mr. Williams."

"Yes, sir," said Jimmy Williams, but all the same, he felt queer. For drinking the toast, somehow, had been very solemn, almost like being in church. But in church you didn't exactly pray for other people's damnation, though the preacher might get right excited over sin.

Well, then the two of them sat down again, and Old Man Cappalow began to talk of the great plantation days and the world as it used to be. Of course, Jimmy Williams had heard plenty of talk of that sort. But this was different. For the old man talked of those days as if they were still going on, not as if they were past. And as he talked, the whole room seemed to join in, with a thousand, sighing, small voices, stately and clear, till Jimmy Williams didn't know whether he was on his head or his heels and it seemed quite natural to him to look at the fresh, crisp Richmond newspaper on the desk and see it was dated "June 14, 1859" instead of "June 14, 1897." Well, maybe it was the wine, though he'd only had a thimbleful. But when Jimmy Williams went out into the sun again, he felt changed, and excited too. For he knew about Old Man Cappalow now, and he was just about the grandest person in the world.

The Negro went a little behind him, all the way to the gate, on soft feet. When they got there, the Negro opened the gate and spoke.

"Young marster," he said, "I don't know what Marse John took in his head to ask you up to the house. But we lives private, me and Marse John. We lives very private." There was a curious pleading in his voice.

"I don't tell tales," said Jimmy Williams, and kicked at the fence.

"Yes, sir," said the Negro, and he seemed relieved. "I knew you one of the right ones. I knew that. But we'se living very private till the big folks come back. We don't want no tales spread before. And then we'se going back to Otranto, the way we should."

"I know about Otranto. He told me," said Jimmy Williams, catching his breath.

"Otranto Marse John's plantation in Verginny," said the Negro, as if he hadn't heard. "He owns the river and the valley, the streams and the hills. We got four hundred field hands at Otranto and stables for sixty horses. But we can't go back there till the big folks come back. Marse John say so, and he always speak the truth. But they's goin' to come back, a-shootin' and pirootin', they pistols at they sides. And every day I irons his Richmond paper for him and he reads about the old times. We got boxes of papers down in the cellar." He paused. "And if he say the old days come back, it bound to be so," he said. Again his voice held that curious pleading. "You remember, young marster," he said. "You remember, white boy."

"I told you I didn't tell tales," said Jimmy Williams. But after that, things were different for him. Because there's one thing about a boy that age that most grown people forget. A boy that age can keep a secret in a way that's perfectly astonishing. And he can go through queer hells and heavens you'll never hear a word about, not even if you got him or bore him.

It was that way with Jimmy Williams; it mightn't have been for another boy. It began like a game, and then it stopped being a game. For, of course, he went back to Old Man Cappalow's. And the Negro, Sam, would show him up to the house and he'd sit in the dim room with the old man and drink the toast in the wine. And it wasn't Old Man Cappalow any more; it was Col. John Leonidas Cappalow, who'd raised and equipped his own regiment and never surrendered. Only, when the time was ripe, he was going back to Otranto, and the old days would bloom again, and Jimmy Williams would be part of them.

When he shut his eyes at night, he could see Otranto and its porches, above the rolling river, great and stately; he could hear the sixty horses stamping in their stalls. He could see the pretty girls, in their wide skirts, coming down the glassy, proud staircases; he could see the fine, handsome gentlemen who ruled the earth and the richness of it without a thought of care. It was all like a storybook to Jimmy Williams—a storybook come true. And more than anything he'd ever wanted in his life, he wanted to be part of it.

The only thing was, it was hard to fit the people he really knew into the story. Now and then Colonel Cappalow would ask him gravely if he knew anyone else in Shady who was worthy of being trusted with the secret. Well, there were plenty of boys like Bob Miller and Tommy Vine, but somehow you couldn't see them in the dim room. They'd fit in, all right, when the great days came back—they'd have to—but meanwhile—well, they might just take it for a tale. And then there was Carrie, the cook. She'd have to be a slave again, of course, and though Jimmy Williams didn't imagine that she'd mind, now and then he had just a suspicion that she might. He didn't ask her about it, but he had the suspicion.

It was even hard to fit Jimmy's father in, with his little black bag and his rumpled clothes and his laugh. Jimmy couldn't quite see his father going up the front steps of Otranto—not because he wasn't a gentleman or grand enough, but because it just didn't happen to be his kind of place. And then, his father didn't really hate anybody, as far as Jimmy knew. But you had to hate people a good deal, if you wanted to follow Colonel Cappalow. You had to shoot at the mark and feel you were shooting the enemy's colors down. You had to believe that even people like General Lee had been wrong, because they hadn't held out in the mountains and fought till everybody died. Well, it was hard to believe a wrong thing of General Lee, and Jimmy Williams didn't quite manage it. He was willing to hate the Yankees and the Republicans— hate them hot and hard—but there weren't any of them in Shady. Well, come to think of it, there was Mr. Rosen, at the dry-goods store, and Mr. Ailey, at the mill. They didn't look very terrible and he was used to them, but he tried to hate them all he could. He got hold of the Rosen boy one day and rocked him home, but the Rosen boy cried, and Jimmy felt mean about it. But if he'd ever seen a real live Republican, with horns and a tail, he'd have done him a mortal injury—he felt sure he would.

And so the summer passed, and by the end of the summer Jimmy didn't feel quite sure which was real—the times now or the times Colonel Cappalow talked about. For he'd dream about Otranto at night and think of it during the day. He'd ride back there on a black horse, at Colonel Cappalow's left, and his saber would be long and shining. But if there was a change in him, there was a change in Colonel Cappalow too. He was a lot more excitable than he used to be, and when he talked to Jimmy sometimes, he'd call him by other names, and when he shot at the mark with the enemy's colors on it, his eyes would blaze. So by that, and by the news he read out of the old papers, Jimmy suddenly got to know that the time was near at hand. They had the treasure all waiting, and soon they'd be ready to rise.

And Colonel Cappalow filled out Jimmy Williams' commission as captain in the army of the New Confederate States of America and presented it to him, with a speech. Jimmy Williams felt very proud of that commission, and hid it under a loose brick in his fireplace chimney, where it would be safe.

Well, then it came to the plans, and when Jimmy Williams first heard about them, he felt a little surprised. There were maps spread all over the big desk in the dim room now, and Colonel Cappalow moved pins and showed Jimmy strategy. And that was very exciting, and like a game. But first of all, they'd have to give a signal and strike a blow. You had to do that first, and then the country would rise. Well, Jimmy Williams could see the reason in that.

They were going into Shady and capture the post office first, and then the railroad station and, after that, they'd dynamite the railroad bridge to stop the trains, and Colonel Cappalow would read a proclamation from the steps of the courthouse. The only part Jimmy Williams didn't like about it was killing the postmaster and the station agent, in case they resisted. Jimmy Williams felt pretty sure they would resist, particularly the station agent, who was a mean customer. And, somehow, killing people you knew wasn't quite like killing Yankees and Republicans. The thought of it shook something in Jimmy's mind and made it waver. But after that they'd march on Washington, and everything would be all right.

All the same, he'd sworn his oath and he was a commissioned officer in the army of the New Confederate States. So, when Colonel Cappalow gave him the pistol that morning, with the bullets and the powder, and explained how he was to keep watch at the door of the post office and shoot to kill if he had to, Jimmy said, "I shall execute the order, sir," the way he'd been taught. After that, they'd go for the station agent and he'd have a chance for a lot more shooting. And it was all going to be for noon the next day.

Somehow, Jimmy Williams couldn't quite believe it was going to be for noon the next day, even when he was loading the pistol in the woodshed of the Williams house, late that afternoon. And yet he saw, with a kind of horrible distinctness, that it was going to be. It might sound crazy to some, but not to him—Colonel Cappalow was a sure shot; he'd seen him shoot at the mark. He could see him shooting, now, and he wondered if a bullet went "whang" when it hit a man. And, just as he was fumbling with the bullets, the woodshed door opened suddenly and there was his father.

Well, naturally, Jimmy dropped the pistol and jumped. The pistol didn't explode, for he'd forgotten it needed a cap. But with that moment something seemed to break inside Jimmy Williams. For it was the first time he'd really been afraid and ashamed in front of his father, and now he was ashamed and afraid. And then it was like waking up out of an illness, for his father saw his white face and said, "What's the matter, son?" and the words began to come out of his mouth.

"Take it easy, son," said the father, but Jimmy couldn't take it easy. He told all about Otranto and Old Man Cappalow and hating the Yankees and killing the postmaster, all jumbled up and higgledy-piggledy. But Doctor Williams made sense of it. At first he smiled a little as he listened, but after a while he stopped smiling, and there was anger in his face. And when Jimmy was quite through, "Well, son," he said, "I reckon we've let you run wild. But I never thought—" He asked Jimmy a few quick questions, mostly about the dynamite, and he seemed relieved when Jimmy told him they were going to get it from the men who were blasting for the new spur track.

"And now, son," he said, "when did you say this massacre was going to start?"

"Twelve o'clock at the post office," said Jimmy. "But we weren't going to massacre. It was just the folks that resisted—"

Doctor Williams made a sound in his throat. "Well," he said, "you and I are going to take a ride in the country, Jimmy. No, we won't tell your mother, I think."

It was the last time Jimmy Williams went out to Old Man Cappalow's, and he remembered that. His father didn't say a word all the way, but once he felt in his back pocket for something he'd taken out of the drawer of his desk, and Jimmy remembered that too.

When they drove up in front of the house, his father gave the reins to Jimmy. "Stay in the buggy, Jimmy," he said. "I'll settle this."

Then he got out of the buggy, a little awkwardly, for he was a heavy man, and Jimmy heard his feet scrunch on the gravel. Jimmy knew again, as he saw him go up the steps, that he wouldn't have fitted in Otranto, and somehow he was glad.

The Negro, Sam, opened the door.

"Tell Colonel Cappalow Doctor Williams wishes to speak with him," said Jimmy's father, and Jimmy could see that his father's neck was red.

"Colonel Cappalow not receivin'," said Sam, in his light sweet voice, but Jimmy's father spoke again.

"Tell Colonel Capalow," he said. He didn't raise his voice, but there was something in it that Jimmy had never heard in that voice before. Sam looked for a moment and went inside the house.

Then Colonel Cappalow came to the door himself. There was red from the evening sun on his white suit and white hair, and he looked tall and proud. He looked first at Jimmy's father and then at Jimmy. And his voice said, quite coldly and reasonably and clearly, "Traitor! All traitors!"

"You'll oblige me by leaving the boy out of it," said Jimmy's father heavily. "This is 1897, sir, not 1860," and for a moment there was something light and heady and dangerous in the air between them. Jimmy knew what his father had in his pocket then, and he sat stiff in the buggy and prayed for time to change and things to go away.

Then Colonel Cappalow put his hand to his forehead. "I beg your pardon, sir," he said, in an altered voice. "You mentioned a date?"

"I said it was 1897," said Doctor Williams, standing square and stocky, "I said Marse Robert's dead—God bless him!—and Jefferson Davis too. And before he died, Marse Robert said we ought to be at peace. The ladies can keep up the war as long as they see fit—that's their privilege. But men ought to act like men."

He stared for a moment at the high-chinned, sculptural face.

"Why, damn your soul!" he said, and it was less an oath than an prayer. "I was with the Ninth Georgia; I went through three campaigns. We fought till the day of Appomattox and it was we-uns' fight." Something rough and from the past had slipped back into his speech—something, too, that Jimmy Williams had never heard in it before. "We didn't own niggers or plantations—the men I fought with. But when it was over, we reckoned it was over and we'd build up the land. Well, we've had a hard time to do it, but we're hoeing corn. We've got something better to do than fill up a boy with a lot of magnolious notions and aim to shoot up a postmaster because there's a Republican President. My God," he said, and again it was less an oath than a prayer, "it was bad enough getting licked when you thought you couldn't be—but when I look at you—well, hate stinks when it's kept too long in the barrel, no matter how you dress it up and talk fine about it. I'm warning you. You keep your hands off my boy. Now, that's enough."

"Traitors," said the old man vaguely, "all traitors." Then a change came over his face and he stumbled forward as if he had stumbled over a stone. The Negro and the white man both sprang to him, but it was the Negro who caught him and lowered him to the ground. Then Jimmy Williams heard his father calling for his black bag, and his limbs were able to move again.

Doctor Williams came out of the bedroom, drying his hands on a towel. His eyes fell upon Jimmy Williams, crouched in front of the chessboard.

"He's all right, son," he said. "At least—he's not all right. But he wasn't in pain."

Jimmy Williams shivered a little. "I heard him talking," he said difficultly. "I heard him calling people things."

"Yes," said his father. "Well, you mustn't think too much of that. You see, a man—" He stopped and began again. "Well, I've no doubt he was considerable of a man once. Only—well, there's a Frenchman calls it a fixed idea. You let it get a hold of you. And the way he was brought up. He got it in his head, you see—he couldn't stand it that he might have been wrong about anything. And the hate—well, it's not for a man. Not when it's like that. Now, where's that Nigra?"

Jimmy Williams shivered again; he did not want Sam back in the room. But when Sam came, he heard the Negro answer, politely.

"H'm," said Doctor Williams. "Twice before. He should have had medical attention."

Marse John don't believe in doctors," said the low, sweet voice.

"He wouldn't," said Doctor Williams briefly. "Well, I'll take the boy home now. But I'll have to come back. I'm coroner for this county. You understand about that?"

"Yes, sir," said the low, sweet voice, "I understand about that." Then the Negro looked at the doctor. "Marse Williams," he said, "I wouldn't have let him do it. He thought he was bound to. But I wouldn't have let him do it."

"Well," said the doctor. He thought, and again said, "Well." Then he said, "Are there any relatives?"

"I take him back to Otranto," said the Negro. "It belongs to another gentleman now, but Marse John got a right to lie there. That's Verginny law, he told me."

"So it is," said the doctor. "I'd forgotten that."

"He don't want no relatives," said the Negro. "He got nephews and nieces and all sorts of kin. But they went against him and he cut them right out of his mind. He don't want no relatives." He paused. "He cut everything out of his mind but the old days," he said. "He start doing it right after the war. That's why we come here. He don't want no part nor portion of the present days. And they send him money from Verginny, but he only spend it the one way—except when we buy this place." He smiled as if at a secret.

"But how?" said the doctor, staring at furniture and pictures.

"Jus' one muleload from Otranto," said the Negro, softly. "And I'd like to see anybody cross Marse John in the old days." He coughed. "They's just one thing, Marse Williams," he said, in his suave voice. "I ain't skeered of sittin' up with Marse John. I always been with him. But it's the money."

"What money?" said Doctor Williams. "Well, that will go through the courts—"

"No, sir," said the Negro patiently. "I mean Marse John's special money that he spend the other money for. He got close to a millyum dollars in that blind closet under the stairs. And nobody dare come for it, as long as he's strong and spry. But now I don't know. I don't know."

"Well," said Doctor Williams, receiving the incredible fact, "I suppose we'd better see."

It was as the Negro had said—a blind closet under the stairs, opened by an elementary sliding catch.

"There's the millyum dollars," said the Negro as the door swung back. He held the cheap glass lamp high—the wide roomy closet was piled from floor to ceiling with stacks of printed paper.

"H'm," said Doctor Williams. "Yes, I thought so. . . . Have you ever seen a million dollars, son?"

"No, sir," said Jimmy Williams.

"Well, take a look," said his father. He slipped a note from a packet and held it under the lamp.

"It says 'One Thousand Dollars,' " said Jimmy Williams. "Oh!"

"Yes," said his father gently. "And it also says "Confederate States of America'. . . . You don't need to worry, Sam. The money's perfectly safe. Nobody will come for it. Except, maybe, museums."

"Yes, Marse Williams," said Sam unquestioningly, accepting the white man's word, now he had seen and judged the white man. He shut the closet.

On his way out, the doctor paused for a moment and looked at the Negro. He might have been thinking aloud—it seemed that way to Jimmy Williams.

"And why did you do it?" he said. "Well, that's something we'll never know. And what are you going to do, once you've taken him back to Otranto?"

"I got my arrangements, thank you, sir," said the Negro.

"I haven't a doubt of it," said Jimmy Williams' father. "But I wish I knew what they were."

"I got my arrangements, gentlemen," the Negro repeated, in his low, sweet voice. Then they left him, holding the lamp, with his tall shadow behind him.

"Maybe I oughtn't to have left him," said Jimmy Williams' father, after a while, as the buggy jogged along. "He's perfectly capable of setting fire to the place and burning it up as a sort of a funeral pyre. And maybe that wouldn't be a bad thing," he added, after a pause. Then he said, "Did you notice the chessmen? I wonder who played that game. It was stopped in the middle." Then, after a while, he said, "I remember the smell of the burning woods in the Wilderness. And I remember Reconstruction. But Marse Robert was right, all the same. You can't go back to the past. And hate's the most expensive commodity in the world. It's never been anything else, and I've seen a lot of it. We've got to realize that—got too much of it, still, as a nation."

But Jimmy Williams was hardly listening. He was thinking it was good to be alone with his father in a buggy at night and good they didn't have to live in Otranto after all.

# THOMAS BAILEY ALDRICH

## *The White Feather*

IN THE THOUSAND AND ONE NIGHTS the vizier's daughter, Scheherazade, told all the stories; but in our single séance the tales were told by five men, gathered round the hearthstone of a New England roadside tavern, in which they had sought shelter from a blizzard and were snowbound for the night. The sleighing party thus circumstanced found themselves, after supper, in a comfortable sitting room with a blazing fire of hemlock logs in front of them, and for lack of more original entertainment, fell to storytelling. Though each of the five narratives which then took shape in the firelight had its own proper *raison d'être*, I shall reproduce only one of them here. The narrative so specialized owes its consequence, such as it is, to the fact that the narrator—nearly a personal stranger to me—was obliged to leave it in a manner unfinished, and that I, by singular chance, was able to supply what might be called a sequel.

This story, which I have named "The White Feather," was related by a Massachusetts veteran of the Civil War, who had left one arm behind him on the field and in the record of his regiment a reputation for great bravery. The Major, as I subsequently learned, had received a military education at a period when the army held out but scant inducements, and had turned aside from it to study law. At the beginning of hostilities in '61, he offered his services to the Federal government, and was placed upon the staff of General —————, with the rank of captain. The grade of major was afterward won in a Massachusetts regiment. Severely wounded at Spottsylvania Courthouse, and permanently disabled, he resigned his commission, and, after a long invalidism, took to the law again.

With the fullest claim to the later title of judge, he prefers to be thought of and addressed as the Major. Today, his sinewy, erect figure and clear blue eyes, gentle and resolute by turns behind their abatis of gray eyebrow, give no hint of his threescore years and ten, especially when he is speaking.

"Some men," began the Major, setting his half-emptied tumbler a little farther back from the edge of the table, "some men have a way of impressing us at sight as persons of indomitable will, or dauntless courage, or sterling integrity—in short, as embodiments of this or that latent quality, although they may have given no evidence whatever of possessing the particular attribute in question. We unhesitatingly assume how they would act under certain imaginable circumstances and conditions. A gesture, a glance of the eye, a something in the intonation of the voice, hypnotizes us, and we at once accept as real what may be only a figment of our own creating. My story, if it's what you would call a story, deals incidentally with one of these curious prepossessions."

The Major paused a moment, and beat a soft tattoo with two fingers on the arm of the chair, as if he were waiting for his thoughts to fall into line.

"At the outbreak of the war, Jefferson Kane was in his senior year at West Point. The smoke of that first gun fired in Charleston harbor had hardly blown away when he withdrew from the Academy—to cast his lot, it was surmised, with that of his native State, as many another Southerner in like circumstances was doing; for Kane belonged to an old Southland family. On the contrary, he applied for service in the army of the North—in the then nebulous Army of the Potomac. Men of his training were sorely needed at the moment, and his application was immediately granted.

"Kane was commissioned first lieutenant and provisionally assigned for duty in a camp of instruction somewhere in Massachusetts, at Readville, if I recollect. There he remained until the early part of '62, doing important work, for the recruits that passed through his hands came out finished soldiers, so far as drill was involved. Then Kane was ordered to the front, and there I fell in with him—a tall, slender young man, with gray eyes and black hair, which he wore rather long, unlike the rest of us, who went closely cropped, Zouave fashion. I ought to say here that though I saw a great deal of him at this time, I am now aware that the impression he produced upon me was somewhat vague. His taking sides with the North presumably gave mortal offense to his family; but he never talked of himself or of the life he had left behind him in the South. Without seeming to do so, he always avoided the topic.

"From the day Kane joined our regiment, which formed part of Stahl's brigade, he was looked upon as a young fellow destined to distinguish himself above the common. It was no ordinary regiment into which he had drifted. Several of the companies comprising it were made up of the flower of New England youth—college seniors, professional men, men of wealth and social rating. But Kane was singled out from the throng, and stood a shining figure.

"I cannot quite define what it was that inspired this instant acceptance of him. Perhaps it was a blending of several things—his judicial coolness, his soldierly carriage, the quiet skill and tact with which he handled men drawn from peaceful pursuits and new to the constraints of discipline; men who a brief space before were persons of consideration in their respective towns and villages; but were now become mere pawns on the great chessboard of war. At times they had to be handled gingerly, for even a pawn will turn. Kane's ready efficiency, and the modesty of it—the modesty that always hitches on to the higher gifts—naturally stimulated confidence in him. His magnetic Southern ways drew friends from right and left. Then he had the prestige of the West Pointer. But allowing for all this, it is not wholly clear what it was that made him, within the space of a month, the favorite of the entire regiment and the idol of Company A, his own company. That was the position he attained with apparently no effort on his part. Company A would have died for him, to a man. Among themselves, round the mess table, they didn't hide their opinion of Jeff Kane, or their views on the situation at large. The chief command would have been his, could the question have been put to vote. "I wouldn't like to lose the kid out of the company,' observed Sergeant Berwick one day, 'but it would be a blessed good thing if he could change shoulder straps with the colonel.' "

Here the Major suddenly remembered the unfinished bourbon and Apollinaris in his glass and interrupted himself.

"The colonel alluded to by the sergeant was a colonel of politics, and ought to have stuck to his glue factory down East. In those days we had a good many generals and colonels, and things, with political pulls. I think there were more than a few of that kidney in our recent little scrimmage with Spain. I don't believe in putting protégés and hangers-on out of employment over the heads of men who have been trained to the profession of arms. Some fine day we'll be convinced of the expediency of stowing the politicians. We ought to have a National Cold Storage Warehouse on purpose. But that's another story, as our friend Kipling remarks—too frequently."

The Major flicked off a flake of cigar ash from the looped-up empty sleeve that constantly gave him the oratorical air of having one hand thrust into his shirt bosom, and went on with his narrative.

"We were as yet on only the outer edge of that lurid battle summer which no man who lived through it, and still lives, can ever forget. Meanwhile vast preparations were making for another attempt upon Richmond. The inertia of camp life with no enemy within reach tells on the nerves after a while. It appeared to be telling on young Kane's. Like the regiment, which hitherto had done nothing but garrison duty in forts around Washington, he had seen no active service, and was ready for it. He was champing on the bit, as the boys said. His impatience impressed his comrades, in whose estimation he had long since become a hero—with all the heroism purely potential.

"For months the monotony of our existence had been enlivened only by occasional reconnaissances, with no result beyond a stray Minié ball now and then from some outlying sharpshooter. So there was widespread enthusiasm, one night, when the report came in that a large Confederate force, supposed to be Fitzhugh Lee's, was in movement somewhere on our left. In the second report, which immediately telescoped the first, this large force dwindled down to a small squad thrown forward—from an Alabama regiment, as we found out later—to establish an advanced picket line. A portion of Company A was selected to look into the move, and dislodge or capture the post. I got leave to accompany Lieutenant Kane and the thirty-five men detailed for duty.

"We started from camp at about four o'clock of an ugly April morning, with just enough light in the sky to make a ghastly outline of everything, and a wind from the foothills that pricked like needles. Insignificant and scarcely noticed details, when they chance to precede some startling event, have an odd fashion of storing themselves away in one's memory. It all seems like something that happened yesterday, that tramp through a landscape that would have done credit to a nightmare—the smell of the earth thick with strange flowering shrubs; the over-leaning branches that dashed handfuls of wet into our faces; the squirrel that barked at us from a persimmon tree, and how Private Duffy raised a laugh by singing out, 'Shut up, ye young Rebil!'' and brought down upon himself a curt reprimand from Kane; for we were then beyond our own lines, and silence was wholesome. The gaiety gradually died out of us as we advanced into the *terra incognita* of the enemy, and we became a file of phantoms stealing through the gloaming.

"Owing to a stretch of swamp and a small stream that tried to head us off in a valley, it was close upon sunrise when we reached the point aimed at. The dawn was already getting in its purple work behind the mountain ranges; very soon the daylight would betray us—and we had planned to take the picket by surprise. For five or ten minutes the plan seemed a dead failure; but presently we saw that we had them. Our approach had evidently not been discovered. The advantages were still in our favor, in spite of the daybreak having overtaken us.

"A coil of wet-wood smoke rising above the treetops, where it was blown into threads by the wind, showed us our nearness to the enemy. Their exact position was ascertained by one of our scouts who crawled through the underbrush and got within a hundred feet of the unsuspecting bivouac.

"On the flattened crest of a little knoll, shut in by dwarf cedars and with a sharp declivity on the side opposite us, an infantry officer and twelve or fifteen men were preparing to breakfast. In front of a hut built of boughs and at some distance from the spot where the rifles were stacked, a group in half undress was sniffing the morning air. A sentinel, with his gun leaning against a stump, was drinking something out of a gourd as unconcernedly as thank you. Such lack of discipline and utter disregard for possible danger were common enough in both armies in the early days of the war. 'The idea of burning green wood on a warpath!' growled the scout. 'If them tenderfoots was in the Indian country their scalps wouldn't be on their empty heads a quarter of an hour.'

"We didn't waste a moment preparing to rush the little post. A whispered order was passed along not to fire before we sprang from cover, and then the word would be given. There was a deathly stillness, except that the birds began to set up a clatter, as they always do at dawn. I remember one shrill little cuss that seemed for all the world to be trying to sound a note of alarm. We scarcely dared draw breath as we moved stealthily forward and up the incline. The attacking party, on the right, was led by Kane and comprised about two-thirds of the detachment; the remainder was to be held in reserve under me. The row of cedars hung with creeper hid us until we were within forty or fifty yards of the encampment, and then the assaulting column charged.

"What happened then—I mean the dark and fatal thing that happened—I didn't witness; but twenty pairs of eyes witnessed it, and a score of tongues afterward bore testimony. I did not see Lieutenant Kane until after the affair was over.

"Though the Confederates were taken wholly unawares, the first shot was fired by them, for just as our men came into the open the sentinel chanced to pick up his musket. A scattering volley followed from our side, and a dozen gray figures, seen for a moment scuttling here and there, seemed to melt into the smoke which had instantly blotted out nearly everything. When the air cleared a little, Kane's men were standing around in disorder on the deserted plateau. A stack of arms lay sprawling on the ground and an iron kettle of soup or coffee, suspended from a wooden tripod, was simmering over the blaze of newly lighted fagots. How in the devil, I wondered, had the picket guard managed to slip through their hands? What had gone wrong?

"It was only on the return march that I was told, in broken words, what had taken place. Lieutenant Kane had botched the business—he had shown the white feather! The incredible story took only a few words in the telling.

"Kane had led the charge with seeming dash and valor, far in advance of the boys, but when the Confederate officer, who was pluckily covering the flight of the picket, suddenly wheeled and with sweeping saber rushed toward Kane, the West Pointer broke his stride, faltered, and squarely fell back upon the line hurrying up the slope to his support. The action was so unexpected and amazing that the men came to a dead halt, as if they had been paralyzed in their tracks, and two priceless minutes were lost. When the ranks recovered from their stupor, not a gray blouse was anywhere to be seen, save that of the sentry lying dead at the foot of the oak stump.

"That was the substance of the hurried account given me by Sergeant Berwick. It explained a thing which had puzzled me not a little. When I reached the plateau myself, immediately after the occurrence of the incident, Kane's men were standing there indecisive, each staring into his comrade's face in a dazed manner. Then their eyes had turned with one accord upon Lieutenant Kane. That combined glance was as swift, precise, and relentless as a volley from a platoon. Kane stood confronting them, erect, a trifle flushed, but perfectly cool, with the point of his saber resting on the toe of one boot. He couldn't have appeared cooler on a dress parade. Something odd and dramatic in the whole situation set me wondering. The actors in the scene preserved their hesitating attitude for only twenty seconds or so, and then the living picture vanished in a flash, like a picture thrown from the kinetoscope, and was replaced by another. Kane stepped forward two paces, and as his sword cut a swift half circle in the air, the command rang out in the old resonant, bell-like tones,

'Fall in, men!' I shall never forget how he looked every inch the soldier at that moment. But they—they knew!

"There was no thought of pursuing the escaped picket with the chances of bringing up against an entire regiment, probably somewhere in the neighborhood. The men silently formed into line, a guard was detailed to protect the rear of the column, and we began our homeward march.

"That march back to Camp Blenker was a solemn business. Excepting for the fact that we were on the double-quick and the drum taps were lacking, it might have been a burial. Not a loud word was spoken in the ranks, but there was a deal of vigorous thinking. I noticed that Second Lieutenant Rollins and three or four others never took their eyes off of Jefferson Kane. If he had made a motion to get away, I rather fancy it would have gone hard with him.

"We got into camp on schedule time, and in less than fifteen minutes afterward Jefferson Kane's name was burning on every lip. Marconi's wireless telegraph was anticipated that afternoon in Camp Blenker. On a hundred intersecting currents of air the story of the lieutenant's disgrace sped from tent to tent throughout the brigade.

"At first nobody would believe it—it was some sell the boys had put up. Then the truth began to gain ground; incredulous faces grew serious; it was a grim matter. The shadow of it gathered and hung over the whole encampment. A heavy gloom settled down upon the members of Company A, for the stigma was especially theirs. There were a few who would not admit that their lieutenant had been guilty of cowardice, and loyally held out to the end. While conceding the surface facts in the case, they contended that the lieutenant had a sudden faint, or an attack of momentary delirium. Similar instances were recalled. They had happened time and again. Anybody who doubted the boy's pluck was an idiot. A braver fellow than Jeff Kane never buckled a sword belt. That vertigo idea, however, didn't cut much ice, as you youngsters of today would phrase it. There were men who did not hesitate to accuse Lieutenant Kane of intending to betray the detachment into the hands of the Confederates. Possibly he didn't start out with that purpose, it might have occurred to him on the spot; the opportunity had suggested it; if there had been more than a picket guard on hand he would have succeeded. But the dominant opinion was summed up by Corporal Simms. 'He just showed the white feather, and that's all there is about it. He didn't mean nothin', he was just scared silly.'

"In the meantime Kane had shut himself in his tent on the slant of a hill, and was not seen again, excepting for half a moment when he flung back the flap and looked down upon the parade ground with its radiating white-walled streets. What report he had made of the expedition, if he had made any report, did not transpire. Within an hour after our return to camp a significant meeting of the captains of the regiment had been convened at headquarters. Of course a court-martial was inevitable. Though Lieutenant Kane had not as yet been placed under actual arrest, he was known to be under surveillance. At noon that day, just as the bugle was sounding, Jefferson Kane shot himself.''

The Major made an abrupt gesture with his one hand, as if to brush away the shadow of the tragedy.

''That was over forty years ago,'' he continued, meditatively, ''but the problem discussed then has been discussed at odd intervals ever since. In a sort of spectral way, the dispute has outlasted nine-tenths of those who survived the war. Differences of opinion hang on like old pensioners or the rheumatism. Whenever four or five graybeards of our regiment get together, boring one another with 'Don't you remember,' the subject is pretty sure to crop up. Some regard Kane's suicide as a confession of guilt, others as corroborative proof of the mental derangement which first showed itself in his otherwise inexplicable defailance before a mere handful of the enemy—a West Pointer! So we have it, hot and heavy, over a man who nearly half a century ago ceased to be of any importance.''

''What is your own diagnosis of the case, Major?'' asked young Dr. Atwood, who always carried the shop about with him.

''Personally,'' returned the Major, ''I acquit Kane of disloyalty, and I don't believe that he was exactly a coward. He hadn't the temperament. I will confess that I'm a little mixed. Sometimes I imagine that that first glimpse of his own people somehow rattled him for an instant, and the thing was done. But whether that man was a coward or a traitor, or neither, is a question which has never definitely been settled.''

''Major,'' I said, hesitating a little, ''I think I can, in a way, settle it—or, at least, throw some light upon it.''

''You?'' The Major, with a half-amused air, looked up at me from under his shaggy, overhanging eyebrows. ''Why, you were not born when all this happened.''

''No, I was not born then. My knowledge in the matter is something very recent. While wintering in the South, two or three years ago, I became acquainted, rather intimately acquainted, with the family of Jefferson Kane—that is, with his brother and sister.''

"So?"

"It was not until after the surrender of Lee that Jefferson's death was known as a certainty to his family—the manner of it is probably not known to them at this hour. Indeed, I am positive of it. They have always supposed that he died on the field or in the hospital.''

"The records at the War Department could have enlightened them,'' said the Major.

"They did not care to inquire. He had passed out of their lives; his defection never was forgiven. The Confederate officer before whose sword Lieutenant Kane recoiled that day was his father.''

"So!"

"Captain Peyton Kane was a broken man after that meeting. He never spoke of it to a living soul, save one—his wife, and to her but once. Captain Kane was killed in the second day's battle at Gettysburg.''

My words were followed by a long silence. The room was so still that we could hear the soft pelting of the snow against the windowpanes.

Then the old Major slowly rose from his chair and took up the empty glass beside him, not noticing that it was empty until he lifted it part way to his lips. "Boys,'' he said, very gently, "only blank cartridges are fired over soldiers' graves. Here's to their memory— the father and the son!''

Other stories, mirthful and serious, were told later on; but the Major did not speak again. He sat there in the dying glow of the firelight, inattentive, seemingly remote in an atmosphere of his own, brooding, doubtless, on

"Old, unhappy, far-off things,
And battles long ago.''

# MARY E. MITCHELL

## *For the Honor of the Company*

THE OLD MAN came slowly up the little graveled path which bisected the plot, and painfully bent himself to one of the ornate iron settees facing the monument. Everything about him, the faded blue suit, the brass-buttoned coat with the tiny flag pinned on its breast, the old army hat, all bespoke the veteran. He wore, also, a look of unwonted tidiness which sat stiffly on his shambling figure. The frayed edges of his clean linen had been clipped, and his thin gray hair neatly brushed. His whole aspect told of a conscientious concession to the solemn rites of Decoration Day.

The bench already held one occupant, small and withered in person, with soft white hair showing beneath a rusty, old-fashioned bonnet. An observer would have pronounced her a contemporary of the newcomer. But it is harder to tell a woman's age than a man's; the way of her life marks her face more than do the years. In this case her deep corrugations bore witness to stress, but behind the furrows lay something which hinted that the owner had overlived the storms, and that the end was peace.

The little green park which they had chosen for their resting place was a fitting spot for old people, for it, too, spoke of battles past and victories won. The monument was one of those misguided efforts by which a grateful community is wont to show its appreciation of heroic service. It rose from the surrounding sward with a dignity of purpose and a pathos of intention quite worthy of better expression. The scrap of ground around it had been promoted from unkempt waste, trampled by children and the occasional cow, to a proud position of national use. On this particular day it fulfilled its duties with an air of special integrity, while the monument fluttered with decorous gaiety in a loyal drapery of red, white, and blue.

The Memorial Day sun was warmly manifesting its patriotism, and the veteran sank into the shaded seat with a sigh of tired content. He took off his hat and mopped his forehead. His part in the program was over, and he had earned his rest. The celebration had been a success; not a threatening cloud had distracted the attention of the audience from the orator of the day. The procession had made an impressive progress to the cemetery, and one more chaplet had been laid upon the grave of the Civil War.

When he had restored his hat to his grizzled head, the veteran straightened up and regarded his seat mate. He was a social soul, and the little cough he gave found no excuse in his bronchial regions; it was a purely voluntary and tentative approach to conversation. The look the woman vouchsafed him did not discourage his advance.

"Sightly place?" he ventured.

"Yes," replied the woman.

"That monument now; it's somethin' to be proud of, ain't it?"

"It's real handsome."

"I ain't been here since it was set up. I belong over Hilton way, but this year the whole county's celebratin' together, you know, an' I thought I'd like to see the boys' names cut up there."

The woman's gaze followed the veteran's to the tablet on the side of the shaft.

"They look good, don't they?" she said softly. "I brought Danny to see them. His gran'father was my husband, an' I give him to his country."

The veteran put his hand to his hat in an awkward gesture of sympathy.

"Well, ma'am," he said, "I often wonder why I warn't taken instead of some better man. I fought right through an' got nothin' but a flesh wound. Lord, but it was the women that suffered; they're the ones that ought to get pensions. I sense as if it was yesterday mornin' I said good-by to my sweetheart."

For a moment the only sound was that of the breeze gently stirring the fresh young maple leaves overhead. Then the woman spoke.

"It seems queer, don't it, for us to be settin' here, an' them never knowin' that we're proud of 'em, an' that the country they died for is doin' 'em honor all over its length and breadth? If they could come back and join in the procession it would make a long line, but, my, wouldn't we make of 'em! I can't help thinkin' how much more they did than just fight."

"That's so," responded the veteran. "There's somebody that says that when you pass out, what you've done don't die, but goes on livin' on after you, an' I guess he's right. If we sensed that all the time we'd be more careful, mebbe."

"It *has* lived after them," approved the woman. "I feel just that way when I'm thinkin' about my husband. He helped break the chains of the slave, but that warn't all or even most of what he done. I guess the war wouldn't have been lost if he hadn't been in it, but he gave the folks that knew him an example of what bein' a hero is, an' you can't calculate what that's meant."

The veteran nodded.

"I never thought of it just that way before, but I guess you're right, ma'am."

"You take Danny, now; he's the only gran'child I've got, an' we set store by him. Well, he's lame, an' the doctor says he won't ever be better. Seems as if it would fair kill his father when he heard that; men take such things hard, you know, and Danny was his eye's apple. But I guess he had some of the fightin' blood in him, for he marched straight up to the sorrer an' looked it square in the face. 'My father faced the music, an' I guess I won't shame him, though it's a different kind of a bullet that's struck me; one you've got to live with instead of die of,' he told Hatty Anne; she's his wife, an' she told me. As for Danny, well, when he was a little mite with a backache a good deal bigger'n he was, he wouldn't cry out because his gran'father was a soldier. We talk to him a lot about it, an' I guess it's given him courage to live."

"Perhaps the little feller'll get over it," said the veteran sympathetically. "Doctors don't know everything."

The woman shook her head.

"There ain't any perhaps about a spine as crooked as Danny's. But he's real sunny dispositioned an' he's got lots of grit. He's just set on playin' soldier, an' it would make you cry to see him drillin', brave as the best, with his poor little back, an' his pipestem legs. He's over there now, waiting for the band to come back; he's just crazy over bands, Danny is."

The veteran strained his dim eyes in the direction of the little figure sitting, crutches by his side, on the broad curb which swept about the curve of the grassplot.

"My husband didn't leave much in the way of worldly goods," continued the woman, "but I guess the legacy he did leave has gone further an' done more'n dollars would have done."

"That's so! That's so!" affirmed the veteran; and again on the two old people fell silence. It was the veteran who broke it.

"I'm thinkin', as I set here, how the real heroes, an' them that ain't heroes, are all mixed up in a war, an' both get equal credit. Here's your husband, now, a brave man who died for his country, an' then again I could tell you a story—but there! My son's wife says my tongue's longer'n the moral law. I guess when I get goin' I don't know when to stop.''

The woman's face expanded in interest as she edged nearer her seat mate.

"I'll be real pleased to hear it," she said.

The veteran painfully crossed his stiff legs, took off his hat and put it on his knee, while with one wrinkled hand he nervously fingered the brim.

"It seems good to be talkin' of old times." The veteran's voice took on an apologetic note. "Young folks don't always know what that means to the old, an' sometimes they get a bit impatient. You can't blame 'em. But this thing I've mentioned I never told but just to one, an' that was my wife; she's dead, now, this twenty year. It ain't a pretty story to tell, or for a woman to hear, but somehow I kind o' feel as if you'd understand. I've never been quite sure I done right; my wife, she thought I did, but you know wives have a way of favorin' what their men do. Perhaps you'll judge different."

The veteran's eyes were fixed on the monument. The woman adjusted herself in an attitude of attention. Now and then there floated over to them the broken sounds of a happy little tune Danny was singing to himself.

"It happened at Gettysburg," said the veteran, "on the second day of the fight. You can't know just how a soldier feels when a battle is in the air. War brings out all that's good in a man, an' right along beside it all that's bad. The thought of the cause you're fightin' for, an' the music, an' the marchin', an' the colors flyin', an' the officers cheerin' the men, all gets hold of somethin' inside of you, an' you could give up everythin' for your country. It's grand, but, Lord, it's no use talkin' about it! You can't put it into words. Queer, ain't it, how many things words can spoil?"

The veteran paused as the woman gave the expected note of assent.

"As for the other side—well, when you're really on the fightin' ground with the bullets flyin' all about you, an' you see the men you've marched with, shoulder to shoulder, shot down, an' you know it's goin' to keep on till one side has to cry quit, then the beast that's in you gets up an' roars, an' you want to kill an' kill; sometimes you turn sick an' want to run—but you don't; no, ma'am! Runnin' is the last thing you do. It takes all kinds of feelin's to make a battle. It's a queer sort of a way to settle troubles, now, ain't it? Seems kind o' heathenish, don't it?"

The woman shook her head.

"I take it we ain't to criticize what the Lord's sanctioned," she said. "The 'God of Battles' is one of his names.''

"Oh, when it comes to the Lord, I ain't takin' exceptions, of course,'' responded the veteran with a slightly embarrassed air. "I wouldn't set myself up to judgin' His doin's, but I shouldn't have thought of introducin' war as a pacifier of nations, myself, or of fightin' as a way to brotherly love. But then I ain't pious. There's a pretty side to war, but it warn't showin' itself that day at Gettysburg.

"It was a gloomy mornin', with a mist like a steam bath, dreary an' drippin'. We couldn't get a sight of anything, an' the fog got into the men's hearts an' wilted them down, like it does starch out of a collar band. There were other reasons for feelin' low. Things looked pretty bad for our side, and every one of us knew it. Our little cap'n danced about for all the world like a war horse; just a bundle of nerves. He said a little speech to us . . . *Said!* It shot right out of him. It hit, too, for the whole company straightened up as if it had got a backbone. 'You do your *damnedest!*' he yelled, 'or by George, I'll shoot every man of you!' You'll have to excuse me, ma'am; I had to repeat it just as he said it, or you wouldn't have understood how wrought up he was; an' 'by George' ain't exactly the words, either.''

The woman nodded indulgently. Her interest outran the amenities.

"Time dragged that mornin',' the veteran went on. "After a while the sun burned off the fog, an' everythin' lay as bright as if there was goin' to be a strawberry festival instead of a bloody battle. The fields was as green as grass an' crops could make 'em, an' the cattle grazed as peaceful as lambs on a May mornin'. One herd of them cows got a taste of what war was before the day was over. It was brought home to them personal, you might say.

"You could hear the cocks crowin' first in one barnyard an' then in another, an' birds was singin' everywheres. Little puffs of far-off smoke was all that told of battle in the air. The mornin' wore on, an' still we waited; there ain't anythin' more wearin' to a soldier's nerves than waitin'. I'd rather fight a dozen battles than spend another mornin' like that.

"It was well on to the middle of the afternoon when the orders was given. There was a racket then, all right! The pretty, peaceful farmyard scene was broke up, an' instead, there was a hell of roarin' guns an' screamin' shells an' blindin' smoke. Talk about slaughter! You've heard of the Devil's Den, I'm thinkin'?''

The woman shook her head.

"It got pretty famous that day. It was a heap of rocks, full of little caves, an' every one of the holes held a Johnny with a sharpshooter. Our men got picked off as fast as they came up. A little ravine ran right by the place, an' the herd of cows I mentioned got penned up right in the range of crossfirin'. Them animals would have learned a lesson that day, if there'd been anything left of them to remember it with. That's generally the way with life, most of us get our experience too late.

"There was a hill called Little Round Top, an' General Warren see right off that was the key to the situation. There didn't seem to be anybody occupyin' it, but it was such a good point, right on the face of it, that he kep' a sharp eye on it. All of a sudden there came a bright flash from near the top, a blindin' flash that made us sit up an' take notice. The truth of it was a company of Rebs were in ambush, an' the sun struck on to their bayonets an' gave them away complete. It's funny how weather steps in sometimes an' balks things. Seems as if it had more to do with winnin' the battle than the whole army did."

"The ways the Lord takes are beyond the understandin' of man," said the woman. "His arm is ever with the righteous."

The veteran meditatively rubbed his rough hand over his shabbily clad knee, as he remarked:

"Mebbe I don't give the Lord credit where it's due. It seems to me we're mighty apt to call it the Lord's arm when it's on our side. I notice them that lose ain't apt to regard it in that light. However, whoever had the managin' of it, that flash saved the day. Our company was one of those sent up to take the hill. In all the war there warn't a finer charge. I don't see how we ever done it with them guns. It was a steep slope, rocky, and rough with tangled undergrowth. We never could have got up in cold blood. We were facin' a hot fire, but our only thought was to get to the top. There warn't a man in the company but would rather have been shot than face our little cap'n after havin' played the coward. I say there warn't a man—there was one, as I found out, but then, Lord, I don't call that thing *a man*.

"Well, up we went, rattlety bang, yankin' them guns over the rocks, stumblin, scramblin, tearin' our faces an' hands an' barkin' our shins, but keepin' right on. An' that ain't mentionin' the bullets whizzin' all about us."

"It must have been awful," interrupted the woman. "It takes a lot of prayin' to keep up courage in the face of danger like that."

"*Prayin'!*" ejaculated the veteran. "If you call it prayin' to be bound to keep on if you had to kill every all-fired Reb in the

Confederate Army to do it, an' to make a road of their dead bodies, then we was all prayin'. I guess men do things different from women. It don't make any odds what we thought; we *did*, and that was more to the point.

"About halfway up the hill, one of the guns got stuck some way, an' I had to stop an' help free it, so I fell behind a bit. As I was hurryin' to ketch up I stumbled on somethin' soft and yieldin'. It was a man, an' he was wearin' the blue. It took me some seconds to sense what it meant, an' then I realized I had run down a skulker, hidin' in the rocks. I just reached out an' hauled him up by the collar of his coat, an' says I, 'What you doin' here?' He was a man from my own company, worse luck. He was tremblin', and his face was white. I shook him just as I would a rat. 'Lemme alone!' he whimpered. 'I was just gettin' my breath!' 'Gettin' your breath!' I yelled. 'You march up that hill as fast as you can go, or you'll get what mean little breath you've got knocked clean out of you, an' it won't be the Rebs that does it either!' With that I give him a kick that sent him flyin' in the right direction. You see, ma'am, I was hot at havin' our company shamed by a thing like that.

"Everybody knows what we did on that hill, an' how our charge saved the day. The names of the officers we lost on Little Round Top are writ up high in the records of the war; an' the men who fought for 'em an' fell with 'em aren't any less heroes, though they may not be in such big print. You can read all about it in any of the histories, but there's just one little story of that day that never got into a book. Nobody knows it but me, an' I saved our company from shame, an' a dead man's name from bein' a byword an' a reproach.

"That evenin', when the firin' had stopped, I was prowlin' around the hillside, lookin' after the wounded and such. I got off the main track of the charge an' blundered about a bit, tryin' to find my way back. I was gettin' a little impatient to know my course, when I saw somethin' black, lyin' on the ground behind a tree. I halted an' got my gun ready; you see, I thought it was a Johnny, skulkin' round to rob the dead. I crept up softly toward the figure. It didn't move. When I got near I see it was a dead body. It was lyin' on its face, an' its heels pointed uphill. Worse'n that, it was wearin' the blue. With my gun as a lever I turned the body over an' looked at the face. It was more because I didn't want to accuse anyone in my thoughts than because I wanted to see who the scamp was, that I turned him over.

"I bent over him to get a good look, an' there, with his white face starin' up at me, lay the man I had kicked uphill that afternoon. He had been shot as he was runnin' away again, shot in the back. That's the biggest disgrace a soldier can earn, I take it. Not an hour before, I'd been braggin' loud about our company, an' there was a man I'd messed with, an' marched with, givin' me the lie as he lay there, the marks of his guilt hittin' me in the face, as it were. It seemed to me as I stood there in the dusk an' stared down at him, as if he was a big, black blot on our fair record, an' as if he marred the glory of the company that had fought so brave. We was the heroes of the day, an' our deed would be in the mouth of every one the country over, an' that rascal spoilt it all. 'Not a man but has done his duty,' our cap'n had said. Oh, well, it ain't any use talkin', but I was mad clean through.

"As I told you, it ain't a pretty thing for you to hear, but I just took aim at that feller's forehead. It's bad enough to shoot a live man, but to send a bullet into a dead face turned up helpless to you—well—it's just plain butchery! But I done it. My shot hit him fair between the eyes. Then I left him."

The veteran paused. The woman's face was turned toward his; both were lost in the interest of the story. The music of the returning band and Danny's shrill little cheers were unheeded. The streamers on the monument fluttered softly, and the shadow of the shaft, lengthening as the sun traveled to the west, fell upon the two old people. Finally the woman spoke.

"It was an awful thing to do. It makes me think of Indians maulin' the bodies they've killed. But I don't know but you was right. It would have been worse for them that loved him to bear a coward's shame. I guess you was right."

"Thank you, ma'am," returned the veteran. "That's the way my wife took it. I'm glad if you can see it in that light. But you mustn't make a mistake about one thing. I warn't thinkin' about that skulker, or them that loved him, when I done what I did. It was for the company I put that bullet into his dead skull, an' I'd do it for the company's sake forty times over—nasty job as it was.

"Of course," he continued, "I'm glad if his family got any comfort out of the thought that he was hit in the front. I never heard anything about him more, I never even heard if he was found, till I just see his name up there, writ in endurin' stone, along with brave men and heroes. Then the whole thing come back to me as plain as day, an' I felt the goose flesh run over me, as I did when I shot into that coward's forehead. Yes, when I see that name, carved deep, Dan'el P. Ol—''

"Stop!"

The cry cut the name short, as clean as a shot. The veteran stared in amazement. His companion had wheeled about on the bench, and was facing him. Her old eyes were blazing. Her withered cheeks flushed dark red; then the color went out and left the white of ashes.

"Why, ma'am!" stammered the old man. "Why, ma'am! I guess you ain't feelin' well. I oughtn't to have told you such a story. 'Tain't fit for ladies to hear. I guess you'll have to excuse me. You see, that name brought it back so vivid."

"Oh stop!" again cried the woman. Her hands were working nervously and she was trembling from head to foot.

A slow conviction dawned upon the veteran's bewildered brain.

"Why, ma'am!" he exclaimed once more. "I'm right sorry if it was any one you happen to know. I'd never—''

"Hush! For God's sake, hush!" The woman was panting and breathless. "Don't you see the child is comin'?"

The band had vanished and Danny, who had watched the last back around the corner, was hastening to his grandmother as fast as his crutches would allow. His eager little face was shining with its past delight. The woman rose quickly, clutching the back of the settee for support. The veteran struggled to his feet.

"*The child!*" he repeated in confusion. Then a light broke on him. He took a step forward, but the woman put out her poor quavering hands as if to push him away.

There they stood, these two old people, and stared dumbly into each other's eyes. The woman read in the man's face the horror of his deed, but she saw nothing to help her misery. The veteran's face was as gray and drawn as that of his companion. His act was beyond recall. What he had smitten was more than life.

Then, as Danny came up and clutched his grandmother's gown, gazing half shyly, half admiringly at the old man in his uniform, the veteran straightened with a martial air. It was as if a call to battle had put new life into long unused muscles. He stretched out a tremulous hand and laid it on the crooked little shoulder. The rapture of being touched by a real soldier overcame the lad's bashfulness, and he smiled up at the old face above him.

"My grandfather fought in the war," he said.

The veteran's voice was grave and steady as he answered.

"Danny," he said, "always be proud of that. When things go hard you just shut your eyes an' think that you're a soldier's boy, an' that your name's his name, an' that he died in battle. Don't ever go back on that, Danny. There ain't any braver thing than a soldier, an' he died in battle."

"He was shot in the forehead. He was the bravest of the brave," said Danny.

# STEPHEN VINCENT BENÉT

## Jack Ellyat at Gettysburg

DRAW A CLUMSY FISHHOOK now on a piece of paper,
To the left of the shank, by the bend of the curving hook,
Draw a Maltese cross with the top block cut away.
The cross is the town. Nine roads star out from it
East, West, South, North.
                              And now, still more to the left
Of the lopped-off cross, on the other side of the town,
Draw a long, slightly wavy line of ridges and hills
Roughly parallel to the fishhook shank.
(The hook of the fishhook is turned away from the cross
And the wavy line.)
                        There your ground and your ridges lie.
The fishhook is Cemetery Ridge and the North
Waiting to be assaulted—the wavy line
Seminary Ridge whence the Southern assault will come.

The valley between is more than a mile in breadth.
It is some three miles from the lowest jut of the cross
To the button at the far end of the fishhook shank,
Big Round Top, with Little Round Top not far away.
Both ridges are strong and rocky, well made for war.
But the Northern one is the stronger shorter one.
Lee's army must spread out like an uncoiled snake
Lying along a fence rail, while Meade's can coil
Or halfway coil, like a snake part clung to a stone.
Meade has the more men and the easier shifts to make,
Lee the old prestige of triumph and his tried skill.
His task is—to coil his snake round the other snake
Halfway clung to the stone, and shatter it so,
Or to break some point in the shank of the fishhook line
And so cut the snake in two.
                              Meade's task is to hold.

That is the chess and the scheme of the wooden blocks
Set down on the contour map.

                    Having learned so much,
Forget it now, while the ripple lines of the map
Arise into bouldered ridges, tree-grown, bird-visited,
Where the gnats buzz, and the wren builds a hollow nest
And the rocks are gray in the sun and black in the rain,
And the jack-in-the-pulpits grow in the cool, damp hollows.
See no names of leaders painted upon the blocks
Such as "Hill," or "Hancock," or "Pender"—

                              but see instead
Three miles of living men—three long double miles
Of men and guns and horses and fires and wagons,
Teamsters, surgeons, generals, orderlies,
A hundred and sixty thousand living men
Asleep or eating or thinking of writing brief
Notes in the thought of death, shooting dice or swearing,
Groaning in hospital wagons, standing guard
While the slow stars walk through heaven in silver mail,
Hearing a stream or a joke or a horse cropping grass
Or hearing nothing, being too tired to hear.
All night till the round sun comes and the morning breaks,
Three double miles of live men.
Listen to them, their breath goes up through the night
In a great chord of life, in the sighing murmur
Of wind-stirred wheat.

                    A hundred and sixty thousand
Breathing men, at night, on two hostile ridges set down.


Jack Ellyat slept that night on the rocky ground
Of Cemetery Hill while the cold stars marched,
And if his bed was harder than Jacob's stone
Yet he could sleep on it now and be glad for sleep.


He had been through Chancellorsville and the whistling
      wood,
He had been through this last day. It is well to sleep
After such days.

                He had seen in the last four months
Many roads, much weather and death, and two men fey

Before they died with the prescience of death to come,
John Haberdeen and the corporal from Millerstown.
Such things are often remembered even in sleep.
He thought to himself, before he lay on the ground,
"We got it hot today in that red-brick town
But we'll get it hotter tomorrow."

                              And when he woke
And saw the round sun risen in the clear sky,
He could feel that thought steam up from the rocky ground
And touch each man.

                    One man looked down from the hill,
"That must be their whole damn army," he said and
    whistled,
"It'll be a picnic today, boys. Yes, it'll be
A regular basket-picnic." He whistled again.

"Shut your trap about picnics, Ace," said another man,
"You make me too damn hungry!"

                         He sighed out loud.
"We had enough of a picnic at Chancellorsville,"
He said. "I ain't felt right in my stummick since.
Can you make 'em out?"
                   "Sure," said Ace, "but they're pretty far."

"Wonder who we'll get? That bunch we got yesterday
Was a mean-shootin' bunch."

                      "Now don't you worry," said Ace.
"We'll get plenty."
                The other man sighed again.
"Did you see that darky woman selling hot pies,
Two days ago, on the road?" he said, licking his lips,
"Blackberry pies. The boys ahead got a lot
And Jake and me clubbed together for three. And then
Just as we were ready to make the sneak,
Who comes up with a roar but the provost guard?
Did we get any pies? I guess you know if we did.
I couldn't spit for an hour, I felt so mad.
Next war I'm goin' to be provost guard or bust."
A thin voice said abruptly, "They're moving—lookit—
They're moving, I tell you—lookit—"

                                          They all looked then.
A little crackling noise as of burning thornsticks
Began far away—ceased wholly—began again—
"We won't get it awhile," thought Ellyat. "They're trying
          the left.
We won't get it awhile, but we'll get it soon.
I feel funny today. I don't think I'm going to be killed
But I feel funny. That's their whole army all right.
I wonder if those other two felt like this,
John Haberdeen and the corporal from Millerstown?
What's it like to see your name on a bullet?
It must feel queer. This is going to be a big one.
The Johnnies know it. That house looks pretty down there.
*Phaëton, charioteer in your drunken car,*
*What have you got for a man that carries my name?*
We're a damn good company now, if we say it ourselves,
And the Old Man knows it—but this one's bound to be
          tough.

*Charioteer, you were driving yesterday,*
*No doubt, but I did not see you. I see you now.*
*What have you got today for a man with my name?"*

The firing began that morning at nine o'clock,
But it was three before the attacks were launched.
There were two attacks, one a drive on the Union left
To take the Round Tops, the other one on the right.
Lee had planned them to strike together and, striking so,
Cut the Union snake in three pieces.
                                          It did not happen.
On the left, Dutch Longstreet, slow, pugnacious and
          stubborn,
Hard to beat and just as hard to convince,
Has his own ideas of the battle and does not move
For hours after the hour that Lee had planned,
Though, when he does, he moves with pugnacious strength.

Facing him, in the valley before the Round Tops,
Sickles thrusts out blue troops in a weak right angle,
Some distance from the Ridge, by the Emmettsburg pike.
There is a peach orchard there, a field of ripe wheat
And other peaceable things soon not to be peaceful.

They say the bluecoats, marching through the ripe wheat,
Made a blue-and-yellow picture that men remember
Even now in their age, in their crack-voiced age.
They say the noise was incessant as the sound
Of all wolves howling, when that attack came on.
They say, when the guns all spoke, that the solid ground
Of the rocky ridges trembled like a sick child.
*We have made the sick earth tremble with other shakings*
*In our time, in our time, in our time, but it has not taught*
    *us*
*To leave the grain in the field.*

                    So the storm came on
Yelling against the angle.

                    The men who fought there
Were the tired fighters, the hammered, the weather-
    beaten, the very hard-dying men.

                    They came and died
And came again and died and stood there and died,
Till at last the angle was crumpled and broken in,
Sickles shot down, Willard, Barlow and Semmes shot
    down,
Wheatfield and orchard bloody and trampled and taken,
And Hood's tall Texans sweeping on toward the Round
    Tops
As Hood fell wounded.

                On Little Round Top's height
Stands a lonely figure, seeing that rush come on—
Greek-mouthed Warren, Meade's chief of engineers.
—Sometimes, and in battle even, a moment comes
When a man with eyes can see a dip in the scales
And, so seeing, reverse a fortune. Warren has eyes
And such a moment comes to him now. He turns
—In a clear flash seeing the crests of the Round Tops
    taken, the gray artillery there and the battle lost—
And rides off hell-for-leather to gather troops
And bring them up in the very nick of time,
While the gray rush still advances, keening its cry.
The crest is three times taken and then retaken
In fierce wolf-flurries of combat, in gasping Iliads
Too rapid to note or remember, too obscure to freeze in a
    song.

But at last, when the round sun drops, when the nun-
     footed night,
Dark-veiled walker, holding the first weak stars
Like children against her breast, spreads her pure cloths
     there,
The Union still holds the Round Tops and the two hard
     keys of war.

Night falls. The blood drips in the rocks of the Devil's Den.
The murmur begins to rise from the thirsty ground
Where the twenty thousand dead and wounded lie.
Such was Longstreet's war, and such the Union defence,
The deaths and the woundings, the victory and defeat
At the end of the fishhook shank.
                         And so Longstreet failed
Ere Ewell and Early struck the fishhook itself
At Culp's Hill and the Ridge and at Cemetery Hill,
With better fortune, though not with fortune enough
To plant hard triumph deep on the sharp-edged rocks
And break the scales of the snake.
                         When that last attack
Came, with its cry, Jack Ellyat saw it come on.

They had been waiting for hours on that hard hill,
Sometimes under fire, sometimes untroubled by shells.
A man chewed a stick of grass and hummed to himself.
Another played mumbledeypeg with a worn black knife.
Two men were talking girls till they got too mad
And the sergeant stopped them.
                         Then they waited again.

Jack Ellyat waited, hearing that other roar.
Rise and fall, be distant and then approach.
Now and then he turned on his side and looked at the sky
As if to build a house of peace from that blue,
But could find no house of peace there.
                         Only the roar,
The slow sun sinking, the fey touch at his mind . . .

He was lying behind a tree and a chunk of rock
On thick, coarse grass. Farther down the slope of the hill
There were houses, a rough stone wall, and blue loungy
          men.
Behind them lay the batteries on the crest.
He wondered if there were people still in the houses.
One house had a long, slant roof. He followed the slant
Of the roof with his finger, idly, pleased with the line.

The shelling burst out from the Southern guns again.
Their own batteries answered behind them. He looked at
          his house
While the shells came down. I'd like to live in that house.
Now the shelling lessened.
                          The man with the old black knife
Shut up the knife and began to baby his rifle.
They're coming, Jack thought, This is it.
                                There was an abrupt
Slight stiffening in the bodies of other men,
A few chopped ends of words scattered back and forth,
Eyes looking, hands busy in swift, well-accustomed
          gestures.
This is it. He felt his own hands moving like theirs
Though he was not telling them to. This is it. He felt
The old familiar tightness around his chest.
The man with the grass chewed his stalk a little too hard
And then suddenly spat it out.
                    Jack Ellyat saw
Through the falling night, that slight, gray fringe that was
          war
Coming against them, not as it came in pictures
With a ruler-edge, but a crinkled and smudgy line
Like a child's vague scrawl in soft crayon, but moving on,
But with its little red handkerchiefs of flags
Sagging up and down, here and there.
                            It was still quite far,
It was still like a toy attack—it was swallowed now
By a wood and came out larger with larger flags.
Their own guns on the crest were trying to break it up

—Smoking sand thrown into an ant-legged line—
But it still kept on—one fringe and another fringe
And another and—

              He lost them all for a moment
In a dip of ground.

                    That is it, he thought with a parched
Mind, It's a big one. They must be yelling all right
Though you can't hear them. They're going to do it this
    time,
Do it or bust—you can tell from the way they come—
I hope to Christ that the batteries do their job
When they get out of that dip.

                        Hell, they've lost 'em now,
And they're still coming.
He heard a thin gnat-shrieking
"Hold your fire till they're close enough, men!"

                          The new lieutenant.
The new lieutenant looked thin. "Aw, go home," he
    muttered,
"We're no militia—What do you think we are?"


Then suddenly, down by his house, the low stone wall
Flashed and was instantly huge with a wall of smoke.
He was yelling now. He saw a red battle flag
Push through smoke like a prow and be blotted out
By smoke and flash.

              His heart knocked hard in his chest.
"Do it or bust," he mumbled, holding his fire
While the rags of smoke blew off.

                    He heard a thick chunk
Beside him, turned his head for a flicker of time.
The man who had chewed on the grass was injuredly
    trying
To rise on his knees, his face annoyed by a smile.
Then the blood poured over the smile and he crumpled up.
Ellyat stretched out a hand to touch him and felt the hand
Rasped by a file.

              He jerked back the hand and sucked it.
"Bastards," he said in a minor and even voice.

All this had occurred, it seemed, in no time at all,
But when he turned back, the smoky slope of the hill
Was gray—and a staggering red advancing flag
And those same shouting strangers he knew so well,
No longer ants—but there—and stumblingly running—
And that high, shrill, hated keen piercing all the flat
    thunder.

His lips went back. He felt something swell in his chest
Like a huge, indocile bubble.
                         "By God," he said,
Loading and firing. "You're not going to get this hill,
You're not going to get this hill. By God, but you're not!"

He saw one gray man spin like a crazy dancer
And another fall at his heels—but the hill kept growing
    them.
Something made him look toward his left.
                          A yellow-fanged face
Was aiming a pistol over a chunk of rock.
He fired and the face went down like a broken pipe
While something hit him sharply and took his breath.
"Get back, you suckers," he croaked. "Get back there, you
    suckers!"
He wouldn't have time to load now—they were too near.
He was up and screaming. He swung his gun like a club
Through a twilight full of bright stabbings, and felt it
    crash
On a thing that broke. He had no breath any more.
He had no thoughts. Then the blunt fist hit him again.

He was down in the grass and the black sheep of night ran
    over him . . .

# JOSEPH ALTSHELER

## *At the Twelfth Hour*

THERE WAS NO PAUSE in the clamor outside, which rose sometimes to a higher key, and then sank back to its level, like the rush of a storm. Every log and plank in the little house would tremble as if it were so much human flesh and blood, when a crash louder than the rest betokened the sudden discharge of all the guns in some battery. The loose windows rattled in their wooden frames alike before the roar of the artillery and the shriller note of the rifles, which clattered and buzzed without ceasing, and seemed to boast a sting sharper and more deadly than that of their comrades the big guns. Whiffs of smoke, like the scud blown about by the winds at sea, would pass before the windows and float off into the forest. Sometimes a yellow light, that wavered like heat-lightning, would shine through the glass and quiver for a moment or two across the wooden floor. In the east there was a haze, a mottled blur of red and yellow and blue, and whether the crash of the artillery rose or sank, whether the clatter of the rifles was louder or weaker, there came always the unbroken din of two hundred thousand men foot to foot in battle,—a shuffling, moaning noise, a shriek, then a roar.

The widow moved the table and its dim candle nearer the window, not that she might see better outside, but there she could have a stronger light on her sewing, which was important and must be finished. The blaze of the battle flared in at the window more than once, and flickered across her face, revealing the strong, harsh features, and the hundreds of fine wrinkles that crossed one another in countless mazes, and clustered under her eyes and around the corners of her mouth. She was not a handsome woman, nor had ever been, even on her bridal morning, but she was still tall and muscular, her figure clothed in a poor print dress,—one who had endured much, and could endure more. As she bent over her humble sewing, the dim light of the candle was reflected in hopeless eyes.

The battle rolled a little nearer from the east, and the flashes of its light grew more frequent. The trembling of the house never ceased. On the hearth-stone some tiny half-dead embers danced about under the incessant rocking, like popping grains of corn, and the windows in their frames droned out their steady rattle.

But the widow paid no heed, going on with her sewing. The battle was nothing to her. She did not care who won; she would not go out of her house to see. If men were such barbarians and brutes as to murder one another for they knew not what, then let them. The more human flesh and blood the war devoured, the greater its appetite grew; for upon such food it fattened and prospered. Her three sons had gone to the man-eater, gulped down, one, two, three, in the order of their age: first the eldest, then the second, and then her youngest, her best beloved. She had thought that he, at least, who would not be a man for years, might be left to her; but the news had come from Shiloh, in a meagre letter written by a comrade, that he had fallen there, mortally wounded, and the enemy who kept the field had buried him, perhaps.

She had the letter yet, but she never looked at it. There was no need, when she knew every line, every word, every letter, and just how they looked and stood on the page. The two older sons, like so many of the men of those wild hill regions, had been worthless,—drinkers of whiskey, tellers of lies, squalid loafers blinking at the sun; but the third, the boy, had been different, and she had expected him to become a man such as a woman could admire, a man upon whom a woman could depend,—that is, one stronger than herself, and as good. He had been both son and daughter to her, for in that way a mother looks upon the youngest or only son when he has no sister; but fair hair and blue eyes and a girl face had not prevented him from following the others, and now she knew not even where his bones lay, save that the mould of a wide and desolate battle-field inclosed them, and, in some palce, hid them.

This woman did not cry; no tears came from her eyes when the news of the boy's death was brought to her, and none came now, when she still saw him, fair-haired and white-faced, lying out there under the sky. She had merely become harsher and harder, and, never much given to speech, she spoke less than before.

The battle rolled yet a little nearer from the east, and the complaining windows rattled more loudly. Above the thud of the cannon and the unbroken crash of the rifles she could hear now the shouting of many men, a guttural tumult which brought to mind the roar and shriek of wild animals in combat. The coming of the twilight did not seem to diminish their ferocity, and, repeating her old formula, she said, "Let them fight on through the night, if it please them."

The earth rumbled and rocked beneath a mighty discharge of artillery, the old house shook, and the heap of coals rolled down and scattered over the hearth. She walked from the window and put them carefully in place with an iron shovel. Thrown back together they sent up little spears of flame, which cast a flickering light over the desolate room,—the bare wooden floor, the rough log walls spotted with a few old newspaper prints, the two pine tables, the cane-bottomed chairs, the home-made wooden stool, the iron kettle in one corner and the tin pans beside it, the low bed covered with a brown counterpane in another corner,—a room that suited the mind and the temper of the woman who owned it and lived in it.

The battle crept still closer; the departed sun, the twilight deepening into night, had no effect on the fury of the combatants. Gun answered gun, and the rifles hurled opposing showers of lead. The difference in the two notes of the battle, the sullen, bass thunder of the cannon with its curious trembling cadence, and the sharper, shriller crash of the small arms, like the wrath of little people, became clearer, more distinct. Over both, in irregular waves, swelled the shouting; the wild and piercing "rebel yell" and the hoarse Yankee cheer contending and mingling and rolling back and forth in a manner that would tell nothing to a listener save that men were in mortal combat.

She heard a shrieking noise, like the scream of a man, but far louder; a long trail of light appeared in the sky, curving and arching like a rainbow until it touched the earth, when it disappeared in one grand explosion, throwing red, blue, green, and yellow lights into the air, as if a little volcano had burst. She almost fancied she could hear pieces of the shell whizzing through the air, though it was only fancy; but she knew that the earth where it struck had been torn up, and the dead were scattered about like its own pieces. Up went another, and another, and the air was filled with them, shining and shrieking as if in delight because they gave the finish and crowning touch to the battle. She watched them with a certain pleasure as they curved so beautifully, and gave herself praise when she timed to the second the moment of striking the earth. Soon the air was filled with a shower of the curving lights, and then they ceased for a while.

Still the dim battle raged in the darkness. But presently a light flared up again and did not disappear. It burned with a steady red and blue flame that indicated something more than the flashing of cannon and rifles, and, looking through a window-pane, the widow saw the cause. The forest was on fire, the exploding gunpowder having served as a torch; the blaze ran high above the trees, adding a new rush and roar to the thunder and sweep of the battle. But she was calm; for the forest did not come near enough to place her house in danger of the fire, and there was no reason why she need disturb herself. She blew out the candle, carefully put away in the cupboard the piece remaining,— economy being both a virtue and a necessity with her,—and returned to her seat by the window, now lighted only by the blaze of the battle and the burning trees. The light from the flaming forest grew stronger, and flared through the window all the way across the room. When the flash of the guns joined it, the glare was so vivid that the widow was compelled to shield her eyes with her hand; she would have closed the shutter of the window and relighted the candle, had there been a shutter to close. Clouds of smoke—some light, white, and innocent-looking, others heavy and black—floated past the window. Such clouds were needed, she thought, to veil the horrors of the slaughter-yard outside. She looked at the little tin clock on the mantel, ticking placidly away, and saw that it was a quarter to ten. She would have gone to bed, but one could not sleep with all that noise outside and so near. She thought it wise to take her old seat by the window and watch the flames from the forest, because sparks driven by the wind might fall on her house and set it on fire. There were two buckets filled with water in the little lean-to that served as a kitchen, and she set them in a place that would be handy in case the dangerous sparks came.

But she did not think the water would be needed, since the wind, though light, was blowing the fire from her. This was indicated clearly by the streams of flame, red in the centre, blue and white at the edges, which leaned eastward. The fire had gathered full volume now, and gave her a gorgeous spectacle, the flames leaping far above the trees, where they united into cones and pyramids, flashing with many colors and sending forth millions of sparks, which curved up, and then fell like showers of fireflies. Under this flaming cloud, the cannon spouted and the rifles flashed with as much steadiness and vigor as ever. It seemed to be a vast panoramic effect in fire planned for her alone, after the fahion of the Roman emperors, of whom she had never heard.

By the light of the fire and the battle she saw, for the first time, some figures struggling in the chaos of flame and smoke. Human beings she knew them to be, though they looked but little like it, being mere writhing black lines in a whirl of red fire and blue smoke. It was a living picture, to her, of the infernal regions, in which she was a firm believer; those ghastly shapes straining and fighting among the eternal flames. She felt a little sympathy for the many—mostly boys like her own boy who had fallen at Shiloh—who were about to pass through the flames of this world into the flames of the next; for she had been taught that only one out of a hundred could be saved, and she never doubted it. If she felt doubt at all, it was about the deserts of the hundredth man.

The thunder of the cannon sank presently to a mutter and a growl, the rifles ceased entirely, and the sudden drop in the noise of the battle caused the fire's roar to be heard above it like a tempest. She could still see the black figures, so many jumping-jacks, through the veil of flame and smoke; but they were not now a confused and struggling heap, without plan or order; they had drawn apart in two lines, and for two or three minutes remained motionless, save for a few figures which strutted up and down and waved what looked through the fiery mist like little sticks, but which she knew to be long swords. She knew enough more to guess that one line was about to charge the other, or more likely, both would charge at the same time, and the sinking of the battle was but a pause to gather strength for a supreme effort.

She was interested, and her interest increased when she saw the opposing lines swing forward a little, as if making ready for the shock. The sudden ebb of the firing had made all other noises curiously distinct. The ticking of the little clock on the mantel became a steady drumbeat. She even fancied that she could hear the commands given to the two lines of puny black figures, but she knew it was only fancy.

This silence, so heavy that it oppressed her, after all she had heard, was broken by the discharge of hidden batteries, so many great guns at once that the widow sprang up from her chair; she thought at first that the house was falling about her, and she clapped her hands to her ears to shut out the penetrating crash, which was succeeded by the fierce, unbroken shrieking of the small arms. The cloud of smoke at once thickened and darkened, but she could see through it the two lines, now dim gray images of men, rushing upon each other. She watched with eager, intent eyes. The whirling smoke would hide parts of one line for a moment, leaving it a series of disconnected fragments; then would drift away, revealing the unbroken ranks again. She could hear the ticking of the clock no longer, for the pounding of the guns was so terrific now that continuous thunder roared in her ears, inside her head, and seemed not to come from anything without. A window-pane broke under the impact of so much sound, and the fragments of glass rattled on the floor, but she did not take her eyes from the battle.

Over the heads of the rushing lines the smoke formed in a cloud so thick, so black, so threatening, and so low that it inclosed them, like a roof. The old likeness came back to the widow. It is the roof of hell, she said to herself; these walls and pillars of flame are its sides, and the men who fight in there, hemmed in by fire, are the damned, condemned to fight so forever.

On they rushed, some of the dim gray figures seeming to dance above the earth in the flames, like the imps they were, and the two lines met midway. She thought she could hear the smash of wave on wave above the red roar of the guns, and figures shot into the air as if hurled up by the meeting of tremendous and equal forces. A long cry, a yell, a shriek, and a wail, which could come only from human throats, thousands of them together, swelled again above everything else,—above the roar of the fire, above the crash of the rifles, above the thunder of the cannon.

In spite of her stoicism the watcher quivered a little and turned her eyes away from the window, but she turned them back again. The cry sank to a quaver, then rose again to a scream; and thus it sank and rose, as the battle surged from side to side in the flaming pit. She thought she could hear the clash of arms, bayonet on bayonet, sword on sword, and all the sounds of war became confused and mingled, like the two lines of men which had rushed so fiercely together. There were no longer two lines,—not even one line,—but a medley; struggling heaps, red whirlpools which threw out their dead and whirled on, grinding up the living like grain in a hopper. The soldiers fought in the very centre of the pit, and the shifting red curtain of flame between gave them strange shapes, enlarging some, belittling others, and then blending all into a blurred mass, a huddle of men without form or number.

Fantastic and horrible, the scene appealed strongly to the widow's hard religious sense. She could no longer doubt that the red chaos upon which she was looking was a picture of life from the regions of eternal torture, reserved for the damned, reproduced on earth for the beneift of men. It was, then, with a feeling of increased interest that she watched the battle as it blazed and shrieked to and fro. The thunder of the cannon and the crash of the rifles were still as steady as the rush of a tempest, and the wild shouting of the men now rose above the din, then was crushed out by it, only to be heard again, fiercer and shriller than before.

The great clouds which lowered over the pit grew blacker and bigger, and rolled away in sombre waves on every side. Their vanguard reached even to her house and passed over it. The loathsome smell of burnt gunpowder and raw and roasted human flesh came in at the broken window. She stuffed a quilt into the open space, until neither smoke nor smell could enter; but some of the droppings of the black cloud, little balls and curls of smoke, came down the chimney and floated about the room, to remind the woman that the whirlwind of the battle whirled widely enough to draw her in, too. Her throat felt hot and scaly, and she took a gourd of water from one of the buckets and drank it. It was cool to the throat, and as smooth as oil. How some of those men lying out there, helpless on the ground, longed for water, cold water! How her own boy, doubtless, had longed for it, as he lay on the field of Shiloh waiting for the death that came! A feeling of pity, a strong feeling, swelled up in her soul. She walked again across the room and looked at the little tin clock on the mantel. Ten forty-five! It was time for the battle to close; it had been time long ago.

Then she went back as usual to the window, and she noticed at once that the roar and blaze of the battle were sinking. The thunder of the guns was not continuous, and the intervals increased in number and became longer. The fire of the rifles was broken into crackling showers, and spots of gray or white, where the air was breaking through, appeared in the wall of flame. The black roof of smoke lifted a little, and seemed to be losing length and breadth as the wind swept off cloudy patches and carried them away. The fire in the forest was dying, and she ceased to hear the rush of the flames from tree to tree. Once the human shout or shriek—she could not tell which—came to her ear, but she heard it no more just then. The men, more distinct now as the veil of flame thinned away or rose in vapor, still struggled, but with less ferocity. The groups were breaking up, and the two lines shrank apart, each seeming to abandon the ground for which it had fought.

It was nearly eleven o'clock, and the moon, able for the first time to send its beams through the battle-smoke, was beginning to cast a silvery radiance over the field. The flames sank fast. The fire in the forest burnt out. The great cloud of smoke broke up into many little clouds which drifted away westward before the wind. The showers of sparks ceased, and the bits of charred wood no longer fell. A fine cloud of ashes blown through the air began to form a film over the window-panes.

The battle died like the eruption of a volcano, which shoots up with all its strength, and then sinks from exhaustion. The human figures melted away, and the last was gone, though the widow knew that many must be lying in the ravines and on the hillsides beyond her view. There were four cannon-shots at irregular intervals, the fourth a long time after the third, a volley or two from the rifles, a pop-pop or two, and the firing was over. Some feeble flames from grass or bush still spurted up, but they fought in a lost cause, for the silver radiance of the moon grew, and they paled and sank back before it.

The ticking of the clock made the cessation of noise outside more noticeable. She opened the window, and the air that came in was strong with a fleshy smell. But so much smoke had come down the chimney, and the room was so close, that she kept the window open and let the air seek every corner. Outside, the unburnt trees were swaying in the west wind, but there was no other noise. The battlefield, unlighted by the fire of cannon and rifles, had become invisible; but she knew that many men were lying there, and the wind sobbing through the burnt and unburnt forest was their dead march.

Fine ashes, borne by the wind from the burnt forest, still fell; some came in at the open window, and fell in a faint whitish powder on the floor. The widow took her wisp broom and brushed the ashes carefully into the fire; but she did not close the window, for the fresh air which blew in had a tonic strength, though there was still about it some of that strange odor, the breath of slaughter.

She resolved to watch the field a little longer, and then she would go to bed; she had wasted enough time watching the struggles of lost souls. The light of the moon was beginning to wane, and the trees and hills were growing more shadowy; their silver gray was changing to black, the sombre hue borrowed from the skies above them. Flecks of fire like smouldering coals gleamed through the darkness, showing where a tree-trunk or a bush still burned in the wake of the battle or the fire. The wind rose again, and these tiny patches of flame blazed before it more brightly for a time, and then went out. But the wind moaned more loudly as it blew among the burned tree-trunks and the dead branches. Some trees, eaten through by the fire, fell, and the night, so still otherwise, echoed with the sound.

All the lights from the fire went out, but others took their place. She could see them far apart, but twinkling like little stars fallen to earth;

probably the lanterns, she thought, of surgeons and soldiers come to look for those whose wounds were not mortal. Why not let them lie there and pay the price of their own folly? They had gone into the battle knowing its risks, and they should not seek to shun them. She would go to bed, and she put up her hand to pull down the window. She heard a prolonged cry, a wail and a sob; distant, perhaps, and feeble, but telling of pain and fear.

It came direct from the battlefield. She would have dismissed the sound, as she had dismissed all other signs of the battle, but it came again and was more penetrating. She thought that she had no fancy, no imagination, and that the battle had passed leaving her mind untouched, but the cry lingered. It rose for the third time, louder, fuller, more piercing than before, and the air ached with it. She was sure now that it was many voices in one, all groaning in their agony, and their groans uniting in a single lament, which rose above that of the wind and filled all the air with its wailing. She tried again to crush down her thoughts, and to hide the scenes that she saw with her mind, and not with her eyes; but her will refused to obey her, and yielded readily to imagination, which, held back so long, took possession of its kingdom with despotic power. Her face and hands became cold and wet at the sights and scenes that her fancy made her hear and see. It was easy to turn this field into the field of Shiloh, and her ready imagination, laughing at her will, did it for her. In that other battle her boy was lying at the foot of a hillock, his white face growing whiter, turned up to the stars; the dead lay around him, and there was no sound but his groans.

She closed the window with a sudden and violent gesture, as if she would shut out the sight, and would shut out too those cries which had stirred her imagination into such life. She walked angrily to the hearth and banked the coals for the last time, firmly resolved to go to bed and sleep. The clock ticked away loudly and clearly, as if to show its triumph over the battle, which was now gone, while it ticked on.

But the cry of anguish from the field reached her there; fainter, more muffled, but not to be mistaken. Whether it came through the glass or how else, she knew not, but she heard it,—a cry to her, a cry that would reach her even in bed and would not let her sleep. It was as if her own son had been crying to her for help, for water. She threw up the window again, and looked toward the battlefield. The air was filled with the cries of the wounded like the chorus of the lost, but of the field itself she could see nothing. The night had darkened fast, and the ground on which the men had fought was clothed in a ghostly vapor. The burnt trees were but a faint tracery of black, and the wind had ceased, leaving the night, hot, close, and breathless. The fine ashes from the fire no longer fell, and the air was free from them, but it was thick and heavy, and the repellent smell of human flesh lingered. It was a terrible night for the wounded. They would lie on the ground in the close heat and gasp for air, which would be like fire to their lungs.

The little clock struck midnight with a loud, emphatic tang, each stroke echoing and reminding her that it was time to go.

The two buckets filled with water, which she had brought to save her house from fire, still stood by the window. She put the drinking-gourd into one of them, lifted both, and passed out of the house. She was a strong woman, and she did not stagger beneath the weight of the water. This, she knew, was what they would want most; for in all that she had ever heard of battlefields the cry for water was loudest. Yet all her pity in that moment was for one,—not one of those who lay there, but her own boy on that other battlefield. She saw only him, only his face; like a girl's it had always looked to her, with its youthful flush and the fair hair around it. It was he, not the others, who was taking her out on the field, and she walked on with straight, strong steps, because he led her.

The mists and vapors seemed to drift away as she approached the battlefield, and the trees, holding out their burnt arms, rose distinct and clear from the darkness. The cries of the wounded increased, and were no longer a steady volume like the moaning of the wind; but she could distinguish in the tumult articulate sounds, even words, and they were always the same,—the cry for water rising above all others, just as she had been told. She reached the ground over which the fire had swept. Some clusters of sparks, invisible from the window, lingered yet in the clefts of roots and rocks, and glimmered like marsh lights.

The strange repellent odor that reminded her of the drippings of a slaughter-house attacked her with renewed strength. She turned a little sick, but she conquered her faintness and went on. Wisps of smoke were still drifting about, and she stumbled on something and nearly fell; but she saved the precious water, and saw that her foot had struck against a cannon-ball, which lay there, half buried in the earth, spent, after its mission. To her eyes the earth upon it was the color of blood, and giving it a look of repulsion she passed on. She saw two or three rifles upon the ground, abandoned by their owners; and here was a broken sword, and there a knapsack, still full, which some soldier had thrown away. Under the half-burned trunk of a tree was something dark and shapeless, and charred like the tree; but she knew what it was, and after the first glance kept her head turned away. She passed more like it, but all were motionless, for the fire had spared nothing over which it had gone.

The smell of roasted flesh was strong here, but the silence appalled her. All the cries came from the further part of the field, and around her no voice was raised. The figures, half hidden in the dark, did not stir. The trees waved their burnt arms, and gave forth a dry, parched sound when a whiff of wind struck them, like the rustle of a field of dead broom sedge.

She crossed the strip over which the fire had swept and burned out everything living, and entered the red battlefield beyond. It was lighter here, for there were fewer trees and the moon had cleared somewhat. She saw many figures of men: some motioness as they had been in the burnt woods; others twisting and distorting themselves like spiders on a pin; and still others half sitting or leaning against a stone or a stump, and trying to bind up their own wounds. The cries were a medley, chiefly groans and shrieks, but sometimes laughter, and twice a song. She had never seen ground so torn, for here the battle had trod to and fro in all its strength and ferocity. Three or four trees, cut down by cannon-balls, had fallen together, their boughs interlaced, and a hole in the earth showed where a huge shell had burst. Some sharp pieces of the exploding iron had been driven into a neighborning tree, and a little further on a patch of bushes had been mowed down like grass in a hayfield.

A man, shot in the legs, who had propped himself against a rock, saw the water that she carrried, and cried to her to come to him with it. He damned her from a full vocabulary because she did not make enough haste, and when she came tried to snatch the gourd from her hand. But with her stronger hand she pushed his away, and made him drink while she held the gourd. He was young, but it did not seem strange to her to hear such volleys of profanity from one who had the splendor of youth, for her older sons had been of his kind. She left him cursing her because she did not give him more water, and went on; for the face of her boy was still leading her, and the one she left was not like his.

The field extended further than she could see, but all around her was the lament of after-the-battle. Lights trembled or glimmered over the field; the surgeons and soldiers holding them were seeking the wounded, and she saw that some wore the blue and others the gray. Such a shambles as this was the only place in which they could meet like brethren, and here they passed each other without comment; nor did they notice her, save one, an old man with the shining tools of a surgeon in his hand, who gave her an approving nod.

She heard a moan which seemed to come from a little clump of bushes spared by the cannon-balls. A man,—a boy, rather,—with the animal instinct, had crawled in there that he might die unseen. He was in delirium with fever, and cried for his mother. The widow's heart was touched more deeply than before, for it was to such as he that her boy's face was leading her. She took him from out the bushes, stanched his wounds, and gave him of the cold water to drink. The fever abated, and his delirious talk sank to a mere mutter, while she stood and watched until one of the wagons gathering up the wounded came by; then she helped put him in, and passed on with the water to the others. She was eager to help; it was true pity, not a mere sense of duty, for she was now among the boys, the slender lads of eighteen and seventeen and sixteen; and very many of them there were, too, and she knew that her own boy had called her to help these. They lay thick upon the ground,—children they seemed to her; yet this war had such in scores of thousands, who went from the country schoolhouses to the battlefield.

Most of them were dead; sometimes they lay in long rows, as if they had been made ready for the grave; sometimes they lay in a heap, their bodies crossing; and here and there lay one who had found death alone. But amid the dead were a few living, and the widow's hands grew tenderer and more gentle as she raised their heads and let them drink. The water in her buckets was three fourths gone, and she was very careful of it now, for a little might mean a life.

The vapors still hung over the field, and the thick, clammy air was often death to the wounded who could not breathe it. The widow wished more than once for a little of the water, herself, but there were others who needed it far more, and she went on with her work among the boys. She thought often, as she looked at the white young faces around her, of that slaughter of the innocents of which the Bible told, and it seemed to her that this was as wicked and fruitless as that.

The lights were growing fewer, and the carts with the wounded rumbled past her less often; the cries, a volume of sound before, became solitary moans. The darkness, cut here and there by the vapors, hid most of the field, and she was forced to search closely to tell the living from the dead. She was tired, weary in bone and sinew, but the face of her boy led her on, and, while any of the living remained there, she would seek. She stumbled once, in the darkness, on a dead body, and springing back with a shudder when she felt the yielding flesh under her feet, walked on into a little hollow.

She heard a boy groan,—very feebly, but still she could not mistake the sound for any of the fancied noises of the battlefield; and then the same faint voice calling his mother. She had heard other boys, on that night, calling for their mothers, but there was a new tone in this cry. She trembled and stood quite still, listening for the groan, which came again, feebler than before. It was so faint that she could not tell from what point it came, and all the shadows seemed to have gathered in the hollow. If she had only a light! She saw one of the lanterns glimmering far off in the field, but even if she obtained it she might not be able to find the place again. She advanced into the hollow, bending down low and searching the thick weeds and tangled bushes with her eyes. One of the buckets she had left behind; the other yet contained a gourdful of water, and she preserved it as if it were so much gold, now more jealously than ever.

She saw nothing. The place was larger than she had thought, and was thick with vines and weeds and heaped-up stones. She stumbled twice and fell upon her knees, but each time she held the water so well that not a drop was spilled. She stood erect again, listening, but hearing nothing. She called aloud, saying that help was there, but no answer came. Her heart was beating violently, but she neither wept nor cried aloud, for she was a woman of strength, and had always been of few words and less show.

Where she stood was the lowest point of the battlefield, and was on its outer edge. It was likewise the darkest spot, and the remainder of it seemed to curve before and above her in a great dusky amphitheatre, broken faintly by a few points of light where the lantern burned. She saw the formless bulk of a single cart moving slowly. In a little while the field would be abandoned to her and the dead.

She turned and continued the search, feeling her way through the mass of vegetation, and listening for the guiding groan. Again she stopped, and her heart was in the grip of fear lest she should not find him. She bent her ear close to the ground, and then she heard a cry so faint that it was but a sigh. She pushed her way through some bushes, and there he lay, his back against a rock, his white girlish face with its circle of fair hair turned up to the sky. The eyes were closed, and the chest seemed not to move. A great clot of blood hung upon his left shoulder and made a red gleam against the cloth of his coat.

Let it be said again that she was not a woman who showed her emotions, though at that first glance her face perhaps turned as white as his. She set the bucket down, knelt at his side, and, putting her face close to his, found that he was not dead, for she felt his breath upon her lips. She raised the head a little, and a sigh of pain, scarcely to be heard, escaped him. She poured some of the water, every drop more precious now than ever, into the gourd, and moistened his lips, which burned with the fever. Then she raised his head higher and dropped a little into his mouth. He sighed again, and his eyelids quivered and were lifted until a faint trace of the blue beneath appeared; then they closed. But she poured water into his mouth and down his throat a second time, and she could feel that pulse and breathing were stronger.

The blood was clotted and caked over his wound, but with wisdom she let it alone, knowing that there was no better bandage to stop the flow. She wet his hands and face with water and gave him more to drink, and saw a trace of color appear in his cheeks. His eyes opened partly two or three times, and he talked, but not of anything she knew, speaking in confused words of other battlefields and long marches; and before a sentence or its sense was finished another would be begun. She wanted no help; she looked around in jealousy lest another should come, and saw how small was the chance of it. The last cart had disappeared from the field, so far as she could see; she could count but four lights, and they were far off. In that part of the field, she, the living, was alone with the dead and the boy who hung between life and death.

Never had she felt herself more strong of body and mind, more full of resource; never had she felt herself more ready of head and hand. She gave him the last of the water, and saw the spot of color in his cheek, which was not of fever, grow. Then she lifted him in her arms, and began to walk with her burden across the battlefield. She looked at the wound, and seeing no fresh blood knew that she had not strained it open in lifting. With that she was satisfied, and she went on with careful step.

She felt her way through the roughness of the hollow, where the bushes and the weeds clung to her dress and her feet and tried to trip her; but she thrust them all aside and went on toward the house. She passed out of the hollow, and into the space which had received the full sweep of the cannon-balls and bullets.

The field was clothed in vapors which floated around her like little clouds. The white faces of the dead looked up at her, and she seemed to be going between rows of them on either side.

She walked on with sure and steady step, not feeling the weight in her arms and against her shoulder, unmoved by the ghastly heaps and the dead faces. She reached the burnt ground, where the little patches of fire that she had seen as she passed the other way had ceased to burn, but the smoke was still rising and the ground was yet warm. She feared that the smoke would get into his throat and choke down the little life that was left. So she ran, and the burnt arms of the trees seemed to wave at her and to jeer her, as if they knew she would be too late. She stumbled a little, but recovered herself. The boy stirred and groaned. She was in dread lest the rough jolt had started his wound, but her hand could not feel the warmth of fresh blood, and, reassured, she hastened through the burnt strip and toward home.

The house was silent and dark; apparently, no one had noticed the log cabin, its secluded position and the clump of woods perhaps hiding it from men whose attention had been devoted solely to the battle. She pushed open the door, and entered with her helpless burden. Some coals still glowed on the hearth, and threw out a warm light which bade her welcome. She put the boy on the bed, and covered the coals with ashes, for it was hot and close in the house. Then she lighted the piece of candle, and setting it where it could serve her with its light, and yet not shine into his eyes, she proceeded with her work.

Women who live such lives as hers must learn a little of all things, and she knew the duties of a surgeon. Twice she had bound up the wounds of her husband, received in some mountain fray. She undressed the young soldier, and as she did so she noticed the scar of a year-old wound under the shoulder,—a wound that might well have been mortal. The bullet of to-night had gone almost through, and she could feel it against the skin on the other side. She cut it out easily with the blade of a pocketknife, and put it in the cupboard. Then she bound up the wound the late bullet had made when it entered, leaving the congealed blood upon it as help against a fresh flow, and sat down to wait.

He was still talking, saying words that had no meaning, and threw his arms about a little; but he was stronger, and she hoped, though she knew, too, that he trembled on the edge.

She sat for a long time watching every movement, even the slightest. The little clock ticked so loudly that she thought once of stopping it; but the sound was so steady and regular that it lulled them, the boy as well as herself, and she let it alone.

He became quieter and grew stronger, too, as she could tell by his breathing, and slept. She spread a sheet over him, and opened the window that a little air might enter the close, warm room. She stood there for a while and looked toward the battlefield, but she could see nothng now to tell her of the combat. The vapors that floated over it hid it and all its ruin.

The wind rose, stirring the hot, close air and cooling the night. It whistled softly through the trees and among the hills, but it did not bring the smell of battle. That had vanished with the combat that had been so unreal itself, as she looked at it from her window. Now she could not see a human figure nor any sign of war. The cabin was just the same lone cabin among the hills that it had always been. She went outside and made the circuit of the house, but there was nothing for eye or ear to note. The night was darkening again, the wind had blown up clouds which hid the face of the moon, and but a few stars twinkled in the sky. The air felt damp, and scattered drops of rain whirled before the wind which was whistling, far off, as it drove away through the hills.

She went back into the house,—for she could not leave the boy more than a minute or two,—and found that he was sleeping well. She prepared some stimulants, and put them where they would be ready to her hand. Then she made over all her arrangements for the morrow, for two instead of one, and placed everything about the house in order, that it might put on its best look in the daylight. She finished her task, and sat down by the bed. Presently the sufferer began to talk of battle and strive to move, thinking he was in action on the field again. When she felt of his wrist and forehead, she saw that the fever was rising, and she thought he was going to die. She did all that her experience told her, and waited. Her bitterness came back, and she called them fools and barbarians once more; she was a fool herself to have had pity upon them.

The boy's wild talk was all of war. She followed him through march and camp, skirmish and battle, charge and retreat, and saw how they had taken their hold upon him, and what courage and energy he had put into his part. In half an hour he became quieter, and the fever sank. A cannon-shot boomed among the hills—so far away that the sound was softened by the distance. But it echoed long; hill and valley took it up and passed it on to farther hill and valley; and she heard it again and again, until it died away in the farthest hills like the last throb of a distant drumbeat. It was as if it had been a minute gun for the dead, and she went in terror to the bed; but the boy was not dead. He had passed again from delirium to sleep, and, fearing everything now, she went outside to see if the cannon-shot, by any chance, foretold a renewal of the battle; but it must have been a stray shot, for, as before, nowhere could she see a light, nowhere a living figure, nor could she hear any sound of human beings. The air was cooler, and, shivering, she went back into the house.

Presently, the drops changed to steady rain, which beat upon the windows; but it was peaceful and sheltered in the little house, and as she looked out at the rain, dashed past by the wind, there was a softness in her heart. The rain ceased after a while, and the trees and bushes dripped silver drops. The boy stirred; but it was some thought in his sleep that made him stir, not fever. She looked at him closely. His breathing was regular and easy, and she knew that he would live.

Going once more to the window, and with eyes to the skies, she gave her wordless thanks to God.

A broad bar of light appeared in the east. The day was coming.

# CLIFFORD DOWDEY

*Weep Not for Them*

NOW IT WAS ALL OVER. The dust was settling in the road again and the smoke had blown away under the tender breeze. Around the house the chickens had come out and were clucking near the well, and between the well and the house the great oak cast its ancient shade. Along the porch, tulips grew and wistaria climbed the columns. Odell paused at the foot of the steps, looking where the meadow rolled to the woods and at the bright trees standing clear against the sky. He had forgotten that Virginia could be so beautiful in the summer.

Hearing his steps, Miss Betty hurried through the door, followed by the half dozen girls who refugeed at her home. Odell knew them all now. But while he was greeting each in turn, he was seeing only Rosalie, and all the words of the others were a choral background to her voice. She was very grave, not excited like her friends, and she seemed studying him all the while in some intent compassion. Then he remembered yesterday, and now all the others' words came separate and distinct, the voices a pattern of questions.

He leaned against the column and knew himself to be extremely tired. The sun was setting, but on a sudden the light seemed to fade fast, and where the July silence had spread over the land, the old noises returned. He heard the sodden hoofbeats of cavalry mounts, the creaking of limbers, the clanging of a swab-bucket chain, and the crunch of rolling wagons. Always there were wagons. . . .

"But what actually did happen, Odell?" Miss Betty was saying. "Can a body go to bed again feeling safe in her own house—or are those people still five miles away at Malvern Hill?"

"No, they've retreated again, ten miles at least beyond Malvern Hill. There're not even any stragglers near by. You're safe enough."

"Then why skulk there like a bump on a log? If they've retreated again, we must've beaten them."

"No. . . . " He knew he had spoken to Rosalie. She had turned away, moving into the house. Odell turned back to old Miss Betty. "No, ma'am, we didn't beat the Yankees. We fought badly. I fought very badly."

"Oh, shucks, Odell," Miss Betty said, "you always took yourself too seriously. Since you've become colonel, anybody would think you had the weight of the war on your shoulders. Here the Yankees have been retreating a week, from in sight of Richmond to down there in the swamps, and all you think about is how you fought badly. Why, man alive, if you'd seen them as we have here—the stragglers, I reckon you'd call them, and those skirmishers off from the main body—passing this house, asking for food and water, and not enough fight left even to try and scare us."

Her words were lost in sudden cries from the girls: "There's Cary! There's Gracchus! Oh, look, there's the general! Ah, there's George!"

Rosalie came through the door with a pitcher of lemonade. Odell moved toward her as the other girls rushed to the top of the steps. Teetering on the porch edge, they waved and called at the passing men, and gave a flurried squeal when the general lifted his hat. Then they began pelting questions at George Frayser, dismounting in the yard.

"Oh, George, tell us about how we beat 'em."

Odell forgot them as he reached Rosalie. She poured a glass of the thin lemonade and said, "We forgot this in all the excitement of you coming back this way. We knew you had won yesterday, but we hadn't heard any real news. You must be thirsty."

"Thank you," he said, looking into the glass, because now that they stood alone and quiet in the midst of other sounds, he could not look at her. "You got my note?"

"Oh, yes, and I was so happy and proud, but, Odell, it's silly of you to think you failed. You mightn't have done as well as you expected to, but lots of others have done worse." She paused then and he had to look at her.

His gaze was held in some sick compulsion, not wanting sympathy, not wanting understanding, but blindly directed to this girl, still under twenty, who saw more than all the others—except one.

About that one, Odell said, "Some of those who failed resent the general because he's new, I reckon, and won't work with him. I believed in him. I'm sure he had the right idea of turning the Union siege of Richmond into a rout of their whole army."

"But you did lift the siege. You've driven them over thirty miles from Richmond. We can tell you, Odell, because we'be been living behind their lines for weeks and now the last of them have passed, three days ago. So, you see—''

"Rosalie. We're not going to win by lifting sieges or driving the enemy thirty miles. We're going to win by destroying his army. The general had plans for that, and we failed him. We let the Yankees get away in five battles. Our last crack at them was yesterday, at Malvern Hill. They not only got away from that. They gave us terrible losses before they retreated beyond our reach. That's where I failed.''

"Please, Odell, I know there are technical things I don't understand, and with your conscientiousness, you might feel you failed at some point—''

He broke in with a gesture of weariness. "Rosalie, you certainly can understand me losing a third of my regiment. You can understand that they fought wonderfully, that they did everything they were asked—but they were asked the wrong things. I did that.''

Studying him silently, as a woman measures a man as she sees him removed from his own personal stress, Rosalie showed that she still did not grasp the essential failure of the campaign just ended, or of his part in the final action of it yesterday. She turned from him and smiled, over his shoulder, to Miss Betty.

The old lady took the lemonade pitcher and said to Odell, "It's a good thing the other men know when a battle is won.''

They had something to do with winning it. How automatically the words came to his mind. He looked at those other men, forming a group with the girls in the yard around happy George Frayser. There would be a big night in Richmond for most of them. Rosalie's hand lay on his arm.

Her smile was warm and young. "Why don't we walk down to the garden like we used to?''

"Isn't it destroyed?'' Then he knew he was afraid of her compassion, of her knowing the inside of him. Rosalie looked at him steadily, in awareness of his feelings of yesterday in the blistering sun of Malvern Hill. "The wall is not destroyed,'' she said. "It's quiet there.''

He glanced over his shoulder. The groups were breaking, men remounting and turning their horses toward camp or on the road to Richmond. In the early twilight the clang and creak of artillery, the muffled thud of hoofs, undertoned the voices on the porch and in the yard. Good-by . . . good-by . . . you come . . . good-by all. . . .

Nobody would think he was running away. Nobody was thinking of him at all. He walked faster than normal, crossing the width of the porch, and they went down the side steps toward the grove. He had played there as a small boy when his parents had come visiting Miss Betty. Then Rosalie had played there as a little girl, visiting her aunt, and he would stop by for coffee when he had been out shooting or going home after a long run on a fox.

The brick wall of the garden had no rambler roses over it now. Yankee skirmishers had fought there when they were covering the retreat of their own wagons down the road toward the river. Retreat from Mechanicsville to Gaines' Mill, from Frayser's Farm to Malvern Hill; and on every field they left more Confederate dead than of their own. McClellan was a name that would live long in this land of Tidewater Virginia. Their own new general might have a name like that, too, if Odell had not failed. . . .

"See, she said, "with the shadows now, you would hardly know the flowers were all gone."

"Yes. I remember them so well from the last time I saw them."

"Three years ago this August the nineteenth."

"You remember that?" A suggestion of a smile stirred in him.

"Of course. It was my sixteenth birthday and, besides, you were going away to New York the next day."

"Better that I had never come back." How automatically those words came, too, but this time aloud.

Rosalie made no sound, moving from his side to the wall. Her pale dress draped along the bricks, she sat straight, a small curve in her back and her dark hair falling below her neck. "Could those two years in New York have changed you so much?"

"So much from what, Rosalie?"

"You came home to fight for your state because it was invaded, and you have risked your life and—"

"And the lives of other men."

She gave him a startled glance, her face white in the deepening dusk. "Then you have changed. In the old days, before we knew we loved each other—"

"I reckon I always knew that," he said gently, feeling even that was offered in amelioration.

"If we talk of that, I know I always loved you ever since I can remember. When I was a little girl, Miss Betty thought that it was hero worship and the silly romances that young girls conjure up for older men. Well, there was real hero worship in it, because then you were a man of faith."

"You've got to have faith in something." That was certainty and he stood straighter, as a condemned man might who could at least accept his fate with dignity.

"There's where you've changed, Odell. You had nothing to have faith in before, except a belief in yourself, and yet you took that reponsible place in New York where you had to learn as you went. It's the same now. You had no previous military training except drilling with Company F, but you've been promoted fast because you believed and you've improved. You're learning as you go, along with everybody else, even the new general. Nobody expects you to be a Stonewall Jackson. They just expect you to keep the faith. When you have something to work with, as you have, faith is worth more than all manner of proficiency. Faith can work miracles."

It was all true, everything she said, just as last night was true, and his youth was true, but they were gone beyond his recapture. He felt that release of her tension when he did not answer. There was a slight sound, like a sigh, and then she moved away.

"Don't go like this," he said.

She paused. "My words mean nothing to you. I can't reach you any more."

He turned, seeing her misty in the lilac evening, her hands making a small white ball where she clenched them together. But he could not reach her either. "I'm sorry, Rosalie, I seem so no-account now, but—please know it's not you. If anybody could—"

"But nobody can." Her voice sounded dried, as if drained of all desire to encompass them in her love. "I must go in now. The others will be wondering."

He watched her walk neither fast nor slow, but, knowing her since she was a child, he knew she sought composure. She had old knowledge of him, too, going back to days when he had not realized she was storing up her wisdoms of Odell Mathis. On this wall, where he leaned now as Rosalie was lost in the grove shadows, he had held her up and pointed out the flowers in Miss Betty's garden so long ago. She had not been that child when he left three years ago, but something of the relationship from those days had still colored their mood together.

Last fall, when he furloughed after the opening actions in Northern Virginia, he had found the child gone. He had found it when they kissed. She was a woman, coming to him as a woman, and then first he was aware of loving her. All her knowledge of him was flattering then, joining them in a special bond, as did the associations of their long-shared pasts. Now, in his failure, it was a cold light revealing him, and he withdrew from her as he did from their friends in the house.

Their voices reached him and the warmth of them seemed reflected in the yellow lights from the windows. If they would only talk frankly of his failure, he could reach again some certainty, something to base his future actions on. But they laughed too heartily and their eyes said, as her words had, "Others have failed too. You're just learning. There'll be other battles."

There'd be other battles when his junior officers would run to him in bewilderment, their voices losing all personality in their frenzy. "We've broken on the right. There's no contact with the next regiment!" That was the regiment of happy George Frayser. George had not been happy then. "In God's name, Odell, where are you?"

He lurched out from the wall, the vividness of the reliving goading him into undirected movement as it had then.

Suddenly he put purpose in his strides. He was going to camp, but not to work. He was going to talk to George Frayser and any other brigade officers around. He was going to put it up to them squarely. Did they think he had failed? He had to know, and from them. His fellow officers woud know. They, not Rosalie, were the ones who had seen him.

They saw his men cutting down trees to clear the obstructed road, so his guns and wagons could pass. General Jackson, to whom they had been attached that day, had warned him to take care of every wagon. "There's too much wastefulness in this country."

"Yeh, be careful," said the officers who had worked with Jackson before. "Old Jack sets great store by them wagons. He'll skin you alive if'n you lose even a wheelbarrow."

He had not lost any wagons—just time. He was bringing the whole train through fine when the aid rode up, flushed as a gobbler, and yelled for the whole world to hear: "Are you trying to build a county pike? You're an hour late and you've turned road engineer! Everybody's going in piecemeal as it is. Get your regiment prepared for action, and get them now!"

Odell left the wagons then, and got the guns through the half-cleared obstructions any which way, a limber breaking an axle. When they did reach the field, the smoke billowed down like fog.

They moved forward in smoke and a storm of shell. They fell in droves. Everywhere voices poked at him, "Your're late." He hurried his men when they should have sought cover. George's regiment took cover and contact was lost. The left regiment veered away from the punishment, and contact was lost there too. Of a certainty he should have stopped then, waiting for orders, but his junior officers were yelling at him for directions and he was late.

They drove ahead. He saw blue uniforms through the swirling fog, and the fire of their guns lashed red and yellow in his face. Not a gray uniform was in sight. His men rocked back and somebody said, "Pull 'em out, pull 'em out, or your regiment will be destroyed."

They reeled down the hill with that gale of shell blowing against their backs and the men kept falling. He could scarcely rouse enough to carry off the wounded, and their moans followed him. From far away a voice he recognized as the brigadier's said, "It's all over. We lost a lot of men. Re-form as best you can."

With merciful night the shocked remnants re-formed and the wounded were brought off, and the officers gathered and the words began. They had a different sound from the words at other messes. They were like men waiting for one of their group to leave. Nobody told him he had done anything wrong, and always before they had. The things before were small.

He heard their voices now, in the old farmhouse where most of the brigade field officers were billeted, and they had the old sound. They bantered with the rough edge of cruelty which only intimates may use. He knew it well, and none of it had been turned on him since he took his regiment up Malvern Hill. This, then, was the time to have it out. They must tell him.

He walked carefully on the grass, taking care that he made no sound. He tiptoed onto the wrecked porch. Laughter rolled freely from the small front room and he crossed to the doorway under its sound. The men could not have heard him until his step in the bare hall, and then he stood blinking in the candlelight, sensing the sprawled uniforms around the floor.

The voices broke off and then, in a tone lower than before he came, the colonel said, "I thought you were staying at the party at Miss Betty's."

He saw most of the majors of the brigade and the young colonel who had spoken. "I thought I had better work. Where's George?"

"Like you, married to his reports." This was quiet and courteous, to someone respected.

Their faces grew clear, showing the evidence of their laughter, suspended, as they waited until he left to laugh again. He could not ask them now. He could not suddenly blurt out, "Do you think I failed?" He needed a sobered occasion, when they were receptive to military conversation.

"George is upstairs," the colonel said.

Odell turned away, leaving the enclosed silence behind him. Not until he was on the stairs did their voices start up again. Then George called, "Is that you, Odell?"

His room was stifling, and night insects swarmed around the candle near him. George seemed not to mind. His coat was off and his collar opened, but his genial neatness was unruffled.

"George," Odell said, and saw the expectant smile fade, the head cock a little to one side as he waited, the eyes warm in sympathy. "I've got to make out my reports and—and I don't know how much to tell, how much to leave out—if to start back with those accursed wagons—"

George became Colonel Frayser, a kind, friendly colonel. "Forget the wagons. You take it too much to heart. You did all right."

"All right, but not good. You called me when I lost contact—"

"I was excited then. The whole thing was a mess anyway; and, besides, nobody expects you to be a Stonewall Jackson."

Odell started, and George, leaning forward, said quickly, "What's the matter? Have I hurt your feelings?"

"No." He could not tell him Rosalie had used those same words. He could not tell any more of anything, and he no longer needed to ask. He knew.

He wanted to be away. "I'll just say in the report I was detained by cutting a road for the wagons, and go on."

"Certainly. I tell you, you did all right. Nothing went as it should. We've all got a lot to learn. You know that."

Odell was no longer listening. All right. They all said that, just as George Frayser said it, revealing sympathy while they studied him, but a little removed, too, standing outside and watching, and waiting to see what he would do. That was the answer and he knew what to do. Why humiliate himself by asking when there was only one thing he could do?

George jumped quicker than he did at the voices raised outside where the sentries paced. They reached the open window together and Odell recognized the strident voice as old Miss Betty's.

"You, Odell Mathis! George Frayser! You come out here and tell this young man who I am. Maybe he's a Yankee spy, not knowing me."

George grinned. For a moment it seemed like the old exchange, and then he was hurrying down the narrow stairs and all the other officers were pushing out of the front room into the hall. By the time they reached the yard, the sheepish sentry had permitted Miss Betty's carriage to pass.

In the pale reflection of light, Odell saw the old lady being helped out by a Negro even more ancient than she, while a young colored boy held the reins. On the darker far side of the carriage, Odell saw the pale blur of Rosalie's dress, and he hurried around behind the carriage. Miss Betty was calling to the officers.

"Help me get this stuff out I brought you over. I hid some blackberry wine in the well from those people. I reckon it's as cold as a julep, but it might cheer you who couldn't stay to the party."

The men rushed the carriage with whoops, very decently taking no notice of Rosalie. Odell found her hands in the night, and knew he was no longer afraid of Rosalie now.

She said, "I just had to see you, Odell, and I got Miss Betty to come. I couldn't go to sleep after leaving you like I did today. Why, there I was talking to you about faith and all the time acting like I had none in you when—oh, Odell, I love you so."

"I'm awfully glad you came, Rosalie, because there's something I've got to tell you." He moved her away from the carriage and, with her close beside him, he felt her gentleness like a palpable thing.

He turned to look directly at Rosalie and, with simple conviction, said, "I never thought you lost faith because, not knowing in detail about the battle, you couldn't know how miserably I failed. But the men know. I came back here tonight to ask them."

Feeling her tense in his arms, he paused, waiting for her to speak. Her breath drew in, but she said nothing.

"Well," he went on, "I didn't need to ask them. They've lost faith in me, I saw that, and that's why I have none in myself."

"No, Odell, you don't know that. You've made it true by believing it. You have a great power of believing. I think it's your belief in our cause that makes you feel your own mistake unfits you for it."

She had not heard their laughter break off. He was wearied of all the doubts and indecision, and he said, "In any event, it's true for me."

Rosalie drew back, her young face uplifted as her eyes searched into him. "Then you're going to resign?"

He held himself still, like a rabbit under a fox, trying to hide from her knowing. She had made it too bald, sheared of all extenuations. She knew.

"That's what it comes down to, Odell. Reasons don't matter."

"Very well." He collected himself again, forcing the decision firm in his brain. "I'll resign tonight. As soon as you go, I'll tell the other officers."

He was aware of time between them before she answered, her voice a little faint, "You'll feel better."

"Yes. I feel better already. I didn't realize what a weight it's been, keeping it all to myself. There's nothing worse than uncertainty." He had added one sentence on another and, when she still remained silent, he said, "Will you want to see me tomorrow and know what happened?"

"Of course. I'll always want to see you and—and know what happens. I love you." she turned to call Miss Betty.

In the hot narrow room he stood before them—George Frayser and the other colonel, five majors, one from his own regiment, and a captain from his regiment who was acting major for the one killed. Two candles burned in empty cans, and the sluggish swamp breeze wavered the light on the eight faces.

"Gentlemen," he said, "it was good of you to come here to listen to the few words I must tell you. I don't want to embarrass you, so I'll say it quickly. I know you've all lost faith in me since I failed at Malvern Hill, and I'm resigning for the good of our army."

He intended to say more, but the outburst drove him back as had the storm of shell yesterday. Every man was speaking, and all the voices were raised.

"Failed? You didn't fail. You just made a mistake. Everybody made mistakes."

Then, clear above the others, came the voice of the third colonel. He was twenty-four years old, just two years out of the Point, and ranking colonel of the brigade. He was saying "—and if everybody who made mistakes yesterday resigned, we wouldn't have an officer left in the army, and that goes for the new commander, General Lee."

"Wait a minute, men," Odell had to shout to make himself heard. "I appreciate what you're trying to do, but, you see, I know how I failed more clearly than any of you do. I foolishly cut that road for wagons, and I held up the whole brigade. Then I went in excitedly and made a bad position hopeless, at a terrible cost to my troops. Believe me, this is not hurt vanity. In fact, I'm hurting my pride now more than I ever knew I could. But, even such a poor soldier as I am, I am enough of one to know that I failed miserably and—''

''Not failure!'' The young colonel scrambled to his feet. He was gripped by an intensity not shown since the battle. Some of the fire of fight shone in his eyes. ''You made a mistake in tarrying on that damn road, yes. But once you got up, you had your men ready to fight, and they fought better than any regiment in the whole division.''

''That's right,'' said the captain from his regiment. He was standing, too, and some of the cold ferocity he had revealed on that hill colored him now. ''I took a company into that fight, and I know your men would have gone anywhere you sent them yesterday, and they'll go again tomorrow.''

'Please, gentlemen,'' Odell said. They were only pouring salt into his humiliation. ''Wait a minute—''

''You wait, Odell.'' George had lunged out from the doorway, standing straight, and there was no kind patience on him now. ''These men are telling you the truth.''

''I know, George, but—''

''But you don't seem to know that this whole campaign, not only yesterday, was the first time this army ever worked together. It was our first test under fire—a sort of trial by fire, if you will. Everybody made mistakes, but out of those mistakes we're learning what we've got. General Hill made a mistake in our opening action at Mechanicsville and lost more men than you had in your command. But he kept hitting and his men kept fighting for him, as yours did for you, and the enemy is thirty miles from Richmond, even if we didn't accomplish all we set out to. Do you think A. P. Hill should have resigned after Mechanicsville?''

''It's not the same.'' The old doubts were churning up again, the old uncertainties. ''He's a trained soldier.''

''Trained soldier maybe, but not with this army. This is a people's army, not professionals, and a peaceful people, at that. We've got to learn about ourselves and each other as we go. What we learned about you is that you have that magical thing, leadership. When your men went on the field they fought, all by themselves, right up to the enemy's cannon, and they didn't stop until you pulled them out. You talk about the men you lost and losing contact with me. If I had gotten my men up the hill as you did, you wouldn't have lost so many and we might have held the position.''

The young colonel said, ''We would've held it if I had gotten up, but my men wouldn't take the fire.''

''That was my fault.'' That came from one of his majors. He had laughed more heartily than all the others during the past day, and broken off at Odell's appearance more quickly than anyone else. Now he was marked by the same driving force as the others. He seemed to feel the same release that Odell had felt when he confessed his mistakes. He was saying, ''I held the flank of our regiments, in contact with Colonel Mathis, and it looked like our men couldn't take the fire. I put them under a little rise—''

''I was the one who made you think we couldn't stand the fire.'' That was the slight, scholarly major who had the other batallion. ''I thought our flank might be turned on the left and we'd be encircled. I dug in to meet the enfilading fire and it was only a few skirmishers falling back. It was like this.'' He got down on his hands and knees. ''I'm my own battalion. You're yours.'' That major got down alongside him. ''George, you're the enemy at the top of the hill.'' George leaned down, his big hands on the floor. ''And your're the skirmishers running around on the flank.'' The captain bent down and moved around beside him, very serious as the enemy skirmishers.

They were all serious and very earnest, and suddenly Odell saw that his fellow officers looked more like themselves than they had since the battle. And for the first time since he stumbled down that hill—in another age, it seemed now—a great slow smile welled up in him. Their laughter had been their escape from facing their own mistakes. Now he had released them, and they had forgotten him. Listening to them all arguing about who had committed the worst mistakes, he knew at last that his was, as Rosalie had said, only one among many.

He started to move slowly around the battle line, now stretched from wall to wall. No one noticed. He tiptoed out onto the porch, and the hot July night felt cool and refreshing. Rosalie would not be asleep yet, not waiting as she was to know what had happened. She probably knew now, with her store of wisdoms of him. She was right that his faith in the cause had been so great that one mistake made him feel unfit. But it was that faith that gave him the magical leadership.

Odell went down the rickety steps and turned across the fields toward Miss Betty's. It must be midnight, but two miles once more was little for a colonel whose men would follow him anywhere. A new sound accompanied him. It was somebody whistling Dixie. It was he.

# THOMAS NELSON PAGE

## *The Burial of the Guns*

LEE SURRENDERED THE REMNANT of his army at Appomattox, April 9, 1865, and yet a couple of days later the old Colonel's battery lay intrenched right in the mountain-pass where it had halted three days before. Two weeks previously it had been detailed with a light division sent to meet and repel a force which it was understood was coming in by way of the southwest valley to strike Lee in the rear of his long line from Richmond to Petersburg. It had done its work. The mountain-pass had been seized and held, and the Federal force had not gotten by that road within the blue rampart which guarded on that side the heart of Virginia. This pass, which was the key to the main line of passage over the mountains, had been assigned by the commander of the division to the old Colonel and his old battery, and they had held it. The position taken by the battery had been chosen with a soldier's eye. A better place could not have been selected to hold the pass. It was its highest point, just where the road crawled over the shoulder of the mountain along the limestone cliff, a hundred feet sheer above the deep river, where its waters had cut their way in ages past, and now lay deep and silent, as if resting after their arduous toil before they began to boil over the great bowlders which filled the bed a hundred or more yards below.

The little plateau at the top guarded the descending road on either side for nearly a mile, and the mountain on the other side of the river was the centre of a clump of rocky, heavily timbered spurs, so inaccessible that no feet but those of wild animals or of the hardiest hunter had ever climbed it. On the side of the river on which the road lay, the only path out over the mountain except the road itself was a charcoal-burner's track, dwindling at times to a footway known only to the mountain-folk, which a picket at the top could hold against an army. The position, well defended, was impregnable, and it was well defended. This the general of the division knew when he detailed the old Colonel and gave him his order to hold the pass until relieved, and not let his guns fall into the hands of the enemy. He knew both the Colonel and his battery. The battery was one of the oldest in the army. It had been in the service since April, 1861, and its commander had come to be known as "The Wheel Horse of his division." He was, perhaps, the oldest officer of his rank in his branch of the service. Although he had bitterly opposed secession, and was many years past the age of service when the war came on, yet as soon as the President called on the State for her quota of troops to coerce South Carolina, he had raised and uniformed an artillery company, and offered it, not to the President of the United States, but to the Governor of Virginia.

It is just at this point that he suddenly looms up to me as a soldier; the relation he never wholly lost to me afterward, though I knew him for many, many years of peace. His gray coat with the red facing and the bars on the collar; his military cap; his gray flannel shirt—it was the first time I ever saw him wear anything but immaculate linen—his high boots; his horse caparisoned with a black, high-peaked saddle, with crupper and breast-girth, instead of the light English hunting-saddle to which I had been accustomed, all come before me now as if it were but the other day. I remember but little beyond it, yet I remember, as if it were yesterday, his leaving home, and the scenes which immediately preceded it; the excitement created by the news of the President's call for troops; the unanimous judgment that it meant war; the immediate determination of the old Colonel, who had hith-erto opposed secession, that it must be met; the suppressed agitation on the plantation, attendant upon the tender of his services and the Governor's acceptance of them. The prompt and continuous work incident to the enlistment of the men, the bustle of preparation, and all the scenes of that time, come before me now. It turned the calm current of the life of an old and placid country neighborhood, far from any city or centre, and stirred it into a boiling torrent, strong enough, or fierce enough to cut its way and join the general torrent which was bearing down and sweeping everything before it. It seemed but a minute before the quiet old plantation, in which the harvest, the corn-shucking, and the Christmas holidays alone marked the passage of the quiet seasons, and where a strange carriage or a single horse-man coming down the big road was an event in life, was turned into a depot of war-supplies, and the neighborhood became a parade-ground. The old Colonel, not a colonel yet, not even a captain, except by brevet, was on his horse by daybreak and off on his rounds through the plantations and the pines enlisting his company. The office in the yard, heretofore one in name only, became one now in reality, and a table was set out piled with papers, pens, ink, books of tactics and regulation, at which men were accepted and enrolled. Soldiers seemed to spring from the ground, as they did from the sowing of the dragon's teeth in the days of Cadmus. Men came up the high road or down the paths across the fields, sometimes singly, but oftener in little parties of two or three, and, asking for the Captain, entered the office as private citizens and came out soldiers enlisted in the war. There was nothing heard of on the plantation except fighting; white and black, all were at work, and all were eager; the servants contended for the honor of going with their master; the women flocked to the house to assist in the work of preparation, cutting out and making under-clothes, knitting socks, picking lint, preparing bandages, and sewing on uniforms; for many of the men who had enlisted were of the poorest class, far too poor to furnish anything themselves, and their equipment had to be contributed mainly by wealthier neighbors. The work was carried on at night as well as by day, for the occasion was urgent. Meantime the men were being drilled by the Captain and his lieutenants, who had been militia officers of old. We were carried to see the drill at the cross-roads, and a brave sight it seemed to us: the lines marching and countermarching in the field, with the horses galloping as they wheeled amid clouds of dust, at the hoarse commands of the excited officers, and the roadside lined with spectators of every age and condition. I recall the arrival of the messenger one night, with the telegraphic order to the Captain to report with his company at "Camp Lee" immediately; the hush in the parlor that attended its reading; then the forced beginning of the conversation afterwards in a somewhat strained and unnatural key, and the Captain's quick and decisive outlining of his plans.

Within the hour a dozen messengers were on their way in various directions to notify the members of the command of the summons, and to deliver the order for their attendance at a given point next day. It seemed that a sudden and great change had come. It was the actual appearance of what had hitherto only been theoretical—war. The next morning the Captain, in full uniform, took leave of the assembled plantation, with a few solemn words commending all he left behind to God, and galloped away up the big road to join and lead his battery to the war, and to be gone just four years.

Within a month he was on "the Peninsula" with Magruder, guarding Virginia on the east against the first attack. His camp was first at Yorktown and then on Jamestown Island, the honor having been assigned his battery of guarding the oldest cradle of the race on this continent. It was at "Little Bethel" that his guns were first trained on the enemy, and that the battery first saw what they had to do, and from this time until the middle of April, 1865, they were in service, and no battery saw more service or suffered more in it. Its story was a part of the story of the Southern Army in Virginia. The Captain was a rigid disciplinarian, and his company had more work to do than most new companies. A pious churchman, of the old puritanical type not uncommon to Virginia, he looked after the spiritual as well as the physical welfare of his men, and his chaplain or he read prayers at the head of his company every morning during the war. At first he was not popular with the men, he made the duties of camp life so onerous to them, it was "nothing but drilling and praying all the time," they said. But he had not commanded very long before they came to know the stuff that was in him. He had not been in service a year before he had had four horses shot under him, and when later on he was offered the command of a battalion, the old compny petitioned to be one of his batteries, and still remained under his command. Before the first year was out the battery had, through its own elements, and the discipline of the Captain, become a cohesive force, and a distinct integer in the Army of Northern Virginia. Young farmer recruits knew of its prestige and expressed preference for it of many batteries of rapidly growing or grown reputation. Owing to its high stand, the old and clumsy guns with which it had started out were taken from it, and in their place was presented a battery of four fine, brass, twelve-pound Napoleons of the newest and most approved kind, and two three-inch Parrotts, all captured. The men were as pleased with them as children with new toys. The care and attention needed to keep them in prime order broke the monotony of camp life. They soon had abundant opportunities to test their power. They worked admirably, carried far, and were extraordinarily accurate in their aim. The men from admiration of their guns grew to have first a pride in, and then an affection for them, and gave them nicknames as they did their comrades; the four Napoleons being dubbed, "The Evangelists," and the two rifles being "The Eagle," because of its scream and force, and "The Cat," because when it became hot from rapid firing "It jumped," they said, "like a cat." From many a hill-top in Virginia, Maryland, and Pennsylvania "The Evangelists" spoke their hoarse message of battle

and death, "The Eagle" screamed her terrible note, and "The Cat"
jumped as she spat her deadly shot from her hot throat. In the Valley of
Virginia; on the levels of Henrico and Hanover; on the slopes of
Manassas; in the woods of Chancellorsville; on the heights of
Fredericksburg; at Antietam and Gettysburg; in the Spottsylvania
wilderness, and again on the Hanover levels and on the lines before
Petersburg, the old guns through nearly four years roared from fiery
throats their deadly messages. The history of the battery was bound up
with the history of Lee's army. A rivalry sprang up among the
detachments of the different guns, and their several records were
jealously kept. The number of duels each gun was in was carefully
counted, every scar got in battle was treasured, and the men around
their camp-fires, at their scanty messes, or on the march, bragged of
them among themselves and avouched them as witnesses. New recruits coming in to fill the gaps made by the killed and disabled,
readily fell in with the common mood and caught the spirit like a
contagion. It was not an uncommon thing for a wheel to be smashed in
by a shell, but if it happened to one gun oftener than to another there
was envy. Two of the Evangelists seemed to be especially favored
in this line, while the Cat was so exempt as to become the subject of
some derision. The men stood by the guns till they were knocked to
pieces, and when the fortune of the day went against them, had with
their own hands oftener than once saved them after most of their
horses were killed.

This had happened in turn to every gun, the men at times working
like beavers in mud up to their thighs and under a murderous fire to get
their guns out. Many a man had been killed tugging at trail or wheel
when the day was against them; but not a gun had ever been lost. At
last the evil day arrived. At Winchester a sudden and impetuous
charge for a while swept everything before it, and carried the knoll
where the old battery was posted; but all the guns were got out by the
toiling and rapidly dropping men, except the Cat, which was captured
with its entire detachment working at it until they were surrounded
and knocked from the piece by cavalrymen. Most of the men who
were not killed were retaken before the day was over, with many guns;
but the Cat was lost. She remained in the enemy's hands and probably
was being turned against her old comrades and lovers. The company
was inconsolable. The death of comrades was too natural and common a thing to depress the men beyond what such occurrences
necessarily did; but to lose a gun! It was like losing the old Colonel; it

was worse: a gun was ranked as a brigadier; and the Cat was equal to a major-general. The other guns seemed lost without her; the Eagle especially, which generally went next to her, appeared to the men to have a lonely and subdued air. The battery was no longer the same: it seemed broken and depleted, shrunken to a mere section. It was worse than Cold Harbor, where over half the men were killed or wounded. The old Captain, now Colonel of the battalion, appreciated the loss and apprehended its effect on the men as much as they themselves did, and application was made for a gun to take the place of the lost piece; but there was none to be had, as the men said they had known all along. It was added—perhaps by a department clerk—that if they wanted a gun to take the place of the one they had lost, they had better capture it. "By——, we will," they said—adding epithets, intended for the department clerk in his "bomb-proof," not to be printed in this record—and they did. For some time afterwards in every engagement into which they got there used to be speculation among them as to whether the Cat were not there on the other side; some of the men swearing they could tell her report, and even going to the rash length of offering bets on her presence.

By one of those curious coincidences, as strange as anything in fiction, a new general had, in 1864, come down across the Rapidan to take Richmond, and the old battery had found a hill-top in the line in which Lee's army lay stretched across "the Wilderness" country to stop him. The day, though early in May, was a hot one, and the old battery, like most others, had suffered fearfully. Two of the guns had had wheels cut down by shells and the men had been badly cut up; but the fortune of the day had been with Lee, and a little before nightfall, after a terrible fight, there was a rapid advance, Lee's infantry sweeping everything before it, and the artillery, after opening the way for the charge, pushing along with it; now unlimbering as some vantage-ground was gained, and using canister with deadly effect; now driving ahead again so rapidly that it was mixed up with the muskets when the long line of breastworks was carried with a rush, and a line of guns were caught still hot from their rapid work. As the old battery, with lathered horses and smoke-grimed men, swung up the crest and unlimbered on the captured breastwork, a cheer went up which was heard even above the long general yell of the advancing line, and for a moment half the men in the battery crowded together around some object on the edge of the redoubt, yelling like madmen. The next instant they divided, and there was the Cat, smoke-grimed and bloodstained and still sweating hot from her last fire, being dragged from her muddy ditch by as many men as could get hold of trail-rope or wheel, and rushed into her old place beside the Eagle, in time to be double-shotted with canister to the muzzle, and to pour it from among her old comrades into her now retiring former masters. Still, she had a new carriage, and her record was lost, while those of the other guns had been faithfully kept by the men. This made a difference in her position for which even the bullets in her wheels did not wholly atone; even Harris, the sergeant of her detachment, felt that.

It was only a few days later, however, that abundant atonement was made. The new general did not retire across the Rapidan after his first defeat, and a new battle had to be fought: a battle, if anything, more furious, more terrible than the first, when the dead filled the trenches and covered the fields. He simply marched by the left flank, and Lee marching by the right flank to head him, flung himself upon him again at Spottsylvania Court-House. That day the Cat, standing in her place behind the new and temporary breastwork thrown up when the battery was posted, had the felloes of her wheels, which showed above the top of the bank, entirely cut away by Minie-bullets, so that when she jumped in the recoil her wheels smashed and let her down. This covered all old scores. The other guns had been cut down by shells or solid shot; but never before had one been gnawed down by musket-balls. From this time all through the campaign the Cat held her own beside her brazen and bloody sisters, and in the cold trenches before Petersburg that winter, when the new general—Starvation—had joined the one already there, she made her bloody mark as often as any gun on the long lines.

Thus the old battery had come to be known, as its old commander, now colonel of a battalion, had come to be known by those in yet higher command. And when in the opening spring of 1865 it became apparent to the leaders of both armies that the long line could not longer be held if a force should enter behind it, and, sweeping the one partially unswept portion of Virginia, cut the railways in the south-west, and a man was wanted to command the artillery in the expedition sent to meet this force, it was not remarkable that the old Colonel and his battalion should be selected for the work. The force sent out was but small; for the long line was worn to a thin one in those days, and great changes were taking place, the consequences of which were known only to the commanders. In a few days the commander of the expedition found that he must divide his small force for a time, at least, to accomplish his purpose, and sending the old Colonel with one battery of artillery to guard one pass, must push on over the mountain by another way to meet the expected force, if possible, and repel it before it crossed the farther range. Thus the old battery, on an April evening of 1865, found itself toiling alone up the steep mountain road which leads above the river to the gap, which formed the chief pass in that part of the Blue Ridge. Both men and horses looked, in the dim and waning light of the gray April day, rather like shadows of the beings they represented than the actual beings themselves. And anyone seeing them as they toiled painfully up, the thin horses floundering in the mud, and the men, often up to their knees, tugging at the sinking wheels, now stopping to rest, and always moving so slowly that they seemed scarcely to advance at all, might have thought them the ghosts of some old battery lost from some long gone and forgotten war on that deep and desolate mountain road. Often, when they stopped, the blowing of the horses and the murmuring of the river in its bed below were the only sounds heard, and the tired voices of the men when they spoke among themselves seemed hardly more articulate sounds than they. Then the voice of the mounted figure on the roan horse half hidden in the mist would cut in, clear and inspiring, in a tone of encouragement more than of command, and everything would wake up: the drivers would shout and crack their whips; the horses would bend themselves on the collars and flounder in the mud; the men would spring once more to the mud-clogged wheels, and the slow ascent would begin again.

The orders of the Colonel, as has been said, were brief: To hold the pass until he received further instructions, and not to lose his guns. To be ordered, with him, was to obey. The last streak of twilight brought them to the top of the pass; his soldier's instinct and a brief reconnoissance made earlier in the day told him that this was his place, and before daybreak next morning the point was as well fortified as a night's work by weary and supperless men could make it. A prettier spot could not have been found for the purpose; a small plateau, something over an acre in extent, where a charcoal-burner's hut had once stood, lay right at the top of the pass. It was a little higher on either side than in the middle, where a small brook, along which the charcoal-burner's track was yet visible, came down from the wooded mountain above, thus giving a natural crest to aid the fortification on either side, with open space for the guns, while the edge of the wood coming down from the mountain afforded shelter for the camp.

As the battery was unsupported it had to rely on itself for everything, a condition which most soldiers by this time were accustomed to. A dozen or so of rifles were in the camp, and with these pickets were armed and posted. The pass had been seized none too soon; a scout brought in the information before nightfall that the invading force had crossed the farther range before that sent to meet it could get there, and taking the nearest road had avoided the main body opposing it, and been met only by a rapidly moving detachment, nothing more than a scouting party, and now were advancing rapidly on the road on which they were posted, evidently meaning to seize the pass and cross the mountain at this point. The day was Sunday; a beautiful Spring Sunday; but it was no Sabbath for the old battery. All day the men worked, making and strengthening their redoubt to guard the pass, and by the next morning, with the old battery at the top, it was impregnable. They were just in time. Before noon their vedettes brought in word that the enemy were ascending the mountain, and the sun had hardly turned when the advance guard rode up, came within range of the picket, and were fired on.

It was apparent that they supposed the force there only a small one, for they retired and soon came up again reinforced in some numbers, and a sharp little skirmish ensued, hot enough to make them more prudent afterwards, though the picket retired up the mountain. This gave them encouragement and probably misled them, for they now advanced boldly. They saw the redoubt on the crest as they came on, and unlimbering a section or two, flung a few shells up at it, which either fell short or passed over without doing material damage. None of the guns was allowed to respond, as the distance was too great with the ammunition the battery had, and, indifferent as it was, it was too precious to be wasted in a duel at an ineffectual range. Doubtless deceived by this, the enemy came on in force, being obliged by the character of the ground to keep almost entirely to the road, which really made them advance in column. The battery waited. Under orders of the Colonel the guns standing in line were double-shotted with canister, and, loaded to the muzzle, were trained down to sweep the road at from four to five hundred yards' distance. And when the column reached this point the six guns, aimed by old and skilful gunners, at a given word swept road and mountain-side with a storm of leaden hail. It was a fire no mortal man could stand up against, and the practiced gunners rammed their pieces full again, and before the smoke had cleared or the reverberation had died away among the mountains, had fired the guns again and yet again. The road was cleared of living things when the draught setting down the river drew the smoke away; but it was no discredit to the other force; for no army that was ever uniformed could stand against that battery in that pass. Again and again the attempt was made to get a body of men up under cover of the woods and rocks on the mountain-side, while the guns below utilized their better ammunition from longer range; but it was uesless. Although one of the lieutenants and several men were killed in the skirmish, and a number more were wounded, though not severely, the old battery commanded the mountain-side, and its skilful gunners swept it at every point the foot of man could scale. The sun went down flinging his last flame on a victorious battery still crowning the mountain pass. The dead were buried by night in a corner of the little plateau, borne to their last bivouac on the old gun-carriages which they had stood by so often—which the men said would ''sort of ease their minds.''

The next day the fight was renewed, and with the same result. The old battery in its position was unconquerable. Only one fear now faced them; their ammunition was getting as low as their rations; another such day or half-day would exhaust it. A sergeant was sent back down the mountain to try to get more, or, if not, to get tidings. The next day it was supposed the fight would be renewed; and the men waited, alert, eager, vigilant, their spirits high, their appetite for victory whetted by success. The men were at their breakfast, or what went for breakfast, scanty at all times, now doubly so, hardly deserving the title of a meal, so poor and small were the portions of cornmeal, cooked in their frying-pans, which went for their rations, when the sound of artillery below broke on the quiet air. They were on their feet in an instant and at the guns, crowding upon the breastwork to look or to listen; for the road, as far as could be seen down the mountain, was empty except for their own picket, and lay as quiet as if sleeping in the balmy air. And yet volley after volley of artillery came rolling up the mountain. What could it mean? That the rest of their force had come up and was engaged with that at the foot of the mountain? The Colonel decided to be ready to go and help them; to fall on the enemy in the rear; perhaps they might capture the entire force. It seemed the natural thing to do, and the guns were limbered up in an incredibly short time, and a roadway made through the intrenchment, the men working like beavers under the excitement. Before they had left the redoubt, however, the vedettes sent out returned and reported that there was no engagement going on, and the firing below seemed to be only practising. There was quite a stir in the camp below; but they had not even broken camp. This was mysterious. Perhaps it meant that they had received reinforcements, but it was a queer way of showing it. The old Colonel sighed as he thought of the good ammunition they could throw away down there, and of his empty limber-chests. It was necessary to be on the alert, however; the guns were run back into their old places, and the horses picketed once more back among the trees. Meantime he sent another messenger back, this time a courier, for he had but one commissioned officer left, and the picket below was strengthened.

The morning passed and no one came; the day wore on and still no advance was made by the force below. It was suggested that the enemy had left; he had, at least, gotten enough of that battery. A reconnoissance, however, showed that he was still encamped at the foot of the mountain. It was conjectured that he was trying to find a way around to take them in the rear, or to cross the ridge by the footpath. Preparation was made to guard more closely the mountain-path across the spur, and a detachment was sent up to strengthen the picket there. The waiting told on the men and they grew bored and restless. They gathered about the guns in groups and talked; talked of each piece some, but not with the old spirit and vim; the loneliness of the mountain seemed to oppress them; the mountains stretching up so brown and gray on one side of them, and so brown and gray on the other, with their bare, dark forests soughing from time to time as the wind swept up the pass. The minds of the men seemed to go back to the time when they were not so alone, but were part of a great and busy army, and some of them fell to talking of the past, and the battles they had figured in, and of the comrades they had lost. They told them off in a slow and colorless way, as if it were all part of the past as much as the dead they named. One hundred and nineteen times they had been in action. Only seventeen men were left of the eighty odd who had first enlisted in the battery, and of these four were at home crippled for life. Two of the oldest men had been among the half-dozen who had fallen in the skirmish just the day before. It looked tolerably hard to be killed that way after passing for four years through such battles as they had been in; and both had wives and children at home, too, and not a cent to leave them to their names. They agreed calmly that they'd have to "sort of look after them a little" if they ever got home. These were some of the things they talked about as they pulled their old worn coats about them, stuffed their thin, weather-stained hands in their ragged pockets to warm them, and squatted down under the breastwork to keep a little out of the wind. One thing they talked about a good deal was something to eat. They described meals they had had at one time or another as personal adventures, and discussed the chances of securing others in the future as if they were prizes of fortune. One listening and seeing their thin, worn faces and their wasted frames might have supposed they were starving, and they were, but they did not say so.

Towards the middle of the afternoon there was a sudden excitement in the camp. A dozen men saw them at the same time: a squad of three men down the road at the farthest turn, past their picket, but an advancing column could not have created as much excitement, for the middle man carried a white flag. In a minute every man in the battery was on the breastwork. What could it mean! It was a long way off, nearly half a mile, and the flag was small: possibly only a pocket-handkerchief or a napkin; but it was held aloft as a flag unmistakably. A hundred conjectures were indulged in. Was it a summons to surrender? A request for an armistice for some purpose? Or was it a trick to ascertain their number and position? Some held one view, some another. Some extreme ones thought a shot ought to be fired over them to warn them not to come on; no flags of truce were wanted. The old Colonel, who had walked to the edge of the plateau outside the redoubt and taken his position where he could study the advancing figures with his field-glass, had not spoken. The lieutenant who was next in command to him had walked out after him, and stood near him, from time to time dropping a word or two of conjecture in a half-audible tone; but the Colonel had not answered a word; perhaps none was expected. Suddenly he took his glass down, and gave an order to the lieutenant: "Take two men and meet them at the turn yonder; learn their business; and act as your best judgment advises. If necessary to bring the messenger farther, bring only the officer who has the flag, and halt him at that rock yonder, where I will join him." The tone was as placid as if such an occurrence came every day. Two minutes later the lieutenant was on his way down the mountain and the Colonel had the men in ranks. His face was as grave and his manner as quiet as usual, neither more nor less so. The men were in a state of suppressed excitement. Having put them in charge of the second sergeant the Colonel returned to the breastwork. The two officers were slowly ascending the hill, side by side, the bearer of the flag, now easily distinguishable in his jaunty uniform as a captain of cavalry, talking, and the lieutenant in faded gray, faced with yet more faded red, walking beside him with a face white even at that distance, and lips shut as though they would never open again. They halted at the big bowlder which the Colonel had indicated, and the lieutenant, having saluted ceremoniously, turned to come up to the camp; the Colonel, however, went down to meet him. The two men met, but there was no spoken question; if the Colonel inquired it was only with the eyes. The lieutenant spoke, however. "He says," he began and stopped, then began again—"he says, General Lee—" again he choked, then blurted out, "I believe it is all a lie—a damned lie."

"Not dead? Not killed?" said the Colonel, quickly.

"No, not as bad as that; surrendered: surrendered his entire army at Appomattox day before yesterday. I believe it is all a damned lie," he broke out again, as if the hot denial relieved him. The Colonel simply turned away his face and stepped a pace or two off, and the two men stood motionless back to back for more than a minute. Then the Colonel stirred.

"Shall I go back with you?" the lieutenant asked, huskily.

The Colonel did not answer immediately. Then he said: "No, go back to camp and await my return." He said nothing about not speaking of the report. He knew it was not needed. Then he went down the hill slowly alone, while the lieutenant went up to the camp.

The interview between the two officers beside the bowlder was not a long one. It consisted of a brief statement by the Federal envoy of the fact of Lee's surrender two days before near Appomattox Court-House, with the sources of his information, coupled with a formal demand on the Colonel for his surrender. To this the Colonel replied that he had been detached and put under command of another officer for a specific purpose, and that his orders were to hold that pass, which he should do until he was instructed otherwise by his superior in command. With that they parted, ceremoniously, the Federal captain returning to where he had left his horse in charge of his companions a little below, and the old Colonel coming slowly up the hill to camp. The men were at once set to work to meet any attack which might be made. They knew that the message was of grave import, but not of how grave. They thought it meant that another attack would be made immediately, and they sprang to their work with renewed vigor, and a zeal as fresh as if it were but the beginning and not the end.

The time wore on, however, and there was no demonstration

below, though hour after hour it was expected and even hoped for. Just as the sun sank into a bed of blue cloud a horseman was seen coming up the darkened mountain from the eastward side, and in a little while practised eyes reported him one of their own men—the sergeant who had been sent back the day before for ammunition. He was alone, and had something white before him on his horse—it could not be the ammunition; but perhaps that might be coming on behind. Every step of his jaded horse was anxiously watched. As he drew near, the lieutenant, after a word with the Colonel, walked down to meet him, and there was a short colloquy in the muddy road; then they came back together and slowly entered the camp, the sergeant handing down a bag of corn which he had got somewhere below, with the grim remark to his comrades, "There's your rations," and going at once to the Colonel's camp-fire, a little to one side among the trees, where the Colonel awaited him. A long conference was held, and then the sergeant left to take his luck with his mess, who were already parching the corn he had brought for their supper, while the lieutenant made the round of the camp; leaving the Colonel seated alone on a log by his camp-fire. He sat without moving, hardly stirring until the lieutenant returned from his round. A minute later the men were called from the guns and made to fall into line. They were silent, tremulous with suppressed excitement; the most sun-burned and weather-stained of them a little pale; the meanest, raggedest, and most insignificant not unimpressive in the deep and solemn silence with which they stood, their eyes fastened on the Colonel, waiting for him to speak. He stepped out in front of them, slowly ran his eye along the irregular line, up and down, taking in every man in his glance, resting on some longer than on others, the older men, then dropped them to the ground, and then suddenly, as if with an effort, began to speak. His voice had a somewhat metallic sound, as if it were restrained; but it was otherwise the ordinary tone of command. It was not much that he said; simply that it had become his duty to acquaint them with the information whch he had received: that General Lee had surrendered two days before at Appomattox Court-House, yielding to overwhelming numbers; that this afternoon when he had first heard the report he had questioned its truth, but that it had been confirmed by one of their own men, and no longer admitted of doubt; that the rest of their own force, it was learned, had been captured, or had disbanded, and the enemy was now on both sides of the mountain; that a demand had been made on him that morning to surrender too; but that he had orders which he felt held good until they were countermanded, and he had declined. Later intelligence satisfied him that to attempt to hold out further would be useless, and would involve needless waste of life; he had determined, therefore, not to attempt to hold their position longer; but to lead them out, if possible, so as to avoid being made prisoners and enable them to reach home sooner and aid their families. His orders were not to let his guns fall into the enemy's hands, and he should take the only step possible to prevent it. In fifty minutes he should call the battery into line once more, and roll the guns over the cliff into the river, and immediately afterwards, leaving the wagons there, he would try to lead them across the mountain, and as far as they could go in a body without being liable to capture, and then he should disband them, and his responsibility for them would end. As it was necessary to make some preparations he would now dismiss them to prepare any rations they might have and get ready to march.

All this was in the formal manner of a common order of the day; and the old Colonel had spoken in measured sentences, with little feeling in his voice. Not a man in the line had uttered a word after the first sound, half exclamation, half groan, which had burst from them at the announcement of Lee's surrender. After that they had stood in their tracks like rooted trees, as motionless as those on the mountain behind them, their eyes fixed on their commander, and only the quick heaving up and down the dark line, as of horses over-laboring, told of the emotion which was shaking them. The Colonel, as he ended, half-turned to his subordinate officer at the end of the dim line, as though he were about to turn the company over to him to be dismissed; then faced the line again, and taking a step nearer, with a sudden movement of his hands towards the men as though he would have stretched them out to them, began again:

"Men," he said, and his voice changed at the word, and sounded like a father's or a brother's, "My men, I cannot let you go so. We were neighbors when the war began—many of us, and some not here to-night; we have been more since then—comrades, brothers in arms; we have all stood for one thing—for Virginia and the South; we have all done our duty—tried to do our duty; we have fought a good fight, and now it seems to be over, and we have been overwhelmed by numbers, not whipped—and we are going home. We have the future before us—we don't know just what it will bring, but we can stand a good deal. We have proved it. Upon us depends the South in the future as in the past. You have done your duty in the past, you will not fail in the future. Go home and be honest, brave, self-sacrificing, God-fearing citizens, as you have been soldiers, and you need not fear for Virginia and the South. The war may be over; but you will ever be ready to serve your country. The end may not be as we wanted it, prayed for it, fought for it; but we can trust God; the end in the end will be the best that could be; even if the South is not free she will be better and stronger that she fought as she did. Go home and bring up your children to love her, and though you may have nothing else to leave them, you can leave them the heritage that they are sons of men who were in Lee's army.''

He stopped, looked up and down the ranks again, which had instinctively crowded together and drawn around him in a half-circle; made a sign to the lieutenant to take charge, and turned abruptly on his heel to walk away. But as he did so, the long pent-up emotion burst forth. With a wild cheer the men seized him, crowding around and hugging him, as with protestations, prayers, sobs, oaths—broken, incoherent, inarticulate—they swore to be faithful, to live loyal forever to the South, to him, to Lee. Many of them cried like children; others offered to go down and have one more battle on the plain. The old Colonel soothed them, and quieted their excitement, and then gave a command about the preparations to be made. This called them to order at once; and in a few minutes the camp was as orderly and quiet as usual: the fires were replenished; the scanty stores were being overhauled; the place was selected, and being got ready to roll the guns over the cliff; the camp was being ransacked for such articles as could be carried, and all preparations were being hastily made for their march.

The old Colonel having completed his arrangements sat down by his camp-fire with paper and pencil, and began to write; and as the men finished their work they gathered about in groups, at first around their campfires, but shortly strolled over to where the guns still stood at the breastwork, black and vague in the darkness. Soon they were all assembled about the guns. One after another they visited, closing around it and handling it from muzzle to trail as a man might a horse to try its sinew and bone, or a child to feel its fineness and warmth. They were for the most part silent, and when any sound came through the dusk from them to the officers at their fire, it was murmurous and fitful as of men speaking low and brokenly. There was no sound of the noisy controversy which was generally heard, the give-and-take of the camp-fire, the firing backwards and forwards that went on on the march; if a compliment was paid a gun by one of its special detachment, it was accepted by the others; in fact, those who had generally run it down now seemed most anxious to accord the piece praise. Presently a small number of the men returned to a camp-fire, and, building it up, seated themselves about it, gathering closer and closer together until they were in a little knot. One of them appeared to be writing, while two or three took up flaming chunks from the fire and held them as torches for him to see by. In time the entire company assembled about them, standing in respectful silence, broken only occasionally by a reply from one or another to some question from the scribe. After a little there was a sound of a roll-call, and reading and a short colloquy followed, and then two men, one with a paper in his hand, approached the fire beside which the officers sat still engaged.

"What is it, Harris?" said the Colonel to the man with the paper, who bore remnants of the chevrons of a sergeant on his stained and faded jacket.

"If you please, sir," he said, with a salute, "we have been talking it over, and we'd like this paper to go in along with that you're writing." He held it out to the lieutenant, who was the nearer and had reached forward to take it. "We s'pose you're agoin' to bury it with the guns," he said, hesitatingly, as he handed it over.

"What is it?" asked the Colonel, shading his eyes with his hands.

"It's just a little list we made out in and among us," he said, "with a few things we'd like to put in, so's if anyone ever hauls 'em out they'll find it there to tell what the old battery was, and if they don't, it'll be in one of 'em down thar 'til judgment, an' it'll sort of ease our minds a bit." He stopped and waited as a man who had delivered his message. The old Colonel had risen and taken the paper, and now held it with a firm grasp, as if it might blow away with the rising wind. He did not say a word, but his hand shook a little as he proceeded to fold it carefully, and there was a burning gleam in his deep-set eyes, back under his bushy, gray brows.

"Will you sort of look over it, sir, if you think it's worth while? We was in a sort of hurry and we had to put it down just as we come to it; we didn't have time to pick our ammunition; and it ain't written the best in the world, nohow." He waited again, and the Colonel opened the paper and glanced down at it mechanically. It contained first a roster, headed by the list of six guns, named by name: "Matthew," "Mark," "Luke," and "John," "The Eagle," and "The Cat"; then of the men, beginning with the heading:

THOSE KILLED.

Then had followed "Those wounded," but this was marked out. Then came a roster of the company when it first entered service; then of those who had joined afterward; then of those who were present now. At the end of all there was this statement, not very well written, nor wholly accurately spelt:

"To Whom it may Concern: We, the above members of the old battery known, etc., of six guns, named, etc., commanded by the said Col. etc., left on the 11th day of April, 1865, have made out this roll of the battery, them as is gone and them as is left, to bury with the guns which the same we bury this night. We're all volunteers, every man; we joined the army at the beginning of the war, and we've stuck through to the end; sometimes we aint had much to eat, and sometimes we aint had nothin', but we've fought the best we could 119 battles and skirmishes as near as we can make out in four years, and never lost a gun. Now we're agoin' home. We aint surrendered; just disbanded, and we pledges ourselves to teach our children to love the South and General Lee; and to come when we're called anywheres an' anytime, so help us God."

There was a dead silence whilst the Colonel read.

"Taint entirely accurite, sir, in one particular," said the sergeant, apologetically; "but we thought it would be playin' it sort o' low down on the Cat if we was to say we lost her unless we could tell about gittin' of her back, and the way she done since, and we didn't have time to do all that." He looked around as if to receive the corroboration of the other men, which they signified by nods and shuffling.

The Colonel said it was all right, and the paper should go into the guns.

"If you please, sir, the guns are all loaded," said the sergeant; "in and about our last charge, too; and we'd like to fire 'em off once more, jist for old times' sake to remember 'em by, if you don't think no harm could come of it?"

The Colonel reflected a moment and said it might be done; they might fire each gun separately as they rolled it over, or might get all ready and fire together, and then roll them over, whichever they wished. This was satisfactory.

The men were then ordered to prepare to march immediately, and withdrew for the purpose. The pickets were called in. In a short time they were ready, horses and all, just as they would have been to march ordinarily, except that the wagons and caissons were packed over in one corner by the camp with the harness hung on poles beside them, and the guns stood in their old places at the breastwork ready to defend the pass. The embers of the sinking campfires threw a faint light on them standing so still and silent. The old Colonel took his place, and at a command from him in a somewhat low voice, the men, except a detail left to hold the horses, moved into company-front facing the guns. Not a word was spoken, except the words of command. At the order each detachment went to its gun; the guns were run back and the men with their own hands ran them up on the edge of the perpendicular bluff above the river, where, sheer below, its waters washed its base, as if to face an enemy on the black mountain the other side. The pieces stood ranged in the order in which they had so often stood in battle, and the gray, thin fog rising slowly and silently from the river deep down between the cliffs, and wreathing the mountain-side above, might have been the smoke from some unearthly battle fought in the dim pass by ghostly guns, yet posted there in the darkness, manned by phantom gunners, while phantom horses stood behind, lit vaguely up by phantom camp-fires. At the given word the laniards were pulled together, and together as one the six black guns, belching flame and lead, roared their last challenge on the misty night, sending a deadly hail of shot and shell, tearing the trees and splintering the rocks of the farther side, and sending the thunder reverberating through the pass and down the mountain, startling from its slumber the sleeping camp on the hills below, and driving the browsing deer and the prowling mountain-fox in terror up the mountain.

There was silence among the men about the guns for one brief instant and then such a cheer burst forth as had never broken from them in battle: cheer on cheer, the long, wild, old familiar rebel yell for the guns they had fought with and loved.

The noise had not died away and the men behind were still trying to quiet the frightened horses when the sergeant, the same who had written, received from the hand of the Colonel a long package or roll which contained the records of the battery furnished by the men and by the Colonel himself, securely wrapped to make them water-tight, and it was rammed down the yet warm throat of the nearest gun: the Cat, and then the gun was tamped to the muzzle to make her water-tight, and, like her sisters, was spiked, and her vent tamped tight. All this took but a minute, and the next instant the guns were run up once more to the edge of the cliff; and the men stood by them with their hands still on them. A deadly silence fell on the men, and even the horses behind seemed to feel the spell. There was a long pause, in which not a breath was heard from any man, and the soughing of the tree-tops above and the rushing of the rapids below were the only sounds. They seemed to come from far, very far away. Then the Colonel said, quietly, "Let them go, and God be our helper, Amen." There was the noise in the darkness of trampling and scraping on the cliff-top for a second; the sound as of men straining hard together, and then with a pant it ceased all at once, and the men held their breath to hear. One second of utter silence; then one prolonged, deep, resounding splash sending up a great mass of white foam as the brass-pieces together plunged into the dark water below, and then the soughing of the trees and the murmur of the river came again with painful distinctness. It was full ten minutes before the Colonel spoke, though there were other sounds enough in the darkness, and some of the men, as the dark, outstretched bodies showed, were lying on the ground flat on their faces. Then the Colonel gave the command to fall in in the same quiet, grave tone he had used all night. The line fell in, the men getting to their horses and mounting in silence; the Colonel put himself at their head and gave the order of march, and the dark line turned in the darkness, crossed the little plateau between the smouldering camp-fires and the spectral caissons with the harness hanging beside them, and slowly entered the dim charcoal-burner's track. Not a word was spoken as they moved off. They might all have been phantoms. Only, the sergeant in the rear, as he crossed the little breastwork which ran along the upper side and marked the boundary of the little camp, half turned and glanced at the dying fires, the low, newly made mounds in the corner, the abandoned caissons, and the empty redoubt, and said, slowly, in a low voice to himself,

"Well, by God!"

# AMBROSE BIERCE

## *An Occurence at Owl Creek Bridge*

A MAN STOOD upon a railroad bridge in northern Alabama, looking down into the swift water twenty feet below. The man's hands were behind his back, the wrists bound with a cord. A rope closely encircled his neck. It was attached to a stout cross-timber above his head and the slack fell to the level of his knees. Some loose boards laid upon the sleepers supporting the metals of the railway supplied a footing for him and his executioners—two private soldiers of the Federal army, directed by a sergeant who in civil life may have been a deputy sheriff. At a short remove upon the same temporary platform was an officer in the uniform of his rank, armed. He was a captain. A sentinel at each end of the bridge stood with his rifle in the position known as "support," that is to say, vertical in front of the left shoulder, the hammer resting on the forearm thrown straight across the chest—a formal and unnatural position, enforcing an erect carriage of the body. It did not appear to be the duty of these two men to know what was occurring at the centre of the bridge; they merely blockaded the two ends of the foot planking that traversed it.

Beyond one of the sentinels nobody was in sight; the railroad ran straight away into a forest for a hundred yards, then, curving, was lost to view. Doubtless there was an outpost farther along. The other bank of the stream was open ground—a gentle activity topped with a stockade of vertical tree trunks, loop-holed for rifles, with a single embrasure through which protruded the muzzle of a brass cannon commanding the bridge. Midway of the slope between bridge and fort were the spectators—a single company of infantry in line, at "parade rest," the butts of the rifles on the ground, the barrels inclining slightly backward against the right shoulder, the hands crossed upon the stock. A lieutenant stood at the right of the line, the point of his sword upon the ground, his left hand resting upon his right. Excepting the group of four at the centre of the bridge, not a man moved. The

343

company faced the bridge, staring stonily, motionless. The sentinels, facing the banks of the stream, might have been statues to adorn the bridge. The captain stood with folded arms, silent, observing, the work of his subordinates, but making no sign. Death is a dignitary who when he comes announced is to be received with formal manifestations of respect, even by those most familiar with him. In the code of military etiquette silence and fixity are forms of deference.

The man who was engaged in being hanged was apparently about thirty-five years of age. He was a civilian, if one might judge from his habit, which was that of a planter. His features were good—a straight nose, firm mouth, broad forehead, from which his long, dark hair was combed straight back, falling behind his ears to the collar of his well-fitting frock coat. He wore a mustache and pointed beard, but no whiskers; his eyes were large and dark gray, and had a kindly expression which one would hardly have expected in one whose neck was in the hemp. Evidently this was no vulgar assassin. The liberal military code makes provision for hanging many kinds of persons, and gentlemen are not excluded.

The preparations being complete, the two private soldiers stepped aside and each drew away the plank upon which he had been standing. The sergeant turned to the captain, saluted and placed himself immediately behind that officer, who in turn moved apart one pace. These movements left the condemned man and the sergeant standing on the two ends of the same plank, which spanned three of the cross-ties of the bridge. The end upon which the civilian stood almost, but not quite, reached a fourth. This plank had been held in place by the weight of the captain; it was now held by that of the sergeant. At a signal from the former the latter would step aside, the plank would tilt and the condemned man go down between two ties. The arrangement commended itself to his judgment as simple and effective. His face had not been covered nor his eyes bandaged. He looked a moment at his "unsteadfast footing," then let his gaze wander to the swirling water of the stream racing madly beneath his feet. A piece of dancing driftwood caught his attention and his eyes followed it down the current. How slowly it appeared to move! What a sluggish stream!

He closed his eyes in order to fix his last thoughts upon his wife and children. The water, touched to gold by the early sun, the brooding mists under the banks at some distance down the stream, the fort, the soldiers, the piece of drift—all had distracted him. And now he became conscious of a new disturbance. Striking through the thought of his dear ones was a sound which he could neither ignore nor understand, a sharp, distinct, metallic percussion like the stroke of a blacksmith's hammer upon the anvil; it had the same ringing quality. He wondered what it was, and whether immeasurably distant or nearby—it seemed both. Its recurrence was regular, but as slow as the tolling of a death knell. He awaited each stroke with impatience and—he knew not why—apprehension. The intervals of silence grew progressively longer; the delays became maddening. With their greater infrequency the sounds increased in strength and sharpness. They hurt his ear like the thrust of a knife; he feared he would shriek. What he heard was the ticking of his watch.

He unclosed his eyes and saw again the water below him. "If I could free my hands," he thought, "I might throw off the noose and spring into the stream. By diving I could evade the bullets and, swimming vigorously, reach the bank, take to the woods and get away home. My home, thank God, is as yet outside their lines; my wife and little ones are still beyond the invader's farthest advance."

As these thoughts, which have here to be set down in words, were flashed into the doomed man's brain rather than evolved from it the captain nodded to the sergeant. The sergeant stepped aside.

## 2

PEYTON FARQUHAR was a well-to-do planter, of an old and highly respected Alabama family. Being a slave owner and like other slave owners a politician he was naturally an original secessionist and ardently devoted to the Southern cause. Circumstances of an imperious nature, which it is unnecessary to relate here, had prevented him from taking service with the gallant army that had fought the disastrous campaigns ending with the fall of Corinth, and he chafed under the inglorious restraint, longing for the release of his energies, the larger life of the soldier, the opportunity for distinction. That opportunity, he felt, would come, as it comes to all in war time. Meanwhile he did what he could. No service was too humble for him to perform in aid of the South, no adventure too perilous for him to undertake if consistent with the character of a civilian who was at heart a soldier, and who in good faith and without too much qualification assented to at least a part of the frankly villainous dictum that all is fair in love and war.

One evening while Farquhar and his wife were sitting on a rustic bench near the entrance to his grounds, a gray-clad soldier rode up to the gate and asked for a drink of water. Mrs. Farquhar was only too happy to serve him with her own white hands. While she was fetching the water her husband approached the dusty horseman and inquired eagerly for news from the front.

"The Yanks are repairing the railroads," said the man, "and are getting ready for another advance. They have reached the Owl Creek bridge, put it in order and built a stockade on the north bank. The commandant has issued an order, which is posted everywhere, declaring that any civilian caught interfering with the railroad, its bridges, tunnels or trains will be summarily hanged. I saw the order."

"How far is it to the Owl Creek bridge?" Farquhar asked.

"About thirty miles."

"Is there no force on this side the creek?"

"Only a picket post half a mile out, on the railroad, and a single sentinel at this end of the bridge."

"Suppose a man—a civilian and student of hanging—should elude the picket post and perhaps get the better of the sentinel," said Farquhar, smiling, "what could he accomplish?"

The soldier reflected. "I was there a month ago," he replied. "I observed that the flood of last winter had lodged a great quantity of driftwood against the wooden pier at this end of the bridge. It is now dry and would burn like tow."

The lady had now brought the water, which the soldier drank. He thanked her ceremoniously, bowed to her husband and rode away. An hour later, after nightfall, he repassed the plantation, going northward in the direction from which he had come. He was a Federal scout.

# 3

As PEYTON FARQUHAR fell straight downward through the bridge he lost consciousness and was as one already dead. From this state he was awakened—ages later, it seemed to him—by the pain of a sharp pressure upon his throat, followed by a sense of suffocation. Keen, poignant agonies seemed to shoot from his neck downward through every fibre of his body and limbs. These pains appeared to flash along well-defined lines of ramification and to beat with an inconceivably rapid periodicity. They seemed like streams of pulsating fire heating him to an intolerable temperature. As to his head, he was conscious of nothing but a feeling of fulness—of congestion. These sensations were unaccompanied by thought. The intellectual part of his nature was already effaced; he had power only to feel, and feeling was torment. He was conscious of motion. Encompassed in a luminous cloud, of which he was now merely the fiery heart, without material substance, he swung through unthinkable arcs of oscillation, like a vast pendulum. Then all at once, with terrible suddenness, the light about him shot upward with the noise of a loud plash; a frightful roaring was in his ears, and all was cold and dark. The power of thought was restored; he knew that the rope had broken and he had fallen into the stream. There was no additional strangulation; the noose about his neck was already suffocating him and kept the water from his lungs. To die of hanging at the bottom of a river!—the idea seemed to him ludicrous. He opened his eyes in the darkness and saw above him a gleam of light, but how distant, how inaccessible! He was still sinking, for the light became fainter and fainter until it was a mere glimmer. Then it began to grow and brighten, and he knew that he was rising toward the surface—knew it with reluctance, for he was now very comfortable. "To be hanged and drowned," he thought, "that is not so bad; but I do not wish to be shot. No; I will not be shot; that is not fair."

He was not conscious of an effort, but a sharp pain in his wrist apprised him that he was trying to free his hands. He gave the struggle his attention, as an idler might observe the feat of a juggler, without interest in the outcome. What splendid effort!—what magnificent, what superhuman strength! Ah, that was a fine endeavor! Bravo! The cord fell away; his arms parted and floated upward, the hands dimly seen on each side in the growing light. He watched them with a new interest as first one and then the other pounced upon the noose at his neck. They tore it away and thrust it fiercely aside, its undulations resembling those of a water-snake. "Put it back, put it back!" He thought he shouted these words to his hands, for the undoing of the noose had been succeeded by the direst pang that he had yet experienced. His neck ached horribly; his brain was on fire; his heart, which had been fluttering faintly, gave a great leap, trying to force itself out at his mouth. His whole body was racked and wrenched with an insupportable anguish! But his disobedient hands gave no heed to the command. They beat the water vigorously with quick, downward strokes, forcing him to the surface. He felt his head emerge; his eyes were blinded by the sunlight; his chest expanded convulsively, and with a supreme and crowning agony his lungs engulfed a great draught of air, which instantly he expelled in a shriek!

He was now in full possession of his physical senses. They were, indeed, preternaturally keen and alert. Something in the awful disturbance of his organic system had so exalted and refined them that they made record of things never before perceived. He felt the ripples upon his face and heard their separate sounds as they struck. He looked at the forest on the bank of the stream, saw the individual trees, the leaves and the veining of each leaf—saw the very insects upon them: the locusts, the brilliant-bodied flies, the gray spiders stretching their webs from twig to twig. He noted the prismatic colors in all the dewdrops upon a million blades of grass. The humming of the gnats that danced above the eddies of the stream, the beating of the dragon-flies' wings, the strokes of the water-spiders' legs, like oars which had lifted their boat—all these made audible music. A fish slid along beneath his eyes and he heard the rush of its body parting the water.

He had come to the surface facing down the stream; in a moment the visible world seemed to wheel slowly round, himself the pivotal point, and he saw the bridge, the fort, the soldiers upon the bridge, the captain, the sergeant, the two privates, his executioners. They were in silhouette against the blue sky. They shouted and gesticulated, pointing at him. The captain had drawn his pistol, but did not fire; the others were unarmed. Their movements were grotesque and horrible, their forms gigantic.

Suddenly he heard a sharp report and something struck the water smartly within a few inches of his head, spattering his face with spray. He heard a second report, and saw one of the sentinels with his rifle at his shoulder, a light cloud of blue smoke rising from the muzzle. The man in the water saw the eye of the man on the bridge gazing into his own through the sights of the rifle. He observed that it was a gray eye and remembered having read that gray eyes were keenest, and that all famous marksmen had them. Nevertheless, this one had missed.

A counter-swirl had caught Farquhar and turned him half round; he was again looking into the forest on the bank opposite the fort. The sound of a clear, high voice in a monotonous singsong now rang out behind him and came across the water with a distinctness that pierced and subdued all other sounds, even the beating of the ripples in his ears. Although no soldier, he had frequented camps enough to know the dread significance of that deliberate, drawling, aspirated chant; the lieutenant on shore was taking a part in the morning's work. How coldly and pitilessly—with what an even, calm intonation, presaging, and enforcing tranquillity in the men—with what accurately measured intervals fell those cruel words:

"Attention, company! . . . Shoulder arms! . . . Ready! . . . Aim! . . . Fire!"

Farquhar dived—dived as deeply as he could. The water roared in his ears like the voice of Niagara, yet he heard the dulled thunder of the volley and, rising again toward the surface, met shining bits of metal, singularly flattened, oscillating slowly downward. Some of them touched him on the face and hands, then fell away, continuing their descent. One lodged between his collar and neck; it was uncomfortably warm and he snatched it out.

As he rose to the surface, gasping for breath, he saw that he had been a long time under water; he was perceptibly farther down stream—nearer to safety. The soldiers had almost finished reloading; the metal ramrods flashed all at once in the sunshine as they were drawn from the barrels, turned in the air, and thrust into their sockets. The two sentinels fired again, independently and ineffectually.

The hunted man saw all this over his shoulder; he was now swimming vigorously with the current. His brain was as energetic as his arms and legs; he thought with the rapidity of lightning.

"The officer," he reasoned, "will not make that martinet's error a second time. It is as easy to dodge a volley as a single shot. He has probably already given the command to fire at will. God help me, I cannot dodge them all!"

An appalling plash within two yards of him was followed by a loud, rushing sound, *diminuendo*, which seemed to travel back through the air to the fort and died in an explosion which stirred the very river to its deeps! A rising sheet of water curved over him, fell down upon him, blinded him, strangled him! The cannon had taken a hand in the game. As he shook his head free from the commotion of the smitten water he heard the deflected shot humming through the air ahead, and in an instant it was cracking and smashing the branches in the forest beyond.

"They will not do that again," he thought; "the next time they will use a charge of grape. I must keep my eye upon the gun; the smoke will apprise me—the report arrives too late; it lags behind the missile. That is a good gun.''

Suddenly he felt himself whirled round and round—spinning like a top. The water, the banks, the forests, the now distant bridge, fort and men—all were commingled and blurred. Objects were represented by their colors only; circular horizontal streaks of color—that was all he saw. He had been caught in a vortex and was being whirled on with a velocity of advance and gyration that made him giddy and sick. In a few moments he was flung upon the gravel at the foot of the left bank of the stream—the southern bank—and behind a projecting point which concealed him from his enemies. The sudden arrest of his motion, the abrasion of one of his hands on the gravel, restored him, and he wept with delight. He dug his fingers into the sand, threw it over himself in handfuls and audibly blessed it. It looked like diamonds, rubies, emeralds; he could think of nothing beautiful which it did not resemble. The trees upon the bank were giant garden plants; he noted a definite order in their arrangement, inhaled the fragrance of their blooms. A strange, roseate light shone through the spaces among their trunks and the wind made in their branches the music of aeolian harps. He had no wish to perfect his escape—was content to remain in that enchanting spot until retaken.

A whiz and rattle of grapeshot among the branches high above his head roused him from his dream. The baffled cannoneer had fired him a ramdon farewell. He sprang to his feet, rushed up the sloping bank, and plunged into the forest.

All that day he traveled, laying his course by the rounding sun. The forest seemed interminable; nowhere did he discover a break in it, not even a woodman's road. He had not known that he lived in so wild a region. There was something uncanny in the revelation.

By nightfall, he was fatigued, footsore, famishing. The thought of his wife and children urged him on. At last he found a road which led him in what he knew to be the right direction. It was as wide and straight as a city street, yet it seemed untraveled. No fields bordered it, no dwelling anywhere. Not so much as the barking of a dog suggested human habitation. The black bodies of the trees formed a straight wall on both sides, terminating on the horizon in a point, like a diagram in a lesson in perspective. Overhead, as he looked up through this rift in the wood, shone great golden stars looking unfamiliar and grouped in strange constellations. He was sure they were arranged in some order which had a secret and malign significance. The wood on either side was full of singular noises, among which—once, twice, and again—he distinctly heard whispers in an unknown tongue.

His neck was in pain and lifting his hand to it he found it horribly swollen. He knew that it had a circle of black where the rope had bruised it. His eyes felt congested; he could no longer close them. His tongue was swollen with thirst; he relieved its fever by thrusting it forward from between his teeth into the cold air. How softly the turf had carpeted the untraveled avenue—he could no longer feel the roadway beneath his feet!

Doubtless, despite his suffering, he had fallen asleep while walking, for now he sees another scene—perhaps he has merely recovered from a delirium. He stands at the gate of his own home. All is as he left it, and all bright and beautiful in the morning sunshine. He must have traveled the entire night. As he pushes open the gate and passes up the wide white walk, he sees a flutter of female garments; his wife, looking fresh and cool and sweet, steps down from the veranda to meet him. At the bottom of the steps she stands waiting, with a smile of ineffable joy, an attitude of matchless grace and dignity. Ah, how beautiful she is! He springs forward with extended arms. As he is about to clasp her he feels a stunning blow upon the back of the neck; a blinding white light blazes all about him with a sound like the shock of a cannon—then all is darkness and silence!

Peyton Farquhar was dead; his body, with a broken neck, swung gently from side to side beneath the timbers of the Owl Creek bridge.

# JAMES WARNER BELLAH
## *How Stonewall Came Back*

IT WAS TOWARD THE last of that second April that Roan Catlett began to ride in the shadow of black doubt. The bright Manassas fight of the summer had tarnished dull under the slow months of falling back to the Rappahannock. In the Shenandoah Valley, Jackson, heavily outnumbered, played fox most of the time, but all the time he'd given ground. From the Potomac patrols, he'd been pushed south to Winchester, only to give up Winchester and pull farther south. With only Ashby's scattered cavalry actions pressuring back on the Northern pursuit and the eternal sharp picket brawls, to give the feeling of any fight left in it at all. Once there had been that brilliant countermarch back to Winchester, for the Kernstown Fight. Thirty-six muddy miles of marching back—for a three-hour slug fight and out south once more, proud, but licked again!

The sawdust runs out of a man and he becomes old inside, with an old man's senile fears close to his heart and an old man's tears drenching his soul. Inside, where he lived, Roan was licked. It hung on him night and morning and wouldn't lift, whatever. Too close to his personal honor to say the word, but too insistent now, to give it the lie.

That last morning in April when Gen. Turner Ashby sabered the Union cavalry back into their own camps at Harrisonburg, it came plain to Roan. There ain't no use. You could always drive them in, in small actions, but still they came acoming. From Harrisonburg north, the Valley was choked thick with Yankees. Solid blocked to the Potomac. Across the Shenandoah Mountains due west, there was Frémont's brand-new Western Army, rumored to come down through Buffalo Gap and take Staunton. Behind Roan's back, across the Blue Ridge Mountains east, there were thirty-three thousand Federals

355

pressing Fredericksburg, to close the northern door on McClellan's siege of Richmond—and if that ain't all four sides but a footpath, what is?

Ashby brought his troopers out of the woods after re-forming them and led them back down the Cross Keys Road toward Port Republic. They said Turner Ashby'd gone a little mad a year ago when they killed his brother. Said when Dick Ashby's body was lowered into the grave at Romney that Turner had snapped his brother's saber across his knee and thrown both pieces in on the casket. Said the two broken pieces striking hollow wood was worse than any curse he might have called. Strange man. Small and dark almost to a Spanish cast. Praying man. Gentle in his words and clean in talk and thought. A man'd do well not to have Ashby's hand against him.

Warm rain soaked them, running down inside, washing the body filth into their steaming boots. Roan felt it good. Miserable—but perversely good—a part of the whole damned business under the mists that hid the great hulking mountains like veils across the faces of mourning women.

*If they killed my brother Buford, I'd never let up on 'em. But I saved Bufe from it for a couple of years till he gets eighteen—and it ain't goin' to last that long. Bufe don't die trailside with the outer air blood-bubblin' through a hole in his chest, pressuring his lungs to slow strangulation. No, sir; he stays at V.M.I. down in Lexington where a drill gun in hand'll give him the feel and a uniform to his back'll lend the cockiness. When pa wrote he'd tried to leave school and enlist, I wrote it strong to Bufe, like deserting his corps. Job was plain. Study and work it out for two more years. No, sir, Bufe, a man don't run away from the job in hand. He works it out to the finish, before he takes on the next.*

Roan skinned his lips back off his teeth in violent mental satisfaction. Bufe was his—out of all the family. Bufe was his own, in some strange way it can happen. There had always been thoughts and laughter between them without words. A piece of the cosmos, divided equally. Each knowing the inner man of the other since the very beginning, when Bufe, toddling on fat uncertain legs, walked from his mother and put his chubby hand in Roan's four-year-old one. "Let go m'brother! I do his fightin' for him, 'til he grows!"

Morning of May first it was still raining. Not in drops you could see, but in heavy drenching sheets that brushed your face like gossamer wash on God's clothesline. The threadbare head of General

Jackson's column came up the Elk Run Valley out of that rain, six thousand all told, but sullen inside from retreating. Men slogging mud to the knees in places, guns bogging down to trunnions, until they were dug free. Horses' legs plastered with the drying mud on their backs corded thick like scabs over saber cuts. But the column didn't cross the Shenandoah into Port Republic town. It turned east on the Brown's Gap Road, heading for the Blue Ridge Mountains.

You couldn't believe that, when you first saw it from Ashby's bivouac. Must be one regiment turning off to secure that side of the crossing, while the rest went on into town. Only it wasn't. Regiment after regiment made the same turn east and the column didn't stop for even a breath. Mechum's Station lay that way—on the Virginia Central Rail Road—with Richmond south and east by steam car. And all the Valley left behind. Harrisonburg, Staunton, Lexington—for the Yankees to pour into if Jackson left. And Jackson was leaving.

You could see the infantry sucking the greasy mud, feel the misty mountains pawing at your shoulders, but you couldn't hear above the snarling river water, white-roaring, so that you had to shout, ''What's that?''

''The Valley jig is up! Jackson's pulling out for the last stand around Richmond. March direction don't lie. He's headin' for the rail road and it's high-low-jack and the game!''

A few minutes later Turner Ashby was crouching roadside with his map on his knee, his milk-white horse beside him, laced thick with the mud. General Ashby hated to have his horse streaked, but there wasn't time. There never was time any more. He had his orders.

He passed them. ''The main screen will be maintained on Harrisonburg,'' he said softly, ''to cover the rear of General Jackson's withdrawal. Two troops will work well over west, and north of Staunton to fend around Buffalo Gap, Lebanon Springs, McDowell and the Bull Pasture River, to feel out the advance elements of General Frémont's Shenandoah Mountain Army.'' Ashby looked up at the handful of his officers and noncoms. There was mud in his black mustache, twisted into it like pomade, but his dark eyes were as calm as if he were planning to plow his north forty, up at Rose Hill. ''Those two troops will be between two Federal armies,'' he said, ''so don't go to shooting up each other through jumpiness. The orders are to fend and scout''—Turner Ashby folded his map and stood up—''and delay fighting where you can without being sucked in and taken. Questions?''

There it was, plain. The last muddy ditch! Throw the cavalry back against them once again to hide the fact of withdrawal as long as possible. Nine hundred of Ashby's troopers against two Federal armies. Feel 'em, fool 'em, fuddle 'em, as long as could be to let Jackson get to Richmond. Stonewall's heart must be broken inside him at the orders calling him down there—and every other Valley heart with it.

Roan's troop rode west for two days. Back toward Cross Keys and down to Bridgewater. Mount Crawford and on to Stabling's Spring. He didn't want to get out of this dreadful break-up alive somehow, and yet he didn't want to die. He'd built up too much credit on the living side. Other men right and left had been killed riding with him and he had lived. To die now was like throwing in a good hand at cards. But there wouldn't be anything to live for afterwards, if you played 'em. The money wouldn't buy. You couldn't even get the last year out of mind, and with the war lost, you couldn't tolerate the awful memory. It would be like the cancerous lumps that grow inside of old folks. Can't cut them out, so they snarl their growing into vitals until the only way left is death. Death becomes academic and the values of life cease to be.

The third day, when they had a sharp skirmish along Mossy Creek with a Harrisonburg vedette, Roan fought with his whole mind and body waiting for a bullet. Hell, it couldn't be long now. There wa'n't nothing left but for it to hit him. He began to quiver in his flesh for it, like a horse twitching flies, and when the fight was done, he had a bad five or ten minutes when he thought he was going to cry—go all to pieces and whimper in his soul. He clawed his sweating face with his dirty fingers. Twisted his hands into it for control. His breath caught in silent sobs and he had no God in that moment to lean upon, because he felt unworthy to call upon Him. It was like he had really died a little bit and was halfway across. Too far to pull clear back and not far enough to go on. Awful.

The troop moved on up into North River Gap in the Shenandoahs, and Roan rode with it like a man in sick stupor. There were almost four troops in the mountains by May sixth, under Ashby's Captain Sheetz. Operating by squads and half troops, feeling out the road to Franklin for General Frémont's advance guard—fending as far north as Brock's Gap Settlement to make sure Frémont wouldn't try to come through the mountains up there to join his army with Banks' at Harrisonburg, instead of south to take undefended Staunton. Roan didn't care what happened. His heart was gone out of it.

He knew he was going home a couple of days before he went. Not deserting, for there was nothing left to desert from—just going home, like a man has to when his work's finished, win or lose. Plugging these mountains, just waiting for it, hopelessly, was fool's business now, with Jackson gone. Sure you could spot 'em first and sting 'em like always, but four troops couldn't stop Frémont. Frémont's army would pour through four troops like spring wash down the creeks and there'd be nothing left but lost hope. But today, tomorrow, there was still time and everything'd be the same at home as before—except in his mind. At least he'd have that sameness to breathe in for a spell, before it happened.

The Catlett place was about six miles from Deerfield in the Short Mountain country. Log cabin it was in Indian times long before. Then built onto as they cleared the land in his great-grandfather's time and more still in his grandfather's. When the Tidewater branch of Catletts died out, the old English furniture and the silver came over the mountains by oxcart, and some of the old Catlett pictures came with it. That was when they built the brick part of the house. Funny hodgepodge of a place really, because the Catletts never tore any of the old parts down. They just built on solidly as they lived solidly. Kept what they had and added to. The women they married did that for them—kept the blood and kept the progression.

It wasn't that Roan really wanted to go home, because he really didn't. There just wasn't anything left for him to do. It was going to hurt bad to go, because he'd have to tell his father all of it and he hated to do that. How they'd whipped the Yankees man for man and troop for troop, every time the fight was joined—and yet lost it all somehow day by day, week by week, until nothing was left now but a handful of tired and ragged cavalrymen in the mountains, between two whole Yankee armies—with Richmond ringed about and the Valley wide open. *Thy will be done—but dear God in heaven, I wish I was a little boy again with my father big to help me*.

Roan hadn't ever wanted to go home since he'd started out for Harper's Ferry last year. He seemed to have a soldier's instinct about that from the start. Turn your back on all that was before and don't come back until the fight's over or it'll weaken you somehow in your mind. It'll soften your bowels against going back to fear and sweat and killing.

He walked slowly down the Green Valley Pike, leading his tired mare, Lady, and breathing the evening air deep for the first smell of his own chimney smoke. Lady touched her velvet lips to his crusted shoulder, slobbered his upper arm and breathed down her nose in soft whispers to him. Frémont's men'd burn the houses and loot off the stuff to send north. A trooper of Ashby's they'd collar like a hoss thief, like as not hang him where they took him. But not Roan. That's what a man's last gunload is for, to shoot it out cold to them for his own kill, standing. He ground his teeth in tired and impotent rage, for all the dead men he'd buried and all the hope that had died with them, for his youth that was gone and his old age that would never sit upon him more heavily than it did this night.

Then roadside, half a dozen yards ahead to the right, a gunlock snicked open sharp. "Stand and stipulate!" Roan stopped in his tracks. It was an old man's voice, cracked slightly in the words, but not with fear—and the sound of it echoed vaguely from the past.

"Friend," Roan said, puzzling the voice.

"Friend to who?"

Roan laughed then. "Friend to Judge Manigault," he said, "and to Gin'ral Turner Ashby and Stonewall Jackson! That enough, sir? I'm Roan Catlett, judge."

"God bless m'soul, Roan"—the judge stepped out of the rhododendron. "H'are you, boy?" and with his old Lefevre rifle in his left hand, he held out his right to Roan. "Yore pappy'll shore be glad t'see you!"

"Yes, sir," Roan said. "Yore boy Forney's all right, last I saw. He's up around Harrisonburg, with Ashby himself."

"Oh, Forney'll get along," the judge snorted. "The Slow Devil's in him and the Devil always looks after his own." He swept an arm back toward the roadside and two more armed figures crawled out of the bushes. One was Tom Ruffin, the hunchback saddle maker from Deerfield, and the other was Davin Ancrum's twelve-year-old brother, Custis. They had rifles, and white kerchiefs were tied to their upper left arms.

"What is it?" Roan asked.

"Law of levée, suh," Judge Manigault said. "Legal as taxes. We heard things weren't turnin' off good just right now and that this yere fellow Frémont was on his way down yere from Franklin with a brand-new Yankee Army to join Banks. Folks don't take kindly to John C. Frémont heah-abouts, even though his wife is Senator Tom Benton's daughter, Jessie—grandniece to Governor McDowell, of Cherry Grove, just south a piece. Bad blood, suh! His mother was Miz Anne Whiting Pryor, who left her husband in Richmond and ran off to

Savannah with a schoolteacher named Frémont, his father. Major
Pryor should've shot the seducer dead, you ask me, but the major was
an old man with a shaky hand. So we aim to shoot the son, he sets foot
in our country!''

"You can't," Roan said; "a citizen fires a shot at a bluecoat,
they'll execute him out of hand.''

"No, suh.'' Judge Manigault drew himself up. "Law of *levée en
masse*, suh. All the old men left—all the boys too young to go. They
ain't firin' any lone, personal shots at Frémont. That's *franc-
tireurin'*—not legal. But *levée en masse* is legal as militia. These yere
handkerchiefs on our arms and the feathers in our caps is uniform.
Every man jack of the Short Mountain Defense Comp'ny has stood up
and sworn to obey me—a regularly sittin' magistrate of the common-
wealth of Virginia, suh. That's command. Uniform and command
make us an armed force under the law of *levée en masse*, same as the
army, suh—and as we stand—not a one of Frémont's men's goin' to
come into our mountain or our valley and live to talk about it!''

"You tell Davin you saw me, Roan,'' young Custis Ancrum said.
"You tell him pappy and me ain't goin' to let 'em burn our house and
barns!''

The tears were so thick in Roan's throat that he choked. "Well——''
he said. "Well, I reckon——''

"Git along, boy,'' Judge Manigault told him. "You'll be late
t'yore suppah.''

A mile farther down, Roan turned in the drive and led Lady straight
to the barn.

There was lantern light up there and after a moment it raised high.
"Who is it?''

Roan stopped and swallowed hard, "Roan, sir,'' and the two men
stood there, twenty yards apart across the darkness, unable to move
for a minute or to say more. What can be said, ever, between a grown
man and his father? That they both lived once, drawn close in child
love and love of child, and that the years have broken the protecting
circle so that no longer can arms fend danger or a son in manhood seek
them? Of the hour before the attack, when the need for older words
and thought becomes so vital, that it is a pain inside like unto nausea?
Or of the older man, roaming the cold house with the haunt upon him,
when the rain beats with the high wind off Short Mountain? *Take care
of yourself, Roan*—like a hoarse, demanding prayer.

Their hands came together, more to keep each from embracing the other than for any other reason, and Thomas Catlett said, "You've thickened through, Roan," and Roan said, "Reckon so," and that was awful, for there was so much more they couldn't say. "Go to your mother, boy. I'll do for the hoss," and Roan said, "Yes, sir"; then he was running blind toward the house, his boots and spurs thundering across the summer-kitchen breezeway and up the steps in back. "Mom!"

He scrubbed himself clean in the great wooden tub in the kitchen and got into clean clothing and it felt wrong on him somehow, like a popinjay strutting uniform in the Richmond Home Guard. It took him back to times before—and there never could be times before—ever again. His campaign smell was gone to his own nostrils and his honor somehow gone with it.

"What's it like, Roan? Do they give you warm food? Do you have chapel service?" The searching, homely questions of mothers, against the things they cannot know.

"Not like yore cooking, mom"—he tried to smile, but the effort twisted his mouth hard—"and not like the Revrund Kinsolving's brimstone preaching."

"What's it like, Roan?"—his sister, Emily, turned fifteen, intense and slendering tall, with burgeoning womanhood. "What's it like, Roan!"—breathless with it almost, as she held his boots, new dubbined by her own hand in fierce love for her older brother. *Tell me of the gallantry and the glory and of some young Lochinvar I cannot yet know, but who rides for me as surely as my heart beats for the sound of hoofs that will someday come. What's it like, Roan!* Her eyes were bright upon him with her delicate nostrils flared to her indrawn breath.

"Boredom mostly, Em. Hurry up—and wait. And measles." He laughed to stem the tears within, for the knowledge was full upon him that his own people were utter strangers to him this night. That what had been so close a part of him was no longer there for him to touch. The year between was like a wall between. The voices he knew so well could not probe his thinking any more. Like a man in a dream he was, who walks eternally through a blank-faced crowd, trying to ask for that which he must seek, with his voice soundless, and deaf ears turned against him.

"What's it like, Roan?" Charlie looked up at him with his chubby boy's face turning man subtly with his tenth year, his eyes wide and his jaw pushed out hard. "You kill a lot of Yankees, Roan? Tell us how!"

Edward half drew his saber and touched a thumb to the cutting edge. "Ask pop, Roan; if I can join the levée. Custis Ancrum's only seven months older than me. Ask him!" . . .

"What's it like, Roan?" That was his father, much later, when Sarah Catlett left them together with a woman's instinct for a man and his first son. It had a different sound from all the others, as if somehow Thomas Catlett knew what it was like full well, but didn't dare to do any more about it than ask. Roan stood up and walked across behind the table, wondering how to tell it; knowing he had to, but wondering how. Then he knew how the only way must be.

"I don't know about Richmond, sir, but we've lost the Valley cold. Gin'ral Jackson's had to pull out at last. Left only Ashby."

"Yes"—his father frowned slightly—"I was afraid so, from what we heard." He nodded once or twice, like a man who finally gets his thinking straight.

"They've sent us over here," Roan said, "four thin troops, to do what we can to harass Frémont joining Banks. That's the story plain"—he shook his head fiercely—"and it's no use!"

"What then, Roan?" his father asked softly.

There it was as Roan had dreaded it. He was the man bringing the news—the man with the immediate experience. He posed the problem. His, then, to make the decision, for it is too late ever to be a little boy again, once the years have passed.

"I don't know, sir," he said helplessly. "What do you think?"

"I don't know," Thomas Catlett said. "You've got older than me, somehow, Roan, since you went off with the army. You know things I don't know. Think things, I reckon, that have never been in my mind. I have never been a soldier, Roan. It is as if I were suspended somehow between Grandfather Catlett and you. Somewhere between Cowpens and Yorktown in that old war and General Jackson in this one. Looking in through a window. Not a part of it." Thomas Catlett smiled wistfully. "It is as if you were my father, in a way; not I yours."

Roan drew in a deep breath. "I'll tell you then, sir"—and the shame was full upon him, but he beat it back with the heavy hand of youth. "We must load the wagons with all we want to save, and take the family out south. Mother and Emily and the two boys."

The words were there between them, and there was no calling them back. Their echo lay in shattered pieces, jagged and ugly with destruction, and the silence that followed after was the silence of things dead.

"Out south—to where, Roan?"

"I don't know," Roan said. "All I know is that the Valley jig is up and I had to come and tell you."

The silence fell again, and it was a dreadful-sounding nothingness that hung in the old room and probed the farthest reaches of its shadows. From the walls, it came back upon them again like tide returning up the beach and held them in its cold import of finality.

"What about Buford, down at Lexington?" His father's voice was steady.

Then it was as if Roan had known all along that his father would ask that question next. As if he had been standing, braced, to meet it, but when it came he had no answer.

"How is Bufe?" he asked quickly. "Have you heard? Tell me!" Too quickly, to buy him time.

Thomas Catlett moved his eyes to look at his oldest son without moving his head. "Last week," he said, "Buford wrote you had written him about not leaving school"—and that was all Thomas Catlett said. For just a second or two his tongue sucked his lips as if he would say more, but he closed his mouth on the impulse and clasped his hands on the table edge. The words he might have said were in Roan's mind, plainer than if he had said them: *Like deserting your corps, Bufe—a man don't run away from the job in hand. He works it out to the finish before he takes on the next.* Deep anger lashed at Roan's vitals, caught as he was between necessity and the shame of meeting it. He was like a man tied up and struck, then, across the face. You couldn't tell this to Buford, for Buford couldn't know it yet for what it really was. He was like Roan had been last year—fresh in his heart for it, eager with the dreams of childhood, but with manhood bursting within him now to make those dreams come true. The trap of glory. The bone-strewn short cut that eternally weaves its bloody snare for youth.

"You know that boy better than I do, Roan," his father said. "His heart is one with your heart. Where you are is where his mind lives. What you do is what he will always try to follow. You might be twins—close in mind as some twins are. But with more than that in it, because you are older. Older enough so that all of Buford's life you will be to him what a father is for the first few years of a boy's life. His god, Roan."

Then the guilt came full upon Roan and hung in his nostrils like the stench of flesh rot. Not his own guilt alone but the guilt of despair that creeps into the souls of men as sickness will take their bodies when plague stalks the land. Rotting their minds with the mass fear that comes of doubt and question. Shriveling their hearts until they are like sheep for the driving, denying them the right to walk in forthright pride as men, destroying the heritage of God's image.

Thomas Catlett reached a steady hand and raised his brandy to his lips. He watched his son's eyes over the rim of the glass as he drank. "What were you planning—to drop by Lexington on the way? To tell Buford and take him along—on south?"

Roan stared at the older man. "I—a—"

Just then the dogs began to give voice down in the runs. Old Bess first, with her heavy bell ringing full to the night. Then the others waking and coming in on the chorus because it was Old Bess and they didn't dare not take her word for whatever stalked the darkness. Close in to the house Splinter woke and growled in his whitening muzzle, like an old man cursing for the sleep he was going to lose now. Roan stepped quickly for his hand gun, pulled it out of holster.

His father watched him for a moment, then he crossed to the door, opened it and stepped outside. Splinter was growling down by the pike now, thrashing angrily around through the brush, circling for what scent there would be to satisfy his sleepwalking. Outside with his father, the darkness seemed to bring the whole place in close on Roan. To ring him about tightly so that he couldn't move his arms. There was too much of it suddenly for one man to live in all alone. Too many people crowding close for a moment, whispering from other years long gone. Buckskin people with long rifles to hand who had known Captain Washington long before General Braddock got to know him—or My Lord Cornwallis. Steady people, forthright to God and stouthearted to living with the fundamentals deep grained in their souls. It was like they had all slowly drifted down from the burial place to stand by this night and watch the Catletts close—with the right the Catletts have to watch their own. Babies born in the old house, who had grown up to those mountains, to call the land theirs in their time—in sweat and worry and heartbreak. In joy and love and living. The gun hung heavy in Roan's hand, like someone pulling on his arm, and in that moment he knew his shame full.

"There is someone on the pike," his father said quietly. They could see old Splinter against the night sky. He had straightened out his circling and was standing braced with his ancient nose up to what wind there was. Then Old Bess in the runs must have told him, for she tore it out of her throat suddenly to shout the others down in a panic of unholy joy and Splinter took off up the road fit to tear his rheumatism out by the roots.

"Lord a'mighty!" Buford said. "Ain't it enough I got to walk all night but Judge Manigault like to shot me down the road, Splinter like to eat me up and m'own brother Roan meets me gun in hand!.... H'are you, dad?... Damn, man, I'm glad t'see you, Roan! What time is it?" And again there the three of them were as Roan and his father had been earlier, with so much to say and no words to say it with. No power to get it out of their inner thinking.

"Past eleven, Buford," Thomas Catlett said.

"Just made it," Buford snorted in disgust, "in time to turn around and mosey straight back!"

"Made it from where, Bufe?" Roan's voice was sharp.

"Staunton, Roan. Where else?"

"What the hell for Staunton!"

"Well——" Buford grinned. "The army must of done something wrong, for they sent word for the Cadet Corps to come on up from the Institute to help. We left Lexington the first of May to march up. General Smith marched us—they say to General Jackson's order. That's all I know."

"That can't be!" Roan said helplessly. "They wouldn't do that—put boys in to hold Staunton!"

"Not so much of the boy talk, Roan," Buford grinned. "They gave us men's shoes and socks down at the Deaf and Dumb Asylum where we're camped, and we're going to get real rifles to replace our smooth bores when we take off west to fight Frémont." He stood on one foot and held up the other to show the issue shoes. His cadet trousers were stuffed in mud-crusted laced leggings and his short jacket was strapped at the waist with the Institute belt—buckle turned to the rear, "Too bright for a target," he said. "Orders are to wear it in back, but polish it bright, don't fear!" and he pulled the Institute *képi* down to his eyes so's just not to hide them, in the selfsame way General Jackson had of doing, and Roan knew suddenly that every man jack of the corps was doing just that to his *képi* forty times a day, because Jackson had that habit, hoping to burr the visor with thumb and finger just as Jackson's was burred. Of such things are schoolboys made forever—and were it not so, there would be no men in the world.

"What you doin' here, Roan? They told us Ashby was screening way up in the mountains. Towards Franklin."

"That's right," Roan growled. "I—just—dropped by. Close enough to."

"Me, too," Buford said. "Got a pass 'til reveille. Reckon I should see ma? Or would it upset her—me havin' to go right back without even time for a snack?"

"Reckon you should," his father said. He stood for a moment looking full at his oldest son in what light there was, and a strange thing came to pass. Just as Thomas had felt for a brief moment that Roan was older in his mind than he was in his for this night, so now Buford, as he stood there slightly puzzled, looking from one to the other, was older than either of them, for manhood isn't years, it is heart, and if the heart be strong in youthful dreams, who shall deny that it still is heart?

"I'll go saddle Lady," Roan growled. He walked across the paddock, icy cold in his whole inner body. How could they do it? How could they order those boys up from Lexington to try to hold Staunton, when Jackson's whole army had pulled out? His fury snarled in his mind liked a treed hill cat—the numb fury a soldier lives in half his time. He cursed General Jackson with his lips drawn thin against his teeth. *They cannot have Buford, I'll go back, but they cannot have Buford.* But he knew now he was only whistling in the dark. Had been, about Bufe, from the first.

When he led Lady up to the house, his mother stood there with a handkerchief crushed tightly in her hand, but no tears. "It seems a shame," she said, "to walk so far to have to start right back! I'll give you some ham and biscuits to take. I——"

"It's only fifteen miles up and fifteen back," Buford said, "by road. Shorter the way I cut across. It's nothing—as long as I saw you for a minute. And none of you are to worry," he said solemnly, "because Frémont ain't goin' to get to pass through those mountains! Take my word for it. *Virginiae Fidem Praesto!*"

Thomas Catlett took down his squirrel rifle. "I'll walk a piece back with you both."

Then they were on the road again north. Three shadowy figures with Lady behind, following Roan close for comfort. The night damp was down full and there was still no talk in it, for there couldn't be. The thinking ran too deep for talk. Old thinking. That these three men were not themselves alone, but only a part of a long dead march behind them to bring them where they were tonight. And that ahead in the shadows of tomorrow lay the further march of their own sons. Caught between, the present tenants of the name, with the power in their hearts to add to it, but no right whatsoever to detract.

After a while Thomas Catlett stopped and pulled a white kerchief from his pocket, circling his upper left arm with it and knotting it with his teeth.

"Judge Manigault's road block is just beyond," he said. "I've got the twelve-to-daylight watch with Doctor Crosset and Senator Ancrum. Good night, boys." He held out his hand to Roan.

Roan stared at his father. "You just let me talk! You weren't goin', whatever!"

"I reckon not," his father smiled. "This Valley is mine—from way back. I wouldn't—have any other place to go." Roan took his father's hand and then he whipped off his hat and leaned and kissed his father's cheek. Bufe took off his hat. Thomas took off his hat. "Take care of yourselves, y'heah?" and they said, "Yes, sir. Take care of yourself, sir."

Out of earshot down the road, Buford said, "Goin' where, Roan? Where you and papa goin'?"

"No place." Roan shook his head. "Just talking, earlier. About—after"—he gestured vaguely to the night.

"Been at Staunton a few days," Buford said. "Drilling and such. Tonight was the first chance I got to ask a pass. Funny, Roan, we should have picked the same night. Makes a man believe strange things—like thinking goin' across space the way telegraphing goes down a wire. We've been like that a lot, in our time." He turned his face toward his brother. "Ever notice?"

"Yes." Roan's throat hurt. "Yes. I have." *Let go m' brother! I do his fighting for him till he grows.*

"Roan," Buford said, "I'm awful proud of you. I couldn't say that to any other living man the way I mean it. Kind of makes me feel inside like you was a girl I wanted to kiss," he laughed. "I ain't agoin' to kiss you, so don't draw back, but I'm awful proud of you, boy. A sergeant of Ashby's Cav'ry! Boy!"

"That's good, huh?" Roan smiled.

"Damn good, for my money." Buford nodded once or twice. Then he said, "I'm turnin' off just beyond, Roan. The road down toward Waller's Creek that follows the railroad in to town. Could I ask you something?'' His voice was solemn soft. For a moment Roan couldn't draw his breath and his heart was white cold within him. *Dear God*, he thought, *don't let the finger be upon Buford like it was on Forney Manigault when he saw death at Manassas. Don't let Buford tell me that he sees it grinning at him now. Don't, God, don't.*

"Go ahead, Bufe, ask."

"Well," Buford said, "what's it like? Just that, I reckon. What's it like, Roan?"

The reprieve in Roan was like a live thing, leaping for joy. It pressed his throat tight so that he could not talk. But he could breathe again and think again, and with the thinking came the hopeless, futile knowledge that no man who's been in it can ever really tell it right. There are no words.

"How do you mean, Bufe?"

"Well," Bufe said thoughtfully, "just that, I reckon. Just what's it like in a battle? I never thought one way or another to fight a man with fists. If he was big, I reckon I fought harder 'cause I was scared. Reckon I never thought if I was brave or a coward. But I'd kind of like to know what it's like—if you can tell me?"

Roan's impulse was to fling his arm tightly across Bufe's shoulders to hold him close, but it was too late for that. Too late now for everything. *I can't do his fighting for him any longer, for he's grown.* With that he laughed, and the sound was horrid against the silence of the night. "That's all it is, Bufe, boy. Just what you said. If he's big, you just fight harder, 'cause yo're scared!" Then Roan did put his hand on Buford's shoulder, not his arm around, but his hand tight, fingers pressing hard. The anger in the paddock was gone from his soul with the faint and distant echo of the past. "I reckon yo're grown, Bufe. Take care of yoreself, y'hear?"

"You, too, Roan. Here's m'turn-off. Good luck."

Roan threw his leg over Lady and sat for a moment looking down at his younger brother, getting the boy's face full in mind as he saw it now. And his heart was quiet within him, for he knew now that, win or lose, you never throw the cards in, for the money never buys anyway—beyond the satisfaction of your own soul for the playing.

Buford stood there in the roadway, his face turned to the sound of the scrabbling hoofbeats, his mouth open still to call good-by once again, but it was too far now for Roan to hear. So, after a moment, he turned his back and put his tired boy's legs into the last ten miles back into Staunton, to the job in hand.

It was lightening for dawn by the time Roan worked his way up into the high country where he'd left his patrol. "All hell's breaking open soon," they told him. "Word's been coming all the way down the line all night. Frémont's man Milroy has got thirty-seven hundred Yankees in McDowell Village, foot of Bull Pasture Mountain right ahead of us, with a regiment deployed on Shenandoah Mountain. Rest of Frémont's army is strung along South Branch Valley. Schenk's Brigade is thirty-four miles north at Franklin, and Frémont himself is still in Petersburg, with Blenker's Division not yet quit of Romney! That's seventy-five miles of stringing out, sarge. There's goin' to be some fancy clobberin' heahabouts before day is done!"

"What with—four cav'ry troops?"

"Hell. Ain't y'heard? Jackson's back!"

Roan was too far upcountry to see. But Buford, jogging fast into Staunton to make reveille, saw.

When the first train rolled slowly into Staunton Station, folks didn't know what for, beyond just a train. Then somebody recognized Clubby Johnson forming up the companies, with his big stick to hand instead of a sword—shouting in that loud voice of his he didn't even soften to say sweet words to the ladies. By that time the next train close behind was clanking to a steam-spitting stop and the third-brigade regiments began piling off—the 10th, 23rd and 37th Virginia—taking it on the double to clear the tracks, forming column in the street beside. "Stonewall's back!" The word smoked through town like brush fire in a quick wind shift and folks came arunning leaving lay what be—death, childbirth and taxes. Down to the depot to see it and breathe it and shout inside with the joy of it.

"Damn if Stonewall didn't march us clean to Mechum's Station, without a word of whereto! Cars come in and marshaled and ev'one swore to hell we're headed for Richmond. Trains were all set to pull—and they pulled. But west and back again—not east! And by Garry, for breakfast, heah we are, to git that bastoon Frémont!" More trains were pulling in, as far down the single track as you could see. Stopping and letting off. First brigade now—the "Stonewall" since Manassas, under that fancy General Winder—2nd, 4th, 5th, 27th and 33rd Virginia, piling down and forming columns.

"What for y'ask?" I'll tell you what for! That Tom Jackson's plenty smart, in spite of what some say. Ev'body in the Valley thought he'd snuck out—so did Banks and so did Frémont! That's why Jackson done it—to make them believe! Between the two, the

Yankees've got forty thousand men, once they jine up. But they ain't agoin' to jine now. Stonewall kept Ashby wedged between, and now he's all between himself with six thousand men to put the clobber on one and one, piecemeal, before they know which side's painted. Hold up theah! Wait fer pappy!''

You could see General Jackson then through the troops forming in the streets and the troops detraining. Here a minute for a quick sight of him putting a word to Captain Hotchkiss. Gone then, walking slow and thoughtful, and there again bending an ear to General Winder's question. Not a smidgin of haste in him, nor excitement, with the crowds cheering him and the little boys yelling shrill. Just tall and calm and quiet, with his beard combed out with morning and his eyes so blue it hurt to look into them. His old overcoat buttoned tight for a while, then draped to his arm as the heat of the day came full. Once in a while, thumb and finger to his cap visor where it was burred, to pull it down firm. Seeing all of it, prodding hard for it to be the way he wanted, oblivious of whatever else but what he had to do—but powerful thankful in his soul that this fight wasn't coming up for Sunday. Stonewall's back!

Upcountry twenty-two miles, the cavalry dismounted to fight on foot. Sent the horses back with horse holders and took the line with carbines to pin the flung-out Yankee pickets. Pinned 'em cold until Old Clubby Ed Johnson came double-quicking his advance-guard march up to take over. Took over and went through, waving his big hickory club like a drum major and shouting blue billy for bumblebees. Yanks recognized him. ''There's old Johnson! Let's flank him!'' and Clubby yelled back, ''Yes, damn you! Flank me if you can!'' and he drove on through the regiment on the mountain, developing the fight around McDowell Village.

It was a rifle fight, Bull Pasture, when the third brigade came up, laid on across jagged, sawtoothed mountains where a cat could hardly cling, let alone wheeled artillery. Four hours of lead drenching, with the barrels hot to frying eggs, and both sides scrambling the steep slopes for position and neither getting it too well. Roan's troop was in part of it, dismounted, when it began to break toward nightfall. Not long, but just enough for him to know he wasn't waiting for it any longer. His flesh was cool in sweat with the mountain winds, but there was no faint quiver of expectation left in it. Firm and hard and slow-triggered.

Then darkness came down and the Yanks in the village began to pull out, heading for the bridge, retiring under cover of what artillery they could bring to bear on the flat. Pulled out about a mile and built a lot of campfires—and pulled out again, leaving the fires to cover for them while they headed north for Franklin, telescoping the whole of Frémont's army back on itself and making sure, for all bets, that there wouldn't be no junction with Banks yet awhile!

Roan found Buford with his jacket off, digging trenches to bury Yankee dead. Whole Institute Corps was burying—to harden the boys up, some said. But the hell with that—Jackson himself had let 'em march upcountry with his own old Stonewall Brigade—and that's enough for a start in war, for any man's money.

"H'are y', Bufe."

"Hello, Roan." Buford sleeved the sweat off his face and came up grinning, shovel in hand. "Some fight, I reckon, by the sound. Didn't get to see much with," he said distinctly, "the Stonewall Brigade held in reserve."

Roan grunted. "Never do see much. Jest what's around you."

"Sure," Buford nodded. "So I reckon we'll go back to Lexington now, what with exams six weeks ahead, and not even see that much."

"I reckon," Roan said.

"But I'll be back," Buford said, and he wagged his head emphatically, "because it ain't no more than just what you said—'if he's big, you fight harder, 'cause yo're scared!'"

The bodies weren't covered. They lay beside the lengthening trench just as they had been littered in, with the earthy smell of death rising from them like swamp mist. Too many of them to give personality back to any. Ohio boys from the Maumee—Western Virginia boys from the coal country. Dead soldiers left behind forever in the backwash of a lost fight, with dirty hands and wrenched faces softening to peace in the quiet nobility that comes upon those who die under God's sky to go down into God's earth as they lie—with no tribal trappings of funeral pomp and circumstance to make them seem asleep—no paint and flowers and music to give the lie to Death.

"It's a little more," Roan said softly. "I couldn't tell you when you asked, for it wasn't in me then, but it is now, Bufe."

"What, Roan?"

Roan looked at his brother closely. "Bufe," he said, "life takes a lot of living, but only one dying. I don't know how it happened"—he shook his head—"but I died a little bit over at Mossy Creek the other day, so now, when it really comes, I've got it all to do over again." He smiled. "Will you remember that, Bufe—if you come back—just don't—die too many times. Bufe, I'm hungry. Let's eat."

# SHELBY FOOTE
## *Pillar of Fire*

# 1

ANKLE DEEP IN THE dusty places, the road led twelve miles from the landing, around the head of a horseshoe lake and down its eastern slope where the houses were. We left the gunboat at eight oclock in brilliant sunlight, two mounted officers wearing sabers and sashes and thirty Negro infantrymen in neat blue uniforms; at noon the colonel halted the column before a two-story frame structure with a brick portico and squat, whitewashed pillars. He sat a hammer-headed roan, an early-middle-aged man with a patch across one eye.

"Looks old," he said, rolling his cigar along his lower lip. He faced front, addressing the house itself. "Ought to burn pretty," he added after a pause, perhaps to explain why he had not chosen one of the larger ones in both directions. I saw that he was smiling, and that was as usual at such a time, the head lifted to expose the mouth beneath the wide pepper-and-salt mustache. Behind us the troops were quiet: so quiet that when the colonel turned in the saddle, leather squeaked. "Walk up there, Mr. Lundy, and give them the news."

The troops stood at ease in a column of fours, the rifle barrels slanting and glinting. Above their tunics, which were powdered with dust except where they were splotched a darker blue at backs and armpits from four hours of hard marching, their faces appeared cracked as if by erosion where sweat had run.

"Orderly," I said. A soldier stepped out of ranks and held the reins near the snaffle while I dismounted on the off side, favoring my stiff right leg. I went up toward the house. When the colonel called after me, something I could not distinguish above the sound of my boots crunching gravel on the driveway, I halted and faced about. "Sir?"

"Tell them twenty minutes!" With one arm he made the sweeping gesture I had come to know so well. "To clear out!" I heard him call.

I went on—this was nothing new; it was always twenty minutes—remembering, as I had done now for the past two years whenever I

375

approached a strange house, that I had lost a friend this way. It was in Virginia, after Second Bull Run, the hot first day of September, '62. The two of us, separated from our command in the retreat, walked up to a roadside cabin to ask the way, and somone fired at us from behind a shuttered window. I ran out of range before the man (or woman; I never knew) could reload, and by the time I got up courage enough to come back, half an hour later, no one was there except my friend, lying in the yard in his gaudy zouave uniform with his knees drawn up and both hands clapped tight against his belt buckle. He looked pinch-faced and very dead, and it seemed indeed a useless way to die.

That was while I was still just Private Lundy, within a month of the day I enlisted back home in Cashtown; that was my baptism of fire, as they like to call it. After that came Antietam and Fredericksburg, where I won my stripes. The war moved fast in those days and while I was in Washington recovering from my Chancellorsville wound I received my commission and orders to report directly to the War Department after a twenty-day convalescent leave. I enjoyed the visit home, limping on a cane and having people admire my new shoulder straps and fire-gilt buttons. "Adam, you're looking fit," they said, pretending not to notice the ruined knee. 'Fit' was their notion of a soldier word, though in fact the only way any solder ever used it was as the past tense of fight.

When I reported back to the capital I was assigned to the West, arriving during the siege of Vicksburg and serving as liaison officer on one of the gunboats. Thus I missed the fighting at Gettysburg, up near home. It was not unpleasant duty. I had a bed to sleep in, with sheets, and three real meals every twenty-four hours, plus coffee in the galley whenever I wanted it. We shot at them, they shot at us: I could tell myself I was helping to win the war. Independence Day the city fell, and in early August I was ordered to report for duty with Colonel Nathan Frisbie aboard the gunboat *Starlight*. Up till then it had all been more or less average, including the wound; there were thousands like me. But now it changed, and I knew it from the first time I saw him.

He looked at me hard with his one gray eye before returning the salute. "Glad to have you aboard," he said at last. A Negro corporal was braced in a position of exaggerated attention beside a stand of colors at the rear of the cabin. "Orderly," the colonel said. The corporal rolled his eyes. "Show the lieutenant his quarters."

Next morning at six o'clock the corporal rapped at the door of my cabin, then entered and gave me the colonel's compliments, along with instructions to report to the orderly room for a tour of inspection before breakfast. I'd been asleep; I dressed in a hurry, flustered at being late on my first day of duty. Colonel Frisbie was checking the morning report when I came in. He glanced up and said quietly, "Get your saber, Mr. Lundy." I returned to my cabin, took the saber out of its wrappings, and buckled it on. I hadnt worn it since the convalescent leave, and in fact hadnt thought I'd ever wear it again.

The troops were on the after deck, each man standing beside his pallet; the colonel and I followed the first sergeant down the aisle. From time to time Colonel Frisbie would pause and lift an article from the display of equipment on one of the pads, then look sharply at the owner before passing on. "Take his name, Sergeant." Their dark faces were empty of everything, but I saw that each man trembled slightly while the colonel stood before him.

After breakfast Colonel Frisbie called me into the orderly room for a conference. This was the first of many. He sat at his desk, forearms flat along its top, the patch over his eye dead black like a target center, his lips hidden beneath the blousy, slightly grizzled mustache. There was hardly any motion in his face as he spoke.

When Vicksburg fell, the colonel said, Mr. Lincoln announced that the Mississippi "flowed unvexed to the sea." But, like so many political announcements, this was not strictly true; there was still considerable vexation in the form of sniping from the levee, raids by bodies of regular and irregular cavalry—bushwackers, the colonel called them—and random incidents involving dynamite and disrespect to the flag. So while Sherman sidestepped his way to Atlanta, commanders of districts flanking the river were insturcted to end all such troubles. On the theory that partisan troops could not function without the support of the people who lived year-round in the theater, the commanders adopted a policy of holding the civilian population responsible.

"They started this thing, Mr. Lundy," the colonel said. "They began it, sir, and while they had the upper hand they thought it was might fine. Remember the plumes and roses in those days? Well, *we're* top dog now, East and West, and we'll give them what they blustered for, indeed. We'll give them war enough to last the time of man."

He brooded, his face in shadow, his hands resting within the circle of yellow lamplight on his desk. I wondered if this silence, which seemed long, was a sign that the conference was over. But just as I was about to excuse myself, the colonel spoke again. He cleared his throat. "Lieutenant, does that knee bother you?"

"Not often, sir, Just when—"

"Never you mind," Colonel Frisbie said, and moving one hand suddenly to the lamp he turned the wick up full and tilted the shade so that the light was thrown directly on his face. His expression was strained, the patch neat and exact. "Theyll pay for that knee, lieutenant. And they will pay for this!" He lifted the patch onto his forehead. The empty socket pulsed as red and raw as when the wound was new.

During the year that followed, the colonel spoke to me often of these and other things. Every morning there was a meeting in the orderly room after breakfast—'conferences' he called them, but he did the talking. I understood how he felt about the eye, the desire to make someone pay for its loss; I had felt it myself about the ruined knee and the death of my friend in Virginia, until I reminded myself, in the case of the knee, that the bullets flew both ways, and in the case of my friend that it was primarily a question of whose home was being invaded. I had more or less put it behind me, this thought of repayment; but with Colonel Frisbie it was different, and for many reasons. He was a New Englander, a lawyer in civilian life, an original abolitionist. He had been active in the underground railroad during the '50s, and when war came he entered the army as a captain under Frémont in Saint Louis. These were things he told me from time to time, but there were things he did not tell, things I found out later.

He had been with Sherman at Shiloh, a major by then, adjutant in an Indiana regiment which broke badly under the Sunday dawn attack. He was near the bluff above Pittsburg Landing, using the flat of his saber on stragglers, when a stray minié came his way with a spent whine and took out his left eye: whereupon he went under the bluff, tore off his shoulder straps, and lay down among the skulkers. There were ten thousand others down there, including officers, and only a few of them wounded; he had better provocation than most. Yet he could not accept it in the way those others apparently could. When the battle was over he bandaged his eye with a strip from his shirt, rejoined his regiment, and later was commended in reports. There were men in his outfit, however, including some of his own clerks, who had also been under the bluff, and he saw them looking at him as if to say, "If you wont tell on me, I wont on you." Soon afterwards he was assigned to courts martial duty with the Adjutant General's Department. When the army adopted its reprisal policy in the lower

Mississippi Valley, he was given another promotion and a gunboat with special troops aboard to enforce it.

Patrolling the river from Vicksburg north to Memphis, two hundred and fifty air-line miles and almost twice that far by water, One-Eye Frisbie and the *Starlight* became well known throughout the delta country. Where partisan resistance had once been strongest, soon there was little activity of any kind. It became a bleak region, populated only by women and children and old men and house servants too feeble to join the others gone as 'contraband' with the Union armies. The fields lay fallow, last year's cotton drooping on dead brown stalks. Even the birds went hungry, what few remained. The land was desolated as if by plague.

The only protest now was an occasional shot from the levee, which was followed by instant reprisal in accordance wit the Army policy. Colonel Frisbie would tie up at the nearest river town, sending word for evacuation within twenty minutes, and then would give the *Starlight* gunners half an hour's brisk drill, throwing explosive shells over the levee and into the empty buildings and streets where chickens and dogs fluttered and slunk and squawked and howled. Or he would tie up at the point where the sniping occurred, lead the troops ashore, and march them overland sometimes as far as a dozen miles to burn an isolated plantation house.

I was with him from the beginning and I remember him mainly as straddled in silhouette before the lick and soar of flames. Dispossessed, the family huddled somewhere in the background. At first they had been arrogant, threatening reprisal by Forrest or Jameson or Van Dorn. "You had better burn the trees as well," one woman told us. "When we first came there was nothing but woods and we built our homes. We'll build them again." But when Atlanta was besieged their defiance faltered, and when Sherman had taken the city and was preparing for the march that would "make Georgia howl," they knew they were beaten and their armies would never return. There had been a time when they sent their plantation bells and even their brass doorknobs to be melted for cannon; but not any more. Now the war had left them. They were faced with the aftermath before the finish.

Colonel Frisbie looked upon all this as indemnity collectible for the loss of his eye and his courage at Shiloh. Saber and sash and gray eye glinting firelight, he would watch a house burn with a smile that was more like a grimace, lip lifted to expose the white teeth clamping the cigar. That was the way I remembered him now as I continued to walk

up the driveway toward the house. Around one of its corners I saw that
the outbuildings had already burned, and I wondered if it had been
done by accident—a not uncommon plantation mishap—or by one of
our armies passing through at the time of the Vicksburg campaign.
Then, nearing the portico, I saw that the door was ajar. Beyond it I
could see into a high dim hall where a staircase rose in a slow curve. I
stood in the doorway, listening, then rapped.

The rapping was abrupt and loud against the silence. Then there
was only vacancy, somehow even more empty than before.

"Hello!" I cried, my voice as reverberant as if I had spoken from
the bottom of a well. "Hello in there!"

I had a moment of sharp fear, a sudden vision of someone crouched
at the top of the staircase, sighting down a rifle barrel at me with a hot,
unwinking eye. But when I bent forward and peered, there was no
one, nothing. I went in.

Through a doorway on the right I saw a tall black man standing
beside an armchair. He wore a rusty claw-hammer coat with buttons
of tarnished brass, and on his head there was what appeared to be pair
of enormous white horns. Looking closer I saw that the Negro had
bound a dinner napkin about his jaws, one of which was badly
swollen, and had tied it at the crown of his head so that the corners
stood up stiffly from the knot like the ears on a rabbit. The armchair
was wide and deep; it faced the cold fireplace, its high, fan-shaped
back turned toward the door.

I said, "Didnt you hear me calling?" The Negro just stood there,
saying nothing. It occurred to me then that he might be deaf; he had
that peculiar, vacant look on his face. I came forward. "I said
didnt . . ."

But as I approached him, obliquing to avoid the chair, I saw
something else.

There was a hand on the chair arm. Pale against the leather and
mottled with dark brown liver spots, it resembled the hand of a
mummy, the nails long and narrow, almond-shaped. Crossing to the
hearth I looked down at the man in the chair, and the man looked up at
me. He was old—though old was hardly word enough to express it; he
was ancient—with sunken cheeks and a mass of white hair like a
mane, obviously a tall man and probably a big one, once, but thin now
to the point of emaciation, as if he had been reduced to skin and
skeleton and only the most essential organs, heart and lungs and
maybe bowels, though not very much of either—'Except heart; there's

plenty of that,' I thought, looking into the cold green eyes. His chin, resting upon a high stock, trembled as he spoke.

"Have you brum to run my howl?" he said.

I stared at him. "How's that?" I asked. But the old man did not answer.

"He hyar you, captain," the Negro said. His enormous horns bobbed with the motion of his jaw. "He hyar you well enough, but something happen to him lately he caint talk right."

This was Isaac Jameson, who was born in a wilderness shack beside the Trace while his father, a South Carolina merchant, was removing his family and his business to the Natchez District as part of a caravan which he and other Loyalists had organized to escape the Revolution on the seaboard. Thus in later years, like so many of the leaders of his time, Isaac was able to say in truth that he was a log cabin boy. But it was misleading, for his father, who had prospered under the Crown back east, became even wealthier in the west, and Isaac grew up in a fine big house on the bluff overlooking the river. From the gallery he could watch Spanish sentries patrolling the wharf where steamboats, up from New Orleans, put in with goods for the Jameson warehouse. He was grown, twenty years old and four inches over six feet tall, when John Adams sent troops to take over for the United States and created the Mississippi Territory. The Republic, which his father had come seven hundred miles to escape, had dogged his heels.

Issac was sixth among eight sons, and he was unlike the others. It was not only that he stood half a head taller; there was some intrinsic difference. They were reliable men, even the two younger ones who followed the removal. But Isaac would not stand at a desk totting figures or checking bills of lading. He was off to cockfights or horseraces, and he spent more evenings in the Under-the-Hill section than he did in Natchez proper. His father, remembering the shack by the Trace, the panthers screaming in the outward darkness while his wife was in labor, believed that his son—wilderness born, conceived in a time of revolution—had received in his blood, along with whatever it was that had given him the extra height and the unaccountable width of his shoulders, some goading spark of rebellion, some fierce, hot distillate of the jungle itself.

Then one day he was gone. He did not say where he was going, or even that he was leaving; he just went. Then ten years later he turned up again, with a bad leg wound from the Battle of New Orleans. He was a year mending. Then he spent another year trying to make up for lost time. But it did not go right. There were still the cockfights and the grog shops and the women under the hill, but the old life had palled on him. He was thirty-nine, a bachelor, well into middle age, and apparently it had all come to nothing.

Then he found what he had been seeking from the start, though he did not know he was looking for it until some time after he found it. Just before his fortieth birthday—in the spring of 1818; Mississippi had entered the Union in December—he rode into the northern wilderness with two trappers who had come to town on their annual spree. This time he was gone a little over two years. Shortly after the treaty of Doaks Stand opened five and a half million acres of Choctaw land across the middle of the state, he reappeared at his father's house. He was in buckskins, his hair shoulder length.

Next day he was gone for good, with ten of his father's Negroes and five thousand dollars in gold in his saddlebags. He had come back to claim his legacy, to take this now instead of his share in the Jameson estate when the old man died. The brothers were willing, since it would mean a larger share for them when the time came. The father considered it a down-right bargain; he would have given twice that amount for Isaac's guarantee to stay away from Natchez with his escapades and his damage to the name. He said, "If you want to play prodigal it's all right with me. But mind you: when youre swilling with swine and chomping the husks, dont cut your eyes around in my direction. There wont be any lamp in the window, or fatted calf either. This is all."

It was all Isaac wanted, apparently. Between sunup and nightfall of the following day—a Sunday, early in June—they rolled forty miles along the road connecting hamlets north of Natchez. Sundown of the third day they made camp on the near bank of the Yazoo, gazing down off the Walnut Hills, and Wednesday they entered the delta, a flat land baked gray by the sun wherever it exposed itself, which was rare, from under the intertwined branches of sycamores and water oaks and cottonwoods and elms. Grass grew so thick that even the broad tires of the Conestoga left no mark of passage. Slow, circuitous creeks, covered with dusty scum and steaming in the heat, drained east and south, away from the river, each doubling back on itself in convulsive loops and coils like a snake fighting lice. For four days then, while the Negroes clutched desperately at seats and stanchions in a din of creaking wood and clattering metal (they had been warehouse hands, townspeople, and ones the brothers could easiest spare at that) the wagon lurched thorugh thickets of scrub oak and stunted willow and over fallen trunks and rotted stumps. It had a pitching roll, like that of a ship riding a heavy swell, which actually did cause most of the Negroes to become seasick four hundred miles from salt water.

They followed no trail, for there was no trail to follow. There was only Isaac, who rode a claybank mare as far out front as visibility allowed, sometimes half a mile, sometimes ten feet, and even in the latter case they sometimes followed not the sight of him but the sound of snapping limbs and Isaac's cursing. Often they had to dismount with axes and chop through. Just before noon of the eighth day, Sunday again, they struck the southern end of a lake, veered right, then left, and continued northward along its eastern shore. Two hours later Isaac reined in the mare, and when the wagon drew abreast he signaled for a halt. A wind had risen, ruffling the lake; through the screen of cypresses the waves were bright like little hatchets in the sunlight. "All right," he said. "You can get the gear unloaded. We are home."

That was the beginning. During the next ten years he was joined by others drawn from the south and east to new land available at ninety cents an acre with few questions asked. The eighteen hundred acres of Isaac's original claim were increased to thirty-two hundred in 1826 when his neighbors north and south went broke in the crash. Two years later, though he had named his ten-square-mile plantation Solitaire in confirmation of his bachelor intentions, he got married. It happened almost accidentally. She was the youngest of four daughters; the other three were already married, and she herself was more or less engaged at the time to the blacksmith's assistant, two doors down the street. Her father kept a tavern, and from time to time she took her turn at the tap. Isaac found her tending bar one warm spring evening when he rode down for a drink. He had seen her before, of course, though he had not really noticed. Now he did. He particularly admired her arms, which were bared to the elbows, and her thick yellow hair, worn shoulder length. That night he had trouble getting to sleep. At last he dropped off, however. He did not dream, but when he woke he thought immediately of her. Whats this? he asked himself. He returned to the Inn that evening, and the next. By then he had decided. He spoke to the father first. "I'm willing if Katy is," the innkeeper said.

The wedding was held at the Tavern and the blacksmith's young assistant was there, bulging his biceps, drunk for the first time in his life. He got into three fights that day, though not with Isaac.

# 2

THAT ENDED THE first phase of his life, the fifty years spent running hard after trouble in any form, first among men—river bullies at Natchez-under-the-Hill, painted Creeks at Burnt Corn, British regulars at New Orleans; he had tried them all—and then against the cat- and snake-infested jungles of the South. Isaac, however, was not aware that it had ended until two years later, after Dancing Rabbit opened the remaining northern section of the state to settlers, when his neighbors, small farmers and planters alike, were selling their claims for whatever they could get, packing their carts and Conestogas, and heading north into the rich new land that lay between the lake and the Tennessee line. It was then, after they had gone and he had stayed, that Isaac knew his wilderness thirst had been slaked.

What bound him finally and forever to this earth, however—and he knew it—was the birth of his son in August, 1833, the year the stars fell. Mrs Jameson named him Clive, not for any particular reason; she just like the name. In the ten following years she bore six more children. They were all girls and were all either born dead or died within a week. They lay in a cedar grove, beneath a row of crosses. She had become a pleasant-faced, bustling woman, rather full-bodied, expending her energy on a determination to keep the Jameson house the finest on the lake.

This took some doing: for, though nowhere near the extent it would reach ten years later in the expansive early '50s, there was already plenty of competition. Cotton was coming into its own, and the lake country was a district of big plantations, thousand- and two- and three-thousand-acre places which the owners ruled like barons. When the small farmers, settlers who had followed Isaac into the region after the Doaks Stand treaty opened the land, moved away to the north after Dancing Rabbit—usually with no more than they had had when they arrived, a wagon and a team of mules or oxen, a rifle and a couple of sticks of furniture, a hound or two and a crate of chickens or shoats, a wife and a stair-stepped parcel of children in linsey-woolsey, and perhaps a widowed mother or mother-in-law—their claims were gobbled up by those who stayed, as well as by others who moved in on their heels. These last, the second wave of comers, were essentially businessmen. They had no gift (or, for that matter, desire) for ringing trees and rooting stumps; their gift was rather for organization. They could juggle figures and balance books and put the profits where they earned more profits. Eli Whitney made them rich and now they began to build fine houses to show it, calling them Westoak Hall and Waverly and Briartree, proud-sounding names in imitation of those in the tidewater counties of Virginia, though in fact the Virginians were few among them. They were mostly Kentuckians and North Carolinians, arrived by way of East Mississippi or the river, and for the most part they were not younger sons of established families, sent forth with the parental blessing and gold in their saddlebags. Many of them did not know their grandparents' names, and some of them had never known their fathers.

Isaac's original L-shaped structure, which he and the ten slaves had put up in 1820 soon after their arrival, had grown now to a two-story mansion with a brick portico and concrete pillars; the roof had been raised so that now all the bedrooms were upstairs. It was still called Solitaire though the name no longer fit. Isaac himself had grown handsomer with age. He was still a big man, six feet four, but he looked slimmer and, somehow, even fitter and more hale. Gray hair became him. Dressed habitually in broadcloth and starched linen, he had a stiffness, a formality that resembled an outward show of self-satisfaction and pride. In 1848, when he was seventy, people seeing him on the street in Ithaca, with his straight-backed manner of walking and his careful way of planting his feet, would point him out to visitors. "Thats Ike Jameson," they would say. "He was the first man into these parts. Fine-looking, aint he. How old would you take him to be?" The visitor would guess at fifty- or fifty-five and his host would laugh. "Seventy. Seventy, by God. Youd never think it, would you? to look at him."

In September of that year he sent his son, who had reached fifteen the month before, to the Virginia Military Institute. This was at the boy's insistence, and Isaac was willing: not because he wanted him to become a soldier (he wanted no such thing; he had known too many soldiers in his time) but because in preparation for the life of a planter it did not much matter what form the schooling took. In fact a military school was probably best, since the boy would be less likely to become seriously involved with books. A young man's true education began when he was through with school and had come back home to learn the running of the plantation, the particular temper and whims of cotton as well as the temper and whims of the people who worked it, meaning Negroes. Besides, the Mexican War was recently over. Young men throughout the South were admiring General Winfield

Scott and old Rough-and-Ready Taylor, Captain Bragg the artillery-
man who "gave them a little more grape," and Colonel Davis from
down near Natchez who formed his regiment, the Mississippi Rifles,
in a V at Buena Vista and won the battle with a single charge.

Early in June, nine months later, when Isaac went to Bristol to meet
him at the station, Clive was in uniform, the buttons bright against
black facings on the slate-gray cloth. All down the platform, people
were looking at him. Isaac was impressed.

"I declare, boy, you look almost grown to me."

"Hello, papa," he said, and extended his hand. Always before that
they had kissed.

Three Junes later, when he came home from graduation, tall, slim,
handsome, blond, nineteen, he was the catch of the lake. It was not
only his looks; he could be amusing, too, as for instance when he gave
an imitation of his mathematics instructor, T. J. Jackson, who wound
up every lecture covered with chalkdust and perspiration and who
sometimes became so interested in solving algebra and trigonometry
problems that he forgot the students were present and just stood there
reasoning with himself and Euclid. Clive had much success with this;
"Give us Professor Jackson," they would beg him in houses along the
lake. Soon, however, his social horizon widened. He was one of the
real catches of the delta. Isaac and Mrs Jameson were impressed, and
so were the various girls; but the ones who were most impressed were
the girls' mothers. They preened their daughters, set their caps, and
laid their snares. At dances and outings he moved among them,
attentive, grave, pleasant, quite conscious of the advantages of his
position.

Isaac was amused, but he was also rather awed. His own youth had
been so different. Past seventy, nearing eighty, he could look back on
a life divided neatly into two unequal compartments, the first containing fifty years of wildness and the second containing twenty-odd—
nearly thirty—years of domesticity, with marriage like an airtight
door between them. Now, though he did not know it and could have
done nothing about it anyhow, he was moving toward another door
which led to a third compartment, less roomy than either of the other
two, with a closer atmosphere, even stifling in the end, and more
different from both of the previous two than those two had been
different from each other. In a sense beyond longevity he led three
lives in one.

Since 1850, the year of the Compromise, planters in the lake region had been talking disunion. As a topic for discussion it had crowded out the weather and even the cotton market. Seated on their verandas or in their parlors, clutching juleps in their fists, they blustered. They had built their fine big neo-Tidewater houses, displaying them to their neighbors and whoever passed along the lakeside road, each as a sort of patent of nobility, a claim to traditions and ancestry which they for the most part lacked. Insecurity had bred a semblance of security, until now no one questioned their right to anything at all. When Lincoln was nominated in 1860 they took it as a pointed insult. Not that they believed he would be elected; no; "Never in all this world," they said. "Those abolitionist scoundrels just want to flaunt this ape in our faces for the purpose of watching our reaction. Yes. Well, we'll show them something in the way of action they havent bargained for, if they dont watch out. Let them be warned," they added solemnly.

They admired the spirit and emulated the manner of the Texas senator, an ex-South Carolinian with a reputation as a duelist, who said to his Northern fellow-senators, smiling as he said it though not in friendliness at all: "The difficulty between you and us, gentlemen, is that you will not send the right sort of people here. Why will you not send either Christians or gentlemen?"

"Wigfall knows how to treat them," the planters said. "A few more like him and Preston Brooks and we'd have this hooraw hushed."

But Isaac, who had fought under Andrew Jackson at New Orleans and followed his politics ever since, believed in the Union in much the same way as Jackson had believed in it. He thought sectional differences could be solved better within the Union than outside it. At first he would say so, with the others watching him hot-eyed over the frosted rim of goblets. Later he saw that it was no use. Like much of the rest of the nation, they were determined to have violence as the answer to some deep-seated need, as actual as thirst.

Clive took little or no part in these discussions which went on all around him. He had come home from the Institute with a soldier's training, but now he was busy learning the life of a planter; the slate-gray uniforms and the tactics texts had been folded away in a trunk with the unblooded sword. He was closer to his mother than he was to Isaac. He was quiet, indeed somewhat vague in his manner, with gentle eyes; his way now was very little different, in fact, from the way in which he had moved among the Bristol matrons and fanned their hopes with his almost casual attentiveness. He loved horses and spent much of his time in the stables. Behind the softness of his eyes and voice there was something wild that matched the wildness of horses, and this was where he most resembled his father.

Then Lincoln was elected—the planters had said it would never happen; "Never in all this world," they said—and South Carolina seceded, followed within two weeks by Mississippi and then the others among the Deep South fire-eater states. That was in January. Moderation was gone now, what little had remained. Clive even heard from the Institute that the chalkdusty Professor Jackson, a Mexican War veteran himself, had stood up in chapel and made a speech; "Draw the sword and throw away the scabbard!" he had cried. It did not sound at all like him, but anything was believable in these times. Two months later, a month before Sumter, Clive rode off as captain of a cavalry troop formed by the lake planters and their sons. With their wagons, their spare mounts and body servants, they made a long column; their ornaments flashed in the sunlight.

Nearly all of them returned within four months, not as a unit but in straggling twos and threes. It was the common end of such 'elite' organizations; they had not expected war to be like that. The excitement lasted not even as long as the glitter of their collar ornaments. Once it was gone they thought they might as well come home. They had seen no fighting anyhow. It was mostly drill and guard mount, patrolling encampments while the infantry slept, moving from place to place, then back again. The glory had departed, and so did they.

When Clive came home, his uniform and saber sash a bit faded from the weather, Isaac came out to meet him in the yard, looking somehow more military in broadcloth than his son looked in uniform. They stood looking at each other. "How did it go?" Isaac asked him.

"It went all right, considering. There just wasnt anything to do."

"You wanted it another way. Was that it?"

"I didnt want it the way it was. We disbanded piecemeal, man by man. They would come and say they were leaving. Then theyd leave. Finally there were less than a dozen of us; so we left too. We made it official."

They stood facing each other in the hot summer sunlight; First Manassas had been fought two weeks ago. Clive was smiling. Isaac did not smile. "And what are you going to do now?" he asked. "Stay here and farm the place?"

"I might."

"So?"

"I might. . . ."

"So?"

"No, papa. I'll go back. But different."

"So," Isaac said.

He stayed ten days, and then he left again. This time he went alone. Within two years Clive Jameson was one of the sainted names of the Confederacy. It began when he came out of Donelson with Forrest, escaping through icy backwater saddle-skirt deep. Then he distinguished himself at Shiloh, leading a cavalry charge against the Peach Orchard and another at Fallen Timbers after the battle; Beauregard cited him as one of the heroes of that field. By the time of Vicksburg, in the summer of '63, newspapers were beginning to print the story of his life. Southern accounts always mentioned hs having been born the year the stars fell; Starborn, one called him, and the others took it up. Poetesses laureate in a hundred backwoods counties submitted verse in which they told how he had streamed down to earth like a meteor to save the South; they made much of the flaming wake. Northern accounts, on the other hand, made much of the fact that his mother had tended bar in her father's taproom.

He never wrote. They did not see him again until late in '63 when he was wounded at Chickamauga, his fifth but his first really serious wound, and was brought home in an ambulance to recover. He was still a young man, just past his thirtieth birthday, but he looked older than his years. It was as if the furnace of war had baked the flesh of his hard, handsome face, which by now was tacked in replica on cabin walls, badly reproduced pen-and-ink sketches clipped from newspapers, and mooned over by girls in attic bedrooms. The softness had gone from his eyes and voice. He did not resemble himself; he resembled his pictures. Having him at Solitaire was like having a segment of some actual blasted battlefield at hand. His mother, after an hour with him, came away shaking her head. "What have they done to my boy?" she asked.

"He's a hero," Isaac said. He had seen and known heroes before. "What did you expect?"

Clive mended fast, however, and soon after the first of the year he rode away. They heard of his raid into Kentucky that spring—'brilliant' was the word that appeared most frequently in the newspaper accounts; the columns bristled with it, alongside 'gallant'—and in June he led his brigade in the attack that crumpled Grierson's flank at Brice's Crossroads and sent the invaders stumbling back to Memphis. The papers were full of it, prose and verse.

Mrs Jameson sealed off the upper story of her house. She and Isaac lived downstairs. She was fifty-six, an active, bustling woman who got things done. She still had the yellow hair and even the beautifully rounded arms, but she was subject to dizzy spells, which she called the Vapors, and during such an attack her mind would wander. She would imagine the war was over and her son was dead. A moment later, though, she would sigh and say, "I'm glad he's doing well, but I wish they would let him come home for a while. I really do."

She never thought of him the way he had been when he was there with his Chickamauga wound. In her mind she saw him as he had been when he rode away that first time, in the spring of '61, with the soft voice and gentle eyes, of as he was in the daguerreotype which she kept on the night table beside her bed. It had been taken when he was a child; he wore button shoes and ribbed stockings and a jacket of watered silk, and there was a small-boy sweetness in his face. Sometimes in the night Isaac would wake to find the candle burning at the bedside and Mrs Jameson sitting bolt upright, propped on three pillows, with the picture in her hands. There would be tears in her eyes, and if he spoke to her at such a time she would turn and look at him with the face of a stranger.

On a hot July morning she was waxing the dining room table—a task she had always reserved for herself because it gave her a particular pleasure—when suddenly she paused and a peculiar expression came over her face, the expression of someone about to sneeze. Then she did; she sneezed loudly. "God bless me," she said, automatically, and went on with her work, applying the wax in long, even strokes. Presently she raised one hand to her forehead, palm outward, fingers relaxed. "I feel so dizzy," she said. She looked frightened. Isaac reached her just as she fell. He carried her to a couch in the living room and knelt beside her, patting her wrists. Her breath came in harsh stertorous groans.

"Katy!" Isaac kept saying. "Katy, dont you know me?"

She did not know him; she did not know anything. Foam kept forming on her lips and Isaac wiped it away with his handkerchief. Two Negroes stood in the background. There was nothing they could do. All the doctors were off to war, but that was just as well since there was nothing they could have done either. It was a cerebral hemorrhage and she died within four hours.

Next day they buried her in the cedar grove, at the near end of the row of small, weathered crosses. Isaac was dry-eyed at the burial; he did not seem to understand what had happened. He was bewildered at last by mortality, by a world in which a person could sneeze and say, "God bless me: I feel dizzy," and then be dead. He was eighty-six years old.

3

ALL BUT THREE of the slaves had left by then, gone on their own or as dish-washers and ditch-diggers with the Union armies which had roamed the district at will and without real opposition since early '64. There was Edward, the butler, who was almost seventy, the last of the original ten who had come with Isaac in the Conestoga north from Natchez. He was stone deaf, a tall, straight-backed Negro, mute and inscrutable behind his wall of dignity and deafness. The other two were women; both were old, one lame (she did the cooking, what there was to cook) and the other half-witted. These three lived in one of the cabins that formed a double row, called the Quarters, half a mile behind the house. The other cabins were empty, beginning to dry rot from disuse, and the street between the rows, formerly grassless, polished by generations of bare feet until it was almost as smooth and shiny as a ballroom floor, was beginning to spring up in weeds. When Mrs Jameson died Edward moved into the house with Isaac. Five weeks later the two women joined them because a Federal platoon, out on patrol, burned the quarters.

That was in August. Near sundown the platoon made bivouac in a pasture near the house. The cooks set up their kitchen and sent out a three-man detail for firewood. They were tearing up the floorboards in one of the cabins, the planks making sudden, ripping sounds like musketry, when one of the soldiers happened to glance up and see a tall yellow woman, her face pitted with old smallpox scars, standing in the doorway watching them. She clasped her wrists over her stomach and watched them gravely. It gave him a start, finding her there like that without having heard her approach.

"Yawl bed not be doing that," she said when the soldier looked at her.

The others paused too, now. They stood leaning forward with half-ripped planks in their hands. Their uniforms were dusty, still sweaty from marching all that afternoon. "Why not, aunty?" the first said. His speech was Southern, though obviously from north of Mississippi.

"I'll tell Mars Ike and he'll tell his boy: thats why. And the genril he'll come back and git you, too, what time he hears you messing with his belongings like you doing."

They resumed their work, tearing up the floorboards with a splintering, ripping sound, and the sunlight slanting through the western window was filled with dust-motes. Then one of them said casually, "What general would that be, aunty?"

"Genril Cli Jameson, Mars Ike's boy. You see if I dont."

Again they paused, once more with the ends of half-ripped planks in their hands. But this time it was different. They looked at her, all three together, and something like joy was registered on their faces. "Does this belong to him, that house and all these shanties?"

"Does indeed, and you best quit or I'll tell him. I'm a mind to tell him anyhow, the way yawl acting."

"Well," the first said, still not moving, still bent forward. "Well, well. What do you know."

Then he moved. He finished prizing up the plank he had hold of, took a jackknife from his pocket, one of the big horn-handled ones the suttlers sold in such volume every payday, and began to peel shavings from the edge of the plank. It was cypress, long since cured, and the shavings came off straight and clean, a rich pink almost red. The other two watched him for a moment, puzzled. Then they understood and began to do the same, taking out their knives and peeling shavings from other planks. They worked in silence, all three together. They were from a Tennessee Union regiment—what their enemies called home-made Yankees. All three had week-old beards.

"That damned butcher," the third said. He had not spoken until now. "Aint it funny what luck will sometimes throw your way?"

The woman watched them without understanding, still with her hands crossed on the bulge of her stomach, while one of the soldiers scraped the shavings into a small pile in one corner of the room. He laid planks across it, first the split ones and then whole ones, building a teepee of lumber. When he had finished this he took a tinder box from the pocket of his blouse, then bent and struck it so that a shower of sparks fell into the heart of the little heaped-up pile of cypress shavings. At first it merely smoked and glowed. Suddenly a flame leaped up, bright yellow, then orange, then rose-colored, licking the wall of the cabin.

"Yawl bed not be doing that," the woman said again, her voice as flat, as inflectionless as at the start.

The soldiers stood watching the fire. When it was burning nicely they gathered up the remainder of their ripped-up floorboards and started for the pasture where by now the cook had begun to beat with a big spoon against the bottom of a dishpan to hurry them along. One paused at the foot of the steps, turning with the bundle of planks on his shoulder. The others stopped beyond him, looking back and smiling as he spoke. "Tell him that for Fort Pillow, aunty. Tell him it's from the friend of a man who was there."

Fifteen minutes later Isaac and Edward and the lame cook, and presently the half-witted woman too, stood on the back gallery and watched the quarters burn. "I told um not to, plain as I'm standing here talking to you right now," the woman said. There was no wind, not a breath, the flames went straight up with a sucking, roaring sound like the rush of something passing at great speed. Even deaf Edward, though he could not hear it, felt its deep murmuring whoosh against his face. He turned his head this way and that, as if he had recovered his hearing after all those years of silence.

The Federal platoon, the men in collarless fatigue blouses and galluses, many of them smoking pipes while they waited for supper, gathered at the back of the pasture to watch the progress of the fire. They leaned their elbows on the top rail of the fence, and as the dusk came on and the flames spread from cabin to cabin along the double row, flickering brighter and brighter on their faces, they made jokes at one another up and down the line. Soon the cook beat again on the dishpan with the spoon and they lined up with messkits in their hands. The fire burned on. It burned steadily into the night, its red glow reflected against the underside of the pall of smoke hanging over the plantation. From time to time a roof fell in, occasionally two together, and a bright rush of sparks flew upward in a fiery column that stood steadily upright for a long moment, substantial as a glittering pillar of jeweled brass supporting the black overhang of smoke, before it paled and faded and was gone.

Next morning when Isaac came out of the house he found the pasture empty, the soldiers gone, with only an unclosed latrine and a few charred sticks of the cookfire to show they had been there at all. He walked down to where the quarters had been, and there were only the foundation stones and the toppled chimneys, the bricks still hot among the cooling ashes. The cabins had been built during the ten-year bachelor period between his arrival and his marriage—six-teen cabins, two rows of eight, put up during the ten-year span by a five-man building team who snaked the big cypresses out of a slough, split them with axes and crosscut saws for timbers and planks and shingles and even pegs to save the cost of nails. They had been good cabins, snug in winter, cool in summer, built to last; they had seen forty years of living and dying, laughing and weeping, arrival and departure. Now they were gone, burned overnight, casualties of the war.

As he turned at the end of the double row, starting back, a great weariness came over him. He stood there for a moment, arms loose at his sides, then returned to the house. He went up the steps and across the gallery. In the kitchen a strange thing happened to him.

The cook was boiling something on the stove, stirring it with a long-handled spoon, and as he came past he intended to ask her, 'Is breakfast ready?' But that was not what he said. He said, "Is breck us riding?"

"Sir?"

He tried again. "Has bread abiding?"

"Sir?" The cook looked at him. She had turned sideways, still bent forward over the pot, and the spoon dripped a thin white liquid. It was cornmeal mush; she would boil it to a thicker consistence, then cook it into cakes to be served with sorghum. With her crooked leg, bowed back, and lips collapsed about her toothless mouth so that her nose and chin were brought into near conjunction, she resembled a witch. "Sir?" she said.

Isaac made a gesture of impatience and went on toward the front of the house. His arms and legs were trembling; there was a pulsing sensation in his head, immediately behind his eyes, a throbbing produced by pressure. Something is happening to me! he thought. He could think the words clearly: 'Is breakfast ready?' but when he tried to say them they came out wrong. Words came out that were not even in his mind as he spoke. Something has happend to me! he thought.

These were the first signs of motor aphasia, the words coming wrong from his tongue. They were not always wrong; sometimes he could speak with no trouble at all. But sooner or later a word or a phrase, unconnected with what he intended to say, would substitute itself. Then the lame cook or the half-witted woman, who was supposed to be the housemaid but who actually did nothing, would look at him with puzzled eyes. "Sir?" they would say, feeling awkward. They did not know whether it was a mishap or a joke; they did not know whether to worry or to laugh. So Isaac avoided them, preferring the company of Edward, who did not hear him anyhow, whether the words were correct or wrong, accurate or garbled.

Mostly, though, he kept to himself, avoiding any need for speech. His favorite pastime now was to walk eastward beyond the burnt-out quarters and on to where a Choctaw village had been, a pottery center with its clay deposit which he in his turn had used for making bricks. He remembered the Indians from fifty years ago, going north in their filthy blankets, braves and squaws, dispossessed by a race of men who were not only more cunning but who backed their cunning with gunpowder and whiskey. They were gone now, casualties not of war but of progress, obsolete, and had left no sign of their passing except the shards of pottery and arrowheads turned up by plowmen, the Indian mounds scattered at random about the land for archeologists to guess at, and an occasional lift to the cheek-bones in a Negro face and a cocoa tint to the skin.

Isaac had never been one for abstract thinking; but now, reft of his vocation by the war, of his wife by death, and of speech by whatever had gripped his brain and tongue, he asked himself certain questions. It was as if, now that he could no longer voice them, the words came to him with great clarity of mind. Remembering the Indian days, the exodus, he applied what he remembered to the present, to himself. Was it all for nothing, the distances, the ambition, and the labor? He and his kind, the pioneers, the land-grabbing hungry rough-shod men who had had, like the flatboat river bullies before them, that curious combination of bravado and deadly earnestness, loving a fight for the sake of the fight itself and not the outcome—were they to disappear, having served their purpose, and leave no more trace than the Choctaws? If so, where was the dignity of man, to be thrown aside like this, a worn-out tool? He remembered the land as it was when he first came, a great endless green expanse of trees, motionless under the press of summer or tossing and groaning in the winds of spring and fall. He ringed them, felled them, dragged them out; he fired the stumps so that the air was hazed with the blue smoke of their burning, and then he had made his lakeside dream a reality; the plowmen came, the cotton sprouted, and he prospered; until now. The earth, he thought, the earth endures. He groped for the answer, dealing with such abstract simplicities for the first time since childhood, back before memory. The earth, he thought, and the earth goes back to the sun; that was where it began. There is no law, no reason except the sun, and the sun doesnt care. Its only concern is its brightness; we feed that brightness like straws dropped into its flame. Fire! he thought suddenly. It all goes back to fire!

At last he gave up the walks and spent his days in a big armchair in the parlor, keeping the curtains drawn. He had nothing to do with anyone but the deaf butler, with whom speech was not only unnecessary but impossible. Edward brought him food on a tray, such as it was—mostly the cakes of boiled-down gruel, with sorghum and an occasional piece of sidemeat—but Isaac scarcely touched it. He lost weight; the flesh hung loose on his big frame; his temples were concave, his eyes far back in their sockets. Sometimes, alone in the darkened parlor, he tried to form words aloud, listening to what came out when he spoke. But it was worse than ever. Often, now, the sounds were not even words. I'm talking in the tongues, he thought, remembering the revivals and sanctifyings he had attended around Natchez as a young man, a scoffer on the lookout for excitement. He had seen and heard whole creekbanks full of people writhing and speaking gibberish—'the tongues' they called it; they claimed to understand each other in such fits. God had touched them, they said.

Maybe God had touched him too, he thought. He had never been religious, never having felt the need for it—not even now, when a general revival was spreading through the armies and the civilian population of the South—yet he knew nothing of aphasia, either by name or contact, and it seemed to him there must be some reason why he had been stricken like the fanatics on the creekbank; there must be some connection. But if it was God it was punishment, since it had not come through faith. He must be under judgment, just as maybe the whole nation was, having to suffer for the double sin of slavery and mistreatment of the land. Presently, however, this passed and he let it go; he stopped considering it at all, and he stopped trying to talk. He went back to his previous conviction. No, no, he thought, alone in the parlor with the curtains drawn. It's the sun and we go back there, back to fire.

In late October, a time of heat—the long hot summer of '64 had held; dust was everywhere over the empty fields—he was sitting in the armchair and he heard footsteps on the driveway. There was a chink of spurs, then boot-heels coming hard up the front steps. They crossed the veranda. For a moment there was silence, then a rapping of knuckles against the door jamb. A voice: "Hello!" Another silence, somehow more pregnant than the one before. And then: "Hello in there!"

To Isaac all this seemed so loud that even Edward must have heard it. But when he turned and looked at him he saw that the butler was still locked behind his wall of deafness; he stood beside Isaac's chair, looking morosely at nothing at all. He had a toothache and the cook had put a wad of cotton soaked in camphor inside his cheek, binding the bulged jaw with a dinner napkin tied at the crown of his head. It was one of Mrs Jameson's best pieces of linen, big and heavy, and the two corners of the folded napkin stood up stiffly from the knot.

While Isaac watched, the Negro turned his face toward the door, his eyes coming suddenly wide with surprise. Then Isaac heard the voice again, the crisp Northern accent: "Didnt you hear me out there?" Footsteps approached and the voice began again, repeating the question, but was cut off by a surprised intake of breath. Then Isaac saw him. A Federal officer, complete with sword and sash and buttons stamped US, stood on the hearth. They looked at one another.

Isaac saw that the officer was a young man—rather hard-looking, however, as if the face had been baked in the same crucible that had hardened and glazed the face of his son Clive—and he thought: It's something the war does to them; North and South, they get this way after a time because nowadays the wars go on too long. Then as they looked at each other, one on the hearth and the other in the chair, Isaac knew why the officer was there. He steadied himself to speak, intending to say, 'Have you come to burn my house?' But it did not come out that way; he spoke again in the tongues.

The lieutenant, whose rank Isaac saw when he bent forward, listened to Edward's explanation of the garbled language, then said carefully: "I have come to give you notice, notification." He paused, cleared his throat, and continued. He spoke carefully, not as if he were choosing his words, but as if from a memorized speech. "In reprisal for sniping, by a party or parties unknown, against the gunboat *Starlight* at sundown yesterday, I inform you now, by order of Colonel Nathan Frisbie, United States Army, that this house has been selected to be burned. You have exactly twenty minutes."

Isaac sat watching the hard young face, the moving lips, the bars on the shoulders. The lips stopped, stern-set, but he still watched. "Fire," he said or intended to say. "It all began and ends in fire."

Full in our faces the big low blood-red disk of the sun rested its rim on the levee, like a coin balanced lengthwise on a knife edge. We marched westward through a wilderness of briers and canebrakes, along a road that had been cleared by the planters in their palmy days to haul cotton to the steamboat landing for shipment to New Orleans.

The column had rounded the head of the lake and turned toward the river where the gunboat waited. Four miles in our rear, beyond the lake, the reflection of the burning house was a rose-and-violet glow to match the sunset in our front.

I rode beside the colonel at the head and the troops plodded behind in a column of fours. They marched at ease, their boots stirring the dust so that those in the center were hidden from the waist down and those at the tail showed only their heads and shoulders. Their rifle barrels, canted in all directions, caught the ruddy, almost level rays of the sun; the bayonets, fixed, appeared to have been blooded. They kept their heads lowered, their mouths tight shut, breathing through their noses. The only sounds were the more or less steady clink of equipment, the soft clop clop of horses' hoofs, and the shuffle of shoes in the dust. It somehow had an air of unreality in the failing light.

While the upper half of the sun still showed above the dark knife edge of the levee we approached a live-oak spreading its limbs above a grassy space beside the road. Colonel Frisbie drew rein and raised one arm to signal a halt. The troops came to a jumbled stop, like freight cars. Then the sergeant advanced and stood beside the colonel's horse, waiting. He was short and muscular, thick-chested and very black, with so little neck that his head seemed to rest directly on his shoulders. "Ten minutes," the colonel told him.

The sergeant saluted, holding it stiffly until the colonel returned it, then faced about. The troops stood in the dust of the road. He drew himself up, taking a deep breath. "De-tail: ten *shut*!" He glared. "Ground—harms!"

Dismounting, the colonel smiled. "Good man," he said. "That comes of having trained him myself."

"Yes sir," I said.

The platoon fell out, coming apart almost unwillingly, like something coming unglued. Colonel Frisbie often declared that, properly trained and led, Negro troops made "the finest soldiers on the planet, bar none," and when he was given command of the *Starlight* he set out to prove his contention by supplying the proper training and leadership. Now he was satisfied; it was no longer a theory, it was a fact. The corporal-orderly took our horses and we crossed the grass and sat with our backs against the trunk of the live-oak. I was glad to rest my knee.

High in the branches a blue jay shrilled and chattered. The colonel looked up, searching, and finally found him. "Isnt today Friday?"

"Yes sir," I said.

"Thought so. Then here's another case of these people not knowing what theyre talking about. They say you never see a jay on a Friday because thats the day theyre all in hell getting instructions from the devil. And they believe it, too—I dont exaggerate." He nodded. Ever since he had heard the fable he had been spending a good part of every Friday watching for a blue jay. It bothered him for a while that he could not find one. But now he had, and he felt better; he could move on to something else, some other old wives' tale to disprove. "I suppose while we're whipping the rebelliousness out of them we'd do well to take out some of the superstition along with it. Hey?"

"Yes sir," I said.

He went on talking and I went on saying Yes Sir every time I heard his voice rise to a question. But I was not listening; I could not have repeated a word he said just then. My mind was back on the other side of the lake, where the reflection of the burning house grew brighter against the darkling sky—remembering, then and now:

When I had finished my recitation—"selected to be burned. You have exactly twenty minutes"—the old man looked up at me out of a face that was older than time. He sank back into the chair. "Far," he said; "It goes back too far," and gave no other sign that he had understood or even heard what I said. I left the house, went back down the driveway to where the troops crouched in loose circles, preparing to eat the bread and meat, the midday meal they had brought in their haversacks.

Colonel Frisbie was waiting. "What did they say in there?" he asked.

"It was an old man. . . ."

"Well?"

"Sir?"

"What did he say?"

"He didnt say anything. He just sat there."

"Oh?" the colonel said, turning to accept a packet of sandwiches from the orderly. This was officers' food. "Well. Maybe for once we've found one who admits he deserves what he's going to get. Or maybe it's not his." He opened the packet, selected a sandwich, and extended the rest toward me. "Here." I shook my head but he insisted. "Go on. Take one." I took one—it was mutton—then sat with it untasted in my hand.

The colonel ate rapidly and efficiently, moving his jaw with a steady sidewise thrust and taking sips from his canteen between bites. When he had eaten a second sandwich he took out his watch, opened

the heavy silver case, and laid it face-up on his knee. Soon afterwards
he picked it up again; he rose, brushed crumbs from the breast of his
uniform, looked hard at the watch for a few more seconds, then
snapped it shut with a sharp, decisive click.

"All right, Mr Lundy," he said. "Time's up."

I reentered the house with the sergeant and ten of the men. From the
hall I saw the butler still standing in the parlor beside the fanback chair
where the old man sat. At a sign from the sergeant, two of the soldiers
took position on opposite sides of the chair, then lifted the old man,
chair and all, and carried him through the hall, out of the door and
across the porch, and set him down at the foot of the lawn, near the
road and facing the front of the house. The butler walked alongside,
his pink-palmed hands fluttering in time with the tails of his claw-
hammer coat, making gestures of caution. "Keerful, yawl," he kept
saying in the cracked, off-key voice of the deaf. "Be keerful, now."
The napkin-end rabbit ears had broken. One fell sideways, along his
jaw, and the other down over his face. He slapped at it from time to
time to get it out of his eyes as he stood watching the soldiers set the
chair down.

What followed was familiar enough; we had done this at many
points along the river between Vicksburg and Memphis, the Walnut
Hills and the Lower Chickasaw Bluff, better than two dozen times in
the course of a year. The soldiers went from room to room, ripping
curtains from the windows and splintering furniture and bed-slats for
kindling. When the sergeant reported the preparations complete, I
made a tour of inspection, upstairs and down—the upstairs had been
closed off for some time now; dust was everywhere, except in one
room which apparently was used by one of the servants. At his
shouted command, soldiers in half a dozen rooms struck matches
simultaneously. (A match was still a rarity but we received a special
issue for our work, big sulphur ones that sputtered at first with a great
deal of smoke and stench till they burned past the chemical tip.) Then
one by one they returned and reported to the sergeant. The sergeant in
turn reported to me, and I gave the order to retire. It was like combat,
and all quite military; Colonel Frisbie had worked out the procedure in
a company order a year ago, with subparagraphs under paragraphs
and a time-schedule running down the margin.

From the lawn, where we turned to watch, the house appeared as
peaceful, as undisturbed as it had been before we entered. But soon,
one after another, wisps of smoke began to laze out, and presently a

lick of flame darted and curled from one of the downstairs windows. As I stood watching the flames begin to catch, I let my eye wander over the front of the house and I saw at an upper window the head and shoulders of a Negro woman. I could see her plainly, even the smallpox scars on her face. She did not seem excited. In fact she seemed quite calm, even decorous, sitting there looking out over the lawn where the soldiers by now were beginning to shout and point: "Look yonder! Look up yonder!"

I ran toward the house. The smoke and flames were mostly from the draperies and splintered furniture, I saw as I entered the hall again, but the smoke was thick enough to send me into a fit of coughing and I saw the staircase through a haze of tears. Climbing at a stumbling run I reached the upper hall. The smoke was less dense here; I managed to choose the door to the proper bedroom. It was not locked, as I had feared it might be. I was about to kick it in, but then I tried the knob and it came open.

The woman sat in a rocking chair beside the window. She had hidden behind some clothes in a closet while we searched and set fire to the house; then she had taken her seat by the window, and from time to time—the gesture was almost coy, coquettish—she raised one hand to wave at all the soldiers on the lawn. "Look yonder! Look up yonder!" they still shouted, pointing, and she waved back, flirtatious. When I stumbled into the room, half blinded by smoke, she turned and looked at me without surprise; I even had the impression that she had been waiting for me to join her.

"Shame," she said solemnly. She wagged a finger at me. "Shame on you, captain, for trying to burn Mars Ike's fine house. *I* seen you."

The tears cleared and I found myself looking into the woman's eyes. They were dark brown, almost black, the yellowed whites flicked with little points of red, and completely mad. Trapped in a burning house with a raving lunatic: it was something out of a nightmare. I was wondering how to get her to leave, whether to use force or try to persuade her, when she solved everything by saying in a hoarse whisper, as if in fear of being overheard: "Sh. Less us git out of here, fo they burns it." I nodded, afraid to speak because whatever I said might cause her to change her mind. I even bent forward, adopting her air of conspiracy. "Wait," she said. "I'll git my things."

While the flames crackled in an adjoining room, really catching now, she got what she called her 'things'—a big, brass-hinged family

Bible and a cracked porcelain chamberpot with a design of overlap-
ping rose leaves about its rim—and we went downstairs together
through the smoke, which was considerably thicker now. "Look to
me like they done already started to burn it," she said. As we came out
onto the lawn the soldiers gave a cheer.

But I did not feel heroic. For one thing, there had been small risk
involved; and for another, even that small risk had frightened me
badly. The house continued to smoulder and smoke, though little
tongues of flame licked murmurous at the sills. This went on for what
seemed a very long time, myself thinking as I watched: Go on, burn!
Get it over; burn! And then, as if in answer, a great billow of flame
rushed from a downstairs window, then another from another and
another, rushing, soaring, crackling like laughter, until the whole
front of the house was swathed in flames. It did not murmur now. It
roared.

Those nearest the house, myself among them, gave back from the
press of heat. It came in a rolling wave; our ears filled with the roaring
until we got far enough back to hear a commotion in progress at the
opposite end of the lawn, near the road. Turning, we saw what had
happened.

The old man in the chair was making some sort of disturbance,
jerking his arms and legs and wagging his head. He had been quiet up
to this time, but now he appeared to be making a violent speech. The
soldiers had crowded around, nudging each other and craning over
one another's shoulders for a better view. Then I got there and I saw
what it was. He was having a stroke, perhaps a heart attack. The
buttler, still wearing the absurd napkin bandage about his jaws, stood
on one side of the chair; he bent over the old man, his hands out toward
him. On the other side were two women. One was lame and witchlike
except that now her eyes were round with fright, the way no witch's
ever were; I had not seen her before. The other was the mad woman I
had brought out of the burning house. She still clutched the brass-
hinged Bible under one arm, and with the other she had drawn back
the chamberpot, holding it by the wire handle and threatening the
soldier onlookers with it. It was heavy and substantial looking, despite
the crack down its curved flank—a formidable weapon. Brandishing
it, she shouted at the soldiers.

"Shame!" she cried, not at all in the playful tone she had used
when she said the word to me in the house a few minutes before. She
was really angry now. Her smallpox-pitted face was distorted by rage,

and her eyes were wilder than ever. "Whynt you bluebelly hellions let him be! Wicked! Calling yourself soldiers. Burners is all you is. Aint you hurt him enough aready? Shame on you!"

By the time I got there, however, the old man was past being hurt by anyone. The frenzy was finished, whether it came from the heart or the brain. He slumped in the chair, his legs thrust forward, knees stiff, and his arms dropped limp at his flanks, inside the chair arms. The only sign of life was the harsh breathing and the wide, staring eyes; he was going. Soon the breathing stopped, too, and I saw in the dead eyes a stereoscopic reflection of the burning house repeated in double miniature. Behind me the flames soared higher, roaring, crackling. The lame woman dropped to her knees and began to wail.

These were things I knew would stay with me always, the sound of that scream, the twin reflection in those eyes. They were with me now as Colonel Frisbie stood over me, repeating my name: "Lundy. Mr Lundy!" I looked up, like a man brought suddenly out of sleep, and saw him standing straddle-legged in high dusty boots.·

"Sir?"

"Come on, Lieutenant. Time to go." He turned and then looked back. "Whats the matter with you?"

"Yes, sir," I said, not having heard the words themselves, only the questioning tone.

He turned back, and now for the first time in all the months I had known him, the pretense was gone; he was a man alone. "Whats the matter?" he said. "Dont you like me?"

It was out, and as soon as he had said it I could see that he had surprised himself even more than he had surprised me. He wished he could call the question back. But he stood there, still naked to the elements.

"Yes sir," I said. "I have come to feel very close to you through these past fourteen months."

I got up and walked to where the orderly held our horses. Colonel Frisbie came on behind me; for a moment I had almost liked him; God knows he had his problems; but now he was himself again. The troops had already fallen into column on the road. We marched, and the sun was completely gone. Behind us the glow of burning had spread along the eastern sky. As we marched westward through a blue dusk the glow receded, drawing in upon itself. The colonel lit another cigar; its smoke had a strong, tarry smell as its ruby tip shone and paled, on and off and on and off, like a signal lamp. When he turned in the saddle, looking back, leather creaked above the muffled clopping of hoofs in the cooling dust.

"Looks lower," he said. He smoked, still looking back. The cigar glowed. I knew he was watching me, thinking about my answer to his question; he hadnt quite understood it yet. Then he turned to the front again. "Catch quick, burn slow. Thats the way those old ones always go."

I did not answer. I did not look back.

As we went up the levee, having crossed the swampy, canebrake region that lay between the river and the lake—a wilderness belonging less to men than to bears and deer, alligators and moccasins, weird-screaming birds and insects that ticked like clocks in the brush—the colonel drew rein and turned his horse aside for the troops to pass. I took position alongside him on the crest, facing east toward where the reflection had shrunk to a low dome of red. Then suddenly, as we looked across the wilderness and the lake, the house collapsed and loosed a fountain of sparks, a tall column of fire that stood upright for a long minute, solid as a pillar outlined clearly against the backdrop of the night. It rose and held and faded, and the glow was less than before, no more than a gleam.

"Roof fell in," the colonel said. "Thats all, hey?"

I did not answer. I was seeing in my mind the dead face, the eyes with their twin reflection; I was hearing the lame woman scream; I was trying to remember something out of the Book of Job: *Yet man is born unto trouble, as the sparks fly upward.* And: *Man that is born of woman is of few days, and full of trouble, He cometh forth like a flower, and is cut down: he fleeth also as a shadow, and continueth not.* I was still trying to remember the words, but could not, when the last of the troops filed past. The words I remembered were those of the mad woman on the lawn. "Calling yourself soldiers," she said. "Burners is all you is." I twitched the reins, following Colonel Frisbie down the western slope of the levee, over the gang-plank and onto the gunboat again.

# ROBERT W. CHAMBERS

## *The Pickets*

"We be of one blood, you and I!"

—KIPLING.

"HI YANK!"

"Shut up!" replied Alden, wriggling to the edge of the rifle-pit. Connor also crawled a little higher and squinted through the chinks of the pine logs.

"Hey, Johnny!" he called across the river, "are you that clay-eatin' Cracker with green lamps on your pilot?"

"O Yank! Are yew the U.S. mewl with a C.S.A. brand on yewr head-stall?"

"Shut up!" replied Connor, sullenly.

A jeering laugh answered him from across the river.

"He had you there, Connor," observed Alden, with faint interest.

Connor took off his blue cap and examined the bullet-hole in the crown.

"C.S.A. brand on my head-stall, eh!" he repeated, savagely, twirling the cap between his dirty fingers.

"You called him a clay-eating Cracker," observed Alden; "and you referred to his spectacles as green lanterns on his pilot."

"I'll show him whose head-stall is branded," muttered Connor, shoving his smoky rifle through the log-crack.

Alden slid down to the bottom of the shallow pit, and watched him apathetically. He gasped once or twice, threw open his jacket at the throat, and stuffed a filthy handkerchief into the crown of his cap, arranging the ends as a shelter for his neck.

Connor lay silent, his right eye fastened upon the rifle-sight, his dusty army shoes crossed behind him. One yellow sock had slipped down over the worn shoe-heel and laid bare a dust-begrimed ankle-bone.

Suddenly Connor's rifle cracked; the echoes rattled and clattered away through the woods; a thin cloud of pungent vapor slowly drifted straight upward, shredding into filmy streamers among the tangled branches overhead.

"Get him?" asked Alden, after a silence.

"Nope," replied Connor. Then he addressed himself to his late target across the river:

"Hello, Johnny!"

"Hi, Yank!"

"How close?"

"Hey?"

"How close?"

"What, sonny?"

"My shot, you fool!"

"Why, sonny!" called back the Confederate, in affected surprise, "was yew a-shootin' at me?"

Bang! went Connor's rifle again. A derisive catcall answered him, and he turned furiously to Alden.

"Oh, let up," said the young fellow; "it's too hot for that."

Connor was speechless with rage, and he hastily jammed another cartridge into his long hot rifle; but Alden roused himself, brushed away a persistent fly, and crept up to the edge of the pit again.

"Hello, Johnny!" he shouted.

"That you, sonny?" replied the Confederate.

"Yes; say, Johnny, shall we call it square until four o'clock?"

"What time is it?" replied the cautious Confederate; "all our expensive gold watches is bein' repaired at Chickamauga."

At this taunt Connor showed his teeth, but Alden laid one hand on his arm and sang out: "It's two o'clock, Richmond time; Sherman has just telegraphed us from your Statehouse."

"Wall, in that case this crool war is over," relied the Confederate sharp-shooter; "we'll be easy on old Sherman."

"See here!" cried Alden; "is it a truce until four o'clock?"

"All right! Your word, Yank!"

"You have it!"

"Done!" said the Confederate, coolly rising to his feet and strolling down to the river bank, both hands in his pockets.

Alden and Connor crawled out of their ill-smelling dust-wallow, leaving their rifles behind them.

"Whew! It's hot, Johnny," said Alden, pleasantly. He pulled out a stained pipe, blew into the stem, polished the bowl with his sleeve, and sucked wistfully at the end. Then he went and sat down beside Connor, who had improvised a fishing outfit from his ramrod, a bit of string, and a rusty hook.

The Confederate rifleman also sat down on his side of the stream, puffing luxuriously on a fragrant corncob pipe. Alden watched him askance, sucking the stem of his own empty pipe. After a minute or two, Connor dug up a worm from the roots of a beech tree with his bayonet, fixed it to the hook, flung the line into the muddy current, and squatted gravely on his haunches, chewing a leaf stem.

Presently the Confederate soldier raised his head and looked across at Alden.

"What's yewr name, sonny?" he asked.

"Alden," replied the young fellow, briefly.

"Mine's Craig," observed the Confederate; "what's yewr regiment?"

"Two Hundred and Sixtieth New York; what's yours, Mr. Craig?"

"Ninety-third Maryland, *Mister* Alden."

"Quit that throwin' sticks in the water!" growled Connor. "How do you s'pose I'm goin' to catch anythin'?"

Alden tossed his stick back into the brush-heap and laughed.

"How's your tobacco, Craig?" he called out.

"Bully! How's yewr coffee 'n' tack, Alden?"

"First rate!" replied the youth.

After a silence he said, "Is it a go?"

"You bet," said Craig, fumbling in his pockets. He produced a heavy twist of Virginia tobacco, laid it on a log, hacked off about three inches with his sheath-knife, and folded it up in a big green sycamore leaf. This again he rolled into a corn-husk, weighted it with a pebble; then, stepping back, he hurled it into the air, saying, "Deal square, Yank!"

The tobacco fell at Alden's feet. He picked it up, measured it carefully with his clasp-knife, and called out: "Two and three-quarters, Craig. What do you want, hard-tack or coffee?"

"Tack," replied Craig; "don't stint!"

Alden laid out two biscuits. As he was about to hack a quarter from the third, he happend to glance over the creek at his enemy. There was no mistaking the expression in his face. Starvation was stamped on every feature.

When Craig caught Alden's eye, he spat with elaborate care, whistled a bar of the "Bonny Blue Flag," and pretended to yawn.

Alden hesitated, glanced at Connor, then placed three whole biscuit in the corn-husk, added a pinch of coffee, and tossed the parcel over to Craig.

That Craig longed to fling himself upon the food and devour it was plain to Alden, who was watching his face. But he didn't; he strolled leisurely down the bank, picked up the parcel, weighed it critically before opening it, and finally sat down to examine the contents. When he saw that the third cracker was whole and that a pinch of coffee had been added, he paused in his examination and remained motionless on the bank, head bent. Presently he looked up and asked Alden if he had made a mistake. The young fellow shook his head and drew a long puff of smoke from his pipe, watching it curl out of his nose with interest.

"Then I'm obliged to yew, Alden," said Craig; "'low I'll eat a snack to see it ain't pizened."

He filled his lean jaws with the dry biscuit, then scooped up a tin cup full of water from the muddy river and set the rest of the cracker to soak.

"Good?" queried Alden.

"Fair," drawled Craig, bolting an unchewed segment and choking a little. "How's the twist?"

"Fine," said Alden; "tastes like stable-sweepings."

They smiled at each other across the stream.

"Sa-a-y," drawled Craig, with his mouth full, "when yew're out of twist, jest yew sing out, sonny."

"All right," replied Alden. He stretched back in the shadow of a sycamore and watched Craig with pleasant eyes.

Presently Connor had a bite and jerked his line into the air.

"Look yere," said Craig, "that ain't no way for to ketch red-horse. Yew want a ca'tridge on foh a sinker, sonny."

"What's that?" inquired Connor, suspiciously.

"Put on a sinker."

"Go on, Connor," said Alden.

Connor saw him smoking, and sniffed anxiously. Alden tossed him the twist, telling him to fill his pipe.

Presently Connor found a small pebble and improvised a sinker. He swung his line again into the muddy current, with a mechanical sidelong glance to see what Craig was doing, and settled down again on his haunches, smoking and grunting.

"Enny news, Alden?" queried Craig after a silence.

"Nothing much; except that Richmond has fallen," grinned Alden.

"Quit foolin'," urged the Southerner; "ain't there no news?"

"No. Some of our men down at Mud Pond got sick eating catfish. They caught them in the pond. It appears you Johnnys used the pond as a cemetery, and our men got sick eating the fish."

"That so?" drawled Craig; "too bad. Lots of yewr men was in Long Pond too, I reckon."

In the silence that followed two rifleshots sounded faint and dull from the distant forest.

"'Nother great Union victory," drawled Craig. "Extry! Extry! Richmond is took!"

Alden laughed and puffed his pipe.

"We licked the boots off of the 30th Texas last Monday," he said.

"Sho!" drawled Craig; "what did you go a lickin' their boots for—blackin'?"

"Oh, shut up!" said Connor from the bank; "I can't ketch no fish if you two fools don't quit jawin'."

The sun was dipping below the pine-clad ridge, flooding river and wood with a fierce radiance. The spruce needles glittered, edged with gold; every broad, green leaf wore a heart of gilded splendor, and the muddy waters of the river rolled onward like a flood of precious metal, heavy, burnished, noiseless.

From a balsam bough a thrush uttered three timid notes; a great, gauzy-winged grasshopper drifted blindly into a clump of sun-scorched weeds, click! click! cr-r-r-r!

"Purty, ain't it," said Craig, looking at the thrush. Then he swallowed the last morsel of muddy hard-tack, wiped his beard on his cuff, hitched up his trousers, took off his green glasses, and rubbed his eyes.

"A he catbird sings purtier, though," he said, with a yawn.

Alden drew out his watch, puffed once or twice, and stood up, stretching his arms in the air.

"It's four o'clock," he began, but was cut short by a shout from Connor.

"Gee whiz!" he yelled, "what have I got on this here pole?"

The ramrod was bending, the line swaying heavily in the current.

"It's four o'clock, Connor," said Alden, keeping a wary eye on Craig.

"That's all right!" called Craig; "the time's extended till yewr friend lands that there fish."

"Pulls like a porpoise,' grunted Connor. "I bet it busts my ram-rod!"

"Does it pull?" grinned Craig.

"Yes, a dead weight!"

"Don't it jerk kinder this way an' that," asked Craig, much interested.

"Naw," said Connor; "the bloody thing jest pulls steady."

"Then it ain't no red-horse; it's a catfish!"

"Huh!" sneered Connor; "don't I know a catfish? This ain't no catfish, lemme tell yer!"

"Then it's a log," laughed Alden.

"By gum! here it comes," panted Connor; "here, Alden, jest you ketch it with my knife; hook the blade, blame ye!"

Alden cautiously descended the red bank of mud, holding on to roots and branches, and bent over the water. He hooked the big-bladed clasp-knife like a scythe, set the spring, and leaned out over the water.

"Now!" muttered Connor.

An oily circle appeared upon the surface of the turbid water,— another and another. A few bubbles rose and floated upon the tide.

Then something black appeared just beneath the bubbles, and Alden hooked it with his knife and dragged it shoreward. It was the sleeve of a man's coat.

Connor dropped his ramrod and gaped at the thing. Alden would have loosed it, but the knife-blade was tangled in the sleeve.

He turned a sick face up to Connor.

"Pull it in," said the older man. "Here, give it to me, lad—"

When at last the silent vistor lay upon the bank, they saw it was the body of a Union cavalryman. Alden stared at the dead face, fascinated; Connor mechanically counted the yellow chevrons upon the blue sleeve, now soaked black. The muddy water ran over the baked soil, spreading out in dust-covered pools; the spurred boots trickled slime. After a while both men turned their heads and looked at Craig. The Southerner stood silent and grave, his battered cap in his hand. They eyed each other quietly for a moment, then, with a vague gesture, the Southerner walked back into his pit and presently reappeared, trailing his rifle.

Connor had already begun to dig with his bayonet, but he glanced up sharply at the rifle in Craig's hand. Then he looked searchingly into the eyes of the Southerner. Presently he bent his head and quietly continued digging.

It was after sunset before he and Alden finished the shallow grave,

Craig watching them in silence, his rifle between his knees. When they were ready they rolled the body into the hole and stood up.

Craig also rose, raising his rifle to a "present." He held it there while the two Union soldiers shovelled the earth into the grave. Then Alden went back and lifted the two rifles from the pit, handed Connor his, and waited.

"Ready!" growled Connor. "Aim!"

Alden's rifle came to his shoulder. Craig also raised his rifle.

"Fire!"

Three times the three shots rang out in the wilderness, over the unknown grave. After a moment or two Alden nodded goodnight to Craig across the river, and walked slowly toward his rifle-pit. Connor shambled after him. As he turned to lower himself into the pit he called across the river, "Good-night, Craig!"

"Good-night, Connor," said Craig.

# JOHN P. MARQUAND

*High Tide*

SOMETIMES, IN THE SULTRY warmth of summer at Deer Bottom, old Scott Mattaye could remember the high tide; and sometimes, when he was feeling in the mood, he might even tell of how he went through a hostile country to find an army which was lost, and how the Battle of Gettysburg might have been wholly different if his horse had not gone lame. At such an hour, after his second glass, the old man would sit straighter at the table, and his voice, slightly cracked, but soft and gently drawling, would rise above the whirring of the moths which kept fluttering around the guttering candles like incarnations of the quiet sounds from the warm, dark night outside.

"Yo' follow me, gentlemen?" he would say. "I'm referrin', of co'se, to the lack of cavalry in the opening phases of that engagement—cavalry, the eyes and ears. And I'm referrin', above all, to the temp'rary absence—an' I maintain the just and unavoidable absence—of our cavalry general, on whose staff I had the honor of servin'. I'm referrin' to that immortal hero, gentlemen, Major General J. E. B. Stuart—Beauty Stuart—Good Time Stuart—in the Army of Northern Virginia of the Confederate States of America— the ve'y greatest cavalry commander in that army, gentlemen, which, of co'se, is the same as sayin' the greatest cavalry leader in the history of the world."

He meant no bathos or exaggeration when he said it. Some impression had been left upon him which transcended time. He would smile beneath his drooping white mustache as though he had a secret, and he had the secret of his days. Strange, unrelated moments were flitting before him like the shadows of the moths upon the wall—plumed hats, boots of yellow leather that came above the knee, girls snipping buttons off gray coats, eggnogs, Virginia hams which glowed like ruby from the silver on the table, black boys dancing the buck and wing beneath the lantern light, a kiss, a lock of hair, the Bower, Frederick, Winchester, high tide.

"High tide," he said; "it all was accident and time."

It was clear what he was thinking, although his words had a way of wandering when his mind was groping in the mazes of his vanished world. He was going back to the hours when the tide of the Confederacy lapped over the Potomac to reach its high-water mark of the war. He was thinking of Rowser's Ford and the captured wagon train at Cooksville—twisted iron rails, staggering horses, men reeling in the saddle, drunk with sleep. He was thinking of a spy, and of Stuart's last great raid. The Army of Northern Virginia was pouring into Pennsylvania. Lee and Longstreet were arguing over plans.

"Sammy," he said to the cook's small boy, "bring refreshment to the gentlemen. . . . Now, Gettysburg—of co'se, we should have whipped 'em if Stuart had been there. I should have fetched him— yes, indeed. If that horse had not gone lame near East Berlin, why, sholy I'd have fetched him. If I had not stopped by the stone house near the road. A matter of a spy, you understand—a foul, ugly matter. . . . I share in the responsibility, gentlemen. It all was accident and time."

He did not add that he had nearly died in cold blood in that square stone house, but his fear was in his face. His fear was like a specter then, just behind his chair.

He could see the beginning, and he knew that the hand of fate was in it, though it was more than sixty years ago. Stuart had been stroking his fine brown beard, as he always did when he was troubled. It was in the cool of an early summer morning, the first day of July. The horses' heads were drooping, and faces were blank from lack of sleep.

"Mattaye," Stuart was saying, "I'm lost. Early's gone. Everybody's gone. I've sent off three officers already. You go out, too, and find the army. You see this map? We're here. Ride out toward that place Gettysburg yonder. Keep riding till you find it."

It was a fine day, he could remember. The fields were green and fresh from early summer, and the land was richer than the land at home. It was a country of fine, rolling fields of pasture and wheat and corn, of neat hedges, neat houses and compact, ungenerous trees. It was a land uncompromising in its plenty, without warmth of welcome. But the dead weight of weariness was what he remembered best. After two days of steady march, men were lying exhausted with bridles in hands, watching horses that stood too tired to eat. There was food in the Yankee wagons they had taken outside of Washington. He could see the white tops of the wagons down the road, but there were many too tired for food.

Scott Mattaye straightened his shoulders. He was made of iron and rawhide then, but he was very tired.

"The army, sir?" he said. "Which army, sir?"

His question made Stuart laugh, and the sound of it came back across the years. He was in a hostile country with his column too tired to move. He was lost and he was worried, and he had not slept an hour in the last three days. Yet the general seemed to feel none of the lethargy of exhaustion. The way he wore his sash, the tilt of the plume in his slouch hat, the angle of his cloak about one shoulder made his equipment look as fresh as when he had started. Nothing ever wilted in the general.

"Which army?" he said. "Well, I'm not aiming to encounter Federal troops in force this minute. I'd prefer to meet the Army of Northern Virginia, Gen. Robert E. Lee commanding, now engaged in invasion of Pennsylvania, and due to end this war. I'm out of touch, and I don't like it—not right now. They're somewhere over there— somewhere."

He waved his arm toward the southwest, but there was nothing. There was no dust or smoke or sound; nothing but open rolling fields, stretching to the horizon in the tranquil light of early morning. The very peace was like a disturbing suspicion that something had gone wrong. It could only have been anxiety that made Stuart speak so frankly.

"The corps should be coming together," he said, "and we should be in front. There should be word, you understand? . . . Your horse all right?"

Scott's horse was a light sorrel, caked with sweat and dust. The general was examining the animal.

"He's worn down, sir," said Scott, "but he's as good as any in the column, I reckon, sir."

"Take your blankets and saddle off," Stuart said. "Kill him if you have to, but report to General Lee, you understand? Ask for orders and a new horse to take you back."

"Yes, sir," said Scott. "Where will I find you, sir?"

"We're resting here two hours," said Stuart. "Then we're moving on Carlisle. Watch out for cavalry, and don't get caught. We've lost too many on the staff. Good-by."

Only the impression of small things was left to Scott Mattaye, and the touch of all the great sights meant much less, until all his memory of camp and bivouac came down to little things. Bodies of men, the sound of marching troops and firing were a part of his life, and were blurred into the monotony of days, but the smell of bacon grease in smoke, a voice or the squeal of a horse would be like yesterday. He remembered how his blankets sprawled over the tailboard of the headquarters wagon, inertly, like a dead man's limbs. As they did so, he had a glimpse of fine gray cloth among them. It was his new uniform coat, which he had planned to wear in Washington City, certain they would take Washington.

An impulse made him put it on which was composed of various thoughts—the idea that he might never wear it, through accident or theft, the desire to appear in an enemy country like a gentleman, and the conviction that a staff officer should look his best. The coat had the buff facings of the staff. Though it was wrinkled and still damp from a wetting in the Potomac, it was very well cut. He strapped his belt over it, with his saber and his pistol—a fine, ivory-handled weapon which he had taken from a Yankee colonel in Centerville. His saddle was a Yankee saddle; even his horse had a U.S. brand, but his coat was Richmond, bought with two hundred and fifty dollars of his country's notes.

"You, Jerry," he said to the horse, "step on. We're bound to go." Then he remembered that the animal sighed almost exactly like a man.

He went down the road past the picket at a trot, and half a mile farther on he met a patrol, riding back. He knew the officer, a friend of his. It was Travis Greene, from Maryland, and Scott had always liked him. He liked the way he handled horses; there was something in him which Scott had always trusted—a candor, a vein of sympathy. He only remembered later that the other's eyes were sharp that morning, and unusually curious.

"Trav," he said, "seen anything out there?"

Trav shook his head and grinned. The corners of his thin mouth wrinkled. He had a disarming way of wrinkling up his nose, like a lean hound dog sniffing at the air.

"No," he answered. "Where yo' headin'?"

"Message," said Scott.

"Seems like the general's getting nervous," Trav said. "Nothing but the staff with messages. Yo' won't get far on that old crock of yours. He's powerful near through."

"Why, boy," said Scott, "this animal can go a week and never drop. Why, he just craves to run. Why, boy, you've never seen a raid. This is only triflin' up to now.''

"Where we headin'?" the other asked. "I reckon you don't know.''

Scott felt the importance of his knowledge and smiled. "Don't you wish you knew?" he said. "Where Beauty Stuart wants. That's where. Come to think of it, seems to me you're always asking questions.''

"Saucy, aren't you?" said Trav. "I reckon you're out calling in that new coat of yours. I'd take you for a damn Yank if it wasn't for that coat.''

"Would you?" said Scott. "Well, you ask Beauty Stuart where I'm going. No doubt he'd just delight to tell you, and call for your advice. I'll be seeing you. Good-by.''

Then, almost without thinking, he pulled his watch from his breeches pocket. It was a fine, heavy repeater.

"You, Trav," he called, "keep this, and if I don't get back, send it on to Deer Bottom, and I'll be much obliged.''

He could still hear the voices, low and pleasant, and could recall the way Trav started as he reached and caught the watch, and the unexpected sharpness of his glance.

"To Deer Bottom? Certain sure! I'm proud of your confidence," he said. "Good-by!"

Scott Mattaye loosened his revolver in its holster and put his horse to a trot again, not fast, for he had the cavalry instinct to save the animal's strength, and the horse was tired.

"You, Jerry," he said, "take your time.''

Then, as he spoke the word, he knew that he had made a blunder. He had three hundred dollars in Confederate bills in his pocket, which would have been more useful at Deer Bottom than a watch; and now, because of a sentimental impulse, he had no way of judging the distance he was traveling, except by instinct and the sun. He had been out before, more times than he could count. He knew that one could conceivably ride all day through an opposing army with a good horse and a knowledge of the road. He had seen enough in the raids around McClellan and Pope to have gained a contempt for Yankee horsemanship. He could get safe away from a regiment of Yankee cavalry.

But now he could detect a difference. He had been in a friendly country on other rides alone, where there had been a careless tangle of woods and grown-over fields. Friendly people had waved to him; girls had brought him milk. His horse beneath him had been like a reservoir

of untapped strength, but now his horse was tired. There was no
spring in the trot, nor a trace of willingness to increase the pace, and
the country itself was foreign. There was a plenty in the Pennsylvania
fields, like the rolling land along the Shenandoah, but there was no
gentility or generosity in that plenty. There was the same sinister
threat in the meticulous furrows and the abundance of that earth which
he had seen in the armies that sprang from it—the same hostile,
careless giving. The blue uniforms were a part of that land, and the
Yankee wagons groaning with beef and ordnance.

There was a menace in that hostile land, for everything was watching him. He could feel a hatred in that country rising against him like a
wave. The sun, glinting on the windows of small farmhouses, made
those windows look like eyes, reflecting the hatred of unseen faces,
staring toward the road. And the uncertainty of time was weighing on
him, because he did not know the time. The uncertainty made him
furtive, and made him remember Stuart's own uncertainty. "Time,"
the hoof beats of his horse were saying, and the humming of the
insects and the rustling of the corn were speaking of that flowing,
unseen principle which connected life and death.

A sound made him draw his reins, and his horse stopped, obedient
and still. It came, a swift, metallic click, from behind a clump of small
trees near a bend which shut out his vision to the right. Before he knew
what he was doing, his revolver was cocked in his hand, while he sat
staring, listening. He did not know that he was speaking until he heard
his voice.

"Pshaw," he heard himself mutter, "it's only someone hoeing."

A man in overalls was hoeing a potato patch just around the bend.
He turned and stared at Scott, leaning on his hoe.

"Morning, friend," said Scott. "It looks like a right fine
morning."

The man spat on a potato hill. "I ain't no friend of yourn," he said,
"nor any of your kind."

Scott laughed. "Why, mister," he said, "I mean you no harm, and
that's why I say 'friend.' I only aim to ask you if you can let me know
the time."

"Would it give you comfort," the other asked, "if you was to
know the time?"

"Why, sholy," Scott said, still smiling. "I'd like right well
to know."

The man's voice became louder. It was like a blow across the face:

"Then I'll die before I tell yer, ye nigger-tradin' thief! Two of my sons has died, and I can die before I raise a hand to give one mite of comfort to your lot! I only hope your time is short, and I may see your carcass rotting! Now git on!"

Scott Mattaye did not answer. He put his horse to the trot and hurried down the road, amazed. He saw other men pause to gaze at him from the roadside. Women stared from doorways. Children, when they saw him, ran screaming. He had never felt the weight of hatred until then. He did not stop again to ask the time.

He did not stop again until his horse went lame. By then a high forenoon sun was beating on his plumed felt hat, and the farming country lay before him as beautiful as a picture, incongruously far from war. The horse went lame so suddenly you might have thought he had been shot—a stumble, a sharp snort of pain, and he was limping. After Scott Mattaye was off the saddle, it did not take a half a minute to convince him that his horse was through, and, though he had grown callous to the suffering of animals, he had a pang of sorrow.

"Boy," he said, "you did the best you could."

The road, he remembered, was sloping down to a ford across a brook. Beyond the ford it wound up again, past a rutted lane, which led to a square house of deep-gray limestone, set back perhaps a hundred yards from the roadway.

That house on its little rise of ground always came back to his memory as aloofly pleasant—heavy chimneys, small-paned windows, a fine, arched doorway of an earlier time. It always seemed to him to speak of kindliness and of sober, decent lives, and to be without a taint of anything sinister or bizarre. A long cattle barn stood behind the house, flanked by young apple trees set in even rows. He looked for half a minute, then hooked the bridle through his arm, walking slowly with his limping horse.

"Jerry," he said, "I'm going to leave you yonder."

The windows were blank and impassive as he walked up the lane, and everything was silent—it seemed to him too silent.

"Hello," he called. "Is anybody home?"

The sound of his voice was like the breaking of a spell. Two shepherd dogs rushed at him, snarling. A door had slammed and an old man ran toward them with a stick, a picture of towering strength, half worn away by age. A white shirt, bare, scrawny arms and a fine white beard halfway down his chest, but his height was what Scott remembered best. He was very tall.

"Grandpa!" he heard a child's voice calling from the house. "Don't take on so, grandpa! You'll have another bad turn if you do!"

The noise of the dogs seemed to ebb away. All his memory of the barnyard seemed to ebb away, leaving only that figure of age, half disturbing, half majestic—something never to forget. The old man was breathing much too heavily. His shirt and knit suspenders and baggy trousers took nothing from his dignity. Something in his face made his beard like ashes over glowing coals—a mobile, powerful face. His forehead was high. His eyes were serene and steely blue. Scott Mattaye took off his hat and bowed, though the man was plain and not a gentleman.

"I'm intrudin', sir," he said. "My horse—he's broken down. I reckon that—"

"Mary Breen!" the old man shouted. "You, Mary Breen!"

A girl—she could not have been above thirteen—came running from the house. Her gingham dress, her face and eyes had a washed-out look; her bleached yellow pigtails were slapping on her shoulders.

"Mary Breen," the old man said, "put up that hoss. . . . I made haste, as I always will, to serve the Lord. . . . Young man, you come with me. This is a day of glory."

Scott Mattaye stared at him, bewildered for a moment.

"Put up that hoss," the old man said, "and put the saddle on the bay that's waiting. . . . You'll need another hoss for sure. Now, please to follow me."

"Sholy, sir," said Scott. "With great pleasure. I'll be pleased to settle for another animal, of co'se. Excuse me. Could you let me know the time?"

He had no premonition, he always said, on entering the house. He had seen enough peculiar people and places in that war. The tide of war had pushed him into mean kitchens and stables for a night, or just as strangely it had whirled him into dining rooms of great plantation houses, where he had touched on lives which he would never touch again. He did not bother to put an implication on the old man's words, except that they were friendly. The friendliness brought back Scott's confidence in inevitable fortune, and he straightened his sash and dusted off his coat.

"Yes," the old man said again, "this is a day of glory. I'm glad I've lived to see it, because I'm gittin' old."

The kitchen was very neat. A kettle was humming on the stove, so that the steam made the air humidly pleasant. There were two strong wooden chairs and a deal table, but what he noticed first was the asthmatic, hurried ticking of a clock above the humming of the boiling water. He turned to glance at it where it stood on a shelf between two windows. A dingy clock in a veneered mahogany case—he could shut his eyes and see it still. The hour was just eleven.

"No," the old man said, "not here. The parlor's just this way."

He had opened a door to the front entry, and Scott began to smile, amused by the formality which led him to the parlor. He had a glimpse of himself in the entry mirror; his face was thin and brown, and his coat, he was pleased to notice, fitted very well.

"Here you be," the old man said, "and we give thanks you're here."

He opened the parlor door as he spoke, and Scott had a whiff of fresh cigar smoke and a blurred vision of a horsehair sofa and of faded floral wallpaper, but he only half saw the room. For a second—the time could not have been long—he stood on the threshold stonily, incapable of motion.

A saber and a revolver were lying on the parlor table, and behind the table, smoking a cigar, his coat half unbuttoned and his black hat slouched over his eyes, a Federal major was sitting. In that instant of surprise Scott could think of nothing. A sharp nose and deep brown eyes, florid cheeks, a drooping black mustache, half covering a lantern jaw, clean linen, dark blue broadcloth, gold on the shoulders—Scott Mattaye saw it all in an instant, and then, before speech or motion could touch him, the major began to smile.

"Howdy, Captain James," the major said. "I saw you from the window. I'm from—you know where. Let's get down to business. I've got a way to ride. Do you want to see my papers?"

"No," said Scott; his voice was hoarse. "No, major."

"No doubt about you," the major said. "New coat, Yankee saddle, Yankee boots. You've got your nerve to go among 'em so, and, by gad, you're young to be in a game like this."

Scott Mattaye did not answer, because the idea which came to him was too grotesque, though already he knew that his intuition had been right. The major was watching him curiously, but not suspiciously, beneath the brim of his black hat, and Scott Mattaye had learned to read the capabilities of an individual. Something told him that this officer was an accurate and dangerous man, and a capable one besides. The major's hand, with thick, blunt fingers, was resting on the table just six inches away from his pistol butt. Scott could see it from the corner of his eye, and he could notice four notches cut in the black walnut of the butt, telling him in silent voices that the chances were the major could shoot him dead if he made a sudden move. Scott was standing in the doorway, with the old man just behind him. If he should make a move to draw his weapon, before his pistol was out of the holster he knew he would be dead.

"A dirty game," the major said with his cigar between his teeth, "a thankless game. You should be more careful, captain. Your uniform's too new."

Scott Mattaye was not a fool. He knew, if he had not known before, what he was supposed to be and why the major was waiting.

"Thank you, sir," said Scott, and he contrived to smile. A little talk, a word, a gesture, and he might have a chance to snatch that pistol from the table. "I agree, sir, it's a right dirty business, and I detest a—scout. . . . But, excuse me, we'd better be alone."

It would help to get the old man out. He turned slowly, until their eyes met—the old man's eyes were as blue as a china plate at home—and he heard the major laughing.

"Don't worry about Pa Breen," he said. "He's as straight as string. . . . Father, you go out and close the door."

"Young man," old Mr. Breen said, "don't fret about me none. I can die for a cause as good as you, I guess. Amen."

When he closed the door, there was no sound outside in the entry, but the farmer must have had the tread of an Indian, because, five seconds later, Scott heard the kitchen door slam shut.

"The old man's cracked," the major said. "You know, one of those fanatic abolitionists—agent in the underground, friend of Garrison and Whittier, leader of the party hereabouts. Why, he'd kill a man in gray as easily as he'd stick a pig, and he's in the butcher business. They had to hide his pants so he wouldn't go to Harper's Ferry with Brown."

"Yes, sir," said Scott. "John Brown, I presume you mean? It's been my observation that he's a right smart old man."

The major tapped his fingers on the table, but some perversity kept them close to the revolver butt.

"Mad," said the major. "Ideas drive men mad, when ideas and religion mix. . . . What's your notion of their strength, James? . . . Sit down. There's a chair."

Scott Mattaye drew his chair carefully to the opposite side of the table. Being an officer of the staff, he had heard enough rumors and secrets to enable him to twist them plausibly into lies. It surprised him how quickly his mind was working, and as smoothly as his voice.

"Major," said Scott, "Marse Bob, he has a heap of men. Reserves have been drawn from the state garrisons. I'm safe saying General Lee's across the river with a hundred and ten thousand. It's high tide."

He tossed out the number glibly, though he knew he was naming twice the strength. He did so from his knowledge of the Yankee obsession of superior numbers, and he saw that his guess was right. The major whistled softly.

"You're high," he said, "I hope. Can you name the strength of corps?"

He had never thought of the meaning of information until he sat there, waiting for the Yankee major to move his hand. As he spoke, he could think of armies moving like blind monsters, each groping toward the other to the tune of lies like his. He paused and leaned a trifle across the table.

"Major," he said, "have you another of those cigars? I'm perishin' for a smoke."

He gathered his feet under him noiselessly. He could not sit there talking. If he could make the major move his hand, he could push the table over.

"Beg pardon," the major said, and reached with his left hand inside his coat and tossed a leather case across the table. "A light?" The major pushed across a silver match safe, still with his left hand. "Believe me, your information's worth a box of those cigars."

A tap on the door made him stop. It was the little girl with the bleached pigtails; she was carrying two glasses and a small stone jug.

"Why," said Scott Mattaye, "hello, honeybee!"

"Grandpop," said the little girl, "he said to fetch you this."

"Set it on the floor," the major said, "and close the door behind you. We're not thirsty, sister."

"Grandpop," said the little girl, "he don't touch it since he was took with spells. Somethin' 'pears to git aholt of him, like a rope acrost the chest. First a pain under his arm, like, and then acrost the chest."

"You tell your grandpop to take a pill," the major said, "and go out and close the door."

The major leaned back in his chair. His deliberation set Scott's nerves on edge, but the major did not move his hand.

"Well," he said, "it's a quaint, strange world. Here you and I are sitting, smoking good Havanas. There an old man is 'took with spells.' And somewhere else two armies are jockeying for position. Suppose they ran into each other blind, neither of them ready. War's like walking in the dark.''

''Believe me, sir,'' Scott said, and he half forgot what he was supposed to be, ''Robert E. Lee is never in the dark. He's the greatest man alive.''

''Youve got the cant,'' said the major. ''But you don't believe that, do you? Where's his cavalry? Off with Stuart, when it should be in front of his army. Either Lee or Stuart's a plain fool.''

Scott Mattaye half rose from his chair, and sat down again. Just in time he remembered where he was.

''Yes, sir'' the major was saying, as though he were reading from a textbook. ''Cavalry should form a screen in front of any army of invasion, as any plebe knows at the Point, instead of being detached on a needless mission, moving northwest when the main body's thirty miles south.''

Then Scott Mattaye forgot, and spoke before he thought. ''Here,'' he asked sharply. ''How did you know that?''

The major's head went forward; his eyes were suddenly sharp: ''Why, you sent us word from Hanover yourself.''

''Hanover?'' said Scott, but the major was not listening. At last he had raised his right hand from the table.

''Hush!'' the major said. ''Hush! Listen!''

For a second Scott forgot the hand. The major had good ears. Through the closed windows Scott became conscious of what the major heard, though it was not a sound exactly. It was rather a very faint concussion, a stirring in the air, which might have been summer thunder if the sun were not shining. Even in the parlor Scott could feel its strength.

''I hear 'em. Guns,'' he said.

Though the major was looking at him, his eyes were blank from listening.

''Yes, he said, ''a scad of guns. We've struck into something heavy. . . . There. You hear?''

Scott could hear, and he could see. In that same instant the officer turned his head toward the direction of the sound, and then Scott moved. He was very quick in those days when a sudden motion might make the difference between life and death. That Yankee moved also, but he was not fast enough. Scott had snatched the pistol up, and he was stepping backward.

"Here, you!" the major shouted. "Set that down!"

"Mister major," Scott told him, "yo' step backward from that table and keep down yo' voice, if yo' want to save yo' skin. . . . That's better, major. . . . You've told me something right valuable. General Stuart will be pleased to know he's got a spy out with him. I'll be surprised if that spy keeps livin' long."

The major was a cool man, Scott always said. He leaned against the wall, twisting an end of his mustache and speaking in a careful nasal drawl.

"All right for now," the major said, "but you listen to me, staff officer. A spy's more valuable than you or me. I hope you realize I'll do my best to stop you if I can."

Scott smiled back at him in perfect comprehension. "I realize," he said. "That's why I beg of you to stand right still. If there's a battle yonder, I'm goin' to it, mister major, and yo' horse is going with me."

"You've got a most consoling voice," the major said.

"Put your hands above your head," said Scott.

Then he knew there was something wrong. The major's eyes had narrowed and he was looking across Scott's shoulder toward the little parlor door.

"Certainly," the major said. "Don't get excited, Johnny."

There was a creak of a floor board behind him. He remembered the impulse to turn and the certainty that something was just behind him, but almost with the impulse a weight landed on his back and he was pitching forward.

Scott fired just as he was falling, so that the crash of the shot and the smell of black powder blended with a taste of sulphur in his mouth. Someone had him by the throat. He kicked to free himself, but someone held his legs.

"Tie his hands," he heard the major say. "Steady. He's all right."

He was choking; flashes of searing light were darting across his eyes.

"Breen"—another voice was speaking—a soft Southern voice— "take yo' hands off him. We've got him all right now."

Then he was struggling to his feet. His hands were tied behind him, and he noticed that a cloud of powder smoke was rising softly toward the ceiling. There was a haze before his eyes and a drumming in his ears.

"Scott Mattaye," someone was saying, "I'm right sorry it is you."

The haze was lifting like a curtain, until he could see the room again. The major was perhaps four feet away, lighting another of his cigars. Old Breen, with one of his braces snapped, leaned against the table. Scott could hear the old man's breath.

"Hush, hush," it seemed to say. "Hush, hush."

There was a fourth man in the room, in Confederate uniform. Scott felt a wave of nausea as he saw him. The man was Travis Greene, whom he had met that very morning.

"Johnny," the major said, "you stand still."

"So it's you, Trav, is it?" Scott Mattaye was saying.

The other cleared his throat, looked at Scott and then away.

"Scott," he said, "I reported to the general your horse looked mighty bad. He sent me on to follow you. I was looking for a chance to get away. Scott, I'm sorry it should be you. I—I always liked you, Scott."

Scott Mattaye answered dully. "Trav," he said, "I won't say what I think."

"I reckon I don't mind," said Greene. "That's part of it."

Scott drew in his breath. He could see the deadliness of logic, and his lack of emotion surprised him. The old man's breathing, with its wheezing haste, was all that disturbed him.

"Trav," he said, "you better keep out of our lines, if once I get away."

"Scott," said Greene again, "it makes me sick it's you."

Then the major was speaking impersonally, almost kindly: "Listen, Johnny. I'd take you back as a prisoner if I dared to run the risk, but we're too close to rebel cavalry for anything like that. This officer"—he waved his cigar slowly and was careful with his words—"this officer is going back where he's useful, son. You see my point. There's no hard feeling in it, but you and I don't amount to shucks. This officer is going back, and there must be no—er—chance of your going. See my point?"

Scott moistened his lips. They were very numb and cold.

"I understand," he said. "Well, I'd be pleased if you get it over with. Perhaps we'd all be pleased."

There was a silence. He heard Greene start to speak, and stop. The old man's breathing was easier. He became aware that the old man was watching him with his steady light blue eyes.

"Gentlemen," said Grandpa Breen, "you leave this yere to me. There's been enough goin's on to attract attention. I'll gladly mind this yere."

There was no doubt of his meaning or any doubt that the major took his meaning. The major was buttoning his coat with steady, rapid fingers.

"There's a time," the old man said, "and a place for everything under the sun. Take him to the kitchen and tie him to the hick'ry chair. I'll fetch rope."

"Major," said Greene, "you take him."

"Oh," the major said, "let's get out of this! Come on."

The major was a good hand with the ropes. He lashed Scott to the kitchen chair so efficiently that there was no chance of moving. Just above his head, where he could not see it, the clock was ticking, and the kettle was bubbling on the stove. Once he was alone, he found himself searching the pine floor for a speck of dust. They were in the parlor, talking. He could hear the murmur of their voices.

". . . soon's it's dark," he heard the old man say.

"Major!" he shouted. "Here, you, major!"

The door from the entry opened, he remembered, and the major stood there pulling on his gloves. The major was a right cool man.

"Johnny," he said, "you keep your nerve."

"Yes, sir," said Scott, "I've got my nerve. I simply wish to ask you, are you leaving me alone?"

"Yes," the major said. "Johnny, keep your nerve."

Their glances met, but only for a fraction of a second, as though they saw something indecent in each other's eyes. Yet, curiously, Scott Mattaye always said that he could understand exactly how the major must have felt.

"I'm not letting your friend come in," the major said.

"You tell him good-by," said Scott.

"Good-by," the major said. "I should have shot you, Johnny, when you were rolling on the floor."

Then the kitchen door opened, letting in warm air that was sweet with the scent of hay. Old Mr. Breen, still in his shirt sleeves, was standing in the doorway with a shovel in his hand. The homeliness of the kitchen and the peaceful warmth from outdoors made everything grotesque.

"Brother," said Mr. Breen to the major, "the hosses are ready. You'd best be gittin' on. . . . And you, young man, I wish you no pain, but I know what you are figurin'. It won't do no good to holler. No one'll hear who cares. It won't do no good to tip over in the chair. I made it. It won't break. But I'll be near if you should call."

Scott Mattaye did not speak again, and the door slammed shut. He tried to move, but he was as helpless as a hog tied by the legs. First the dogs were yelping, and then there was a sound of hoofs outside the door, and then the place was still except for the humming of the kettle and the ticking of the clock. It was saying, "Time . . . time . . . time," and in back of everything was that almost soundless vibration of cannon a long way off. He closed his eyes, but even when he closed them he could see Mr. Breen.

He had no proper sense of sequence, for his mind was like a sick man's; but there was one thing in his thoughts, Scott Mattaye remembered. He could not divide an hour from the next when his mind was carrying him to a hundred places. Bits of his life would whirl about him. He was shooting wild turkey at Deer Bottom; he was with the cavalry again; but there was one thing on his mind. He must not let the old man know that he was in deathly fear. He could tell that if he let the old man know, the structure of decency would go toppling. His control and self-respect would go.

"Time," the clock was gasping. "Time . . . time . . . time."

The light was growing softer outside the kitchen windows when the kitchen door opened again and Mr. Breen came in. Clay was smeared on his hands and over his gaunt, bare arms. He walked past the chair and began washing at the kitchen sink.

"Young man," said Mr. Breen, "do you need water?"

"No," said Scott. . . . "So you're going to kill me, mister?"

The old man walked in front of him with a clean towel in his hands.

"Yes," he said, "I'm the Lord's poor instrument. Young man, are you afraid?"

"No," said Scott, "but if I were you, I reckon I'd be afraid."

Old Mr. Breen stared down at him and began to wipe his hands.

"Did your people fear," he asked, "when they sent an anointed saint to heaven?"

"Mister," said Scott—and he kept his voice even—"I'd be pleased to know, for the comfort of my mind, when you propose to kill me."

"After dark," said Mr. Breen. "I don't aim to lug you out for burial in daylight. I'm pleased you ain't afraid. I ain't afraid, and I'll die presently. There's somethin' gits me—here."

Suddenly his eyes were childlike, Scott remembered. He was drawing his hand across his chest.

"Mister," said Scott quickly, "I've seen a heap of illness. Step here and show me where."

"Young man," said Mr. Breen, "I can read your mind, I guess. You want to tip your chair and yourself atop of me. No, young man. I'll be goin', but I'll be ready in case you call."

The light outside the kitchen windows was growing soft and mellow, and he could hear the cannon. The time was going past him like a flood again, leaving him motionless like a rock against that flow. No one disturbed him. For a long while he was entirely alone. As the dusk came down he heard the lowing of cows and the clatter of the milk pails which had stood beside the barn. It must have been when the old man had started milking that the little girl came in through the doorway from the entry. The door squeaked and opened just a crack at first.

"Why, hello, honeybee," said Scott. "Come in. Don't go away. Sholy I can't hurt you, honeybee."

She came tiptoeing toward him. He did not blame her for being frightened.

"Honeybee," he said—the child was not attractive, but he could see she liked the name—"I'm powerful thirsty. Could you fetch a cup of water from the sink?"

"I'm scared," the little girl whispered. There was no doubt she was scared.

"Why, shucks!" said Scott. "You scared—a saucy girl like you? You fetch that cup now, honeybee. Isn't your grandpop milking? How'll he know? . . . There. . . . And I've got something for you in my coat. Just ease this rope off my hand so I can reach—"

"No," she whispered, "I'm too scared." But he could see that greed was gleaming in her eyes exactly like a voice.

He could hear his own voice still, not like his own, with its undercurrent of appeal beneath its ridiculous pretense at playfulness, as he pleaded for life. He was ashamed of that moment always—his begging from a child so that one hand could be free.

"I dassent," she whispered, but he knew better. She would dare, because there was something inside his coat. All the repression of her life gleamed in her pale blue eyes in little points of light. She would dare, not through any liking but from acquisitive desire.

"Honeybee," said Scott, "it's something mighty fine—something you won't guess."

There was no sound which made him look up, but he had the sense that there was something different in the gathering of the dusk. The dusk seemed to settle over him like a blanket thrown about his head.

He looked up to see the old man, standing in the doorway, watching. There was something in the way he stood that made Scott sure that he had planned that scene for his own pleasure. He must have been there for several minutes, as inevitable as the figure with the hour glass and the scythe.

"Mary Breen," the old man said, "you step away. Now, Mary Breen, you fetch the papers by the wood box. . . . So. Now lay 'em on the floor around the chair—under it. . . . You'd best lay on some more. And now go up to your chamber and close your door tight shut."

They were silent for a while. Old Mr. Breen seemed taller in the dark—more like an immense abstraction than a man.

"It's gittin' dark," he said. "Young man, I'll leave you five minutes to say your prayers."

He turned on his heel silently, walked out and closed the door.

"Time," the clock was whispering, "time!"

Inside the stove a piece of wood snapped sharply. He could see the glow of coals through the lids on top. The homely smells of the kitchen came around him in a rush. He strained sideways at his ropes, and the heaviness of his breathing drowned every other sound.

"Help!" he shouted.

The dogs in the yard began to bark, so that his shout mingled with the wave of barking. He was always ashamed of the rest of it, when he gave way to fear.

"Help!" he shouted. "Murder!"

He hitched forward, and the chair fell forward, throwing him head first into the dusky whiteness of the papers on the floor. The blow on his head must have stunned him, but he could not have been out long. There was still a little daylight when he found himself, lying sideways, still lashed to the kitchen chair.

"Mister soldier!" someone was calling. "You hear me, mister soldier?" It was the little girl in the gingham dress again.

"Yes," he said, "I hear you, honeybee."

"It's grandpop," she was sobbing. "He's took again. He's flopped flat down right on the parlor floor. When you hollered, he flopped down."

"Yo' get a knife and cut me loose," said Scott. "I reckon I can help your grandpop then."

"Mister," she sobbed, "please, you won't hurt him?"

"No," he answered, "I won't hurt him."

Once he was loose, his arms and legs were useless for a while. They burned and ached, once the blood came back, until tears stood in his eyes.

"Strike a candle light," he said, "and help me up. I'm very pressed for time."

He hobbled through the entry. It was true what she had said. Old Mr. Breen was lying on the parlor floor, face up, flat out. The candle which the girl was holding made a frame about the high head and the flowing beard. He was conscious, in great pain, staring up at Scott Mattaye. Scott's own ivory-handled revolver was lying on the floor, where it must have fallen from old Breen's hand. He stooped painfully and picked it up, but for half a minute no one spoke.

"Your heart, sir?" said Scott. He was incomprehensibly courteous and polite, but the old man did not speak.

"Something gits him right across the chest," said Mary Breen. "It pulls him down."

"Set that candle on the table," Scott was speaking gently. He saw his belt and saber in the corner. He walked over and strapped on his belt.

"Sir," he said still gently, "I'm sorry to leave you in distress, but you and I don't matter. I know, and it's consolin' if you know. You've a horse in the barn, I recall yo' saying. I'm leaving you a hundred dollars on this table for the horse. I'll call at a neighbor's to send you help. . . . And now good night."

He was in the barnyard among the snarling dogs, holding a stable lantern. There was a heavy smell from hay and from the soft, warm breath of cattle. There was a drumming in his ears like the hurry of the clock.

"Time," it was saying, "time."

He heard himself speaking to Mary Breen, and then he was mounted and in the yard again. The horse was coarse and wild.

"Scuse me," Mary Breen was calling. "Ain't you forgot—somethin' in your pocket?"

He pulled out the rest of his bills. "There," he said, "take 'em, honeybee."

He saw the house like a sharp, ungainly blot against the sky where a deep red gash of something burning in the west made the outline clear.

As he moved down the lane toward that distant glow, he did not know what he felt or thought, except that he must hurry, but suddenly he leaned forward on the neck of the farm horse. He felt sick—deathly sick.

There he was, sitting at his table at Deer Bottom, too old by any right to feel the force of memory, but there was an ugliness and simplicity which still could make him ill. The wings of death were hovering near him, but no such death as that. He only had the consolation from the knowledge he had gained that life meant very little, for life was all dirt cheap.

"Only two things," he said, "matter—accident and time. Now, Gettysburg—all that mattered were accident and time."

His mind was back on that night again. It always seemed to him that most of the Gettysburg affair was night—mistaken roads and Union pickets, and other roads choked by ammunition trains and infantry, and wounded moving back—two crawling, passing lines. Though the discipline was good, roads were always confused in the rear of a line of battle. There was the vagueness of a dream when one rode at such a time. There was no hope in haste or wishing.

"You come from Stuart?" someone said. "Well, it's too late for cavalry until we drive 'em. Where've you been? We've been fighting here since yesterday."

The night was never clear, but when he saw the leader of the army, that was clear enough. He reported to General Lee at a quarter before ten in the morning, outside a half-demolished house on the outskirts of the town of Gettysburg.

Couriers were holding horses, and staff officers were standing a few paces back, so that he always thought of the general as entirely alone. He could remember a tall, solitary man with a graying beard and deep, dark eyes, whose face was passionless, almost gentle. He was looking, Scott remembered, across a valley of fine green fields to a long, gentle slope, which was held by the Union lines about half a mile away.

He was speaking to a dusty, worried officer, Scott remembered, unhurriedly, except for one short gesture, and Scott could hear the words:

"Is he ready to attack, sir?"

"No, sir."

"Very well," the general said. "Hurry back; tell him he's very late already."

He stared back across the valley as Scott stood waiting. The stones of a cemetery were visible upon the ridge opposite, and an ugly building, which would be some sort of school. The ridge was heavy with troops, throwing up lines of earthworks. Beyond were the dust clouds of more troops moving up, and more. That ridge was a fine position, which was growing stronger every hour. Now and then there would be a burst of rifle fire, but there was no forward movement.

He stood waiting while the general looked, forgetting his fatigue as he watched, and he knew what the man was thinking. He was thinking of the time, while the time was running by him. Then Scott saw him strike his hands together in a sudden, swift motion, and he heard him say:

"It's too bad—too bad."

He was thinking of the time. Scott had a wish to be somewhere else. He felt like an eavesdropper who had heard a dangerous secret, but the general was turning toward him slowly.

"Well," he said, "what is it, captain?"

"Captain Mattaye, sir," began Scott, "from General Stuart's staff. A message from General Stuart, sir—"

"Yes," the general stopped him; "when did you leave the general, captain? How far is he along?"

"Six o'clock yesterday morning, sir," said Scott. "General Stuart was at Dover then."

For a moment the general looked at him, and it seemed to Scott that the general was very tired, though his expression did not change.

"Captain," the general said, "you're very late."

Scott felt his face grow red. "Sir—" he began, but the general stopped him.

"Never mind," he said. "Of course, you were delayed."

"Sir," said Scott, "will the general send me back with orders?"

"No"—the voice was tranquil and very courteous—"General Stuart has his orders. It's too late to make it better. . . . No fault of yours, captain. It would have been too late unless he had come yesterday—a simple matter of time and distance." He raised his voice, and Scott knew again that he was thinking of the time: "Colonel, send another officer to General Longstreet to find out his delay. And give this officer food and rest. He's too tired to go on."

# PAUL JONES

*Beautiful Rebel*

ON A SHARP, diamond-bright morning in March of 1862, young Andrew Woodley turned a familiar corner in Philadelphia, and came to the house of his legal preceptor, Henry Durham. A wrought-iron handrail in a leaf-and-tendril design helped Andy's game leg up three snowy marble steps. Everything was just as he remembered it in April, 1861, when he had put on a uniform and gone off to war. Now he was back in the dark civilian suit of a law student.

He had to smile, recalling the Frenchified shakos and cocks' plumes of his militia regiment, to fit the name their political colonel had chosen, Davidson's Voltigeurs. They'd had time for only sketchy drill on the cricket grounds in Germantown. By June they were encamped outside Arlington. One Sunday in July they were near a stream in Virginia called Bull Run. A battle was making up, like a summer thunderstorm, but Davidson's Voltigeurs remembered that their three months' enlistment had expired. Colonel Davidson rejected the brigadier's appeal, and marched his men away from the sound of guns.

With a few others, Andrew Woodley stayed behind when the regiment retired. He and his friends held strong views on how far a legal point could justify gentlemen who backed away from danger. Andy's combat service, on that occasion, was brief. They were still on the camp site, among the raked-out cook fires, hearing only desultory firing, when he felt a heavy blow on his right leg above the knee, as if he had been struck with a club. A shell fragment had hit him. As he fell, he saw a jet of blood spurting through a rip in his uniform trousers.

One of his friends put a tourniquet above the wound. Then they helped him to the side of a road, where they hoisted him into the wagonette of a tipsy sight-seer driving back to Washington with a lady friend no better than she should be, but kind-hearted. She propped

441

Andy's leg up on a champagne basket and saw him safely into the hospital at Alexandria. All that autumn and winter he was in bed or on crutches. The wound was a long time healing, but in another month his leg would be as good as ever and he could enlist again.

He found Henry Durham in the book-lined back parlor that served as his law office. Andy's preceptor was a thin, elderly man with white hair like a lion's mane, in the fashion of his youth under Jackson.

"How is the war going, in your judgment, Andrew?" Mr. Durham asked presently, with some deference, as to a learned associate.

Andy had no real idea. Civilians were always asking questions he couldn't answer. He had given no thought to issues or strategy since the day he put on his uniform.

"We're bound to win," he said, "but I haven't any notion when or how. Meanwhile, I thought I might help with the settlement of the Carey estate. You'll remember they're cousins of mine."

"Ah, yes. Richard Carey died while you were away. His wife, Harriet, inherits everything except a few keepsakes."

"I lived with them, you know, after my mother's death. She's extremely pinched for money. I wondered why."

"A matter for formal releases," said Mr. Durham. "I must have the signatures of the Maryland branch of the family. They have ignored my letters. I understand Henry Carey is very bitter about the war. He and his wife, your Cousin Phoebe, have a place on the Maryland side of the Potomac, beyond Harpers Ferry. Lancelot, the son, retired from the Army three years ago to help his father. Then there's Lucinda."

"I remember Lucinda," Andy said. "Very pretty girl, but rather shy and silent. Is she still here in boarding school?"

"She was expelled from Miss Chauveau's last November," Mr. Durham said testily. "I can't think why you call her shy and silent. The A.P.M. gave me twenty-four hours to get her out of the jurisdiction, provided she went South. Otherwise, he intended to jail her."

"A child of sixteen?"

"She is now eighteen, Andrew, and has decided ideas about the rebellion. The day the Fire Zouaves marched to the Prime Street Depot, a riot broke out in Locust Street when they saw the Stars and Bars flying from a bedroom window at Miss Chauveau's Academy. Lucinda had sewn the flag herself, in secret. She did not deny it. She gloried in it."

"Her father can't be Secesh. He was chairman of an Anti-Slavery Convention three years ago."

"He is a States' rights man by conviction. Lucinda, naturally, is loyal to her father. I sent her home."

"Couldn't I go see them and get their signatures? You always said, sir, that a lawyer's true function is to compose differences. I can't believe they'd let Cousin Harriet starve, if they knew."

"You have certain advantages," Mr. Durham admitted. "Getting an Army pass would would be easy for a convalescent soldier. And you're kinfolk, which counts a lot, I believe, in Maryland. I'll have the papers prepared for you. And there's one other thing. Under the will, Lucinda inherits a breastpin made of a miniature portrait of her Great-grandmother Carey. You'd better take that with you."

It was a handsome little picture, painted on ivory, in an oval setting of gold fretwork. Riding toward Baltimore on the afternoon train, Andy looked at it a dozen times. He had his documents and a change of linen in a small carpetbag, but the portrait fascinated him, and he kept it in his pocket. It showed the head of a charming woman, with her hair dressed away from the pure line of her forehead. "Remarkable thing," Henry Durham had said. "That could be an exact picture of Lucinda herself." The lawyer in Andrew Woodley argued that no one had ever fallen in love with a portrait. Still, something kept drawing his thoughts back to the miniature.

At Baltimore, Andy changed to the B. & O. for Harpers Ferry. There he had to wait overnight, before he caught a morning ride on an Army wagon headed toward Sharpsburg. The driver, Cpl. Joe Voigt, barrel-chested, with mighty arms, wore the plain new blues of the Army of the Potomac. The war had passed through the fancy-dress stage. Joe knew the Carey place well. "I got a detail right down the hill from their house," he said. "Watching a rope ferry, in case the Rebs get cute. Easiest duty I ever drew since I started soldiering."

That was ten years ago, he explained. He'd had seven years with the 2nd Dragoons on the plains, most of it escorting the Santa Fe mail. Some hard fighting against the Cienaguilla Apaches. Then back East, a civilian again, working on the B. & O. around Martinsburg.

"This fuss began, and Old Jack stole all our locomotives. Made wooden wheels for them, hitched them up to forty horses apiece and hauled them over dirt roads to the Manassas Gap line at Strasburg. He did me out of a job, and it made me mad, so I joined up with the infantry. Had enough stables in the Dragoons. You visiting the Careys?"

"On business."

"Old Mr. Carey's practically under house arrest. And that Miss

Lucinda! She treats a Union man like he was a toad. The one I feel sorry for is Miz Phoebe, eating her heart out for her boy, Lance.''

"What happened to Lance?" Andy asked, suddenly alert.

"He's over the river, a captain in the C.S.A. Every afternoon for the past three weeks he's been riding his little mare, Rowena, down to the meadow across the Potomac, like he wanted to make sure the old place was still there. On detached service, I reckon.''

"You seem well posted on the Careys.''

"Lance was my C.O. for five years in the Dragoons. Resigned and came East to help his old daddy with the farm, the year before I bought out my enlistment. He's a hard man, even for a West Pointer, but you don't want a better cavalry officer. And a real good Indian fighter. Tough. I wish I had a five-dollar gold piece for every time he took my stripes away. But he was fair. I'd get them back when I earned them.''

Pride echoed in Joe Voight's tone, the feeling of an old regular for the stern, just, inflexible, all-knowing commander. He and Lance would be opposite sides of the same clear-stamped medallion.

The corporal pulled his team of Army mules up to a halt at the beginning of a steep downward turn in the road. "If you're going to Careys',''" he said, "you better cut through their woodlot. The house ain't more than a quarter mile. When you finish your business, come down and visit. I always got coffee for a comrade.''

"I'll drop by,'' said Andy, stepping down to the wheel and then to the rutted country road.

At the woodlot's end there was a length of open meadow, and then an orchard screening the long, low stone house. Across the valley, Virginia was a long sweep of brilliant green pasture.

Three hundred yards away, Andy saw a horseman in gray ride suddenly out of nowhere from a fold in the terrain.

Nearly at the same moment, Andy was conscious of a flash of white under the apple trees. A girl was running toward him from the house, both hands holding the fullness of her skirt. It was Lucinda. She saw him and gave a startled gasp, letting her dress fall into place.

"Why, it's Cousin Andrew,'' she said, her hands going automatically to her wind-blown hair. "You're very welcome.''

"Thank you, Cousin Lucinda.'' She was even more beautiful, he thought, than the mintature, with a shapely body, finely turned wrists and ankles, lustrous blue eyes and a magnetic vitality. She put her arm under his and turned him toward the river.

"That's Lance,'' she said, raising her free hand in a salute to the distant horseman. "Mother watches from the kitchen, but I always come down here to wave at him, so he'll know we're all right."

Before vanishing behind a screen of trees, the gray rider flourished his hat.

"One day," Lucinda said indignantly, "one of those blue-belly sneaks at the ferry fired a shot at Lance. Their corporal came up afterward and apologized to mother. He said it was a Massachusetts man did it and he gave him a thrashing, because he had served under Lance in the Dragoons, and, anyhow, pickets aren't supposed to fire on casual targets. It was just hypocrisy. Corporal Voigt was really afraid mother would stop giving them fresh eggs and butter and home-baked bread. She's so kind she can't bear to see men hungry, even if they are Feds. Come into the house. You know, I'm not sure you even remember me."

"I couldn't forget our polka at Cousin Harriet's party."

They were walking through the orchard and she smiled at him. "It wasn't a polka. It was a schottische, and the music was Listen to the Mocking Bird. You had a blue dress coat with brass buttons, and a white neckcloth that I longed to straighten, because it was all under one ear after you waltzed with that odious Fenton girl. You see, you made an impression on me. You were the first man that ever asked me to dance." All this came out impetuously, in a manner that confirmed the complete trust in her brilliant eyes.

They went through a puzzle of passageways and steps up or down, to reach a large, comfortable family room, where a man with white hair sat by a wood fire.

"We have a visitor, father," said Lucinda. "It's Cousin Andrew Woodley, from Philadlephia."

Henry Carey looked at Andy with sad, tired eyes. It was plain that the times had defeated him. "You must be Cousin Mary's boy," said the old man. A spark glittered. "Have you come here to spy on us?"

"I came," Andy said in an even voice, "on business, to get the signatures of your branch of the family in connection with your Cousin Richard Carey's estate. And also to give Lucinda a breastpin which she inherits under the will. I have the forms here."

When he had arranged the documents on the marble-topped center table, Andy took the miniature from his pocket and handed it to Lucinda.

She gave a cry of delight. "Mother! Come look!"

A stout, handsome, flustered woman with a kind face and smiling eyes entered from a door beyond the fireplace. Her hands were white with flour.

"Why, your're Mary's boy!" she said. She kissed Andy affectionately. "You have her eyes. I remember when you were a baby. And now you're a grown man, and a fine lawyer, so Lucinda tells me. My, since she came back from Philadelphia last year, she's never stopped talking about her Cousin Andrew. I declare, you made a conquest, honey."

"Mother!" said Lucinda, suddenly scarlet.

"And how *is* Cousin Harriet bearing up?" Mrs. Carey said.

"Well enough, ma'am, but poor as a churchmouse. That's why I'm here to get you to sign these papers, so she can have her money."

"That's easily fixed. . . . Run and find the pen and ink, Lucinda, like a lamb, while I fix Andrew something to eat."

Andy had a warm, comforting sense of being welcome among his own people. Mr. Carey seemed more relaxed. Lucinda, he saw, had scarcely heard her mother. She was standing before a mirror, candidly comparing her reflection with the minature.

Henry Carey shifted his position in the chair by the fire. "Stay where you are, Lucinda," he said. "We won't need any pen and ink."

Lucinda and her mother exchanged troubled glances. Andy said, "It's only a legal form, sir. I'm sure you don't contest Cousin Harriet's right to the property of her late husband."

"It is not a question of property, but of principle, sir, if you can apprehend the difference. My son is in the field, defending his state. As long as you cannot get his signature, you shall not have ours."

"I believe we might dispense with Lancelot's signature," Andy said. "The President's proclamation on nonintercourse last year included Virginia, but omitted Maryland, which has not seceded. Your son is serving with Virginia troops.I believe a contention would hold that by joining the rebellion Lancelot has brought himself under the provisions of the decree. That is—" Andy faltered, appalled by the sudden fury in the old man's face and by the cold contempt in Lucinda's eyes.

"Why, damn it," Mr. Carey shouted, struggling to get up, "you're nothing but a pettifogging Philadelphia lawyer! My son, sir, is serving his state, and his family will do nothing even remotely acknowledging Lincoln's fancied right to brand us as rebels! . . . Mrs.Carey! Show your cousin out!"

"I can find the door," said Andy.

Mr. Carey looked at him with disdain. "A young man your age," he said, "should have no trouble meeting Lance face to face."

Andy picked up his carpetbag. "I got this limp," he said furiously, "from a Confederate shell fragment at Bull Run!"

The old man was darkly entertained. "Nicked you, did they?" he crowed. "By thunder, you were one that couldn't skedaddle!"

Mrs. Carey showed her distress. Andy followed her outside to a bricked area under a wide porch by the kitchen. "You mustn't mind Mr. Carey," she said tearfully. "It's this awful war."

"Let Cousin Henry sleep on it," Andy said. "I'll spend the night with Corporal Voigt." Tomorrow, he thought, he could try again.

"I'll fix you some food. Give me your carpetbag."

As Mrs. Carey went into the kitchen, Lucinda came out. Her chin was high, her eyes hostile, and Andy's heart sank when she gave him the miniature, quickly, as though it cost her a great effort.

"You must take this back," she said coldly. "Papa says we must have nothing to do with the estate as long as Lance is over the river."

"Lucinda!" he protested. But she turned sharply, without another word, and went back into the house.

Waiting for Mrs. Carey to come back, Andy walked up and down the brick pavement with the miniature still in his hand. He felt deeply depressed. By some unhappy inspiration, he had gone directly to the one point that would enrage Mr. Carey. And then there was Lucinda, of the once warm eyes and dazzling smile, who had been so tender until he attempted to rule Lance out of any consideration. Now he had lost her. His one hope was Mrs. Carey. But when she came out of the kitchen and returned his carpetbag, much heavier, she was in a dispirited mood.

"If I were you," she said, "I think I'd start back to Philadelphia now. Mrs. Carey's on his high horse."

"But what can I tell Cousin Harriet?"

"I'm just as sorry for her as I can be, you know that."

He gave her the miniature. "Would you keep this for Lucinda? You needn't mention it until you think best."

"Of course, dear."

Andy, preparing to walk down to the ferry, paused at the edge of the porch. "Suppose," he said, "Lance came here with me tomorrow and was willing to sign. Then you could all sign, couldn't you?"

"You know right well that's impossible, child." She searched

Andy's face with anxious eyes. "Or could he? Is there someway I could see him, even for a minute?"

"I don't know. But I can try."

At the ferry, where a narrow road angled downhill to the riverbank, he found Joe Voigt in the small stone ferry house. A shabby scow, just big enough for a single horse and wagon, lay against the near shore. Two cables hung slack above the river crossing.

For a field soldier, Corporal Voigt lived in luxury. There was a brisk fire on the hearth, he had a broken armchair to sit in, and a white pine table, at which he was playing euchre with a bony private.

"Evening, Andy," he said. "Help yourself to some coffee. This here's Ellery Channing Peacock. Came all the way down from Lowell, Mass., to help preserve the glorious Union and hang Jeff Davis. . . . That's another two bits you owe me, Ellery. Put the cards away now and get moving with the rations."

After Peacock had gone, Andy said, "You didn't have to send him out on my account."

"I didn't," said Joe. "I notice your gripsack's a lot fuller than it was. I can read sign. You got some food in there. Enough for two, maybe."

Mrs. Carey had been generous. Unfolded, a huge linen napkin disclosed a loaf of bread, a lump of fresh butter wrapped in a cabbage leaf, half a dozen eggs and a lordly slice of ham. Joe got out the skillet and they dined sumptuously. But even in a relaxed mood over fresh coffee, the corporal scoffed at Andy's first hint that they might lure Lance across the river.

"You're losing your mind," he said. "Talk sense. You can't disrupt a whole war just so one girl can see her darling brother."

"I'm thinking about one signature that will keep an old lady from starving. That's what I came here for, and I want it."

"That's civilian stuff," said Corporal Voigt flatly.

Andy got up for another cup of coffee, dawdling deliberately, before taking a flanking approach. "Maybe you're right, Joe," he said. "Why should you care about a widow you never saw? But how about Miz Phoebe Carey? She'll be awful disappointed in you."

"Why, what'd I do?"

"Lance is her son, isn't he? You know how mothers are. The last thing she said to me was, she'd give anything just to see and talk to her boy, even if it was only for a minute. I said I'd ask you. And you told me yourself she's pining away for him."

"She is, for a fact," Joe admitted, deeply impressed.

"But never mind. If you can't, you can't."

"Wait a minute," Joe said. "I don't suppose a little visit between a mother and her son is going to bust up the Union. The thing is, will Lance cross the river? If he will, he's got to do it tomorrow, when there's no chance of an officer turning up from our company headquarters. They're all going to a wedding over by Sharpsburg."

"We can try, can't we?"

"I reckon so," the corporal agreed.

It was as simple as that, Andy thought, to move people to action, if you touched the right spring.

Joe planned the enterprise. For one thing, he would send Private Peacock back to Harpers Ferry early in the morning. "Ellery wouldn't approve of this operation," he said. "He worries a lot because nobody wants to win this war except him and Senator Sumner."

They needn't bother about the other men, strung out at posts up and down the river. The corporal and Andy would pull the ferry into midstream, fly Mrs. Carey's white napkin for a signal and invite Lance Carey to a parley.

"The flag'll fetch him," Joe said. "He's cavalry, and just naturally curious, like a Plains Indian or an antelope."

By a fitful change in the weather morning brought them a warm, sunny day. Private Peacock was dispatched with the wagon, and, while Joe Voigt inspected his posts, Andy shaved and put on a fresh shirt.

They whiled away the time playing euchre, Joe's passion. At two o'clock, when they hauled the ferryboat into the river by its overhead cables, Andy had won a dollar and sixty cents. That was reason enough to take the cards with them and to resume the game afloat.

The sun was hot on the water. Joe unbuttoned the collar of his tunic and bent to the task of winning his money back. Andy could not keep his mind on the hands. His thoughts concentrated on the desperate importance of persuading Captain Carey to cross the river. Not only for the settlement of the estate but because he found it so urgent to see Lucinda again.

"I'll order you up," Joe said, inspecting his cards. At just that moment, Andy, facing the Virginia side, saw a man ride down to the ferry landing. It was a civilian wearing a tightly buttoned black coat and fine gray trousers strapped under polished black boots. His dark slouch hat shaded a wary, resolute face with a wide mouth and a big chin. The horse was an ugly roan.

"Somebody's hailing the ferry," Andy said.

"Just when I got the right and left bowers," Joe complained. He turned, and, after a long look, said, "Why, it's the captain! What's he doing in civvies?"

"You mean Lance Carey?"

"Nobody else." Joe gathered up the playing cards, tied a string around them and slipped the pack into the top of his boot for safe-keeping.

The horseman had dismounted, and the roan was drinking from the river. "Pull that ferry over here!" he called in a strong voice.

As soon as the flatboat touched the bank, Carey led his mount on board, and they pulled the ferry back into the river.

At midstream, Joe demanded, "Now then, what's going on?"

The captain looked at him coolly. "Button your tunic, corporal. An old dragoon ought to set an example of smartness. I don't know why I should be cross-questioned. You signaled for a parley, not I." His head inclined toward Andy. "Who's this gentleman?"

"You can talk in front of him. He's your Cousin Andrew, down from Philadelphia to see your family on legal business."

Lance Carey offered his hand. "A pleasure, Cousin Andrew," he said. "Davidson's Voltigeurs, wasn't it? A time-expired regiment at Manassas. You stayed behind and fought like a man. It made me proud of my kin."

"I don't know how you heard that," Andy, expanding under the praise.

"We get very good intelligence from the district. Naturally, I followed your name with particular interest. How is the family?"

"They're in good health," Andy said, and went on to explain about the settlement of the estate. "That's why we asked for a parley. I thought you might talk to your father."

"I'll do what I can. Cousin Harriet was always very good to me. But you must remember, father's a civilian, and civilians can be difficult in wartime."

"Will you come up to the house with me now?"

"Now?" said Captain Carey dubiously. "I'm on a special mission at the moment. I hadn't even planned to come this way until I saw your signal." He turned to Joe Voigt, who was staring with disgust at the roan horse. "Not much to look at, but he'll take me where I'm going and bring me back. I'm not risking Rowena today."

"And just where might the captain be going?" Joe asked.

"I can't tell you that. But, for your information, I have a fixed rendezvous inside your lines in an hour and a half."

"You got a pass?"

"I have." The captain took a folded paper from his pocket. Andy looked over Joe's shoulder as the corporal examined it closely. Everything was in order. For twelve hours, from two P.M. to two A.M., Lancelot Carey, Esq., had permission to cross the lines of the Army of the Potomac on urgent business, using any available transportation, north and west of Harpers Ferry. By order of the provost marshal. Signed, stamped and perfectly regular, as Joe admitted, returning it.

"I wish I knew what's going on," he muttered.

"It doesn't concern you," said Lance, "and meanwhile, now that you've seen my pass, suppose you pull this ferry over and let me complete my mission."

"You going up to see your mother?"

"Naturally, since I'm here. I can take ten minutes."

Lance was his idea of a soldier, Andy thought, pulling on the cable. Just the way he stood by his horse's head, resolute but relaxed; the air of mystery and danger given him by his secret assignment and his reputation as an Indian fighter on the Great Plains; all these things, plus ten years' difference in their ages and his acceptance of Andy as a fellow fighting man, made a profound impression.

The ferry touched the Maryland shore and Captain Carey led his horse to firm ground. Then there was a sound of wheels on the curving hill road, and a light wagon came into view. Mrs. Carey held the reins, and beside her, with a shawl wrapped around his shoulders, was her husband. Lucinda jumped from the back seat before the wagon stopped and fairly flew across the ferry landing.

"Lance, Lance!" she cried, and threw her arms around her brother. "Are you all right? We didn't know what to think!"

There was a high pitch of excitement for the next five minutes, while Lance made the situation clear. Old Mr. Carey broke into an actual smile and looked ten years younger as he wrung his son's hand. Mrs. Carey dissolved in happy tears and kissed everybody all around, including Joe Voigt. First and last, there was a great deal of embracing. At one point, Andy found Lucinda's lips pressing his. He noticed she was wearing the miniature pinned at the throat of her dress.

"You're not angry?" he said, retaining her hand.

"I couldn't be mad at anybody now," she said. "Not even you. Let me go. I want to talk to Lance."

The corporal had retired to the doorway of his stone hut, and Andy joined him there. "It does a man good just to see Miz Carey's face," Joe said. "You going back home now?"

"Long enough to settle the estate. I figure I might re-enlist down here. Maybe in your regiment."

"You'd get a bigger bounty in Pennsylvania," Joe said practically. "But I reckon you're thinking of something else. Glad to have you along any time. You'll do."

Lucinda interrupted them. "Cousin Andrew," she said, "you're to come up to the house with us. Father says he'll be pleased to sign, as long as Lance is willing." She turned to Joe. "You, too, Corporal Voigt, if you'd care to take some refreshment."

"That's right kind of you, but I'm on duty," Joe said. "The war's still on, last I heard. I got to inspect my posts."

Riding up the hill road, with the horse laboring in the shafts, Andy and Lucinda sat together in the back seat. His hand tightened on hers, and she did not withdraw it. He had a wonderful sense of pleasure and security. A soldier, he thought, needed only a few simple things. A warm, dry shelter, enough to eat and drink; some hope of staying alive with honor; and the knowledge that somewhere a girl is specially concerned about him in a way that no one else can be.

"What I don't understand," Mr. Carey said to his son, who rode by the front wheel, "is why you're in civilian clothes, Lancelot, and with a special pass. Is your mission too secret to talk about?"

"As a matter of fact, sir," said the captain, "now that it's all in the family, so to speak, I don't suppose there's any harm telling you. I'm going to a wedding."

Andy was thundersturck. The ladies uttered cries of astonishment and delight. "A wedding!" Lucinda repeated. "Who's getting married?"

"Friend of mine, fellow I roomed with at the Point. You remember, Shorty Willets. He's a major now, in the Michigan cavalry. The bride is one of the Hilary girls over by Sharpsburg. Things are slow around here. The action's down in the Peninsula. My general saw no objection to a visit incognito, considering the occasion. And neither did his brother-in-law, who happens to be Shorty's commanding officer. At any rate, the pass came through, and here I am."

Mr. Carey cleared his throat. "It seems an odd way to make war," he said dubiously.

"Yes, sir. It's an odd war. I reckon there'll be plenty of time for fighting, sooner or later. There always has been, in any campaign I can remember."

Mrs. Carey was lost in thought, checking through her extensive acquaintanceship in the countryside. "That must be Evaline Hilary," she decided. "Such a pretty girl. . . . You remember her, Lucinda."

"I don't remember anybody anymore," Lucinda said forlornly. "It's ages since I've been to a party."

They had reached the house, and Andy helped her to the ground with his hands around her waist. "I wish we were going to the wedding," he said, "and you were wearing a blue dress with a wreath of flowers in your hair, the way I remember you at Cousin Harriet's dancing party."

I still have that dress," she said. "Oh, Lance, could Andrew and I go?"

"In ten minutes I'll have to be riding on," said Captain Carey. "I'm standing up with Shorty and I have to be early. But I reckon a best man can invite two guests. Why doesn't Cousin Andrew drive you over in the wagonette, and we can all come back together? That is, unless he's in a hurry to get up to Philadelphia with the papers we're signing."

"Of course he's not," said Mrs. Carey. "Lawyers are never in a hurry. . . . Run, Lucinda, and put on your prettiest dress."

"The blue one," Andy said, "with a wreath of white flowers in your hair."

# ROBERT EDMOND ALTER

*Bummer's Roost*

JUST OFF THE ROAD to Stafford Hall, in the new, tall green weed, Yorky Towne sat, his back against an oak root, corncob in his mouth. He felt drowsy, peaceful in the warm mid-day air, translucent with sleep. A soft clip-clop rhythm entered his drowse, lulling him further from reality. Then, as it grew louder, it startled him and he half-sat up. Horsemen were thundering down through the arched tunnel of white oaks, coming for the Hall.

At first he thought maybe Sherman had come with his soldiers, but then decided that it wasn't likely. The Yank army was too far north. Besides, everyone knew they were striking for Savannah. Disappointment mingled with relief as he rolled over, pawed aside a belt of weed and looked out at the road.

Ten horsemen pounded past him. Only one of the riders was in full Confederate uniform, though all of them were armed. Home Guard-Yorky recognized them. The man in uniform was Lt. Woodward. . . . He had lost an arm at Malvern Hill. The boy reckoned something was up. The irregulars had looked downright serious.

He came to his knees, put his corncob inside an old tin box, and pushed it into the weeds. Old Mrs. Stafford would kick up a fuss if she caught him smoking. She claimed a man shouldn't smoke at all until he was at least sixteen, and he was only fourteen. Well, he reckoned that what she didn't know wouldn't hurt her. He started down the road at a jog.

Jem Woodward had pulled his troop up before Stafford's pillared gallery, and he sat limply in his saddle for a moment rubbing at his dusty face with his good hand. None of the men made a move to dismount. Yorky edged past the rear horseman, touching the mare's flank with his hand, making it quiver. One of the men looked down at him and nodded.

Brutus Brown, a giant Negro, came around the corner of the gallery and stared at the mounted men with surprise.

Jem Woodward lowered his hand and stiffened his sitting position.

"Brutus, you-all fetch Mizz Stafford my compliments. Tell her we'd like kindly to see her. . . . Tell her we ain't got much time," he ordered.

The great front door swung open noiselessly, and Mrs. Stafford, thin, tiny, straight and proud as a new rifle, stepped out onto the gallery. Yorky wedged himself between two horses, where he hoped she wouldn't take notice of him. She'd be after him about his chores.

Mrs. Stafford's stiff, grayish face turned up to Jem Woodward. "I'll thank you to remember, Lt. Woodward, that I don't allow my field hands to come clattering through my house to call me . . . I still have a house servant for that. Now, may I offer you gentlemen some refreshment?"

Jem Woodward made a left-handed salute, bowing his head slightly.

"Sorry, mam, we're in a hurry today—thank you kindly. We're after a bunch of Sherman's bummers. . . . They come down this way two nights ago an' started raidin'. Burnt ol' Will Mickle's place down to Pine Crossin' last night, an' been doin' all sorts of mischief. They ain't been round here have they, mam?"

Yorky knew what bummers were—armed Yankee stragglers who had started out as army foragers but had become thieves, incendiaries, and murderers. They were rough, lawless men, looked down upon by even their own combat comrades. Yorky would like to see them all dead. He sighed, feeling frustrated and impotent. He didn't see why the war had to come along when it did. Seems like it could have held off for a couple of years . . . then he would have been old enough to fight with the men.

"Yankees this far south?" Mrs. Stafford was saying. "It would seem they have more courage than brains."

"Yes, mam," Jem Woodward agreed. "I reckon we'll catch this bunch proper, now that they've isolated themselves from their army. Well, we got to git. . . . If you hear anythin' of them bummers, mam, I'd deeply appreciate it if you'd send one of your hands down to Parkins Corner; we're keeping a small detachment there jus' in case. Reckon you could send Yorky here."

Yorky flinched as Mrs. Stafford's cold eyes leaped for him. She stared at the boy for a moment, then nodded. "Yes, of course."

The one-armed soldier smiled, touching his hat again. "Obliged, mam," he said. Then the troop went thundering down the road, leaving a swirling wake of beige dust behind them.

Yorky, alone in the yard, hung his head, shuffling his bare feet in the dirt. He always felt slightly awed and insignificant under the shadow of the great house. The mansion had been beautiful once—before the war, but now it had a sort of chapped, stained look about it, and two of the upstairs shutters had an ugly sag to them. If he could find a way to get ahold of some whitewash he would like to give the Hall a coat, get old Brutus to help him. That might cheer Mrs. Stafford up some. He kicked thoughtlessly at a stone and frowned. He doubted it, though . . . Since the death of old Mr. Stafford and young Farrel Stafford, she didn't seem to care about anything; just wandered through the great rooms of the Hall and stared at memories with cold eyes.

He started edging off toward the corner of the gallery.

"Yorky—what are you about now?"

"Nothin', mam . . . jus' goan try to catch some fish for supper."

She sniffed and looked down the long shaded avenue as though she expected someone to come riding home, someone who would never come again. Her eyes lowered, and when she spoke her voice was ringed with weariness.

"Well, there isn't much strength in fish, but I imagine it will keep us living."

Yorky glanced at her again, covertly. "Reckon if you'd let me have the loan of Mr. Farrel's Sharps rifle I could get us some squirrels," he suggested. "I seen some nice fat ones near Humpback Hill yester. . . ."

Her head came up quickly, her cold eyes sparking with unexpected life. "I've told you before that no one will ever use that rifle. I want you to stop pestering me about it."

Yorky bit at his lip and nodded. He shuffled off toward the ragged formal gardens. Brutus scratched at his ear, made a sympathetic tsk with his mouth, and fell in step with the boy.

"Why come ol' Mistus won' let you have de borry of dat gun, Misto Yo'ky?"

Yorky scowled and snatched a crepe myrtle stem from its bunch. "'Cause she don't like me, that's why!" But he knew that wasn't true. Mrs. Stafford didn't like or dislike him, she simply didn't care one way or another—and he amended the statement:

" 'Cause I ain't a Stafford; 'cause the gun belonged to Mr. Farrel, an' she's keepin' it for him—even though he ain't never comin' back to use it."

Brutus sounded the sympathetic tsk again, shook his head dolefully. "Well, Misto Yo'ky, I 'spect I could make some traps an' you an' me could cotch dem fat squirrels. . . . I got nothin' else to do since most de field han's run off to jine Sherman."

Yorky nodded disinterestedly. "Awright, Brutus—iffin you want to." He walked on down the path, leaving the Negro standing aimlessly in the tattered splendor of the unkempt garden.

Down at the creek, Yorky scrambled over the patine rocks until he gained his favorite fishing spot and sat himself in a warm island of sun. A bumblebee buzzed past him and droned away, leaving a thinning wake of sound behind. He sighed and slid his line down into the still amber water. He didn't have much heart for fishing—the business about the Sharps rifle still rankled him.

He reckoned that all in all the war had been pretty unfair to him. It wasn't enough that he was too young to fight, but his pa . . . Linkton Towne had been Stafford's overseer before the war. He had gone off with the two Stafford men in '61, with the understanding that Yorky would live in the Hall with Mrs. Stafford until his return. But he had fallen with the two Stafford men at Shiloh, at a site the Confederates had fondly nicknamed The Hornet's Nest. Now Yorky and Mrs. Stafford lived together in the great silent Hall, waiting for nothing.

Yorky had a little room off the kitchen. It was nicer than what he'd had in the shack he'd been born in, the shack where his mother had died when he was two, and yet it wasn't nicer—somehow.

Shiloh, he thought. That was a place in the Bible, wasn't it? Funny that his Pa and the two Staffords should all get killed at a place in the Bible. He rubbed his nose, then gave his eyes a swipe while he was at it.

"Ain't no call for her to treat me like trash," he muttered. "Ain't my fault that Mr. Farrel got hisself kilt." Then a stab of contrition hit him and he looked up. She didn't really treat him like trash. He reckoned she couldn't help the way she felt; her son had been her whole life.

A thin twist of pale smoke coiled wanly above Humpback Hill. He stared at it puzzledly, couldn't imagine who would be building a fire up there. He stood up and ran a practiced eye over the familiar landmarks, lining up certain trees and boulders. The short study convinced him that the smoke was coming from the vicinity of Chigger Cave.

Some runaway field hand, he decided. Then he felt a sudden wave of righteous indignation. Whoever it was had no call making a fire on Mrs. Stafford's property. He hid his pole and bait-can, and set off through the woods to chase the transgressor away.

He knew the hill like the back of his hand; and when he heard a horse's sudden whinny, he paused in cautious consternation. Horses, since the war, were hard come by. He doubted that a runaway would have one. Maybe he best move soft. A rock-ribbed pass, he knew, ran into Chigger Cave, forming a small cleared enclosure before the cave's entrance. Aside from the pass there was only one other way to enter or leave the cave, and that was a hard, dangerous scramble straight up a serrated gully in the wall of the enclosure. He remembered a sort of trail that ran along the rock-roof of the pass. A man could climb that path and look right down into the enclosure . . . So could a boy—he'd done it before.

He approached the hill, running silently through the warm weed, and went at a solidly packed rock pile. He began scrambling.

From the rock path he could look down into the pass on his left. There was nothing there but cool shadow. He dropped to his hands and knees and continued on up the incline. He wasn't quite certain what it was that he was afraid of, wasn't even sure that he was afraid, still . . .

He approached a great outcropping of rock cautiously, knowing that the drop into the enclosure lay just beyond. And then he heard a cough . . . He hunched in on himself, waited. A moment later a voice came up to him.

"Parks—hand me that cider jug."

"You dry, Bill?"

"Well, you could light matches on my tongue without strikin' 'em—that's how dry I am. Thankee, mate."

Yorky frowned, a vague sense of uneasiness edging in on him. The voices had a harsh, foreign twang to them . . . And then, even though he had never heard their cacophonous sounds before, he knew they were Yankee voices. Chigger Cave had become a bummers' roost.

He wiggled nearer to the parapet of rock and peered over the edge. Three Yank cavalrymen were grouped around a small fire in the center of the clearing. Four hobbled horses stood a little to one side of the cave-mouth, nibbling at green weeds. Two of the soldiers were sitting on the ground; one, a small brittle man with sly winky eyes; the other, a great swollen-bodied sergeant with a pink, moist moonface. The third Yank was standing, arms akimbo on slim hips. A tall, darkly handsome man with quick eyes and a thin, tight mouth.

The fat sergeant was drinking from the jug. He jerked it from his mouth abruptly and lowered it heavily to the ground, making a resounding th-uung. "Way hay, Stormalong, John!" he cried, grinning.

The tall man's dark face twisted slightly as though in amused disdain. "If you're done with your burping and swilling, Bullock, we might get down to cases. There's a plantation near here I'd like to strike tonight. I talked with a contraband and he said there's no one there but an old lady and a kid. Tomorrow we can head south again."

The fat man made a pouchy frown with his face and spat lustily in the dust. "I don't like it," he said. "We're too far south as it is to suit me. If we get in trouble they ain't no army to fall back on."

"You know the pickings weren't any good as long as we stayed with the army . . . Everyone and his brother was out foraging and looting. We've done all right by following my advice so far, haven't we?"

"Oh, my yes, we done fine, *jus'* fine," Bullock replied. "We got a whole cave full of junk that I don't know what we'll do with. . . . We got Rebs out-the-barrel chasin' us. . . . An' if we get too cute, Sherman is gonna frown an' say 'I think these boys need a spot of punishment'. I ain't hankerin' to have myself strung up by the thumbs to dry in the sun. I seen a fella in the 30th Indiana get that cure once. . . . He weren't lookin' so spry when they cut him down."

He reached for the jug again and patted its plump side with his hand. "I think we better call it quits, Sim, an' strike back for the army. I'm in favor of a good lootin' jus' like any soldier . . . But there weren't no call to burn that old man's house last night."

Sim brought his hands together, working a fist in a palm. "I don't like Rebs," he said tonelessly.

"They's people, jus' like anyone else. Oh, I'll fight 'em ifn I got to, but I want 'em to have a muskit in their claw when they come again' me. I ain't no woman or kid fighter. I reckon mebbe we'll head north tomorrow."

Sim smiled without humor. "I think we'll leave that up to the rest of us," he said softly.

Bullock blinked, sighed, and struggled up to his feet. For the first time Yorky felt that he looked as dangerous as Sim. The fat man took one step forward, his face suddenly mean. "I guess mebbe you forget, Sim, that I'm leadin' this bunch? I guess mebbe because I'm fat you think I don't know how to fight? Well, my son, you name yer poison an' I'll see you drink it—fists, feet, by'net, pistol. . . ."

"Bill—" the little man, Parks, whined, "Bill, tone down, Bill."

Yorky began edging back. He had to get to Parkins Corner, fast; had to get the detachment of Home Guard before the bummers got away. He started to turn, then froze. . . . A long shadow was spilling over his left hand, staining the ground beyond him. His head jerked up and he looked into the grinning face of a Yankee soldier.

"Just rest easy, sonny," the Yank said. "Reckon I'd just as soon kick in a Reb civilian's face as I would a Reb rifleman's." Then he turned his head slightly and called:

"Bill! Got me a young Johnny up here!"

"Well," Bullock's voice replied gruffly, "fetch hin down. Seems like this is my trouble day."

Sergeant Bill Bullock stared at Yorky with little snapping eyes, grunted, then swiped at his moist chin with a beefy hand. He snatched the hand away abruptly and leaned his gleaming face in close to the boy. "Well," he roared suddenly, "this is jus' what I need—a punk Johnny to set the Rebs on me!"

Yorky reckoned he hated Yankees as much as any good American boy did, and hated bummers more; and suddenly all his hate bunched in his brain and gave him wild courage. "I know what you are!" he shouted. "You're dirty bummers! I hate your dirty guts!"

Bill Bullock blinked, looked slightly foolish, then began to smile.

"Say, Sim," he said over his shoulder, "talkin' about guts; here's a bucko what's got his share, an' him jus' a little bitty Johnny."

Sim's cold eyes flicked over the boy. He nodded and stooped down to rummage through a pile of equipment at his feet. His hand cleared a bayonet from its scabbard. "There's no sense in putting a bullet in the Johnny and letting the whole country know we're here," he said. "I'll take him back in the cave and use this."

Yorky flinched back into the waiting arms of the soldier who had captured him. The Yank grabbed him tight by the elbows.

Bullock looked baffled. "You don't mean you want to *kill* him?" he whispered. "You don't mean *that*, do you, Sim? A boy?" Then, seeing the evident meaning in Sim's dark face, his pouty mouth grimaced and his hand dropped to his holster and rested on the flap. "Well, if you do—you got to put that pig sticker in me first."

For the first time anger flared in Sim's eyes. "Bullock, when are you going to wake up and realize we aren't playing for marbles? You want that kid to scoot out of here and fetch the Rebs on our trails? We're traveling too heavy to be chased."

Bullock kept his eyes on Sim when he spoke. "Mick—let the kid go. Johnny, you step over to the cave there an' set down. . . . . Move now."

Yorky felt the pressure relax on his elbows. He moved hesitantly past the soldiers and over to the cave-mouth. When he looked back he saw Bullock and Sim still facing each other over the fire.

"Well, gambler," Bullock said, "you gonna pick up the chips or let 'em lay? Make up yer mind; I feel a thirst comin' on me."

Sim smiled crookedly, lowered his hand, and shot the bayonet into the dirt point-first. "We'll try this again, Bullock . . . when I have my hand on my holster."

Bullock nodded his thick head, his voice matching the grim slant of his eyes. "Sure—I imagine it'll be one of those times when I have my back to you." Then he turned with a contemptuous grunt and waddled over to the boy.

Yorky knew he should hate the fat man, because Bullock was a Yank and a bummer, and yet he couldn't ignore the fact that Bullock had saved his life, and that was worth something—even between enemies.

"I—I got to thank you, Mr. Bullock, fer standin' up fer me . . ."

But the fat sergeant smiled and waved his hand unconcernedly. "Twern't nothin', Johnny. Sit down." He lowered his own ponderous bulk to the ground with a long grunt. "If—" he began reflectively, "there's one thing I like it's a boy with nerve. . . . Yessir, I like that. 'Minds me of the time I was young an' out in the Californy gold field. . . ." He glanced sideways at the boy. "Yep, a bucko had to have guts them days to get by, I can tell you!"

Yorky's interest was tickled. He sat down and looked at the fat man searchingly. "Was you with the '49ers, Mr. Bullock, truly?"

Bullock seemed unimpressed with his own past. He shrugged and shot a thoughtful eye at the turquoise sky. "Yes, them times were interesting I guess, what with fightin' Injuns, Spanish buckos, claim-jumpers, findin' gold and losin' it, gettin' snowed in in the mountains

... Course none of it was half as excitin' as the battles I been in ... An*tee*dum, and Bull Run, Fred'sburg, Seven Days, Chancellor'ville. . . ."

Yorky's mind was too busy building up an image of this great, brawling soldier of fortune to realize that if Bullock was with Sherman's Western Army, the chances of his having fought with the Army of the Potomac at the named conflicts were doubtful. He wished, secretly—rather guiltily—that his Pa had been like Bullock. And then he asked, hesitantly, "Was you—at Shiloh, Mr. Bullock?"

It seemed for a split-second that Bullock was going to nod his head, but then he paused and ran his eyes over the boy's face quickly, searching. "No—" he muttered. "No, I missed that one." He hunched forward, cradling the jug between his crossed legs, smiled, and somehow his beefy, good-natured countenance put Yorky at ease.

"But bein' a soldier ain't too much fun, by an' large," and again his eyes slid sideways toward the boy, "—not half the fun of bein' a seaman in the South Seas is," he added suggestively.

Yorky wetted his dry lips, tasting the bait. "Was you a sailor, too?"

"Haw!" Bullock crowed, and gave his meaty thigh a great slap. "Was I ever! Yessir, Johnny, had me my own schooner. Captain I was. Why, boy, there's a new world out there beyond the horizon—a world of deep blue water, coral, palms an' coc'nuts. There's islands out there that might be jewels dropped out of heaven—an' I been to most of 'em, an' there's few white men that can say the same! I was a sandalwooder, do yuh see? I traded with an' fought with head-hunters for that wood; an', boy, the profits was tremenjus!"

Yorky's eyes glazed with new visions. He forgot that he was a captive in a bummer's roost, that a tall dark man was waiting to kill him. He thought about savage islands and their weird people, about a new world beyond the horizon, and about having a friend.

Bullock's eyes were still searching the sky, sliding down from time to time to take in the boy's enchanted face. "Yessir," he said, "from all I can hear an' see this ol' war is jus' about over. You know what I'm gonna do then, Johnny? Gonna take my share of this loot an' my discharge pay an' buy myself another schooner. I—I might even put in at Savannah on my way to the Horn. Might even find I need a brave young fella to go 'long with me as cabin boy. . . . I don't know, it's worth thinkin' about. . . ."

Yorky hunched forward, all of his loneliness crowding into his pounding heart. He touched Bullock's plump knee with his hand.

"You—you mean you might consider takin' me along, Mr. Bullock? You might let me go with you to the South Sea? I ain't got no folks, Mr. Bullock—I'm all alone, nearly. Would you really stop by fer me?"

Bullock smiled kindly. "Well, now, Johnny—I reckon that depends on whether or not you let me outa this hole you got me in. If I thought I could trust you I'd let you waltz right on out of here; then I could head north without no Rebs chasin' after me. Then, when the war's over, I could buy that schooner . . . Dirt cheap, I figure."

Yorky hesitated. This Yank was asking him to turn against the Southern Cause. *This bummer, this* . . . This Yank had befriended him, saved his life, was almost offering to take him to the South Seas. He came up to a kneeling position and grabbed Bullock's arm. "You got to promise not to raid no more plantations. . . . You got to promise that!"

Bullock's moon-face bunched into a gigantic smile. He patted Yorky's thin shoulder. " 'Course I promise! All you got to do is not tell nobody you seen us here. 'Member now—nobody! Else I won't be able to get that schooner. Now you skeedaddle out of here, an' I'll come look for you." He lurched up, lifted the flap of his holster and wrapped his hand around the pistol butt. He looked at his three comrades with flat eyes.

"This here boy give me his word he ain't gonna split; that's good 'nuff for me. He's goin' outa here now in one piece. I reckon I don't want no argyment about it . . . I ain't ready to turn my back jus' yet. Scoot, Johnny!"

All the way down the pass and through the woods, Yorky's brain was full of Bullock. All of his war-hate was obscured by his fascination for the fat man who was going to take him to a new world. He didn't even stop to think that Bullock hadn't asked him what his name was.

The raiders struck Stafford Hall just before dawn. The first thing Yorky heard was the smashing of the tall French windows along the gallery front. Then he heard voices shouting, and he left his bed in his nightgown, barefooted. He was in the center of the dark kitchen when he heard the shot.

It was over by the time he reached the gallery. Brutus, with the Sharps rifle, was lying in the dirt drive, and down the black avenue he could hear the sharp clippity-clop of fleeing horses.

Mrs. Stafford stepped down into the drive and picked up the rifle, and she stood that way, holding it in one hand, clutching a wrapper about her narrow body with the other. Then she came back to the house, walking past Yorky without looking at him.

"Brutus tried to protect me," she said, her voice a thin thread of sound. "The gun wasn't even loaded . . . He'd never fired one in his life . . . He just slipped in through the rear and snatched it out of the cupboard and tried to frighten them away. A tall, cruel looking Yank shot him down . . . and then they ran."

Yorky turned numbly and re-entered the house with Mrs. Stafford, leaving something fragile broken on the gallery behind him. She placed the rifle in a corner of the drawing room and sat down wearily in a rose-brocaded chair.

Yorky stood in the doorway staring at the rug with burning eyes.

"I found them bummers this afternoon—yesterday," he blurted suddenly. "I didn't tell nobody 'cause one of 'em saved my life . . . He promised they wouldn't do no more raidin' . . . he promised he'd come fer me at the end of the war . . . that we'd go to the South Seas together on his schooner . . . He *promised* me!"

Mrs. Stafford turned and looked at the boy, startled, as though just now aware of his existence. A soft look of realization crept into her eyes, touched the thin line of her mouth. "Yorky," she said, "come here—please." Then she put her brittle hands on his shoulders and looked at his bowed, tousled head.

"Poor little fellow. . . . I haven't been much of a friend to you, have I? I thought because I let you live here in the Hall with me you were content. I forgot that a boy needs someone to talk to, someone to bring his troubles and questions and hurts to. In my grief I forgot that all little boys are like my boy once was. Yorky—forgive me."

He caught her hands, pulled them away from his shoulders and held them tight. "You got to let me take the Sharps rifle, Mizz Stafford. I know where them bummers are. . . . I got to go at 'em. You send one of the boys after the detachment at Parkins Corner, tell 'em to come hightailin' to Chigger Cave. . . ."

Mrs. Stafford's face was alive with new life, with concern. She shook her head rapidly. "No, Yorky, no . . . I can't."

He dropped her hands, stepped back. "I ain't goan hurt the ol' gun!" he cried angrily. "But I got to have me a weapon!"

"No, you don't understand. I don't care about the rifle now . . . It's you, Yorky, you can't go fight men, you're just a boy. . . ."

"*I got to!* It's my fault this happened. I *trusted* him. I let 'em go, an' now Brutus is dead. I jus' got to, Mizz Stafford!"

She sagged visibly before his eyes, no longer stiff and haughty, just old and tired. "Little boys," she murmured, "little boys and war. . . . Do you know where the ammunition is?"

Yorky paused at the doorway and looked back at the huddled, silent figure. "I don't want you should feel bad, Mizz Stafford—you always been kind to me." He hesitated, biting at his lip.

"You always been like a ma to me, mam," he lied.

It was nearly seven in the morning when the raiders returned to Chigger Cave. They came down the pass single-file on their over-burdened mounts, clinking and clattering with plunder. Yorky had been waiting on the ledge for over an hour. He checked them off as they entered the rock-enclosure; One—Sim; two—Parks; three—Mick; four . . . He bit at his lip, watching the fat sergeant bring up the rear.

Bullock, strangely, had little to say. He turned his horse over to Parks, went to the cave-mouth and sat down heavily. He put his chin in his hands and stared at the ground, ignoring the jug.

Yorky eased the rifle barrel over the parapet and took a sight on Sim. *A tall, cruel looking Yank shot him down. . . .* His finger squeezed back on the trigger. Sim turned away abruptly as the Sharps exploded sound into the enclosure. Mick had been standing directly behind Sim; he doubled over with a half-scream and toppled into the dead fire.

Sim sprang sideways, clawing for his pistol. Out of the corner of his eye Yorky saw Parks swinging a carbine up. Then Yorky ducked as a bullet flattened solidly against the rock. He worked frantically trying to reload the rifle with trembling hands; slid the breech-block down and shoved a paper cartridge, containing a conical bullet and powder, into the chamber. He snapped the block closed, shearing the base of the cartridge, and placed a cap over the flashhole nipple.

He came up in a half-crouch and snapped his second shot down at the blue soldiers. Two bullets splattered near his head. He ducked again, sobbing now. He reckoned that war wasn't such a much after all—too mean. He was scared—real scared, and he knew it. He could run; hit back along the ridge and down into the woods; they'd never catch him . . . He came up and fired again, dodged to the left as rock fragments needled his cheek and the back of his neck. No, he couldn't run . . . had to hold them there for the detachment.

He crawled further along the ridge to a fresh firing position; ran the rifle out, and he and Parks fired at each other simultaneously. The

Yank tipped over backwards without a sound. Bill Bullock was standing between two horses, holding a pistol in his hand, peering up at the rocks. Yorky could pick him off just as easy. . . .

"Ain't no sense in him showin' hisself thataway," he whispered angrily, and he swiped at his burning eyes quickly. "Darn ol' fool! *Fat ol' Fool!* Why don't he take better cover?"

He raised his head again and looked hurriedly over the enclosure. Where was Sim? Why wasn't anyone shooting at him? Bullock was looking up again, but not at Yorky's position. The fat sergeant pushed on the flank of the off horse, making it step aside; then he turned and waddled quickly for the cave. Yorky swung the rifle in line with him . . . Then, as he squeezed the trigger, he jerked the barrel down, spitting up dirt at Bullock's heels.

"Run you fat bummer," he sobbed as he reloaded the rifle.

Rocks were clattering downward somewhere. Yorky raised his head trying to discover the cause of the slide. Who was doing it? Where? Then he remembered the steep serrated gully . . . it was to the right of the overhang—he couldn't see it from his position. *Sim!*

The boy looked around desperately. Where would he come from? Where was he right now? A stone clinked near his knee. He gasped and looked up. . . .

On a great overbrow of smooth rock, directly overhead, Sim rose into standing position and pointed his pistol down at Yorky. His thin, tight mouth jerked into a smile.

Yorky didn't even think to use the rifle, he rolled back against the parapet and raised one hand. "No!" he cried.

A shot cracked a clear, lonely sound in the pass. The dark soldier took a step aimlessly, seemed to miss his footing, and pitched head-long over Yorky. The cowering boy could still see the grin of Sim's face as the Yank jackknifed in the air and plunged for the enclosure floor.

Yorky peered cautiously over the parapet. He couldn't see Sim's body. But he could see Bullock standing just outside of the cave, a smoking pistol in his hand. Old Fool! the boy thought. Don't he know I could pick him off jus' as easy as pie? Then he pulled back behind the parapet and wiped at his moist face. No; I reckon he knows I can't do her . . .

For a full minute Yorky wasn't worth anything. He just sat with his back to the rock and watched his hands tremble. He was glad it was over—awful glad.

Bullock was rifling through Sim's pockets when Yorky entered the enclosure. He looked up and smiled, and something clinked in his hand. "Sim owed me some money," he explained. Yorky said nothing. He glanced at the still forms of Parks and Mick. They must have owed Bullock money also—their pockets had been turned out.

Bullock gave a grunt and lurched to his feet. "Well, shipmate," he said easily, "I reckon this evens us; you didn't tell the Rebs on me, an' I took care of Sim for you. You know, Sim was a gunfighter afore the war, fast too. . . . But I always reckoned I could handle him."

"I did tell on you-all," Yorky said abruptly. "—This mornin' after you killed Brutus . . . After you broke yer promise."

Bullock looked startled. "You mean there's Rebs waitin' for me beyond the pass?"

"No, not yet, but they're a'comin'."

The fat sergeant nodded shortly and turned for the cave. "Just got to get me somethin' outa here, then I'll be on my way." He came back out into the enclosure a moment later with a plump canvas bag that clinked when he moved it. "For the schooner," he explained, and he dropped the bag into one of the horse's saddle bags. Then he turned to the boy and put out a plump moist hand.

"I didn't want to make that raid last night, Johnny," he said apologetically. "But them boys just wouldn't listen to reason, Sim got 'em all riled up. It was Sim that killed that field hand. I—I was gonna pay Sim back for that later. . . . Well, it don't matter now. It don't change nothin' between you an' me. . . . We're still goin' to the South Seas when the war ends. What's wrong? Don't you want to shake hands with me, Johnny?"

Yorky nodded and took the soldier's hand. Bullock was right, it didn't matter now—it didn't matter that he knew Bullock was lying, that he knew Bullock would never come for him to take him to the South Seas. Bullock had saved his life, and that was worth something—between soldiers.

Bullock laughed and heaved himself up into the saddle. "Remember, Johnny—Savannah!" he called. Then he waved a pudgy hand and started down the pass.

"Savannah," the boy murmured after him. He smiled and shook his head. For a moment he stood in the quiet enclosure and looked at the three dead soldiers. Then he shouldered the Sharps rifle and started down the pass for the Hall. He reckoned Mrs. Stafford was going to need him now.

# STEPHEN CRANE

*The Little Regiment*

THE FOG MADE the clothes of the men of the column in the roadway seem of a luminous quality. It imparted to the heavy infantry overcoats a new colour, a kind of blue which was so pale that a regiment might have been merely a long, low shadow in the mist. However, a muttering, one part grumble, three parts joke, hovered in the air above the thick ranks, and blended in an undertoned roar, which was the voice of the column.

The town on the southern shore of the little river loomed spectrally, a faint etching upon the grey cloud-masses which were shifting with oily languor. A long row of guns upon the northern bank had been pitiless in their hatred, but a little battered belfry could be dimly seen still pointing with invincible resolution toward the heavens.

The enclouded air vibrated with noises made by hidden colossal things. The infantry tramplings, the heavy rumbling of the artillery, made the earth speak of gigantic preparation. Guns on distant heights thundered from time to time with sudden, nervous roars, as if unable to endure in silence a knowledge of hostile troops massing, other guns going to position. These sounds, near and remote, defined an immense battle-ground, described the tremendous width of the stage of the prospective drama. The voices of the guns, slightly casual, unexcited in their challenges and warnings, could not destroy the unutterable eloquence of the word in the air, a meaning of impending struggle which made the breath halt at the lips.

The column in the roadway was ankle-deep in mud. The men swore piously at the rain which drizzled upon them, compelling them to stand always very erect in fear of the drops that would sweep in under their coat collars. The fog was as cold as wet cloths. The men stuffed their hands deep into their pockets, and huddled their muskets in their arms. The machinery of orders had rooted these soldiers deeply into the mud, precisely as almightly nature roots mullein stalks.

They listened and speculated when a tumult of fighting came from the dim town across the river. When the noise lulled for a time they resumed their descriptions of the mud and graphically exaggerated the number of hours they had been kept waiting. The general commanding their division rode along the ranks, and they cheered admiringly, affectionately, crying out to him gleeful prophecies of the coming battle. Each man scanned him with a peculiarly keen personal interest, and afterward spoke of him with unquestioning devotion and confidence, narrating anecdotes which were mainly untrue.

When the jokers lifted the shrill voices which invariably belonged to them, flinging witticisms at their comrades, a loud laugh would sweep from rank to rank, and soldiers who had not heard would lean forward and demand repetition. When were borne past them some wounded men with grey and blood-smeared faces, and eyes that rolled in that helpless beseeching for assistance from the sky which comes with supreme pain, the soldiers in the mud watched intently, and from time to time asked of the bearers an account of the affair. Frequently they bragged of their corps, their division, their brigade, their regiment. Anon they referred to the mud and the cold drizzle. Upon this threshold of a wild scene of death they, in short, defied the proportion of events with that splendour of heedlessness which belongs only to veterans.

"Like a lot of wooden soldiers," swore Billie Dempster, moving his feet in the thick mass, and casting a vindictive glance indefinitely. "Standing in the mud for a hundred years."

"Oh, shut up!" murmured his brother Dan. The manner of his words implied that this fraternal voice near him was an indescribable bore.

"Why should I shut up?" demanded Billie.

"Because you're a fool," cried Dan, taking no time to debate it; "the biggest fool in the regiment."

There was but one man between them, and he was habituated. These insults from brother to brother had swept across his chest, flown past his face, many times during two long campaigns. Upon this occasion he simply grinned first at one, then at the other.

The way of these brothers was not an unknown topic in regimental gossip. They had enlisted simultaneously, with each sneering loudly at the other for doing it. They left their little town, and went forward with the flag, exchanging protestations of undying suspicion. In the camp life they so openly despised each other that, when entertaining quarrels were lacking, their companions often contrived situations calculated to bring forth display of this fraternal dislike.

Both were large-limbed, strong young men, and often fought with friends in camp unless one was near to interfere with the other. This latter happened rather frequently, because Dan, preposterously willing for any manner of combat, had a very great horror of seeing Billie in a fight; and Billie, almost odiously ready himself, simply refused to see Dan stripped to his shirt and with his fists aloft. This sat queerly upon them, and made them the objects of plots.

When Dan jumped through a ring of eager soldiers and dragged forth his raving brother by the arm, a thing often predicted would almost come to pass. When Billie performed the same office for Dan, the prediction would again miss fulfilment by an inch. But indeed they never fought together, although they were perpetually upon the verge.

They expressed longing for such conflict. As a matter of truth, they had at one time made full arrangement for it, but even with the encouragement and interest of half of the regiment they somehow failed to achieve collision.

If Dan became a victim of police duty, no jeering was so destructive to the feelings as Billie's comment. If Billie got a call to appear at the headquarters, none would so genially prophesy his complete undoing as Dan. Small misfortunes to one were, in truth, invariably greeted with hilarity by the other, who seemed to see in them great reinforcement of his opinion.

As soldiers, they expressed each for each a scorn intense and blasting. After a certain battle, Billie was promoted to corporal. When Dan was told of it, he seemed smitten dumb with astonishment and patriotic indignation. He stared in silence, while the dark blood rushed to Billie's forehead, and he shifted his weight from foot to foot. Dan at last found his tongue, and said; "Well, I'm durned!" If he had heard that an army mule had been appointed to the post of corps commander, his tone could not have had more derision in it. Afterward, he adopted a fervid insubordination, an almost religious reluctance to obey the new corporal's orders, which came near to developing the desired strife.

It is here finally to be recorded also that Dan, most ferociously profane in speech, very rarely swore in the presence of his brother; and that Billie, whose oaths came from his lips with the grace of falling pebbles, was seldom known to express himself in this manner when near his brother Dan.

At last the afternoon contained a suggestion of evening. Metallic cries rang suddenly from end to end of the column. They inspired at once a quick, business-like adjustment. The long thing stirred in the mud. The men had hushed, and were looking across the river. A moment later the shadowy mass of pale blue figures was moving steadily toward the stream. There could be heard from the town a clash of swift fighting and cheering. The noise of the shooting coming through the heavy air had its sharpness taken from it, and sounded in thuds.

There was a halt upon the bank above the pontoons. When the column went winding down the incline, and streamed out upon the bridge, the fog had faded to a great degree, and in the clearer dusk the guns on a distant ridge were enabled to perceive the crossing. The long whirling outcries of the shells came into the air above the men. An occasional solid shot struck the surface of the river, and dashed into view a sudden vertical jet. The distance was subtly illuminated by the lightning from the deep-booming guns. One by one the batteries on the northern shore aroused, the innumerable guns bellowing in angry oration at the distant ridge. The rolling thunder crashed and reverberated as a wild surf sounds on a still night, and to this music the column marched across the pontoons.

The waters of the grim river curled away in a smile from the ends of the great boats, and slid swiftly beneath the planking. The dark, riddled walls of the town upreared before the troops, and from a region hidden by these hammered and tumbled houses came incessantly the yells and firings of a prolonged and close skirmish.

When Dan had called his brother a fool, his voice had been so decisive, so brightly assured, that many men had laughed, considering it to be great humour under the circumstances. The incident happened to rankle deep in Billie. It was not any strange thing that his brother had called him a fool. In fact, he often called him a fool with exactly the same amount of cheerful and prompt conviction, and before large audiences, too. Billie wondered in his own mind why he took such profound offence in this case; but, at any rate, as he slid down the bank and on to the bridge with his regiment, he was searching his knowledge for something that would pierce Dan's blithesome spirit. But he could contrive nothing at this time, and his impotency made the glance which he was once able to give his brother still more malignant.

The guns far and near were roaring a fearful and grand introduction for this column which was marching upon the stage of death. Billie felt it, but only in a numb way. His heart was cased in that curious dissonant metal which covers a man's emotions at such times. The terrible voices from the hills told him that in this wide conflict his life was an insignificant fact, and that his death would be an insignificant fact. They portended the whirlwind to which he would be as necessary as a butterfly's waved wing. The solemnity, the sadness of it came near enough to make him wonder why he was neither solemn nor sad. When his mind vaguely adjusted events according to their importance to him, it appeared that the uppermost thing was the fact that upon the eve of battle, and before many comrades, his brother had called him a fool.

Dan was in a particularly happy mood. "Hurray! Look at 'em shoot," he said, when the long witches' croon of the shells came into the air. It enraged Billie when he felt the little thorn in him, and saw at the same time that his brother had completely forgotten it.

The column went from the bridge into more mud. At this southern end there was a chaos of hoarse directions and commands. Darkness was coming upon the earth, and regiments were being hurried up the slippery bank. As Billie floundered in the black mud, amid the swearing, sliding crowd, he suddenly resolved that, in the absence of other means of hurting Dan, he would avoid looking at him, refrain from speaking to him, pay absolutely no heed to his existence; and this, done skilfully, would, he imagined, soon reduce his brother to a poignant sensitiveness.

At the top of the bank the column again halted and rearranged itself, as a man after a climb rearranges his clothing. Presently the great steel-backed brigade, an infinitely graceful thing in the rhythm and ease of its veteran movement, swung up a little narrow, slanting street.

Evening had come so swiftly that the fighting on the remote borders of the town was indicated by thin flashes of flame. Some building was on fire, and its reflection upon the clouds was an oval of delicate pink.

## 2

ALL DEMEANOR OF rural serenity had been wrenched violently from the little town by the guns and by the waves of men which had surged through it. The hand of war laid upon this village had in an instant changed it to a thing of remnants. It resembled the place of a monstrous shaking of the earth itself. The windows, now mere unsightly holes, made the tumbled and blackened dwellings seem skeletons.

Doors lay splintered to fragments. Chimneys had flung their bricks everywhere. The artillery fire had not neglected the rows of gentle shade-trees which had lined the streets. Branches and heavy trunks cluttered the mud in driftwood tangles, while a few shattered forms had contrived to remain dejectedly, mournfully upright. They expressed an innocence, a helplessness, which perforce created a pity for their happening into this cauldron of battle. Furthermore, there was under foot a vast collection of odd things reminiscent of the charge, the fight, the retreat. There were boxes and barrels filled with earth, behind which riflemen had lain snugly, and in these little trenches were the dead in blue with the dead in grey, the poses eloquent of the struggles for possession of the town, until the history of the whole conflict was written plainly in the streets.

And yet the spirit of this little city, its quaint individuality poised in the air above the ruins, defying the guns, the sweeping volleys; holding in contempt those avaricious blazes which had attacked many dwellings. The hard earthen sidewalks proclaimed the games that had been played there during long lazy days, in the careful shadows of the trees. "General Merchandise," in faint letters upon a long board, had to be read with a slanted glance, for the sign dangled by one end; but the porch of the old store was a palpable legend of wide-hatted men, smoking.

This subtle essence, this soul of the life that had been, brushed like invisible wings the thoughts of the men in the swift columns that came up from the river.

In the darkness a loud and endless humming arose from the great blue crowds bivouacked in the streets. From time to time a sharp spatter of firing from far picket lines entered this bass chorus. The smell from the smouldering ruins floated on the cold night breeze.

Dan, seated ruefully upon the doorstep of a shot-pierced house, was proclaiming the campaign badly managed. Orders had been issued forbidding campfires.

Suddenly he ceased his oration and, scanning the group of his comrades, said: 'Where's Billie? Do you know?''

"Gone on picket."

"Get out! Has he?" said Dan. "No business to go on picket. Why don't some of them other corporals take their turn?"

A bearded private was smoking his pipe of confiscated tobacco, seated comfortably upon a horse-hair trunk which he had dragged from the house. He observed: "*Was* his turn."

"No such thing," cried Dan. He and the man on the horse-hair trunk held discussion in which Dan stoutly maintained that if his brother had been sent on picket it was an injustice. He ceased his argument when another soldier, upon whose arms could faintly be seen the two stripes of a corporal, entered the circle. "Humph," said Dan, "where you been?"

The corporal made no answer. Presently Dan said: "Billie, where you been?"

His brother did not seem to hear these inquiries. He glanced at the house which towered above them, and remarked casually to the man on the horse-hair trunk: "Funny, ain't it? After the pelting this town got, you'd think there wouldn't be one brick left on another."

"Oh," said Dan, glowering at his brother's back. "Getting mighty smart, ain't you?"

The absence of camp-fires allowed the evening to make apparent its quality of faint silver light in which the blue clothes of the throng became black, and the faces became white expanses, void of expression. There was considerable excitement a short distance from the group around the doorstep. A soldier had chanced upon a hoop-skirt, and arrayed in it he was performing a dance amid the applause of his companions. Billie and a greater part of the men immediately poured over there to witness the exhibition.

"What's the matter with Billie?" demanded Dan of the man upon the horse-hair trunk.

"How do I know?" rejoined the other in mild resentment. He arose and walked away. When he returned he said briefly, in a weather-wise tone, that it would rain during the night.

Dan took a seat upon one end of the horse-hair trunk. He was facing the crowd around the dancer, which in its hilarity swung this way and that way. At times he imagined that he could recognize his brother's face.

He and the man on the other end of the trunk thoughtfully talked of the army's position. To their minds, infantry and artillery were in a most precarious jumble in the streets of the town; but they did not grow nervous over it, for they were used to having the army appear in a precarious jumble to their minds. They had learned to accept such puzzling situations as a consequence of their position in the ranks, and were now usually in possession of a simple but perfectly immovable faith that somebody understood the jumble. Even if they had been convinced that the army was a headless monster, they would merely have nodded with the veteran's singular cynicism. It was none of their business as soldiers. Their duty was to grab sleep and food when occasion permitted, and cheerfully fight wherever their feet were planted until more orders came. This was a task sufficiently absorbing.

They spoke of other corps, and, this talk being confidential, their voices dropped to tones of awe. "The Ninth"—"The First"—"The Fifth"—"The Sixth"—"The Third"—the simple numerals rang with eloquence, each having a meaning which was to float through many years as no intangible arithmetical mist, but as pregnant with individuality as the names of cities.

Of their own corps they spoke with a deep veneration, an idolatry, a supreme confidence which apparently would not blanch to see it match against everything.

It was as if their respect for other corps was due partly to a wonder that organizations not blessed with their own famous numeral could take such an interest in war. They could prove that their division was the best in the corps, and that their brigade was the best in the division. And their regiment—it was plain that no fortune of life was equal to the chance which caused a man to be born, so to speak, into this command, the keystone of the defending arch.

At times Dan covered with insults the character of a vague, unnamed general to whose petulance and busybody spirit he ascribed the order which made hot coffee impossible.

Dan said that victory was certain in the coming battle. The other man seemed rather dubious. He remarked upon the fortified line of hills, which had impressed him even from the other side of the river. "Shucks," said Dan. "Why, we—" He pictured a splendid overflowing of these hills by the sea of men in blue. During the period of this conversation Dan's glance searched the merry throng about the dancer. Above the babble of voices in the street a far-away thunder could sometimes be heard, evidently from the very edge of the horizon—the boom-boom of restless guns.

# 3

ULTIMATELY THE NIGHT deepended to the tone of black velvet. The outlines of the fireless camp were like the faint drawings upon ancient tapestry. The glint of a rifle, the shine of a button, might have been of threads of silver and gold sewn upon the fabric of the night. There was little presented to the vision, but to a sense more subtle there was discernible in the atmosphere something like a pulse; a mystic beating which would have told a stranger of the presence of a giant thing—the slumbering mass of regiments and batteries.

With fires forbidden, the floor of a dry old kitchen was thought to be a good exchange for the cold earth of December, even if a shell had exploded in it and knocked it so out of shape that when a man lay curled in his blanket his last waking thought was likely to be of the wall that bellied out above him, as if strongly anxious to topple upon the score of soldiers.

Billie looked at the bricks ever about to descend in a shower upon his face, listened to the industrious pickets plying their rifles on the border of the town, imagined some measure of the din of the coming battle, thought of Dan and Dan's chagrin, and, rolling over in his blanket, went to sleep with satisfaction.

At an unknown hour he was aroused by the creaking of boards. Lifting himself upon his elbow, he saw a sergeant prowling among the sleeping forms. The sergeant carried a candle in an old brass candlestick. He would have resembled some old farmer on an unusual midnight tour if it were not for the significance of his gleaming buttons and striped sleeves.

Billie blinked stupidly at the light until his mind returned from the journeys of slumber. The sergeant stooped among the unconscious soldiers, holding the candle close, and peering into each face.

"Hello, Haines," said Billie, "Relief?"

"Hello, Billie," said the sergeant. "Special duty."

"Dan got to go?"

"Jameson, Hunter, McCormack, D. Dempster, Yes.—Where is he?"

"Over there by the winder," said Billie gesturing. "What is it for, Haines?"

"You don't think I know, do you?" demanded the sergeant. He began to pipe sharply but cheerily at men upon the floor. "Come, Mac, get up here. Here's a special for you. Wake up, Jameson. Come along, Dannie, me boy."

Each man at once took this call to duty as a personal affront. They pulled themselves out of their blankets, rubbed their eyes, and swore at whoever was responsible. "Them's orders," cried the sergeant. "Come! Get out of here." An undetailed head with dishevelled hair thrust out from a blanket, and a sleepy voice said: "Shut up, Haines, and go home."

When the detail clanked out of the kitchen, all but one of the remaining men seemed to be again asleep. Billie, leaning on his elbow, was gazing into darkness. When the footsteps died to silence, he curled himself into his blanket.

At the first cool lavender lights of daybreak he aroused again, and scanned his recumbent companions. Seeing a wakeful one he asked: "Is Dan back yet?"

The man said: "Hain't seen 'im."

Billie put both hands behind his head, and scowled into the air. "Can't see the use of these cussed details in the nighttime," he muttered in his most unreasonable tones. "Darn nuisance. Why can't they—?" He grumbled at length and graphically.

When Dan entered with the squad, however, Billie was convincingly asleep.

# 4

THE REGIMENT TROTTED in double time along the street, and the colonel seemed to quarrel over the right of way with many artillery officers. Batteries were waiting in the mud, and the men of them, exasperated by the bustle of this ambitious infantry, shook their fists from saddle and caisson, exchanging all manner of taunts and jests. The slanted guns continued to look reflectively at the ground.

On the outskirts of the crumbled town a fringe of blue figures was firing into the fog. The regiment swung out into skirmish lines, and the fringe of blue figures departed, turning their backs and going joyfuly around the flank.

The bullets began a low moan off toward a ridge which loomed faintly in the heavy mist. When the swift crescendo had reached its climax, the missiles zipped just overhead, as if piercing an invisible curtain. A battery on the hill was crashing with such tumult that it was as if the guns had quarrelled and had fallen pell-mell and snarling upon each other. The shells howled on their journey toward the town. From short-range distance there came a spatter of musketry, sweeping along an invisible line and making faint sheets of orange light.

Some in the new skirmish lines were beginning to fire at various shadows discerned in the vapour—forms of men suddenly revealed by some humour of the laggard masses of clouds. The crackle of musketry began to dominate the purring of the hostile bullets. Dan, in the front rank, held his rifle poised, and looked into the fog keenly, coldly, with the air of a sportsman. His nerves were so steady that it was as if they had been drawn from his body, leaving him merely a muscular machine; but his numb heart was somehow beating to the pealing march of the fight.

The waving skirmish line went backward and forward, ran this way and that way. Men got lost in the fog, and men were found again. Once they got too close to the formidable ridge, and the thing burst out as if repulsing a general attack. Once another blue regiment was apprehended on the very edge of firing into them. Once a friendly battery began an elaborate and scientific process of extermination. Always as busy as brokers, the men slid here and there over the plain, fighting their foes, escaping from their friends, leaving a history of many movements in the wet yellow turf, cursing the atmosphere, blazing away every time they could identify the enemy.

In one mystic changing of the fog, as if the fingers of spirits were drawing aside these draperies, a small group of the grey skirmishers, silent, statuesque, was suddenly disclosed to Dan and those about him. So vivid and near were they that there was something uncanny in the revelation.

There might have been a second of mutual staring. Then each rifle in each group was at the shoulder. As Dan's glance flashed along the barrel of his weapon, the figure of a man suddenly loomed as if the musket had been a telescope. The short black beard, the slouch hat, the pose of the man as he sighted to shoot, made a quick picture in Dan's mind. The same moment, it would seem, he pulled his own trigger, and the man, smitten, lurched forward, while his exploding rifle made a slanting crimson streak in the air, and the slouch hat fell before the body. The billows of the fog, governed by singular impulses, rolled between.

"You got that feller sure enough," said a comrade to Dan. Dan looked at him absent-mindedly.

# 5

WHEN THE NEXT morning calmly displayed another fog, the men of the regiment exchanged eloquent comments; but they did not abuse it at length, because the streets of the town now contained enough galloping aides to make three troops of cavalry, and they knew that they had come to the verge of the great fight.

Dan conversed with the man who had once possessed a horse-hair trunk; but they did not mention the line of hills which had furnished them in more careless moments with an agreeable topic. They avoided it now as condemned men do the subject of death, and yet the thought of it stayed in their eyes as they looked at each other and talked gravely of other things.

The expectant regiment heaved a long sigh of relief when the sharp call "Fall in," repeated indefinitely, arose in the streets. It was inevitable that a bloody battle was to be fought, and they wanted to get it off their minds. They were, however, doomed again to spend a long period planted firmly in the mud. They craned their necks, and wondered where some of the other regiments were going.

At last the mists rolled carelessly away. Nature made at this time all provisions to enable foes to see each other, and immediately the roar of guns resounded from every hill. The endless cracking of the skirmishers swelled to rolling crashes of musketry. Shells screamed with panther-like noises at the houses. Dan looked at the man of the horse-hair trunk, and the man said; "Well, here she comes!"

The tenor voices of younger officers and the deep and hoarse voices of the older ones rang in the streets. These cries pricked like spurs. The masses of men vibrated from the suddenness with which they were plunged into the situation of troops about to fight. That the orders were long expected did not concern the emotion.

Simultaneous movement was imparted to all these thick bodies of men and horses that lay in the town. Regiment after regiment swung rapidly into the streets that faced the sinister ridge.

This exodus was theatrical. The little sober-hued village had been like the cloak which disguises the king of drama. It was now put aside, and an army, splendid thing of steel and blue, stood forth in the sunlight.

Even the soldiers in the heavy columns drew deep breaths at the sight, more majestic than they had dreamed. The heights of the enemy's position were crowded with men who resembled people come to witness some mighty pageant. But as the columns moved steadily to their positions, the guns, matter-of-fact warriors, doubled their number, and shells burst with red thrilling tumult on the crowded plain. One came into the ranks of the regiment, and after the smoke and the wrath of it had faded, leaving motionless figures, every one stormed according to the limits of his vocabulary, for veterans detest being killed when they are not busy.

The regiment sometimes looked sidewise at its brigade companions, composed of men who had never been in battle; but no frozen blood could withstand the heat of the splendour of this army before the eyes on the plain, these lines so long that the flanks were little streaks, this mass of men of one intention. The recruits carried themselves heedlessly. At the rear was an idle battery, and three artillerymen in a foolish row on a caisson nudged each other and grinned at the recruits. "You'll catch it pretty soon," they called out. They were impersonally gleeful, as if they themselves were not also likely to catch it pretty soon. But with this picture of an army in their hearts, the new men perhaps felt the devotion which the drops may feel for the wave; they were of its power and glory; they smiled jauntily at the foolish row of gunners,and told them to go to blazes.

The column trotted across some little bridges, and spread quickly into lines of battle. Before them was a bit of plain, and in back of the plain was the ridge. There was no time left for consideration. The men were staring at the plain, mightily wondering how it would feel to be out there, when a brigade in advance yelled and charged. The hill was all grey smoke and fire-points.

That fierce elation in the terrors of war, catching a man's heart and making it burn with such ardour that he becomes capable of dying, flashed in the faces of the men like coloured lights, and made them resemble leashed animals, eager, ferocious, daunting at nothing. The line was really in its first leap before the wild, hoarse crying of the orders.

The greed for close quarters which is the emotion of a bayonet charge came then into the minds of the men and developed until it was a madness. The field, with its faded grass of a Southern winter, seemed to this fury miles in width.

High, slow-moving masses of smoke, with an odour of burning cotton, engulfed the line until the men might have been swimmers. Before them the ridge, the shore of this grey sea, was outlined, crossed, and re-crossed by sheets of flame. The howl of the battle arose to the noise of innumerable wind demons.

The line, galloping, scrambling, plunging like a herd of wounded horses, went over a field that was sown with corpses, the records of other charges.

Directly in front of the black-faced, whooping Dan, carousing in this onward sweep like a new kind of fiend, a wounded man appeared, raising his shattered body, and staring at this rush of men down upon him. It seemed to occur to him that he was to be trampled; he made a desperate, piteous effort to escape; then finally huddled in a waiting heap. Dan and the soldier near him widened the interval between them without looking down, without appearing to heed the wounded man. This little clump of blue seemed to reel past them as boulders reel past a train.

Bursting through a smoke-wave, the scampering, unformed bunches came upon the wreck of the brigade that had preceded them, a floundering mass stopped afar from the hill by the swirling volleys.

It was as if a necromancer had suddenly shown them a picture of the fate which awaited them; but the line with muscular spasm hurled itself over this wreckage and onward, until men were stumbling amid the relics of other assaults, the point where the fire from the ridge consumed.

The men, panting, perspiring, with crazed faces, tried to push against it; but it was as if they had come to a wall. The wave halted, shuddered in an agony from the quick struggle of its two desires, then toppled, and broke into a fragmentary thing which has no name.

Veterans could now at last be distinguished from recruits. The new regiments were instantly gone, lost, scattered, as if they never had been. But the sweeping failure of the charge, the battle, could not make the veterans forget their business. With a last throe, the band of maniacs drew itself up and blazed a volley at the hill, insignificant to those iron entrenchments, but nevertheless expressing that singular final despair which enables men coolly to defy the walls of a city of death.

After this episode the men renamed their command. They called it the Little Regiment.

# 6

"I SEEN DAN shoot a feller yesterday. Yes sir. I'm sure it was him that done it. And maybe he thinks about that feller now, and wonders if *he* tumbled down just about the same way. Them things come up in a man's mind."

Bivouac fires upon the sidewalks, in the streets, in the yards, threw high their wavering reflections, which examined, like slim red fingers, the dingy scarred walls and the piles of tumbled brick. The droning of voices again arose from great blue crowds.

The odour of frying bacon, the fragrance from countless little coffee-pails floated among the ruins. The rifles, stacked in the shadows, emitted flashes of steely light. Wherever a flag lay horizontally from one stack to another was the bed of an eagle which had led men into the mystic smoke.

The men about a particular fire were engaged in holding in check their jovial spirits. They moved whispering around the blaze, although they looked at it with a certain fine contentment, like labourers after a day's hard work.

There was one who sat apart. They did not address him save in tones suddenly changed. They did not regard him directly, but always in little sidelong glances.

At last a soldier from a distant fire came into this circle of light. He studied for a time the man who sat apart. Then he hesitatingly stepped closer, and said: "Got any news, Dan?"

"No," said Dan.

The new-comer shifted his feet. He looked at the fire, at the sky, at the other men, at Dan. His face expressed a curious despair; his tongue was plainly in rebellion. Finally, however, he contrived to say: "Well, there's some chance yet, Dan. Lots of the wounded are still lying out there, you know. There's some chance yet."

"Yes," said Dan.

The soldier shifted his feet again, and looked miserably into the air. After another struggle he said; "Well, there's some chance yet, Dan." He moved hastily away.

One of the men of the squad, perhaps encouraged by this example, now approached the still figure. "No news yet, hey?" he said, after coughing behind his hand.

"No," said Dan.

"Well," said the man, "I've been thinking of how he was fretting about you the night you went on special duty. You recollect? Well, sir, I was surprised. He couldn't say enough about it. I swan, I don't believe he slep' a wink after you left, but just lay awake cussing special duty and worrying. I was surprised. But there he lay cussing. He—"

Dan made a curious sound, as if a stone had wedged in his throat. He said: "Shut up, will you?"

Afterward the men would not allow his moody contemplation of the fire to be interrupted.

"Oh, let him alone, can't you?"

"Come away from there, Casey!"

"Say, can't you leave him be?"

They moved with reverence about the immovable figure, with its countenance of mask-like invulnerability.

# 7

AFTER THE RED round eye of the sun had stared long at the little plain and its burden, darkness, a sable mercy, came heavily upon it, and the wan hands of the dead were no longer seen in strange frozen gestures.

The heights in front of the plain shone with tiny campfires, and from the town in the rear, small shimmerings ascended from the blazes of the bivouac. The plain was a black expanse upon which, from time to time, dots of light, lanterns, floated slowly here and there. These fields were long steeped in grim mystery.

Suddenly, upon one dark spot, there was a resurrection. A strange thing had been groaning there, prostrate. Then it suddenly dragged itself to a sitting position, and became a man.

The man stared stupidly for a moment at the lights on the hill, then turned and contemplated the faint colouring over the town. For some moments he remained thus, staring with dull eyes, his face unemotional, wooden.

Finally he looked around him at the corpses dimly to be seen. No change flashed into his face upon viewing these men. They seemed to suggest merely that his information concerning himself was not too complete. He ran his fingers over his arms and chest, bearing always the air of an idiot upon a bench at an almshouse door.

Finding no wound in his arms nor in his chest, he raised his hand to his head, and the fingers came away with some dark liquid upon them. Holding these fingers close to his eyes, he scanned them in the same stupid fashion, while his body gently swayed.

The soldier rolled his eyes again toward the town. When he arose, his clothing peeled from the frozen ground like wet paper. Hearing the sound of it, he seemed to see reason for deliberation. He paused and looked at the ground, then at his trousers, then at the ground.

Finally he went slowly off toward the faint reflection, holding his hands palm outward before him, and walking in the manner of a blind man.

# 8

THE IMMOVABLE DAN again sat unaddressed in themidst of comrades who did not joke aloud. The dampness of the usual morning fog seemed to make the little camp-fires furious.

Suddenly a cry arose in the streets, a shout of amazement and delight. The men making breakfast at the fire looked up quickly. They broke forth in clamorous exclamation: "Well! Of all things! Dan! Dan! Look who's coming! Oh, Dan!"

Dan the silent raised his eyes and saw a man, with a bandage of the size of a helmet about his head, receiving a furious demonstration from the company. He was shaking hands, and explaining, and haranguing to a high degree.

Dan started. His face of bronze flushed to his temples. He seemed about to leap from the ground, but then suddenly he sank back, and resumed his impassive gazing.

The men were in a flurry. Then looked from one to the other. "Dan! Look! See who's coming!" some cried again. "Dan! Look!"

He scowled at last, and moved his shoulders sullenly. "Well, don't I know it?"

But they could not be convinced that his eyes were in service. "Dan, why can't you look? See who's coming!"

He made a gesture then of irritation and rage. "Curse it! Don't I know it?"

The man with a bandage of the size of a helmet moved forward, always shaking hands and explaining. At times his glance wandered to Dan, who saw with his eyes riveted.

After a series of shiftings, it occurred naturally that the man with the bandage was very near to the man who saw the flames. He paused, and there was a little silence. Finally he said: "Hello, Dan."

"Hello, Billie."

# AMBROSE BIERCE

## *One of the Missing*

JEROME SEARING, a private soldier of General Sherman's army, then confronting the enemy at and about Kennesaw Mountain, Georgia, turned his back upon a small group of officers with whom he had been talking in low tones, stepped across a light line of earthworks, and disappeared in a forest. None of the men in line behind the works had said a word to him, nor had he so much as nodded to them in passing, but all who saw understood that this brave man had been intrusted with some perilous duty. Jerome Searing, though a private, did not serve in the ranks; he was detailed for service at division headquarters, being borne upon the rolls as an orderly. "Orderly" is a word covering a multitude of duties. An orderly may be a messenger, a clerk, an officer's servant—anything. He may perform services for which no provision is made in orders and army regulations. Their nature may depend upon his aptitude, upon favor, upon accident. Private Searing, an incomparable marksman, young, hardy, intelligent and insensible to fear, was a scout. The general commanding his division was not content to obey orders blindly without knowing what was in his front, even when his command was not on detached service, but formed a fraction of the line of the army; nor was he satisfied to receive his knowledge of his *visà-vis* through the customary channels; he wanted to know more than he was apprised of by the corps commander and the collisions of pickets and skirmishers. Hence Jerome Searing, with his extraordinary daring, his woodcraft, his sharp eyes, and truthful tongue. On this occasion his instructions were simple: to get as near the enemy's lines as possible and learn all that he could.

In a few moments he had arrived at the picket-line, the men on duty there lying in groups of two and four behind little banks of earth scooped out of the slight depression in which they lay, their rifles protruding from the green boughs with which they had masked their small defenses. The forest extended without a break toward the front, so solemn and silent that only by an effort of the imagination could it be conceived as populous with armed men, alert and vigilant—a forest formidable with possibilities of battle. Pausing a moment in one of these rifle-pits to apprise the men of his intention Searing crept stealthily forward on his hands and knees and was soon lost to view in a dense thicket of underbrush.

"That is the last of him," said one of the men; "I wish I had his rifle; those fellows will hurt some of us with it."

Searing crept on, taking advantage of every accident of ground and growth to give himself better cover. His eyes penetrated everywhere, his ears took note of every sound. He stilled his breathing, and at the cracking of a twig beneath his knee stopped his progress and hugged the earth. It was slow work, but not tedious; the danger made it exciting, but by no physical signs was the excitement manifest. His pulse was as regular, his nerves were as steady as if he were trying to trap a sparrow.

"It seems a long time," he thought, "but I cannot have come very far; I am still alive."

He smiled at his own method of estimating distance, and crept forward. A moment later he suddenly flattened himself upon the earth and lay motionless, minute after minute. Through a narrow opening in the bushes he had caught sight of a small mound of yellow clay—one of the enemy's rifle-pits. After some little time he cautiously raised his head, inch by inch, then his body upon his hands, spread out on each side of him, all the while intently regarding the hillock of clay. In another moment he was upon his feet, rifle in hand, striding rapidly forward with little attempt at concealment. He had rightly interpreted the signs, whatever they were; the enemy was gone.

To assure himself beyond a doubt before going back to report upon so important a matter, Searing pushed forward across the line of abandoned pits, running from cover to cover in the more open forest, his eyes vigilant to discover possible stragglers. He came to the edge of a plantation—one of those forlorn, deserted homesteads of the last years of the war, upgrown with brambles, ugly with broken fences and desolate with vacant buildings having blank apertures in place of doors and windows. After a keen reconnoissance from the safe seclusion of a clump of young pines Searing ran lightly across a field and through an orchard to a small structure which stood apart from the other farm buildings, on a slight elevation. This he thought would enable him to overlook a large scope of country in the direction that he supposed the enemy to have taken in withdrawing. This building, which had originally consisted of a single room elevated upon four posts about ten feet high, was now little more than a roof; the floor had fallen away, the joists and planks loosely piled on the ground below or resting on end at various angles, not wholly torn from their fastenings above. The supporting posts were themselves no longer vertical. It looked as if the whole edifice would go down at the touch of a finger.

Concealing himself in the débris of joists and flooring Searing looked across the open ground between his point of view and a spur of Kennesaw Mountain, a half-mile away. A road leading up and across this spur was crowded with troops—the rear-guard of the retiring enemy, their gun-barrels gleaming in the morning sunlight.

Searing had now learned all that he could hope to know. It was his duty to return to his own command with all possible speed and report his discovery. But the gray column of Confederates toiling up the mountain road was singularly tempting. His rifle—an ordinary "Springfield," but fitted with a globe sight and hair-trigger—would easily send its ounce and a quarter of lead hissing into their midst. That would probably not affect the duration and result of the war, but it is the business of a soldier to kill. It is also his habit if he is a good soldier. Searing cocked his rifle and "set" the trigger.

But it was decreed from the beginning of time that Private Searing was not to murder anybody that bright summer morning, nor was the Confederate retreat to be announced by him. For countless ages events had been so matching themselves together in that wondrous mosaic to some parts of which, dimly discernible, we give the name of history, that the acts which he had in will would have marred the harmony of the pattern. Some twenty-five years previously the Power charged with the execution of the work according to the design had provided against that mischance by causing the birth of a certain male child in a little village at the foot of the Carpathian Mountains, had carefully reared it, supervised its education, directed its desires into a military channel, and in due time made it an officer of artillery. By the concurrence of an infinite number of favoring influences and their preponderance over an infinite number of opposing ones, this officer of artillery had been made to commit a breach of discipline and flee from his native country to avoid punishment. He had been directed to New Orleans (instead of New York), where a recruiting officer awaited him on the wharf. He was enlisted and promoted, and things were so ordered that he now commanded a Confederate battery some two miles along the line from where Jerome Searing, the Federal scout, stood cocking his rifle. Nothing had been neglected—at every step in the progress of both these men's lives, and in the lives of their contemporaries and ancestors, the right thing had been done to bring about the desired result. Had anything in all this vast concatenation been overlooked Private Searing might have fired on the retreating Confederates that morning, and would perhaps have missed. As it fell out, a Confederate captain of artillery, having nothing better to do while awaiting his turn to pull out and be off, amused himself by sighting a field-piece obliquely to his right at what he mistook for some Federal officers on the crest of a hill, and discharged it. The shot flew high of its mark.

As Jerome Searing drew back the hammer of his rifle and with his eyes upon the distant Confederates considered where he could plant his shot with the best hope of making a widow or an orphan or a childless mother,—perhaps all three, for Private Searing, although he had repeatedly refused promotion, was not without a certain kind of ambition,—he heard a rushing sound in the air, like that made by the wings of a great bird swooping down upon its prey. More quickly than he could apprehend the gradation, it increased to a hoarse and horrible roar, as the missile that made it sprang at him out of the confusion of timbers above him, smashing it into matchwood, and bringing down the crazy edifice with a loud clatter, in clouds of blinding dust!

When Jerome Searing recovered consciousness he did not at once understand what had occurred. It was, indeed, some time before he opened his eyes. For a while he believed that he had died and been buried, and he tried to recall some portions of the burial service. He thought that his wife was kneeling upon his grave, adding her weight to that of the earth upon his breast. The two of them, widow and earth, had crushed his coffin. Unless the children should persuade her to go home he would not much longer be able to breathe. He felt a sense of wrong. "I cannot speak to her," he thought; "the dead have no voice; and if I open my eyes I shall get them full of earth."

He opened his eyes. A great expanse of blue sky, rising from a fringe of the tops of trees. In the foreground, shutting out some of the trees, a high, dun mound, angular in outline and crossed by an intricate, patternless system of straight lines; the whole an immeasurable distance away—a distance so inconceivably great that it fatigued him, and he closed his eyes. The moment that he did so he was conscious of an insufferable light. A sound was in his ears like the low, rhythmic thunder of a distant sea breaking in successive waves upon the beach, and out of this noise, seeming a part of it, or possibly coming from beyond it, and intermingled with its ceaseless undertone, came the articulate words: "Jerome Searing, you are caught like a rat in a trap—in a trap, trap, trap."

Suddenly there fell a great silence, a black darkness, an infinite tranquillity, and Jerome Searing, perfectly conscious of his rathood, and well assured of the trap that he was in, remembering all and nowise alarmed, again opened his eyes to reconnoitre, to note the strength of his enemy, to plan his defense.

He was caught in a reclining posture, his back firmly supported by a solid beam. Another lay across his breast, but he had been able to shrink a little away from it so that it no longer oppressed him, though it was immovable. A brace joining it at an angle had wedged him against a pile of boards on his left, fastening the arm on that side. His legs, slightly parted and straight along the ground, were covered upward to the knees with a mass of débris which towered above his narrow horizon. His head was as rigidly fixed as in a vise; he could move his eyes, his chin—no more. Only his right arm was partly free. "You must help us out of this," he said to it. But he could not get it from under the heavy timber athwart his chest, nor move it outward more than six inches at the elbow.

Searing was not seriously injured, nor did he suffer pain. A smart rap on the head from a flying fragment of the splintered post, incurred simultaneously with the frightfully sudden shock to the nervous system, had momentarily dazed him. His term of unconsciousness, including the period of recovery, during which he had had the strange fancies, had probably not exceeded a few seconds, for the dust of the wreck had not wholly cleared away as he began an intelligent survey of the situation.

With his partly free right hand he now tried to get hold of the beam that lay across, but not quite against, his breast. In no way could he do so. He was unable to depress the shoulder so as to push the elbow beyond that edge of the timber which was nearest his knees; failing in that, he could not raise the forearm and hand to grasp the beam. The brace that made an angle with it downward and backward prevented him from doing anything in that direction, and between it and his body the space was not half so wide as the length of his forearm. Obviously he could not get his hand under the beam nor over it; the hand could not, in fact, touch it at all. Having demonstrated his inability, he desisted, and began to think whether he could reach any of the débris piled upon his legs.

In surveying the mass with a view to determining that point, his attention was arrested by what seemed to be a ring of shining metal immediately in front of his eyes. It appeared to him at first to surround some perfectly black substance, and it was somewhat more than a half-inch in diameter. It suddenly occurred to his mind that the blackness was simply shadow and that the ring was in fact the muzzle of his rifle protruding from the pile of débris. He was not long in satisfying himself that this was so—if it was a satisfaction. By closing either eye he could look a little way along the barrel—to the point where it was hidden by the rubbish that held it. He could see the one side, with the corresponding eye, at apparently the same angle as the other side with the other eye. Looking with the right eye, the weapon seemed to be directed at a point to the left of his head, and *vice versa*. He was unable to see the upper surface of the barrel, but could see the under surface of the stock at a slight angle. The piece was, in fact, aimed at the exact centre of his forehead.

In the perception of this circumstance, in the recollection that just previously to the mischance of which this uncomfortable situation was the result he had cocked the rifle and set the trigger so that a touch would discharge it, Private Searing was affected with a feeling of uneasiness. But that was as far as possible from fear; he was a brave man, somewhat familiar with the aspect of rifles from that point of view, and of cannon too. And now he recalled, with something like amusement, an incident of his experience at the storming of Missionary Ridge, where, walking up to one of the enemy's embrasures from which he had seen a heavy gun throw charge after charge of grape among the assailants he had thought for a moment that the piece had been withdrawn; he could see nothing in the opening but a brazen circle. What that was he had understood just in time to step aside as it pitched another peck of iron down that swarming slope. To face firearms is one of the commonest incidents in a soldier's life— firearms, too, with malevolent eyes blazing behind them. That is what a soldier is for. Still, Private Searing did not altogether relish the situation, and turned away his eyes.

After groping, aimless, with his right hand for a time he made an ineffectual attempt to release his left. Then he tried to disengage his head, the fixity of which was the more annoying from his ignorance of what held it. Next he tried to free his feet, but while exerting the powerful muscles of his legs for that purpose it occurred to him that a disturbance of the rubbish which held them might discharge the rifle; how it could have endured what had already befallen it he could not understand, although memory assisted him with several instances in point. One in particular he recalled, in which in a moment of mental abstraction he had clubbed his rifle and beaten out another gentleman's brains, observing afterward that the weapon which he had been diligently swinging by the muzzle was loaded, capped, and at full cock—knowledge of which circumstance would doubtless have cheered his antagonist to longer endurance. He had always smiled in recalling that blunder of his "green and salad days" as a soldier, but now he did not smile. He turned his eyes again to the muzzle of the rifle and for a moment fancied that it had moved; it seemed somewhat nearer.

Again he looked away. The tops of the distant trees beyond the bounds of the plantation interested him: he had not before observed how light and feathery they were, nor how darkly blue the sky was, even among their branches, where they somewhat paled it with their green; above him it appeared almost black. "It will be uncomfortably hot here," he thought, "as the day advances. I wonder which way I am looking."

Judging by such shadows as he could see, he decided that his face was due north; he would at least not have the sun in his eyes, and north—well, that was toward his wife and children.

"Bah!" he exclaimed aloud, "what have they to do with it?"

He closed his eyes. "As I can't get out I may as well go to sleep. The rebels are gone and some of our fellows are sure to stray out here foraging. They'll find me.

But he did not sleep. Gradually he became sensible of a pain in his forehead—a dull ache, hardly perceptible at first, but growing more and more uncomfortable. He opened his eyes and it was gone—closed them and it returned. "The devil!" he said, irrelevantly, and stared again at the sky. He heard the singing of birds, the strange metallic note of the meadow lark, suggesting the clash of vibrant blades. He fell into pleasant memories of his childhood, played again with his brother and sister, raced across the fields, shouting to alarm the sedentary larks, entered the sombre forest beyond and with timid steps followed the faint path to Ghost Rock, standing at last with audible heart-throbs before the Dead Man's Cave and seeking to penetrate its awful mystery. For the first time he observed that the opening of the haunted cavern was encircled by a ring of metal. Then all else vanished and left him gazing into the barrel of his rifle as before. But whereas before it had seemed nearer, it now seemed an inconceivable distance away, and all the more sinister for that. He cried out and, startled by something in his own voice—the note of fear—lied to himself in denial: "If I don't sing out I may stay here till I die."

He now made no further attempt to evade the menacing stare of the gun barrel. If he turned away his eyes an instant it was to look for assistance (although he could not see the ground on either side the ruin), and he permitted them to return, obedient to the imperative fascination. If he closed them it was from weariness, and instantly the poignant pain in his forehead—the prophecy and menace of the bullet—forced him to reopen them.

The tension of nerve and brain was too severe; nature came to his relief with intervals of unconsciousness. Reviving from one of these he became sensible of a sharp, smarting pain in his right hand, and when he worked his fingers together, or rubbed his palm with them, he could feel that they were wet and slippery. He could not see the hand, but he knew the sensation; it was running blood. In his delirium he had beaten it against the jagged fragments of the wreck, had clutched it full of splinters. He resolved that he would meet his fate more manly. He was a plain, common soldier, had no religion and not much philosophy; he could not die like a hero, with great and wise last words, even if there had been some one to hear them, but he could die "game," and he would. But if he could only know when to expect the shot!

Some rats which had probably inhabited the shed came sneaking and scampering about. One of them mounted the pile of débris that held the rifle; another followed and another. Searing regarded them at first with indifference, then with friendly interest; then, as the thought flashed into his bewildered mind that they might touch the trigger of his rifle, he cursed them and ordered them to go away. "It is no business of yours," he cried.

The creatures went away; they would return later, attack his face, gnaw away his nose, cut his throat—he knew that, but he hoped by that time to be dead.

Nothing could now unfix his gaze from the little ring of metal with its black interior. The pain in his forehead was fierce and incessant.

He felt it gradually penetrating the brain more and more deeply, until at last its progress was arrested by the wood at the back of his head. It grew momentarily more insufferable: he began wantonly beating his lacerated hand against the splinters again to counteract that horrible ache. It seemed to throb with a slow, regular recurrence, each pulsation sharper than the preceding, and sometimes he cried out, thinking he felt the fatal bullet. No thoughts of home, of wife and children, of country, of glory. The whole record of memory was effaced. The world had passed away—not a vestige remained. Here in this confusion of timbers and boards is the sole universe. Here is immortality in time—each pain an everlasting life. The throbs tick off eternities.

Jerome Searing, the man of courage, the formidable enemy, the strong, resolute warrior, was as pale as a ghost. His jaw was fallen; his eyes protruded; he trembled in every fibre; a cold sweat bathed his entire body; he screamed with fear. He was not insane—he was terrified.

In groping about with his torn and bleeding hand he seized at last a strip of board, and, pulling, felt it give away. It lay parallel with his body, and by bending his elbow as much as the contracted space would permit, he could draw it a few inches at a time. Finally it was altogether loosened from the wreckage covering his legs; he could lift it clear of the ground its whole length. A great hope came into his mind: perhaps he could work it upward, that is to say backward, far enough to lift the end and push aside the rifle; or, if that were too tightly wedged, so place the strip of board as to deflect the bullet. With this object he passed it backward inch by inch, hardly daring to breathe lest that act somehow defeat his intent, and more than ever unable to remove his eyes from the rifle, which might perhaps now hasten to improve its waning opportunity. Something at least had been gained: in the occupation of his mind in this attempt at self-defense he was less sensible of the pain in his head and had ceased to wince. But he was still dreadfully frightened and his teeth rattled like castanets.

The strip of board ceased to move to the suasion of his hand. He tugged at it with all his strength, changed the direction of its length all he could, but it had met some extended obstruction behind him and the end in front was still too far away to clear the pile of débris and reach the muzzle of the gun. It extended, indeed, nearly as far as the trigger guard, which, uncovered by the rubbish, he could imperfectly see with his right eye. He tried to break the strip with his hand, but had no leverage. In his defeat, all his terror returned, augmented tenfold. The black aperture of the rifle appeared to threaten a sharper and more imminent death in punishment of his rebellion. The track of the bullet through his head ached with an intenser anguish. He began to tremble again.

Suddenly he became composed. His tremor subsided. He clenched his teeth and drew down his eyebrows. He had not exhausted his means of defense; a new design had shaped itself in his mind— another plan of battle. Raising the front end of the strip of board, he carefully pushed it forward through the wreckage at the side of the rifle until it pressed against the trigger guard. Then he moved the end slowly outward until he could feel that it had cleared it, then, closing his eyes, thrust it against the trigger with all his strength! There was no explosion; the rifle had been discharged as it dropped from his hand when the building fell. But it did its work.

Lieutenant Adrian Searing, in command of the picket-guard on that part of the line through which his brother Jerome had passed on his mission, sat with attentive ears in his breastwork behind the line. Not the faintest sound escaped him; the cry of a bird, the barking of a squirrel, the noise of the wind among the pines—all were anxiously noted by his overstrained sense. Suddenly, directly in front of his line, he heard a faint, confused rumble, like the clatter of a falling building translated by distance. The lieutenant mechanically looked at his watch. Six o'clock and eighteen minutes. At the same moment an officer approached him on foot from the rear and saluted.

"Lieutenant," said the officer, "the colonel directs you to move forward your line and feel the enemy if you find him. If not, continue the advance until directed to halt. There is reason to think that the enemy has retreated."

The lieutenant nodded and said nothing; the other officer retired. In a moment the men, apprised of their duty by the non-commissioned officers in low tones, had deployed from their rifle-pits and were moving forward in skirmishing order, with set teeth and beating hearts.

This line of skirmishers sweeps across the plantation toward the mountain. They pass on both sides of the wrecked building, observing nothing. At a short distance in their rear their commander comes. He casts his eyes curiously upon the ruin and sees a dead body half buried in boards and timbers. It is so covered with dust that its clothing is Confederate gray. Its face is yellowish white; the cheeks are fallen in, the temples sunken, too, with sharp ridges about them, making the forehead forbiddingly narrow; the upper lip, slightly lifted, shows the white teeth, rigidly clenched. The hair is heavy with moisture, the face as wet as the dewy grass all about. From his point of view the officer does not observe the rifle; the man was apparently killed by the fall of the building.

"Dead a week," said the officer curtly, moving on and absently pulling out his watch as if to verify his estimate of time. Six o'clock and forty minutes.

# O. HENRY

## *Two Renegades*

IN THE GATE CITY of the South the Confederate Veterans were reuniting; and I stood to see them march, beneath the tangled flags of the great conflict, to the hall of their oratory and commemoration.

While the irregular and halting line was passing I made onslaught upon it and dragged forth from the ranks my friend Barnard O'Keefe, who had no right to be there. For he was a Northerner born and bred; and what should he be doing hallooing for the Stars and Bars among those gray and moribund veterans? And why should he be trudging, with his shining, martial, humorous, broad face, among those warriors of a previous and alien generation?

I say I dragged him forth, and held him till the last hickory leg and waving goatee had stumbled past. And then I hustled him out of the crowd into a cool interiour; for the Gate City was stirred that day, and the hand-organs wisely eliminated "Marching Through Georgia" from their repertories.

"Now, what deviltry are you up to?" I asked of O'Keefe when there were a table and things in glasses between us.

O'Keefe wiped his heated face and instigated a commotion among the floating ice in his glass before he chose to answer.

"I am assisting at the wake," said he, "of the only nation on earth that ever did me a good turn. As one gentleman to another, I am ratifying and celebrating the foreign policy of the late Jefferson Davis, as fine a statesman as ever settled the financial question of a country. Equal ratio—that was his platform—a barrel of money for a barrel of flour—a pair of $20 bills for a pair of boots—a hatful of currency for a new hat—say, ain't that simple compared with W. J. B.'s little old oxidized plank?"

"What talk is this?" I asked. "Your financial digression is merely a subterfuge. Why were you marching in the ranks of the Confederate Veterans?"

"Because, my lad," answered O'Keefe, "the Confederate Gov-

507

ernment in its might and power interposed to protect and defend
Barnard O'Keefe against immediate and dangerous assassination at
the hands of a blood-thirsty foreign country after the United States of
America had overruled his appeal for protection, and had instructed
Private Secretary Cortelyou to reduce his estimate of the Republican
majority for 1905 by one vote.''

"Come, Barney," said I, "the Confederate States of America has
been out of existence nearly forty years. You do not look older
yourself. When was it that the deceased government exerted its
foreign policy in your behalf?''

"Four months ago," said O'Keefe promptly. "The infamous
foreign power I alluded to is still staggering from the official blow
dealt it by Mr. Davis's contraband aggregation of states. That's why
you see me cake-walking with the ex-rebs to the illegitimate tune
about 'simmon-seeds and cotton. I vote for the Great Father in
Washington, but I am not going back on Mars' Jeff. You say the
Confederacy has been dead forty years? Well, if it hadn't been for it,
I'd have been breathing to-day with soul so dead I couldn't have
whispered a single cuss-word about my native land. The O'Keefes are
not overburdened with ingratitude.''

I must have looked bewildered. "The war was over," I said
vacantly, "in—"

O'Keefe laughed loudly, scattering my thoughts.

"Ask old Doc Millikin if the war is over!" he shouted, hugely
diverted. "Oh, no! Doc hasn't surrendered yet. And the Confederate
States! Well, I just told you they bucked officially and solidly and
nationally against a foreign government four months ago and kept me
from being shot. Old Jeff's country stepped in and brought me off
under its wing while Roosevelt was having a gunboat painted and
waiting for the National Campaign Committee to look up whether I
had ever scratched the ticket.''

Isn't there a story in this, Barney?'' I asked.

"No," said O'Keefe; "but I'll give you the facts. You know I went
down to Panama when this irritation about a canal began, I thought I'd
get in on the ground floor. I did, and had to sleep on it, and drink water
with little zoos in it; so, of course, I got the Chagres fever. That was in
a little town called San Juan on the coast.

"After I got the fever hard enough to kill a Port-au-Prince nigger, I
had a relapse in the shape of Doc Millikin.

"There was a doctor to attend a sick man! If Doc Millikin had your case, he made the terrors of death seem like an invitation to a donkey-party. He had the bedside manners of Piute medicine-man and the soothing presence of a dray loaded with iron bridge-girders. When he laid his hand on your fevered brow you felt like Cap John Smith just before Pocahontas went his bail.

"Well, this old medical outrage floated down to my shack when I sent for him. He was built like a shad, and his eyebrows was black, and his white whiskers trickled down from his chin like milk coming out of a sprinkling-pot. He had a nigger boy along carrying an old tomato-can full of calomel, and a saw.

"Doc felt my pulse, and then he began to mess up some calomel with an agricultural implement that belonged to the trowel class.

"'I don't want any death-mask made yet, Doc,' I says, 'nor my liver put in a plaster-of-Paris cast. I'm sick; and it's medicine I need, not frescoing.'

"'You're a blame Yankee, ain't you?' asked Doc, going on mixing up his Portland cement.

"'I'm from the North,' says I, 'but I'm a plain man, and don't care for mural decorations. When you get the Isthmus all asphalted over with that boll-weevil prescription, would you mind giving me a dose of pain-killer, or a little strychnine on toast to ease up this feeling of unhealthiness that I have got?'

"'They was all sassy, just like you,' says old Doc, 'but we lowered their temperatures considerable. Yes, sir, I reckon we sent a good many of ye over to old *mortuis nisi bonum*. Look at Antietam and Bull Run and Seven Pines and around Nashville! There never was a battle where we didn't lick ye unless you was ten to our one. I knew you were a blame Yankee the minute I laid eyes on you.'

"'Don't reopen the chasm, Doc,' I begs him. 'Any Yankeeness I may have is geographical; and, as far as I am concerned, a Southerner is as good as a Filipino any day. I'm feeling too bad to argue. Let's have secession without misrepresentation, if you say so; but what I need is more laudanum and less Lundy's Lane. If you're mixing that compound gefloxide of gefloxicum for me, please fill my ears with it before you get around to the battle of Gettysburg, for there is a subject full of talk.'

"By this time Doc Millikin had thrown up a line of fortificatons on square pieces of paper; and he says to me: 'Yank, take one of these powders every two hours. They won't kill you. I'll be around again about sundown to see if you're alive.'

"Old Doc's powders knocked the chagres. I stayed in San Juan, and got to knowing him better. He was from Mississippi, and the red-hottest Southerner that ever smelled mint. He made Stonewall Jackson and R. E. Lee look like Abolitionists. He had a family somewhere down near Yazoo City; but he stayed away from the States on account of an uncontrollable liking he had for the absence of a Yankee government. Him and me got as thick personally as the Emperer of Russia and the dove of peace, but sectionally we didn't amalgamate.

"'Twas a beautiful system of medical practice introduced by old Doc into that isthmus of land. He'd take the bracket-saw and the mild chloride and his hypodermic, and treat anything from yellow fever to a personal friend.

"Besides his other liabilities Doc could play a flute for a minute or two. He was guilty of two tunes—'Dixie' and another one that was mighty close to the 'Suwanee River'—you might say one of its tributaries. He used to come down and sit with me while I was getting well, and aggrieve his flute and say unreconstructed things about the North. You'd have thought the smoke from the first gun at Fort Sumter was still floating around in the air.

"You know that was about the time they staged them property revolutions down there, that wound up in the fifth act with the thrilling canal scene where Uncle Sam has nine curtain-calls holding Miss Panama by the hand, while the bloodhounds keep Senator Morgan treed up in a cocoanut-palm.

"That's the way it wound up; but at first it seemed as if Colombia was going to make Panama look like one of the $3.98 kind, with dents made in it in the factory, like they wear at North Beach fish fries. For mine, I played the straw-hat crowd to win; and they gave me a colonel's commission over a brigade of twenty-seven men in the left wing and second joint of the insurgent army.

"The Colombian troops were awfully rude to us. One day when I had my brigade in a sandy spot, with its shoes off doing a battalion drill by squads, the Government army rushed from behind a bush at us, acting as noisy and disagreeable as they could.

"My troops enfiladed, left-faced, and left the spot. After enticing the enemy for three miles or so we struck a brier-patch and had to sit down. When we were ordered to throw up our toes and surrender we obeyed. Five of my best staff-officers fell, suffering extremely with stone-bruised heels.

"Then and there those Colombians took your friend Barney, sir, stripped him of the insignia of his rank, consisting of a pair of brass knuckles and a canteen of rum, and dragged him before a military court. The presiding general went through the usual legal formalities that sometimes cause a case to hang on the calendar of a South American military court as long as ten minutes. He asked me my age, and then sentenced me to be shot.

"They woke up the court interpreter, an American named Jenks, who was in the rum business and vice versa, and told him to translate the verdict.

"Jenks stretched himself and took a morphine tablet.

"'You've got to back up against th' 'dobe, old man,' says he to me. 'Three weeks, I believe, you get. Haven't got a chew of fine-cut on you, have you?'

"'Translate that again, with foot-notes and a glossary,' says I. 'I don't know whether I'm discharged, condemned, or handed over to the Gerry Society.'

"'Oh,' says Jenks, 'don't you understand? You're to be stood up against a 'dobe wall and shot in two or three weeks—three, I think, they said.'

"'Would you mind asking 'em which?' says I. 'A week don't amount to much after you are dead, but it seems a real nice long spell while you are alive.'

"'It's two weeks,' says the interpreter, after inquiring in Spanish of the court. 'Shall I ask 'em again?'

"'Let be,' says I. 'Let's have a stationary verdict. If I keep on appealing this way they'll have me shot about ten days before I was captured. No, I haven't got any fine-cut.'

"They sends me over to the *calaboza* with a detachment of coloured postal-telegraph boys carrying Enfield rifles, and I am locked up in a kind of brick bakery. The temperature in there was just about the kind mentioned in the cooking recipes that call for a quick oven.

"Then I gives a silver dollar to one of the guards to send for the United States consul. He comes around in pajamas, with a pair of glasses on his nose and a dozen or two inside of him.

"'I'm to be shot in two weeks,' says I. 'And although I've made a memorandum of it, I don't seem to get it off my mind. You want to call up Uncle Sam on the cable as quick as you can and get him all worked up about it. Have 'em send the *Kentucky* and the *Kearsarge* and the *Oregon* down right away. That'll be about enough battleships; but it

wouldn't hurt to have a couple of cruisers and a torpedo-boat de-
stroyer, too. And—say, if Dewey isn't busy, better have him come
along on the fastest one of the fleet.'

"'Now, see here, O'Keefe,' says the consul, getting the best of a
hiccup, 'what do you want to bother the State Department about this
matter for?'

"'Didn't you hear me?' says I; 'I'm to be shot in two weeks. Did
you think I said I was going to a lawn-party? And it wouldn't hurt if
Roosevelt could get the Japs to send down the *Yellowyamtiskookum* or
the *Ogotosingsing* or some other first-class cruisers to help. It would
make me feel safer.'

"'Now, what you want,' says the consul, 'is not to get excited. I'll
send you over some chewing tobacco and some banana fritters when I
go back. The United States can't interefere in this. You know you
were caught insurging against the government, and you're subject to
the laws of this country. Tell you the truth, I've had an intimation from
the State Department—unofficially, of course—that whenever a soldier of fortune demands a fleet of gunboats in a case of revolutionary
*katzenjammer*, I should cut the cable, give him all the tobacco he
wants, and after he's shot take his clothes, if they fit me, for part
payment of my salary.'

"'Consul,' says I to him, 'this is a serious question. You are
representing Uncle Sam. This ain't any little international tomfool-
ery, like a universal peace congress or the christening of the *Shamrock
IV*. I'm an American citizen and I demand protection. I demand the
Mosquito fleet, and Schley, and the Atlantic squadron, and Bob
Evans, and General E. Byrd Grubb, and two or three protocols. What
are you going to do about it?'

"'Nothing doing,' says the consul.

"'Be off with you, then,' says I, out of patience with him, 'and
send me Doc Millikin. Ask Doc to come and see me.'

"Doc comes and looks through the bars at me, surrounded by dirty
soldiers, with even my shoes and canteen confiscated, and he looks
mightily pleased.

"'Hello, Yank,' says he, 'getting a little taste of Johnson's Island,
now, ain't ye?'

"'Doc,' says I, 'I've just had an interview with the U.S. consul. I
gather from his remarks that I might just as well have been caught
selling suspenders in Kishineff under the name of Rosenstein as to be
in my present condition. It seems that the only maritime aid I am to

receive from the United States is some navy-plug to chew. Doc,' says
I, 'can't you suspend hostilities on the slavery question long enough
to do something for me?'

"'It ain't been my habit,' Doc Millikin answers, 'to do any painless
dentistry when I find a Yank cutting an eyetooth. So the Stars and
Stripes ain't landing any marines to shell the huts of the Colombian
cannibals, hey? Oh, say, can you see by the dawn's early light the
star-spangled banner has fluked in the fight? What's the matter with
the War Department, hey? It's a great thing to be a citizen of a
gold-standard nation, ain't it?'

"'Rub it in, Doc, all you want,' says I. 'I guess we're weak on
foreign policy.'

"'For a Yank,' says Doc, putting on his specs and talking more
mild, 'you ain't so bad. If you had come from below the line I reckon I
would have liked you right smart. Now since your country has gone
back on you, you have to come to the old doctor whose cotton you
burned and whose mules you stole and whose niggers you freed to
help you. Ain't that so, Yank?'

"'It is,' says I heartily, 'and let's have a diagnosis of the case right
away, for in two weeks' time all you can do is to hold an autopsy and I
don't want to be amputated if I can help it.'

"'Now,' says Doc, business-like, 'it's easy enough for you to get
out of this scrape. Money'll do it. You've got to pay a long string of
'em from General Pomposo down to this anthropoid ape guarding
your door. About $10,000 will do the trick. Have you got the money?'

"'Me?' says I. 'I've got one Chili dollor, two *real* pieces, and a
*medio*.'

"'Then if you've any last words, utter 'em,' says the old reb. 'The
roster of your financial budget sounds quite much to me like the noise
of a requiem.'

"'Change the treatment,' says I. 'I admit that I'm short. Call a
consultation or use radium or smuggle me in some saws or something.'

"'Yank,' says Doc Millikin, 'I've a good notion to help you.
There's only one government in the world that can get you out of this
difficulty; and that's the Confederate States of America, the grandest
nation that ever existed.'

"Just as you said to me I says to Doc; 'Why, the Confederacy ain't
a nation. It's been absolved forty years ago.'

"'That's a campaign lie,' says Doc. 'She's running along as solid as the Roman Empire. She's the only hope you've got. Now, you, being a Yank, have got to go through with some preliminary obsequies before you can get official aid. You've got to take the oath of allegiance to the Confederate Government. Then I'll guarantee she does all she can for you. What do you say, Yank?—it's your last chance.'

"'If you're fooling with me, Doc,' I answers, 'you're no better than the United States. But as you say it's the last chance, hurry up and swear me. I always did like corn whisky and 'possum anyhow. I believe I'm half Southerner by nature. I'm willing to try the Ku-klux in place of the khaki. Get brisk.'

"Doc Millikin thinks awhile, and then he offers me this oath of allegiance to take without any kind of chaser:

"'I, Barnard O'Keefe, Yank, being of sound body but a Republican mind, hereby swear to transfer my fealty, respect, and allegiance to the Confederate States of America, and the government thereof in consideration of said government, through its official acts and powers, obtaining my freedom and release from confinement and sentence of death brought about by the exuberance of my Irish proclivities and my general pizenness as a Yank.'

"I repeated these words after Doc, but they seemed to me a kind of hocus-pocus; and I don't believe any life-insurance company in the country would have issued me a policy on the strength of 'em.

"Doc went away saying he would communicate with his government immediately.

"Say—you can imagine how I felt—me to be shot in two weeks and my only hope for help being in a government that's been dead so long that it isn't even remembered except on Decoration Day and when Joe Wheeler signs the voucher for his pay-check. But it was all there was in sight; and somehow I thought Doc Millikin had something up his old alpaca sleeve that wasn't all foolishness.

"Around to the jail comes old Doc again in about a week. I was flea-bitten, a mite sarcastic, and fundamentally hungry.

"'Any Confederate ironclads in the offing?' I asks. 'Do you notice any sounds resembling the approach of Jeb Stewart's cavalry overland or Stonewall Jackson sneaking up in the rear? If you do, I wish you'd say so.'

"'It's too soon yet for help to come,' says Doc.

"'The sooner the betterr,' says I. 'I don't care if it gets in fully fifteen minutes before I am shot; and if you happen to lay eyes on

Beauregard or Albert Sidney Johnston or any of the relief corps, wig-wag 'em to hike along.'

"'There's been no answer received yet,' says Doc.

"'Don't forget,' says I, 'that there's only four days more. I don't know how you propose to work this thing, Doc,' I says to him; 'but it seems to me I'd sleep better if you had got a government that was alive and on the map—like Afghanistan or Great Britain, or old man Kruger's kingdom, to take this matter up. I don't mean any disrespect to your Confederate States, but I can't help feeling that my chances of being pulled out of this scrape was decidedly weakened when General Lee surrendered.'

"'It's your only chance,' said Doc; 'don't quarrel with it. What did your own country do for you?'

"It was only two days before the morning I was to be be shot, when Doc Millikin came around again.

"'All right, Yank,' says he. 'Help's come. The Confederate States of America is going to apply for your release. The representatives of the government arrived on a fruit-steamer last night.'

"'Bully!' says I—'bully for you, Doc! I suppose it's marines with a Gatling. I'm going to love your country all I can for this.'

"'Negotiations,'" says old Doc, 'will be opened between the two governments at once. You will know later on to-day if they are successful.'

"About four in the afternoon a soldier in red trousers brings a paper round to the jail, and they unlocks the door and I walks out. The guard at the door bows and I bows, and I steps into the grass and wades around to Doc Millikin's shack.

"Doc was sitting in his hammock playing 'Dixie,' soft and low and out of tune, on his flute. I interrupted him at 'Look away! look away!' and shook his hand for five minutes.

"'I never thought,' says Doc, taking a chew fretfully, 'that I'd ever try to save any blame Yank's life. But, Mr. O'Keefe, I don't see but what you are entitled to be considered part human, anyhow. I never thought Yanks had any of the rudiments of decorum and laudability about them. I reckon I might have been too aggregative in my tabulation. But it ain't me you want to thank—it's the Confederate States of America.'

"'And I'm much obliged to 'em,' says I. 'It's a poor man that wouldn't be patriotic with a country that's saved his life. I'll drink to the Stars and Bars whenever there's a flagstaff and a glass convenient.

But where,' says I, 'are the rescuing troops? If there was a gun fired or a shell burst, I didn't hear it.'

"Doc Millikin raises up and points out the window with his flute at the banana-steamer loading with fruit.

" 'Yank,' says he, 'there's a steamer that's going to sail in the morning. If I was you, I'd sail on it. The Confederate Government's done all it can for you. There wasn't a gun fired. The negotiations was carried on secretly between the two nations by the purser of that steamer. I got him to do it because I didn't want to appear in it. Twelve thousand dollars was paid to the officials in bribes to let you go.'

" 'Man!' says I, sitting down hard—'twelve thousand—how will I ever—who could have—where did the money come from?'

" 'Yazoo City,' says Doc Millikin: 'I've got a little saved up there. Two barrels full. It looks good to these Colombians. 'Twas Confederate money, every dollar of it. Now do you see why you'd better leave before they try to pass some of it on an expert?'

" 'I do,' says I.

" 'Now, let's hear you give the password,' says Doc Millikin.

" 'Hurrah for Jeff Davis!' says I.

" 'Correct,' says Doc. 'And let me tell you something: The next tune I learn on my flute is going to be "Yankee Doodle." I reckon there's some Yanks that are not so pizen. Or, if you was me, would you try "The Red, White, and Blue"?' "

# ROBERT EDMOND ALTER

## *The Centennial Comment*

THEY PROPPED THE OLD man up in his bed where he could look into the room. It took four of them to do it: his granddaughter, great-granddaughter, great-great-granddaughter, and Mr. Morris, the newspaperman from the North. It wasn't that he was heavy—he weighed less than a hundred—but he was brittle and a great deal of care had to be exerted when shifting him about.

He liked the upright position, liked to see what was going on. It hurt his back some, but he was used to that and he said nothing. He studied Lois, his great-great-granddaughter, with his one good eye. She was seventeen and something to look at. She was a fool for tight sweaters, and with good reason; she stuck out like knobs on a smooth log. Fant liked that fine. Red fire, it didn't hurt any to look, did it? He grunted and reckoned not.

They all stopped talking and looked at him when they heard his sound. And that made him angry. *Bosh*, he thought, *now they're going to hang around and wait for me to speak.*

Like *a bunch of early birds looking at a worm,* Fant thought sourly. He ran his rheumy eye over Lois again and chuckled without sound. They didn't make 'em that way when he was that age. He remembered the girl by the turnpike on the march to Shiloh. She had been pretty enough, but you couldn't tell much about her figure from that Mother Hubbard her ma made her wear.

It had been a crazy march; the troops untrained, undisciplined, whooping and hollering through the woods, banging off their muskets . . . Beauregard had been so disgusted with them he'd damn near called off the attack. But the fellas could tell right off about that girl. She was the I-like-boys-like-crazy kind.

She stood beyond the split rail, bare-footed in the yard with the chickens scratching around her, hands on her hips, smiling at the troops, giving them a sort of under-and-around look. Why, she had them so excited they were ready to forget the war and let the Yanks have Tennessee.

It was young Hank Stanley—the boy who later became famous by presuming—who had talked Fant into it. "Go on. Slip in there and see if you can make off with a kiss. She's begging for it. There's not an officer in sight . . ." Hank had said.

Fant had been scared—he was just eighteen—but he didn't let on, couldn't, not with a couple hundred of his friends watching. He hopped the rail and approached the girl with a sort of salute.

"Mornin', Miss. I—them fellas there bet me I wouldn't take a kiss off you . . ."

"What did they bet?" she asked quick as a whip.

"Well—I dunno, a plug of tobacco or somethin', I guess."

She smiled, shy-like, and yet he knew it wasn't so. And she put her mouth up to his and kissed him hard. Didn't those fellas hoot and holler? By juckies, they nearly took the split rail apart.

"You win," she said coyly.

Fant was so embarrassed he didn't know what was happening. It wasn't until after he'd landed in the scrub weed and felt the pain in his backside, and turned to look at the big bewhiskered man standing over him, that he realized he was in trouble. It was the girl's pa, angrily vowing to kill him then and there. Fortunately Hank led a sortie against the old man and chased him and his daughter back into the house. But even so, Fant took an awful ribbing all the rest of the way to Shiloh, and he had to limp the first three miles.

Yes, it had been a pure-out circus. But the battle on April 6th, at Shiloh, changed all of that. It changed the thinking of every man in both armies, from the generals down to the drummer boys. The days of whooping and hollering and musket-banging on march was gone. War had become a grim business.

Old Fant looked at Mr. Morris. The newspaperman didn't want to hear about the girl and her pa by the turn-pike. No, he wanted words of wisdom, a summing up of the great war that the present world could only read about. He didn't want facts. For a week now radio and TV had been feeding that to the public. Fant had even heard some of it himself, but it hadn't meant much to him. He'd been living with the facts of his life for one hundred and seventeen years.

One hundred years ago on this very day a group of South Carolina hotheads had fired the first shot on a square-block fort in the mouth of Charleston Harbour. The shot had marked the ending and the beginning of a new nation that had split in blood before it could understand the essential power of unity.

Fant had been seventeen. In March of the following year he had turned eighteen and had joined the Confederate forces, just before the battle of Shiloh. Now, on the day of the Centennial year, he was the only survivor of all those millions of boys who had gone off to the throb of drum and squeak of fife to fight for the blue and gray.

What could he say to this man who was waiting patiently to transmit his words to a curious public? The summing up was for historians of the time, not for the lone man who had been there. For that man it had been horror, boredom, fatigue, hate, mood . . . And how do you transmit a mood to people of the Twentieth Century?

That long-drawn, flat ridge of hill on the way to Antietam Creek, say. Thousands of men strung along the summit in double file, and with the curve of the hill you could look back as far as the eye could reach and see the tiny silhouettes—like ants walking on their hind-legs—pictured and moving against the vivid backdrop of turquoise sky. Dust and silence, punctuated by the gurgle of canteens, the clink and clank of equipment, the squeak and give of harness, the thud of thousands of boots. And then the sudden clear rise of Jimmy Nough-ton's Irish tenor, knifing into the dead air like a bugle call, singing of the minstrel boy who had gone to war.

And Fant had thought it the most glorious moment he'd ever known, had wished it could endure forever, because soldiering beat farming all hollow; soldiering was camaraderie, glory . . . And later in Bloody Lane, between Sharpsburg and Antietam Creek, he had cowered in terror under the whine and slam of shot, with dead men under his knees, with going-to-be dead men stumbling and coughing away from him, trying to say *God, God,* with cursing men rising over him to shoot and shout and . . . And how do you hand that to Mr. Morris of the Twentieth Century?

He sighed, wondering what to say to this man of another world. Should he tell him of the difference between a Yankee and a Secesh charge? That was fact. When the Yanks charged they shouted "Hur-rah boys!" This encouraged them to go on but had no demoralizing effect on the enemy. But a Secesh charge went to the tune of the Rebel Yell, and this wailing scream struck terror into the hearts of the enemy; and whoever heard of a Reb needing encouragement to charge? Not that there was anything wrong with the Yanks when they finally got there; they would toe-the-mark like fighting demons, and you had to hammer 'em right down into the ground before their weaker sisters would call Uncle and run.

He thought fondly of the Rebel Yell, wishing he could hear it wailing discord once more, seeing in his mind the thousands of tanned, greasy necks stretching upward, the wet, dirty faces lifted to the sky, the whisker-rimmed mouths open, and the long reaching *Y-Yo-Yo—Wo-Wo-Wooo!* of the scream.

But he couldn't tell that to Mr. Morris from the North. Mr. Morris would smile politely, nod his head and say, "Very interesting, Mr. Austin. But can you give us a—uh—well a sort of summing up . . . You know, your interpretation of the Civil War from the viewpoint of a century later?"

A century later? He could tell of a boy he killed at Gettysburg . . .

The Yank had gotten twisted around in the confusion after Pickett's Bloody Angle had broken and had started to retreat with the Secesh troops instead of standing pat where he had belonged.

Young, scared half to death, too frightened to even lift his rifle and fight his way out, he had turned suddenly and faced Fant, screaming, "No! No, Reb! Don't shoot, damn you!" And Fant—not thinking, rattled—swung up his percussion carbine from the hip and blasted the Yank into a bloody somersault.

You don't forget something like that. You don't forget the boy's face, words, or even the new brass buttons on his tunic. You remember it even a century later. You wake up in the middle of a vast night in a damp bed and find yourself running and screaming with men who have been dead and forgotten for years, across furrowed and equipment-littered fields, and you hear again the blast and heave of the shells, and the whine of the minie balls, and you see the Yank before you, screaming and waving his hand, and you feel the tug of the trigger, the jar of the carbine going *ca-blam!* taste the powder . . .

And you sit bolt-up in bed and you cry into the dark room:

"I didn't know! Godamn it, I didn't know! How could I have known at that moment, at that place? I was frightened too, I tell you! I was callow and scared! I didn't think—couldn't." And then your wife or daughter, or granddaughter or great-granddaughter, came to you and mothered you back down into the damp sheets and told you it was all right, that you were only having a bad dream. But it wasn't a dream—it had been dying by living again.

But he couldn't tell that to Mr. Morris and to the people of Mr. Morris' world. Neither the North nor the South of today wanted to hear that the only surviving soldier of the Civil War had killed a Yankee boy that he could have taken prisoner, ninety-eight years ago . . .

He looked at the newspaperman again and frowned. *What is it you want to hear from me?* he asked himself. *What is it they all want to hear?* What would satisfy them? His granddaughter was showing Mr. Morris the Brady picture book of the war, pointing to the picture of the sunken road at Sharpsburg that Brady took right after the battle.

"This was the very spot that Grandfather fought at, Mr. Morris. Here in the centre—between those dead men and all that rubbish there."

Fant grimaced. He didn't know what part of Bloody Lane he had fought in. When he looked at the picture it all seemed the same to him—a ditch full of dead soldiers. Besides, Mr. Morris didn't give a hoot about where he fought; he wanted the summing up.

What would satisfy the man and send him on his way? Should he tell about Appomattox, about Lee's face at the end when he looked down at his men and said, "Men, we have fought through the war together. I have done my best for you. My heart is too full to say more." And how, with a final wave of his hat, he rode through the weeping army; and how they had followed him on foot, crying and slobbering in his wake; how Fant, overcome with emotion, had pushed his way frantically through his comrades to gain the general's side, and Lee's sad, fatherly face had turned down and he had murmured, "Let the boy through," and Fant had laid his hand on old Traveller's quivering flank and found that he was unable to say anything.

No, that wouldn't do. That meant nothing to the people of today. They hadn't been there, they hadn't seen him; they hadn't been a part of it—and he was the only part left.

Mr. Morris had set the book aside. He was smiling at Fant.

"Do you feel like talking now, Mr. Austin? Can you tell us anything? Your thoughts or emotions on the war? Just any comment for the Centennial?" he asked quietly.

Fant stared at the man from the North . . . And suddenly he smiled, because suddenly he knew that he had it—what they all wanted to hear, what would satisfy them when it was recorded.

None of them could see the smile; it was buried deep in the wrinkles of his face, lost in the folds of loose flesh. It was his secret laughing place. He opened his mouth and cleared his rusty throat and tried to fix a fierce aspect to his one good eye.

"Get the hell out of here, you damn Yankee," he commented huskily.

# ABOUT THE EDITORS

MARTIN H. GREENBERG, who has been called "the king of the anthologists," now has some 120 of them to his credit. Greenberg is professor of regional analysis and political science at the University of Wisconsin – Green Bay, where he teaches a course in American foreign and defense policy. With Augustus R. Norton, he is the co-editor of *Touring Nam: The Vietnam War Reader.*

BILL PRONZINI is one of America's finest mystery/suspense/espionage writers, as well as one of its leading critics. He has published some 34 novels and more than 280 stories. His fiction has been translated into 17 languages and he has edited or coedited some 40 anthologies, including *A Treasury of World War II Stories, Baker's Dozen: 13 Short Mystery Novels,* and *Baker's Dozen: 13 Short Espionage Novels.* A long-time resident of San Francisco, he possesses one of the larger collections of pulp magazines (including a large number of war-related ones) in the world.